Drawing his dagger, Will stepped to the lamp behind him stabbed a wedge of yellow lg picking out the figure hunched and huddled in the lurid sca

His first emotion was one of pure elation; the trap he and Kerrigan had set had functioned far better than he could have hoped. But the second emotion completely smothered that.

Pure fear poured into Will as he saw what they'd caught. The creature had the bulk of a large dog or a small bear, and its body and head and legs bristled with four-inch-long hairs, with a thick down covering its back. Its shoulders were hunched as it tugged mightily to free its right hand, its legs bunched and pushing.

All eight of its legs!

The creature turned and looked at him with bubbled eyes and wickedly curved mandibles. The mouth parts worked and Will heard something that almost clicked and growled its way into a semblance of human speech.

Will brought the dagger up and whipped it forward. The hilt smashed the creature in the middle of the back, then bounced back down onto the bed. Sprinting into the room, Will dove for the dagger. As his right hand closed on the hilt, something grabbed his jacket right between his shoulder blades. Then the spider thing hauled Will up and smashed his head against the rafter.

Stars exploded, and the world faded from Will's sight . . .

WHEN DRAGONS RAGE

Book Two of the DragonCrown War Cycle

Michael A. Stackpole

BANTAM BOOKS

fantasy

WHEN DRAGONS RAGE
A Bantam Spectra Trade Paperback / December 2002

SPECTRA and the portrayal of a boxed "s" are trademarks of
Bantam Books, a division of Random House, Inc.

Map by Elizabeth T. Danforth.

Library of Congress Cataloging-in-Publication Data
Stackpole, Michael A, 1957–
When dragons rage/Michael A. Stackpole
p.   cm. (DragonCrown war cycle; bk. 2)
ISBN 0-553-37920-8
PS3569.T137 W48 2002   2002027811
813/.54 21

Published simultaneously in the United States and Canada

Bantam Books are published by Bantam Books, a division of Random
House, Inc. Its trademark, consisting of the words "Bantam Books"
and the portrayal of a rooster, is Registered in U.S. Patent and Trademark Office and in other countries. Marca Registrada. Random
House, New York, New York.

PRINTED IN THE UNITED STATES OF AMERICA

RRH   10 9 8 7 6 5 4 3 2 1

To the memory of
Austin H. Kerin
(If not for his book, I'd not be a writer today.)

Acknowledgments

Anne Lesley Groell has the patience of a saint and was quite kind with me as this book groaned along well past deadline. The errors herein are mine, and the dearth of them is all her doing. The author would also like to thank all of those readers who made good their promise to read some fantasy while awaiting their next BattleMech or lightsaber fix.

THE NORRINGTON PROPHECY

A Norrington to lead them,
Immortal, washed in fire
Victorious, from sea to ice.

Power of the north he will shatter,
A scourge he will kill,
Then Vorquellyn will redeem.

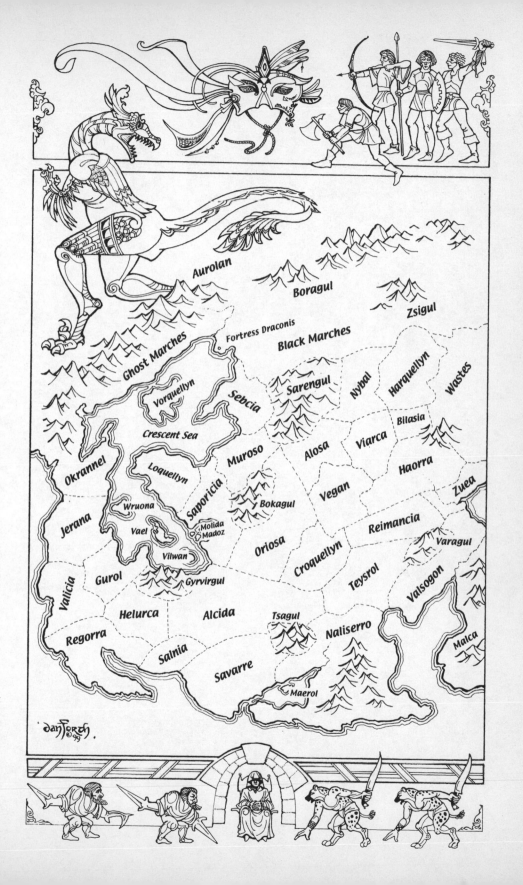

CHAPTER 1

A misty blue curtain descended over Princess Alexia of Okrannel, obscuring her surroundings. Save that something felt solid beneath her feet, she would have had no way of discerning up from down. *Not that there really is any ground here—or up or down.*

She lifted her head and gazed forward, trying to see the mountain she knew loomed afar. In accord with her thought, the cerulean mist swirled and parted, bleeding down and away into low fog that tugged at the hem of her gown. In the distance she did see the sharp-peaked mountain blotting out a wedge of starry night sky.

Though the mountaintop lay miles away, she reached it in three long-legged strides. She smiled, for melting of both the mist and the miles were not the only changes wrought as she moved forward. She had arrived in the mist in a simple white gown with a short cape, but by the time she reached the mountain and the arched mouth of the cavern near its top, her clothing had shifted to a warrior's tunic, simple trousers, and a good pair of boots.

She recognized her clothes as those she had last seen Crow wearing. This surprised her because though she was operating in a magickal realm where her whim could shape reality, she had not consciously chosen Crow's raiment. Either her mind was betraying her, or other forces held a certain sway in the Communion's domain.

Alyx glanced up at the stone arch defining the cave's mouth, and gathered her long, white-blonde hair over her shoulder. Unconsciously plaiting it, she read, "The secrets within are secret without, for the good of all the world." While hardly lyrical or powerful, the words described what would happen to discussions held beyond the arch. Nothing she said or heard could be shared in the waking world.

She shivered and set her shoulders. In Yslin—mere months previous, though it seemed like years—she had been invited to join the world's eldest and most elite secret society: the Great Communion of Dragons. Any Communicant could access their enchanted meeting place in a trance that would appear to be simple sleep to observers. Alexia had tucked herself into bed at the Scarlet Mask Inn before she traveled here. This was her first conscious journey to the Communion, so a touch of fear fluttered in her belly.

Still braiding her hair, she entered the cavern, occasionally ducking her head around low-hanging stalactites. She threaded her way along a dimly glowing curved path that led down to a vast arch that bridged a crevasse. She could not see the bottom of it and suspected it had none. The span linking one side to the other was narrow, and try as she might she could not make it appear any broader. On the other side, the cavern closed into a twisting, serpentine tunnel that worked its way down, and finally opened into a vast chamber filled with moist air and the gentle ripple of water washing up on a shore.

A boat waited at the end of a pier that jutted into the dark underground lake. The boat had no masts and had been styled after a dragon, with a fearsome head curving up from the bow. Back on the wheeldeck stood a steel construct, animated by magick, that appeared to be the marriage of human and dragon forms. Its massive, clawed hands rested on the wheel. Its dark eyes did not show any light, nor did it acknowledge her as she boarded amidships.

She glanced at it. "Maroth, take me forth."

The ship lurched slightly, then began to move across the lake. Alexia strode to the bow. Water flowed noisily by under the keel, and some splashed up to sprinkle coldly on her face. She felt the rush of the passage in the breeze upon her face, but the ship sped into a starless void that provided few visual clues as to movement. Glancing back she saw nothing of the pier, but when she turned to look forward again, an island had appeared, towering over the boat as it moved to a small quay.

The boat glided to rest, bumping only slightly, and Alexia leaped effortlessly to the granite quay. She turned and tossed the pilot a salute. "Thank you, Maroth."

The mechanical creature made no response.

Alexia mounted the steps and slowly began to recognize the places from which bits and pieces of the island had been drawn. The steps reminded her of the seaside entry into Fortress Draconis, though she saw none of the dragonel ports that had defended its small harbor. And the island still boasted the soaring cylindrical towers typical of strongholds predating Chytrine's creation of weapons that could raze them. The island also bore no scars of battle, and though Fortress Draconis had yet to fall the last time she saw it, she imagined Chytrine's assault had by now reduced it to smoking, corpse-ridden ruins.

Up the steps she went, then crested the island's rim and began a steep descent to its interior. A lush garden greeted her, rich with blossoms that bloomed despite the twilight. The scented symphony of their nocturnal perfume exceeded their beauty. Some of the trees bore fruit and her mouth began to water.

Alyx smiled, wondering if her mouth was watering in this illusion, or back in the tavern. *Could I pluck some of the fruit? Would it taste delicious when I bit into it?*

"It would, in fact, daughter."

She spun, dropping into a combat stance, then relaxed and straightened. "You surprised me."

"My apologies." The rough figure of a man materialized from a shadowed grove. Thickly and powerfully built, he wore a black surcoat worked with a scale pattern reminiscent of dragon flesh. His gauntlets and boots—both of which were armored and ended in talons—continued that theme. The elaborate helm he wore fully hid his face, but the golden eyes glowed and moved as if they were real, and even the ears seemed to function.

Alyx knew the man chose to wear that form here, and had enough ease with his surroundings to look however he chose. What she was able to do with clothing, he could do with his whole person. *And more.*

The Black Dragon reached up and plucked a ripe, red apple from the tree above him. "It will provide no nutrition, but will be pleasing nonetheless."

Alyx straightened up and pressed a hand to her stomach. "I am not certain I could keep food down at the moment."

The Black's eyes narrowed. "What news of the world, then? What has happened?"

Alexia rubbed a hand over her forehead before she graced him with a violet-eyed glance. "After last I spoke with you, much, very much. Because of your warning, Adrogans sent some of us to Wruona to wrest the Jeranese fragment of the DragonCrown from the pirates. We got it and got away. What little remained of their fleet after the raid on Vilwan was laid to waste by Kerrigan."

"I knew you had met with some success, but I don't know Kerrigan."

She hesitated for a moment. "Kerrigan Reese. He is from Vilwan, and not more than seventeen. He's tall, but a suet-ball that could easily be dismissed as some overindulged noble's-child. He's smart, however, and has incredible power. He can command spells that no human has ever mastered, and yet others that have not been employed since the time of Yrulph Kirûn."

The Black nodded solemnly. "He who was Chytrine's mentor. So young a man wielding such power could be dangerous. He's mature beyond his years, is he?"

Alyx looked at the apple in the Black's hand and imagined it in hers. It appeared in her hand, and then evaporated. "I wish he were, but he's not. His last teacher, Orla, tried to make him grow up, but she died on Wruona. He's pushed himself hard since then, and worked diligently for the Draconis Baron, but without something to give him direction, I don't know what he's going to do. The impact of Orla's death has yet to sink in, and if he loses control, he could be extremely dangerous."

The man began to pace. "The Norrington. He was with you, too?"

"Yes. Will." Alyx smiled. "He's a thief, and very good at it. He has little in the way of conscience, though one seems to be growing. Peri—Perrine, my sister from the Gyrkyme—thinks he is good-hearted. I trust her judgment. After we escaped from Wruona we went to Loquellyn. The elves weren't about to let Peri set foot there, but Will made them reconsider. He can be surprising that way. He's young, too—younger than Kerrigan—and can be very childish. But he's game in a fight and capable of great cleverness."

"Cleverness will be important, since he is the key to the prophecy that will destroy Chytrine. We once thought it was his grandfather, or his father, Bosleigh. When they joined Chytrine and became her *sullanciri,* that focused hopes on someone else."

Alyx sighed. "We've met some of the *sullanciri* and even killed a few. You know I slew one at Svoin. Resolute later killed Ganagrei south of Fortress Draconis, after we evacuated with refugees. Do you have news of the Fortress?"

The Black Dragon shook his head. "Nothing reliable, except that news from there is rare. That suggests the worst: that Chytrine's forces have completely laid it to waste. Balancing that, however, is the fact that her armies have not yet moved south, so she still may be searching for the DragonCrown fragments there."

"Or the defenders so chewed up her army that she needs to wait for reinforcements." Alexia tapped a finger on her chin. "A mix of the two is also possible. That was a big place, with lots of tunnels and warrens. There could be survivors holding out, still fighting. It might have been broken, but crushing it completely would be difficult."

The Black faced her. "I shall hope your assessment is accurate. I suspect you will learn sooner than I if it is. But how is it that you are not there?"

"Chytrine allowed Oriosans and noncombatants free passage to the south. I did not want to go, but Dothan Cavarre asked me to safeguard his wife and children as they returned to Oriosa. I didn't know until earlier today that he had an ulterior motive." Alexia hesitated for a second. "The Draconis

Baron had gotten Kerrigan to create a duplicate for one piece of the Dragon-Crown, which was left behind as he smuggled the real one out. Chytrine was deceived, though she still sent troops after us. We held them off—that's when Resolute killed Ganagrei."

"There's nothing wrong with killing *sullanciri*. How long ago was that?"

"Two weeks? No, only eighteen days. Once we reached Sebcia we got relays of fresh horses and pushed hard to reach Oriosa with Ryhope. When we crossed the border, Kerrigan told us he had the fragment. He also said he'd worked a spell on another fragment. He's not sure whether Chytrine will detect it, but if not, it will feed her sense of paranoia, and that will be to our advantage."

The Black Dragon nodded. "It will, very much so." The figure's head came up as he turned to regard her. "You did not come here while on the road—despite having left Fortress Draconis and having seen a *sullanciri* destroyed."

Alexia blinked. "I didn't realize there was . . ."

The Black shook his head. "No, there is no requirement for you to share anything, daughter. What I was leading to was this: these things were quite momentous, and seeking perspective on them would be understandable. It was not until you were out of danger, however, that you came here. What else has happened?"

She frowned. "You told me, when first I met you, that I could trust Crow. When we reached Oriosa his countrymen arrested him. They have him in custody. You knew who he was, didn't you?"

The dark figure slowly nodded, and clasped his hands at the small of his back. "I have known his identity for a long time."

"How could you tell me I could trust him? He's Tarrant Hawkins, the man who betrayed the last expedition sent to destroy Chytrine. Kenwick Norrington became a *sullanciri* because of him." Her hands closed into fists. "There are some who say he even got my father killed."

"You feel betrayed."

"Yes!" The emotions coursing through her surprised Alexia. She hadn't completely taken the Black Dragon at his word, but his comments pertaining to Crow had disposed her well toward the man. To find out that he was the most evil man outside Chytrine's legions had hurt.

"You feel a bit betrayed by me, since I told you to trust him, but more by Crow, isn't that it?" The Black cocked his head slightly. "You perhaps wonder why he didn't tell you who he was, and yet you react with the same revulsion anyone would. Yes, Tarrant Hawkins has been painted as an evil man, but you have had experience of him. Is Crow evil?"

"It doesn't matter. A man cannot change from his past."

The Black Dragon snorted, puffs of cool blue flame jetting from each nostril. "Then, I would suggest, daughter, that you have a choice of two explanations. The first is that Crow is as evil as Hawkins is in legend, and that Crow managed to deceive you. The second..."

Alexia's eyes narrowed. "...The second is that Hawkins was as courageous as Crow, and the legends about him are wrong. But, if that were true, why would he allow such lies to be spread?"

The Black's jaw opened in a dragonish grin. "That was not a choice given to him, Alexia. People saw him as a threat. They neutralized him. He is lucky to yet be alive. Enduring lies is better than lying in a grave."

"What threat could he have been?"

"He told the crowned heads that Chytrine would come for their realms in a generation, and this was a message they did not want to hear or have heard by others."

"They knew she would come back?" Alexia raised her fists to her temples. "Amid the Gyrkyme it was supposed that someday Chytrine would return, but no one knew she had vowed to do so. You're telling me the crowned heads *knew* she would return and did not prepare? That no one prepared save the Draconis Baron and King Augustus? How could they?"

"A crown on the head does not guarantee brains in the skull."

"But to ignore the threat is criminal!"

"Yes, but recall they lived in fear. A *sullanciri* slew Queen Lanivette in Meredo, in her castle, with all of her troops waiting to oppose him."

She nodded. "Leaving Scrainwood as king, and likely a willing collaborator with Chytrine."

"Of course, and what other ruler could not fear the same fate for himself and his nation?" The Black's eyes half-lidded. "For many, the assumption was that if they did nothing, Chytrine would not see them as a threat. What they did not realize was that to do nothing to oppose a tyrant in fact aids that tyrant."

Alexia opened her mouth for a second, then closed it. "And Crow and Resolute have spent two and a half decades opposing her."

"They've not been alone. And they are trusted." The Black Dragon began pacing again. "The Draconis Baron would never have allowed Crow to travel with you if he did not trust him."

"You're saying Cavarre knew?"

"He must have, yes."

"Who else?"

The Black shrugged. "Augustus, certainly; a few others. Once Hawkins was believed dead, he passed from notice. Some of the Vorquelves know, but the Vorquelves would never betray Crow, since he is a key to getting their homeland back."

Alyx shivered. The revelation of Crow's true identity had shaken and confused her. He was a comrade in arms, a friend. She liked him. He had risked his life to save her. He had opposed and destroyed *sullanciri*. He had given her good counsel. He *had* lied to her, but only to hide his identity.

"Crow knew my father, then?"

"They were well acquainted, for a time. Hawkins impressed your father with his honesty and courage."

She raised an eyebrow. "You knew my father?"

"I never had the pleasure of embracing him and calling him brother, but I did know him and certainly knew of him. He was a good man, and he would be inordinately proud of you." The Black grinned again. "But we can reminisce about your father another time, because it was your concern over Crow that brought you here."

His comment brought her up short. "Can you read my mind?"

He shrugged. "As you get more practice here, you will become more comfortable. I am not really reading your mind; there are just some things you are thinking rather loudly. For example, you are correct in supposing that Crow should not be executed for the crimes he was accused of so long ago. You will think of a plan to rescue him, though I urge caution in executing anything that would put you on the wrong side of authority. You are a princess, albeit of a nation still occupied by Aurolani forces, but you can use your station."

She smiled. "Even though I'd rather just break him out of the root cellar where he's being held and disappear?"

"I like the direct approach as much as you do, but that's a plan that will label you nothing more than a strong arm with a sword. You will need a different plan: one to confuse your enemies and keep them off balance."

"Chytrine will not care."

"It wasn't of her that I was speaking." The Black gave her a golden-eyed stare. "Chytrine is not the only one who desires power in the south. As you become powerful, others will find reason to oppose you. They are a cautious lot, however, and the more you give them to think about, the slower they act."

"And now you've given me something to think about." She smiled, hearing in the Black's words something Crow had told her back in Yslin. "Yes. I think I have a plan to save Crow. All I need to do is . . ."

The Black held a hand up. "Don't say anything, or you will be unable to mention it in the physical world. If what I glean in flashes from your thoughts is at all accurate, however, this plan will do as much to confuse your enemies as it will to save Crow—both of which I applaud heartily."

"Thank you. And, belatedly, thank you for the warning about the theft of the Jeranese fragment of the DragonCrown. If you had said nothing, Chytrine would now have it."

The Black shook his head. "No thanks are required. Telling you was all I could do. You did the hard work, and all the praise is deservedly yours. And now you will save Crow, for which I shall also be grateful. Go now, daughter, and do what you must. The world requires it."

The Black gestured, and a wave of dizziness washed over Alexia. She blacked out for a moment, then reappeared in her bed, the din of the tavern's common room buzzing up through the wooden floor. The plan she'd formulated had crystallized in her mind. Throwing back the blanket, she swung her long legs from the bed and began tugging her boots on.

"Crow, you've spent a lifetime saving other folks. Starting now, that investment gets paid back."

CHAPTER 2

Will Norrington paced the floor at the foot of the bed, shooting venomous glances at the powerfully built Vorquelf leaning back against the headboard. "They're going to kill Crow. How can you just sit there? Some friend you are."

Resolute blinked once, slowly, then regarded the youth with a cold, argent gaze. "Choose your words carefully, boy."

A shiver ran down Will's spine, but the hot fury racing through him didn't let that chill get far. "Are you going to kill me because of what I'm saying?"

"No." The single word came husky and low, more growled than spoken. Because he was of elven stock, Resolute had long limbs. And, were he standing, the brush of white hair that ran in a stripe over his skull would have touched the ceiling. Moreover, the Vorquelf lacked the slender build of most elves. His arms rippled with muscle, and the flesh sheathing them was amply decorated with arcane tattoos. Scars likewise crisscrossed his skin, with thick knots standing out on his knuckles.

The Vorquelf's eyes tightened. "You should choose your words carefully, because you'll be eating them if you continue. Out with what you're really thinking."

Will, who was Resolute's physical antithesis—being small, slender, and relatively unmarked in his youth, with grey eyes and brown hair—planted his fists on his hips and frowned. "I *am* saying what I think. I think we should go out there, pull Crow out of that turnip-bin they're keeping him in, and get away from here."

"Really?" The Vorquelf's silver eyes had no whites, no pupils, so Will couldn't be sure when he was being stared at or not. "Let us play with your scenario, shall we? Not with the obvious things, though."

"Such as?"

"Such as having no place to go. Such as being outnumbered by the troops on hand."

"Local militia. We could slip past them and spirit Crow away, and you know it."

Resolute did allow a faint flicker of a smile to flash over his face for a heartbeat. "Regardless, they would come after us."

"So we kill them."

"Really?" The Vorquelf's expression tightened. "For what?"

"They are going to kill Crow. Did you miss that when Call Mably met us out on the road? They think Crow was this Hawkins, and he's under a death sentence. They'll take him to Meredo, King Scrainwood will pretend to listen to him, and then he'll kill him. It's wrong!"

"Why?"

Will's eyes widened. "Because Crow isn't Hawkins. He isn't the Traitor, and there's no way we can let them take him. If some of them have to die because they're too stupid to see the truth, well, sometimes stupidity is a fatal disease."

"It is, at that. I'd be careful, though."

Something in Resolute's tone sliced into Will's outrage. "What is it?"

The Vorquelf arched an eyebrow. "All your posturing is built on your belief that they have mistaken Crow for Hawkins."

"They have."

Resolute shook his head. "No, they haven't. Crow *was* Hawkins."

Will's jaw dropped and he hunched forward, grabbing the foot of the bed. He felt as if he'd been gut-punched, for no breath could come. He knew from the Vorquelf's voice that there was no deception, no hidden meaning in those words—and try as he might, he could find no way to twist them.

But that's impossible! Everyone knew the story of the Traitor, the one who betrayed the world's heroes to Chytrine. In songs he had become Squab, always conniving and craven, always defeated. It was common knowledge that the real Hawkins had killed himself in shame over what he had done.

"No, it can't be. Not Crow." Will looked up and caught Resolute's unwavering gaze. A lump rose in his throat and tears began to leak from his eyes. *Crying? No, no, no.* He covered his face with one hand and slammed his right fist down on the bed. "You're wrong. You have to be."

Resolute kept his voice even. "You're smarter than that, boy. Think, boy, think the way I know you can."

The youth looked up and swiped at his tears. "What's there to think,

Resolute? Crow can't be Hawkins. Hawkins was a coward and a schemer. Crow isn't."

"You were there, Will. Crow gave himself over without a fight."

"Sure, sure, but he did that to protect the rest of us. He's like that, trusting the mistake would be straightened out." Will smiled, nodding. "He's *too* trusting, and you know it."

"Yes, he is. So was Hawkins." The Vorquelf drew his knees up and rested his arms on them. "That was why Hawkins had to die."

Will leaned heavily on the foot of the bed and shook his head. "I don't believe it. How could Crow be Hawkins?"

"Because he was too trusting. The basic story is true. Hawkins accompanied Lord Norrington, your grandfather, and Leigh Norrington, your father, on the last war against Chytrine. That was a quarter century ago. Along the way your father found a terrible sword, Temmer. It made him invincible in battle, though not invulnerable. The price the wielder paid was that he would lose his last battle.

"That last battle came at Fortress Draconis. Chytrine had one ancient *sullanciri*—an undead hoargoun. You saw some of the frost giants at Svoin, though this one had been dead long before I was born. It used fear the way a skunk uses stink. The warriors who faced it broke and ran, your father among them. Only two men stood to oppose it."

Will looked up. "At that interior gate?"

Resolute nodded solemnly. "Your father had run, and Scrainwood with him. Hawkins ran, too, but his fear was for your father. He found him, took Temmer from him, and slew the *sullanciri*."

"Really?" The young thief frowned. "I never heard that."

"Those who were there knew it, but many had been so fear-mad they seldom wanted to think about that whole battle."

"You said two men stood against it. The other was Princess Alexia's father, wasn't it?"

The Vorquelf nodded. "You saw the plaza at Fortress Draconis. You saw where he died. Hawkins couldn't save him, but he saved many others. Because of that, he was selected to go north with your grandfather and King Augustus, to chase after Chytrine's retreating army. When Chytrine split off from the army, Hawkins was allowed to join the band heading after her."

"Of course; he had Temmer."

"No. Temmer was shattered killing the *sullanciri*." The Vorquelf's head turned toward the sword with the keystone pommel. "That is Tsamoc, and the sword Hawkins carried as he went after Chytrine."

Will nodded. He'd seen Crow use the sword in battle. It had a glowing, opalescent gem set in the blade's forte. The sword had enough magick in it to kill a *sullanciri* on the battlefield of Svoin, though Princess Alexia had been using it at the time.

"That band of heroes knew they were off on a suicide mission, but they went anyway. Only it turned out to be worse than that, for Chytrine trapped them. She slew some, hurt others badly, but turned all to her will. She made them into her new *sullanciri,* since the old ones had been slain. And she tortured Hawkins, physically and mentally. She offered to make him her consort, to give him all of the Southlands if he would lead her troops.

"Hawkins refused and survived her attempt to kill him. He came south and reported to the crowned heads what Chytrine had told him: that the children of that day would never live to see their own children mature. She vowed to invade again, and everyone knew her threat was a potent one."

Will frowned. "But if things are as you say, then Hawkins did nothing wrong. Why does Scrainwood want him dead?"

"Scrainwood's hatred for Hawkins runs deep. Scrainwood wanted Temmer for himself. He wanted to be a hero, but instead he proved a coward. Hawkins knew it. But, more importantly, the kings and queens faced a problem. Okrannel had fallen to Chytrine, and that scared a lot of people. They knew that if Chytrine's threats were made common knowledge, there would be panic. People would revolt. The safety people craved would mean their sons and daughters would be sent off to die fighting for Okrannel. It was the same reasoning they have used when they refuse to liberate my homeland, Vorquellyn. Hawkins had to be destroyed so he would never be believed."

Resolute's chin came up. "In Yslin, in Fortress Gryps, Hawkins' father stripped him of his mask. His father told him he had no son named Tarrant. It wasn't quite then that Crow was born, but that was surely when Hawkins died. We Vorquelves took him in, because we know what it is to be without a home. And we knew Hawkins couldn't be the person they said he was."

Resolute smiled, his eyes narrowing at the same time. "Not long after I met Hawkins, he vowed he'd see Vorquellyn liberated in his lifetime. Just as Oracle knew you were part of a prophecy, part of the web of events that would lead to Vorquellyn's redemption, so we knew Hawkins was part of it, too. Because of that, we knew the rumors had to be false."

Will blinked. "You're telling me all this, and yet you're not helping me to free him? Fat lot of good his execution will do your island's redemption."

Resolute shook his head fiercely. "You're missing it, boy; think. For over two decades Crow never set foot in Oriosa. Why? Because we knew, at some point, someone would let the truth slip. Vorquelven minstrels started the Squab songs. They started the rumor that Hawkins had killed himself, and people believed it because they thought a traitor ought to have the decency to kill himself in shame. Later, the same minstrels started the Kedyn's Crow songs—all of them true, mind you. Despite all that, though, we knew that coming to Oriosa would be too risky."

"Why did he do it, then?"

"You can answer that question."

Will closed his eyes and concentrated. Crow had spent a quarter century fighting Chytrine. He had searched the world for Will, knowing he was the last of the Norrington bloodline, which was prophesied to destroy Chytrine. He'd fought to destroy her troops and to keep her from obtaining a fragment of the DragonCrown. And, coming south, they'd killed another *sullanciri* and returned Princess Ryhope and her children to Oriosa.

The thief opened his eyes again. "Crow felt that getting here, delivering Ryhope, was worth the risk of his life?"

"Ryhope? *You* were more important, Will. You are *the* Norrington."

Will rolled his eyes. "That's beside the point. We can't let Crow rot in that pit they've got him in."

"We won't, but breaking in and pulling him out isn't going to work, either. You can be smart, Will, so use your head."

"I am. Getting him out of jail here will be easier than in Meredo."

Resolute shook his head. "Think more deeply. Crow's freedom will be won by something other than a sword."

Will shifted his shoulders uneasily. "Maybe, but sticking a blade into someone like Call Mably would be fun."

"And cause more trouble than it would prevent." The Vorquelf stretched out again. "Think of a solution that would work for a shadow, not a blade."

The youth sighed mightily. "You're no help at all."

"When you have a plan that will work, I will help."

"The help I need is in making a plan." Will frowned. "So until then, you're going to do nothing?"

"No, I'm going to sleep." Resolute yawned. "Not the whole time it will take you to come up with a plan, however. I doubt I need much more than a week's sleep."

The thief stuck his tongue out at the elf. "Well, I'm going down to the common room for inspiration."

Before Will could reach the door, Resolute called out. "Don't forget your mask."

Will stiffened, then pulled it from the peg on the wall. The simple mask of green leather had an orphan's notch cut beneath the right eyehole. The Oriosan king's seal had branded the mask above and between the eyes. Will pulled it on. The leather felt cool on his face. As he knotted it, he made sure to catch a strand of hair in the knot, to make the mask a part of him.

He turned and opened his hands. "Satisfied?"

"For now."

Will slipped from the room and down the short corridor, passing Alexia's room on the right and Kerrigan's on the left. He found it annoying that both of them had retired for the evening; he would have thought that they wanted to free Crow as badly as he did. His irritation passed, however, when he thought about what Resolute had forced him to consider.

Maybe they're working on their own plans. Will smiled as he began to descend the stairs. Alexia could figure out a way to free Crow. Kerrigan, well, Will wasn't all that certain about the magicker, but Kerrigan had shown some spine on the retreat, so anything was possible.

Will's descent carried him into the inn's small common room and, for a moment, the familiar din of tavern chaos made him smile. Then, slowly, the noise died as people turned to look at him. Most of them wore masks, save for a bunch of pig farmers back in the cold-corner. While the masks hid much of their expressions, Will did see some eyes widen, then smiles begin to blossom.

Applause erupted spontaneously, then one corpulent man who seemed to have gained a pound around his middle for every hair he had lost from his crown, stood and waved Will forward. "My friends, this is Will Norrington—*the* Norrington. He's the one who will destroy Chytrine. He led Princess Ryhope right here to our town. Even more importantly, he's the one who finally delivered the Traitor to justice."

Will's eyes widened in horror. "No, no, that's not it at all."

The man's smile grew, his rosy cheeks piling up around the corners of his mouth. "See, and modest, too! A true Oriosan hero."

The applause grew and the insanity of it hit Will in increasing waves. These people had it all wrong about Crow. More importantly, they were ignoring the fact that he was there because Chytrine had crushed Fortress Draconis and before spring she could be sacking Tolsin.

The joy on their faces stopped him from wanting to yell at them. These people knew full well how he had come to be there. To dwell on that, however—to think about their homes being burned, their children slain, their town and their nation vanishing—would drive them insane. They were taking joy in a small victory, a small act of defiance, because it gave them hope.

My presence gives them hope.

Will shivered. A quarter century ago the rulers of the world had destroyed Hawkins to preserve hope for their people. Now these people would raise Will up as a symbol of hope. He had done nothing and would be exalted, whereas Crow, who had done so much, had been vilified.

The bald man took Will by the arm and led him to a table. "An ale for our hero. Please, Lord Norrington, sit, sit. Join us."

Will sat mechanically, staring at the sloshing wooden mug of ale that appeared before him.

His host called to the minstrel by the fire. "Songbird, play us something good." The man hesitated for a moment, then slapped Will on the back. "Sing to us of Squab. You'd be liking that, wouldn't you, m'lord?"

Will's eyes narrowed, as the hints of a shadow plan began to collect in his mind. "Yes, yes, I would like that." The young thief smiled up at his host. "Sing to me of Squab. There is much I want to learn."

CHAPTER 3

Kerrigan Reese shivered in his bed, huddled beneath a thick woolen blanket that smelled of sour sweat. The corpulent youth had pulled the blanket up over his head. He endeavored to keep still, so that the crackling scrunch of the mattress' straw couldn't drag him back to reality.

The shivers betrayed him, however. The tremors coaxed little sounds from the straw. The scrabbling of rodents, perhaps, or of insects. Or of beetles burrowing into a grave, devouring the flesh of the dead . . .

He shook his head, letting the resulting thunderclap of sound banish those thoughts. For a moment or two it worked, then the sounds returned. And beneath them, the buzzed roar of the common room's rabble: laughing, shouting, and singing some stupid song.

Kerrigan wondered how they could sing at a time like this. Everything had come crashing in on him. The world he had known in his first seventeen years had exploded like an alembic in a failed spellcasting. His life on Vilwan had been one of peace and comfort—though he had failed to recognize that at the time. His tutors had been severe taskmasters, but had taught him all manner of spells that no Human sorcerer had mastered in centuries. *If ever!*

He had known the way of the world, of the evil that was Chytrine. The grand history of Vilwan had informed him of the wars that had been fought against her. He had read of the loss of Vorquellyn and of the war before his birth. Okrannel had fallen to Chytrine's forces then, but she had been stopped at Fortress Draconis. The clear assumption had been that the last war had put a stop to her predations, but her renewed attacks against the Southlands gave lie to that idea.

And her attacks had destroyed his life.

Chytrine had formed an alliance with Vionna, the Pirate Queen of Wruona. The pirates had sent a fleet to attack Vilwan, complete with dragonels mounted aboard the ships. There was even a dragon. A fierce battle had raged at the northern tip of the island. The pirates had failed in their invasion, but not without exacting a terrible price.

Kerrigan did not know of that battle firsthand. He, like so many sorcerers his age and younger, had been evacuated from Vilwan. As the ships that had brought troops to Vilwan took Apprentices and Adepts away, the true focus of Chytrine's plan was revealed. Pirates attacked the evacuation fleet—destroying ships, devastating a whole generation of magickers. Kerrigan himself had been sorely wounded, and save for luck and circumstance would have died.

From there he had been made a plaything of Panqui juveniles, traveled to Yslin and on to Okrannel, where he had helped with the preparations for the siege of Svoin. He'd then been sent to steal a portion of the DragonCrown that Vionna's consort, the Azure Spider, had stolen from Jerana. On that quest his last tutor, Orla, had been slain.

And then there was the siege of Fortress Draconis and a second evacuation to the south. In that one, he had taken charge of a small company of children. He'd been unable to protect the young sorcerers who had been on the ship with him, but he vowed he would not let these children—the scions of the fortress' brave defenders—come to harm.

He'd borne up bravely through it all. He was able to acknowledge that, but once they'd reached Oriosa and he was freed of the vow he'd given the Draconis Baron, things had spiraled down into him. Orla, as she was dying, told him to have nothing further to do with Vilwan and to follow Crow and Resolute. Resolute clearly had nothing but contempt for him—it helped very little that Resolute seemed to hold *everyone* in contempt. Crow, who had been kindly and gentle, now languished in prison, leaving Kerrigan very much alone.

Strains of a melody leaked up from below and Kerrigan recognized it, which rather surprised him. Though he could wield great magicks, he couldn't carry a tune in a bucket. One of his mentors had a weakness for common tavern songs, and performers had come to Vilwan to entertain him—all for Kerrigan's benefit, of course. Kerrigan remembered none of the verses of this song, but the refrain came back strongly as the audience below joined in.

Now Squab is dead,
They've cut off his head,
And plied torch to his heart.

Garlic in his mouth,
Head buried facing south,
His body torn apart.
'Tis the way,
To treat cowards, they say.
'Specially those who think they're so smart.

The song would continue with some Squab misadventure or other, showing him a fool. Kerrigan did not doubt that Crow had been Hawkins. When the Oriosan authorities came to arrest him, Crow had warned Kerrigan to keep the secret the Draconis Baron had entrusted to him. Crow's cryptic and secretive behavior at that point had told Kerrigan that he was guilty as charged. But as for Crow's being *Squab,* that had surprised Kerrigan— primarily because Squab had always been a simpleton and Crow had been anything but.

The secret he'd been entrusted was now all he had. Reaching inside his layers of tunics, he fished out a leather sack heavy and bulging as if it housed an apple made of metal. As he opened it he did catch the glint of gold, but one that flashed scarlet after a moment. He poured the object into his right hand, then cupped his left beneath it, too.

Fortress Draconis had once housed three fragments of the DragonCrown Yrulph Kirûn had fashioned centuries before. After his defeat the Crown had been broken apart and the pieces scattered. The Draconis Baron had asked Kerrigan to fashion a decoy for the ruby fragment, then had given the true fragment to him, to let him carry it away during the evacuation.

The ruby set in gold glowed with a rich red light that slowly pulsed. The young magicker had once held another DragonCrown fragment, but it had remained lifeless and cold to his touch. This one had warmed while in his possession and as he brushed fingertips over it, the glow intensified where flesh touched stone.

Kerrigan had not noticed the light in the stone when he was at Fortress Draconis; he would have told the Draconis Baron if he had. It had first appeared on retreat from the fortress and had grown steadily since. He didn't know what it was, or why it was happening.

He probably should have been frightened, but he wasn't.

The ruby's glow suffused the tight, dark space beneath the blanket. Kerrigan studied it and it slowly pulsed. He could feel some warmth in his fingers—at least he thought he could—so he brought the gem closer to his face, to see if he could feel heat there.

He did, a little, but then the glow stopped pulsing and instead expanded into a scarlet tunnel that drew him in. Quick panic rose in him, throbbing through his stomach. A tingle ran over his body—the same sensation that prickles the hair at the nape of the neck when being watched unseen. Kerrigan tried to pull his head back, push his hands down, but found his body locked in a rictus as hard as the magickal armor that would rise through his flesh to protect him.

You are but a boy.

The words came softly, whispered and insubstantial, yet seeming to pierce the red haze that defined his world. He had no sense of his body, and yet no sense of freedom. It was as if his entire being drifted amorphously behind the point of his vision. He wanted to turn and look, to see if he could find whoever it was that spoke to him, but he couldn't.

There is nothing to see, boy, because you are within.

Two things came to Kerrigan immediately. First, he knew that whoever was speaking was reading his thoughts. He tried to shield them, but even the most rudimentary protection was knocked aside like a dry leaf before a gust of wind.

The second thing would have set him to trembling except that his body could not move. The words filled his mind like the swell of a wave, but they were but the foam at the crest: translated, distilled, strained, and predigested so he could grasp them. Beneath surged unprecedented power.

A million questions raced through his mind. Though he could make no sense of the chaos, the speaker—a female, of this he was certain—sorted through them as if they were a handful of coins. Trickles of something that might be amusement caressed him. He sought to concentrate.

More amusement met this effort. *You are quite learned, boy, but not yet wise. You are a child in your father's clothing, playing at being a man.*

The words—"boy," "child," "father," and "man"—rolled around in Kerrigan's mind. They had some of the nuances conferred on them by common convention, but there was more as well. He would have expected a sharper contrast between boy and man, yet both came tainted with a sense of youth, even infancy. Father and child should have possessed a greater affinity for each other, but instead there was a dislocation. It was as if father was used to acknowledge a biological connection with child, but hinted at none of the nurturing and education a parent would provide.

Kerrigan again focused. *Who are you?*

Mirth came full, but carried with it a whiplash sting. *Names have power, as well you know. But names have no power now, for us. We are players being played. Pawns. Our destinies intersect and spin away, then curl back again to fuse or destroy.*

He less heard the words than got a sense of soaring, wheeling, looping, and diving, as a bird might, riding the buffeting winds above a cliff. The sensation initially left him feeling light and quick, then, at the last, hit hard and he spun out of control.

A gentle presence caressed his mind and peace returned. *Forgive me, boy, for I have long been without company and have forgotten my strength.*

Kerrigan shivered. *I'm not a boy. And not a pawn.*

No pawn ever sees himself as a pawn.

Who controls me?

'Tis not so simple a game, Kerriganreese. Many play, many exert control. Ours is not to resist, but to know when we are being controlled. We cannot determine where we will fall, but perhaps how we will fall.

Confusion ripped through his mind. He had grown up with cryptic remarks galore on Vilwan; such was the way of wizards. He had always assumed these things were largely bluff, but here he was reading ripples on the surface of a deep ocean. While he wanted to know more, he also knew he'd drown.

Perhaps wiser after all. The words warmed him. *You know much must be done. You cannot do it alone. You are stronger than even you think, but your strength comes from your friends. Forget this, and the world will suffer.*

The sting came swift and brutal, stabbing deep into his belly. The paralysis released him. His body snapped forward and he rolled onto his left side, clutching the DragonCrown fragment to his belly. The flesh quivered and he tried to pull himself more tightly into a ball, but his girth prevented it. The agony in his middle cast lightning into the rest of him, but after a moment it evaporated, leaving him sweaty and cold.

As cold as the stone in his hands.

Kerrigan cast the blanket off and gulped down cooler air. He rolled onto his back and lay there gasping. He stared up at the shifting shadows and streaks of light cast up through the ill-fitting floorboards. Sweat stung his eyes, and he swiped at it with his hand before returning the fragment to the leather bag and tucking it back inside his shirt.

He had no idea what had just happened to him—no concrete idea, though he did have fragments. A mind had touched his. He knew it wasn't Chytrine, since she would have scourged him. This mind bore him no malice. The pain he'd known at the end had come because this mind's use of the word "suffer" carried with it far more import than the human word.

The word resurfaced in his mind and he saw it in fine script, as if a mask behind which something hid. *The way the Oriosan King hides his cowardice behind a mask.* In this case, however, the word covered something more terrible. It concealed a horror so overwhelming that were it to be unmasked it would shatter his mind.

Logic suggested that he had been speaking with a dragon. After all, the DragonCrown had been fashioned to make them subject to the owner. The one gem that Chytrine possessed gave her control over at least one dragon. Had he touched the mind of an enslaved dragon?

Kerrigan shifted his shoulders and sat upright. *That doesn't matter.*

Whether it was an enslaved dragon or some trick Chytrine had played upon him was immaterial. The suffering that mind knew would become a daily occurrence if Chytrine won.

The young magicker shook his head. With the help of his friends, he was determined this would never happen.

CHAPTER 4

With his arms flailing unsuccessfully to control his flight, the Tolsin guardsman landed hard on the round wooden table, shattering it completely. The short drop to the ground forced a grunt from him and caused his tin-pot helmet to bounce off. It clunked and danced across the floor, striking Call Mably full in the knee, which was, for Alexia, a consequence unintended but hardly unwelcomed.

Mably—a scrawny man with brown eyes and thin lines of hair covering his pate—hissed and clutched at his knee. He glanced up at her with a hot glare. He wore a leather mask of Oriosan green that had been festooned with a variety of marks and little badges to stress his authority as Tolsin's magistrate, and its gaudy display only served to undermine the glare's heat. He straightened up at his table in the Thistledown Tavern, and did his best to keep his voice even.

"To what do I owe this honor, Princess Alexia?"

Alexia took one step forward, pinning the guardsman's right hand to the floorboards. "I came to visit Crow, but this man was under the mistaken impression that no such visit would be allowed."

Mably's nostrils flared for a moment, then he picked up a small steaming bowl of mulled wine. "He was not mistaken. The Traitor is to be allowed no visitors."

Alexia frowned and turned her head partway to the left. She let her own gaze fall over a few of the tavern's patrons near the fireplace. As they abruptly looked down, pretending to mind their own business, she spoke softly. "If I heard you correctly, Magistrate, you said Crow would be allowed no visitors."

"I did, Princess."

"And you are under the mistaken impression that rule would apply to me?"

"I am."

Alyx walked over to him, the golden mail surcoat she wore rustling as she went. She leaned down, her gloved hands pressed firmly to the table, her nose a gnat's length from his. "I noted your impression was 'mistaken.'"

Mably's eyes hardened as much as they could, which meant they avoided looking as runny as soft-boiled eggs—but not by much. His voice tightened, rising in register. "I recall that. It was not."

"Ah, very good. Then consider this. I am a Princess of Okrannel. I am of the same rank as your King Scrainwood. King Augustus is married to a cousin of mine. If I were to choose to deem your prohibition an insult, then demand satisfaction of you, what do you think would happen? Do you think any of your people would stand against me? And do you think that if I slew the lot of them, you included, I would be censured or punished in any way at all? Don't nod, Mably. You might not be the smartest man alive, but you are not that stupid. I want to see Crow. I *will* see Crow. *Now!*"

She straightened up and hooked her thumbs behind the round buckle of her belt.

Mably reached for his wine coolly, but the ripples in the liquid as he grasped the bowl revealed his fear. He raised his left hand, flicking it casually toward the back of the tavern. "The princess wishes to see the prisoner. Let her pass."

"You are most kind."

Mably's voice grew cold. "Even you would not imagine you would be allowed to wear a weapon."

Her eyes tightened. "You have my word of honor . . ."

"Yours, yes, but not his. You see my predicament, Princess. Your sword belt, please."

Alexia unbuckled it and slid it off. Then she rebuckled it and hung it from a peg on one of the tavern's wooden columns. Unrestrained by the belt, the mail hung on her like a girl's summer shift, rustling loudly as she crossed to the back corner. There, a corpulent guard struggled to his feet, pried a wooden chair off his ample buttocks, then moved it aside from the trapdoor leading down into the cellar.

As the man opened the door, she took a lantern from a wall peg and turned the wick up. The opened trapdoor revealed a steep set of ladderlike steps, and cold and moist air washed over her as she descended. The guard closed the door over her head and the scraping sounds from above indicated he'd resumed his post. She listened closely to see if Mably was ordering him to keep her imprisoned, but she heard nothing. A pity. While she hoped the magistrate would do something stupid, he was too much of a coward to strike openly.

Since it was a small town, Tolsin didn't have much need of a gaol to house prisoners. When Crow had arrived someone had decided they needed a place to keep him—and the best option turned out to be the root cellar below the Thistledown. Alexia was fairly certain that Mably owned the tavern or had an interest in it, and that the Oriosan government would be charged for keeping Crow safe.

As nearly as she could tell, the preparations for housing Crow had been kept to a minimum. A corner of the cellar had been cleared and a patch of straw had been spread out. An eyebolt had been hitched to a rafter and from it hung chains that ended in manacles. The chains were long enough that Crow could lie down, and that surprised Alexia.

The light from her lantern finally touched Crow himself, bleeding some color into what had been the white ghost of a figure huddled in the corner. He'd been stripped of his clothing, and while his long white hair and beard suggested antiquity, his body was still that of a younger man. His left leg remained slightly swollen from broken bones that had only been partially healed by magick. A single scar started at his hairline to the right side of his face, came down over his cheek, then picked up two companions at his collarbone, which then traced down past his hip and thigh to his knee. A plethora of other scars, all white with age, crisscrossed his body.

Alexia gasped—not because of his nakedness or the scars, but because of the new livid bruises on his chest, his arms, legs, and face. His lower lip had been split and his left eye was all but swollen shut. A crust of blood matted the hair at his right temple and one bruise on his chest clearly bore the imprint of a bootheel.

Her gasp snapped his good eye open. Anger rather than fear flashed through it, then the right corner of his mouth tugged back in a smile. "Princess. I am honored. Forgive me for not getting up."

Alexia shook her head and crouched down, setting the lantern at the edge of the straw. "They beat you?"

"They were provoked."

She frowned. "You went with them peacefully. You wouldn't do anything stupid."

He snorted, and his smile stretched the split lip. "Your confidence in me is gratifying. I am afraid I did provoke them."

"How?"

He raised his hands. "They'd looped the chain high enough that I couldn't lie down." His right eye sparkled as he separated his hands, then, quickly, slammed his wrists together. The manacles hit hard with a muffled clang, then the right one sprang open. "A manacle is only as good as the spring that keeps the catch shut. I unwound a bunch of the chain from around the rafter. After that I helped myself to some of the provisions down here. They have some passable wine in that cask over there, and there is some good cheese in that wooden box."

Alexia smiled in spite of herself. "So, I shouldn't have been worried about you at all?"

He winced as he shifted more fully onto his left hip. "Not concerning my hunger. As it was, they decided I had some sort of key in my clothes, so they took them. Then they decided I needed a lesson."

"I'll make sure they get you some clothes. I'm freezing myself down here, and I've got a quilted gambeson on under this mail." She rubbed her gloved hands over her arms. "You won't have to endure the cold tonight."

He shrugged. "I've been in far colder climes and survived, but your kindness is appreciated, Highness."

"Crow, you should call me Alyx."

"Highness, we have been through this before."

"Times are different, Crow. Before you didn't want any familiarity because you said our causes would someday force us apart. You didn't want to be a liability. I didn't know what you were talking about then, but now that I do, it doesn't matter."

Crow snapped the manacle back around his right wrist. "Highness, I wasn't thinking about who I had been when I said that. And I must apologize for misleading you. I would have gladly shared with you all I knew of your father. I didn't know him long or well, but I respected him. That I could not act to save his life is the single greatest regret of my life."

"Crow, I said none of that mattered." Alexia sank forward onto her knees and pressed her palms to her thighs. "Yes, I do want to hear from you about my father, but we have a more pressing problem. Mably's intention is to take you to Meredo, where you will be executed."

Crow nodded slowly, then rested his head against the corner. "He's taken pains to let me know my fate. In great detail, in fact. I gather he's hoping to ride one of the horses they use to tear me apart."

"Crow, I'm not going to let that happen."

"Princess, there is nothing you can do to stop it. We are in Oriosa. Scrainwood has hated me for a very long time, and he has cause to do so. I knew, coming back here, that I risked my life. The simple fact of it was, though, I had to. I had to get Will to safety, return Ryhope, and get whatever it was the Draconis Baron wanted gone from the fortress away."

The scrabbling of a rat in the straw caught her attention for a moment, then she looked back at him. "You're wrong that I can't do anything to save you."

"Highness, I have no doubt you could save me." He laughed lightly. "You could toss me over your shoulder as if I were some lace-laden damsel in a bard's song and cut your way out of here, but then what? It's not that you can't save me, it is that you *should not*. Remember, you're here to convince the crowned heads to commit to fighting Chytrine. Allying yourself with me will not help you.

"Scrainwood hates me because I know he's a coward. Twenty-five years ago I told the crowned heads that they were cowards. I told them Chytrine had vowed to return. For them to follow the plans of anyone associated with me will make people question their leadership and judgment."

"If they were that foolish or cowardly, it should be called into question."

He shook his head. "I won't debate that point. You have to remember that if you are going to lead forces to oppose Chytrine, you *need* forces to lead. If you make rulers choose between you and the appearance of competence, what choice do you think they will make?"

"That doesn't hold for all of them, Crow. Queen Carus of Jerana is fairly new to her throne. She's not bound by her father's judgment. What's been done to you is an injustice."

"Yes, but an injustice that has endured for over two decades. The men who beat me weren't even born when I was stripped of my mask, but they believe every single thing they've been taught about me since they were children. Even if you and King Augustus and Queen Carus stand up and say it was a mistake, they won't believe you.

"But, Highness, you are right. Queen Carus can claim she was deceived about me. You have to take a lesson from her and claim that, too. You have to walk away from me. You have to claim that I fooled you, and you have to be angry about it. Don't let my efforts here be wasted. You'll gain by renouncing me, and your gain will be Chytrine's discomfort."

Alexia shook her head so adamantly that her thick blonde braid lashed past her shoulder and almost whipped his cheek. "No, I'm not going to do that. I've thought about this. A lot. You're a friend. You saved my life. I care about you, and I don't abandon people who matter."

"Princess, I won't drag you down with me."

"You won't drag me down. As you said before, I am strong enough to carry you, Crow." She stood and looked down at him. "I have a plan. It will save your life, and it is frightfully simple. I'm going to marry you."

Crow knelt there, his mouth open, then slowly began to chuckle. His shoulders shifted, then he sagged back into the corner. "Oh, very good, Princess. Cruel to joke with me like that, but very good."

"It's not a joke, Crow."

His head came up, his right eye a crescent slit full of fear. "It had better be a joke."

"No. It works perfectly. I marry you and you become my Prince Consort.

This raises you to such a level of nobility that Scrainwood cannot carry out a summary execution. You will get another trial, since a trial *in absentia* is not recognized as binding in any treaty between Okrannel and Oriosa. Moreover, you were tried on charges of treason, and since you will become a citizen of Okrannel when we marry, the charges will no longer apply. The best they could do would be espionage and that would fail because you would have to be tried before your peers, and no royal would want that sort of precedent set. Scrainwood *could* demand personal satisfaction for any insult you gave him, but we both know he won't do that."

"Forgive me, Highness, but are you insane? Your plan might be clever, but it is wasted. You will burn a lot of political capital and for no good reason."

"I hardly think you are 'no good reason.'"

"Highness, listen to me, please." Crow's hands curled into pale fists. "Your loyalty to me . . . I can't tell you what that means, but it is misplaced. You have to make sure Will can oppose Chytrine. You have to see that Kerrigan fulfills his potential. You have to raise an army to destroy Chytrine. You can't let yourself be distracted by my fate."

Alexia stepped toward him and crouched again, her shadow spilling across his scarred flesh. "What I see clearly is that *your* fate is tied up with mine, Will's, Kerrigan's, Vorquellyn, and Chytrine. If I let you die, I'm letting the world die." She reached out and stroked her right hand over the left side of his face, keeping her thumb from touching his black eye. "I'm not letting either die. We'll get a priest in here and have him marry us this afternoon."

"No." Crow shook his head. "Even if we did marry, no one would believe it. It would be assumed to be a trick, which it would be."

"They would have to believe it. We would have witnesses."

"They would say they lied."

She snorted. "They would not dare say *I* lied."

"They would, just not to your face. Before you they would say that I tricked you into it. No, Highness, abandon this plan."

"Crow, it will save your life."

"And ruin yours." He reached up and took her hand in his. "Princess." His voice dropped to a whisper. "Alexia, promise me you won't do this. I won't agree, so the effort will be wasted. Don't. Please."

She squeezed his fingers. "You will resist, won't you?"

He nodded.

"Then I will have to find another plan." She stood slowly, then leaned over and picked up the lantern again. "I am not letting you die."

Crow's right eye sparkled. Was that a tear forming in the corner? "Just worry about the world, Highness. The world you can save. Nothing else matters."

CHAPTER 5

Will awoke muzzy-headed. It wasn't that he'd drunk too much the night before but that he'd stayed up much too late, and Resolute's dawn rising had left him perilously short of sleep. While he had managed to burrow back into the blankets and tried to use them to shut out the light, his efforts failed. He dozed and awoke a half-dozen times before surrendering, slipping from bed and getting dressed.

Despite being half-asleep, he did pull on his mask, tying it into place before he left the room. Prior to the previous night, he'd seen that mask as silly. As a thief he'd always known the value of wearing a mask, but that was to preserve anonymity. An Oriosan mask did just the opposite, proclaiming all manner of details about the person behind it. It struck him as not a little ironic that the customary tool of a thief here allowed him to scout out potential targets by interpreting mask decorations that indicated prosperity or nobility.

And while he'd worn his mask since Yslin, he'd been wearing it to humor those backing the army. But the previous night in the common room, he'd watched how common folk were treating him. They were reading the mask and believing what it proclaimed. They knew it had been given to him by the king, and that he was *the Norrington*. To them, it didn't matter that he'd been a thief. The simple fact was that he had been given a mask that elevated him, and it made all the difference.

Part of him wanted to dismiss the mask as nonsense, but he didn't. First—and it pained him to admit it—was the fact that the people really were looking to him as their hope against Chytrine. Their faith surprised him, for in the den of thieves where he grew up, having faith in someone was the first step to being betrayed. Had he wanted to wring money from those who believed in him, he could have had whatever they possessed in a heartbeat.

He didn't want their money, however. He wanted their good wishes and hopes. He had a mission—saving Crow—and his mask told those in Tolsin that he was to be trusted. It gave him a legitimacy he never would have had otherwise, and he was determined to use that power to save his friend.

And while it surprised him that he was employing so valuable a tool for someone else's benefit, he also acknowledged that the world was no longer as it had been just six months earlier.

Will wandered down the stairs and through the inn's common room. He nodded in response to the innkeeper's greeting, then headed out into the town. The coming winter had left a chill in the air, but the sun's caress warmed him. The sun had long since climbed above the Bokagul Mountains to the south, and somewhere between that and Tolsin lay the city of Valsina, the home of the Norrington family. His father's wife controlled the estates, holding it for her children—allegedly his half brothers. Bosleigh Norrington had acknowledged the two boys as his, but dark rumors suggested he had not sired them.

Tolsin itself wasn't very impressive, though it was large enough to support two inns and a third tavern, as well as a smith and several carpenters and woodwrights. It had a market square in the heart of town, with farmers and traveling merchants selling their wares.

As Will wandered, eyeing the Thistledown Tavern for any signs of easy ingress, he recognized some folks from the inn's common room the night before. He exchanged a kind word or a wave, and noticed they warmed to his attention. Six months previous he would have been calculating how much he could take them for, but now he found himself thinking about how his failure would mean doom for them all.

"Good morning, my lord." The voice remained soft, despite a certain keenness of tone. Sephi slipped her hand through the crook of his right arm and smiled at him. "I need to speak to you."

Will kept his expression impassive as he looked at her. She'd pulled her black hair back into a thick braid, and her hazel eyes shone from within the depths of a dark brown mask. It had an orphan's notch cut at the bottom of the left eyehole, indicating her father was dead. Will wondered for a moment if Distalus, the man she had been traveling with in Alcida, had been her father. *No question that he's dead.*

Sephi pressed her lips into a flat line when he failed to greet her immediately. "Please, Lord Norrington. I know you think I have done you a grievous wrong."

You betrayed Crow! He wanted to shove her away. He might have done just that, save for two things. The first was that, since she had been a spy in the employ of the Oriosan government, she might be of use. *To save Crow I will use anyone and anything at hand, and not regret a moment of it.*

The other was that hint of pleading in her voice. She wanted him to understand why she had done what she did, and that meant she could give him information—trading it for forgiveness. Information he desperately wanted, so he answered her with a nod.

"Yes, Sephi, if that is your name, what you did hurt me." He drew in a deep breath, then slowly exhaled. His voice remained even, but his tone was cold. "Crow saved your life and you turned him over to enemies who will kill him."

Her shoulders slumped. "That is how it seems, I know. And, yes, I am Sephi. Please, my lord, I would have you know why I acted as I did."

"It doesn't matter."

"But it matters to me. You are the Norrington, and I've hurt you."

Will stopped and turned to face her, placing his left hand over hers. He let a little warmth filter into his voice, promising a healing of the rift. "I'm sure you did what you did because you thought it was right."

"Yes, that's it exactly." She nodded solemnly, then lowered her voice. "I feel I can confide in you, my lord, because we have seen each other naked."

A small jolt ripped through Will. Back during the summer Crow, Resolute, and he had run into Sephi in Alcida. They'd rescued her from a band of gibberkin. Her companions had been slain and she had been hurt. While they had traveled together for a number of days, he'd never seen the tall, slender girl naked. Will was certain he'd have remembered that.

Then it struck him. *When we met, she had no mask!* For her to be without a mask was to be as vulnerable as he might have felt without clothes. *And Crow had his mask stripped from him!* Will couldn't even begin to imagine how much that must have hurt his friend.

He nodded slowly to the girl and began his manipulation. "Yes, Sephi, you can trust me. Since being made aware of who I am, well, considerations wear on me, but I know how important trust is. And, I will admit, I did feel betrayed by you."

"But, Will, I mean, Lord Norrington, I didn't . . . that wasn't my intent." She sighed heavily. "My lord, you have to understand, I grew up here in Oriosa. I grew up with tales of the Traitor, and Oriosans felt his betrayal more keenly than others. The Norrington Prophecy, the one that predicted your coming, had previously been taken to refer to your grandfather, and then to your father. When Lord Norrington went out to fight Chytrine, there was much rejoicing, and when he failed and went over to serve the Aurolani Empress, we knew despair. Worse yet, he had been betrayed by Hawkins, the coward. And then, to expunge the evil of your grandfather murdering Queen

Lanivette, your father headed north to do what that proud band of heroes failed to do.

"You know well what happened. Your father, brave though he was, fell prey to the blandishments of Chytrine." She lowered her voice again and led him down into an alley between the town's main stable and carpentry shop. "Distalus said that your father had tried to get Chytrine to free those who had become her *sullanciri*. She tricked him, and his father talked him into joining her."

Will shivered. He'd met his father. He was now a twisted creature serving Chytrine as herald or ambassador. From stories it was obvious that his father had not been well when he went north, and whatever Chytrine had done to him had not healed him.

Sephi continued. "You know the tale of Nefrai-kesh killing Queen Lanivette—I was there when Distalus told it to you. He didn't tell the whole thing, though. When the *sullanciri* grabbed her, he held her head in his hands before he twisted it off. He told her how Chytrine hated the Traitor, and that Oriosa was going to be the first nation she destroyed, since it was Hawkins' home. He told her that Hawkins was still alive, and that while he lived, Oriosa would always be in jeopardy. Then he killed her by twisting her head off."

Will frowned. "How did Distalus know this?"

"Because the king was there, my lord. Prince Scrainwood was there, beating on the *sullanciri,* trying to get him to free the queen. He could not, and Nefrai-kesh placed the queen's severed head in the prince's hands, then promised to come back for him. He said he would come back if Hawkins was not dead.

"This is why, my lord, when the king ascended to the throne, Hawkins was tried *in absentia* and sentenced to death. Chytrine took that as a sign, and that is why Oriosa was spared, even temporarily. King Scrainwood then sent agents out, agents like me, to scourge the Southlands to find Hawkins—and to find you. He wanted you safe, so you could destroy Chytrine and save our nation."

"He wanted me found? He already had the Norringtons in Valsina."

Sephi shook her head. "They're big enough to look the part of heroes, but they don't look the part of your father's son. You fit perfectly, and I know you will fulfill the prophecy."

The thief had no difficulty reading sincerity in her words. He couldn't explain exactly why he knew she was telling the truth, but years of dealing with the best liars in Yslin's underworld had let him sort fact from fiction. She wanted him to believe her, and he did.

"How is it, then, Sephi, that you managed to identify Crow as Hawkins? You weren't even born when the Traitor was exiled."

She shifted her shoulders uneasily. "I didn't, not really. After you rescued me, there were things that had been taken from my possessions. Distalus had been keeping notes and I had to assume they had fallen into the wrong hands. I didn't know who any of you were, but I took some things while we were together. From you I had a gnawed bone, a piece of bloodied cloth from Resolute, a lock of Crow's hair. When I got to Yslin, I turned them over to the king's sorcerers and they used magick to identify them. They actually didn't figure out Crow was the Traitor until they returned to Meredo. By then Crow was in Okrannel and they lost track of him until they received a message saying he was escorting Princess Ryhope south from Fortress Draconis. I was sent here to Tolsin to identify him."

Will nodded, knowing she'd left out some details, but that hardly mattered at the moment. "When you saw Crow again, Sephi, did you remember he had saved your life? Did you remember how he cared for your wounds?"

Her hand tightened on his forearm. "My lord, you have to understand. All my life I had been taught to hate the Traitor and love my king. When I entered the crown's service, bringing him to justice and ending the threat to our nation was a sacred goal. And then, when the sorcerers made the match, I was summoned to the capital. I was feted and praised. The king himself told me he was so proud of me. I was . . . well, I did not think clearly. I didn't think at all until I had identified him and had told his brother who he was. The pain in Colonel Hawkins' eyes, the hatred I knew I would see in yours . . ."

She hesitated for a moment. "I know that what I did was not wrong. I had been trained to it. I had to do it to save my nation. But I also know what Crow did on Wruona. I know now what he did at Svoin . . ."

Will nodded. "Last night they were singing Squab songs. In them, he's a coward. He's the first to run, the first to snivel, always deserving of a boot in the rear. Listening to the songs, all I could think was that this wasn't Crow."

Sephi nodded slowly, and Will gave her a smile. "Sephi, I know—Crow knows—that you were only doing your duty. You had no choice, but I also think you know that Crow isn't Squab. There is no way anyone who was such a coward would spend a quarter century fighting Chytrine. And there is no way such a coward would inspire such fear in Chytrine that she would blackmail a whole nation into trying to kill him. The fact that she so wants him dead should tell you everything you need to know about him."

Her eyes widened with the full import of his comment and her hand rose to cover her mouth. "Oh! What have I done?"

"It's not what you have done, Sephi, that is important. It is done." Will let warmth flood his voice and he began to offer her a way to rectify her errors. "And I would not ask you to betray your beliefs or your friends. The simple fact of things is this. Since we now know how much Chytrine fears Crow, we know that he is a key to her defeat. If Crow dies, she wins—and we can't allow that."

"Oh, my lord, I will do anything..." Sephi clutched his arm, then loosened her grip, her voice shrinking to a whisper. "You do not trust me, and with good cause. If I thought I deserved it, I would beg your forgiveness."

Will smiled and reached up to stroke her cheek. "Sephi, the last thing I would want is for you to get into trouble. I do not want you to compromise your beliefs. There *is* something you can do to help, though, if you would be willing."

She nodded solemnly. "Anything, my lord."

Will aped her nod, then glanced about conspiratorially before lowering his voice. She leaned closer in anticipation and he knew he had her. He'd shown her how actions she thought would save her nation were actually going to do it harm. She would do anything to fix that, as he intended. In Yslin he'd not have cared one whit about using her, but here it made him a bit uneasy. *Still, she got Crow into trouble, so she can help get him out again.*

He spoke just above a whisper. "Just keep your eyes and ears open. I know you are good at that. If you hear or see anything that would help Crow's situation, let me know. This is especially true in Meredo, since you know the city."

"Yes, Lord Norrington, I will. I promise." She sighed again. "When I met you, I knew you were special. I just didn't know how special. I am glad my judgment then was good, and you have proven it here. Thank you, my lord."

He gave her a wink. "Your keeping faith with Oriosa tells me a lot about my new nation, Sephi. Now, if we work together, we can guarantee its future."

"Yes, my lord, exactly." She slid her hand from his arm, then pulled away and headed back toward the street. "You will hear from me."

Will nodded and watched her go. That minor pang of guilt over having manipulated her sparked in him again, but his sense of betrayal smothered it effectively. He wasn't certain what she would do to help Crow, or how helpful she would be in accomplishing that task, but it didn't hurt to have her on his side.

And if she was playing me, as she tried to do before? Will shrugged and stalked back toward the street. He was Lord Norrington. If she chose to spy on him and betray him to Scrainwood, well, she'd have to work hard to find something to betray. *By the time she could have anything good, I'll have learned enough to protect myself.*

Smiling, Will returned to his stroll through Tolsin and could see, from the expressions others wore, his smile was a good omen indeed.

CHAPTER 6

Kerrigan Reese huddled as best he could in the shadows and shivered. The cool night air had little to do with his discomfort, as he was bundled up against it and swathed in black woolen clothes that rendered him invisible. He even sank to one knee, as did the expedition's leaders, though he knew he'd be at a sore disadvantage when called upon to move quickly.

Kerrigan shivered because the last time he had engaged in this sort of secret operation, Orla had died. Granted, the streets of Tolsin were not the streets of the Wruonin pirate haven, and the local constabulary was not a band of bloodthirsty cutthroats who just happened to have a *sullanciri* visiting them. Still, he'd made a mistake then, and his mentor had paid dearly for it.

Well, at least the princess thinks this is a good idea. He let his shoulders slump a little. *Then again, she's not here.*

In front of him, shrouded in black, Resolute and Will knelt to study the Thistledown Tavern. The squat, two-story building didn't look like much, with its thick thatched roof and tiny windows. The dim light leaking out from behind the warped glass suggested the miserly distribution of candles, but that suited their purpose perfectly.

Two men stood beside the door on guard duty, stamping their feet against the cold. The two of them might have been enough to daunt Tolsin's criminal element, but not the crew that had assembled that night. Resolute could have slain either of them in an instant, and Will was no slouch in combat. Dranae—a massive human warrior, with dark hair, a full beard, and blue eyes—crouched beside Kerrigan. The man towered over him and weighed more than he did, despite not having an ounce of fat on him. Kerrigan would have loved to be that strong, but his life on Vilwan had not exactly been physically demanding. Dranae carried a short wooden staff that hardly looked like much of a weapon, but in a strong man's hands it could break bones.

The last two members of the company carried no weapons. Qwc, a Spritha, clung to the eaves of the building against which Kerrigan huddled. The lack of light made his green carapace look black, but his four wings still managed to flicker as if trapping starlight. His upper pair of hands smoothed his antennae while the lower pair and his feet kept him anchored to the wall. Though only a foot tall, Qwc's speed and ability to fly made him useful.

His voice buzzed low. "Just two, just two there."

Resolute nodded. "Lombo?"

Kerrigan glanced back over his shoulder at the creature hulking there. The Panqui was an intelligent beast who had once been a Wruonin pirate until he had been betrayed and almost slain. Huge, with bony plates armoring his flesh, long retractable claws, and a jutting muzzle full of teeth, he looked more than sufficient to tear the town apart, much less two guards before some tavern. In battle against Chytrine's forces the Panqui had gleefully attacked and killed Grand Temeryces, coming away without a scratch.

Lombo raised his muzzle and sniffed, his ears flattening back along his skull. "Two outside. More inside. And Crow."

The Vorquelf nodded, then turned back to look at Kerrigan. "Your turn, Adept. Can you do it?"

Kerrigan frowned for a moment, then flicked fingers at the building. The spell he cast sped unseen at the tavern, then raced back to him, allowing him to view it with *mageyes*. For him, the night's gloom vanished and the building lit up, with each living creature glowing more brightly than the candles. Aside from the two men by the door, three more people occupied the upper floor. One was sleeping and the other two were . . .

Kerrigan blushed and refocused on the ground floor and the basement. Four men remained in the tavern itself, and he picked up two more individuals in the cellar. They were very close, but one lay on the ground while the other fairly blazed with activity. "Someone is down there with him and is kicking him."

Will turned, eyes narrowing. "Stop him."

The young mage opened his mouth to explain that while casting the spell in question was simple, focusing it to hit the people in the basement would be trickier. But the look in Will's eyes indicated that an explanation would be wasted. While Kerrigan knew his Vilwanese tutors would have berated him soundly for using his skills in an illegal activity, he drew in a deep breath, set his shoulders, then opened his palms and let the spell ripple out.

The magick flowed out effortlessly, moving through the night like fog. The two guards collapsed in boneless heaps by the door. Within the tavern itself, the sleeper upstairs burrowed deeper into the covers and the other two relaxed into sleep; even falling out of bed didn't waken the one of them. The guards on the ground floor toppled to the floor or sagged in their chairs. And in the basement, the man who had been kicking Crow dropped to the ground as if he had been poleaxed.

Kerrigan smiled and Will began to head toward the building. The magicker grabbed his wrist. "Wait."

"Why?"

A series of staccato thumps sounded from around the building. Plump little creatures fell from the eaves and a couple more plopped down from the roof. Will craned his head forward, then shivered. "Rats?"

"There will be more inside, so be careful."

The Vorquelf raised a hand and pointed to the building. Qwc flew straight away to it, then keened a high tone. The others followed in his wake, with Lombo hefting the two fallen guardsmen. Dranae and Kerrigan appropriated their spears and helmets, then took up the guard positions while Will unlocked the tavern door with a click. Lombo, the Vorquelf, and Will disappeared inside. The Spritha then launched himself into the air and began a circling patrol.

Kerrigan really didn't expect much trouble. Princess Alexia and her Gyrkyme companion, Perrine, had hosted a dinner for Call Mably and the other local nobility. They'd all been seated well above the salt, while the present company had lurked below it, pretending to drink far too much and stumbling off to bed while the others engaged in discussions of world affairs and other important events. None of the guests would be allowed to leave until Alexia declared the festivities at an end, and she'd not do that until Qwc returned and let her know the night's adventure had succeeded.

Dranae fitted the dented helmet on his head. "Your control of magick is impressive, Adept Reese."

Kerrigan blinked. "Oh, no, I was very sloppy." He toed one of the sleeping rats. "If I had concentrated, I could have gotten just the men. Oh, and the dog in the corner, too. I just let the spell go and got everything in there. I should have been more precise."

"But Adept Reese, I was under the impression that outside the realm of combat magicks, humans did not have the discipline necessary to work magick on living creatures. In fact, isn't the spell you used part of an elven healing regime to make the injured sleep while other healing spells take effect?"

"Well, yes, but . . ." Kerrigan frowned. "On Vilwan I had elven instructors. I just did what they taught me to."

"You learned your lessons very well."

"How is it that you know about magick?" Kerrigan tried to keep his voice even. "No disrespect intended, but..."

"But I hardly seem like a scholar?" The big man shrugged and tapped the helmet over the left side of his head. "You know that Crow, Resolute, and Will rescued me from a squad of gibberkin. They had made me a prisoner and hit me in the head. I don't remember anything from before I joined with Crow, so I can't answer. Could be it was something I overheard while on Vilwan, fighting the pirates. There were elven healers there, so that's probably the answer."

Kerrigan nodded easily. "Elven magick is very difficult to learn because it is different than human magick. Human magick you construct, whereas elven magick flows and grows."

Any further discussion of magick ended with the tavern's door opening. Resolute emerged first and Lombo followed, dragging a guardsman in each hand. He sat them beside the door, with their backs against the building. Will exited last and relocked the door while Dranae and Kerrigan returned the helmets to their respective owners.

Resolute frowned as he took the helmet Kerrigan had put on the man's head and turned it around properly. "It's done."

Kerrigan smiled. "It worked?"

Will laughed. "Perfect, Kerrigan. When all this is over, you and me are going to be unstoppable. You drop the guards, and I'll get the goods."

The Vorquelf glanced down at the thief. "You didn't steal anything, did you, boy?"

Will's nostrils flared. "That wasn't part of the plan. No."

"Good. Then move."

The five figures hustled away from the tavern. Kerrigan hesitated in the shadows from which he had cast the spell. "Do you want me to wake them up?"

"No."

"Yes."

Kerrigan looked first from Resolute to Will. "Which?"

The Vorquelf shook his head. "Let them wake at dawn as they normally would."

Will groaned. "But that means the guy in the basement will stay sleeping."

"Let him. It just postpones things."

Dranae raised an eyebrow. "The one who was kicking Crow? What did you do to him?"

Resolute shrugged. "The ladder down into the cellar is steep. He fell. Broke his leg."

Will nodded. "A really nasty break, too, with the bone poking out and everything."

Kerrigan blanched. "You broke his leg deliberately?"

"I wanted to break both of them, and then stuff his thumbs up..."

"Enough, Will." Resolute urged them on through the town, pressing a hand over Kerrigan's spine. "There are times, Adept Reese, when petty evils need to be met with painful retribution. The man will recover, but anytime he goes to kick someone else, he will remember. It's not much of a victory, but for this night's work, it will do."

The rustle of feathers that announced Perrine's arrival came more quietly than the dawn's scrabbling of waking pigeons in the eaves. Alyx smiled and leaned out the window as the Gyrkyme folded her wings. Perrine had the coloration of a falcon, which was common for the Gyrkyme warrior caste, with dark brown feathers over shoulders and back, which shaded to cream over her breasts and belly and were dappled with brown. Large amber eyes flickered with intelligence, though the brown fletching around them did make her look as if tears had stained her face. The fierce grin belied any sadness, however.

"You were right, sister, they gathered at the far end of the town, thinking to go around as they headed to the capital. Lombo has squatted in the gate, and seems oblivious to the two guards beating him with sticks."

Alyx shook her head. "I'd best get down there in case he decides to notice. Will you...?"

Perrine screeched happily and launched herself into the morning air with a powerful beat of her wings. "Not too much blood, I promise."

"Thank you, my sister."

Alexia turned and stalked through her room, leaving her baggage and sword behind. As was her custom, she had braided her hair into a thick queue and tied it off with a black leather thong. She'd attired herself in a simple doeskin tunic and trousers to match, though they had been dyed black. She'd tucked them into her boots and belted the tunic with a wide belt into which she had tucked her gloves. Accustomed as she was to wearing her coat of mail, she felt light and almost naked without it as she flew down the stairs and out into the street.

It didn't take her long to cross the distance from the inn to where Call Mably and his squad of guards had gathered. Lombo still squatted in the gateway, with the splintered bits of sticks littering the ground around him. Perrine perched on top of the gate, gazing balefully down at Mably, and Qwc had lighted on Crow's shoulder. Around them, various townfolk had begun to assemble.

Alexia smiled as she broke into the circle and grabbed hold of Mably's horse's bridle. "Magistrate Mably, had you told me you intended to leave at this hour, I would have adjourned our celebration earlier."

Were it not for the green mask he wore, Mably's face would have had no color. Alexia revised her initial assessment quickly, for his eyes were rather red and his skin actually hinted at the color of his mask. She resisted the temptation to spook his horse, which easily would have spilled him from the saddle and quite probably induced vomiting.

"Princess, I thought not to trouble you with such a mundane thing as moving the prisoner."

"You might not think I have an interest in that, Magistrate, but where my husband goes, so go I."

Mably's red eyes all but bugged from his mask. "What?"

Even Crow's head came up. "Princess, don't." He clearly wanted to offer more of a protest, but lacked the energy. He'd been set in the saddle and tied there; his wrists were also heavily bound. A threadbare grey blanket had been thrown over him, but fell only to mid-thigh, letting everyone see his bare, bruised legs.

Mably raised his head. "You claim this man is your husband?"

Alexia nodded. "He is."

"She's lying."

Mably smiled. "He denies it, Princess."

"He's delirious, and no wonder, after the treatment he's had at your hands." Alexia smiled warmly. "As well you know, Oriosan custom does allow a wife to travel with her husband while he is being taken for judgment."

"Judgment has been rendered, he is bound for punishment. The custom does not apply." Mably snorted. "Besides, he denies you are married."

"And you have maintained he is Hawkins, the Traitor, who is a notorious liar, so how can you believe him?" She held up her left hand and thumbed a gold ring around her fourth finger. "We are wedded. We were wedded in a ceremony in Kedyn's Temple at Fortress Draconis. Prince Erlestoke was a witness."

Crow growled. "Mably, you are not so much a fool as to believe this, are you?"

"Hush, beloved." The princess looked from Crow back up to Mably. "Look at his hand, Magistrate; you'll see his ring. Even the most simple of magickers could tell you our rings are linked as they should be after such a ceremony."

The bureaucrat snarled. "He had no ring when we took him into custody."

"Your search of his person failed to find it."

"You had no ring on last night."

"You simply failed to see it." Alyx snorted. "A consequence of being blind drunk, it would seem."

Mably shook his head once, hard, then hissed in pain. "Princess, you know the only magicker worth the name here in Tolsin is Adept Reese, and I would trust what he says about those rings. You are lying."

"She's not lying."

Alexia turned and saw a slender, dark-haired woman emerge from the crowd. Anger flashed through her, and above the gate Perrine's wings unfurled. *That is Sephi, the woman who betrayed Crow to Scrainwood. What is her game?*

Mably's head came up. "What are you prattling on about, girl?"

Sephi's eyes blazed. "I said she is not lying. They are wed."

"More nonsense."

"Is it?" Sephi's voice took on an edge. "You know well who I am, Call Mably. I am the king's eyes and ears. I was sent here to confirm the Traitor's identity. I know all about him, and I know they are wed."

The magistrate shifted his shoulders. "Why didn't you tell me this before?"

"Magistrate, you are only meant to know that which the king wishes you to know. Are you smarter than he is? The king's answer to that question would differ from yours, I am certain." Sephi shook her head. "I reveal this knowledge to prevent you from doing something stupid, like parading a Prince of Okrannel through Oriosa naked. I will not have you embarrassing our nation."

The magistrate slumped in his saddle. "This is not right. There was no ring on his finger."

"That's because the princess is lying."

"Shut up!" Mably's shout silenced Crow, but clearly cost him mightily. He breathed hard for several seconds, then glared down at Alexia. "This *is* trickery, I know it. I will not be made a fool."

The princess stepped back and opened her hands. "If you choose to call me a liar, I will demand satisfaction of you. You may choose between that and believing the king's spy here and letting me accompany my husband to Meredo."

"Just you, Princess."

"Of course, just me. And my bodyguards."

Mably groaned.

Alyx smiled. "You know they will be there regardless, Magistrate. Do not fight a battle you cannot win."

"This is a skirmish, Princess, and one you have won." Mably drew himself up in the saddle again. "In Meredo the battle shall be decided, and it shall not be in your favor."

CHAPTER 7

The group rode from Tolsin at noon and Alyx was pleased at how well the morning's events had worked out; though she did acknowledge that her feelings might not be shared by all. Call Mably clearly was not happy; she could feel his hot stare burning into her back. Mably rode at the head of the rear guard, having been chased there by Resolute. The Tolsin magistrate had left the town at the head of the procession but as some of the guardsmen moved out to scout along the route, Mably found himself in the middle of her group and beat a hasty retreat.

It did not help Mably at all that the guardsmen had seen him faced down by Sephi. This left him weak enough that the guards seemed to tolerate him instead of look to him for direction. The further from Tolsin he got, the less power he wielded and Resolute stepped forward to fill that void.

Resolute's de facto assumption of leadership further discomfited Mably. The Vorquelf, with Dranae as his lieutenant, dispatched scouts and otherwise organized the guardsmen's rotations. Only one of the Tolsin guardsmen offered resistance to Resolute's orders—until Will quipped that defying Resolute was stupid, and that stupid people often break their legs in horrible accidents. The guardsman quickly acquiesced and found that Resolute actually knew what he was about.

Alexia would have been quite happy about events had Crow not worn so dour an expression. "Crow, you cannot actually think I was going to allow them to haul you off, can you? Do you think you would have made it all the way to Meredo?"

Crow frowned heavily. "Chances are I'd have made it a mile closer to the capital than Mably, but that's not important. I didn't want you caught up in what will happen to me. I asked you not to do this."

He held up his left hand and thumbed the gold ring on his finger. "Kerrigan fashioned the rings, I take it, the way he was able to fashion the duplicate of the fragment?"

"He had to borrow the rings from the innkeeper and his wife to get the right sense of them, but yes."

The white-haired man shook his head. "And then Will stole into the tavern and slipped it on my finger."

Alyx nodded. "I was not there. I was serving to distract Mably and a few others. It all went off very easily."

"Unless you had your leg broken."

"I understand he was kicking you."

Crow shrugged. "It didn't hurt. He kicked like a girl."

Her violet eyes opened wide. "If I kicked you, you'd not say that."

"Like as not." He glanced over at her, the flesh surrounding his left eye a sickly yellow with purple streaks. "But the fact is, you have kicked me. By doing this."

"Crow, you're not saying that being rescued has hurt your vanity!" Alyx threw her head back and laughed. "If that's what you're saying, you've been beaten more soundly in the head than I imagined."

Crow raised himself, straightening his spine proudly. It was not easy for him to do, but the only hint of the difficulty came as the flesh around his eyes tightened. "You do know me better than that, Princess. I wanted you to walk away. I wanted to keep you safe from what will happen to me. I've been prepared for years for this, but you were taken by surprise. My doom is of my own making, and you shouldn't be caught up in it."

"You wanted to keep me safe. Why is that?"

"Because you are important. The world is depending upon you."

She leaned forward, resting both hands on the saddlehorn. "If that were it, you'd have insisted I never go into combat."

Crow sighed. "Combat is different. What will come is not something you've trained for. And there is more. You are a friend. I also told Resolute to walk away when this happened."

Alyx narrowed her eyes. "How is it, Crow, that you can be loyal to your friends—that you can ride into combat with them and save their lives, that you can endure decades of shame searching for the one person who will rescue a world that has condemned you—and yet fail to understand why your friends would stand beside you? Do we seem that shallow to you?"

He raised a hand and the sleeve of his leather jerkin fell enough that she could see the bruises the manacles had left. "No, no, it's not that at all. I just..." He swallowed hard and glanced away, catching his lower lip between his teeth. He started to speak again, then blew the words from his tongue in a huff of air.

She reached out and laid a gentle hand on his left shoulder. "Crow, it's okay."

"No, it's not, Princess." He drew in a deep breath and exhaled slowly. "I've known, from the moment they stripped my mask from me, that I was doing the right thing. Even so, when they took my mask—when they had my *father* strip my mask from me, it crushed me. I felt as if my face had been clawed bare of flesh. I had always sought to be worthy of wearing a mask, and here I had been stripped of it. Tarrant Hawkins was dead.

"After that, for the next few months anyway, I don't remember much. I drank to oblivion, but always woke *barefaced*. I would have lost myself in the pleasures of the flesh, but no one would have me. I was turned out of inns. I was battered and beaten, spat upon, tossed into cesspits and sewers. Had I been on fire, people would have pissed on me, but only so I could suffer with the burns."

His voice came barely above a whisper. A shiver ran through him as he spoke. Alexia felt it through her hand and thought her touch an invasion, but she could not bear to take her hand away. She really wanted to rub her hand over his shoulder, along his back, but refrained by reminding herself of his bruises.

The desire to comfort him confused her. Anyone else she'd have clapped on the shoulder and told to bear up. Among the Gyrkyme confession of this sort was unknown. There were so few of them, and they all lived in a small area, that everyone simply knew all there was to know. While the Gyrkyme held confidences sacred, secrets became news and spread swiftly. Sins were not hidden and were easily forgiven. Since coming into the wider world she had, on occasion, had comrades who felt the need to unburden themselves, and she listened for as long as seemed polite before escaping.

This was different, however. The pain in his voice slowly slid into her, tightening her stomach. His words defined a burden he had carried for as long as she had been alive, and she wished she could do something to help lift it from him.

In that regard, squeezing his shoulder seemed a wholly inadequate effort.

Crow continued speaking, his eyes focusing on the road. "Resolute had been north, scouting Boragul for any signs of Chytrine. How he found me, I'm not certain, but he took me out of Yslin, away from men, and into the mountains near Gyrvirgul. Why he put up with me, I don't know. I did nothing but sleep or cry, and hated doing both. He just sat with me, silent when I needed, bracing when I needed, and often speaking of the future, which I needed most of all."

Alyx squeezed his shoulder again. "Resolute is your friend."

Crow nodded. "Yes, and a better friend than I had ever known. He built me back up. He created Kedyn's Crow—citing some elven prophecy which I think he made up. But mostly he reminded me that I'd pledged that Vorquellyn would be redeemed in my lifetime. I resisted that idea for a bit, but eventually it took. I still knew, though, that this day would come, and I made him promise to walk away when it did."

"How could he if you're going to redeem Vorquellyn?"

"I just said it would be redeemed in my lifetime. The sooner I die, the sooner it's done."

Alyx shot him a sidelong glance. "I suspect Resolute doesn't quite see it that way."

"He only sees things *his* way." Crow's head came up and he glanced at where Resolute rode well ahead of him. "Resolute Faithbreaker!"

The Vorquelf half turned, cupped a hand to a pointed ear, then quickly pulled his hand away and shrugged.

Crow growled. "He can hear a gnat breathing twenty leagues away, but is damnably deaf other times."

"It could be, Crow, he just doesn't think that charge worth answering." She gave him a quick smile. "Or it could be that he feels abandoning you would be a greater breach of faith."

He shot her a sidelong look. "He doesn't need defending."

"I wasn't defending him. I was defending me and my choice." Her eyes narrowed. "You recall refusing to promise to slay me, were I to go over to Chytrine? You told me you refused because you didn't want to give me any possible sense of security. You didn't want my defenses to flag so I would become susceptible to her offers. Do you remember that?"

"I do."

"You weren't telling me what I wanted to hear. You were telling me a truth I *needed* to hear. Well, here is one for you. We are your friends, and we *need* you with us. That might conflict with your plans, but you'll just have to live with it."

Crow closed his eyes for a moment, then nodded. "Thank you."

"You're welcome."

He cleared his throat. "Still, couldn't you have found another way to do this, Princess? It's such a transparent strategy, no one will believe it."

"They'd not believe I could succumb to your charms?"

"If I had any." Crow smiled. "Don't evade the point. By claiming to be married to me, you have completely destroyed your value as a dynastic marriage partner."

"An added benefit."

"Be serious."

She let her hand trail down his arm before returning to her saddlehorn. "I am serious. You know that I was trained to lead armies. This was what my father wanted, and he told Preyknosery Ironwing. The Gyrkyme honored my father's wishes, and King Augustus saw to it that I had the help and training needed. They and he know my value to the world. My grandfather and my great-grandaunt, however, do not. They see me as a brood mare to be married off to some prince to strengthen alliances so we'll have support in taking back Okrannel. They'd put me in a bed to earn more troops, when I could lead *fewer* and take Okrannel myself."

"That may be as you say, Princess, but no one will believe we are wed."

Alyx smiled. "The Norrington and Perrine stood as witnesses to our nuptials. Prince Erlestoke was there, may the gods keep his soul."

"Two friends and a dead man as witnesses? No one will accept their word."

"But they will accept mine. They have to because that is the way of the nobility. To accuse me of lying has consequences."

"But when it is shown you are, Princess..."

She shook her head adamantly. "You listen to me, Crow, and listen well. I know your story; I've known it all my life. The shame, the lies, how they painted you are all irrelevant, I've met you. You have saved my life; I have saved yours. We have shared a wineskin after a battle, we've stormed a pirate haven, and we've killed a *sullanciri*. I know that the Hawkins of legend, of infamy, is not you."

"Yes, but..."

"No, Crow, no buts." She swallowed hard as a lump rose in her throat. "I would like to think, had my father lived, he would have been there when they tried you and would have raged against the injustice. Had King Augustus not been in Okrannel, I'm certain he would have as well."

Crow shook his head. "They would have had no choice."

"We'll never know, but I know Augustus and know he'd not have sanctioned such an injustice. My point, however, is simply this: the crowned heads, in order to preserve their realms, chose to destroy your life. They created a lie and used it to destroy you. You said your father stripped your mask from you. Do you think he would have done that if he knew the truth?"

The man shivered for a moment, then his voice sank low. "He knew a truth, and that made him take my mask. He didn't need their lie."

She frowned, not understanding. *Time for that later.* "Crow, the world's leaders are the ones who did this to you. I will not stand for it. This lie has done enough damage."

"So you'll fight it with another lie?" The words formed an accusation, but the grin tugging at the corner of his mouth softened it.

She nodded. "It stops your summary execution and buys us time. Many will work hard trying to talk me out of the marriage. I could trade an annulment for a pardon and we would be done with it. After all, everyone knows that Hawkins killed himself. You were just mistakenly identified as him. Remember, among the Vorquelves, the stories of Kedyn's Crow predate the last war."

Crow laughed. "Oh, you have this all thought out."

"Had to. Will and Kerrigan ask the most annoying questions. Of course, as with any plan, it will come apart when we engage the enemy." Alyx shrugged. "But we have to win, so we will."

He looked over at her, then shook his head. "Scrainwood isn't an imbecile, but he thought he was just picking a fight with me. He's going to get far more than he ever bargained for."

"He called this tune a quarter century ago, and has been dancing to it for a good long time." Princess Alexia squeezed Crow's shoulder again. "The time has come to pay the piper."

CHAPTER 8

The column of snowflakes swirled across the Aurolani landscape moving toward her as if with intelligence and intent. Isaura reached out with an ungloved hand. Long, slender fingers sheathed in flesh barely darker than the snow itself sank into the whirlwind. At her touch the snow-ghost flew apart, small flakes lighting on her long hair and gown, hidden there as completely as if they had fallen back to the snowfield beneath her feet.

The breeze that had animated that tiny cyclone spawned others that raced toward the Conservatory as if Southlands warriors mounted an assault on the building. The Conservatory had been built into the side of a mountain. The magicks the *sullanciri* Neskartu had used to create it had molded molten rock into towers and chambers. Even the exterior walls, having been battered by a quarter century of fierce northern storms, still retained their pristine, glassy surface.

Students stood in the white field before the Conservatory, for those who had studied there for years had become at least partially inured to the cold. Those trained in combat dueled each other, male and female alike stripped to the waist, their bodies adorned with colorful tattoos. Magicks crackled between them, the sounds carrying crisply through the cold air. If the combat mages even noticed the rising breeze, they did not seek shelter from it.

Other longtime students wore more clothing, but likewise ignored the wind. The newest students, however—most children and all facing their first winter—huddled together, their backs to the wind. As distant as she was, she could feel them attempting to summon a warming spell. Having been trained on Vilwan, their methods were awkward, their efforts stunted, and their results meager.

Isaura tilted her head slightly to the left and watched them. The Vilwanese students had been plucked from the sea and brought to Aurolan to be trained by Neskartu, but they resisted him and his methods much as they tried to resist the cold. And suffered equally for both.

Isaura did not resist the wind and cold, but embraced it. The Vilwanese saw cold as the absence of heat, but she knew this was merely shortsightedness. There was still heat in the wind, for heat was merely energy, and if there was no energy, there would be no wind. *Heat is there; one merely has to know where to seek it.*

Another whirlwind bore down on her, and she sensed its intent immediately. She turned, looking back at the frosted fortress of black stone that dominated the high-walled mountain valley. Where the Conservatory had been shaped of stone, the fortress seemed like a tooth that had erupted from the snowy landscape, strong and sharp.

She caught a flash of white in a window of an upper chamber and smiled. Isaura began to walk swiftly toward the castle, the whirlwind tugging at the skirts of her gown, urging her on. She flicked a hand at it, reweaving the threads of energy running through it, and it collapsed into a small cloud of ice dust.

From it rose another whirlwind, this one more powerful. It circled her once, eliciting a shriek of delight as her hair danced on its teasing tendrils. The storm lunged at her, surrounding her in its fury. The wind howled inarticulately, then lifted her up and bore her on an icy pedestal to an upper balcony of the castle.

Isaura laughed aloud, her silver eyes flashing as she soared above the landscape. Outside the valley, far to the north and again to the west, she could see the distant, dark cones of volcanoes with steam rising from them. Vast fields of pure white lay between them, stippled here and there with small clusters of domed buildings. Most of the Aurolani citizenry lived in vast cavern complexes. The buildings she could see largely consisted of shelters for the various flocks and herds raised on the tundra.

The whirlwind set her down gently on the balcony, then swirled tightly into a slender column. She bowed her head graciously. "Thank you, kind sir."

With barely a sound, the column of ice convulsed and then dissipated.

Smiling, Isaura entered the open arched doorway. Her skin tingled as she passed through the threshold spell that retained the castle's heat. A few flakes of snow fell from her shoulders and hair, but only the most hardy hit the stone floor. Those that did melted quickly, then evaporated.

She stopped three feet inside the threshold of the grand chamber. It extended on into darkness far ahead of her, easily three times as long as it was wide or high. To the right, in the middle of the wall and opposite the main doors, stood a hearth tall enough for a man to march through and wide enough to accept a whole company. A fire raged therein, bathing the woman standing before it in undulating light.

The woman stood easily as tall as Isaura and had the same slightly pointed ears. Her hair was golden, however, matching her gown, in contrast to Isaura's snowy mane. Clean-limbed, though heavier than Isaura, the woman had a calm elegance about her that appeared to quiet the riot of flames in the hearth. The fire continued to burn hot, but the flames slowed, twisting and floating like silk on a light breeze.

Isaura smoothed her gown and raked fingers back through her hair. She allowed herself a smile and the barest flash of strong, white teeth, then approached the other woman. "Mother! You've returned from the Southlands. Did you succeed?"

"Yes, daughter, I did." The woman looked over at her with blue-green eyes alive with reflected firelight. "I have some of what I want from Draconis, but a puzzle as well."

"A puzzle?" Isaura wrinkled her brow. "Is there something wrong?"

"No, my child; do not frown like that. Yours is a face too beautiful to be marred with worry lines." The woman raised her right hand and beckoned. "Come closer, Isaura. You will help me solve this problem, then all will be well."

Isaura's heart leaped in her breast as she moved to her mother's side. She did know that the Empress Chytrine was not truly her mother. Chytrine had adopted her when she was just a babe, since she had been abandoned by her mother, and of her father there was no record. Her bastardy had not concerned Chytrine, however, who took her in and raised her as if her own, giving her every appropriate benefit as a child legitimately born to the throne.

"I do want to help, Mother. Please, I will do anything I can."

"Of course you will, child." Chytrine smiled in a kindly manner, but the smile died quickly, bespeaking concerns that only an empress could bear. "In the south, daughter, they vex me. They slew Anariah in a cruel trap. They lured him into it by using decoys, and linking them to the real fragments of the DragonCrown. The imitations were not good, but Anariah was young and not schooled in lesser magicks. He was unaware of the danger until too late."

Isaura closed her eyes and lowered her head. Anariah had been a golden dragon with which she had only a passing acquaintance, but he had been one of her mother's favorites. He had first been drawn to Chytrine because of the one fragment of the DragonCrown she had possessed before the fall of

Fortress Draconis. She told him of her plans for the re-created crown and the dragon allied himself with her cause, becoming a fervent supporter of Chytrine's campaign against the south.

"Oh, Mother, you have my deepest sympathy."

"Of course, yes, child. You are most kind."

The pressure of a finger under her chin lifted her head and Isaura opened her eyes. "I can imagine he was very brave."

Chytrine nodded solemnly. "He was. His dedication to our cause never wavered. Anariah never hesitated in the cause of liberating the DragonCrown from the southern tyrants. Their possession of it imperiled his kin, even himself, but it was not for dragonkind alone that he acted. He fought to stop the rot of the south from poisoning us."

Chytrine's hand fell away and she again gazed into the fire. "Oh, daughter, you have no idea the corruption of the south. This is my fault, and you must forgive me. I have kept you here, in our land, to preserve you. There are times—and I do not mean this as criticism—that you are so sensitive."

"I know you only want the best for me, Mother." Isaura smiled. "I am quite content to be here in your realm."

"It is beautiful, isn't it? Whenever I travel to the south, I long for it, not just because I hate the oppressive heat, but the stink, the moisture, the way things grow and drag on you." Chytrine frowned. "You see, Isaura-sweet, the world of Aurolan is simple and it is the way it was meant to be. It is cold; it is unforgiving. Weakness is dispatched in favor of strength. Here we live in accord with the dictates of the world, as it should be.

"But there, in the Southlands...Oh, Isaura, you would not believe it. They think they can harness rivers, diverting water into fields. They build dikes to steal land from the sea, then wonder why the sea shatters the dikes and reclaims its property. And then their cities..."

Chytrine shook her head slowly. "Our people reside in caverns, in living rock. We find a space within which to exist, but in the south they use rock to wall away space, to make it smaller. They are so afraid of the world that they encyst themselves in these festering artificial caverns. Here, when something dies, it is harvested, rendered, every bit of it used for the common good. Our nightsoil is collected and feeds our gardens. Nothing is wasted, but there, they pour their chamber pots in the streets. Dead animals lie in the gutter and vermin crawl about, fighting over corpses and worse, getting into storage houses, eating until they are corpulent. And if they are found out and killed, are they eaten? No, just discarded in the streets to feed a new generation of pests."

The Aurolani Empress' eyes blazed. "I have insulated you from that, daughter, for it causes my stomach to churn. I hate telling you of it, and I would shield you forever from it, but circumstances will not permit this."

"Why? What is happening, Mother?"

"Many things, Isaura, many things." Chytrine reached into one sleeve of her gown and produced a green-and-gold gem set in gold. With a flick of her free hand, the empress summoned a small table, which flew across the room and tottered for a moment beside her. As it settled, she placed the stone on it.

Isaura recognized the first fragment of the DragonCrown that had been liberated from Svarskya before her birth. Her mother had possessed it since then, and wore it on occasion. Isaura had always liked the stone because of the play of colors through it. There were times, when she was just a child, that she had imagined the stone winking at her like some jeweled eye.

Chytrine's hand again emerged from the sleeve and held a yellow stone. The fire's light created a luminous cross that shifted through the gem's face. Chytrine set it down on the table, then brushed her fingertips over it.

"That one is from Draconis, Mother?"

"Yes, it is the first we recovered. We found its duplicate and used that to trace the original. We also found a duplicate of the ruby and it led us to this."

Chytrine's right hand dipped into the left sleeve and produced a gold-bound ruby that, at first glance, appeared to match the others in terms of workmanship and setting. It even radiated power, though on a more muted scale than the other two. Still, had she not been looking for the differences, Isaura was uncertain she would have noticed them with a casual examination.

She held a hand out. "May I?"

"Yes, Isaura, this is the puzzle I want you to help me with." Chytrine gave her the ruby, then looked down and stroked her fingers over the yellow stone. "Tell me what you think of it."

Isaura let both hands enfold the stone, then clutched it to her bosom. She closed her eyes and lowered her head. She forced away the sound of the fire and any sense of its heat. She willfully isolated her mind from all physical sensations and focused on the stone. Isaura felt resistance at first, then suddenly blasted past it.

"Oh!" She gasped aloud and recoiled, her hands opening. The stone dropped toward the floor, but before it could hit, a wave of sorcery caught it up and lifted it into the air again.

Isaura immediately dropped to her knees. "Forgive me, Mother."

"Child, I am the one who needs forgiveness. I did not warn you." Chytrine gestured fluidly and the ruby floated to the table. "What did you feel?"

Isaura concentrated. "Several magicks, Mother. It is linked to the True-stone, and strongly. There is a spell there that would take any magick seeking the stone and convert it into energy that feeds the link. It is as if tugging on a string here rings a bell further away. This decoy would call all the more loudly when searchers neared the Truestone."

Chytrine smiled. "Yes, that spell was quite interesting and rather unexpected. And of the magick that created the fragment?"

The young woman frowned. "That is difficult to get a sense of. It is a very complex spell, because the duplicate really does carry with it some of the resonance of the original. It combines elements from four different themes of magick, but that's not the most interesting thing. It seems constructed along the lines of a human spell, but there are elven and urZrethi elements in it. What is it?"

Chytrine shook her head. "I do not know, save that it indicates that the Southlands have a new champion, or the potential for one. It would be too much to hope he had been slain at Draconis. He is out there, I can feel it."

Isaura glanced up, her eyes widening with horror. "Is it the Norrington, Mother?"

The Aurolani Empress arched an eyebrow. "What brings the Norrington to mind, daughter?"

"Only my concern for you. Nefrai-laysh said he had seen the Norrington, and that you had sent Myrall'mara to destroy him. I know you do not want me to worry about you, but I do. I cannot help it. I fear for you because of him."

Chytrine strode to her and raised a hand to caress Isaura's cheek. "Pet, you need not worry. This Norrington is but a pup. He will come to see reason as his father and grandfather did before him. There is danger, however. I need someone I can trust to help me deal with it. You, Isaura, shall be my agent."

"Yes, Mother." The girl's face blossomed with a smile. "I won't fail you. Whatever you need done, I shall do it."

Chytrine took Isaura's hands in her own. "I know you will, child. You must listen very carefully. You know there is a chance that events will cost me my life. Yrulph Kirûn knew as much and groomed me to carry his mission forward. I must prepare against that eventuality, so I will send you south, that you may see the conditions there for yourself. You will know what I have told you is true."

"I already know that, Mother. I know it in my heart and mind."

"Isaura, dearest, you know better than to assume that untested ice is strong. And though you accept every word I have said about the south, what you see will make the urgency of my mission that much more clear to you." Chytrine nodded slowly and gave her hands a squeeze. "Soon enough, daughter, you shall repair to the south and see for yourself. Once you are finished there, I shall have more work for you. With your willing aid, this coming winter shall be the Southlands' last."

CHAPTER 9

Will didn't even turn to look back toward the fire as the stick snapped. "Couldn't sleep, Kerrigan?"

The other's breath caught in his throat. "Oh, the stick cracking told you someone was here. None of the others would have stepped on it, would they?"

A tiny part of Will wanted to reply, "No, you stone-footed oaf," but he withheld that comment. He shrugged and pointed to a moss-saddled portion of the log he sat on. "Only me, but that's because I'm the only person less suited to being in the woods than you. Resolute's worked hard to learn me things, but not all of it takes."

Kerrigan sat and pulled his blanket tight around his shoulders. "You don't have to humor me, Will."

"I wasn't."

The jowly mage nodded. "You are a thief. Stepping on something like a stick would alert householders, so you would have learned long ago not to do that. Moreover, I've seen you in the woods, but I've not *heard* you."

The thief couldn't suppress his smile as he glanced at Kerrigan. Off to the left, twenty yards back, the fire around which Princess Alexia's bodyguards slept blazed merrily. At the southern end of that circle, a tent had been pitched to provide the married couple some privacy. A stake had been driven into the ground in front of it, and twin chains that led to anklets snaked in through the flaps. Beyond it, another twenty yards on, lay the Tolsin campfire, with Mably and his men positioned between the prisoner and the horses.

Out away from the fire only a fragment of its light and none of its heat touched them. "I really didn't mean to be humoring you, Ker."

The mage looked up. "Care?"

"Ker, like the first part of your name? I know you don't want to be called Keri, but Kerrigan is kind of a mouthful. It's a nickname, you know?"

Kerrigan shook his head. "No, I don't. I've never had one."

Will blinked. "Never? I've had lots, and even get called by one. Okay, look, Will is my nickname." He lowered his voice. "My real name is Wilburforce."

Kerrigan nodded solemnly. "That's a good, strong name."

"Now you're humoring me."

"Oh, no, I'm being quite sincere. In the Twilight Campaign, there was an Oriosan cavalry commander, Wilburforce Eastlan, who helped drive Kree'chuc north. Surely you know that, and know that is why your name is taken as a particularly good omen." Kerrigan looked at him with innocent, green eyes. "When we passed through the Valsina area, that's what people were saying."

"You know this history stuff, and you don't know what a nickname is?"

The mage shrugged. "On Vilwan we did not use nicknames." He hesitated for a moment, then frowned. "I must amend that. On Vilwan I never had one. I don't know about the others."

Something in Kerrigan's voice piqued Will's curiosity. He turned, bringing his left shin to lie across the trunk of the fallen tree. "You didn't have any friends who called you stuff? Sometimes, like in the winter, some of the other kids would call me Chill because it rhymes with Will, and is another word for 'brrrr,' which is part of my name and because my feet were cold in the bed. I hated that. The 'Chilly-willie' name."

The mage canted his head to the right and nodded a couple of times. Will knew he was taking apart the nickname, studying it the way Resolute had him study tracks in the dirt. Finally, Kerrigan looked at him again and blinked a couple of times. "I see how they got it, yes. And, no, I didn't really have friends. I remember, when I was very young, that there were some other students who studied with me, but pretty soon we were split up and I was given to tutors like Orla, though none of them was her equal."

"You had no friends?" Will tried to keep the surprise out of his voice, but failed completely. "No one to joke with, to tease, nothing?"

Kerrigan recoiled from the questions. "Vilwan is a different sort of place."

"I remember. I was there." Will stopped short of pointing out that while he was there, he had seen plenty of mages who had friends, who fought together in teams, who could joke. Even Orla had had a sense of humor at times. "I was there at the siege."

"Well, then, you know. They got me away during the siege." The corpulent youth sighed. "I wish they had left me alone. I wouldn't be here, and Orla wouldn't be dead."

"Yeah, and Chytrine would have the piece of the DragonCrown you're carrying."

Kerrigan's eyes grew wide and a hand shifted beneath the blanket. "How did you . . . Did Crow tell you?"

Will shook his head and picked with a thumbnail at a piece of bark trapped in the triangle of his legs. "I'm a thief, remember? You're guarding that thing as well as a gem merchant with a hoard, or some swain mooncalfing over a locket with a curl of his lover's hair. No one else would have noticed. Well, probably Resolute—he sees everything. But you're big enough that most'll just figure you have chiggers in your armpit."

"I do not."

Will shrugged. "Just scratch like you do and it'll keep folks away."

"So you knew I was hiding something, but how did you know it was a fragment?"

The thief pursed his lips. Instead of telling Kerrigan he'd not known for certain until he'd seen Kerrigan's reaction to his bluff, he decided to lie. "You've been hiding it since we left Fortress Draconis. Now, aside from the people we got out, the only things of worth there were fragments. The Draconis Baron had to try to get at least one piece out and if there was anyone who could hide it with magick, it would be you. I just kind of figured it out from there."

"He made me promise not to say anything, not to tell anyone but Crow and the princess. Will, you can't say anything."

Will shook his head. "I won't say a word, but you have to let me help you hide it. Here, on the road, it's not so important. Strikes me, though, that given what folks think about Crow, Meredo is pretty much going to be enemy territory. Chytrine had *sullanciri* in Yslin last autumn, so you know she could have them in Meredo."

The magicker nodded slowly. "Yes, that makes sense. How will we hide it?"

"Easily. We'll start on the road." Will shivered. Kerrigan was leaning forward, hanging on his every word. Not having had friends growing up, and with Orla dead, Kerrigan was desperate for someone to talk to. Had Will been setting him up to be robbed, well, it would have been too simple.

The small part of Will that had absorbed all Marcus' lessons wanted to laugh at Kerrigan. Here he was, a powerful mage, in possession of an item so priceless that the Aurolani Empress would destroy nations to possess it. Kerrigan had already seen the riches that she'd offered the Pirate Queen Vionna for the Lakaslin fragment, so he knew just how much it was to be treasured. Yet despite all that, here he was listening to Will's advice as to how to safeguard it. In a heartbeat the fragment could be Will's—the reward for it, too.

Will snorted. "Starting tomorrow, put all your stuff in one of your saddlebags, then fill the other up with junk." He leaned over and picked up a pine cone. "Things like this, and little animal skulls, funny-shaped rocks. Have Qwc and Lombo find things for you, and spend time looking at them. Offer to show them to the Tolsin men. Let them think you're a little crazy."

Kerrigan nodded. "They think that already. And that I'm useless, even though I started their fire for them, wet wood and all."

"I'd have left them cold. 'Cept maybe Mably. I'd start a fire with him."

"No, Will, don't think that. It didn't work with Wheele and Orla died because of it."

"Hey, Ker, stop right there."

"What?"

"Orla's death isn't your fault." Will held up a hand to prevent a protest. "I know you said I wasn't good at being a mind reader when I said that before, but you remember back in Yslin? Orla came with Crow and Resolute and the princess and we went after a *sullanciri*. And that Dark Lancer had made my friends into monsters, and we had to kill them. We didn't have any choice 'cuz they would have killed us. But when it was all over, they were dead and they were just kids again. And I couldn't help thinking, somehow, that there was a way we could have not killed them.

"But, you know, I worked out that it wasn't my fault. You trace it back, and it's all Chytrine. She's the one who made the *sullanciri,* and she's the one who wants me dead, and she's the one who had the pirates attack Vilwan, which meant you had to go away and Orla with you." His head came up. "You and me, we're not doing this. We might not do everything right, but we have to do something because if we don't, then she wins and folks will be dead. Lots of them."

Kerrigan sat there for a bit, his thick lips pursed. Will wasn't sure how long the magicker thought, but it was long enough that the cold and the silence began to gnaw at Will. If not for the steam drifting from Kerrigan's nostrils, he could have imagined the mage had turned to stone.

"That is it, though, Will," he finally said. "You and I might not do everything right, but at least you're doing some things right. I..." Kerrigan's voice failed for a moment, then returned muted and cool. "All the training I had was meant to prepare me for something great. What, I don't know, no one ever told me. They just made me do more and more and more. And then, when I was leaving Vilwan, the pirates tried to stop us. I destroyed their ship, but the people on the boat with me were hurt and then the ship capsized, and that was my fault, so that those who weren't dead already drowned. And then I used the wrong spell on Wheele..."

"But, Kerrigan, your spell let Orla's spell work. And you're forgetting all the stuff you did during the Svoin siege, and figuring out those spells when we were in Loquellyn, and your lighting up the firedirt that killed Chytrine's troops and saved the people we were getting out of Fortress Draconis. You've done good, lots of good.

"And I know I haven't been fair to you." Will sighed. "I let Scabby Jack and Garrow's gang beat you up. I said you froze when that big frostclaw came after you. I never told you I was sorry Orla died. I guess, growing up, I had friends, but I never had people I could trust like you could her. I saw how she was, and I envy you knowing her. She was a good person."

"I know, and I miss her."

They both sat there quietly for a moment. Will thought about Orla for a bit, then about Resolute and Crow. They were the first real friends he'd ever had, and the first people he could trust, because they trusted him. Granted, they had drawn him into things without telling him who he was, but time had let him see that they were trying to protect him, preparing him to accept his responsibility as the person who was prophesied to bring an end to Chytrine's invasion of the south.

Kerrigan's voice came soft through the night. "Did you ever think you'd be here, Will?"

"Here, in some forest in Oriosa, wearing a mask, freezing, while the most evil man in the world is sleeping with a beautiful princess and the most evil woman in the world is sending vast armies south to kill me? Not specifically, no."

"You know what I mean." The magicker's hands emerged from beneath the blanket and he stared down at his open palms. "When I was growing up, I used to imagine things. I thought maybe I would become Grand Magister of Vilwan and invent new and wonderful spells. And other times I'd dream about opposing Chytrine, but in those dreams it would be the two of us in some wizards' duel and I'd batter her down and save the world.

"But here I am, in a cold wood, talking to someone who is younger than me and, no disrespect intended, about as ill prepared to save the world as I am."

"And don't forget that we're being hunted."

"I haven't." Kerrigan glanced over at the tent. "Orla told me to follow Crow and Resolute, and now Crow turns out to be Hawkins and King Scrainwood will probably kill him. And I have a fragment, and you are a pawn of destiny, and Fortress Draconis has fallen, and my mentor is dead. Have I forgotten anything?"

Will grinned. "General Adrogans took Svoin, then burned it to the ground."

"Oh, yeah." Kerrigan winced. "Things are not going well."

"When you look at it that way, yeah. I mean, if I'm the hope of the world, then the world ought to be feeling pretty worried." Will shrugged. "Then again, we aren't dead yet, we've killed a couple of Chytrine's Dark Lancers, and there are two fragments that are not in her hands. The fact that Fortress Draconis has fallen means some folks are going to have to start doing things to stop Chytrine, so we have a chance."

"Yes, we do at that." Kerrigan nodded slowly. "And we will make the best of it. Pursuant to which, when I get this collection of things, I hide the fragment in it?"

Will shook his head. "Nope, but you'll treat the collection as if it does contain something valuable. You'll show folks some things, but never let them examine the collection itself. When we get to Meredo, that collection will be the thing they go after. And when they find there is nothing of value, they'll just think you are crazy and have nothing to hide. And so they will stop looking."

"That makes sense." But despite his words, Kerrigan sounded uncertain. "In Meredo, you will help me hide it so no one will get it?"

Will stood, stretched, and stamped his feet. "Yes, we'll find a place for it that no one will ever discover."

Kerrigan's brows furrowed and his jowls quivered. "But, logically, if we can find it, then it can't be a place no one would ever . . . Oh, sorry."

"We'll find a place." The thief smiled. "Trust me, Ker. You owe Chytrine for Orla, I owe her for my friends and more. Keeping that fragment from her is just the first part of paying her back."

CHAPTER 10

The rage radiating off King Scrainwood was colder than the north wind swirling snowflakes through the sky over Meredo. Alexia let it beat at her back as she looked out one of the throne room windows. She allowed herself the hint of a smile, imagining both the expression on Scrainwood's face and the grin her describing his anger would put on Crow's face. She very much looked forward to sharing that with him.

Fuming, Scrainwood sat on his throne, his right fist tight and pounding the arm, while his Minister of Protocol, Cartland Gapes, and the unctuous Cabot Marsham attempted to employ their brand of reason on the Okrans Ambassador, Vladoslav Svoinyk. She wished Perrine had accompanied her to the meeting, but she could have easily imagined her Gyrkyme sister grabbing Marsham and soaring into the room's vaults before dropping him.

"No disrespect intended to the House of Svarskya, the Kingdom of Okrannel, or the Princess Alexia herself," Marsham offered, oozing contempt from each word, "but we all know this marriage is a sham. Clearly the Traitor deceived her into saying they had married to selfishly save his own worthless skin. His propensities for deception are the stuff of legend. His victims are known for their innocence. If the princess would merely give some indication of having been fooled, we shall..."

Gapes, who was tall with a thick mane of white hair, cut Marsham off. "What we meant, Ambassador, is this: we fully acknowledge the strength of Okrans nobility and their pride, for it is that pride which has kept them honed and ready to destroy Chytrine. Clearly that pride drove them to liberate Svoin, your family's home city, and without such fierce pride, the princess could not have successfully led her companions on the daring raid that liberated the DragonCrown fragment from the Wruonin pirates. And that same pride and strength and overwhelming courage was what enabled her to bring our Princess Ryhope home again to Meredo, saving her life and those of her countrymen.

"This pride, however, must be balanced against the vaunted Okrans honor—the sort of honor displayed by her father as he gave his life at Fortress Draconis to save his boon companions from the *sullanciri* in Chytrine's employ. It is certain that the princess must see how her liaison with the Traitor would bring shame upon her nation. Now, we have taken steps to assure that news of this supposed marriage will spread no further, but unless she denounces it, the rumors will foment and there will be no hope of killing them. While the princess might feel she has to stand by a judgment made in haste, since it was a commitment made, she must also acknowledge that haste is seldom conducive to reason. If she so desires, a judicious comment at this time would save the honor of Okrannel."

Alyx kept her face impassive as she turned to face those in the room again. She positioned herself so that the glow of the window would backlight her and make her face more difficult to read. She had chosen not to attend in full armor, but instead opted for her Alcidese uniform, albeit without rank insignia. She wore a dagger at her right hip and had been allowed to retain it as a courtesy of her rank.

Vladoslav Svoinyk had a medium build and his soft face and dark hair made him appear far too youthful for a position of importance at the court of Oriosa. Still, the sharpness of his dark-eyed gaze, and the way he nodded gravely in response to the minister's words, showed cautious deliberation before he spoke. Alyx had seen his like among warriors. Enemies misjudged him easily, and would pay a terrible price for their error.

"Minister, your kind words about the pride and honor of Okrannel are heartwarming, for all too often we have been dismissed as a once-was nation. At the Council of Kings last autumn in Alcida, it was King Scrainwood's insistence that the Oriosan delegation be introduced before the delegation from Okrannel, which could easily be taken as an indication that our nation is nothing more than phantasy."

"Ambassador, that error was the result of misinterpretations by the Alcidese Protocol Minister of casual remarks I had made concerning the beliefs of *other* nations. That my remarks were attributed to my liege has caused me no end of heartache. The responsibility for any discomfort caused you or your nation is mine to bear alone."

Svoinyk nodded solemnly. "Minister Gapes, your love of the Okrans people is not unknown to us. It does puzzle me, however, why you neglected to mention one of our more famous attributes: our intelligence. You have noted the courage and pride with which Princess Alexia saved your people and defeated the Wruonin pirates, but you don't acknowledge how intelligent she must have been to do that."

Gapes bowed his head. "Again, I have offended you, and I have no desire to do so. Her intelligence is manifest in all these things, as well as her resilience and drive. If you have felt I have slighted her in this regard, I abase myself with apology."

Svoinyk smiled. "I find it curious, then, Minister, that you acknowledge how intelligent she is, and yet maintain she was duped."

Gapes' eyes widened, but before he could recover from his shock, Marsham snapped quickly. "The Traitor has fooled many, including those who are far smarter than Princess Alexia."

Svoinyk's face froze, and in his words Scrainwood's cold fury met its match. "You present me a paradox, then, Count Marsham. I know you were fooled by Hawkins, and I cannot help but imagine you believe yourself smarter than my princess. But she tells me that she was not deceived. Which, if intelligence is to be measured based on who was fooled and who was not, would make her your superior. Moreover, we have ample evidence of her courage, wit, pride, and honor; whereas I have yet to learn of anything so illuminating about you. Princess Alexia may not deign to notice the slights you offer her, but I have. While my position in service to my king prevents me from demanding satisfaction from you, I would cast all that aside to do so."

Svoinyk's words staggered Marsham. The man's face turned purple, but before he could say anything, the king snapped his fingers. "That will be all, Marsham."

"But, my liege . . ."

"Do not make me tire of you so early in the day." Scrainwood passed a hand over his eyes, more as if hiding his mask from Marsham's sight, than blocking his vision of the subordinate. "Go, find my son. Help him do . . . *something.*"

The room remained quiet save for the heavy footsteps of Marsham's retreat. Door hinges creaked. Outside the wind whistled as it picked up, coaxing heavier flurries from the grey clouds cloaking the sky. Scrainwood's head came up as the door closed, then he waited several seconds longer, before letting his words slither beneath the silence.

"Let us end this polite game, for I tire of it." Scrainwood looked over at Alyx. "I have never liked Hawkins. He was a lowborn schemer from the start and I saw this instantly. I knew what he wanted: power. I was there when he stole Temmer from Bosleigh Norrington."

Scrainwood's right hand played over his jaw. The fact that Hawkins had slapped the king was part of the Traitor's legend, and Alexia had no doubt that Scrainwood was reliving the sting of those blows.

"Now, Princess, I accept that you are brave and honorable, prideful, intelligent, and courageous. I also accept that you are of the weaker sex, and your emotions hold more sway over you than they should. But it is evident that when it comes to combat you set the frailties of your nature aside. I would ask you to look beyond your emotions now and realize that even your best effort will avail you in no way here. The Traitor will be slain for treason. That *is* the way it must be."

Alyx's nostrils flared and red nibbled at the edges of her vision. She would have happily marched over to that throne and plucked Scrainwood from it, then beat him senseless. Two things restrained her, the first being her certainty that Scrainwood would take her offense at his insult as proof of the insult's validity.

The second was Svoinyk raising his left hand. "Highness, the princess would dispute your view of things. The fact of her marriage to Crow casts your statement into doubt. Minister Gapes will agree that as a Prince Consort, Crow is due a new trial, since his station calls into question whether or not he is even capable of committing treason against Oriosa."

Scrainwood snorted at that suggestion. "We have borne the shame of him. He is Oriosan."

"I would beg to differ, Highness. In Yslin, his father stripped his mask from him, and declared in public that he had no son named Tarrant. In my study of your laws, a father may exile his son in this manner, and his name shall be struck from the rolls of Oriosa for all time. Since you brought the elder Hawkins to Yslin, this exile must be seen as being sanctioned by you. Moreover, Crow's trial for treason happened years *after* this exile. In your own history, the rebel Prince Lehern was similarly exiled by his father at the conclusion of the rebellion precisely to prevent his brother from having him tried for treason and killed."

"Do *not* seek to lecture me on my own history, Ambassador. You go too far."

"No offense intended, Highness, for the princess merely intends to honor your history and knows that by it, Oriosa will be fair to the man she has taken as her husband." Svoinyk glanced at Gapes. "The new trial will have to be conducted before a tribunal of his peers, of course. King Augustus is already on his way here to serve. Queen Carus of Jerana is also coming to Meredo. Oriosa will, of course, be represented on the tribunal. Perhaps the king himself will stand in judgment?"

Alyx bit the inside of her cheek to keep from smiling as Scrainwood fidgeted. Svoinyk had warned her as they rode through the snowy streets, that he would inform the king that plans had already been set in motion. Augustus and Carus would be beyond reproach, which put Scrainwood in the minority. Whether or not Scrainwood would join them would be a decision that would be made after a lot of agonizing thought. The expression on Scrainwood's face, albeit half-hidden by his mask, did mark the start of that process.

"Moreover, Minister, the trial will be, of necessity, secret. We shall not want to poison the relations between our nations through any parades or other demonstrations that would suggest Okrannel is harboring and protecting a national enemy. While the trial will allow you to present evidence that Crow is indeed Hawkins, these charges must undergo rigorous scrutiny and, therefore, should not be reduced to fodder for gossipmongers."

Gapes frowned. "Surely, Ambassador, you cannot expect that news of the capture of Hawkins should be kept a secret?"

"Ah, but Minister, did you not already assure me that you were taking steps to see that this was indeed going to be the case?"

The white-haired minister hesitated for a moment, then glanced back at King Scrainwood. "My lord, I have failed you."

"Indeed, you have, Gapes, most tragically." The king looked at Alexia. "Shall we dismiss these two to work out the details, Princess? Your man is more than capable of winning what you desire, and Gapes will give it to him."

Alyx nodded. "And your Marsham shall try to steal it back. You know he will spend secrets faster than a sailor spends gold on shore."

"I will deal with Marsham."

"Or I shall."

Scrainwood's eyes narrowed, then he nodded. "And likely would do me a favor in doing so. Gapes, take the ambassador to your chambers; do what must be done."

Svoinyk looked at Alyx imploringly, but she just nodded. "Go. You know what we want."

"Yes, Highness." Svoinyk left in Gapes' wake.

Scrainwood sat back in his throne, then steepled his fingers, his elbows resting on the arms. "It might appear I have underestimated you."

"You're not convinced?"

The Oriosan King slowly smiled. "My remark about your being of the weaker sex stung, didn't it?"

The sly tone of his voice would have surprised her, had not Crow told her in midnight whispers about Scrainwood and his actions on the first Norrington campaign. *Crow's right, the man thinks he is smarter by half than anyone else.*

Alyx lifted her chin. "I did take offense, yes."

"But you held your tongue. That was good." Scrainwood gestured toward the far end of the room, whence the two men had recently exited. "That earned you your victory, though it was effort spent needlessly. This alleged marriage is to protect Hawkins. You needn't have resorted to trickery. You could have come to me. Accommodations could have been made."

"I don't believe you, Highness." She regarded him coldly. "I believe Crow would have been slain attempting to escape from Call Mably somewhere on the road to the capital. It would have denied you a public execution, which would be difficult to engineer in any regard, since he saved your sister's life by leading her from Fortress Draconis."

"That is a point with merit, though no orders were issued to have Crow slain."

"Not by you, but I would be more than willing to bet Cabot Marsham would have managed to get word to Mably in time."

Scrainwood smiled much too easily. "Your concern for Crow is almost enough to make me believe you do love him. How can you love a man like that?"

"He is a good man. He is brave, loyal, and selfless." Alyx frowned. "Why do you hate him so? Because he slapped you? Because he denied you a sword and a place in history? You know what happened to Leigh Norrington. You were there. I only know it from the songs, but I know enough of songs to know the tragedy was true, though details are lost. Would you truly have wanted that?"

The king's voice sank into a growl. "Are you Okrans all intent on scourging me with history? It was a different time then, different demands."

"I've fought Chytrine. I've slain *sullanciri*. I know what you knew then."

"No, *no*, you don't. I never grew up under the threat of Chytrine. She was a monster from the past. She was something used to frighten children. Her minions, the vylaens and gibberers and frostclaws, they were real enough, but rare—so rare that they seemed things lost from an ancient time when we found them roaming our lands. We were unprepared for the threat thrust upon us."

And you found yourself wanting. Alyx shivered. The man she saw before her had grown bitter and afraid through the decades, but she also knew he had been weak before his generation ever went out to fight Chytrine. She remembered the message his son Erlestoke had asked her to deliver to him, and knew it had been born in a boy's view of his father—before Hawkins had earned Scrainwood's ire.

"By the gods, is that it, then?" Alyx began to pace back and forth before the throne. "You, the prince of the realm, are thrust into a conflict for which you are not prepared, and here come Bosleigh Norrington and Tarrant Hawkins and Kenwick Norrington, an obscure march lord of your realm. They've found gibberers. They've found a magic sword. There is a prophecy concerning them. Your nation is at the forefront of the effort to save the world and defeat Chytrine, and you are not part of it. You go along, of course, but you shy from the work, hiding behind your status as the crown prince."

"No!" Scrainwood rose quickly, his fists balled, his protestation echoing through the hall. He looked as if he would attack her. His eyes blazed beneath his mask, then he coughed and his eyes tightened.

He sat back down. "I am not now as I was then. It was a different world, and I had been raised to deal with that world. Alliances, secrets, trade... These things I knew and could master. It had been a century since the last invasion, and with each year we allowed ourselves to believe Chytrine had died or lost interest. I knew I had nothing to fear, and then the world changed. My rightful role was usurped and I was shamed by some marcher-stripling.

"But in the death of the heroes, I read the future, Princess. I was back in my realm of alliances and secrets, politics and trade. I was in the world of power, and I could see what would happen if word of Chytrine's survival, of Chytrine's threat to the world, were known. Upheaval. Refugees fleeing. What happened to Okrannel happening on a grand scale. I made the others see it. I was truly the one who saved the world, because the mere threat of Chytrine would have destroyed it."

Alyx shook her head. The logic worked, but it was predicated on a complete disregard for reality. A man who could not rise to the challenge on the battlefield shifted everything onto an arena where he was the master. He had convinced himself—perhaps not wrongly—that he had saved the world. The problem was that he had saved it only for a time—the time Chytrine had granted him. Her return threatened everything, and the truth about Crow and his delivering her warning revealed Scrainwood's efforts to have been corrupt.

A spark of fury flashed through her, and Scrainwood toyed with his ring. Alyx recalled having been told the ring had an enchantment that picked up the hostile intent of those near him. She smiled. *He'd not intuited that his remark made me angry; the ring warned him of my anger. The snake.*

She kept her voice calm and even. "There is something you have to understand, Highness. You were not ready for the things thrust upon you a generation ago. I *am*. Crow is very important to Chytrine's defeat, and if you thought about it, you would see that clearly. But since I doubt you will think clearly on it, I shall give you something else to think about."

"A threat, Princess?"

"No, not a threat." She kept her face impassive. "When last I saw your son at Fortress Draconis, Erlestoke asked me to pass on to you a message. He asked me to tell you that, for the sake of your nation, you shouldn't live your whole life as a coward."

The words shook him, but not as strongly as she would have hoped. "There was a time he viewed me as a hero."

"So, perhaps, what you want to think on is whether or not you can have him see you that way again."

Scrainwood shook his head. "He's dead. What he thinks does not matter."

"If that is what you think, then you truly are in luck." She nodded to him once. "Against the threat we face, if you are a coward, your nation will perish. There will be no one left to think on you at all."

CHAPTER 11

I'm dead. Erlestoke harbored no illusions about his chances for survival. For over a month the remnants of the Fortress Draconis garrison had fought running battles with the Aurolani horde. Control of the ruins varied depending upon the time of day. The invaders held sway during daylight and the defenders at night. Sporadic reports of draconette shots and the screams of the wounded filled the darkness as ragged bands of defenders ambushed their enemies.

Erlestoke knew that their strikes at the Aurolani troops were little more than flea bites. The most they could do was pick off patrols, destroy supplies, and otherwise make the occupation of the fortress unpleasant. By day the defenders hid in the warrens beneath the city, and repeated attempts by Chytrine's troops to flush them out had ended badly for the Aurolani.

Chytrine's troops never recoiled from employing even the most blasphemous methods to force the defenders from their sanctuaries. Fortress Draconis' tallest tower still stood. The Crown Tower had been decorated with the skull of a dragon that had died there decades before. To that skull had been tied the body of Dothan Cavarre, the late Draconis Baron, and day by day carrion birds had feasted upon him.

At least two resistance squads had attacked the tower in futile attempts to rescue the baron's remains. They had been cut down ruthlessly, and now their bodies hung from the remaining sections of walls. Chytrine meant for that display to intimidate the remaining defenders, but instead the survivors just took it as a challenge.

Erlestoke had stopped his own squad from making a similar rescue attempt by pointing out that their jobs at Fortress Draconis had not changed. The reasons they had been stationed there—men, elves, *meckanshii,* and urZrethi alike—was to protect the Southlands from invasion and to safeguard the fragments of the DragonCrown. "The best way we show respect for the Draconis Baron is not in saving his bones, but in continuing to perform the task to which he had devoted his life."

The others had agreed, and their dedication to that mission had resulted in Erlestoke's current predicament—one that was likely to cost him *his* life. Prior to its fall, Fortress Draconis had been positioned to prevent Aurolani troops from heading south. The garrison might not have been large enough to destroy any army itself, but cutting off the lines of supply would have been simple. Chytrine had to eliminate Fortress Draconis before any southern invasion could take place.

She had, and her troops streamed southward day and night. Erlestoke's company watched the troop movements, tallied the information, then relayed it south via *arcanslata*—a magical slate that would send to its twin any information written upon it. Erlestoke had no idea where the twin of his unit's *arcanslata* was—though Jilandessa was leaning toward Alcida or Valicia based on some of the brief replies to their information. His squad only sent troop information and had not let anyone know he lived, for fear that information might cause Chytrine to hunt him down for use against his father.

Two days earlier Erlestoke's people had taken up one of their usual vantage points to watch troop movements and had seen new banners appearing within the ranks of the Aurolani hosts heading south. They'd gotten used to the large banners proclaiming the identity of a unit, but of late smaller pennants had flown above these. As they were studying the units, a storm had rolled in from the north, bringing with it a quantity of snow, which drove the troops into Fortress Draconis for shelter and sent Erlestoke's people down into the warm bowels of the earth.

When the storm let up a day and a half later, passing to the south with its fury unabated, Erlestoke had led Ryswin and Pack Castleton up to scout things out, entering a nearby ruin they used as a lookout. As was common, a patrol of gibberers came through. All would have been fine, except that they paused to use the building Erlestoke sheltered in to protect them from a rising breeze.

Even their waiting there would not have been a problem, for the gibberers often lingered until the coming dawn signaled the change of a watch. The man-sized beasts had jutting muzzles and stout fangs, with mottled-fur coats of tan and black that served them poorly for hiding in the snow. Their tufted ears rose from thick skulls and flicked forward and back, though they seemed to rely on their sense of smell more than sight or hearing. The way they snorted in the room below him suggested to Erlestoke that the falling temperature was hard on the delicate tissues, helping to hide his scent from them.

He expected them to move on while it would be dark enough to get his men to safety, and their enthused yips seemed to indicate they would be doing that. But then a harsh bark that echoed down the street cut them off.

Their gibbering died quickly, and Erlestoke chanced to look out, barely peering around the corner of a shattered window casement. He saw a tall, slender creature stalking down the center of a snow-choked avenue. The wind swirled around it, dancing snowflakes curling its wake. It wore a white cloak that matched its snow-white fur. The being stalked forward slowly, turning its head side to side. While the strong jaw gave it the illusion of a muzzle, the creature's face appeared far less bestial than that of the gibberers.

And the eyes. Erlestoke knew he'd seen their like before because they had no color to them. They were akin to a Vorquelf's eyes, with no whites, no discernible pupil, but in this case they were entirely black. Even as he made that determination, however, he caught movement in those eyes, as if some malevolent force were trapped in their inky depths.

The creature's head came up and Erlestoke jerked back, but he knew he'd been seen. As the creature hissed a command, Erlestoke blew on the slow-match of his four-barreled draconette. In response to the order, the gibberkin snarled and started up the snow-strewn steps to the building's second floor. Carrying an unsheathed longknife in its right hand, the lead beast came up and around the corner, charging straight at him.

Erlestoke pulled the trigger on the quadnel and the weapon belched flame and lead. A ball the size of an olive shot from the thick cloud of grey smoke and smashed into the gibberer's belly. The impact spun the creature around and the longknife flew from its hand. Red blood splashed over white snow, then the creature crashed against the second gibberer.

The Oriosan Prince rose from his crouch and drew the saber he'd worn strapped across his back. The blade came easily to hand and weighed far less than it appeared because it once had belonged to one of Chytrine's *sullanciri* and had been enchanted. Erlestoke cast the quadnel aside and engaged the onrushing gibberers.

The blade's magick made fighting the gibberers all too simple. In his sight, color drained from the world, save where a golden glow, or red or blue, suggested the flow of energy. As a gibberer drew a longknife back before a thrust, red power would gather in the muscles needed to make the attack. Forewarned by the shift of color, Erlestoke could counterattack.

And countcrattacking, or just attacking, was something the blade made easy. The edge did not seem sharp, and the blade's light weight would have suggested it could not deliver a heavy blow, but it sheared through thick limbs as if they were bundled straw. A quick cut would sever a wrist, flicking the paw and longknife away, and a blow with the saber's handguard would crush a face.

His first slash spun a gibberer away with its face half-cloven, then a return cut stroked open another gibberer's belly. It pitched through an open hole in the floor, crashing below while another leaped up the stairs at him. That gibberer had a two-handed grip on its longknife, looking to use it like an ax.

Erlestoke moved in toward the gibberer and ducked down so that the blow carried the creature over his back. It crashed down hard, but bounced up quickly, regaining its feet on his left with its back at the window. As he flicked his saber out to the right, the sword cut bit deep into another gibberer's hip, dropping him to slide back down the stairs and ball up at the first snowy landing.

The prince turned toward the unharmed gibberer, but remained low, with his right foot actually a step down the stairs. The saber told him that a quick slice as the beast attacked would cut its legs from under it and send it through the hole in the floor. There was a chance he would be wounded, but the sword's sense of the matter was that his foe would be dead, so personal injury was immaterial.

Erlestoke's resistance to that last idea stayed his hand for a moment, but it did not matter. Starting far to the left and working right, little blasts suddenly opened holes in the wall, one after the other. Plaster and lath cracked and sprayed from four of the holes, and smoke rose from their blackened edges.

The fifth hole did not burn through the wall. Whatever magick had caused it had flown through the window and smashed the gibberer square in the back, lifting the creature from the floor. Erlestoke ducked as the gibberkin flew forward, one of its feet catching his left shoulder. The gibberer spun in the air, then its chest exploded, filling the air with a vapor of viscera, blood, and bone.

As his head came up, gibberer blood still running down his skin, Erlestoke caught sight of the white creature. From beneath the cloak it had produced a wand. The creature's gaze locked with his for a moment, then the wand came up and, his sword abandoned, Erlestoke dove low for his quadnel.

The prince scooped the weapon up and quickly worked the lever that rotated the barrels, seating a loaded one against the firing mechanism. Above the metallic clicks and clanks of the gears, the report of another draconette rang out, then a terrific explosion shook the building. What little wall there had been a dozen feet away had vanished, carrying away the stairs, the landing, and splashing the wounded gibberer into a red stain over the debris.

With the automatic motions that had been trained into him through hours of drilling, Erlestoke primed the new barrel and rolled to his knees at the window. He drew a bead on the slender figure, noting already that its left shoulder was matted with blood, and that more ran in rivulets down its useless left arm.

Its right arm came up, however, and a fiery blue dart shot from the wand. It hit the snowy street three feet in front of Castleton, who had dropped into a crouch and was priming his quadnel. The explosion lifted the soldier and whirled him loose-limbed into the air. He crashed down into the snow twenty feet away, disappearing in a cloud of drifting powder snow.

Erlestoke shot and hit the creature high in the chest. A sharp jet of arterial blood squirted into the cold air, then the thing flopped back into the snow. It shook heavily and its limbs twitched violently. Then Ryswin reached it and beheaded it with a short stroke of a gibberer longknife.

The prince leaped from the window and landed in the snow with a crouch. "Ryswin, bring that thing with you!"

"Yes, sir."

Erlestoke ran to where Castleton lay and turned him over. The blast had torn the Oriosan's mask off and had taken with it most of his face. The man's lipless mouth worked for a second, but produced only bloody froth, not words. His back bowed, then he slackened.

The prince reached down and closed the one remaining eye, then searched for the man's quadnel. He slung the draconette over his shoulder, then returned to his fallen comrade and dragged his body off. Ryswin joined him quickly, and the two of them descended through hidden passages that opened before them and closed after, to reach their haven.

Erlestoke gave the two quadnels to their weapons-master, Verum. A couple of other people had taken Castleton's body from him and, off in a corner, were busy washing him and sewing him into a shroud. Across the room, on a table that had seen many a use in their campaign, the raven-haired Harquelf Jilandessa and the *meckanshii* colonel from Murosa, Jancis Ironside, had stretched out the creature. Even without its head, it was tall enough that its feet hung off the edge.

The prince crossed to them. "What is it?"

The elf shook her head. "I've not seen its like before, nor have I heard of anything similar. I could make guesses, but I like them not at all."

Erlestoke rested a hand on her shoulder. "It wields magick more capably than a vylaen. It took two quadnel shots and still did not cease moving until beheaded. It gave orders to gibberers and they obeyed instantly. It's bad enough as it is. Your guessing can't make it worse."

The elf healer nodded, then ran her hand over the creature's belly, rucking up its fur. Beneath the white fur she exposed pink flesh and then a dark tattoo of some arcane symbol. "Do you recognize that?"

"Not really, though I've seen similar on Vorquelves."

"Exactly." She pointed to the creature's head. "I worked magick on the body, just a simple diagnostic spell to get a sense of it. There is vylaen there, clearly, but also elf. Elves don't really differentiate in sense depending upon their homeland, but if one is talented, you can pick up slight variations. This creature has a Vorquellyn taint to it."

The prince nodded. "I noticed the eyes."

Jancis Ironside reached over with her left hand and pried one of the thing's eyes open. Being a *meckanshii*—one of the warriors whose useless limbs had been replaced with mechanical parts—her left hand only had two fingers and a thumb, yet moved with a singular delicacy. "Very hard to miss, these eyes. The look of them sends a shiver through even my metal limbs."

The creature's eyes had begun to cloud in death, but Erlestoke could still imagine something lurking in their depths. He looked at the elf again. "You think these things come from Vorquellyn?"

She nodded. "You know that Yrulph Kirûn, centuries ago, forcefully crossbred *araftii* with elves to create the Gyrkyme. I fear that Chytrine honors her master once more in creating these things. They feel as if they are a cross between vylaens and Vorquelves, born on Vorquellyn. She took the homeland, now she uses it to breed a population of warmages to lead her gibberers against us."

That idea sent a chill down the prince's spine. "Is there any way we can tell for certain?"

"I will make measurements, map the tattoos, look for other clues. If we had more of them, it might help."

Erlestoke nodded. "I'll see what we can do."

Jancis hugged her flesh-and-blood hand to her mechanical shoulder. "Highness, we know Chytrine left a week ago, maybe twelve days, and we assumed she had found and carried away all the pieces of the DragonCrown."

"Yes, that's what we concluded. And we decided she kept troops here to prevent anyone from reoccupying the fortress and threatening her lines of supply."

"Both logical assumptions. But why, then, would she bring creatures so adept at magick here?"

The prince adjusted his mask. "I see your point. If she has a reason for bringing them, it must be an important one. Perhaps she's missing a piece of the Crown, or there is something else of value here. So, just as vital as learning what they are will be learning why they are here. Good thinking, Colonel Ironside; I would have missed that."

Ryswin walked over and nodded to the prince. "Highness, Castleton is in his shroud. Nygal and I shall carry him deep into the tunnels and find a spot to wall him up."

"Ryswin, come quick!" Nygal Tymtas, the young soldier from Savarre, shouted from the corner where Castleton had been laid. "Something very strange is going on."

The elf and the prince dashed toward the corner, then stopped. The stones in the floor upon which Castleton's body rested had begun to glow; heat pulsed out from them. Nygal leaped back and the tips of his boots smoked, though oddly the white canvas of the shroud showed not a scorch or wisp of vapor. The rock became fluid and a thin crust crumbled, revealing a red-gold puddle of stone. The body floated there for a moment, then began to sink, starting at the head and shoulders, then gradually settling in at the feet. His toes were the last to go and when they disappeared, a small golden wave of rock lapped over them, then the stone darkened and cooled.

Erlestoke stared at the flat stone where his comrade's body had lain. "No one here did anything? Said anything? Somehow invoked magick?"

A chorus of negative answers echoed through the chamber.

"Okay, I believe that, which means I don't know what just happened. Inside the hour we're vacating this place. Pack up everything we can. We're going deeper." He turned and studied all of their faces. "I don't know if what just happened was for good or ill, but until we know, it's reason enough for us to keep moving."

CHAPTER 12

It didn't occur to Kerrigan that trying to catch a snowflake on his tongue might not be dignified until he heard someone behind him clearing his throat, and a hissed whisper accompanying it.

Until that point, Kerrigan had been out, knee deep in snow, not far from the inn in which he was being housed, marveling at how the snow softened the city of Meredo. It muted the gay colors splashed on houses and hid the red of the tiled roofs. Thick garlands of it covered the skeletal branches of the trees and little drifts had collected in corners. The thick flakes fell slowly, then swirled and eddied, sometimes dancing down the street, other times falling from branches and eaves in a puff of snow.

Kerrigan had seen snow before on Vilwan. Still, the warmth of the ocean tended to ensure that any snow that fell did not last very long. He'd certainly never seen the quantity that had fallen in Meredo, nor had he been allowed to go out in it.

Just raising his face to the sky and feeling flakes melt against his cheeks had made him laugh. His delight mirrored that of children playing in the snow, launching snowballs at each other, building forts, shrieking as they closed and threw, then ran as a volley from playmates chased them back. Other children lay on their backs, flapping their arms, making snow-Gyrkyme, while yet others crawled into barrels and careened wildly down hills, screaming all the way.

Yet Kerrigan's smile had not been for the snow alone. His previous experience in cities had been something less than positive. In Yslin he'd gotten waylaid by a gang of street urchins and beaten up. And Fortress Draconis had been a city of war. There were few children and less laughter.

The thing that made the difference here was the attitude displayed. As he wandered into the snow-choked street, he had impulsively hand-packed a snowball and thrown it at a hitching post—missing horribly—a man gathering wood smiled at his effort. Some kids threw at the same post from further away, and they cheered and laughed as one hit it. A woman brushing snow from the steps looked at him and nodded, smiling as frosty breath wreathed her face.

None of them knew him, since he had arrived in Meredo with no fanfare. He was just a person and even in a city where those who wore masks considered themselves superior to others, everyone still smiled and was polite. There was a cheerful civility to the interaction of strangers that he'd never really known before, and he liked it.

The voice and the whisper, however, had none of the same friendliness. Kerrigan turned slowly and saw a trio of figures, two male and one female. He did not recognize any of them, but the cadaverous man in the lead wore the grey robes of a Magister, despite his seeming youth. The man's shaved head, beaked nose, and prominent larynx conspired with the grey pallor of his flesh to reinforce the impression that he was dead or close to it. The woman and the other man, who made up in bulk what their leader lacked, both wore the blood-scarlet robes of Adepts, though without any other decorations that might cue him as to their areas of expertise.

The Magister nodded solemnly and drew his hands to the small of his back. "You are Kerrigan Reese."

Kerrigan felt a shiver run up his spine. Orla had admonished him to stay away from Vilwan, and this trio represented his old home. Part of him wished running were an option, but even if there were no snow, he could not have moved fast enough to escape a spell.

And running would be thinking like prey.

Kerrigan nodded slowly. "I am."

"I am Magister Syrett Kar. I am here to take you home."

"Take me home?"

"To Vilwan."

Kerrigan shook his head. "Vilwan is not my home."

The woman leaned in to whisper something to Kar, but the Magister raised his left hand to silence her. "Adept Reese, you have been through a great deal. The Grand Magister is pleased with all you have accomplished. You are now required to return to Vilwan with us to complete your training."

"There is nothing more for me to learn at Vilwan, Magister." Kerrigan tugged on the sleeves of the sheepskin coat he wore, then stripped off his mittens. "I have things that need to be done here, and I will do them."

"You are mistaken, Adept Reese."

The man snaked menace into his voice and it found an ally inside Kerrigan. *My whole entire life has been spent being mistaken, learning, training, trying to do things no one else could do, being told I was wrong, and being made to do it over and over again until I got it right and got another task.* None of his teachers had ever told him *why* he was being asked to do the things he was, why he was getting the training he was. All they told him was that he was wrong or stupid or too slow or too sloppy. They had used the same tone of voice over and over, and part of him bent to respond to it.

Another part, however, rebelled. It was the part of him that had been reinforced by countless little things. Since leaving Vilwan he had done many things right. Perhaps not everything, but he had done enough things right, and those successes drained Kar's voice of some potency.

Kerrigan brought his chin up. "By what authority do you command me?"

The Magister's composure broke for a heartbeat, but he narrowed the surprise out of his brown eyes quickly enough. "How dare you question me?"

"How dare I not, Magister? I know that I am engaged in the struggle to defeat Chytrine. I know she will stop at nothing to stop me. How do I know you are not students of her academy masquerading as officials from Vilwan? In fact, I do not believe you are *from* Vilwan, but instead serve at the consulate here."

While Syrett Kar kept his face impassive, the chunky Adept at his right did not. That man looked surprised. His female compatriot's blue eyes darkened as she stared hard at Kerrigan. She took a couple steps to the left and removed her gloves.

Kar glanced in her direction and frowned. "Adept Tetther, no melodramatics. Adept Reese will not be attacking us." Kar's gaze returned to Kerrigan. "Your questions are well asked. We should go to the consulate to get the answers. I do know you've not visited there yet. That should prove I am genuine."

"Chytrine surely has agents watching our consulate." Kerrigan fought to keep his nervousness out of his voice. "You may return to the consulate, and when you have sufficient authorization to compel my return, then send me a message and I shall come. Not before."

The woman snarled. "We do have 'sufficient authorization.'"

Kerrigan turned his head, slowly and fluidly, imitating the look of contempt he'd seen Resolute use. "Sufficient for you, perhaps, but my concerns dwell in spheres far above your petty interests."

He knew he'd been pushing it with that last, and she reacted hotly. Power began to course through her as her fingers clawed. Kar turned toward her, snapping a command, but her eyes had tightened into angry slits. The other Adept began to withdraw, a look of horror widening on his face.

Time began to move oddly for Kerrigan. Part of him—the scared child that wanted to comply with Kar's commands—recognized the danger. Just from the traces of the magick radiating out from Tetther, Kerrigan deduced she was a combat specialist and had been ready to deal harshly with him. Part of him wanted to drop to his knees and beg for mercy, but the fear remained muted and controllable.

Another part of him, that which had studied magick, likewise recognized the threat. He analyzed it in an instant, knew the spell, and had a choice of a half-dozen spells that would counter it. A couple he could have cast quickly enough to stop her spell from even being cast. Her effort would have been bottled up in her body, and would have savaged her. As an exercise in magery, he viewed his counter and the consequences in a completely clinical matter—the human cost merely a minor abstraction.

A third part of him, the part tempered by all he had seen and done since leaving Vilwan, won out. He ignored the fear. He acknowledged the cost. Then he gestured with his right hand, simply and easily, triggering a spell he knew so well that using it was hardly an effort.

It was the telekinetic spell he'd used to pluck books from a library shelf and, just as easily, had used to pluck a ship from the ocean. In this case he used it to tickle snow from a roof and brought it sliding down upon her in a small avalanche. The snowfall slammed heavily into her back, pitching her forward and burying her. It knocked the wind from her and shattered the concentration she needed to cast her spell.

Kar leaped back a step. He looked at her, then carefully brushed a dusting of snow from his chest and arms before turning toward Kerrigan. "You took a chance dealing with her that way."

Kerrigan shook his head. "No chance at all." He looked up at the roofline and Kar turned to follow his gaze. Up there, at the peak of the red tile wedge, squatted Lombo. "If I hadn't done something, he would have. Please tell Vilwan I am well protected."

The Magister blinked, then glanced at Tetther struggling to free herself from the mound of snow. "You are not what I was led to believe you would be."

"And what was that?"

Kar started to answer, then snapped his mouth shut. "It doesn't matter. I shall get the authorization. But I suppose I should ask what you will consider sufficient."

Kerrigan shrugged. "I suppose that is a point I can discuss with the Grand Magister when he arrives."

"You can't honestly believe..."

Kerrigan held a hand up. "My last mentor was slain by Chytrine, but she was your senior by decades. You know enough about me to know I am assigned to no one school of magick, so I have no Magister over me. With Orla dead, the Grand Magister is the only one to whom I should answer. That is the way of Vilwan. It is the system from which you derive your authority."

Kar frowned. "Now you have me puzzled, Adept."

"About what?"

"You have concluded that I am not sufficiently versed in combat magicks to apprehend you. If I were, I'd not have brought Adept Tetther along, and had I had any inkling of this outcome, I would have brought more people. You are powerful enough to ignore me, but you provide me this reasonable request to give me a way to preserve my dignity and avoid having to explain how I failed to bring you in."

Kerrigan fought mightily to keep any expression off his face. Will had recently confessed to Kerrigan that he didn't really know what Kerrigan had been carrying until Kerrigan himself had confirmed his guess. *Will called it a bluff.* Just as Kerrigan had assumed Will had known something he did not, Kar was assuming Kerrigan had drawn certain conclusions and Kerrigan clearly saw it was in his best interest to let the Magister go right on believing them.

"Magister, no disrespect intended, but I've been at Svoin and Port Gold and Fortress Draconis. I've lived with Panqui. I've fought pirates. I've fought bandits in Yslin and gibberers in the woodlands of the Black Marches. There are events unfolding that are more important than the orders you've been given. If I have to choose between obeying you and defeating Chytrine, well, my choice is clear. As should yours be."

Kar nodded slowly; then walked to the half-buried Tetther. With the help of the other Adept, he dragged her clear. Kar sent the two Adepts off, then turned and bowed in Kerrigan's direction. "I would like to say I shall see you shortly, but I do not feel I will. My school, by the way, is Clairvoyance—this is how we knew where to find you."

"Clairvoyance is one of the most difficult schools to master." Kerrigan glanced at the pile of snow. "You said you had no idea that she could not handle me. Your visions stopped with meeting me here?"

"One did. Others, well..." The man sighed out a cloud of steam. "Your path, Adept, moves through more darkness than light. Be wary, but of stout heart."

Kerrigan nodded, then bowed respectfully. "Thank you, Magister. If our paths do cross again, I hope it will be in the light."

"As do I, Adept Reese, as do I."

The grey-robed mage departed and a heartbeat after he turned a corner and disappeared from sight, Lombo leaped from the roof and landed in the snowpile that had buried Tetther. His claws raked through the snow, then he smiled up at Kerrigan. "Good no kill."

"Sorry for robbing you of your fun, my friend. She didn't deserve to die."

"More smart live longer."

"True enough." Kerrigan smiled. "Had you not been up there, I'd not have thought of bringing the snow down on her."

"Kerrigan no kill." Lombo shrugged. "No kill hard."

"No. It's just that killing is a lot easier for some. I just can't..."

"No need." Lombo ambled over to him and draped a long arm over his shoulders. "Kerrigan make Will-talk. But less."

The magicker laughed. "Yes, Will can talk a lot but sometimes, what he says is useful. It was here. It saved a lot of trouble. That's good, I guess."

Lombo nodded. "Much trouble coming."

"So Magister Kar said." Kerrigan sighed out a misty cloud. "Let's just hope it's not so much trouble that Will-talk and no kill can't get us out of it."

CHAPTER 13

Will did his best not to gawk as Count Marsham led him into the palace throne room. While the building had the external architecture of a fortress, with narrowed windows and thick walls, parts of the interior had clearly undergone extensive renovation. For while the throne room did still feature thick columns that supported a vaulted ceiling, the walls had been covered with wooden panels framed in gilt. Wonderful murals covered the panels, and while a quick glance suggested a few hid secret doors, they were obviously there for decoration more than utility.

A thick green carpet led from the doorway to the throne. On either side of it a marble mosaic floor with grand patterns in white, black, and red spread out. It looked fairly new based on the lack of wear. The throne itself sat on a small dais and consisted of a high-backed chair and canopy, with two extensions on either side for Scrainwood's sons. The fact that their seats were little more than a green velvet cushion over a slab of wood would do nothing at all to encourage them to attend court.

Marsham stopped just inside the door. "Highness, I present Lord Norrington."

Scrainwood looked up from the small book he had been perusing. Though Will himself couldn't read and hadn't much studied the habits of readers, he knew Scrainwood had affected the pose to make himself seem smarter. The light slanting in from the windows didn't fall close enough to the throne actually to let the king read. This realization put Will further on his guard as he composed a smile for the king.

Scrainwood snapped the book closed and smiled, then rose. "Of course,

Marsham, I know my friend Lord Norrington by sight. Who does not? He's quite taken our city by storm. Our people love him as I do, as the world does."

"Of course, Highness. As I love him as well."

"As well you should, Marsham." The king nodded once, then shooed Marsham off with a flick of his hand. The gesture seemed small at so long a range, but it shook Marsham. The man clearly did not like being dismissed, especially in so casual a manner.

He turned to go, but Will reached a hand out to stop him. "Count Marsham, your service to us is so dear." Will grasped the man's right hand in both of his and pumped it fiercely, then half turned and waved the man toward the door.

Marsham departed, but glanced covertly at his hand, just to make certain all his rings were still there. He bowed as he exited, then closed the doors. Before they clicked shut, Will did see the man glaring at him, and the thief suppressed the desire to stick out his tongue.

Cabot Marsham had found him at the Rampant Panther Inn where Alexia's companions had taken rooms. The man's speech had been flowery and *unctuous*—a word Will got from Kerrigan and, while he didn't know what it meant, it just sounded right. Marsham had spoken of the honor it would be to conduct him to the king, and the hope and love he had for Will. Despite that, Will noted that the man wore far fewer rings than the lines on his fingers suggested he preferred, had chosen older clothing for his journey, and carried a purse with no serious weight of coin in it.

If trust were measured in gold, Marsham's couldn't have bought sour beer and moldy bread meant for swineslop.

But, as far as Will was concerned, swineslop would have been too good for Marsham, and probably for the king as well. In spite of that belief, Will adjusted his mask, then bowed deeply.

"Will, no need for formality between such as us. While you may be only a lord, you and I are cut of the same cloth. Great times demand great efforts from the great, and we are great." Scrainwood beckoned him forward as casually as he had dismissed Marsham, though it struck Will that dismissal came far more naturally to him than summoning. "Come here, Will. There are things we must discuss."

The thief marched straight down the carpet, glancing at the panels and the windows. Wearing his mask did not bother him, save where it trimmed a little off his peripheral vision. Still he did spot many things that would be of great value, were they not far too large to be carried off easily.

A flashed vision of fire and of gibberers hauling things away shook him. *The only way any of this will leave here is if the palace is looted.* At first that struck him as a good thing, since it would punish Scrainwood. That thought, however, died as Will realized that the sacking of the palace would mean the city had fallen. The smiling faces of those who had greeted him, of those who had seen him as a savior, melted into tortured reflections in bloody pools.

Will focused on the king as he stopped a dozen feet from the dais. "What would you have of me, Highness?"

"First, my hearty greeting and best wishes. I apologize for taking so long to bring you here. I simply insist that you move from your current lodgings and stay here in the palace."

The thief nodded. "Your invitation is most kind, Highness, but I shall remain where I am. The people like having me there. We sing and tell stories. It makes them happy and less afraid."

Scrainwood hesitated for a moment, as if weighing Will's argument. "But your safety is in question."

"You've never taken a good look at Resolute, have you?"

"He is your Vorquelf?"

The thief winced. "He and Crow found me and have kept me safe. He's killed a *sullanciri*. They both have. I'm safe with him."

The king nodded in acquiescence, but Will thought his surrender was a bit too quick. "I shall abide by your wishes in that matter, though I should point out that, as a Lord of the Realm, you do have certain incomes that mean you can afford better lodgings."

Will's expression did brighten at the mention of money, but the quick flash in the king's eyes cautioned him. "I didn't know that, Highness."

"Indeed. You are not the richest of nobles, but Valsina does produce rents and incomes. The merchantman Playfair has been administering the holdings ever since your father ... went away. He keeps a good accounting, steals little, and delivers the taxes on time. It would not be an exaggeration to say you could buy the tavern where you dwell now without a significant diminution of your wealth."

The thief frowned with concentration and slowly divined the meaning of the king's words. "That much, huh? That's a lot, because they're charging us a blind a night."

Scrainwood stiffened as Will used the slang term for the realm's gold coin. Officially known as a crown, it had Scrainwood in profile on the face. Almost without exception, the coins in circulation had that single eye punched, gouged, scraped, or scratched out. Some said it was because Scrainwood used magick to watch them through the coins, but Will had the feeling that most folks just wanted the king to turn a blind eye on them and their dealings.

Will continued, letting his words flow quickly and his voice betray a lack of sophistication. "So that would make ten blinds for a week and in a month thirty, so for a year that would be, um, well, that is more money than I've ever had before. Are you sure it is mine?"

"Yes, Will, it is. It belongs to you as right of your blood and"—the king injected gravity into his voice—"because of the responsibilities you acquit to the crown. You do wish to observe and maintain the responsibilities of a noble, do you not, Will Norrington?"

The thief nodded because that was the response the king wanted.

"Very good." Scrainwood stepped down from the dais and wandered off toward the windows. Snow still came down. In the last four days there had been one day of sunshine, but all it did was melt a crust onto the snow and coat roadways with ice, then two more days of snow had fluttered white over the city. Just getting Will to the palace had been a chore for Marsham's cursing coachman and in another couple of days, the city would be immobilized.

"As you know, Will, the trial of Hawkins for treason against your nation and against your family soon will begin. King Augustus and Queen Carus will be arriving late today or early tomorrow and the trial will begin a half-week from now. Your participation in that trial will be vital. Hawkins, being from Valsina, is one of your vassals. He owes a duty to you and your family that he failed to acquit."

The king turned and the light from the window lanced down to outline him in silver fire, darkening his face. "You have spoken affectionately of Crow. I know the songs you sing in the tavern, songs of your own making, praise him. I've heard 'The Lay of Ganagrei,' and found it quite stirring though clearly fanciful. Your attachment to Hawkins is understandable, but you are young and even now growing into adult responsibilities. Do you understand what I am saying?"

Will nodded. "I think I do, Highness."

"Then let us make certain there is no mistaking it. You were given a man's mask years ahead of your time. Destiny has chosen you, Will, and destiny will require that you do many things that you might otherwise wish to avoid. Hawkins, years before you were born—years before you met him—betrayed this nation. He betrayed me. He betrayed your father and grandfather and barely avoided bringing ruin upon the world. All that you fight now is his fault, and his efforts on your behalf spring from remorse, nothing more.

"As a noble of this realm, it is your sworn duty to protect your nation from treason. For this reason, you have a duty to preserve lawful order. Hawkins was convicted of treason before, but because of maneuvering by Princess Alexia, we need to try him again. Your word, as a noble and his lord, will carry much weight in court. If you denounce him, he will be condemned. If you do not, your nation will crumble, for all order and discipline will collapse."

The thief scratched at the back of his head. "So you are telling me that unless I help condemn a man who hasn't done anything wrong, I'll destroy Oriosa?"

"Exactly, Will." Scrainwood came forward enough that Will could see his face. "There are forces that are balanced around Oriosa. Only by maintaining that balance do we survive. It is the life of one man—a man far from innocent—for the lives of all Oriosans. Once Hawkins would have offered himself gladly for this trade, but now, like the coward he is, he fights the inevitable."

"So you want me to do my duty as a noble of the realm?"

"Yes."

"And you want me to denounce Crow?"

"Yes." Scrainwood smiled. "You have it, my boy."

"No, Highness, I don't think I will do it."

The king canted his head and returned to his throne. "What do you mean?"

Will shifted his shoulders, then brought his head up. "Well, Highness, while I've been here I've been studying this duty thing, and my duty is to the nation."

"That's what I have said."

"Yes, but you're confusing *yourself* with Oriosa. They're not the same."

The king barked a laugh. "Civics lessons from a whoreget street-child? You will do what I tell you."

"I will do my duty as a noble of the realm, and that means speaking the truth about my vassal. I don't know what he did so long ago, but I know what he's done now and killing a *sullanciri* ain't the half of it. I'm not lying about Crow for you or anybody."

Scrainwood's eyes blazed angrily. "Do you not understand? I made you; I can unmake you!"

Will snarled. "That won't happen. You made me a noble, but Crow made me *the* Norrington. I've spent the last week letting everyone know I am the Norrington. They've seen me. They've heard my stories. They like me, which is more than can be said of you. If I walked out of here today and started saying that you were Chytrine's body-slave, the people would believe me. And they'd believe it on up to and past the time they hung you with your own guts."

"You go too far!" Scrainwood sprang from the dais and aimed a backhanded slap at Will. The blow caught the thief over his ear and spun him toward the window. He'd not expected Scrainwood to actually attack him, but he'd known forever that a coward was one step removed from a bully.

And it hadn't taken Resolute to train him how to deal with bullies.

With rage purpling his face, the king rushed forward and aimed a kick at Will's body. The youth twisted aside, then grabbed the king's leg and did a quick half turn before releasing. Scrainwood, off-balance and flailing, smashed back against the wall, then slid to the floor. His simple coronet spun off, flashing and whirling in the sunlight, then rang as it ran down and clattered on the cold stone.

Will danced back, rubbing his ear, then peered down at the Oriosan leader. Scrainwood rubbed one hand at the back of his head. Will didn't see any blood on the wall or the man's hand and that disappointed him. For a moment he consoled himself by listening to the painful groans coming from the king.

Then the full realization of what he'd done slammed into him. *I've assaulted the king. Whatever he had in mind to do to Crow, that will be nothing compared to what he does to me. Oh, and if he doesn't kill me, Resolute will!*

Scrainwood snarled. "There can be a treason trial for you, too, whoreget. I shall have you torn apart before Crow, since that will hurt him more."

"Um, aren't you forgetting something? I'm the Norrington. You can't kill me."

"This is my realm, there is nothing I cannot do."

"I can think of one. You can't give your people hope." Will drew hair down to cover his red ear. "Without hope, without a belief in the prophecy that will save them, your nation will die. Like it or not, I am that hope."

"Little boy, I have given my people more than hope. I have kept them safe."

"By betraying Oriosa. Everyone knows it, but is afraid to act because you balance Chytrine off against everyone else. Once that slips, you are dead."

"Was that a threat?" The king snorted. "How dare you threaten me?"

"Hey, who started the hitting here? Who's talking about having me torn apart? I'm giving as good as I get, so, yes, I'm a threat to you." Will folded his arms over his chest to keep his pounding heart inside his ribs. "And if you don't think I'm a credible threat, just be thinking on the last time a Norrington paid a visit to this room. I'm not my grandfather, but I'm just as dedicated to my duty as he was."

The thief stepped toward the king, then stooped and picked up the coronet. He turned it over in his hands, then rolled it back to Scrainwood. "I will do my duty to Oriosa, to my friends, and to the world. So leave me alone to do it."

Without looking back, Will stalked from the room, slamming a fist against his hip so it hurt. It had been stupid to let anger get the better of him. Scrainwood had viewed him as a pawn to be manipulated, and now saw him as an enemy. *Not like I need another one.*

He shrugged. *Let him get in line. If Chytrine leaves anything of me behind, he's welcome to it.*

CHAPTER 14

Alexia had a commander's dislike for surprises. She guarded against them as much as possible, but the political maelstrom that was Meredo gave her a difficult battlefield. King Augustus had arrived from Alcida and was ensconced in Scrainwood's palace. Queen Carus had taken up residence in the home of a noble, and Alexia had spoken with representatives of both leaders. Since they were going to serve on the tribunal along with Prince Linchmere, it would have been untoward for her to speak with them directly, but she was able to let their people know how vital Crow was to the war against Chytrine.

Wave after wave of blizzards had delayed the start of the trial, since snow-clogged streets made movement through Meredo almost impossible. Alexia had appreciated Kerrigan's apparent delight with the snow—and Will's hatred of it, since it made tracking a thief easy and the rooftops a treacherous route. The snow made the city pretty by hiding garbage middens and making things more quiet, which Alexia enjoyed. Still she resented the storms since they meant Perrine could not fly.

So, the princess and her earthbound sister contented themselves playing chess in her chamber. They both agreed to play by Gyrkyme rules, which stated that the Gyrkyme piece—which could leap other pieces because it was airborne—could only be brought down by archers that shot along the board's diagonals. That variation normally outraged players, but both of them had grown up using it, so it would have seemed unnatural to play any other way.

A heavy pounding on the door interrupted their game. Even before Alexia could bid the caller to enter, the latch tripped and the door opened. Alexia had already moved from her chair and slid her sword from its scabbard, leveling it at the door.

The slender, hatchet-faced woman standing there raised an eyebrow. "Prepared to spill your own blood, Alexia?"

The princess did not lower the blade immediately. "Aunt Tatyana, I had no idea you were in Meredo. How did you get here?"

The white-haired woman shrugged and flicked her cloak off. Before the dark woolen garment could hit the floor, one of the two huge men behind her caught it. Both of them wore the same black uniforms with white piping on the sleeves and trouser legs. Alexia did not recognize them, but knew their uniforms. The Crown Circle Guards were revered among the Okrans exiles and known for their devotion to the royal family in general and Grand Duchess Tatyana in particular. Had she ordered them to get her to the moon, they would have found a way and been quick about it.

"My carriage until the snow, then a sleigh. We knew much snow in Okrannel, Alexia. It was no hardship."

"I suppose it was not." The princess resheathed her sword in the scabbard hanging on the back of her chair, then pointed with her left hand to Perrine. "You remember my companion, Perrine."

The old woman looked the Gyrkyme up and down, as if viewing a dullard servant who had just broken a valuable dish. "Yes, of course. You are well?"

"Yes, Grand Duchess."

"Splendid. You will leave us now."

Alexia snarled. "She is not a servant. She is my sister."

That comment brought an answering snarl to Tatyana's thin upper lip, which was only calmed with apparent effort. "Your *sister,* indeed, child. Well, I need to speak with you, and I would save you the embarrassment of doing so before your . . . *sister.*"

Peri just blinked her big amber eyes innocently and Alexia wanted to laugh. Anyone else would have withered under Tatyana's frigid blue gaze, but Perrine paid her no attention. She would only leave if she desired to be absent, or if Alexia asked her to go. That her presence would irritate the Grand Duchess was ample inducement for her to want to stay.

The princess shook her head. "Anything you say to me she will be told. I have no secrets from her."

Tatyana's eyes widened for a moment. "None?"

Alyx hesitated. She'd not told Peri about the Communion of Dragons, primarily because she could not. That inability to share did eat at Alyx a little, but if Peri noticed anything was wrong, she said nothing.

Tatyana's question was not directed at the Communion, however, but something the old woman found far more important. The Crown Circle, based on a vision Tatyana had had, decreed that every Okrans noble in exile should, at the age of fifteen, undertake a "dream raid," in which they entered Okrannel and spent a night on their native soil. The dreams they had that night were viewed as having the clairvoyant power of the Norrington Prophecy. Raiders, when they returned to Yslin and the Crown Circle, were bid to share their dreams only with the circle of elders. For Alexia to have told Perrine about her dreams would have been a treason more serious than Crow's in the eyes of her great-grandaunt.

Alexia nodded slowly. "I share with her my heart, my mind, my hopes, and *many* of my dreams, but not all."

Tatyana appeared to be momentarily mollified. She raised a hand and one of the Guards entered the room, secured the chair Alyx had been using, then offered it to the Grand Duchess. She sat demurely, then looked up at her great-grandniece. "I came as soon as I heard the absurd claim that you have married this Crow. Who is he?"

Alyx folded her arms across her belly and leaned back against the wall. "You met him in Yslin, Aunt Tatyana. The night of the reception for General Adrogans. The man who fetched me wine."

"Your *servant*? Alexia, how could you do that? He is not a noble; he is nothing. And then he turns out to be the Traitor Hawkins? He murdered your father, you know."

"He did nothing of the kind."

The old woman's eyes became bitter. "You were barely alive then."

"And you weren't at Fortress Draconis."

"No, but I *was* present when the world's rulers learned what happened there. Only your father stood against a *sullanciri*. Hawkins could have saved him, but he ran. After your father died, he returned with the sword that slew the *sullanciri*, but it was too late. And he delayed, deliberately, because he hated your father for being all the things he could not be."

The venom in Tatyana's voice shocked Alyx. She'd long thought of her great-grandaunt as bitter, but never before had she heard such vitriol coursing through the woman's words. Tatyana had taken Prince Kirill's death hard. But while she was a bitter woman, she had previously reserved her bile for those who stood between her and the plans to liberate Okrannel.

Tatyana's nostrils flared angrily. "Some will say he was but a child then. Others will excuse things because of the nature of the time or the *sullanciri*'s magick, but Hawkins himself said he regretted your father's death. Had you heard him, Alexia, heard him *then*, not now—not after he has had a quarter century to practice his lies and justify things in his mind—you'd have known he regretted his actions at Fortress Draconis."

"Enough!" Alyx pushed off from the wall and slammed her closed fist on the table, making the chess pieces dance and topple. "I will not have you saying that of Crow. I will not have you saying that of my *husband*."

Tatyana's eyes grew huge. "By the gods, Alexia, you are *not* carrying his child!" The old woman held a skeletal hand out toward her, the fingers clawed and trembling.

"Enough, Aunt Tatyana, enough!" Alexia gave in to temptation and rubbed a hand over her belly as she had seen many a pregnant woman do. "If you came here to hector me, you've made a fine start."

The old woman's voice did not soften, but shrank to a whisper. "I came here to remind you of your duty to your nation. You know, as do I, that when we liberate Okrannel—when *you* liberate our homeland—you will be placed on the throne. While our nation has prospered somewhat in exile, we both know that our resources are insufficient to allow us to rebuild. Svoin is gone, and re-creating it will bankrupt us. You, however, are the gateway to a dynasty. Your union with a Southlands princeling would bring us what we need to rise again."

Alexia laughed and Peri joined her, though softly. "Who would you have me marry, Aunt Tatyana? Linchmere? King Augustus has no eligible sons. Savarre might, but is too far away to trade; likewise for any nation save Saporicia, Jerana, and Gurol. The first two of them are without possibilities, and while Prince Joachim of Gurol is an option, Gurol is almost as poor as Okrannel."

Her aunt shook her head. "You overlook the obvious: Erlestoke of Oriosa."

"He remained behind at Fortress Draconis. His father says he is dead."

The old woman shrugged her shoulders. "Scrainwood is not all-seeing, Alexia."

Whereas you are? Alexia swallowed the barb. "And you think my being married to Crow will prevent a liaison? Erlestoke, praise the gods if he yet lives, has a lover and a child by her. Would that not make him even less desirable than me?"

"Don't be a silly girl, Alexia. You know the way of the world. Arrangements can be made. Annulments may be had."

Alexia let her violet eyes harden. "Very well, let arrangements be made, if I survive the war. If I liberate Okrannel."

Tatyana hissed and darted a hooded glance at Peri. "You *will* liberate Okrannel. You *know* that."

A shiver ran down Alexia's back. The emphasis in her great-grandaunt's words took her back to her meeting with the Crown Circle after the dream raid. She had stood there and explained to them, in exquisite detail, the series of battles she would lead against Chytrine's troops. She had told them of new warmages that she would field, and how the battles would run. She insisted she would be victorious and had impressed them all with her knowledge of warfare. They had taken heart in her dreams and in her skills, hence the hope of all Okrans exiles rested with her.

"Yes, Aunt Tatyana, I *do know;* therefore, I know there will be time to make these arrangements of which you speak. I am not mindless of my duty to my nation, but I am also very mindful of my duty to my friends."

The old woman's thin lips pressed together into a line, then she slowly nodded. "I see. So this is a sham?"

Alyx lifted her chin. "We have slept together. Scrainwood's people will tell you that."

"Yes, but have you *lain* with him?"

Tatyana's question shouldn't have surprised her, but it did. The nights on the road had brought her into physical contact with Crow. It hadn't been the sort of intimacy her question asked after, but it had been more than casual. Comfortable described it in part, but insufficiently. Her inability to name it frustrated her as much as her missing it now did.

The princess put her frustration into a snort. "Would you inspect my loins, Grand Duchess?"

The old woman flicked a finger and one of the guards started forward until Peri's furious shriek split the air. "Touch my sister and the witch will be opened throat to belly." The Gyrkyme held her left hand out, wickedly hooked talons ready to strike.

"Peri, hold." Alexia glared at the guard, backing him into his place. "You have forgotten one thing, *Grand Duchess.* You may lead the Crown Circle, you may have the ear of your brother, but I am the *crown princess.* Nowhere amid your edicts or pronouncements do you have the right to touch my person. You forgot that once and paid a small price for it. Neither you nor your agents will get off so lightly this time."

Tatyana clutched her hands back to her breast and rubbed the fingers that Alexia had bitten at their first meeting, when Tatyana had pried her mouth open to inspect her teeth. "And have you forgotten, Crown Princess Alexia, that while you have been off being trained to win our nation back, I have held it together? The debts owed to our house are owed to *me.* Arrogance and disregard for me and my wishes will cost you terribly."

The old woman stood and reached back for the cloak that was quickly draped over her shoulders. "But go on and play your little game to save this Crow. Just remember, in your dreams, you never had a husband. Consider carefully which way you influence the future. So much rests on your shoulders. I would not have you ruin things on a whim."

"Not a whim, Aunt Tatyana, but for a friend and a man who will much annoy the enemy."

Tatyana raised an eyebrow. "Indeed. Then, perhaps, he will be worth a look, this Crow. I hope for your sake he is, else he will be a distraction and all shall fall to ashes for your folly."

CHAPTER 15

General Markus Adrogans, leader of the Jeranese Horse Guards and commander of the Southlands expedition liberating Okrannel, stood on a windswept hill to the north of the city of Guraskya. He granted that it was a city, for it was the capital of the Guranin Highlands, but compared to the sophisticated cities to the south and east—cities of stone and soaring towers—it seemed little more than a village grown beyond all proportion.

Though the Guranin highlanders did pay allegiance to the Okrans crown, having long ago been conquered, they did hold themselves as a people apart. Younger sons and daughters of the Okrans conquerors had married into the highland clans and instead of bringing city sophistication to their new home, the Okrans nobility were seduced by the strength of highland bloodlines and custom. For generations, lesser nobles fled to the highlands when cities could not contain their dreams and rebellious spirits, and the Guranin welcomed them openly.

Guraskya had been laid out in highland fashion, which meant it really had not been planned at all. Rectangular longhouses of wood, with thatched roofs and smoke holes, provided shelter. The buildings did not rise above a single story, nor were wings built onto them when a clan grew beyond that single structure. Other buildings would be raised, some nearby, some far, none connecting and all canted at angles that made them look like debris left from tossed jackstraw.

From the hilltop Adrogans could see two or three marketplaces, but from their size and location he assumed they had sprung up over what had been a longhouse that had burned down. Stockyards dotted the settlements south, west, and east, with barns and warehouses nearby. To the north a "foreign quarter" had been created, but until the arrival of his troops, it had consisted of two inns and a single tavern, since visitors were rare and accommodations were not meant to encourage long stays.

That foreign quarter had expanded rather quickly in the last month. He and the Alcidese general, Turpus Caro, had stationed their troops in Guraskya, along with a fifth of the Svoin refugees. Other units had trekked further to the north and west, stationing refugees in villages and hamlets, small towns and clan centers. The highland clans, while normally having nothing but contempt for lowlanders, showed incredible compassion for the wretched people who sought sanctuary in their land. The clans had vied to house the people, and Adrogans' early days in Guraskya had been spent listening to clan leaders explain all they had to offer.

In accord with their sizes and wealth, Adrogans had scattered his charges. The vast majority, a thousand of the sickest and most malnourished, had remained in Guraskya. The Tsuvo, Bravonyn, and Arzensk Clans shared the city and had been more than generous in dealing with the refugees. While they had not opened their longhouses to the foreign troops, they went to great pains to sort through genealogies to pair refugees with families that might share even a drop of blood, and he'd been assured that a lot of common links had been discovered in a very short time—much to everyone's satisfaction.

Snow blanketed the city, but still people moved about. The troop staging areas, which ringed the hill on which he stood, showed the most activity. It might have seemed an illusion because the round tents housing troops fluttered and twitched in breezes, though the snow built up around the sides did help insulate those within. The troopers had plenty to do, however, drilling, organizing woodcutting expeditions, and scouting the various approaches the Aurolani might take to attack.

Adrogans stroked his chin with a mittened hand. On the plains before Svoin he had met with Nefrai-kesh, the *sullanciri* who had been Kenwick Norrington and who, in Chytrine's name, commanded the Aurolani garrison in Svarskya. Chytrine's general had promised Adrogans that he would not attack until spring, but the Jeranese leader knew better than to take the *sullanciri* at his word. If Nefrai-kesh needed an excuse to cover a treacherous attack, he could hide behind the fact that he'd been referring to a campaign against Svoin, not against Adrogans' troops.

As a Gyrkyme might fly, less than a hundred miles separated Guraskya from the Okrans capital, so the threat of attack remained almost constant. While the approaches to the highlands were few and easily guarded, Okrans troops without the benefit of Chytrine's magicks and dragonels had been victorious centuries before. Lack of an active threat from the highlands before this had saved them from any concerted Aurolani effort to conquer them, but Adrogans refused to repay the highlanders' kindness by permitting an Aurolani invasion.

Ideas and strategies rolled through Adrogans' mind, but two things distracted him from studying them too closely. The first was the slow filtering of people onto a training field down to his left, on the east side of the encampment. He counted a hundred and a half—a task made easy as they organized themselves into companies of thirty. A week previous, a quarter of that number had been on the field. The people, men and women alike, still had a skeletal thinness to them, but in their eyes he saw the lean hunger of human wolves.

He was not at all certain how many of the thousand who remained in Guraskya would train and join the Svoin Infantry. The people below were the strongest of his refugees and, in many ways, it surprised him that a legion and a half were able to take the field. While putting food in a man's belly can make him content, there is no easy way to put fire in his soul. Those below were mostly bent on revenge, for the Aurolani rape of Svoin had cost everyone at least a relative, friend, or lover.

Fight they would, and fiercely. But Adrogans entertained no illusions about their efficacy, for even three months of training would not prepare them for the sheer savagery of warfare. They would have to be held back like a fierce dog on a short lead and then released at that single point where they could do the most damage. The enemy would destroy them—of that he had no doubt—but he suspected the Svoinyki cared less about living than inflicting death on their former tormentors.

The second thing that served to distract him huffed and puffed up the hill. The white of the snow contrasted sharply with the little man's brown flesh. More oddly, the wizened creature wore only a loincloth and a threadbare cloak. His lack of clothing made it easy to see the various talismans hanging from piercings in his leathery flesh. His spare locks of grey hair floated on the breeze, adding to the jocularity of his lopsided grin.

Adrogans found himself unable to resist returning that grin. "Uncle, it must be momentous news that brings you all the way up here."

Phfas broadened his smile to display yellowed teeth. "You will feel the change. Try."

"I have not the time."

The Zhusk shaman shook his head. "Until you do, all time is wasted."

Adrogans drew in a deep breath and closed his eyes to concentrate. The Zhusk, a primitive people who lived on a plateau in southeast Okrannel, cared little for the gods of the modern era and instead allied themselves with the primal and elemental spirits of the world. The Zhusk, through arcane rituals, bound themselves to these *yrûn*, as the spirits were called. The talismans that Phfas wore indicated his alliance with the *yrûn* of the air, and that spirit often brought information or wispy hints of it, trading speed for weight of information.

Adrogans had grown up in Jerana not knowing he was a half-Zhusk bastard until Phfas had recognized it and had invited him to enter into the Zhusk community. Adrogans had based many of his anti-Aurolani operations in the Zhusk Plateau, with his adopted people supporting his efforts. He had not, however, undergone the rituals that bound him to *yrûn* until the first battle on the plains of Svoin. While the battle raged, he underwent an agonizing ritual that bound several *yrûn* to him.

Turning within, he found a calm place and shut out all sound and sensation. He ignored the wind and the sound of Phfas' breathing. He closed his ears to the shouts of the training refugees, the barking of dogs and the lonely cry of a soaring hawk. He pushed past physical sensation, which allowed him to focus on his spirit and the *yrûn* who were his companions.

Earth and air, water and fire were there, but their fast strength denied them the delicacy he needed. Others he swept his mind past until he came to his mistress, the single *yrûn* to whom he was most tightly bound. She appeared as naught but a mere slip of a girl, with soft new-budded breasts, barely past the gangly stage that presaged her womanly beauty. She took form in luminous white, almost a ghost, save that as he drew closer her body hardened and ragged, tearing edges, as serrated as the teeth she flashed in her mirthless smile, defined her. Those edges glittered coldly, and he felt the nibbling of frostbite on his toes and face.

He pushed that sensation away. *I will not be distracted.*

She knew his thoughts and reached for him, her hands clawing sharply into his scalp. She drew him to her, crushing her body to his. Where she touched him, pain ignited in his piercings. Then she raised her face to his in a kiss that stung. She parted her lips and sucked his tongue into her needle-filled mouth.

A jolt ran through him but he fought past the pain. Beyond it, he got a sense of the whole of Okrannel. It was not as if he were a distant hawk, soaring, able to look down on the nation. That would have been very helpful, but his mistress—the *yrûn* of pain—instead gave him a sense of being a layer of thunderheads covering the nation. Where lightning struck, there pain dwelt, and certain loci had more than their share.

Laughing, he pulled himself from her torturous embrace and flowed out into his own flesh again. His eyes flicked open, then he raised a hand to cover them as the light from the snow blinded him. "So he has moved troops south?"

"As you said." Phfas nodded so emphatically his talismans shook and rattled. "Spring will come early."

The white-haired general shook his head. "Not as quickly as you would like, Uncle."

Adrogans detested any parallels between warfare and games—precisely because a game was an abstraction that in no way encompassed war's frightful cost in lives. Still, a certain amount of playing at warfare had to be done. Each side needed to conceal their strength, while retaining the ability to strike at the enemy or counter his moves. A game of cat and mouse it could be, in which both sides hoped their cat would not run into a hundred-pound mouse with sharp teeth and a scorpion's sting.

In the battle for Svoin, Adrogans had succeeded in concealing just such a sting. He'd hidden troops from the Aurolani scouts and from his own people, then brought them in at a crucial moment to strike at the Aurolani rear. The surprise shattered the Aurolani host. Princess Alexia had slain the *sullanciri* that led them, and his troops crushed the Aurolani. The victory, in which he had been aided by his *yrûn* allies, had given him the time he needed to liberate Svoin.

Common wisdom concerning warfare indicated that nothing could happen during the winter. Snows made travel difficult, both because roads and passes would be impassable; and because the snow would cover any forage for man or beast. Even if an army were to venture into the field and survive the frostbite and desertions that would come from hardship, a single blizzard could swallow them whole. Worse yet, a storm or avalanche could wipe out a supply caravan, leaving the army to starve.

Adrogans could not take refuge in the common wisdom, however, because the Aurolani troops were bred in a boreal realm where the worst winter in the south would be considered a mild spring day. While gibberers, frostclaws, and vylaens might not have been the most mentally flexible of troops, they did come in large groups, were used to the cold, and had a casual disregard for their own lives. Nefrai-kesh, therefore, had the ability to move troops down from Svarskya, infiltrate them into the highlands, and cause trouble.

The Jeranese general had predicted Nefrai-kesh would do just that for two reasons. The first was to sow terror in the countryside and erode any confidence won during the victory at Svoin. Besides, the Aurolani seemed to revel in cruelty for the sake of cruelty. The *sullanciri* had the troops, he could make use of them, and therefore he would.

Second—and of greater strategic importance, as long as Nefrai-kesh was on the offensive—was that he forced Adrogans to react. With hamlets scattered all over the highlands, there was no way to protect everyone. Adrogans would have to field a force that could be kept traveling hither and yon, trying to catch up with raiders who could fade away like ghosts. The effort to stop the raiders would exhaust his people, destroy morale, and possibly even build up resentment among the highlanders for his inability to stop the attacks.

Nefrai-kesh was operating under two disadvantages, though, and Adrogans was certain the Aurolani leader would have acknowledged neither of them as significant. The first was that while he was still human, he had been a formidable military commander. Adrogans knew that Kenwick Norrington had not been his equal even at the best of times, but he did accept that Norrington had known a great deal about warfare. This meant that Norrington might well accept the common wisdom about winter warfare. He would expect Adrogans would retire for the winter, and this gave the Aurolani an advantage since his troops *could* fight in winter.

The second fault compounded the error of underestimating his enemy. Nefrai-kesh likely knew nothing of the *yrûn,* and certainly knew nothing of Adrogans' connections with them. Wizards—as evidenced by the Vilwanese warmages in his army—tended to view the Zhusk as magickal curiosities, and Chytrine likely shared that view. Had she seen the Zhusk as any sort of a threat, she would have tried to wipe them out over the last quarter century.

Because his enemy was assuming his troops could not fight in winter, and because Nefrai-kesh was unaware that the *yrûn* gave him enough information about where enemy troops were moving to position his own forces, Adrogans had no choice but to find a way to fight in the winter. The road to Svarskya had several key points that would cost him dearly to take, were they defended. By spring they would be, so if he could strike quickly and deep into Aurolani-occupied territory, he would save troops without which he could not possibly lay siege to Svarskya.

While the vast majority of his army was not well suited to operations in snowy highlands woods, he did have two groups who excelled at just that sort of thing. The Nalisk Mountain Rangers came from the central mountains of Naliserro and had even impressed the highlanders with their stoicism in the face of hardship. And the Loquelven Blackfeathers had fought hard and well at Svoin. Their leader, Mistress Gilthalarwin, still smarted from a disagreement with Adrogans, so she and her troops would take any opportunity they could to prove their worth.

Adrogans nodded slowly. He would use the Rangers and the Blackfeathers to track and destroy the forces Nefrai-kesh sent into the highlands. Striking out from there would be more difficult, but it could be done. If he could take the northern ford of the Svar River and then the Three Brothers Citadel guarding the road through the South Gorge, he'd be at the doorstep to Svarskya before spring rains came.

Phfas cackled. "If not early spring, a mild winter?"

"Not mild in terms of trouble, Uncle." Adrogans slowly smiled. "Just one full of surprises for those who hate us."

CHAPTER 16

Will smiled as Crow unwrapped the parcel and revealed the sweetcake. "And I didn't steal it, neither."

Crow glanced up and raised an eyebrow. "But you didn't pay for it, did you? The baker thought he was giving to *the* Norrington as a gift."

The thief blinked. "How did you know?" No one could have told Crow, since Will's visit to the gaol had been unannounced. Will had assumed that arriving by surprise would allow him to use his status as the Norrington to bluff his way past guards, and it had. None of them were prepared to stop him, especially after he promised he had no weapons and said that his visit was vital for the defeat of the enemy.

The sweetcake had been obtained in a nearby shop where Will had loitered while studying the gaol and its guards. The shopkeeper, an older man with rosy cheeks and a roundness that made him waddle as he walked, had wrapped the sweetcake up and presented the parcel to Will with a touch of ceremony. Since they had been alone in the shop, Will knew the formality was sincere, not meant as a show that might impress others.

Will had thanked him, then headed to the gaol. A couple of guards questioned him, but armed with an imperious tone and a mask that he'd received from the hand of the king, he was not seriously hindered. He'd been ushered up rather than down, which surprised him a bit, and found Crow in a small room, but one that was clean, warm, and had a window that—despite being barred—admitted sunlight. The minimal furnishing consisted of a cot and straw mattress, a chamber pot, a single small table, and two chairs, but every-thing was in good repair and the chamber pot had a lid.

Crow smiled at him. "Well, I could tell you that it was the knot in the string, which was a gift-knot, but it could have been that you'd retied it that way by accident."

Will raised an eyebrow. "So, what was it?"

"You have no purse. You carry no money."

The thief's mouth opened in an O, then he closed it. "Guess old habits die hard."

"It matters not, Will. The gift is appreciated." Crow set it on the table. "I heard that you had a talk with King Scrainwood."

"The princess must have told you about it."

"On her last visit, yes." Crow smiled brightly. "I got the impression it did not go well."

Will shifted in the chair, then leaned forward. "He wanted me to lie about you and say evil things. I told him no."

The older man's smile contracted into a sharp look. "Only told him?"

Will shrugged. "He hit me. He's stupid. I couldn't help it. I was defending myself and things got out of hand."

Crow frowned heavily, then rose from his chair to look down at the boy. "He's not as stupid as you think, and if you assume he is, he will hurt you. Up to now he thought he could control you, so he didn't have to worry about you. Now he does. He is not a good enemy to have, as is evidenced by my present situation."

"I know, I know." Will held his hands up. "It's been a week since all that happened..."

"But you only told the princess two days ago."

The thief winced. "Well, I was lying low, being good and everything. The king has calmed down; otherwise, they'd not have let me in here."

"They may not let you out."

That sent a shiver through Will, but before he could protest that he could get himself out pretty easily, a key ground in the lock. The thief turned to look and gasped.

The barred door swung open, and through it walked a tall man in simple huntsman garb save for a silver gorget worked with a half-horse, half-fish en-sign, and a slender gold band around his balding head. The man's sun-kissed flesh had gathered into wrinkles at his eyes, and white predominated in what hair he still possessed, yet he moved with an economy of motion that sug-gested he was younger than his years.

Crow dropped to a knee and bowed his head. "Highness."

Will, blinking, slipped off his chair and to a knee as well. "Highness."

"Rise, the both of you." King Augustus of Alcida turned and looked at the gaoler. "That will be all; you may retire." The two bodyguards who had accompanied the king waved the gaoler further down the hallway and out of earshot.

Crow brought his chair around for the king, then pointed to the sweetcake. "I have not much to offer, Highness, but it is yours."

"No, my friend, that is all right. You have given much already to the world, with no thanks. I'll not rob you of even the smallest pleasure you could find here." The king waved Crow to the cot, then leaned heavily on the back of the chair. "I have been greatly remiss. I have owed you an apology for a quarter century."

Crow looked up at him but said nothing. The man's eyes tightened and Will saw a quiver in his lower lip. The king's words had clearly had an effect on Crow.

Augustus looked up and focused distantly. "What I tell you now, Hawkins, will seem self-serving. If you judge me harshly, I can accept that, for I deserve it. I played you false, and while I could protest that I was not on the spot to defend you, I should have been. What was done to you in Yslin was unforgivable, and I should have been there."

Crow looked down at his open hands and slowly shook his head. "You were with the army in Okrannel, saving people. That was more important than dealing with one man. You had other things to think of."

"You forgive me too easily, Hawkins. *Arcanslata* were able to inform me of your situation. I didn't know all the details, but I knew that you had not betrayed the others. I remember that last night around the campfire. What I said then *was* true; I would have been happy to have you with me in Okrannel. I was very happy to have your brother, Sallitt. I didn't know, though, that the charges against you were manufactured."

The king sighed. "When I returned from Okrannel I married, and there was much fanfare. And then in setting up the Okrans court in exile and starting a family, there was much I had to do and there was no sign of you. I did not want to forget you, but I was not reminded."

Crow nodded and started to speak a couple of times before words actually came. When they did, they were soft despite the strain in his voice. "After they took my mask, I, well, I don't remember much of what I did. I wandered. The Vorquelves, because of the prophecy, harbored me in the Downs. If I drew a sober breath, it was by accident. If words came without tears..."

The king dropped to a knee before Crow and rested his hands on the other man's sagging shoulders. "Had I known, my friend..."

Crow weakly patted the king's right hand. "Highness, you had the world to worry about. I was beneath your notice and unworthy of your concern. I was no one. I was nothing. Then Resolute returned to Yslin and found me."

Augustus nodded. "I know. After he found you, he came to find me. He explained many things to me, and I questioned my father, who told me what had happened. I protested that what had been done to you was as evil as anything Chytrine had done. He said to me, 'One man's blood is a puddle, but Chytrine would drown us in oceans.' Sacrificing you seemed a small price to pay to preserve the stability of the world."

Crow's head came up. "Then you have known for twenty-five years who I was?"

"Yes." The king drew in a deep breath. "As prince there was not much I could do, but I did what I could. I arranged favorable trade status for your friend Playfair's trading company, and Resolute was named as my representative to collect the fees needed to keep these arrangements in force. You renewed acquaintance with your friend, and his company provided you with transportation and money. Playfair does not know that *I* know who you are, so he could never tell you of my patronage."

Crow slowly nodded. "Things begin to make sense. Rounce was more than generous, and there were times I feared for his ruination. He would have given me anything, I know that, but it is good to know that he was amply rewarded for his action."

"He has not suffered and you are right; he would have done anything for you. You do know that he is a patron of a number of bards who sing of Crow's exploits?" Augustus rose and seated himself in the chair. "I have followed those songs keenly, often wishing to hear the true story behind them. You and Resolute were able to continue a war I wished we had never abandoned. I could do little save support the Draconis Baron."

"It is well you did." Crow frowned. "He knew who I was. I don't know for how long, but he recognized me at the end. He gave me a sign."

The king nodded. "He did know, though we never spoke openly of you. Whom else he might have told, I do not know. Secrecy was the best way to keep you safe."

Will, who had been sitting and listening, began to twitch. "How can you say that?"

Augustus glanced at him. "Those were dangerous times, Will."

"And that excuses you?" Will stood up and glared at the king. "You come in here and tell Crow that you've known for years and years and years that he was unjustly accused? You knew it destroyed his life, and you didn't do anything?"

"Will." Crow's nostrils flared. "This is the king!"

"I don't care." Will planted his fists on his hips. "King Scrainwood wanted me to lie for him, and here *you* are saying you didn't say anything to counteract the lie that hurt him? You call him friend? And *you,* you let him call you friend?"

Both men stared at him wide-eyed.

"Everyone makes things so complex. Everyone plays at manners just to hide their true feelings. I see people out there who would have beaten me to death for being a thief, but because I'm the Norrington, they'd give me everything I'd have stolen. *And* they still hate me for being a thief, but they lie and say they don't in case I won't save *them* when it comes down to it.

"And you know what? I've heard everyone say that Hawkins had to be sacrificed because if everyone had heard that Chytrine was coming back, they'd have been scared and nations would fall and stuff. Now, you have no trouble putting these same people in your armies and send them out to die without knowing why. So, how come they're frightened sheep when some nighthaunt says she'll be back, but brave and stalwart and courageous when you give them a spear and point them at something that will kill them dead?"

Will pointed a finger at King Augustus. "I know you are brave and everything. I know you're a good king. And you're my king, no matter what Scrainwood says. Nobody pokes your eyes out on coins, but you turned a blind eye to Crow. Through him, Chytrine warned everyone she was coming, but you all decided that to save your own heads, you would not let anyone know what she said, and so no one was prepared for her to come back. And did it ever occur to anyone that if you *had* gotten ready for her to come back, maybe she wouldn't have?"

"*Will!* That's enough." Crow stood and opened his hands to the king. "Highness, I apologize."

"No, no, that's all right." Augustus raised his hands and waved Crow back down on the cot. As Crow resumed his place, Augustus turned and looked up at Will. "Do you really want me to reply, or do you just wish to scourge me with your indignation?"

Will bit back a harsh reply and shivered. "I'll listen."

"Good. I'll answer you, then, but not because you're a noble or the Norrington or even because you are a citizen of my nation. I'll answer you because you are the first person to ask me questions that have plagued me through the years."

Augustus' voice retained its deep tone, but sank in volume to something just shy of a whisper. "You may well be right, Will, that the common folk would not quake in fear at the threat of invasion from the north. Perhaps that is true of most of them, but even you have seen how panic or worry in one can infect others. There are ways to counter that, but at the time Hawkins was sacrificed, worry had infected the crowned heads. Reason did not prevail, and while they accepted a solution that allayed their initial fears, they all knew they had treated a symptom, and not the disease.

"Until I came to the throne—until Queen Carus replaced her father, until others who could think clearly took their places at the heads of their nations—that whole question could not be reexamined. To try to raise the issue of Hawkins would have caused kings to admit they were wrong, or caused their heirs to cast doubt on the legends of their predecessors. Hawkins and his fate became a minor sidelight to the whole problem of preparing for Chytrine's return."

Will frowned. "That's easy to say."

"But it is true, and Hawkins knew it, too." The king glanced at Crow. "He set out to continue the fight against Chytrine, leading by example. Others might have protested, launched petitions to get their name cleared, but he put his old persona to rest and focused on the important problem: defeating Chytrine.

"Now, I will admit to being a coward. I knew what he was doing, and I knew his actions would prove he was not what he had been accused of being. I took refuge in his actions, telling myself that there would come a day when that injustice could be corrected, but that day would have to come *after* Chytrine was defeated. In that way, Hawkins, I did fail you and failed you terribly. Will is right, I really was no friend to you."

Crow smiled. "No, Highness, you were. You were looking to my mission, which is far more important than I am. Had you asked, that is what I would have told you. Better an hour fighting Chytrine than a thousand hours in my defense."

Will shook his head adamantly. "There you go, there you both go. Evil is evil. Hurting Hawkins helped Chytrine. Chytrine is evil, so hurting Hawkins was evil. All this being polite doesn't change that."

Augustus' voice took on an edge. "So I was evil in that moment, and can be judged harshly for it? Yes, Will, you have so judged me, but you have judged me no more harshly than I have judged myself. My only solace has come in knowing that my efforts against Chytrine are the best I can muster. I have not compromised in that, and never shall.

"Hawkins may forgive me, or may not. I may be able to set things to rights for him, and I may not. I *will*, however, accept no compromise in fighting Chytrine. It is by no means a perfect solution, but it is the best solution circumstances permit."

The thief hesitated for a moment. He wanted to let his outrage at the king's treatment of his friend override the practicality of the man's words. *If I do that, though, it will be as bad as the kings who let fear destroy Hawkins.* That realization twisted his guts around and soured his mouth.

Will sighed. "You're right about fighting Chytrine. Doesn't mean that what was done to Crow was right."

"No, it doesn't, and we will find a way to resolve it. If I have to bankrupt Alcida paying for bards to sing of how Hawkins' shame was a trap that caught Chytrine, I will." The king smiled ruefully. "That's provided we defeat her. If we don't, those left alive won't care, and the only songs they will sing will be of misery."

CHAPTER 17

Kerrigan Reese shivered, and it was not from walking through the cold, snowy streets of Meredo. He found the temperature rather bracing. It helped him clear his head, and clear thinking was what he needed.

He had encountered Magister Syrett Kar almost two weeks earlier, and that morning he'd gotten a summons to the Vilwanese consulate. The document had been politely worded, and the wards sealing it had been carefully worked. More important, they had been cunningly cast by a Magister who clearly had studied for decades at Vilwan. Though Kerrigan could not recognize the spells as having been cast by any of his former tutors, he was pretty certain that he would recognize the person waiting for him.

He'd tried to talk to Will about the message when his friend returned to the Rampant Panther after a visit to see Crow, but the thief had been irascible. Will had asked why the person who sent the note hadn't just signed it and left off with all sorts of subtle things that didn't amount to anything but masks to cover evil anyway.

Kerrigan wasn't certain what Will was talking about, but tried to explain that names have power in the realms of magick. For a wizard to sign his name to something was dangerous. If a wizard told you his true name, it was a sign of great trust since another spellcaster could use his name to craft spells of devastating power against him.

But Will wanted no part of explanations and wandered off to his room. Kerrigan couldn't find Resolute or Dranae, and Lombo and Qwc would likely listen to him, but he wasn't certain any insights they provided would be worth much. Lombo, having been deprived of a chance to kill a mage, had taken to hunting through the city for other prey and was off on an expedition and the Spritha just seemed, well, *flighty*.

Kerrigan found himself trapped between two conflicting notions. Orla had told him to stay away from Vilwan, and he took her request very seriously. She said there were people there who would want to destroy him because they feared his power. He was slowly coming to realize that he did have a lot of power. On Vilwan, while he was being trained, he had been so isolated that he really had no perspective on what he could do. But Magister Syrett's surprise at his abilities, and the man's admission that he couldn't have compelled Kerrigan to do anything, provided Kerrigan with a glimmer of what others might see in him.

While on Vilwan he had been sheltered from a lot of things. Since leaving, however, the litany of events he'd mentioned to Syrett had abraded the aura of security. He'd seen people die and he'd even killed some, though indirectly. He'd lost his mentor and friends and felt pains he'd never had before, both physical and emotional.

Just as important, there had been a shift in how he was treated. While Will still regarded him as a kid sometimes, others had begun to deal with him mostly as an adult. The Draconis Baron had charged him with a secret duty to carry a fragment of the DragonCrown from Fortress Draconis. General Adrogans had given him great responsibilities. Regardless of how he saw himself, they saw him as an adult, and gave him adult tasks to perform.

Though Kerrigan didn't see himself as an adult, he knew he was fast becoming one. He wasn't sure if those on Vilwan who feared him did so because he was a child with incredible power or not, but that did seem a distinct possibility. And, if that were so, wouldn't it be the responsible and adult thing to go to the consulate and let them see he was not the thing they feared?

It would have been, and he knew that. He also knew, however, that course of action was predicated on their being afraid of his immaturity. But what if there was another problem? Could they be afraid that his training had warped him to the point where he would become another Yrulph Kirûn? If so, no amount of protestation, no demonstrations, would be sufficient to convince them otherwise. If they were thinking he was insane, or was going to go insane, their fears would force them to lock him away or otherwise neutralize him.

And that is exactly the reason Orla would have warned me away. He shook his head as he wandered along the winding North River Road. The way he'd dealt with Tetther had really been an inventive, mature, and nonlethal manner of employing magick to solve a problem. He was proud of that solution, but could see how others might read it as contemptuous of her and her efforts. Instead of engaging her in a straightforward duel, he'd employed a trick. Since he'd never really been allowed to duel anyone else, he had no idea what the rules were for that sort of thing. But if there *were* rules, he was pretty sure dumping a load of snow on your enemy wasn't covered by them.

In acting innocently to preserve a life, he might have proved to his enemies how dangerous he was.

Kerrigan sighed out a plume of vapor. Had Orla not warned him off, he'd not have been having any of those thoughts. He'd have assumed the summons was benign. It very well could be. It might even contain a congratulations from the Grand Magister himself for all he had done so far. In fact, had she not warned him off, he'd probably have brought the DragonCrown fragment with him and given it over to his superiors.

The various motives for the summons swirled and danced through his head like the snow whirling on the wind as he walked. From his right, in the shadow of a building, a child's voice called for help and he turned to look just in time for a thrown snowball to loom larger in his sight. There was no time for ducking. The surprise was complete, and accompanied by a child's malicious laughter.

The snowball hit, but Kerrigan felt no shock, no cold, no sting nor pain. A bony plate rose through his flesh, armoring his face with an ivory mask any Oriosan would have envied. The plate's thick ridges channeled the snow away from his eyes so effectively that he never even blinked.

Which allowed him to see the expression of horror on the child's face as the snowball exploded against the armor. The boy's eyes grew wide and the laughter choked off. A second snowball fell from his hands as he turned to run. The boy slipped once, falling facefirst into a snowbank, then scrambled up and ran away.

As the plate sank back into his skin, Kerrigan wiped away the lees of snow with his left mitten. The spell that armored him had been worked at the behest of Vilwan to protect him. It had previously been mastered by only one other human mage: Yrulph Kirûn. *Could it be that they have twisted the protection they gave into a threatening sign?*

Kerrigan was determined to make a mature decision concerning the summons, but competing scenarios kept him on the north bank of the Reydo River. Crossing the river would take him to the consulate, and he'd resolved that once he crossed the river, he would not turn back. The decision to cross it, however, had not yet been made.

If Orla was right, then every step he made toward the consulate brought him into greater danger. If she was wrong, staying away denied him more education and support, and the support of Vilwan would be very useful in the fight against Chytrine. In heeding Orla's words, he wasn't sure if he was giving in to a child's fears or being prudent.

Staying away from Vilwan would cut him off from more than just support. His whole life had been spent in training, but he knew not for what. He was pretty certain it had been to help defeat Chytrine, but he had been provided with no direction concerning how he might do that. That he was meant to oppose her was suggested by Vilwan's allowing Orla and him to accompany General Adrogans' expedition to Okrannel; but he also had to allow for the possibility that minds might have been changed on Vilwan.

Once again it came down to having too many questions and no clear source for answers. He didn't want to give in to fears, but where a child's fears ended and an adult's prudent caution began was not a clear line. Moreover, his questions all revolved around Vilwan; what had been intended for him and what would be required of him. Only by visiting the consulate would he have a chance of learning the answers to those questions.

He had to go.

Kerrigan nodded once and turned to the left, marching onto a narrow footbridge over the slowly moving river. The unseasonable cold had not yet frozen a crust over the dark water, but ice was growing out from the shores and already encrusted some of the pylons that supported the bridge's shallow arch.

As he glanced down at them, he saw something glint gold in the water. He shivered and peered closely, then came around the end of the bridge's railing and scrambled awkwardly down the steep shoreline. He squatted in a most ungainly manner at the base of the bridge, and in its dark reflection he could see clearly into the shallows.

There, half-covered by silt, lay the ruby fragment of the DragonCrown!

He had no idea how it had gotten there, but there was no way he could possibly allow it to remain. He moved forward, snow crunching beneath his booted left foot, then dragged his right knee behind him. He inched out onto a little ledge of ice, then stripped off his mittens and prepared to cast the levitation spell he knew so well.

He stared hard into the water, trying to fix the shifting image in his mind so he could grasp the fragment. As he focused, he felt magick and suddenly realized the fragment didn't exist at all, but was part of a spell. *Part of a spell that is using my mind and memories to project that image.*

Something moved in the bridge's reflection, something lurking beneath the span. Kerrigan started to turn and look up, but a heavy weight slammed hard into his back. The armor rose and intercepted the attack, but what hit him carried considerably more force than a snowball. The impact shook him and pitched him forward, sliding him out on the thin ice which, with a rippling thundercrack, disintegrated.

Kerrigan plunged into the frigid water. The shock of it made him gasp. He sucked in water, then coughed out bubbles of valuable air. The mage started to panic and struck for the surface, but his heavy winter clothes dragged him down. He fought to shuck his coat, but even as he tore at the buttons, the light from above began to dim.

He heard something else splash into the water. Kerrigan turned his face upward, hoping for succor. An odd dark shape descended, flashing past his back, then something grabbed him, taking firm hold of his coat and his waist. He felt power in the limbs and for a moment his spirits soared.

Then, whatever had him just took him deeper.

CHAPTER 18

Isaura arrived at the Conservatory and made her way to the Grand Thaumatorium as bidden—less because she wanted to be there than because she felt it her duty to attend. Her mother, again away fighting for the life of her nation, had impressed upon her the necessity for Isaura to act in her stead. Neskartu, the headmaster of the Conservatory and the most magickally adept of the *sullanciri,* had sent a message saying he required her help with a project. Because his summons had indicated she should join him in the Thaumatorium, she assumed it would be another display of magick for his students, and she did enjoy teaching them.

She found herself surprised, then, when she reached the chamber deep in the school's heart. She entered through the tall archway at the head of a long, steep stairway that led down onto the arena floor. Stone terraces set with long wooden tables and chairs provided both seating and work spaces for students, but the room's key feature was the round dais upon which great magicks were wrought for the edification of the audience. Most students looked forward to the time when they would be called upon to perform there, because success could result in their being sent forth to serve the empress in the war.

But this time, no eager faces greeted her, for all the seats were empty. In the arena waited three people, only one of whom she knew. He took the shape of a smallish man, clean-limbed but indistinctly formed. While he had depth, height, and breadth, discerning these dimensions was not easy since his entire body shifted in hue, akin to the reflections from coal oil spread over black water. He remained largely dark, save where lines of iridescent blue or green, red or gold flowed through him or shot like lightning along a limb.

Only Neskartu's eyes remained constant. Witchlight purple orbs, they burned with a feral intensity that completely belied the *sullanciri*'s wisdom. Once he had been known as Heslin and had been schooled on Vilwan. Since swearing allegiance to the empress, he had been shown great magicks and given great power. By himself he had created the Conservatory and helped Chytrine shape other *sullanciri*.

His mouth did not open, and his words did not actually sound in the room. *I am pleased that you have come so swiftly, Isaura.*

"As my mother wishes, Lord Neskartu." Isaura slowly descended the stairs, heedless of the stone's cold on her bare feet. She lifted her skirts enough that she would not trip on the hem, but not a bit higher than modesty would permit.

One of the other two studied her as if he wished she would divest herself of her skirts altogether, and not for the sake of safety. Tall and lean, with fine dark hair and a rakish smile that suggested he knew how handsome others found him, the man wore a blue blouse embroidered with a spiderweb pattern. He lifted his chin, then nodded in greeting, but Isaura gave no sign that she had noticed him at all.

The woman with him held more interest for Isaura. Wisps of brown hair peeked out from beneath a sheepskin hat, and the bulky coat she wore hid her form, but Isaura guessed that her thickness was more coat than body. Her eyes, a deep blue, flicked warily. The man with her was shivering because of the cold, but she was shivering because of her dislike for the place in which she stood.

Neskartu let a hand stretch from his form to point at them. *These are the Azure Spider and Vionna, the Pirate Queen of Wruona.*

Isaura let no emotion pass over her face as she stepped onto the dais beside Neskartu. She simply turned to face the visitors and nodded solemnly. "Welcome to Aurolan."

The man started to speak, but Vionna stopped him by pressing a gloved hand to his chest. "Chytrine summoned us and we have traveled a long, difficult road to get here. The summons was urgent, so we should be speaking with her, shouldn't we?"

"My mother is not in a position to greet you herself, so I have come in her stead." Isaura's reference to Chytrine surprised Vionna, but the girl suppressed a smile at that result. "As you are aware, the war with the Southlands demands great attention. Shifting circumstances have embroiled her in pressing matters."

The Azure Spider snarled. "So, then, I am supposed to stay here and freeze?"

Isaura gave him a thin smile. "You will only freeze if you try to leave."

"Is that a threat?"

Neskartu's form swelled and color moved through him more swiftly. When his words appeared in her mind, they had become brambles. *This child provided you a courteous warning about the hazards of peregrinations in Aurolan. Take pains to apologize now.*

The man winced, having borne the full brunt of Neskartu's comment. The Azure Spider did bow his head in Isaura's direction. "Please forgive my misunderstanding."

The snowy-maned beauty nodded slowly because her upbringing demanded it, but she did not really forgive him. The look in his eyes told her much. He, a Southlander, believed in his heart that her mother was evil. His own greed had pushed him past his fear of her, but also never let him see the true Chytrine, the one who was fighting to save the world from the corruption of the south. Her mother had suggested she might be betrayed, and Isaura found a prime candidate in the Azure Spider.

Neskartu shifted his gaze to Vionna. *My mistress bids me to give you a message. She forgave your inability to destroy Vilwan because you did bring her a cargo of students. She continued to trust you, but you failed her when you allowed the sapphire Truestone to be stolen. Had you just given it to her agent, it would not have been lost. You cost her something she held most dear.*

Vionna's chin came up and her eyes slitted. "And she wishes me to atone for my failure?"

There is a way, yes. The *sullanciri*'s form sank back to normal. *However, you are required to pay a price to earn the chance to atone. As you cost her something dear, so she demands something dear of you.*

"And that would be?"

Your paramour.

Even before the realization that Neskartu was talking about him had registered on the Azure Spider's face, Vionna had nodded her assent. A thread of blue energy rose within the *sullanciri*'s form, then lashed out. It slapped against the Azure Spider's chest and melded itself to his blouse, stiffening it so the man's arms shot out straight to his sides at shoulder level.

"You can't do this to me! Vionna, darling, you can't let them do this to me!" His hazel eyes widened as blue webwork flowed down over his trousers and boots, further restraining him. "Vionna, think of what we mean to each other!"

The pirate queen regarded him coldly. "You or death? Choices, choices. You were fun, but a blanket can keep me warm at night and doesn't become petulant when it's not the center of attention."

"Vionna!"

The woman backhanded her lover, and Isaura recoiled from the violence. The man began to sob. Bloody spittle mixed with tears and ran down to drip off his chin.

Be still, Vionna, for you have given him to my mistress. Damage her property no more. The energy tendril thickened and lifted the Azure Spider from the dais and hung him in the air as if he were bound to some unseen crucifix. *Now, for you, who shall become known as Spyr'skara, you have been fancied a legend. From this point forward you shall join the greatest of legends. My mistress has decided that despite your failures, you will be allowed to join the* sullanciri *and serve her. You will be more than the sum of all your past. Do you wish to serve her?*

Isaura watched the man and waited for him to agree. She had studied the spells that had to be worked to transform a being into one of her mother's elite. While they could be worked on someone who was reluctant, that reluctance blocked them from enjoying their full power. A *sullanciri* created by Neskartu, as was evidenced by Ganagrei and the other lesser *sullanciri*, would not be as powerful as those transformed by her mother. Myrall'mara, Nefrai-kesh, Nefrai-laysh, Neskartu, and Ferxigo had been blessed among her generals and fashioned by her hand alone. The lessers had been worked in concert with Neskartu, but Spyr'skara would be the first he had done without her.

And this is why he needs me. While Neskartu was extremely powerful, his core humanity hampered him. Though he had learned much since his transformation, certain concepts about dealing with the Aurolani school of magick eluded him. Isaura, whom Chytrine had tutored personally for decades, had grown up understanding that system. She could work the grander spells that would contain and reinforce the transformation.

As she had been taught, magick itself flowed through reality in a massive, surging river with eddies and currents, rapids of varying severity and deadly sinks that could suck down even the most careful of mages. Human magick did not recognize the river for what it was, but thought magickal energy just a pool from which the substance to work spells could be drawn. Human mages did recognize dangers in dipping magick from the pool, so their spells were arranged to be a series of handholds and belay lines that would prevent them from slipping too far into the pool and drowning.

While their prudence doubtlessly saved many a foolish mage, it also prevented them from accessing deeper, purer power. A thirsty man might settle for any water, but given a choice would go for cooler. Human magick never allowed its practitioners a chance to find that cooler water and, hampered as they were, they remained unable to truly grasp that they were dealing with a river.

The elves and urZrethi had progressed enough to know that the pool did have motion in it, and that some energy was better than others, but still the idea of the river escaped them. Neskartu had learned enough to perceive motion and different currents of different values, but the vastness of the river escaped even him. Isaura suspected he was afraid of how much power could be had, and afraid that he might just dive into it and never surface again.

That latter fear was one she had known when she first had her eyes opened to the true nature of magick. Her mother allayed that fear by showing her how to read the river. Isaura now could follow the flows. She could look forward and back, spot eddies and sinks. With a thought here or there she could navigate across the flow to reach those currents she required to perform her magicks.

The Azure Spider lifted his head. "I accept." He glared sidelong at the pirate queen. "I move beyond you."

The blue energy flared, and the man's clothing instantly combusted into an azure flame. The man writhed, though the fire he breathed in so seared his throat that he could make no sound. He fought for a moment, then the flame closed around him in a tight blue shroud. His feet rose, his arms came in. For a moment or two his elbows, head, heels, and knees stretched the shroud, then the shape solidified and flowed into something akin to an egg, retaining the blue hue and exhibiting a spiderweb pattern in black over the surface.

The egg hovered in the air and Vionna pulled back. "What are you doing to him?"

That which will please my mistress. That which will allow him to fulfill her desires. Neskartu shifted his gaze to Isaura by floating his eyes around to the left side of his head. *You know your part, Princess.*

Isaura drew in a deep breath and let it out slowly, then closed her eyes. She invoked a simple spell that allowed her to see things in the realm of magick. By this sight, Vionna did not register at all. Neskartu appeared to be much the same as always, and the Thaumatorium glowed green with the residual effects of countless magicks.

The man inside the egg had taken on the grey of ash. Stepping forward, Isaura invoked another spell. She reached her hands up, and they passed through the sides of the shell as if it were not there. Had she desired to do so, she could have reached into the Azure Spider's chest and with the brush of a finger stilled his racing heart. She knew that could be done because she had seen it done with animals, but her mother had only done that so Isaura could learn to set it to beating again before the soul had left the body.

With her hands in place on his head and heart, she concentrated and felt the river flowing around her. There was little for her to see and less to hear, but currents raced past, teasing and buffeting—at times playful and at others resentful. The most violent she let slip past, then found one that suited her needs. Isaura drew it into her, then projected it into the man.

Pure magickal energy flowed into him, dissolving his physical nature as quickly as boiling water dissolves inkstone powder. The energy flooded into the shell, roiling and rising, fighting the confines. Surges shot to the apex, then dripped back down again, unable to escape and seeking a place to run.

A surge of energy from Lord Neskartu injected itself into the mix. It provided direction through a complex series of spells. Isaura caught hints of urZrethi magick, but since the object was transformation, that hardly was a surprise. Other bits and pieces, elven and human, swirled past, then odd things joined them. Neskartu had clearly been fashioning some magicks of his own. They came from human roots, but had been woven differently and were unrecognizable.

Is this the betrayal my mother fears?

Though no answer came to that question, the magicks the *sullanciri* employed did their work. The Azure Spider shook and twitched. His spirit clawed at the new shape in which it was imprisoned. She could feel the man's outrage and shock, but she did not pity him. She could understand fear, but she knew the rewards her mother would grant for serving her. In the world free of southern tyranny, he would be among the most grand heroes, worshipped for all time.

It is done, Princess.

Isaura nodded and drew her hands back, then returned to her place. She blinked, canceling the spells she'd cast, and slowly smiled at Vionna. "It went well."

The pirate queen had paled and stared wide-eyed at the floating egg. "What did you do?"

One last burst of power flowed from Neskartu and toward the egg. The floating ovoid blazed blue, then began to shrink. From the size of a man's torso, it shrank slowly and silently to something barely larger than a hen's egg. At the last it drifted to Vionna and she cupped it in both hands. The magickal cord connecting it to the *sullanciri* snapped and she almost dropped the egg.

He will rest now. You shall keep him close to you, nestled against you, for warmth—his, not yours.

She shook her head. "I am not some hen to incubate an egg."

Neskartu's thoughts lashed her. *You are what my mistress wishes you to be. And not a hen, a courier. Spyr'skara is required in Meredo a day hence.*

Vionna frowned. "Impossible. That journey would take months."

My mistress knows you fail at the possible, so she would not set before you the impossible. You will be conducted there. When you are, open the egg and release him.

"Will it be safe?" The pirate queen looked at the egg. "He was not pleased with me before, and I suspect he will be less so now."

He will do as bidden and, for now, he is bidden not to harm you. You have a more important task, for you shall take the princess with you.

Isaura's silver eyes grew wide. "To the Southlands? I am going south?"

It is as your mother desires, Princess. You will go and observe. She wishes this. She wishes you to bring the ruby replica so you may aid in the recovery of that Truestone. A certain pleasure drifted through the *sullanciri's* thoughts. *In Meredo you will learn, Princess, learn much that will determine the future.*

Isaura started to smile, then a shiver shook her. She had never ventured outside Aurolani domains. While she hungered to see the world her mother had described—no matter its faults—the prospect daunted her. She feared her reactions but, far worse, she feared disappointing her mother.

She nodded. "I shall do as I am bidden, Lord Neskartu."

Of course you shall, Princess. The swirling of colors in his form quickened. *And you, Vionna?*

The pirate looked at the egg, then sighed. "It seems the custom to do as one is bidden. I shall not disappoint."

Very good. The alternative would have been unpleasant. The *sullanciri* let an arm flow out to the left. *Come and enjoy the rewards the empress offers her allies. Tonight you shall be feasted, and tomorrow you shall earn even greater favor.*

CHAPTER 19

Princess Alexia smiled carefully as she sat in the audience chamber where Crow's trial had begun. The room was not exactly small, but was far smaller than the palace's throne room. Unlike the throne room, this chamber had not undergone extensive restoration. While it still featured strong columns upholding a vaulted roof, the walls had not been covered with wooden panels. Tapestries depicting ancient history, a few in serious need of repair, covered them instead.

At the narrow end of the rectangular room, a set of three thrones had been placed, with the centermost pushed slightly back. In it sat Prince Linchmere. Though Alexia knew him to be in his mid-thirties, the man's soft and unremarkable features belied his age. Of average height and on the considerably rounder side of lean, even the fierce visage into which his mask had been worked could not supply him strength or presence. When he listened to evidence, he listened distractedly, and the princess was fairly certain that at least once he had fallen asleep.

Augustus, wearing a thin, black courtesy mask, took the throne at Linchmere's right hand, placing him closest to Alexia. Furthest was Queen Carus of Jerana, a small woman with black hair and restless dark eyes. She wore an embroidered gown of light blue, and had been given a lacy courtesy mask dyed to match. In direct contrast to Linchmere, she listened to things closely and questioned witnesses sharply. She savaged Cabot Marsham as the man testified to things he had said before the Council of Kings a quarter century before, and clearly had studied Jeranese records of the proceedings as she called for constant clarifications of his statements.

Crow sat in the prisoner's docket, with iron shackles securing his feet. He'd been washed and had pulled his white hair back into a tail knotted with black leather. He'd only been allowed simple clothing, but did not appear at all uncomfortable in it, save when a cold draft touched him.

So far the trial had been going well. Marsham had clearly been the cornerstone of the prosecution, but Queen Carus pointed to inconsistencies between what he had said before and what he was telling them now. Moreover, she pointed out, correctly, that his only knowledge of events had come through conversations with Hawkins. This reduced the whole of his testimony to the level of hearsay, which she was not inclined to countenance.

While early testimony by two court mages—one Vilwan-trained—had strongly linked Crow with Hawkins and suggested they were one and the same, beyond that the prosecution faltered. It seemed unlikely that the primary witness against Hawkins would testify. To take the stand would have left Scrainwood open to the sort of close questioning Queen Carus had given Marsham. And since Augustus had been present during the siege of Fortress Draconis where the treason had occurred, he could correct or counter exaggerations. Without that testimony, and since no one save Crow could testify to what had happened in the warrens of Boragul, the Oriosan case against him began to crumble.

Alexia watched Crow as the queen tore into Marsham and felt a bit surprised. Marsham clearly loathed Crow. The venom in his voice, the anger in his eyes, made his hatred of Crow readily apparent. Alexia had not liked the little man from the first time she'd met him, and was taking great delight in his squirming. Likewise, deeper amid the spectators, Will seemed to be enjoying Marsham's discomfort.

Crow was not. He kept his face impassive and listened. She couldn't tell if he felt sorry for the man, or hated him. Alexia found her gaze again and again drawn to his strong profile and the sense of peace Crow possessed. In some ways it calmed her and, yet, in others, it excited her.

Crow's face remained still, save the couple of times when he turned slightly to glance at her. His head would incline forward, tucking his chin down until his beard touched his chest, then he would give her just the hint of a smile. That left eye would close just a whisker shy of a wink, then he would look back up and pay attention again to the court proceedings.

Every time he smiled at her Alexia had to fight to hide her own smile. It was not that she was unused to smiling at Crow. In the time leading up to the trial, she had smiled much at the mention of his name, and had even taken to toying with the gold band around her ring finger. She visited him as often as she could, and hours talking with him flew past. There were even times when she completely forgot where they were, and the reality of his captivity surprised her. At all times she pushed to portray the image of a woman deeply in love with her husband, and did not admit to anyone that all was a pretense, though many suspected and even more were certain.

She had played the role to the hilt and despite the desperation that had prompted her to fashion that solution, there had been many a pleasant moment. Alexia sorely missed the nights on the road, when she and Crow had shared a tent. The two of them had whispered together, at first telling simple things, relating stories and remembrances. They were all of the nature of campfire stories, and quite harmless. Indeed, at first their interaction was nothing more than what the two of them had shared while on the Okrannel campaign together, or on the flight from Fortress Draconis.

Things slowly had begun to shift. She recalled the question she'd asked, one she had immediately withdrawn, but Crow had answered it nonetheless. "No, Princess, this is not how I had anticipated my life running." He went on to share what his dreams had been, his hopes, and revealed to her some of the pain he'd felt when his mask had been torn from him. His voice had tightened as it had when his broken leg had pained him, though the agony must have been much greater.

His willingness to open himself to her had surprised her. She and Perrine had shared much, but they were sisters. They had been raised together, and amid the Gyrkyme confidences were treated as sacred trusts. The Gyrkyme would prefer death to violating such a trust. Betrayal of secrets was considered a very human thing to do, so she had grown up very wary of trusting any human.

Her great-grandaunt Tatyana's scheming nature had reinforced her unwillingness to trust men, though her uncle and cousin, Misha, had begun to erode those walls. Still, Alexia's aloofness inspired few people to confide in her, and she felt little impetus to share with them.

Crow's sharing fed straight back into her sense of kinship with the Gyrkyme. He trusted her implicitly. While he had protested what she had done to save him from a summary execution, his gratitude had shone forth in the confidences he shared with her.

They had been friends before the marriage charade, each having saved the other's life several times during their brief adventures. Traveling together had deepened that friendship. Spending night after night with him, availing herself of his warmth, or just listening to him breathe, she began to find the ordinary in a man who was extraordinary. More than once she'd awakened to find herself pressed tight against his back. She'd pulled away immediately, but more slowly each time it happened, and always with growing reluctance. Visiting him in the Meredo gaol, she regretted the lack of that intimacy and more than once had awakened clutching a pillow to herself.

Crow looked in her direction and smiled again as the tribunal dismissed Marsham. Her heart leaped in her breast, and the corners of her mouth curled up into a smile. There was something in his look, something about his pleasure, that seemed contagious. It wasn't a sensation totally foreign to her, for she knew it with Peri; that pride and happiness at the well-being of a friend. And, as with Peri, she wanted to reach a hand out to touch him.

And she wanted more, to have that smile broadened, to have that pleasure increase on his face...

Before she could think further on those lines, Wroxter Dainn, the Oriosan Justice Advocate Supreme, rose and looked to call another witness. Past him, however, against the far wall, a time-faded tapestry began to smoke. A scorch mark darkened it in the center, near the base, and extended up to the height of a man. The smoke thickened, then popped into a flame that exploded upward to engulf the entire tapestry and sent licking tongues up into the cavernous ceiling vaults.

Sparks and glowing embers fell softly as snow amid the throng. There, in the wall, a previously hidden panel opened and a figure stepped forward to be greeted with gasps. He wore a hooded cloak fashioned after the skin of a Grand Temeryx, save that the varicolored plumage consisted not of feathers but a rainbow of flames.

His eyes seemed alive. Mostly blue, they had wisps of white drift through them like thin clouds in a windy sky. In his left hand he raised a white kerchief, at the same time moving his cloak back enough to show the empty scabbard at his left hip. Within the shadow of his mask his mouth opened, revealing white teeth that contrasted sharply with the ebon of his flesh.

"I am Nefrai-kesh. I come beneath a flag of truce. I demand the Oriosan right to speak at the trial of a vassal of mine."

Augustus had risen from his seat. Linchmere cowered in his, as did most of the spectators. Dainn had recoiled and the queen covered her mouth with her left hand. Crow remained seated, but had outstretched his left hand in Alexia's direction, to keep her back and safe. She'd also gained her feet, and her hand had fallen to where the hilt of her sword should have been.

The first to act, however, was Will Norrington. He shot to his feet and pointed a wavering finger at the *sullanciri*. "H-he's not your vassal, he's mine."

Nefrai-kesh's head came around quickly. The Aurolani general smiled, then he nodded once, solemnly. "Now *you* are the son I wish I'd had."

"Maybe if you'd been a better father, he would have been." Will's grey eyes tightened beneath the mask and he drew the dagger he'd been allowed to carry. "Where he failed, I won't."

The *sullanciri* opened his arms. "You will come to my embrace. Now, later. The timing does not matter. You are my true heir, and there is much I will give you."

Crow rose. "Will, stay back."

"I'm not afraid of him."

"You should be." Crow looked at the *sullanciri*. "And you, baiting children?"

"He wears a mask. He is a man, with a man's responsibilities and duties. You remember those, don't you, Tarrant?" Nefrai-kesh stepped to the Throne of Truth. "King Augustus, you will recognize the truce and my right to speak. My heir presumptive has asserted a claim that is invalid, since neither I nor my son is deceased, and the formalities to dispossess us have not been observed."

Will brandished his dagger. "Don't listen to him."

Augustus frowned. "This is a legal proceeding, Lord Norrington. Rules must be observed. I believe you can be seated, Nefrai-kesh, if you will be sworn to tell the truth."

The young thief snarled. "He works for Chytrine. She made him into a monster! A snake can slither a straight line easier than he'll tell the truth."

Linchmere uncoiled timidly. "We have to hear him. It is the Law."

"Then it's stupid!" Will reached up, ripped off his own mask, and tossed it into the well of the court before turning and stalking out of the chamber. "When Chytrine comes to kill you, you'll give her a courtesy mask and say 'please' and 'thank you.' Rot the lot of you!"

Only the tiny snapping of the flames on the *sullanciri*'s cloak filled the silence in the wake of Will's departure. The assembled Oriosans stared at the flaccid mask lying on the floor. Even Crow looked stricken as he slowly sank back into his chair.

Nefrai-kesh raised his right hand. "I swear to tell the whole of the truth, accepting Kedyn's retribution if I lie."

Wroxter Dainn, whose florid face streamed with sweat, struggled to compose himself. "You have come to testify about the conduct of Tarrant Hawkins?"

"From afar, yes, I have come." Nefrai-kesh's rich voice filled the chamber, but Alexia felt as if she was hearing him with more than her ears. *Magick is at work here.* Even knowing she was being manipulated, she could not shake the sense that his words were sincere and truthful.

"I led the expedition into Boragul. Once there we did encounter the Empress Chytrine, but none of us knew it at the time. We accepted the hospitality of the urZrethi and only discovered too late that we were in a trap. The woman we had pursued had us at her mercy."

The *sullanciri* opened his left hand toward Crow, letting the handkerchief flutter to the ground. "I would first speak in praise of Hawkins. Of all the accusations against him, the most foul are those of cowardice. On the day of our damnation he was the most courageous. He alone fought his way back to our chambers. There he found me, he succored me, and did all he could to safeguard me, as a vassal should. I was sorely wounded—mortally so, save for the intervention of magick. Let no one who hears me ever think he was anything but a hero.

"Once a hero, however, and once a knave. He did commit treason that day. He defied me. Thrice I asked him to do me a service. I demanded it of him as was my right."

Dainn mopped his brow with a handkerchief. "What was that duty?"

Before the *sullanciri* could answer, an agonized groan twisted from Crow's throat. "I could not *kill* you."

"Oh, but would that you had, Tarrant." Nefrai-kesh laid his hand against his breastbone. "Had you done that, I would not be here. Queen Lanivette would not have died by my hand in this very place. Fortress Draconis would not have fallen and the Southlands would not be in jeopardy. You had, in your power, the means to protect your homeland and your friends, but you defied me. You committed treason, against me, against your nation, against the world."

"You know why I could not."

The *sullanciri* slowly shook his head. "The reasoning of a vassal is nothing when it contradicts the order of your lord. So, Augustus, you see what it is? He could have saved you all this, but he did not."

King Augustus shook his head. "Being dead does not preclude one from joining the ranks of the *sullanciri*."

"True, but everyone on that expedition knew the qualitative difference between those who had become *sullanciri* pre- and postmortem. He knew."

Crow looked at his hands. "I didn't believe you would be so weak."

"But I told you, Hawkins. I trusted you, and you failed me." The *sullanciri* stood. "Despite what my grandson charged, I have spoken the truth, and Hawkins has verified it. I know Oriosan law and custom. You may have many speak for him, and more speak against him, but your duty is clear."

Linchmere sat forward. "Do not presume to lecture us, changeling!"

Nefrai-kesh's smile flowed into a predatory display of teeth. "Oh, someone thinks he has a spine. It can be torn out, you know, bone by bone, so numb death slowly spreads through you. I would enjoy that, my prince. Will you indulge me?"

The Oriosan Prince squeaked and curled into a ball in his throne.

Augustus stepped forward. "Enough, Nefrai-kesh. Preserve the illusion that a bit of the man I respected resides in you still."

"If you wish to believe in illusions, Augustus, feel free to delude yourself as long as you like." The *sullanciri* stood, then raked the clawed fingers of his left hand through the air. Black slits appeared as if he had rent some canvas. "The man you respected is no more, but the man you know to fear is yet here. And shall be for a long, long time."

As he spoke his gaze shifted from Augustus to Crow and then her. Their eyes locked for a second and a huge jolt ran through Alexia. It did not feel as if he'd read her mind, but she felt certain he knew it. That realization shook her, but before she could act or speak, he slipped through the rents and they vanished behind him.

Crow turned toward her. "Are you hurt?"

She shivered and shook her head. "No, not at all. You?"

He shifted his shoulders stiffly. "In no real sense." He fell silent for a moment, then shook his head. "I couldn't kill him."

Alexia did lean forward and rest a hand on his shoulder. "He knew that when he asked you to do it. Just as I did when I asked you to promise to kill me if I ever looked to go over to Chytrine. You were right in what you told me, and you were right in denying him then."

"But he's right, I could have saved everyone."

Alexia gave him a brave smile and squeezed his shoulder. "And yet you shall, Crow. And yet you shall."

CHAPTER 20

The sharp, raw, torn sensation in the back of his throat remained with Kerrigan Reese even after the echoes of the harsh cough that awakened him had faded. Curled up as tightly as his girth would allow him, he lay naked, in complete darkness, on his left side. The cold, hard stone beneath him had leached a lot of his body heat. In his mouth was the sour taste of old vomit, and his head ached.

As he tried to straighten out, two more things added to his discomfort. The first was the aching in his back. Whatever had hit him had done so very solidly. Battered muscles protested, and the fatty flesh covering them provided a chorus accompaniment. Even his kidneys ached, and Kerrigan dreaded the damage he'd find if he cast a diagnostic spell.

He would have been tempted to do that, but had a more immediate concern: he was fettered. Stout manacles surrounded his wrists and ankles. Reaching down, he could easily grasp the heavy chains to which his bonds had been joined, though when he took up the slack, the wrist chains did not pull at his ankles. The chain did tighten, though, and one wrist did pull against the other, so he imagined some ring in the floor of his prison to which he was fastened.

The magicker lay very still and thought for a moment. That he was a prisoner was obvious. Having been taken by the Vilwanese was a possibility, and that only indicated how seriously they wanted him back. They would have had to bring in someone or something that could neutralize him. While he was certain that could happen, wouldn't the apprehension have taken place in a more controlled area? He was on his way to the consulate where they could have taken him at their leisure.

And he doubted that, in taking him, they would have seen a benefit in his being half drowned.

The other alternative that left open was Chytrine. He wracked his brain to see if there was anything he had done to attract her attention. He had created a duplicate of one fragment of the DragonCrown and had tampered with another fragment, but he sincerely doubted she could track him through that magick. And other than that covert work, he had done nothing to make her see him as a threat. Any attack would have been better executed on Princess Alexia or Will.

It was entirely possible, of course, that the duplicate he had made would let her track the fragment. But having the means to go after the fragment made it unlikely she would have had him attacked. Once she had the fragment, he was immaterial, so the attack made no sense. More important, if she had seen him as a threat, why she would leave him alive?

But if not Vilwan or Chytrine, then who?

Aside from the sound of his own breathing and the irregular pit-pat of water dropping on stone, the chamber had remained quiet. Because of the darkness Kerrigan could see nothing and couldn't even begin to guess how big the room was. The *mageyes* spell would take care of that problem, so he gathered himself to cast it.

Before he could get the spell off, however, something clicked in the darkness. It came from behind him, but tiny and distant. As sounds went, it wasn't much. Just a simple click.

Kerrigan held his breath. He waited, straining his ears. More water dripped, sometimes one drop on top of the other, but no more clicks. Kerrigan slowly let his breath out, then drew one in through his nose, forcing himself to be quiet even though his lungs wanted cool air to quench the fire in them.

Click.

It came louder this time, and in front of him, down toward where he imagined that ring was set in the floor. *Could it have been a link hitting the ring?* He let the sound run through his mind again, but caught no metal in it. No, it was more like stone on stone.

Or claw *on stone.*

For a heartbeat, then two, the terrible image of a temeryx lurking out there, circling him, shook Kerrigan and made the links rattle. Temeryces served Chytrine the way dogs served huntsmen. The feathered beasts had narrow heads with lots of sharp teeth, huge, sickle-shaped claws on their feet, and smaller grasping clawed hands that they clutched tightly to their breasts.

He'd seen the sort of bite they could leave on a man, and had no desire to see if he could heal himself with magick faster than it could devour him.

He fought back panic for two reasons. The first was that he couldn't cast a spell if he couldn't think, and he had to think to get out of his current situation. And the second was that he did have the magickal armor that would reward the temeryx with a mouthful of bony plates.

His invulnerability heartened him. He calmed himself again and forced himself to breathe more regularly. He remained quiet and listened, but focused more on choosing a spell to cast. He really had two choices: either a spell that would allow him to see in the dark, or a spell that would actually illuminate the place. The light spell he had managed to employ in a similarly dark place had blinded his assailants and facilitated his escape but, chained up as he was, he wasn't going to be running off fast. He chose to save that spell for a reserve and instead prepared to cast the night vision spell.

Kerrigan set himself and limbered his fingers. He pulled his awareness away from the world for a moment, forgetting how cold he felt. Into the realm of magic he plunged, weaving together the various elements that would fashion him an ethereal veil that would enhance his vision. The spellcasting progressed quickly and easily; though he had not used the spell that much, he had always liked it and found it simple to work.

Thwock!

Something hit him and hit him hard, on the right shoulder, and bounced off to clatter in the darkness. *That sound definitely was stone on stone; I was hit by a rock.* The bony plate that had risen to protect him sank away again, taking with it all but the faintest hint of pain from the impact.

Kerrigan groaned. The invocation of the protective spell also shredded the weaving of the night vision spell. The armor took precedence and was cast subconsciously. Its urgency demanded all of his abilities, so the delicate spell he'd been working on evaporated.

He began to cast it again, but before he could complete the working another stone clipped him.

"Hey!"

The sound that replied almost convinced him that there *was* a temeryx present. It started as a hiss, then descended into a mad little laugh. It alternated between serpentine sibilance and a giggle. Kerrigan found nothing benign about it. A shiver slithered up his spine, then he levered himself up on his left elbow and twisted around to sit facing the location of the sound.

The chain on his feet stopped him short of his goal.

The undulating sound stopped for a moment, then another rock smacked Kerrigan square in the chest. It rebounded to his lap. After a moment's bobbling, the magicker grabbed it, then raised his right hand back to throw it.

The chain rattled, but before he could start to throw, the chain was yanked hard.

The stone flew off into the darkness as Kerrigan spun around to the right. Another yank on the foot chain continued to spin him on his bare rump across the floor, and no bony plates appeared to save him the chafing abrasions. Tipping off-balance, he rolled, tangling his legs in the chain, and finding himself suddenly half-buried nose first in a bed of dry straw.

He pulled his head up, then sneezed violently, smacking his forehead into the ground. The straw did cushion the blow, but the magick didn't stop him from hurting himself. "Ow!" He rolled onto his back and brought his hands up to his forehead, whacking his jaw with the left manacle in the process.

He felt the lump growing on his forehead and the tightness of the chains on his legs. The hissed giggling continued, at a higher pitch now, and another rock clicked off his thigh. Instinctively he turned to the right to protect himself, but another rock hit his stomach hard. He twisted away from that line of attack, got hit again, then rolled away and landed on a rock that jabbed him good and solidly in the back.

"OW!" He arched his back and dug away at the stone. Grasping it in both hands, he pushed himself up onto his right hip and went to raise his hands to throw it, but with his legs bound he flopped over awkwardly. To make matters worse yet another stone skipped off his head, sending a hideously sharp sound through his skull.

He ducked his head and pulled his legs up. He had to get free, but the only way he could do that would be by using a spell. The rocks kept invoking the armor, which destroyed any spells he was trying to cast. *I'll have to cast the spell very fast.* He frowned. *Faster than I've ever cast a spell before.*

He went through a catalogue of spells he could use to get the shackles off. Most involved heating the metal until it melted, which would have melted his hands off as well. He knew there were some basic lock-picking spells, but he'd never been taught them. This had not prevented him from fashioning some of his own, based on healing spells. A diagnostic spell would show him how the lock had been constructed, then a modified levitation spell would let him manipulate the pieces of the lock to open it.

These shackles can't be that different in construction than a door lock.

He gathered himself to cast the diagnostic spell quickly, but the rocks kept coming in a steady stream. He tried to ignore them, but it didn't matter. The magick meant to save his life was preventing him from escaping. *There is nothing I can do!*

Howling with frustration, he raised the rock in his right hand and smashed it down on the manacle on his left wrist. It rang loudly and produced a quick spark that died on the prison's damp stone floor. The light hadn't been much, revealing only grey stone and blond straw chaff, but he had seen it.

The rocks stopped flying.

It took Kerrigan a moment or two to accept that this was truly the case. Once he did, he smiled and started to cast the diagnostic spell.

Thwock!

"Stop it!"

"Soppit, soppit, soppit..." The sibilant voice repeated the mocking word in a pitiful tone. The origin point for the voice shifted around and around, with little clicks occasionally accompanying it, as his tormentor circled him. "Soppit, soppit, soppit."

Kerrigan again tried to cast a spell, but a rock stopped him. He tried again and again, hoping that one rock might miss him and he might get his spell to work, but at that range his assailant never missed. In fact, from the high angle of some of the attacks, Kerrigan knew the invisible creature had raced in and hurled the stone *down* at him.

Not being stupid, Kerrigan realized that he wasn't going to cast a spell unless he had respite from the stones. *The only time he stopped was...* Quickly the magicker hammered a manacle with a stone. It rang loudly, but the stones still came. Kerrigan hit it again, glancing it, and striking a spark.

The rocks stopped and silence again reigned.

Kerrigan hit the manacle again and another spark ignited. No stone flew. The youth allowed himself a smile that broadened quickly. With his left hand he swept straw dust into a little pile and struck a spark into it.

The spark survived just long enough for a small thread of smoke to drift up.

Again and again Kerrigan pounded the manacle with the rock. It didn't matter to him that the glancing blows tore at his skin. His wrist was soon slick with blood, but still he struck, flicking spark after spark into his pile of tinder. He blew gently on it, getting sparks to glow brightly before they died. He learned now to avoid scattering the tinder, and between sparks he grabbed straw and crumbled it into more dust.

The hail of stones had stopped, but Kerrigan didn't give a thought to casting a spell. Somehow the creature knew when he was invoking magick. How, he didn't care. He just wanted the torment to stop, and it had. He didn't know if the creature was afraid of fire, or fascinated by it; but if producing it would keep the thing occupied, he was determined to do it.

As he worked he thought back to the Okrannel campaign and the trip south from Fortress Draconis. Though Kerrigan knew very well the spell that would kindle fire, he'd not been allowed to do it on the trip. Orla had not wanted him to become some hedge-wizard in the eyes of the soldiers. On the retreat from Fortress Draconis the princess had noted that he had more important things to be doing than worrying about making fires since others could do that.

Others could. He'd even watched children kindle fires. *Yet here I am, and I can't do that.* He wished he'd watched more closely, for it would have made the whole task easier. Still, as smart as he was, he slowly reconstructed the procedure.

Finally, a spark caught. He blew gently on it and got embers. Another breath and a little flame popped into life. Kerrigan fed a small piece of straw into it, then another. Carefully, gently he fed it, letting it grow. The fire ate the straw quickly, so he twisted stalks and knotted them to make them burn more slowly.

He smiled when he felt heat. It wasn't much, but it was enough to remind him how cold he was. Still, it was heat, and there was light, some *real* light. Staring across the fire limited his vision, but he caught faint hints of the walls and clearly saw the iron ring into which his chains had been slipped.

Kerrigan sat up, his smile very broad as his little fire guttered merrily.

A wave of magick swept into the room. Kerrigan felt it and tried to study the spell, but its complexity defied casual observation. The spell sank into the chains that held him and locked their links. The chains tightened on his legs and held his arms to his thighs.

A very cool and low voice spoke from above and behind him. "Very good, Adept Reese, you have learned your first lesson. Magick is not life."

"Who are you? Where am I? What do you want with me?"

"Three very good questions." The voice remained even and calm. "You will have the opportunity to earn the answers to them."

"Answer one now. I made a fire. That's what you wanted me to do, wasn't it?"

"No." Another spell sped through the room and Kerrigan recognized it instantly. It was the first spell taught to every apprentice. It was the spell they learned before they learned how to make fire.

His fire went out.

"No, no! Not fair. I did what you wanted."

"Listen, Kerrigan Reese. Very little in life is fair. You were born with vast potential for working magick. The world needs you, but you have been held apart from it. And because of your distance, you could easily do more damage than help. This must be determined."

Something hit Kerrigan in the back. It was soft and slid down against his buttocks. He couldn't see it, but it felt like a blanket.

"You now have some idea how desperate a man can be to create a fire when he is cold. Imagine those were not stones, but were raindrops or snowflakes. Imagine that the cold in your limbs made your hands numb. Imagine that huddled in the darkness was your family. Your wife, hungry and cold, your children terrified. The baby probably already dead. When you saw that spark, hope would soar. When it died, hope would die, and you would know your family was going to die along with it.

"You, Kerrigan Reese, might be that spark. If you don't understand how important you are, you will be far too dangerous to be allowed to live." The voice did not rise on that point, making it less a threat than a simple fact. "Think on what I have said. Cast no magick or you will be punished."

"But I'm bleeding."

"And how would one who has no magick deal with that, Adept?" The voice grew distant. "Remember first you are a man and then, perhaps, you will be able to save mankind."

CHAPTER 21

Will snarled and cursed as he kicked his way through brown slush. He didn't care if it splashed up on him—his anger insulated him from the cold. As for the state it left his clothes in, he didn't care about that, either. The clothes, titles, all that stuff was stupid and he hated it.

He spun around and looked back at the palace. The tops of the towers already hid beneath fluffy white blankets of falling snow. It looked very peaceful, which was ridiculous given who was in there at the moment. And the guards, all of them, should have been rushing to the palace to kill the *sullanciri*. That much seemed blatantly obvious to Will, but everyone else seemed to think a flag of truce meant something.

It means you're missing a chance to kill Nefrai-kesh, that's *what it means.*

Growing up in the Dimandowns wasn't easy, but at least he'd learned some hard lessons. The slums of Yslin were a place where truces lasted for as long as it took someone to get more people on his side. If Nefrai-kesh had shown up there the way he showed up in Meredo, he'd have been ripped apart. And, given what he was, even if they hadn't killed him, they certainly wouldn't have believed anything he had to say.

Will turned his back on the palace and continued trudging through the snow. The way nobility acted never ceased to surprise him. On one hand you had folks like King Augustus, who were good and noble most of the time, but who admitted they didn't act well toward a friend. On the other hand you had Scrainwood, for whom Will actually would take a bucket of warm piss in exchange. And in between you had folks who could be greedy and grubby, or who would tell you whatever they thought you wanted to hear, or just had folks who had no idea what life was like in the world of the streets. They all seemed stupid.

He frowned because he didn't want to classify Princess Alexia as a noble in that regard. She really was different, but even she hadn't done anything about Nefrai-kesh. He did allow as how she didn't have a magick sword with her to kill him—Resolute had one, but he wasn't there. And Crow's sword, Tsamoc, now resided in the princess' room, where it was no help. Still and all, he was pretty sure she had to have seen the stupidity of leaving Nefrai-kesh alive.

A shiver ran down his spine. He really had been ready to shove his little dagger into the thing that had been his grandfather, but that hadn't scared the *sullanciri*. He'd just opened his arms and said that Will could come to him. Nefrai-kesh had said that Will would be his heir.

"I don't want to be your heir." Will snarled loudly and stamped his feet. "It's because of you I'm in this mess!"

The absurdity of his complaint struck Will and made him laugh for a moment. He looked up, seeing if anyone else thought things were as silly as he did; but what he saw surprised him because most folks were completely ignoring him. They just paid him no mind, and that astonished him because even walking to the palace to attend the trial he had constantly been subjected to profuse wishes of good will by folks he didn't even know.

But now, now everyone treats me as if I don't exist! He wondered at that for a moment, then his jaw dropped open. *Of course, the* mask! The mask he'd left lying in the court had been the thing people recognized. Oriosans could read masks as easily as Will could calculate the worth of a purse by how it bulged. He might be Will Norrington, but Lord Norrington wore a specific mask and without it he was nothing.

He mulled over the irony that meant *not* wearing a disguise made him invisible, but realized it was just a reversal of the sort of misdirection he and his companions had used when cutting purses in Yslin. Working a crowd, he'd find a target. At a signal two of his confederates would start a fight, jostling people, including the target. As they bumped into him, Will would clip his purse and slip away quietly. All the attention had been drawn to the fighting kids and since no one was watching him, he got away cleanly.

Here the lack of a mask meant that you were beneath notice or, if not that, certainly below the interest of those who could wear masks. Will knew enough of history to know that Muroso, Alosa, and Oriosa had, at one time, been provinces that rebelled against an empire. The rebels had worn masks to disguise themselves as they fought against the empire, and when they won independence, those who had fought for it became the new nobility. To them and their descendants went the right to wear a mask, and the decorations on their masks marked their importance.

Because of the masks, the Oriosans constantly seemed to be looking for symbols and significance in things. Will was certain that tugging off his mask and throwing it on the floor would be seen as having all sorts of portents and meaning, while he'd just done it because he wanted to throw something and wasn't going to throw the dagger, which he liked.

He shook his head, imagining them thinking it was a rejection of his citizenship. Since the masks of the dead were often kept by the family, tossing it toward Nefrai-kesh could be taken as a sign that he was saying that the *sullanciri* should just consider him dead. Or it could be taken as a gesture of his rejecting the niceties of the court and vowing to wage his own war against Chytrine.

There were many more things, and he assumed that gossip mills would be grinding away long hours making them up. He didn't like the idea that some folks would think he was walking away from the war with Chytrine. That would probably be the darkest of the omens read in what he had done. There had to be a way to put that to rights, but exactly how to do it, he wasn't certain.

More symbols, and the Oriosans will believe in me again. They all do things with reasons, and as long as I have a good one, they'll believe me. Will sighed. He knew he'd have to figure things out. He'd have liked to talk to Kerrigan about it, since the mage's perspective on things was even weirder than that of the average Oriosan. Kerrigan, however, had gone missing, and Lombo was out hunting him. The Vilwanese consulate had reported back to Princess Alexia that they didn't know where he was, and their courier sounded nervous enough that Will believed the Vilwanese didn't have him.

The idea that Oriosans always do something for a reason began to bounce around inside Will's skull. He started to wonder what purpose Nefrai-kesh would have for showing up at the trial. Sure, his appearance in the palace was likely to scare a lot of folks—Scrainwood first among them. But a better way to scare a lot of folks would have been for the *sullanciri* just to kill Scrainwood. Having Linchmere on the throne would have terrified everyone in Oriosa and well beyond its borders.

The *sullanciri* couldn't actually have intended to come to give testimony. That made no sense whatsoever. Crow's fate really didn't matter, and if Chytrine wanted Crow dead, she could have sent the *sullanciri* into his cell. Making folks use the laws of a nation to kill an innocent man might strike some nobles as a horrible thing, but Will was fresh from war and knew that anything Scrainwood might have done to Crow would be, odds on, more pleasant than the sort of death found on a battlefield.

By the gods—I should have seen it immediately! Will began to run through the streets, dodging carts, slipping in muddy slush, going down, splashing, getting up again, and continuing as fast as he could. He leaped over snow-drifts, ducked, and twisted through the middle of a snowball war and shoved slower people aside. Ignoring the cries of the few who went down, he sped on, ever faster, toward the Rampant Panther.

There was only one reason that Nefrai-kesh would risk showing up at the trial, and that was *misdirection*. If there was going to be any alarm sent up, it would summon all of the guards to the palace. *And the false flag of truce makes folks believe he means no harm, but I don't believe that at all.* Putting Nefrai-kesh in the palace was a risk, but Chytrine would only undertake that risk for a greater gain, and there was only one thing in Meredo that she wanted that badly.

The ruby fragment of the DragonCrown!

Will burst through the inn's door and bolted immediately for the stairs to the rooms. He held his left hand up beside his face, half in a wave, but mostly to hide the fact that he had no mask on. He hit the landing and doubled back to the second floor, then dashed along the corridor toward the last room on the right.

Time slowed for Will despite his haste. He studied the floor at that end of the corridor, for Kerrigan's room was right across the hall from his own. Before leaving that morning he'd checked Kerrigan's room and had placed a thread between the door and the jamb that would fall out if the door had been opened. More important, Will had used lampblack to darken a couple of knots in the wooden flooring. Had a boot brushed over them, the scuff marks would have showed clearly. Will had avoided them himself, and Resolute had been warned, so only a thief would run afoul of it.

Or Kerrigan, which would be a big help.

As he neared the door he picked the dark thread out against the blond wood. That allowed him a touch of relief, then he slowed and dropped to one knee to survey the knots. Two remained black as puddles of ink, but the third had changed. No streaks, as if anyone had stepped on it, but it had a big flat splash of grey in it.

Dust.

Will looked up at the short rafter running across the width of the corridor. The dust up there had to be thicker than the snow in the streets, and it was possible a cat had wandered along that beam, but Will wasn't of a mind to be considering cats when a thief might be about. Glancing at the wall above the door, he saw a couple of faint marks, the origin of which he couldn't imagine, but he knew they'd not been there earlier. Which meant someone was stealing his DragonCrown fragment.

Drawing his dagger, Will stepped to the door and opened it. The oil lamp behind him stabbed a wedge of yellow light into the tiny room that had housed Kerrigan. The thief's line of sight was drawn upward, to the rafter's continuation in the room, and the figure hunched and huddled in the lurid scarlet glow. What he saw sent two emotions through him, the first quickly being subsumed by the second.

The first emotion was pure elation as he saw that the trap he and Kerrigan had set had functioned far better than he could have hoped. To hide the DragonCrown fragment they searched the room and in that rafter found a rot-hollow right where the beam had been reinforced by two other pieces of lumber. Kerrigan had used magic to strengthen the beam, melding those two sections of wood into the original. At the same time he reshaped the hollow to fit the DragonCrown fragment snugly inside. At Will's suggestion Kerrigan narrowed the hole a thief would reach through, so it would be too small to let him slip a hand back out when he had the gem in it.

Kerrigan had enhanced this situation further by casting another spell on the fragment that would make it as sticky as a spider's web, guaranteeing that any thief who wanted to get away would have to leave his hand behind.

Worked like a charm.

The second emotion completely smothered his elation at success. Pure fear poured into Will as he saw what they'd caught. The creature had the bulk of a large dog or a small bear, and its body bristled with four-inch-long hairs on its bare body and head and legs, with a thick down covering its back. Its shoulders were hunched as it tugged mightily to free its right hand, with its legs bunched and pushing.

All eight of the legs!

With a moment's retrospect Will realized he should have recognized the thing as a spider, for the body came in segments and the four pairs of legs from the middle looked like spider's legs. The fact that the creature was huge beyond all imagining could have fooled him, but it wasn't the deciding factor.

Aside from being blue, save for the bristles of black hair, what forced away the judgment was the human torso that rose from the creature's middle. While the chest was smaller than it should have been for the arms and head, and while blue down did carpet that section of the body, it was unmistakably human.

Then the creature turned and looked at him with bubbled eyes and wickedly curved mandibles. The mouth parts worked and Will heard something that almost clicked and growled its way into a semblance of human speech. An angry hiss capped the remark and the creature gave another hard tug on the fragment.

"You're caught now, thief!"

Will brought the dagger up to his ear and whipped it forward. Though entirely unbalanced for throwing, the dagger sped to its target. The hilt smashed the creature in the middle of the back, wrenched a clicked howl from its throat, then bounced back down onto Kerrigan's bed.

Sprinting into the room, Will dove and grabbed for the dagger. As his right hand closed on the hilt, something grabbed his jacket right between his shoulder blades. Will twisted around to slash at whatever had him, and discovered the thing had shifted to the bottom of the rafter and had grabbed him with its left hand. Will cut at the arm, drawing blood, but failed to win his release.

The spider-thing hauled Will up and smashed his head against the rafter. Stars exploded, and Will must have blacked out for a moment, because when the world swam back into focus, he found his legs wrapped in webbing and the left arm holding him by the front of his jacket. Black blood oozed from the wound and began to soak into his clothing. It had an acrid scent akin to burning nutmeats.

The creature thrust its face to his and snarled. That close to it, Will caught some hint of familiarity that told him who his captor was. The realization shook him. *The Azure Spider!*

The young thief's mouth dropped open. "You are the Azure Spider. You're one of her things now."

The *sullanciri* hissed, then jerked its head to the trapped hand.

Will shook his head. "Not even if I knew how to undo it." He breathed in through his nose, then spat a huge gobbet of spittle, hitting the creature in the left eye cluster.

The mandibles parted, the *sullanciri*'s head dipped, and pure fire pierced Will's neck right and left. His body shook as molten agony poured into him. He tried to scream, but found his throat paralyzed. Then the pressure vanished and he felt himself falling. It seemed to take forever. He watched the *sullanciri*'s left hand get smaller, watched a droplet of that black blood chase him down, and he hoped, somehow, that Kerrigan's bed was still beneath him.

Then the world began to shift. First Will thought his hearing was going bad because while he caught sounds that had the cadence of speech, they made no sense to him. The spider-thing tried to shift to the left, hissing loudly, but since the spittle had half-blinded it and its hand was still trapped, its range of motion was limited.

Then a needle, silver-grey, stabbed up through the *sullanciri*. It drove through the center of the legs, emerged, then spitted the manspine. The creature shook once, hard, then the legs released and curled in. The body started to fall, then hung there by one hand as it went limp save for the rhythmic, pumping contractions of the abdomen.

"Will. *Will!*" Resolute's face appeared above his. The thief couldn't see well enough to read any concern in the Vorquelf's expression, but it came through in the voice. "Will, are you with me, boy?"

Will nodded, or thought he did. Fire burned through his veins and his body bowed as muscles contracted. He tried to open his mouth and speak, but before he could do that, another convulsion hit him and the world dissolved into nothingness.

CHAPTER 22

Nineteen days had passed since the advent of the new Aurolani troops in Fortress Draconis, yet for Erlestoke, it seemed as if the winter had already lasted a year. So many things were different. Since the fall, Fortress Draconis had changed, and well beyond anything ordinary.

Enemy activity had increased and discipline had gotten better. That was due to the new creations, which Ryswin had designated *kryalniri* based on some distant elven tale of when the world was young, winters were long, and fierce beasts hunted through the snows for game that was trapped or travelers who were lost. Jilandessa suggested that Chytrine might have modeled her new creatures on those legends, so the name fit. But the humans just called them "crawls" for ease of understanding, and the elves took that bastardization without umbrage.

The crawls had replaced vylaens as the leaders of gibberkin, and had proven very effective in tightening up on lax patrols and inattentive sentries. Patrols were doubled in size and frequency, which made setting ambushes very difficult. Erlestoke's people had taken to setting snares and other traps to make the gibberkin cautious. While their kill rate dropped, the efforts did slow the enemy progress in their operations.

The Aurolani forces certainly seemed to have some very specific goals in mind. The vylaens had been reorganized into little cadres of magickers. Each one had a crawl in charge of things. The fortress' ruins had been gridded off, as nearly as the prince could determine, and a full-scale magickal survey was under way.

He had to assume they were looking for a fragment of the DragonCrown.

Once their survey indicated there was something in the area, work crews of human captives and gibberkin were brought in to excavate. The digging would last for as little as a couple of hours to a maximum of two days. He'd inspected some of the abandoned digs, and the effort seemed to be pretty well focused at the start, then developed into a broader, more systematic approach that opened a hole in layers.

It did strike the prince as bizarre that their magickers were having trouble locating the fragment they wanted. While Erlestoke himself was completely unable to work magick of any sort, he did have an understanding of it. Somehow the search parties had something that allowed them to focus on the item they were searching for. They worked spells based on the link between that thing and the target, and the magick revealed a location to them.

The link between objects had been made quite apparent to him the first day he'd seen a crawl. In his haste to get to Castleton and to get the crawl's body away for examination, he'd abandoned Malarkex's sword in the ruins. They'd left their headquarters and plunged deeper into the undercity but, somehow, when he awoke the next morning, the saber was once again in his scabbard. Jilandessa had cast a couple of spells and detected some sort of a link between the blade and the scabbard, and while Erlestoke really didn't like the sword, he could see the virtue of having a weapon that returned to him.

He'd smiled at her and extended his right hand. "Would be much nicer if it would come to my hand when I commanded."

The elf had nodded. "It would, but do you really want to be linked to that blade that way?"

The prince agreed he did not.

The appearance of the crawls was not the only adjustment of Aurolani forces at Fortress Draconis. A *sullanciri* had been left in charge with Chytrine's departure. Ferxigo had actually spent time at Fortress Draconis with the urZrethi garrison before she joined the Aurolani tyrant. Her knowledge of Fortress Draconis was dated, but having an urZrethi in charge of operations that involved excavating a mountain made perfect sense.

Between her and the crawls a new layer of leadership appeared. Erlestoke had seen one and Ryswin the other: two tall, humanoid creatures that wore thick woolen cloaks of red with massive hoods that hid their faces. No one who had seen them was sure what they were, but the bumps and spikes concealed rather poorly by their cloaks suggested that either they were very tall men wearing unusual armor, or yet another new concoction of creature. They had been seen giving orders to crawls at various digs, but nothing provided clues as to their true identities.

The mystery of what they were would doubtlessly have consumed Erlestoke's time, save that Fortress Draconis itself was proving to be a challenging enigma. Erlestoke, in the five years he had spent in the garrison, had learned everything he could about the place. The Draconis Baron, Dothan Cavarre, had been quite generous in providing him with information. Erlestoke had even gone so far as to imagine that Cavarre might be grooming him as a replacement—though he also assumed that only death would sever the baron's association with Fortress Draconis.

The prediction had proven true, and his body had been hung from the Crown Tower's dragon skull until picked clean by carrion birds. Aside from the pangs of his friend's death, Erlestoke regretted the loss of the Draconis Baron's wealth of knowledge about the place. While the baron had told Erlestoke much of the fortress' secrets, he clearly had not told him everything.

In vacating their hideout, Erlestoke and his people had moved deeper and discovered a variety of chambers, both worked and natural, where they could take refuge. They'd chosen a likely one that first night and the sentries reported nothing unusual on their watches. Erlestoke's had passed uneventfully; but when they gathered to move on, they discovered that the passage they'd used to reach their haven had been cut off with huge blocks of stone.

Magick was the only explanation for how the stone had moved, but Jilandessa had a hard time identifying the spells used. "Shuffling blocks that big and so silently would take an incredible amount of power. I don't know of a sorcerer capable of doing that."

Ryswin smiled. "If there is, and he's here, we have to hope he'll be on our side."

They left their sanctuary and explored along the other pathways that had opened up. In the depths they discovered a large amphitheater with a semicircular arrangement of stone terraces. In the center stood a raised circular platform. It clearly had once been a meeting place, and Erlestoke speculated that it had belonged to one of the various secret societies. That one or more had facilities at Fortress Draconis made sense, since the garrisons were drawn from all over the world.

This one, however, had been transformed. The terraces would normally have served as seating for the society's members and, at six feet in width, could have accommodated a considerable crowd. As Erlestoke studied the place, he could easily imagine the hearty shout of assent to some proposal, or the bass murmur of a ritual invocation echoing through the place.

Now the terraces did, in fact, accommodate a crowd, but one of far different sort than intended. On each level, with their feet pointing inward, lay stone effigies of Fortress Draconis' defenders. The images had been exquisitely crafted and showed each person in serene repose. Walking down the stairs Erlestoke saw a few individuals memorialized there whom he'd seen blown to bits by Chytrine's thunderballs. On the side of the slabs upon which they lay their names had been inscribed in their native script.

The dead all lay together, unsegregated by nation or race. Ryswin knelt beside a comrade, laying a hand on her cold stone forehead and using the other to hood his eyes. Others spread out, finding comrades and weeping, or noting the presence of others just to confirm their fate.

Toward the top Erlestoke found Pack Castleton. His effigy showed him carrying a quadnel, which brought a smile to the prince's face. He traced a finger over the man's mask and along the stone representation of a ribbon Erlestoke himself had affixed to it. "Rest well, my friend. You have earned it."

Jullagh-tse Seegg, a rust-red urZrethi, shifted her shape so a pair of long, slender legs let her step easily up the stairs to reach him. "I see many here, but not the Draconis Baron."

Erlestoke shook his head. "Perhaps whoever has done this needs his bones." He surveyed the room, estimating numbers, then frowned. "This place could hold four thousand, maybe, and it's only three-quarters full. That means a lot more have survived."

Ryswin joined them. "That, Highness, or the caretakers are behind in their work. If you are right, that would mean there are a thousand of us still lurking in little groups here in the fortress. That's fewer than Chytrine's troops, but far more than I would have ever imagined."

"Highness, over here!" Jancis Ironside beckoned him with her mechanical left arm. She stood on the steps leading up to the central dais. "You have to see this."

The whole of their company moved toward the center of the chamber and mounted the steps. As Erlestoke's eyes came even with the platform, they widened, because where he expected a flat surface he found something entirely different. As he approached, the platform shifted, the flat disk suddenly developing lumps that slowly resolved themselves into walls and the ruins of buildings. Toward the center rose the Crown Tower. At various points the rock retreated to form pits and within a couple of minutes, a miniature model of the fortress had laid itself out.

Even more oddly, the stone took on a transparency that allowed the prince to look deep into the model's foundations. There, far below, he found a simulacrum of the chamber in which he stood. *And there, I can see tiny figures staring down at a model of this model and in it they would see tiny figures...*

He shook his head, then glanced at Jancis. "Is this something you understand?"

She shook her head, too. "No more so than I understand the blocks moving. I've never seen anything like it."

Jilandessa's raven braid snaked over her left shoulder. "Actually you have. There are traces of *arcanslata* magick being worked here. Likewise in the spells that took Pack's body and deposited it here beneath that effigy. They are probably urZrethi in nature, but there is something else. My knowledge is limited in that area."

"Understood, Jilandessa, and not a concern." Erlestoke frowned. "The magick was triggered when Jancis mounted the steps?"

"It would seem that way, but I have no way to be certain."

"Highness, there, in the fortress." Nygal pointed at a blue-green glow near the Crown Tower. "That's near where the crawls are digging right now."

As the prince moved closer, other details painted themselves on the model. Little red lines described paths snaking in and out of buildings. They connected large red dots with a white dot at the center. The dig site likewise had a red tinge to it, though it covered a larger area than one of the circles.

Suddenly the earth shook. The tremor was far from violent enough to topple them, but Erlestoke felt the short, sharp shock easily enough through his boots. On the model, a ruin near the site of the dig collapsed into nothing.

A heartbeat later the entire model wavered and vanished.

Erlestoke crouched and pressed his right hand to the platform's smooth stone surface. It felt as cool as the effigies, and had Nygal and Jilandessa not been staring at the stone with surprise on their faces, he could have believed he imagined it.

He stood and folded his arms over his chest. "We agree we saw a map of the fortress, right?"

Ryswin nodded. "The red lines and spotted dots looked like patrol routes and garrisons."

"Agreed." The prince ran a hand over his jaw. "The glow at the dig would have been a DragonCrown fragment?"

"That would be likely." Jancis frowned. "Were we only being shown one because we're being given a mission, or is that the only one left in the Fortress?"

Nygal's eyes widened further. "If there is only one here, then Chytrine has two."

Erlestoke thought for a moment, then smiled. "I think time is long past when this sort of information about a fragment could do Chytrine good. Before her assault, another fragment was evacuated. If that is a fragment, then she's only gotten one away from here. Jilandessa, any idea why the model went away?"

The Harquelf's dark brows arrowed down over her slender nose. "A spell of that size would require a very powerful sorcerer to cast and a lot of energy to maintain. It could be that he got tired or it is possible that when that building collapsed, he was injured or killed."

The prince nodded. "If I were to guess, I would say the Aurolani used firedirt to bring that building down. They would seem to be getting more desperate in their hunt for this fragment."

Jancis walked up over to where the glow had been. "Here is the problem, Highness. They are digging here right now." She took two steps to the left. "Two days ago, they finished digging here. And last week, they were digging over there."

"You think the fragment is being moved?"

"It's a logical conclusion to draw. Either it's being moved, or something is making them dig in the wrong places." The *meckanshii* shrugged her shoulders. "I think we have to ask if we can get to it before they do and then somehow get it out of Fortress Draconis. The difficulty is going to be that wherever it is, it will be defended. We'll have as hard a time getting at it as they will, and then we have to get it away."

Ryswin knitted his fingers together at his belt. "Perhaps we let them get it, then take it away from them."

Erlestoke shook his head. "That plan has merit, save that they could give it to an *araftii* and have it flown away before we can crawl up from below."

Nygal smiled. "We'll just have to kill all the *araftii*. I've got plenty of shot and firedirt."

The prince nodded. "Good idea, but what if a dragon is sent to get it?"

The Savarese soldier let his smile broaden. "They make bigger targets."

Everyone laughed for a moment, then Erlestoke frowned. "I think the colonel is right, we have to find it first. If we can't, then we have to fall back on Ryswin's plan and make sure the Aurolani don't haul it off."

Verum, the grizzled *meckanshii* who served as their weapons-master, crouched at the edge of the platform. "Begging your pardon, Highness, but how do we know this model wasn't a trick of Chytrine's? If we plan based on it, we could be running into a trap."

"That's a good point, so we will have to be careful. I am inclined to trust it, though, because I don't see the Aurolani venerating our dead like this. All the information given to us was such that it would help us and yet we have nothing that, if revealed to the enemy, would help her." The prince nodded to him. "Your caution is laudable, though, so we will be careful. We can verify the patrol routes with some scouting and, if we are fortunate, we will find our way back here to learn more."

Ryswin jerked his head at the tiers of effigies. "I think, Highness, we might all find our way back here, by one means or another."

"I'm sure you're right, but I hope that in one sense you are wrong." Erlestoke looked around and sighed. "This is an august company, but I don't want to join it. And if we can find that fragment and steal it away from Chytrine, I think our comrades here would be more than pleased to forgo our joining them."

CHAPTER 23

Alexia shivered as she looked at Will. The flame of a half-burned candle flickered and shifted the shadows on the youth's face and chest. He lay very still in the bed, with his hands crossed over his stomach, the sheets and blankets pulled down to his waist and folded neatly. Peri had seen to that, and now lurked back in the shadows between Dranae in the corner and Resolute's brooding presence in the chair beside the door.

The wan candlelight did nothing to disguise the seriousness of Will's condition. His flesh had an alabaster hue to it that brought into sharp relief the network of angry red veins that radiated out and up from the wound. Bandages swathed his neck, though the bleeding from the punctures had mostly stopped. Sweat dappled his brow and gathered in the small hollow at the base of his throat.

Worse than how he looked was how he sounded. His breath came ragged and wet. He would breathe in, then silence would reign for a moment before a labored exhalation. She feared each breath would be followed by silence unbroken.

Qwc sat on Will's pillow, carefully plaiting a temple lock. The small Spritha beat his wings to cool the boy, and kept murmuring things in his ear. Alexia could catch none of the words, but she hoped they brought Will some peace. She even imagined seeing his mouth twitch in an effort to smile, and refused to admit she was just deceiving herself.

A gentle knocking came at the door and she opened it. "You came, Highness."

King Augustus nodded. "Thank you for sending for me. No progress?"

"None. He lives but we don't know for how long." Alexia closed the door behind Alcida's monarch and waved him to the chair beside the bed. "We've sent word out to healers, but without elven magick, we have little hope."

At her comment, Resolute growled, "This is my fault."

"How, Resolute?" Augustus regarded him with a serious expression. "You could not have anticipated this turn of events."

The Vorquelf's silver eyes became cold crescents. "But I could have. I heard him rush into the corridor. I was here, resting, right there in that bed. I knew his tread. I heard him hesitate and assumed he was playing some game. By the time he burst into the room and shouted at the arachnomorph, I should have been on my feet with Syverce in hand. I was late, seconds late. He'd been bitten before I could act."

Dranae growled from the corner. "You did what you could, Resolute. I was in the common room below, warming myself with ale and fire. I saw him rush in, but thought him up to childishness, too. Not only did we mistake him, but we remained unaware of the theft."

Augustus raised an eyebrow. "Theft? I had assumed the attack had been an assassination attempt."

Alexia shook her head. "The Draconis Baron entrusted a portion of the DragonCrown to Kerrigan. Kerrigan told no one but Crow and me—though later he must have entrusted Will with the information. They hid it in Kerrigan's room and set a trap for a would-be thief. It worked, but Will got hurt when he discovered the theft in progress. Chytrine sent one of her creatures. Resolute thinks, and I agree, it was likely a new-formed *sullanciri* created out of the Azure Spider."

"It's dead now; it doesn't matter." Resolute snorted, then stretched out his arms. "My failing is writ here in my flesh. All these sigils. All this magick, and not a healing spell to be found. Just one and he would be well."

The king frowned. "What of Kerrigan?"

Alexia shrugged. "He's missing. Lombo is searching for him."

"And the Spritha?"

Qwc's head came up. "Here, here, Qwc belongs here. Noplace else but here."

The adamance in the little creature's voice underscored the desperation they all felt. The Spritha were known to have a magickal ability to be at the very place they were meant to be, at the given time they were meant to be there. That ability did not dictate every aspect of their lives, but if Qwc knew he was meant to be there with Will, suggesting he be anywhere else was for naught.

The door opened again, this time with no knock to preface it. King Scrainwood slipped into the room and two mailed guardsmen crowded in the hallway behind him. They sought admittance, but Resolute reached out and slammed the door in their faces. Scrainwood opened his mouth to complain, but Resolute towered over him, glaring.

Augustus stood and looked at Scrainwood. "Did you bring Crow?"

The Oriosan King shook his head. "I took your request under advisement and decided to investigate myself. I brought soldiers to keep him safe."

"We don't need them."

Scrainwood snorted in response to Resolute's comment. "His current state would indicate otherwise. Had you been enough to keep the Norrington safe, he'd not be here like this, would he?"

Resolute raised an eyebrow. "And your soldiers would be more effective keeping a *sullanciri* out of here than they were keeping one out of your palace?"

Scrainwood's eyes blazed with outrage. "How dare you?"

The Vorquelf continued. "Did you choose to have your son lead the Tribunal before or after Chytrine told you she was sending Nefrai-kesh to testify at Crow's trial?"

The masked king pointed a trembling finger at Resolute. "Beware, Vorquelf, for this is *my* nation and I will not be impugned."

Augustus reached out and laid a hand on Scrainwood's right shoulder. "Easy."

"No!" Scrainwood's nostrils flared. "I am sick of this, I am sick of all of it. The lies, the innuendo. I am the king. Oriosa's welfare is mine to safeguard and I need no homeless elfwhelp to suggest impropriety in things he knows nothing about. He's fighting for his homeland, but he's late come to all this. Had he been with us a quarter century ago, we'd not be in this fix. We would have been done with Chytrine."

Augustus shook his head. "It is unfair and simplistic to blame this on Resolute. He could not see the future. None of us could. You could just as easily accuse me of having abandoned Norrington when I went to Okrannel."

Scrainwood's lip curled in a sneer. "I've never made that accusation, my friend."

"No, *my friend,* you have not, which is why I still consider you a friend, though you sorely tax my patience."

"What do you mean by that?"

"You know quite well."

"Enough!" Qwc buzzed into the air and hovered there between both kings' faces. "Go, go, go, now. Go, now, now, now. Out, out, out."

Scrainwood flicked a hand out to swat the Spritha from the air, but missed as Qwc dodged back swiftly. The little creature pointed all four of its hands at the Oriosan king, then it spoke. Whereas its voice previously always had a high, keening quality, it dropped several octaves and throbbed out in bass tones.

"*Drotha car est jynda pros!*"

"Aaahhhhh!" Scrainwood screamed hoarsely and dropped to his right knee. He clutched his right hand to his chest, his left hand around his wrist. The ring of state on his right hand pulsed red, as if molten. Scrainwood had a spell worked into it that would warn him of another's hostile intent, and the magick clearly was working.

Resolute rested a hand on Scrainwood's shoulder and let his voice slide into a whisper. "Anger not the wee ones, Highness. When a Spritha laughs, all is right with the world, but when one snarls, even the most mighty is brought low."

"Out, out, everyone out!" Qwc's voice returned to its normal soprano pitch as he flew around the room. He drove the others before him. Peri crowded in behind King Augustus, and Alexia squeezed close to Resolute as the Vorquelf opened the door and propelled the king into the hallway. They exited the room and Qwc managed to shut the door. Peri opened the door to Kerrigan's room and they entered it, with Scrainwood's two guards leading the way.

The two men gasped and drew back as they saw the arachnomorph hanging there by one hand. The light from the DragonCrown fragment still splashed against the inside of the roof, painting it red save where black splotches of *sullanciri* blood had been sprayed.

Scrainwood rubbed at his hand. "That is the thing?"

"Yes." Alexia stepped closer to the *sullanciri*'s remains—not because she had any real desire to do so, but because she knew Scrainwood would keep his distance. "We think Chytrine fashioned it out of the Azure Spider."

"The thief." Scrainwood looked up. "To what is it clinging?"

The princess hesitated, then looked at King Augustus. The Alcidese leader nodded. "It is a portion of the DragonCrown, Highness. It was brought from Fortress Draconis by Kerrigan Reese."

"A portion of the crown *here*, and no one told me?" He flexed the fingers on his right hand. "I *am* the king, and this is most important. Why was I not informed?"

Alexia lifted her chin. "The information was imparted to me in strictest confidence. I deemed that the fewer the people who knew about it, the better."

"I am not *people*, Princess Alexia, I am the *king*." Scrainwood shook his head and flicked a finger toward the fragment's hiding place. "Get it for me."

The two guards looked at each other, each one shaking his head at the other. They hesitated, then slowly moved forward, as carefully as if they were crossing thin ice over the Reydo River.

"Hold for a moment." Alexia's raised hand stopped them. "Highness, there are spells worked on the fragment to prevent its theft. They stopped a *sullanciri*. They will stop these men."

The guards took two big steps back.

Scrainwood tapped a finger against his lips. "No, no, this will not do. You have sorely used me, all of you, and I will not stand for it. I will have to confiscate the fragment of the Crown and make sure it is safely kept."

Augustus shook his head. "My friend, do not look upon the secrecy here as an affront to you, but see it for what it was. Princess Alexia determined, quite rightly, that the fewer people who knew of the fragment, the less chance it would be taken. We already know your palace is not proof against the predation of *sullanciri,* so her caution was not misplaced."

The Oriosan's head came up and he blinked at Augustus. "Oh, my friend, I think you mistake things. This fragment is doubtless what provoked the aggression against my realm. Had I known of it, had I taken charge of it, the Norrington would not be dying across the hall. By deciding that she knew better than I, she placed my realm in jeopardy. She is as much a threat to Oriosa as is her supposed husband."

Alexia watched an iron expression settle over Augustus' face. The Alcidese king looked past Scrainwood at his two bodyguards. "You are dismissed. Fetch Crow here."

"Move and I'll have you slain."

Muscles bunched at the corners of Augustus' jaw. "He'll do nothing of the sort. You have my word. Go. Get Crow, bring him here."

Resolute loomed forward and Peri flashed talons, convincing the two guardsmen to leave their liege.

"Come back here! Cowards! Your livers will be feeding crows before the week is out."

Peri closed the door behind the two men.

Augustus kept his voice even and strained almost all of his fury from it. "Understand something, my friend. While I appreciate the desperate situation in which Oriosa finds itself, and while I have appreciated your information about the activities of Chytrine's troops, her armies are moving south and have already plunged into Sebcia. If Muroso falls, she will race through Oriosa and then into Alcida. I will *not* fight her on my land. I will meet her in Sebcia or Muroso or, if I must, Oriosa. One word on an *arcanslata* and the southern third of Oriosa is mine. I can cut Meredo off against Bokagul, then fight Chytrine in your northeast corridor. Croquellyn will secure my flank."

Scrainwood shivered and toyed with his ring. "You threaten my nation."

"No, Scrainwood, I threaten *you,* because *you* threaten *my* nation. Will you listen to reason, or must I weep as I tell your son that the *sullanciri,* regrettably, still had life in it and killed you? I shall be most eloquent in delivering your eulogy."

"You cannot do this! I am king!"

"Oh, I know, my friend, and I *am* your friend. I shall give you a chance to prove that you are yet mine." Augustus pointed toward the arachnomorph. "You will be given custody of the Crown fragment."

"Yes!"

Scrainwood's avaricious hiss twisted Alexia's guts around. "Sire, are you certain that is wise?"

Augustus nodded. "In exchange for it..."

Scrainwood's eyes tightened. "Exchange? It is my right!"

"A right that shall not confer to your heir, Scrainwood." The Alcidese king sighed impatiently. "You will deliver Crow to his wife, and you will cease your persecution of him. You will support the efforts against Chytrine. You can no longer play one side against the other. The time for that is well past. You have to be with us, in opposition to the Aurolani. You have no choice."

Scrainwood looked up at the fragment. "I am not stupid, Augustus."

"No, but you are not nearly as clever as you believe you are. This is the bargain I offer you. Accept it and I shall not feel the need to invade your nation. What say you, my friend?"

Scrainwood's nostrils flared with a snort. "I accept, *my friend,* and I shall remember. You will get Crow, though formalities need to be observed. You do understand the need for that, yes?"

Augustus nodded. "I do."

Alexia frowned. "Sire, is this really the time for little political games?"

"It is just one point in a grander game, and we are winning that." The Alcidese leader sighed. "Grant him his point."

Alexia nodded reluctantly. She knew well enough that politics at the highest levels required exquisite manners to cover vicious uses of power. Augustus had openly threatened to murder Scrainwood and take his nation. The choice he offered Scrainwood was to accept a portion of the DragonCrown and to turn over Crow. Scrainwood had no choice but to agree, but the illusion of power parity needed to be maintained.

Augustus clearly did not want to invade Oriosa. The Oriosans, despite their current king, were known for their fighting spirits. If Alcida invaded, the Oriosans would oppose them, sapping both nations' strength when they both needed to be fighting Chytrine.

Likewise, the offer to entrust Scrainwood with the DragonCrown fragment was one that really cost Augustus nothing. Because Scrainwood knew of it, there was no way to prevent him from getting his hands on it. All he had to do was cordon off the inn, have his troops take possession of the place, and it was his. And while it might have been a mistake to reveal its presence directly to him, Augustus had to have assumed that since Chytrine knew it was here, she would pressure Scrainwood to get it for her regardless.

The bargain did work. Alcida would keep its army intact and could be later invited into Oriosa to preserve the nation. They got Crow back and elation filled her at this prospect. What she hated about the bargain was that she knew Scrainwood had in mind to fashion some trap for Crow that he could spring later. The very idea that someone would hurt him, and that someone would pull them apart, angered her.

Scrainwood's right hand convulsed down into a fist and he glared at her. "Something not to your liking, Princess? You are getting all you want. We are all working together now."

"Now, yes. I fear for the future."

"As do we all." Scrainwood gave her an oily smile. "A black bargain today, for a brilliant tomorrow. It is not what we would wish, but in dark days like this, we could not have done better."

CHAPTER 24

Her mother had been correct. Even with the thick layer of snow blanketing Meredo, the city's stench proved strong enough to bring tears to Isaura's eyes. Cart wheels churned horse dung, mud, and snow into a soupy brown sludge that spattered pristine snow and passersby alike, then slowly froze as night came on.

The people unsettled Isaura. She had traveled with Nefrai-kesh and Vionna via arcane ways that left her and the pirate queen on the verge of exhaustion. Nefrai-kesh, being a *sullanciri,* did not suffer from the journey and had been about his appointed tasks. Likewise, Spyr'skara weathered the journey well in his shell. Vionna released him and he quickly grew from the size of a large spider into a man-sized arachnomorph. Isaura linked Spyr'skara to the decoy fragment, letting magick direct the *sullanciri* to its target. Spyr'skara snapped its mandibles at his former lover, then leaped away to the rooftops.

They watched the new *sullanciri* for a while, then Vionna led Isaura off to secure rooms in the King's Masque Inn. The place appeared, as nearly as Isaura could determine, to be largely populated by Okrans refugees in service to some noble or other. They were to wait there for the return of Spyr'skara and the ruby fragment of the DragonCrown.

The innkeeper did have two rooms available, though he was reluctant to rent them both to Vionna. The pirate found this curious, since Isaura, wearing a hooded cloak of whitest ermine, stood behind her as she made her request. The innkeeper refused to acknowledge Isaura's presence, but acquiesced when Vionna paid double the night's rate in gold and in advance.

Isaura felt no compunction to tell the pirate that she was using magick to conceal her presence. It was not a spell that prevented people from seeing her per se, for that would be impractical at best and was, as nearly as she knew, impossible. Instead the magick just made it simple for people to forget they had seen her. Her mother had taught her the complex spell and had worked with her until she had perfected its casting and maintenance.

Chytrine had explained it rather simply, despite the spell's being quite a twisted confluence of magickal energies. Most individuals, men chiefly among them, take every bit of information they learn in a day and sort it like with like. What the spell did was to soften the points used to make such matches. Anyone looking at her would see a woman in a hooded cloak of white, but as they sought a similar image to compare her against, they might lose white or cloak or woman. As they tried to find another point, it, too, would vanish. Chytrine had likened it to trying to identify a wine by taste. After four mouthfuls, you might think you had it, but by then the wine would be gone. In the mind of the observer, there would be nothing to remember.

Vionna could see her because Isaura chose to permit it. Aside from not wanting to be rude to a traveling companion, Isaura did need someone who had experience of the Southlands to help her. Anytime she wished Vionna to forget she existed, well . . . The girl smiled; the pirate queen was not possessed of so sharp a mind that she could pierce the spell unaided.

The inn's common room held both horror and delight for Isaura. The acrid scent of unwashed bodies, sour beer, urine, and woodsmoke from the huge hearth assaulted her. Even the heat was oppressive, with the blazing fire raising temperatures to a hedonistic level that would have consumed a week's cooking wood in Aurolan in a night here. The fire's ashes, from what little she had seen of the city, would not be used to fertilize a field, but would be tossed into the streets to darken snow and hasten its melting.

The people also surprised her. They presented a panoply of humanity, with hair of every hue and length. People tall and lean spoke with the short and fat. Twisted, humpbacked old women huddled in a corner, rocking, talking, watching with squinted eyes in puckered faces. Young men said things to a servant that made her stop, and her return comment made one of them turn a hot red. Clothing, most of it filthy, covered them in layers and seemed less meant to keep them warm than to make some sort of display.

She found it all repellent, and would have dashed away up the stairs in Vionna's wake save for one thing. The old women, and the companions of the reddened youth, and most everyone else, laughed. Some were hearty laughs, some giggles, and some cackles of triumph or disgust, but they were laughs. Isaura could identify it as laughter easily enough, but had never heard so much in one place. And it made her smile.

Vionna tugged on her arm. "I said, come on."

Isaura blinked her silver eyes. "Yes, forgive me."

The Aurolani princess followed quietly, less hoping for useful instruction from Vionna than to catch any further laughter from below. The pirate led her up the stairs and down a narrow corridor. She pushed open a door, then took a candle from a wall sconce and used it to light the lamp on the small table beside the bed.

Isaura shivered. While she approved of the room's size—small enough to be a proper Aurolani room built to warm easily—the low pallet on which she was to sleep had a thin blanket and a thinner mattress. The scent of moldy straw filled the room, though the lamp's burning oil competed for domination. The tall ceiling bothered her, since all the warm air rose there, but a constant supply could stream up through the gaps between the floorboards from the common room below.

She pointed to the mattress. "This is soiled."

Vionna bent over and took a deep sniff. "Only a couple of weeks old. There's nothing here that will hurt you."

"But I do not wish to sleep on it."

Vionna straightened up, quickly covering the contempt flashing over her face. "Then I shall take this room and you may have the other."

They crossed the hallway and found another similarly snug room, and the mattress did, indeed, have more and fresher straw. Vionna made a big show of sniffing the straw, then waving a hand toward it. "Perhaps more to your liking, Princess."

"Perhaps." Isaura sat on the edge of the bed. "I am fatigued. You may call upon me later."

The pirate nodded. "As you wish." The disdain she kept off her face still seeped into her words. "Later we shall explore, if that is what you want."

Isaura nodded, then waved her out of the room with a light flick of her right hand. "That would please me."

The pirate covered a yawn with her hand, then wandered out and closed the door behind her. Isaura heard the other door close and slowly smiled. The gesture of dismissal had spawned a spell that created a current linking the two of them. It eroded Vionna's energy and brought to Isaura the fleeting impression of the pirate's intent to find other ways to make the youths in the common room blush. Yet because of the spell, Vionna received Isaura's fatigue, and the Aurolani Princess stood, refreshed as if she had napped for hours.

She acknowledged that using the spell on Vionna without her consent was not the sort of thing done to a friend, but Vionna was not a friend. Isaura had exaggerated the displeasure at the straw to provide Vionna a reason for disliking her. The pirate clearly had no desire to be her escort and saw her as a delicate rime-blossom that had no business being in the south at all.

Isaura harbored no illusions about her own lack of experience, but she also knew that did not make her a fool. She had learned much and would learn much more, but Vionna's contempt hardly made her a good instructor. Moreover, Isaura's mother had desired her to visit the Southlands to learn about them, and being toured around by a renegade-in-heat would hardly provide her with the sort of information she wanted.

With the wave of a finger Isaura extinguished her lamp and entered the hallway. She drifted past Vionna's door, suppressing a smile at the snores echoing from within, then descended the stairs. A man coming up twisted his back to the wall to let her pass, though by the time he reached the hallway above he had forgotten her. She passed out the door and into the darkened street, leaving a shivering couple near the common room door wondering where the draft had come from.

Knowing the track of her boots in the snow would betray her presence, Isaura kept to the streets and walkways on which the snow had been tamped down by the feet of passersby. She saw well enough at night that she eschewed magick to enhance her sight. She did regret the way snow covered everything, for she wished she could see what lurked in the alley middens. From what little she could see as two tatterdemalions dug through one mound, each would have been a treasure trove in Aurolan, with useful bits of wood and food and scrap metal.

Wandering through the city as night fell and the day's warmth fled, she found a city slowing as if moving toward hibernation. People hurried along the streets and crowded into common houses that rang with laughter. Yellow light and flickering shadows splashed over snow, and while the night was not nearly cold enough to discomfit her, Isaura still felt a chill.

She recognized it immediately for it was no stranger to her. In Aurolan she felt it often. Distance existed between her and the others. The *sullanciri* viewed her with a reverence that invited no intimacy. Nefrai-laysh might joke with her, or compose simple rhymes, but she knew that to be a compulsion with him, not anything born of affection. Neskartu, while praising her skills at magick, did not show her even as much fondness as he did his students.

The students never got a chance to form any sort of attachment to her, nor she to them. They differed from her in so many ways that even if she had been allowed to spend much time with them, the chances that they would have liked her were small. She knew that, and used that realization to insulate her from disappointment.

She did know there were people out there who would like her and welcome her as wanderers were welcomed into warm taverns. That much she had been told and she believed those predictions. It surprised her that she wanted such acceptance. In Aurolan she was known and revered by all because of her mother, but here she would be accepted for being herself. That would be as novel an experience as was her trip to the Southlands.

Isaura continued wandering, but refrained from making conscious decisions about where she would go and what she would do. Instead she opened herself to the vast river of magick and let it carry her along. She invoked no spells, but let the eddies and currents nudge her this way and that. Forces outside her control, be they spells cast by others, the whims of the gods, or oaths and truths that once uttered became living entities themselves, were breezes to the sails that were her spirit.

A small ripple sent a tingle through her. She turned left and drifted through the falling snow to another inn. She entered and ascended the stairs and came to a vacant hallway. She strode along quickly, clutching her cloak tightly to quiet her dress' rustle. Loud voices sounded from behind the door on the right, but that was not her destination.

She opened the door on the left, entered, then pressed it closed behind her. In the room's bed lay a youth to whom clung a foul miasma. Though the room was dark, she could see clearly the translucent white hue of his sweaty flesh and the livid red of the venous webwork in his skin. His breath rasped in and out as his chest rose and fell. Short and sharp came his breaths, labored and weakening. She could tell they were weakening.

A Spritha stood on the pillow beside the young man's left ear. The little creature looked up at her and froze. "Go, out, go out."

Isaura raised her left index finger, circled it toward the ceiling, then plunged it straight down. The Spritha dropped the hair he had been braiding, spun on the pillow, and plopped down hard. He sprawled there facefirst, his arms and legs splayed out.

She crossed to the bed and eased her hood down before she folded the cloak back at her shoulders. As she neared the youth she could feel the heat rising from him. She closed her eyes and cast a simple spell, then recoiled at the vehemence of the sensation that came back to her. She gasped aloud and raised a hand to cover her mouth.

The young man had a virulent poison running through him. It ate at him like acid. It was digesting him, slowly, inexorably, and had already done severe damage. He had perhaps hours to live, maybe a day.

Just learning that was abhorrent enough, but Isaura found the poison familiar. She wanted to deny it, but she could not. It had come from Spyr'skara. She had helped Neskartu create the *sullanciri,* so she could feel its influence and taint in the venom. She even knew the *sullanciri* had been given that sort of weapon, but for self-defense.

It was meant for self-defense, but how could this boy threaten a sullanciri? He could not have, clearly—and just as clearly Spyr'skara had bitten him out of spite or a desire to inflict pain, or just a desire to confirm his newfound power. His action had been a betrayal of everything her mother held dear.

Isaura shook her head slowly and refused to let her mother's efforts be tainted by the actions of a flawed creation she had worked to build. She reached out and plunged her spirit into the river while laying her hands, left and right respectively, on the boy's fevered brow and breastbone. She drew to her deep magick, then flooded it cold and pure into the youth.

His body bucked and tensed. His back bowed violently, then slackened and fell back hard enough to bounce the Spritha into the air. Another tremor shook the youth, then his eyes snapped open and his hands clawed at the blankets. His head craned back and his mouth opened, but he said nothing.

He just stared at her, wide-eyed and half-insane from pain and fear.

The magick she coursed into him did not take the shape of a spell per se, but instead flushed through his body and veins, diluting the venom. Where the poison had been molten, the magick was cool. Where the poison had irritated, the magick soothed. The magick cleansed his body of the venom and swept it swirling out into the river, where it would be neutralized.

Half the job is done. Isaura set herself to cast a spell that would repair the damage. She would begin with his neck, for his thrashing had peeled away the bandages, revealing two weeping, necrotic holes, one beneath each ear.

"Your part is done, little sister." The voice rumbled from the darkness to her right, but she could not turn her head to see who spoke. She felt old magick holding her still; she knew its nature and nodded because she knew she would be permitted that motion.

"You are in danger here. Leave before you are detected. The rest shall be attended to. He will live and you will know him when you meet again."

Isaura looked down on the youth's face and into his grey eyes. "I will know you when we meet again."

His lids grew heavy and his eyes slowly closed. His breathing came more regularly and the rattles from his chest had all but vanished. She smiled, then exited the room, trailing in the wake of two guardsmen who, though one held the door to the inn for her, had forgotten her before the door had swung shut.

Across the hall from Will's sickroom, Scrainwood's assessment of the deal they'd made left Alexia uneasy, but anything she might say could break their agreement. In the shadow of the dead *sullanciri*, she turned her attention to the one remaining problem. "Now we have to figure out how to save Will."

The Oriosan king nodded. "I have already sent summonses to mages from throughout the kingdom. I will not lose the Norrington!"

The door to Kerrigan's room swung open and Will slumped against the casement. "Lose me?" His voice came raw, hoarse and wet. "How will you lose me?" The naked youth's eyes rolled up in his head, and he fell back into a startled Dranae's arms.

CHAPTER 25

Kerrigan awoke with the rumble of his empty stomach. Still in darkness, with only the growling of his bowels to compete with the dripping of water, he found himself disoriented for a moment. As it slowly came back to him where he was—though he had no idea where *there* was or why he was there—he began to wonder how long he had slept. The hollowness in his middle suggested he'd missed a meal.

He frowned. He liked to eat, and did it often, so his missing a meal might have meant he'd been gone for two hours or four, or two days. He made a mental note that he didn't know of any spell that would inform him of the time or date, and began to consider how he would go about creating one.

As he thought, he heaved himself up off the straw-strewn ground and tightened the blanket around him. He coughed a little, but it was from a scratchy dry throat, not the wet cough he'd had before. While he was young and healthy, he was also aware that such coughs usually lingered for several days, and he refused to believe he'd slept that long. He played a hand over his jaw and felt little patches of stubble, that suggested he was less than a day and a half out from his last shave.

That means they used magick to clear my lungs.

The realization pleased him for two reasons. The first was that it indicated his captors did not intend to destroy him immediately. Healing spells were not easy to cast and, aside from himself, he knew of no human capable of doing so. This meant the person he'd spoken with had to be one of the elder races: elves or urZrethi. Since neither of them was known for being overly homicidal, Kerrigan gained some confidence.

The latter half of his realization—that his captor had to be a member of an elder race—gave him heart that his captivity actually had purpose. Few urZrethi or elves were in service to Chytrine, so the chances of his being turned over to her were diminished. Exactly what would be expected from him, on the other hand, he had no clue.

A click sounded off to his right. He turned to look and discovered a rectangle of light outlining a doorway. One of the horizontal shafts widened as the door opened. He struggled to his feet and staggered forward, but waited well shy of the portal. He expected another test and listened for noises that might reveal a trap.

"Please, Adept Reese, enter."

Kerrigan crept closer and felt cooler air moving from the prison into the lighted room. He had to push the door open more fully to accommodate his bulk, even when he twisted to the side, then he pressed it closed behind him. The door shut with a muffled click and Kerrigan hoped he would never be required to pass back through it again.

The chamber into which he entered felt smaller than the prison and was an absolute farrago of priceless treasures and filthy trash. Barely twelve feet wide, and perhaps eight high and twenty long, its interior dimensions were defined by the forward edges of deep shelves, which contained rows of books running floor to ceiling. In some places the books had been recessed and trinkets arranged on the shelves—varying from oddly shaped rocks and the mounted skeletons of birds and beasts to artifacts of an arcane and unknowable nature.

Unknowable without the use of magick.

A wagon wheel had been made into the chandelier and it hung above the long, narrow table that filled the center of the room. Thick candles guttered on the wheel, and companions dripped wax in thick icicles from the shelves. Chairs had been arranged at Kerrigan's end of the table, and the opposite. A mélange of crockery and silver had been set on the table and steam rose from some dishes that Kerrigan could not recognize by sight or scent.

He shared the room with two other occupants. The first was seated across from him, with the high-backed chair turned so the person sat looking diagonally off to Kerrigan's right. He appeared to be slender, and wore a gorgeous crimson robe of silk that had been painstakingly embroidered with golden thread, depicting dragons scrolling through an intricate knotwork. Thick gold cord covered seams, finished the sleeves, and rimmed the opening in the hood. The hood itself came low on the person's face, shadowing most of it, and revealing little more than a highly stylized mask that completely covered the person's face. The figure even wore leather gloves and a bright gold scarf, which meant not an inch of its flesh was revealed.

By contrast, the other figure in the room was all but naked. It squatted in the corner, rump on the ground at its heels, knees poking up above its shoulders, which were hunched forward, with its hands pressed to the floor before its groin. Kerrigan recognized it immediately for an urZrethi, but its shaggy black mane covered its shoulders and its beard bled down into a thick mat of chest hair. That hair continued down over its belly and thickened over its loins. Kerrigan couldn't tell if the urZrethi was wearing some sort of furred loincloth or not, and did not study it long enough to find out. Where hair did not cover it, malachite flesh showed through, though in the candlelight it took on a sickly color.

Kerrigan immediately amended his assessment. The urZrethi had to be male—at least, it looked more bulky and wider than any female urZrethi he'd ever seen. What surprised him was seeing it at all. While he did not know much about urZrethi males, he had been under the impression that they were never seen outside the mountains. While Meredo's proximity to Bokagul made it possible for Kerrigan to have been transported there, the young mage thought that unlikely.

His host waved his left hand casually. "I apologize for the poverty of our surroundings, and the paucity of the victuals, but my means for treating with a guest are lamentably strained."

Kerrigan nodded politely, then held his dirty hands up. "I am hardly much of a guest."

Without turning his head, Kerrigan's host raised his left hand and beckoned. "Bok, his hands."

The urZrethi hunched his shoulders further and narrowed his black eyes. He made a little chortling sound deep in his throat, managing to rob it of any melodic content at all, then scuttled forward. Bok extended his left hand up, reaching for a silver basin on a high shelf, but without rising from that crouch, the basin remained a good foot beyond his reach.

Then the urZrethi's arm stretched. Just the forearm bones lengthened, thinning the limb somewhat. The fingers nimbly caught the lip of the basin and brought it down, though Bok had to raise his elbow at an awkward angle to swing the vessel into his right hand.

Kerrigan watched the creature and failed to hide his surprise. He knew urZrethi could shift shape and had seen urZrethi who had changed their shapes, but he'd never seen the process taking place. Moreover, those he had seen in an altered form had kept their limbs symmetrical, which made their odd shapes easier to understand.

Bok reached to another shelf and got a small towel, which he clapped over the top of his head. He continued forward, then squatted at Kerrigan's feet. He raised the bowl in one hand and warbled hoarsely. At the invitation, the mage dipped his hands into the cool clear water, instantly darkening it, then the creature pulled the bowl away and soiled the towel scrubbing Kerrigan's hands down.

Kerrigan's host gestured, and the bowl floated from the floor to his end of the table. He took it in both hands while the urZrethi dried Kerrigan's hands and swirled the dirty water around. He peered into it as if reading it for portents and signs. Kerrigan watched, straining to catch any phrases of a mumbled spell, but he saw or heard nothing to indicate what his host was doing.

His host set the bowl on the table, then pointed to the chair, which slid back from the table. "Please, be seated."

Bok moved away, returning to his corner, and Kerrigan sat, pulling his blanket tight around him. His stomach complained about being empty again, but the mage reached for no food. He had waited for a specific invitation to enter, and would wait for another to dine.

His host nodded. "I shall be known to you as Rym Ramoch. My servant is Loktu-bok Jex. I do not know how much you know of the urZrethi, but from your reaction to him I do suspect you know that finding a male urZrethi outside the mountains is exceedingly rare. In urZrethi society, which is a matriarchy, males are segregated and used for work or breeding. They are little more than chattel, though capable of reasoning. The suffix 'bok' indicates he is an outcast. I found him lurking in the Bokagul foothills and discovered he had potential as an aide. Alas, away from urZrethi society he becomes more and more feral, but is yet loyal and quite strong."

Bok looked up at Kerrigan and gave him a toothsome grin.

Rym tapped his gloved index finger on the table, then drew a small circle with it. "You wonder why you are here, of course; any sapient creature would. You have determined that Bok was the one who stalked and captured you. He is quite at home beneath bridges and you fell for the snare we devised. You are, as you know, quite powerful and have a taint about you and your magick."

"A taint?"

"Indeed, a taint, a stain. I thought it was of one source—the dragonbone armor—but it is more than that."

Kerrigan blinked his eyes. "Dragonbone armor?"

Rym's head came up, but the hood's shadow hid his eyes. "You did not know that the armor that rises through your flesh is composed of dragonbone?"

Kerrigan thought back. The spell had used three fluids, all thick. The first had been ruby red and the second ivory. He'd not seen the third, but it had smelled of mint. "The ivory liquid, that was of dragonbone?"

"It was. Used first was earthsblood, a rare concoction known to few and fewer yet are those who can prepare it. It changed you enough to allow the binding of the dragonbone to you."

"And the third? It smelled of mint." Kerrigan shivered. "It numbed the pain from the other two."

"Some unguent. It is not vital, but recommended so the recipient can concentrate enough to cast the spell. I will say, to have one as young as you cast it is remarkable."

Kerrigan started to smile, but thought better of it. "I did what was required of me. They just asked if I could cast it, then had me do so."

"So, you cast the spell without thought of the consequences?"

"Well, I . . ." Kerrigan frowned and hunched his shoulders. "I had ventured into Yslin, into the bad section of that city, and had been beaten badly. I could have been killed. And before that, pirates had tried to kill me and had shot me with an arrow. My masters decided I needed protecting. They showed me the spell, asked me to cast it, and I did. I didn't know what it would do to me."

Rym canted his head slightly to the right. "And if you had, would you have cast it?"

Kerrigan shrugged. "I was afraid then, so I probably would have. Your demonstration before, with the rocks, reminded me that even protected, I'm pretty vulnerable."

"It disturbs me that you were given this spell to cast without being told its consequences, but your answer does please me. You are honest about your fears. It also speaks well of you that none of the spells you were preparing to cast earlier were of a violent nature."

The young mage's head came up. "How do you know that? I never cast any of them. You could not know what was in my mind."

"Ha." It came as a single low sound, not as much ridicule as surprise. Bok echoed it deeply, chuffing along insensibly until the flick of a finger silenced him.

Rym turned in the chair and brought his hands together, resting his elbows on the table. "You have been trained on Vilwan and you should know that Vilwan now is not as it always was. In the time of Yrulph Kirûn, the way in which magick was taught, and the understanding of it, was different. Because of the methods and understanding, someone like Kirûn could do the things he did. He understood enough of magick to be able to create that spell, and you know it had elven and urZrethi components to it.

"Think on this, Kerrigan Reese. While you are very special and quite adept at magick, how is it that a man, centuries ago, could have created that spell and yet, now, on Vilwan, you are the only man who has mastered the art of healing spells? You have not yet seen a score of years, yet can do something that learned mages four times your age cannot. Do you know why?"

Kerrigan started to answer that they just couldn't grasp that sort of magick, but he knew that was not true. "They are not given the knowledge needed?"

"Not only that, but they are taught to believe it is impossible for them to learn such spells. After Kirûn, after the bloodshed, Vilwan knew it had to police its own or the world would destroy it. They denied to men things that men had done before, and within two generations the hobbling of human mages was complete."

"Then why am I able to do these things?"

"To fight fire, they decided to set a fire. Now, however, they fear you." Rym pressed his hands flat to the table. "And I have cause to fear you, for that second taint on you. How far down the path of Kirûn have you ventured?"

"None. I haven't." Kerrigan raised his hands and the blanket slipped off his shoulders. "Aside from that spell, which I didn't know was his, I've done nothing."

His host's head came up. "If this is true, why do you bear the stink of the DragonCrown about you?"

Kerrigan hesitated. "I don't know . . ."

Rym rose to his feet, his hands still on the table, but flames wreathed them, blackening the table around them. "Do not lie to me, child. You do not want to try me or my patience. Tell me what you know."

"But if you are working for Chytrine . . . !"

The masked mage snarled in some guttural language and the urZrethi became very agitated. Bok bounced in his corner and that long left arm suddenly sprouted spikes from its hand. The urZrethi started to creep forward.

"Bok, no!" The mage looked his servant back into its corner. Once he had retreated, cradling his mace-hand to his chest, Rym looked up at Kerrigan again. "Adept Reese, either you have come in contact with pieces of the DragonCrown—prolonged and personal contact—or you are working on creating your own DragonCrown. Either is madness for someone of your youth. The former might slay you, the latter certainly will and by my hand. Tell me now, do I kill you, or do I help you remain alive so we can end this madness?"

CHAPTER 26

Will's first sensation upon waking was the searing pain in his throat. He tried to swallow, which didn't help. Then the tickle in his throat made him cough, which amplified the hurt and brought him upright, snapping his eyes open. His left hand rested on the straw-tick mattress and his right hand clutched at this throat.

A high, keening wail filled the room. Qwc, who had been holding a half-completed braid of a temple lock, was jerked from the pillow and whipped through the air. He tumbled as he let go, the braid lashing the left side of Will's face, then crashed down between Will's ankles. He landed awkwardly, half on his head and shoulders, then slumped to the side.

The Spritha quickly regained his feet and tried to look dignified as he smoothed his antennae. The effort failed miserably, which sparked laughter from Dranae, Lombo, and Peri. The three of them, arrayed around the room, tried to stifle their mirth, but happy sounds burst out from behind their hands.

Will laughed once, sharply, which sent a dagger through his throat. He groaned and flopped back on the bed, his chest heaving with chuckles, his body twisting, and both hands on his throat. He wanted to stop laughing and stop the pain, but he couldn't.

Qwc scrambled up onto his chest and stood there balancing like a sailor on a pitching deck. "No hurt, Will, no hurt, no. Sorry, so sorry. Stupid Qwc, stupid."

Will screwed his face down tightly to fight the pain, then snorted and let his body ease. He opened one eye and saw the green Spritha standing there, all four hands pressed to his cheeks, and almost started laughing anew. He closed that eye again and swallowed, finding the pain slightly lessened.

Dranae spoke from his corner. "Qwc, come off his chest and let him breathe. If he is able to laugh, he is in no mortal danger."

A whirring buzz filled the room and the Spritha hovered in the air for a moment before flying off toward the foot of the bed. Will listened for the sound to diminish, then risked opening his eyes again. He saw Qwc half-hidden behind Lombo's head, peeking out through his dark mane as if it were underbrush.

Peri crouched beside the bed and smiled at him. "You don't have to talk, Will. Probably best for you not to."

The thief nodded, but hazarded a whisper. "Lady Snowflake. Where?"

The Gyrkyme blinked her big amber eyes. "Who?"

Qwc again launched himself into the air. "The lady. Qwc saw the lady. White, white, white."

Will nodded. "Lady Snowflake."

"There's none such here, Will." Dranae eased himself out of the chair in the corner and approached the foot of the bed. "King Scrainwood came and an argument began, so Qwc sent us from the room. Next thing we knew, you appeared at the door to Kerrigan's room, your neck healed, and you collapsed. We tucked you back into bed and you've slept well past noon."

Lombo sniffed the air, his nostrils widening. "Traces. People here, aside from us."

"Yes, yes." Qwc looped once, then landed with great élan between Will's knees. "Beautiful lady came. Saw her, Qwc did. Beautiful."

Dranae smiled. "And what did she do, Qwc?"

The Spritha sat down abruptly. "Don't know. Qwc slept."

Will nodded. "Touched me. Healed me."

"Healing requires a lot of magic." Peri scratched with a talon right beside her right ear. "You had poison in you, and a horrid wound. It left scars."

"Scars?" Will winced as he spoke more loudly than he should have.

Peri reached over on the bedside table and handed him a small hand glass. Will took it and held it back and away so he could inspect his throat. Qwc lightly leaped over his right knee and helped support the small mirror.

Will got a good look at his throat. Two scars stood out on his neck, each with the fluid patterning of severe burn marks, yet they had regular edges and could each have easily been covered by a small silver coin. When he swallowed, the pain did run from one scar to the other.

He released the mirror, and Qwc toppled backward with the thing on top of him. As the Spritha struggled from beneath it, the thief looked up. "I saw her." He wanted to say more. He wanted to describe this winter vision of loveliness, with her white hair and pale skin and silver eyes. He wanted to tell them of her touch, which was at once gentle and firm. He wanted to share that all with them, but he realized that even if his throat had been fine, the words to explain would be elusive and insufficient.

Dranae folded his arms across his chest. "That you were healed magickally is beyond question. Resolute was able to detect some basic magick, but could not determine how your healing took place. King Scrainwood sent some of his mages, and someone named Syrett Kar came from the Vilwanese consulate. They said a lot, but told us nothing more than Resolute."

Will shivered and drew the bedclothes up around him. "Cold. Thirsty."

Lombo moved to the door. "Thirstbane for Will."

"Lombo, something hot." Peri opened the door for him. "Soup if they have it, nothing too strong. And nothing too solid."

Will nodded and gave the Panqui a smile. The Gyrkyme closed the door, then quickly told Will what little had happened since he had been wounded. She started by assuring him that the ruby fragment was safe, and that Resolute had said that but for Will, it would have been long gone.

Will knew that for a lie, but a kindly one. Resolute would have cursed him for a fool for going after a *sullanciri* with nothing more than a dagger. Will also caught a hint of hurt in Peri's voice that Alexia had kept a secret from her, but that she understood why it had been done.

Will was glad to hear that Nefrai-kesh had not been seen again in Meredo, and even more glad that Crow would be released. While he did not like the idea of Scrainwood getting control of a fragment of the DragonCrown, he agreed with the reasoning. It was better to get Crow free and preserve Alcida's strength than to fight a battle they were destined to lose.

The only true negative was learning that Kerrigan was still missing. Will remembered the trouble Kerrigan had gotten himself into when wandering through the Dim in Yslin. Will had once felt Kerrigan was about as useless as a thief's promise, but he'd come to see just how powerful he was. He admired Kerrigan's pluck in getting the fragment out of Fortress Draconis, and very much wanted his opinion on the business of the healing magick.

Dranae draped another blanket over Will and the thief pulled it tight around him. His flesh developed goose pimples and his body began shivering, but that helped him warm up. As he did, the pain in his throat began to slip away. "Feeling better. Thanks."

Lombo returned with a huge steaming pewter tankard of fragrant soup. Peri eyed it suspiciously because carrot chunks floated within the creamy liquid. She clearly intended to have Lombo take it back, but Will reached for it, so she transferred it from the Panqui to him. "Be careful, Will, it's hot."

The thief nodded, then sipped. The steam filled his head and the soup went down easily. It was hot, no doubt about it, but didn't sear his tongue. He got a piece of carrot, but it had been so well cooked that it just fell to mush in his mouth, and he swallowed it with ease. Easier, in fact, because the soup's warmth helped soothe his throat further.

He lowered the tankard and Qwc helped steady it, then pulled back and shook his hands. "Hot, hot, hot."

"Be careful, Qwc." Will smiled, then turned to the others. "There was a Lady Snowflake."

Dranae looked at Peri, then shook his head. "I saw nothing. Supposing for a moment that you were seeing things because of the poison . . ."

The Gyrkyme raised a hand. "Since he was healed, we have to assume someone did it. If Kerrigan had done it, he would have stayed."

Lombo snorted, then tapped his snout with a finger. "No Kerrigan spoor. Lombo seeking, not finding."

"Agreed, it was not Kerrigan." Dranae raked fingers through his dark beard. "The questions are then simple: who did this, why did they do it, and why did they not remain? There was nothing that should have scared them off."

"Unless it was the sound of us in the other room and the king's guards leaving."

"That's possible, Peri." The man frowned. "Elves and Vilwanese would have taken credit for saving the Norrington. Wanting to keep the work secret would suggest someone who worked for Chytrine."

"*Not* Nefrai-kesh." Will shook his head adamantly. He refused to believe his grandfather would have saved him. He thought for a moment and realized it was more complicated than that. He was afraid his grandfather might have saved him just so he could recruit him to Chytrine's service. That idea sent a chill through him, so he drank more soup.

Peri shook her head. "Unlikely. He seems to like to make his presence known and having you die would advance Chytrine's cause. Dranae, your explanation for why they did not remain to take credit makes sense. That means there is someone in Chytrine's camp who opposes her."

Dranae frowned. "It's not as simple as that, Peri. Assume, for a moment, that the *sullanciri* are scheming against one another to gather power. The arachnomorph could have decided to kill Will to win approval for itself. Another *sullanciri* might want Will alive as a potential rival for his grandfather and father."

He looked down at Will. "You called her Lady Snowflake. Could it have been Myrall'mara? She can heal, and she is very white."

Will thought about that for a moment. Myrall'mara had once been a Vorquelf, and certainly was beautiful and slender and even glowed with light. Lady Snowflake had been similar in form, but had a real quality to her that Myrall'mara never had. And Will recalled very well the hateful expression the *sullanciri* wore when she made an abortive attempt to kill him in Yslin.

"No. Not her." He swallowed more soup, then licked his lips. "She was not a *sullanciri*. Even with the poison, I know that."

"So, another player." Dranae intertwined his fingers, then hooked his hands over the back of his neck. "We don't know who. We don't know if she represents a faction or not. We do know she wanted her work hidden."

Peri nodded. "And we know she is very powerful."

Will tipped the tankard up and drained the last of the soup from it. He smiled and wiped his mouth on the back of his left hand. "Thanks, Lombo."

The hulking Panqui nodded solemnly.

Will threw back the bedclothes, catching Qwc in a woolen tidal wave, then swung his legs off the edge of the bed. He'd have slid off it and onto his feet, but Peri firmly planted a hand in the middle of his chest. "Where do you think you are going?"

"I'm fine now." Will tried to keep his voice light, but a bit of rawness still came through. "I am."

"That wasn't the question Peri asked, Will." Dranae settled a hand on his right shoulder and drew him back around. "Soup and sleep will help you recover, and you need that. We don't know what the poison did, or how well you have been healed."

Will rubbed at the scars on his neck. "There are things that need to be done. The fragment..."

The Gyrkyme shook her head. "Scrainwood's mages cut that section of the rafter out and have conveyed it to the palace. Tomorrow there will be one final formal hearing before Crow is released. There is nothing for you to do."

"Well, there must be things you need to be doing. I am fine here. You don't have to worry about that."

Dranae lifted up the corner of the blanket and let Qwc free himself. "Will, we *are* concerned for you, but that is only part of the reason we're here."

Lombo stretched, flashing claws. "Kerrigan missing. Will stays *found*."

The thief blinked. "You're here *guarding* me?"

"Not needed. Told them no help needed." Qwc shrugged wearily. "Not listening, not listening at all."

Will laughed. "Thank you, I guess."

"No guessing about it, Will. You are the Norrington. You were very nearly killed." Peri reached down and stroked a downy finger against his right cheek. "You are the hope of the world. Hope can't die."

He rubbed his throat again. "I wish Chytrine shared that opinion."

Dranae laughed. "She will, eventually. For her, though, it will just come too late to save her."

CHAPTER 27

Though he sat astride his horse alone, Adrogans could feel the Mistress of Pain clinging to him. She hugged his back to her chest, her claws raking down his chest. Her jagged teeth gnawed at his shoulder and neck. Though her distraction was mighty, Adrogans' concentration was greater. As she used him, he used her, and he got the better of the bargain.

Around him swirled an early-morning blizzard, and the flakes fell thick and fast. Fading into the distance on either side of the Svar River's western shore was the forest through which his troops had moved. Below his position, the land sloped down for five hundred yards to the river's northern ford. The water appeared as a dim black snake, and beyond it lay vague grey-and-white mounds that had once been a small stronghold guarding this important crossing.

Though he could not actually see any movement down there, the *yrûn* allowed him to *feel* the presence of the enemy. Adrogans could not determine how many there were, for he was too young in his power to do so. All he could tell was that there were a lot of them and that both hunger and cold assailed them.

He glanced left at Phfas. The diminutive Zhusk sat the back of a shaggy brown mountain pony. "Your impressions, Uncle?"

Phfas sniffed at the air. "They will not smell worse dead. Gibberkin, vylaens, hoargoun, and something else."

"Something else?" Adrogans focused his perception and Pain lanced a hand deep into his side. He blinked, then refocused, using the clarity that pain gave him. He nodded. There, deep in the knot of bodies that were hungry and shivering, there were others.

"I have them, but do not know them."

The little shaman tightened his grip on the thin woolen blanket he wore over his shoulders. The dark blue and green plaid seemed out of place, though the Guarnin family who gave it to him had been proud he'd carried it with him. Phfas hunched forward in his saddle, as if he were going to whisper to his mount, then slowly shook his head.

"New. A surprise."

"In one sense, yes." Adrogans had taken pains to deploy his light units against the raiders that the Aurolani were sending into the highlands. He would have been content, as his troops trained, to do nothing more than deal with the raiders. When Nefrai-kesh showed up in Meredo, however, his plans changed. He learned instantly of the *sullanciri*'s presence in the Oriosan capital via *arcanslata* and decided to strike fast—before Chytrine's general could return to direct his soldiers.

Adrogans raised his right hand and felt his mistress slip her fingers through his to rake agony down into his armpit. When he let his arm fall again, a mounted trumpeter on his right sounded a call. The Jeranese Horse Guards, resplendent in their brown tabards over ringmail, emerged from the forest and began the descent to the river valley. Off to his right the Jeranese Light Horse came down the hills in a column two abreast and on the left the elite Valician White Mane cavalry rode into position. The three cavalry units gave him three hundred mounted troopers and a force that would sweep swiftly over the ford.

Their ride had not been easy because Guraskya lay nearly sixty miles from the ford. They moved out quickly and changed mounts several times on the journey. The cavalry had not enjoyed pushing their horses so hard in the winter, but they were less inclined to squander an opportunity to strike at the enemy.

While Adrogans could not get an accurate count of the enemy via the *yrûn*'s senses, he could tell that the garrison was not that big. He estimated that his forces had a two-to-one advantage, which would have boded well were he not fighting across a river in the midst of a blizzard and attacking a fortified position.

As expected, the trumpeter's call had done more than summon up the Southlands troops. Dark forms began to stir in the enemy camp. Adrogans studied them, matching what his eyes showed him with what he sensed through pain. Everything seemed to fit save for one rather large anomaly.

"That is a hoargoun down there, yes?"

Phfas nodded solemnly.

The frost giant plodded forward through the snow, dragging a club made from the bole of a tree behind it. Though it moved ponderously slowly, it waded into the river. Water boiled around its broad feet, rising to cover its ankles when Adrogans knew the frigid water would come up to his own knees.

Adrogans concentrated, then shook his head. "I can't feel it, and that water has got to be cold. It must hurt."

The Zhusk shaman again sniffed the air. "That one is beyond hurt."

"Reanimated?"

"Not alive."

"That would mean some fairly powerful magicks at play."

"You're surprised."

The Jeranese general shook his head. With the frost giant contesting the ford, getting a massed formation past would be tough. That club would crush warriors and scatter horses. Adrogans knew the creature would go down eventually; alive or undead it could be chopped to bits. His concern was for how much damage it would do before it was brought down.

Down below, the cavalry units drew themselves up just two hundred yards from the river's far shore, which put them outside the effective range of arrows and draconettes. It would put them in jeopardy from a dragonel shot or even the thunderballs he'd heard about from Fortress Draconis. It was a danger he had to accept, because without massing his troops for a charge, he wouldn't get past the ford. And while that did make them more vulnerable to ranged weapons, for them to spread out would have been a disaster.

Adrogans glanced to his right. "Signal slow advance."

The trumpeter blared out another call and the heavy cavalry began a slow advance toward the ford. The general urged his horse forward. Phfas followed on his left and the signalman on his right. They pulled in behind the Horse Guards and moved forward.

Adrogans drew his saber. "For queen and country!"

The hundred Horse Guards echoed his call, underscored with the skirl of steel being unsheathed. Horses stamped, blowing out jets of steam. Tack jingled, and the mail of restless warriors rustled. Muscles quivered on man and beast alike, and a hundred and a half yards ahead of them, the hoargoun heaved its club into the air and began spinning it slowly.

Adrogans nodded to the signalman. "Blow charge."

The notes for charge blasted out and the Horse Guards surged forward. Hooves devoured the ground. Snow sprayed up, dappling chests and legs, hiding limbs as if the horses were wading through a sea of fog. Men screamed and, awaiting them, the gibberers hooted. Snowflakes stung Adrogans' cheeks as he spurred his horse forward.

Off to his left a new cry was voiced. Springing up from beneath blankets and cloaks of white, the Loquelven Blackfeathers revealed their presence. The light infantry had already been ranging far to the northeast of Guraskya, so were able to make it to the Svar River ford before the cavalry. Under cover of the blizzard they had advanced to the edge of the river and waited there for the trumpet calls.

Even over the pounding of hooves, Adrogans could hear that deep groan of silverwood longbows being drawn. Black arrows a yard long and as thick as a finger sped through the air. On a snowy hill a gibberer spun and fell with two shafts crossed in his chest. A vylaen running toward them took one in the throat and slid face forward to disappear beneath the snow. Another gibberer who stood and hooted defiantly as two arrows fell short of his position had his head snapped back by a shaft that pierced his right eye and burst through the back of his skull.

The vast majority of the arrows flew at the hoargoun. The elves shot from the giant's right, sticking him from calf to crown. Some of the arrows passed through the meat of limbs, ripping holes in his flesh. Others sank deep into muscles and joints. A half-dozen pinned his right ear to his skull and one vanished within his ear canal.

The sheer shock of that many arrows hitting it did seem to affect the giant. Broadheads had cut through muscle, and even reanimated, the creature did need those muscles to move and strike. Tissue hung in shreds from the ravaged right arm, changing the arc of the club.

This did not, on the first pass, seem to matter much.

The club caught the first cavalryman and his horse on the right flank. The club's head had just splashed through the water and was on the upswing, so it lifted the horse and rider into the air. The horse's chest collapsed under the assault, wrapping the beast around the club. The blow jolted the rider from the saddle and he would have flown free save that his right foot caught in a stirrup. As the horse whirled off the club, the man spun around it. His leg twisted in all manner of impossible angles, then he flew apart from the horse and smashed down to the ground before a group of gibberers.

The Aurolani troops fell upon him with longknives. Their howls of triumph shrank to gurgles as a second volley of arrows ripped through them. Shaft-stuck gibberers capered and spun, dark blood spraying. Bodies fell, twitching. And sometimes, in a grotesque display, others could not fall because so many arrows had transfixed them together.

But the majority of arrows sank into the giant's flesh. The club's weight had turned the hoargoun more toward the elves, so this second set struck it full front from groin to throat. More important, the elves had switched arrows. The first they'd used had heavy heads designed to punch through armor. While very effective on the gibberers, they did not do as much damage to the hoargoun as they could have.

The new arrows, however, were designed to carve up tissue. The razored edges had been twisted into a spiral, so as the rotating arrows hit their targets, they drilled in, and an inordinate number of archers went for the giant's neck. Shaft after shaft stabbed into it, paring away the thickly corded muscles that connected the giant's head to its body.

The giant staggered, then the club's momentum twisted the body around. The head didn't turn at the same rate. About the time the hoargoun was left looking back over its own left shoulder, the heavy head flopped forward. Scored tendons parted with whip cracks and the head tumbled free.

The body crashed down moments later. It landed heavily enough to shake the ground and topple some gibberers. Several of the cavalry also went down as the giant's feet swept through their ranks, but the vast majority splashed on past, driving their horses at the gibberers. They rode through the cloud of snow the giant's body had raised, hiding them from Adrogans' sight, but the harsh rasp of steel and the tendrils of pain told him what was happening.

A savage roar erupted from the left as Adrogans' horse vaulted one of the hoargoun's legs. A red-gold fireball careened down from the high point on one snowy mound and engulfed a rider. Man and mount vanished in flame, then reappeared as blackened, skeletal figures that fell to dust as the flames evaporated into greasy smoke.

Up on the hilltop stood a creature Adrogans had not seen before. Tall and slender enough to be mistaken for an elf, it had white fur covering its body save for a scarlet loincloth. It bore a small wand and its head came around, searching. Their gazes met for a second, then the wand came up and another fireball blossomed.

The roiling sphere of burning gases roared as it raced toward him. Adrogans' horse squealed and reared, nostrils flaring. The Jeranese general kicked free of the stirrups as his horse leaped away. He landed on his feet and went down to one knee, raising his saber in a futile attempt at a parry.

Just for a heartbeat, the fireball paused and hung there in the air. Adrogans wondered if the spell had been cast at him and his mount as a unit, and if their splitting had created a problem. It struck him as ironic that he would be trying to puzzle this out in the last seconds of his life. It saddened him that he'd not have a definitive answer before he died.

Then the air stiffened around him and the fireball glanced into the sky. It exploded loudly, shooting tentacular streamers of fire above the battlefield. The blast was enough to knock Adrogans to the ground, and he was not alone. He rolled to his feet amid rising mist from melting snow, then dodged as a fallen horse struggled upright again.

He turned to face the creature that had tried to kill him. Though he realized he would never likely get to it, he fully intended to try to kill it. Steel against magick didn't give him good odds of success, but someone had to destroy it or more warriors would die.

The creature, and two more flanking it, raised their wands to cast more spells, but never got a chance to complete their magery. Blackfeather arrows flew thicker than the snow, and struck with the impact of an ax chopping wood. The coring broadheads drilled inch-wide holes in their targets and sailed on through, leaving a bloody red mist hanging in the air. Two of the creatures went down immediately, collapsing as if their bones had been reduced to pulp. The last, though—the one who had sent the fireball at Adrogans—had time enough to look down at the holes in its middle. Its eyes were coming back up when a shaft slammed into the side of its head. It whirled in a circle, the wand flying from limp fingers, then the creature slid down the mound, leaving a bloody smear in its wake.

The two light horse legions raced across the ford and spread out, driving the gibberers before them. Arrows struck here and there, as the elves chose specific targets. Some of the Horse Guards dismounted and swarmed over the mounds, rooting out hiding gibberers, and quickly the resistance came to an end.

Mistress Gilthalarwin, the leader of the Blackfeathers, waded through the ford. "I saw you go down. Are you hurt? I have a healer."

Adrogans shook his head. "I am fine, though some of my people could likely use help. I thank you and your warriors. If not for you, this would have been much worse."

The elf laughed. Her black hair had been drawn back into a long braid that slithered snakelike over her shoulders. "Ever arrogant, Adrogans. Without us you might not have taken the ford."

"We would have because we had to. And that is not arrogance speaking. I know my people as well as you know yours." He turned and looked at Phfas. "Thank you, Uncle, for saving my life."

The shaman sat on the ground, his chest heaving, but he managed a weak smile. "Armoring you with air had to be done. That magick was strong."

The general nodded. "Mistress, have you any idea what those were?"

"Another Aurolani abomination?" She shook her head. "I shall have it investigated. I will put some of my trackers on them, too, and see if there are more about."

"Very good, thank you." Adrogans waved the trumpeter over. "Sound a recall. Then get me two riders and send them back to the infantry. I want them here in three days to hold the ford."

"Yes, General."

The man stepped away and blew the recall. Troops began to return to their units and the officers began to take a toll of the casualties. Men helped battle-broken comrades, staunched wounds, and set bones. The first

Blackfeathers crossing the river started to move among the cavalry, directing the most seriously wounded to the edge of the river, where their healer would begin casting spells to help them recover.

Adrogans squatted beside Phfas and felt Pain crowding against his back. "Well, Uncle, we've hurt him. I don't know how long it will take him to learn that fact, but when he does he'll react. Do I wait here and make him pay dearly to take this ford back or..."

The old man shook his head. "Ever forward; ever forward. If you remain here, you are a target. If you go on, he has to find you first."

"Yes, and in war it is much better not to be hit at all." Markus Adrogans stood again and bowed his back, feeling a crackling running from waist to neck. "On to Svarskya, then. I remember it having been pretty in the spring. Perhaps this year it shall be again."

C H A P T E R   2 8

Will hated people treating him as if he were sick, because he really felt fine. Well, fine as long as he was bundled up in warm clothing. Growing up as a thief he'd preferred looser-fitting things, since he could slip out of them if someone made a grab for him, and because they provided ample hiding places for loot. Those same loose clothes suited him well now because he could wear thick woolen undergarments beneath them and have a chance of staying warm.

Despite the cold, he had been determined to leave his face bare. It still angered him that the court had chosen to listen to Nefrai-kesh speak against Crow. He'd have refused to attend the court that morning, even though Crow was supposed to be released, but Princess Alexia had some ambassador guy explain why it was important for him to be there.

And why it was important for him to wear a mask.

Will balked at the mask and was surprised to hear Resolute agree with him, but the ambassador pointed out that by being present, Will would again assert his claim to the title of Lord Norrington. Since Crow's release would likely be conditional, having his liege lord there to accept custody of him would be important. In order to show respect for the customs of Oriosa, Will would need to wear his mask.

Sitting there in the court chamber beside Princess Alexia, Will did his best to kill a smile. The assembled spectators from Oriosa had seen him come in and a buzz had run through the crowd. Reactions varied, but he did see some firm nods of respect for his gesture.

Will reached up and adjusted the mask he wore. It was not the one King Scrainwood had given him, but a white lace courtesy mask, of the sort that King Augustus, Queen Carus, and Princess Alexia had been given. They were worn by non-Oriosans in respect for their station. The courtesy masks showed a respect for customs by the visitor, but also marked him as an outsider.

The mask the king had given him he wore on his upper right arm. Its dark green showed up nicely over the red velvet jacket he'd picked out, and the red in the eyeholes was perfect. He'd thought that solution up all by himself, and having both the ambassador and Resolute agree with it had pleased him no end.

When he'd taken his place beside the princess, Crow had looked over at him from the prisoner's docket and knitted his brows with concern. Will winked at him and lifted his chin just enough for Crow to see the twin scars. The older man's eyes tightened in a wince, but Will shook his head to dismiss the concern.

The sharp rap of a staff on the floor up on the tribunal's dais quelled the chatter in the room. Through the open doors at the far end came the three judges. Queen Carus came first, wearing a gown of deep scarlet with triangular ivory panels pointing toward her waist in an hourglass formation. Her black hair had been pulled back and pinned up with golden sticks festooned with rubies.

Augustus came next, more martial than regal in bearing. His clothes mixed green and white with some gold trim, and had a military cut about them without being hopelessly severe. The half-horse, half-fish creature he'd chosen as his insignia appeared as the buckle on the wide white leather belt he wore around his waist. His courtesy mask had been cut from white lace and properly notched at the eyes to reflect the death of his parents.

Linchmere brought up the rear—and while Will knew this was because he was the most important figure in the tribunal, he found it fitting that the prince should be last. His slouched shoulders betokened a general sagging of his body, which resulted in a paunchy belly that jounced as he walked. Linchmere even moved each hip forward as he walked in a fat-man's stroll, though he was not really that heavy.

Even Kerrigan carries himself better.

The tribunal took their places, then Linchmere stepped forward to address the court. Wroxter Dainn and his aides slipped from their seats and dropped to one knee, but Crow stayed in his chair. Will waited to see what Princess Alexia would do, and when she remained seated, he sat there with her.

The Oriosan Prince cleared his throat once, and once again. "Lord and Ladies, King and Queens, distinguished visitors, citizens. This proceeding has been conducted in a solemn manner. We have listened. The evidence has been weighed and we have discussed the truth of this matter."

The prince spoke slowly and had lowered his voice for the sake of authority, but right from the first, right when he realized he should have said "Kings and Queens" before "Lord and Ladies," anxiety beset him. Will could read it in his eyes and the nervous quiver running through Linchmere's lower lip.

"The charges against Crow were charges made against Tarrant Hawkins a long time ago. He was charged with treason and tried. He was sentenced to death but that sentence was never carried out. This man, Crow, was identified as being Tarrant Hawkins. Because of his marriage to Princess Alexia, a new trial was required. A new verdict was sought."

The prince chewed his lower lip for a moment. "In our deliberations, a flaw was noted in the prosecution case. The events took place twenty-five years ago, so the value of eyewitness testimony is questionable. Court sorcerers said their spells established a link between Crow and Hawkins, but the material alleged to have belonged to Hawkins has now gone missing, so their conclusions cannot be reviewed and proven to the satisfaction of the court. The only positive identification offered was that of Nefrai-kesh and, as an enemy, it is expected he lied."

Will frowned, utterly confused. King Augustus had greeted Crow as an old friend, and they had talked about knowing each other. Will hadn't heard Crow admit that he was Hawkins, but he'd never denied it either. The whole question of Crow's identity should have been beside the point.

As Will had understood things, Linchmere was supposed to get up and say that the charges hadn't been proved and that Crow was free to go provided someone would assume responsibility for him. Will would do that, then slip his real mask on, everything would be fine, and they would be free to fight Chytrine.

"I don't understand," he mumbled under his breath.

Alexia leaned slightly in his direction, her shoulder pressing against his. "I was afraid of this. Scrainwood is playing games. The wizards' evidence that has vanished can reappear at any time and the charges can be reinstated. If Scrainwood gets his way, Crow will never be free from the threat of execution. He won't do anything right now, though. King Augustus wouldn't be here if King Scrainwood had gone back on his agreement."

Will snorted. "Scrainwood is a snake."

The princess smiled. "You've insulted snakes."

Linchmere continued. "It is the opinion of the tribunal, then, that insufficient evidence exists to convict this man, Crow, of crimes ascribed to Tarrant Hawkins. You, sir, are free to . . ."

The doors at the far end of the room sailed open, shoved wide by a woman in red riding leathers and a billowing scarlet cloak. She wore a red leather mask that covered her from cheeks to forehead and right up to her hairline, though a lock of her long red hair did curve down over her right eye. The flesh of her lower face likewise was red with cold and windburn. Melting snow glistened on her cloak.

"Where is he?" She stopped in the center aisle and her cloak splashed against her back like a woolen wave. "Where is he?"

"W-who?" Linchmere started to take a half step forward, but he saved it when his voice broke. He lowered it to the serious tone from which it had risen. "Who are you?"

She thrust a finger at him. "You, *sit*. You're not the one I want." She looked around the room, her pale blue eyes lighting on Will for a second, then shifting away again before returning. "You, you're the Norrington, aren't you?"

Will stood slowly. "I am."

She came forward, quickly, not as forcefully as before, and swept past the prisoner's docket. She sank to one knee and took Will's right hand in hers. Raising it to her mouth, she kissed it, sending a jolt through Will.

She glanced up and her gaze met his, sending another jolt through him. Her eyes burned with an intensity that threatened to ignite him. The woman was beautiful, there was no denying that, but it was something else in her, running deep in those eyes, that captivated him.

Will swallowed hard. "Who are you?"

"My lord, I am Princess Sayce of Muroso. I've come from Caledo to beg you to save my nation." Desperation arced through her words. She bowed her head again, touching her forehead to his hand. "Please, my lord, you are our only hope."

"I, um, I . . ." Will looked hopelessly at Alexia, Crow, and then King Augustus.

The Alcidese King rose to his feet. "Princess Sayce, you have interrupted a proceeding, one of some importance."

The young woman stood abruptly and let Will's hand slip from hers. "Important? This is important? You're Augustus of Alcida and she's Carus of Jerana. I have seen you before with my father. Finding Oriosa bound up with nonsense does not surprise me, but you? How could you be here?"

Her voice rose and bitterness crept into it. "Have you no idea of what is happening? Sebcia has collapsed. Chytrine's troops laid siege to Lurrii with dragonels. They shattered the gates, toppled the walls, and the slaughter was beyond imagining. Refugees have been streaming south, but the snows catch and overwhelm them. Come spring, if there ever *is* a spring, we will find families who lay down in the cold together and died. Roads will be strewn with bodies. Yet here you sit, listening to people prattle on about little things that matter not when people are dying. Dying in the hundreds. In the thousands."

Sayce turned and pointed a finger at Will. "I've come for the Norrington, to bring him to Caledo, so he can lead our troops and destroy Chytrine."

"Wait a minute." Will held his hands up. "I may be the Norrington, but you need Princess Alexia to lead the troops." He nodded at Alexia. "She will win the fight for you."

Sayce sniffed at the air, then cocked her head slightly. "You're Alexia? Hmm. What a perfectly lovely *dress*. I hardly thought I would find you here when Aurolani needed killing. My nation will not fall as yours did."

Alexia stood slowly. "I would not wish that on you, Princess, and will do all I can to prevent it." Alexia raised her voice. "Prince Linchmere, I believe you were about to set Crow free."

Linchmere roused himself from his throne and unsteadily took to his feet again. "Yes, Crow, you are free to go."

Will clapped his hands. "Yes!"

Sayce turned and watched as Will and Crow shook hands, then embraced with much backslapping. "I am pleased for your friend, Lord Norrington, but every moment we delay makes the situation more grave."

Will slipped out of Crow's hug, then looked up at her. She stood about a fist taller than he and was lean like a wolf. Over the right breast of her leathers had been burned the bear rampant crest of the Murosan royal house. Her mask hid the upper half of her face, but her strong jaw and full lips suggested the beauty that hid beneath it.

"Princess, if you want me to head north with you, then Crow and Alexia and everyone else will have to come, too."

"Everyone else?"

"My friends. Resolute and Dranae and Peri. There are more, they'll help. We all got the DragonCrown fragment from Wruona."

Sayce nodded solemnly. "Yes, we shall have all your companions. My men are out rounding up more horses—we fair killed ours on the ride here. Once we have fodder for them, and provisions for us, we must go."

"I'll be ready." Will smiled at her, but beyond her Linchmere stiffened. The thief turned to follow the prince's gaze, then began to snarl as he saw a familiar figure framed in the doorway.

King Scrainwood stood there smiling. "Ah, there you are, Princess Sayce. You shall be forgiven the affront of not visiting me first, since I understand you were under the impression the Norrington was to be found here."

Sayce's eyes tightened. "Forgive me, Highness, I meant no disrespect. The Norrington *is* here, so I have accomplished my purpose."

"Alas, you have not. I would not have you or my sister nation to the north labor under the impression that this fraud is the Norrington."

Will's jaw shot open. "What?"

Scrainwood smiled. "Bosleigh Norrington did not go away without issue. *Legitimate* issue. His son shall arrive here in Meredo in a day or two. As it should be, an Oriosan *noble,* loyal and true, shall lead the world against Chytrine."

CHAPTER 29

Isaura breathed deeply of the crisp, clean air of her homeland. She drew it in as best she could, feeling it cool her head and throat and lungs, then exhaled slowly. She let the outgoing breath carry away as much of the taint of the Southlands as possible, though she secretly feared she would never be fully free of the stink of Meredo.

Slowly she wandered through the rime garden behind the citadel in which she lived. No walls separated it from the white tundra that stretched to the north. No vermin would wander in to nibble delicacies, for the treasures of the garden, while they did grow, sustained naught but the spirit of those who wandered amid its splendors.

Several times a year Neskartu's students used magick to form a pellet of ice into which they worked a spell. The magick itself was something Isaura found fascinating because it used the imagery of an illusion and combined it with constructive elements to create wonderful things. Many young students, for example, might imbue their creation with the form of a creature—either realistic or an imagined beast. Once that ice seed was planted in the garden, it would mature and grow up into the image the magicker had envisioned.

The more advanced students could do much more, and often competed for the most complex creations. As she walked through the garden she smiled and reached a hand out to caress the glassy petals of a rose. Made of ice, they had none of the softness of real flowers, but still they had the same delicate construction. A light flick of her finger would shatter the blossom, but Isaura refrained from doing the damage.

She turned from the bush that produced those flowers to another creation, which took on the form of a tree with outswept branches. It differed greatly from the bush, for that rosebush had been shaped by one of the students who had spent much of his life in the Southlands. He had seen rosebushes and was able to recall their details from life, which he then worked into his creation.

The tree, on the other hand, had been created by Corde, a woman barely older than Isaura herself. She'd been brought up as a babe from the south and had no memories of anything other than the Conservatory—at which her parents had studied until their deaths. Corde's creation reflected her intelligence, as it had a tree's shape but was formed from a lacey lattice of snowflakes. Each one of the snowflakes, which ranged in size from the palm of Isaura's hand to something as large as a warrior's shield, appeared to be unique. Moreover, if one peered closely at any one, it would be made up of smaller flakes, and they made up of smaller and smaller until Isaura could not detect them without the aid of magick.

Corde was one of Neskartu's few students who began to get a glimmer of the true nature of magick. Her creation constantly shifted itself, as if the branches were swaying in an unfelt breeze. As Isaura drew closer to it, blossoms slowly opened, and in the flat blades of ice, Isaura's image was magickally graven.

As wondrous as that tree was, it could have been so much more if Corde truly understood that magick was a river. The sorceress had been able to imbue her creation with a lot of energy, and energy from a very pure source, but there would be a point where that would be all used up. The tree would become nothing more than ice. Sunlight would evaporate branches and the winds would tear it apart.

Isaura turned away so as not to invite more displays of imagery from it and hasten its death, but not quickly enough. The image in the petals shifted from her to the face of the youth she had saved in Meredo. It showed him resting and no longer in pain, for which she rejoiced, and she hoped the image was not drawn from her memory but somehow reflective of him at the current time.

That confused her, her hope. She did not know who the youth was or why she had saved him. Yes, she had wanted to undo what Spyr'skara had done. She had not liked the way the Azure Spider looked at her, so frustrating him had given her pleasure. Even after her return to the inn and reunion with Vionna and Nefrai-kesh, when she learned that the new *sullanciri* had been slain, she did not regret having undone his work.

It was only after Nefrai-kesh had taken her and the pirate back home that she began to think more deeply about what she had done. The possibility that her action might have been the very betrayal her mother hinted at did not escape her. She should have felt horrified about that possibility, and she was—at first. But something had shielded her from regret.

She felt as if, somehow, she had been compelled to heal the youth. She had cast herself onto the river of magick and had allowed it to carry her wherever she was meant to go. It had sped her to him and, once there, helping him was imperative.

Isaura shook her head. She did not like at all the idea that she was not responsible for her actions. At the very least, she had been the one to abandon herself to magick, so everything that flowed from that decision was her fault. If she angered her mother by her actions, she had no one to blame but herself.

The problem was that she felt no shame. She could rationalize it through her knowledge that her mother never would have wanted to see a young innocent in such pain. But ultimately, her mother's concerns were not her own. Isaura felt that what she had done was right. The other presence in the room had confirmed this. She was some part of a grander scheme, but she had chosen to act. That she had acted as she did felt right, but for the life of her she could not figure out why.

A hissing sound came to her ears and she looked up. A whirling cylinder of ice and snow drifted to and fro as it slowly wended its way into the garden. It dodged around the larger creations, then drifted past smaller, pausing as if to caress the harmless little animals. Once it had worked its way to the heart of the garden, it swirled over her and around her, and she spun, laughing, in its midst.

It drew away, then tightened and congealed into the form of an older man, with a beard and flowing hair, wearing simple garb complete with a furred cloak. His flesh remained translucent and flowed into a smile as his head came up. His hands worked through a series of gestures and punctuated them with a raised eyebrow.

Isaura bowed to him. "Yes, Drolda, I have been away, but no more. I am here again, my friend, and wish never to leave."

He signed through the secret language they shared.

"The Southlands are strange, Drolda, as well you know." She sighed. "There was much there I still do not understand."

Drolda frowned as his finger wove through a question.

Isaura hesitated. "It is not so much that I am bothered. I am puzzled. Yes, puzzled." She much preferred the idea of being puzzled rather than worried, because a puzzle could be solved.

His head spun around on his shoulders, so he seemed to be peering behind him at the snowflake tree. His head came all the way around, then he exhaled into a cloud that solidified into the youth's image.

"Yes. He was hurt, gravely hurt. I saved him from poison, but I do not know who he was or why I saved him. He could have been an enemy whose life threatens that of my mother."

Her friend's expression soured. Drolda did not like her mother, but for reasons that had never been explained.

Isaura gave him a sad expression. "Do you know who that was?"

The rimeman shook his head, then shrugged, mitigating a portion of the denial. His hands formed a reply.

Isaura laughed. "Forces at play, you say? You are cryptic today, my friend. Gone are the days when you would delight me with simple antics and simple tales."

The creature of ice caressed her shoulder lightly, then contorted his features into an absurd mask that was meant to make her laugh.

She did, but caught the distinct impression that Drolda was hiding something from her. Before she could inquire, however, he went to pieces as if a handful of powder snow in a gale, and she felt the cold kiss of some ice on her cheek. She had seen him disappear like that many times before, and it always betokened one thing. Though she could have turned and been waiting for them, she instead strode deeper into the garden.

"Princess, a moment please."

She turned at Nefrai-kesh's call. "Yes, my lord?"

The leader of the *sullanciri* stood beside Neskartu's scintillating form. "In your mother's absence, I am tasked with your safety. There is a situation in Okrannel that demands my attention."

"Am I to accompany you, Lord Nefrai-kesh?"

Bands of blue streaked through the *sullanciri's* white eyes. "Your company would be most welcome, Princess, and I would be honored by it. You would find Okrannel much to your liking. Vast tracts have been returned to their unsullied state. Alas, what I shall be doing would create hardship for you."

Isaura frowned. Nefrai-kesh, above all the others, showed her respect. The rest of the *sullanciri*, save perhaps Myrall'mara, deferred to her out of fear of her mother. Myrall'mara, while respectful, tended to avoid her. Isaura did not mind their distance, for Myrall'mara always seemed sorrowful, and Isaura had never been able to reach past that sadness.

Nefrai-kesh, on the other hand, had been much of what she imagined a father would be. He had, over the years, introduced her to many things. He taught her how to ride a Grand Temeryx. Newly returned from his journeys, he would give her gifts. The one she treasured most highly was a sapphire ring he said the Queen of Oriosa had insisted he bear to her. Other things, from small bone carvings to exotic teas, had brought her hints of the Southlands and expanded the world beyond the white disk that surrounded the Citadel.

"You know, my lord, that I am not as delicate as you might imagine."

"I know, Princess. Your peregrinations through the streets of Meredo alone tell me you are capable of many things." Neither his body or voice betrayed any hint of suspicion. His face she could not read because of the mask he wore, but had he thought she'd done anything wrong, she'd have known long before this.

"It is that I need to engage an enemy who has proved rather crafty."

"But I would enjoy seeing my mother's enemies vanquished."

"Indeed, I believe that." Nefrai-kesh nodded toward Neskartu. "Resistance to your mother's army has crumbled in Sebcia. Her forces advance into Muroso, and Neskartu will be leading a group of his students to join them. Your mother does want you to see her enemies fall, so you will do so in Neskartu's company."

Isaura tugged lightly on her lower lip with the thumb and forefinger of her left hand. "Will we be going to fight, or just to observe, Lord Neskartu?"

Your mother desires you to observe. My students will fight if they have the opportunity.

Nefrai-kesh raised his right index finger. "It is important that you understand something, Princess. Muroso, before it was part of the great revolt, had been home to the empire's own school of magick. The Academy at Caledo rivaled Vilwan for a time, and Murosan sorcerers are very proud. It is their tradition to engage in duels. They do this for their own pleasure, though they say it is to save the simple folk from suffering. They will challenge our magickers, but you are not to allow yourself to be drawn into one of these duels.

"I need you to observe, and report back to me. While your mother wishes you to see her enemies collapse, I desire this favor of you: use your eyes and senses to tell me how best to continue to defeat her enemies. Will you do this for me?"

"Of course, my lord." Isaura nodded solemnly. "Shall I send to you by *arcanslata,* or is there another means I should use?"

The *sullanciri* stepped forward boldly. Snow crunched beneath his boots. He stopped in front of her, then raised his right hand. "Close your eyes, Princess; open yourself to me."

She did as she was bid. She felt him press three fingers to her forehead. For a moment her flesh tingled, then she shivered. It felt as if something had, just for a heartbeat, frozen the river of magick. It rushed on immediately after that, but the pause shook her.

She opened her eyes as his fingers left her flesh. "What did you do?"

"A trickle of magick, Princess, linking us. When you wish to speak with me, just concentrate and I shall find you. You will tell me what you know, and I shall be obliged."

Isaura nodded. "Yes, my lord, and I shall be pleased to be of service."

"Excellent." Nefrai-kesh turned quickly and peered at Neskartu. "And you, my old friend, you know that if any harm comes to her, you had best be dead. In fact, your last act should be to send her home. Your failure to keep her safe will result in untold miseries."

Of this we are aware, my lord. Even death will not prevent me from keeping our beloved empress' daughter safe.

Isaura felt the confidence in Neskartu's thought, but the creature's colors had dulled and slowed while his outline lost some of its crispness.

The king of the *sullanciri* nodded. "Very well. Princess, you will be traveling south by conventional means. Do not feel you need overburden the drear-sleigh with chests of clothes or an overabundance of supplies. Anything you need shall be given to you on the journey. By its end, you shall be bedecked in the finery of Sebcia and Muroso, honoring your mother's new subjects with your choices."

"How soon do we leave, my lord?"

"Tomorrow evening." Nefrai-kesh waved her back toward the Citadel. "Servants will come and aid you in packing. It is not much time, I know, but to delay would deprive you of learning what your mother desires you to know."

"It is enough time, my lord, thank you." Isaura smiled, then turned in a circle to survey the garden one last time. The snowflake tree chose that moment to fall to pieces, and its swordlike branches sheared through a family of rabbits as they descended, but it did not seem to her an ill omen. It would occur to her later that it should have, but by then events were moving so swiftly that even with this warning, disaster could not have been averted.

CHAPTER 30

Kerrigan Reese felt better, though still uneasy. Before he left the chamber, Rym Ramoch had instructed Bok to bathe and clothe Kerrigan after the young mage ate. The meal had proved filling though not terribly appetizing. Kerrigan suspected the meat in the gravy was really rat, but at that point he was so hungry he didn't care.

After that came a bath. The urZrethi wrestled a half-tun cask into the small room and filled it with water. From a shelf he took a small piece of volcanic rock, whispered over it, then tossed it into the water. Bubbles rose quickly and steam drifted, then the urZrethi pulled the rock out, bounced it from hand to hand, and finally set it steaming on the shelf.

Kerrigan slipped into the warm water and prepared to relax, but Bok took the orders to bathe him seriously. The urZrethi scrubbed him up one side and down the other, leaving his skin red and tingling. Kerrigan had never felt so much a child as he did in that bath. With one hand Bok was able to shift him this way and that, and Kerrigan had no doubt the urZrethi could have hauled him bodily from the bath without difficulty.

Once he'd been bathed, Bok brought him warm clothes of a very utilitarian nature. Though Kerrigan had grown up wearing robes, he had since gotten used to trousers and tunics. Moreover, he associated them with adventure. And because his wearing of them would be frowned upon by his superiors on Vilwan, that sort of minor rebellion thrilled him.

Once Bok had cleared away the wash basin, he brought bedding and bid Kerrigan lie down. As the mage did, the urZrethi stretched an arm up until it was thinner than a spear haft, and pinched the chandelier candles dark.

Kerrigan lay back and considered what Rym had told him. The simple fact that Kerrigan could perform the magicks that he did meant that men could learn them. While Kerrigan loved to think of himself as special, it did seem curious that someone like the Grand Magister could not cast even the most simple of healing spells. And yet, the Grand Magister did know that it was possible for a man to cast those spells.

Either Yrulph Kirûn had been a genius and figured out a lot of things about magick for himself, or he had been taught a great deal and expanded upon it. Or both. Perhaps he so outstripped his superiors that they really had no idea what he was capable of doing.

Just like me.

It made sense, in the aftermath of it all, for leaders on Vilwan to institute changes in instruction that hobbled their charges. If the greatest threat the world had ever known had come from Vilwan, without concessions and safeguards Vilwan would have been destroyed. Nations would refuse to send their talented sorcerers to Vilwan to be trained, shutting down the island and its culture.

Kerrigan's mind reeled as things began to fit into place. Nations had no real desire to have strong magick academies because the first one of them to produce a Kirûn could begin a war of conquest against its neighbors. What the world leaders needed was stable magick in the human nations—magick that would help do many things and make life a bit easier, but nothing that would allow the atrocities that Kirûn had committed when he fashioned and used the DragonCrown.

The leadership on Vilwan, then, would have approached the world leaders with a plan to curb their own magickal power in return for continued support. They purposely stunted the people they trained, while keeping alive the fact that men could handle more powerful spells. He wasn't sure when someone was told the truth about magick, but it was likely after one had attained the rank of Magister—and even then probably only after they had proved their loyalty to Vilwan.

But when Chytrine made her first drive south a quarter century earlier, the Vilwanese leaders realized they'd made a mistake. They had no one who could counter her abilities, for she had been Kirûn's apprentice. Given a generation's respite, they endeavored to train someone who could rival her in power. While they didn't want to produce someone who could threaten the world the way Kirûn had, only Vilwan could produce someone who could defeat her.

At least that would have been their thinking.

So Vilwan created Kerrigan.

And now they fear what they created.

The implications of that realization sent a shiver through him. Would they hunt him down? They had sent one group after him already. What would they bring once they knew how powerful he truly was?

He shook his head in the darkness and consciously shunted those ideas away. Instead he focused on another thing Rym Ramoch had mentioned: the taint on his magick. Kerrigan had long known that different spells had different sensations. A human spell felt rather crude and angular when compared to the living flow of an elven spell. And urZrethi magick had an evanescent quality. Their magick shifted like smoke and shadows, difficult to grasp, but easy to manipulate and use to foster changes.

Thinking about that led him to two questions. The first actually begged an answer. Because he could identify a spell by its casting, he wondered if there were other characteristics that would allow him to learn more about the spell and its caster. Orla had told him that the wand Wheele had carried had somehow allowed the sorcerer to identify her, and to tailor a spell to kill her. Wheele had even taunted her by saying his master, the *sullanciri* Neskartu, had given him the wand for use against "Vilwan spawn." Wheele's comment suggested that there was an identifiable aspect to the magick cast by someone trained on Vilwan. Moreover, Orla had once implied that elements in a spell could help someone identify the individual spellcaster.

Kerrigan accepted the idea that something in how he cast a spell might allow someone to identify him. It was similar to oration: the same speech given to a hundred different people will sound largely the same, but each speaker would bring something new to it that would allow people to differentiate one speaker from another. Identifying the individual speaker would be more difficult, but with sufficient study and good observation, it could be done.

His acceptance of those ideas brought him to the idea of taint. He fully accepted that magickal items of great power were identifiable. The notion that some of their essence might rub off on those who came in contact with them did not surprise him. Not only had he carried a portion of the DragonCrown, but he had worked magick on it and another fragment, and had actually touched yet a third portion of it. For him to be tainted by that contact did not surprise him, and Rym Ramoch had accepted his explanation for the taint without question.

The more curious idea, however, was that Rym had talked about the taint of Kirûn's spell. Kerrigan knew that when he worked magick he drew energy into himself and used it to make spells work, but he had never dwelt long on where that energy came from. He did know some students had trouble accessing it, but that had never been his problem. In fact, many of his tutors had envied the facility with which he was able to draw power to him and infuse it into his spells.

What if, however . . . and here he sought an analogy that might suffice. If drawing power to him were really akin to mining coal, would it be possible that his hands would remain dirty? Would his hands be stained? Would his nails be black? Moreover, if the very act of casting a particular spell left some trace of it on him, would that mean he would bear that taint? Again, Rym's recognition of Kirûn's magick on him would suggest this was true.

And if that is true... Kerrigan hugged his arms to his chest. If a spell or item could leave a trace on an individual, then couldn't that trace be detected? Such a spell, if attuned to the DragonCrown, for example, might be able to let him fix Chytrine's location, so they could strike at her.

He groaned aloud. "If I weren't such an idiot!" When he had magicked the yellow fragment of the DragonCrown, he'd put a spell into it that would slowly warp Chytrine's views of the world. He wanted it to make her paranoid, so she would think those around her were plotting. At the time he thought it was subtle and a fitting revenge for the death of his mentor.

How much simpler it would have been if he'd just stuck a spell into it that would kill her. Or, barring anything that direct, a more subtle spell that would allow him to locate the fragment of the DragonCrown.

He scrubbed his hands over his face. *There are times when I am too smart for my own good. I am smart, but inexperienced. I don't know enough to be able to do all that I could.*

Kerrigan smiled and thought about Orla. The grey-haired woman had once told him as much. When she said to listen to Crow and Resolute, and to avoid Vilwan, it was because she knew that what Vilwan wanted him to be wasn't going to be what the world needed him to be. He was capable of being more than a dragonel, but like a dragonel he needed to be brought to a target and aimed. Crow and Resolute would do that, since they were intent on one thing: stopping Chytrine.

He sat bolt upright on the straw-filled mattress. Off to his left a spark flashed to life, then arced over to a candle on a shelf. The candle caught, then glowed brightly. More sparks exploded from it and flew around the room, igniting more candles and more until all were merrily ablaze.

The initial spark had come from Rym Ramoch's left index finger, which he had casually flicked toward the candle. The masked thaumaturge drew his finger back into his fist and peered down at Kerrigan. "You have been restless, Adept Reese."

"I've been thinking about things you said."

"As I have about things you told me." The robed wizard steepled his fingers. "This ability to duplicate items out of like items intrigues me. We have no time for a demonstration at the moment, but I shall demand one later. And I wonder how well the duplication works. If I asked you to duplicate an enchanted item, would the enchantment come through completely, or would it fail to work?"

Kerrigan shrugged. "I don't know. I don't believe the fragment of the

DragonCrown that I left behind would be useful in the Crown itself. I didn't seek to understand the magick there, so I cannot believe I made a duplicate that would work."

"A pity, though probably for the best, all things considered." Rym canted his head slightly. "Upon what did you think, Adept?"

"Traces and taints in magick, and why Vilwan is the way it is."

"Quite a lot to think about. Did you come to any conclusions?"

"Things you already know, I think, since you detected the taints on me." The rotund mage shifted a bit and drew his legs in under him. "If I could learn to identify the sort of taint the DragonCrown left on me, I might be able to fashion a spell that could locate that same taint in others or on others. If an item like that leaves footprints, then we might be able to follow them."

"Very good. That would be most useful." Rym nodded solemnly. "We shall start you learning how to do that. Once you can see the taint, however, you have to learn to do something before you can track it."

"What's that?"

"Erase it. If the taint allows you to track others, others might track you because of yours."

Kerrigan frowned. "But the need to erase the taint suggests others can identify it. Wait. I already know you can do that. Are you telling me that others might be hunting me because of it?"

"I do not know if they are or not. The simple fact is this: if you were hunting an animal, you would approach it from downwind, so your spoor would not alert it to your presence. Anyone who has a portion of the DragonCrown could be powerful enough to detect your approach."

The young mage nodded thoughtfully. "Yes, of course."

"Good, a first lesson learned." Rym clapped his gloved hands and Bok appeared at his shoulder. "Bok, a meal for Adept Reese, then warm clothes. We will be going out."

Kerrigan's eyes brightened. "Out?"

The hooded mage nodded solemnly. "Yes, to reunite you with your companions. I have determined to my satisfaction that you are not a threat to the world. With my instruction, however, you will become a threat to Chytrine. The sooner your training begins, the better events will be for us all."

CHAPTER 31

King Scrainwood's announcement had stunned Will. After a moment's re-flection, the transparency of the king's strategy made itself manifest. Will had refused to do Scrainwood's bidding, so Scrainwood found someone who would. *He's a scheming snake who will wriggle after a year and a day in the grave.*

Will had known such people in the Dimandowns, but there it was ex-pected. In the Dim you trusted people only when you could see them, and still you assumed they were plotting against you. There wasn't much to be had in the Dim in terms of wealth or power, but folks were still greedy no matter what.

Greed, it struck Will, was a universal vice. Chytrine clearly was greedy for all the south offered. Scrainwood was greedy for the power that went with controlling the Norrington. Others had their own motives for wanting things done, and nobility seemed no proof against greed.

Will had returned to the Rampant Panther in something of a daze, and news of what had happened had clearly preceded him. While the innkeeper was still respectful, Will had gone from being "my lord" to "sir." When he asked for a mug of steaming wine to warm him, the man told him the price. Will overpaid, then crossed to the fire. He sat closer than anyone else could bear, and did not mind that the heat kept others at bay.

Can it be that I am not *the Norrington?* All he had been through seemed to substantiate his claim. His mother had died in a fire from which he'd been rescued. He'd recovered a piece of Vorquelven treasure. In the mountains of Gyrvirgul he'd been tested and the *sullanciri* that was his father had been drawn to him. Even his grandfather had claimed him. That he was a Norrington was not in question.

His being *the* Norrington, on the other hand, suddenly wasn't so clear. The prophecy was a thing of magick, and just by seeing part of a mural Oracle was painting of her vision of the future, he changed things enough that her vision shifted. Had being bitten changed things? Had Lady Snowflake's healing him changed things?

Before him his father, Bosleigh Norrington, had been believed to be *the* Norrington. Resolute had even warned him that he might not be the person named in the prophecy—that lot might fall to one of his children. Could it be that the mantle was shifting, and might land on someone else's shoulders?

He didn't think so, but the hint of doubt plagued him.

Sitting there, drinking the burning liquid, he thought back on all he'd endured. The battles, big and small, against gibberers and pirates, vylaens and dragons. He had almost been slain, twice, by *sullanciri*. He'd seen dragonels and draconettes. He'd been to Gyrvirgul and seen the Gyrkyme at home. He'd been to Okrannel and Wruona and Loquellyn. He'd been to Fortress Draconis and fought on the long retreat. He'd done so many things in the name of the prophecy, and now it was all a mistake?

It can't be. He started to growl, but the scars on his neck hurt. *I can't let Scrainwood's games make me doubt the truth.*

"I must speak with you, Will Norrington."

The thief looked up slowly. Princess Sayce stood there, the heat steaming snow off her cloak and boots.

"I need your help."

Will frowned. "Didn't you hear King Scrainwood? I'm not the Norrington. I'm not the one you're looking for."

"Ha!" She snorted and drew a crude chair from a table, then sat in it, with the chair's back against her chest. "Do you think I'm so feebleminded that such a denial could drive me off?"

Something in her voice, something in the way she offered that challenge, stopped Will from snapping off a smart remark. He would have preferred to be left alone but, at the same time, he didn't want her to go away. He needed time to get himself back under control or he needed perspective to look at his situation anew. Since she'd not grant him the former, he'd look to her for the latter.

He leaned forward, keeping his hands wrapped firmly around the tankard's barrel. "Princess, I am an illiterate thief from Yslin. I can make a rhyme as easy as I can tell you that you have no more than twenty gold crowns in your purse. I know you rode a long way to come find the Norrington and bring him north to save your nation. No one who is feebleminded could or would do that."

She nodded and the firelight danced golden highlights over her red mask. "Then you know I don't care about the games King Scrainwood is playing."

"How do you know it is a game?"

"It's obvious." Sayce waved all other possibilities away lightly. "By morning we will have horses and provisions and can be away for Caledo. Gather your friends and we shall be off."

"That is not going to happen."

Her pale blue eyes narrowed. "I thought you understood how important this is to my people."

"I do, but you've got to understand why it's so important that you make the right choice here." Will looked over at her, meeting her stare openly. "You came to get *the* Norrington. King Scrainwood says I'm not it. You say that's nonsense but let's suppose, just for a moment, that things have changed and he's right. For a while my father was the Norrington. Maybe my turn in that role is over. You take me away, and it could be I'm not the one who will save your nation. You didn't come here for just a symbol, you came here for the fulfillment of a prophecy. What if I'm not it?"

His question stopped her for a moment. "You must be, though. Don't you know?"

"It's magick! How am I supposed to know?" Will swept a thick hank of hair back. "It's not like I have a scar on my forehead or some weird birthmark or anything. Just because my father is a henchman for an evil empress doesn't mean I'm a hero. I mean, I know the songs. I know the legends. It's just easier in the legends."

He lifted his chin and pulled at the collar of his jacket to expose the two round scars there. "See these? I got these because a *sullanciri* tried to kill me. Look like burns, don't they? Soon someone is going to start singing about how the burn marks point to the 'washed in fire' part of the prophecy, and the fact that I survived the attack to the 'immortal' part of it."

Sayce started to say something, but Will rose from his chair and looked past her at all the other people in the room before returning his gaze to her. "Look, I know why you came. The prophecy says someone, a hero named Norrington, is going to vanquish Chytrine. That's great, but whoever he is, he isn't going to do it alone. Sure, people want heroes. I'd love to be one, but I can't be the hero for everyone. And while folks are looking at me, they're missing all the others out there.

"Look at you, Princess. You and your men rode all the way here from Caledo in the nastiest winter anyone's seen in almost forever. If that's not heroism, what is? And look at Crow. Since he was of an age to wear a mask, he's fought Chytrine. He's crisscrossed with scars from battles. He's killed *sullanciri*. There's a hero for you. And Resolute and Alexia, they're heroes. Everyone who was at Fortress Draconis was a hero."

Will felt the eyes of the assembled crowd upon him, and certainly no one was speaking save for him. "You know, having a prophecy just means that everyone assumes that someone else will take care of things for them. And that's just wrong.

"Princess, you've ridden a long way to find someone to help you. I wish I could be that person, but I don't know that I am. What I do know is this: hero or not, fated or not, I'd be able to help you more easily if everyone who *could* do something to help *would.*"

Will shrugged and looked down at her. "I know you wanted more. You deserve more. I don't know that I can help you. I will, if I can, but I need to sort some things out. I'm sorry."

He sighed and threaded his way through the crowd. His feet felt leaden as he mounted the stairs and made his way down the hallway to his room. Suddenly exhausted, he tugged his boots off, then slipped into the bed and shivered himself into a restless sleep.

The next morning came late and Will couldn't tell if Resolute had slept in the other half of the bed or not. There was no sign of him, or that he had even been in the room. The thief knew there was a small Vorquelf community in Meredo, and while Resolute seemed to hold most of his countrykin in little more than contempt, he imagined that spending time with them would be more pleasant than with him.

He huddled in bed trying to think of nothing, which he managed fairly well given that he was very cold. He eventually decided that if he remained in bed he would freeze to death, so he pulled on cold boots and made his way down to the common room. There he ordered a hot tankard of mulled cider and went over to sit by the hearth.

Will had only just begun to feel warm when Dranae entered the inn and stamped the snow off his feet. He started up the stairs, but the innkeeper pointed toward the hearth. The big man smiled as he crossed the room. "Good, you are awake."

"What's good about it?"

Dranae shook his head. "Can't have that now, Will. Not now. Not today. Today is too important."

Will's head came up and the cider's steam caressed his throat. "What's special about today?"

"The Norrington pretender has arrived. He's at the palace, with his mother and the king. King Augustus, Queen Carus, and Princess Sayce are there, along with Princess Alexia and Crow. I was sent for you."

Will shrugged. "You don't need me. The lot of you can just take him and finish the fight against Chytrine. I've done a fat lot of good so far."

Dranae crouched and lowered his voice. "I heard reports of what you said in here last night. Do you believe what you said?"

"That I might not be the Norrington?" Will nodded. "You bet."

"Not that, Will, the other part." The massive man's expression contained a bit of bemusement, but more of respect. "You told everyone that they already had heroes; that what would make the war against Chytrine go better was more folks doing what they could."

"Yeah, something like that."

"So, then, if you are *not* the Norrington, are you going to do your part?"

Will tapped one of his scars with two fingers. "I've done my part."

"But Chytrine's not gone yet." Dranae canted his head. "You remember how you found me, Will? Gibberers had made me a captive and I couldn't remember who I was."

"I know."

"So, don't you wonder why I'm here? It's not because I don't know where I belong, because there are plenty of places I could go. I'm here because what you and Crow and Resolute are doing is very important. I may not know who I am, but I know what I am not. And I am not someone who is going to lie down and cower before some ice queen from the north."

The thief glanced down in his tankard. "But you could die."

"Better that than living a slave, or letting others become enslaved." Dranae stood back up again. "Come on, Will."

Though reluctant to leave the hearth and its warmth, Will bundled himself up against the cold. He tied his formal mask to his upper right arm and even donned a lacy courtesy mask though it did nothing to protect him from the cold. Then he followed Dranae to the palace, using the big man as a windbreak. He would have resisted Dranae's entreaty to accompany him, but the man's referring to the new Norrington as the "pretender" had kindled Will's desire to see him.

They arrived at the palace quickly enough and made their way to the throne room. As big as it was, there was no way it could be warmed enough to suit Will. More important, tension filled the air. Princess Alexia and Crow stood near the windows in close conversation with King Augustus. All three of them wore thick winter clothes more suited to utility than fashion. Princess Sayce hung back from them a bit, but had abandoned her riding leathers for something a bit warmer.

Across the room from them, Queen Carus looked beautiful as always, though Will suspected she had spent a sleepless night. She spoke politely to Linchmere and he nodded, though he looked as if his mind were suffering from frostbite. With them stood an old woman with so cold an expression that Will found it painful to look at her. He dimly recalled her being Princess Alexia's ancient aunt.

In the center of the room, however, was the tableau that he had been brought in to witness. King Scrainwood stood talking to a tall, handsome woman with white-blonde hair and eyes as pale as Princess Sayce's. Between them was a tall, clean-limbed man wearing a green leather mask. He had the thin line of a beard running about his jaw, so Will guessed he was old enough to legitimately be wearing a mask.

Scrainwood let a smile slither onto his face. "Ah, Will, there you are. Please, meet your father's wife, Lady Nolda Norrington. This is your half brother, your *elder* half brother, Kenleigh Norrington. He is, obviously, *the* Norrington."

Kenleigh smiled down at Will as the thief approached. The man's big brown eyes watched him closely and his left hand moved to cover his purse. The clothes he wore were quite stylish, but Will had learned enough about fine clothes to realize these had likely been taken from Linchmere's wardrobe, since they did not quite fit correctly.

Will's gaze flicked up to meet Kenleigh's, and he was surprised to see the man flinch because Kenleigh had to have five inches and forty pounds on him. Will looked at Kenleigh's hands and saw how rough they were, and scarred. They weren't the hands of a noble or even a warrior.

They were the hands of a farmer.

A chill that ran bone deep shook Will, and he looked up at King Scrainwood. "I know why you are doing this. I've defied you. You hate me. Fine. I have to ask, though, do you realize what you are going to do to Kenleigh?"

Kenleigh spoke up in a soft voice. "I'm not afraid."

"No?" Will looked up at him. "I bet you're not. And you know why? Because you're a good man. You believe in hard work and honesty, right? And you're here because the king sent for you and your mother and told you that you have a duty to your nation?"

His half brother nodded solemnly. "The prophecy calls, and I am here to do what must be done."

"Of course you are." Will sighed. "The problem is that those things that need to be done might just be beyond you."

Scrainwood hissed. "Some gutterkin telling an Oriosan noble that he is inferior?"

"Inferior? No. He's just too nice." Will shook his head, then looked up at Scrainwood. "If you were a coin with your eyes put out, you couldn't be more blind, could you? Let me suppose some things. Once my father went over to

Chytrine, you confiscated the Norrington holdings and wanted to forget the family and the prophecy. My father's wife and her sons were reduced to poverty. You couldn't punish Norringtons, so you punished these people. And when I was brought forward as being *the* Norrington of prophecy, suddenly you wanted me to be *your* Norrington. You gave me a mask, the lands that should have belonged to them, and you wanted me to be your pet."

The thief glanced up at Lady Nolda. "You'd always clung to the idea of the prophecy as a way to redeem your life and you assumed one of your boys would be *the* Norrington. You remained ignored until a week ago, when you were sent for because I would not do King Scrainwood's bidding. He promised you your lands again if your son would be the Norrington."

The woman raised her chin imperiously. "It is for the good of the nation."

Will scrubbed a hand over his face. "No. It's good for you. It's also insane."

Will's voice rose. Yes, he was angry with Scrainwood for being a greedy manipulative toad, but he was also angry with everyone else for not seeing what Princess Sayce had said: that they were wasting time. Every moment that was not spent fighting against Chytrine only allowed her to grow stronger.

Most of all, though, he was angry with himself. Deep down inside, when Scrainwood had announced that there was another Norrington, Will had felt happy. The burden that had been thrust upon him had been lifted. He was free. He'd had enough adventures to be drinking off them forever. He might have not killed any *sullanciri,* but he'd survived their attacks. He'd done countless things that would satisfy a lifetime's desire for adventure.

The problem was, of course, that those things were not enough. Chytrine was still out there. He had to do more, and what he had to do wasn't going to be pretty, and a lot of folks would die—including folks who never should have been involved.

Starting with Kenleigh.

Will looked past him to his mother. "You want lands and titles? Before I leave Meredo I will sign over to you all the Norrington lands. They're yours."

Lady Nolda's eyes half lidded with contempt. "They are already my son's."

"Not for long. The king will only let you keep them if your son proves to be the Norrington."

"He is."

"Trust me, Lady Nolda. Your son may be brave and kind and considerate and a hard worker, and he may love you more than he loves his country, but *the* Norrington he's not."

Kenleigh reached out and settled his left hand on Will's right shoulder. "I know who I am."

Will's body tensed. In the blink of an eye he could have plucked the hand from his shoulder, then rotated beneath it, twisting the arm around. A quick wrench and a kick to the back of Kenleigh's left knee, and the man would have been driven to the floor. Then the thief sighed and let his body relax. He didn't need to resort to physical violence.

"Kenleigh, I know who you are, too, and that's why I know you're not the Norrington. If you were, you'd kiss your mother good-bye right now, because you'll never see her again. I don't know how they'll do it, but they'll kill her. Ask the king; he knows. Can you imagine it, Kenleigh, standing here, with your mother's head new-plucked from her body and placed in your hands? Can you see her expression as she stares up at you? Can you feel her blood seeping between your fingers?"

As Will spoke, Scrainwood's face drained of color. "How dare you!"

Will pointed his left index finger at Scrainwood. "Going to hit me again? I dare because you are a coward."

Stars exploded before Will's eyes and he suddenly found himself sitting on the ground. He looked up at Kenleigh and saw Dranae restraining his half brother. Will blinked; his left eye was already beginning to swell shut. And Kenleigh's angry expression had already begun to melt into one of horror at what he had done.

"Nice punch." Will drew himself to his feet carefully, but still staggered back a step. He shook his head again, then snorted a spray of blood. "Really, nice punch."

"I'm sorry."

"So am I." The thief wiped his nose, then flicked the blood on the ground. "You see, King Scrainwood? I insult you, but you don't dare hit me now. Your son didn't dare hit me. It took one of your countrymen to do it. If you were worthy of such loyalty from stouthearted men, Oriosa would be a bulwark against Chytrine. Oriosa is *not* because you *are* a coward and fool."

He looked back over at his half brother. "And you didn't hit me just for what I said about the king, did you? You hit me because you didn't want your mother to die. You love her and your country so much that you'd become the Norrington if she and the king told you to. And when you learned that she'd die because of it, you were torn, right?"

Kenleigh glanced down, not meeting his gaze.

"Well, here is the thing of it." Will wiped a bloody smear on his sleeve. "I don't know if I'm really the Norrington or not, but Chytrine and her *sullanciri* seem to think I am. They've killed my friends because of it. They've tried to kill me. So, until we can convince her different, I'm the Norrington."

He walked over to Kenleigh and patted the man on the shoulder. "You're a good man, too good for this business. Use the lands well and wisely. Lands and titles don't make me the Norrington, and they'll be in good hands with you."

Scrainwood hissed. "You're not the Norrington, whoreget, unless *I* say you are."

The thief shook his head. "But you have, Highness, time after time. Your denials of it now aren't going to be taken seriously, especially outside Oriosa, which is where I'm planning on being as fast as possible."

"You'll never set foot in my nation again."

"Now, *there* is a prophecy I'll guarantee will come true." Will turned and looked at Crow. "I can't imagine why you'd want to be stuck in Oriosa for one moment longer. Princess Sayce says she has horses and supplies, and needs some heroes. I don't expect fighting for Muroso will pay much, but you're fresh out of gaol and any job should be welcome."

Crow laughed lightly. "I'll bear that in mind."

"Good, and bring the wife."

Will looked away before Alexia's surprised expression had fully formed. He reached up and tore off the lacy courtesy mask, then wiped his nose on it before tossing it at Scrainwood's feet. "In the future, all they're going to re-member is that Chytrine was stopped by an Oriosan. You, King Scrainwood, won't be mentioned at all."

CHAPTER 32

Alyx's shock at Will's comment to Crow had not yet worn off as she and Crow had led the way from the palace—with Will, Dranae, and Princess Sayce bringing up the rear. They moved easily through the streets, though Alexia found herself casting eyes back toward the palace. She half suspected Scrainwood would send troops after them, and she did not much like the fact that her great-grandaunt had remained behind.

The journey to the Rampant Panther did not take that long, but before they entered, Alexia stopped, turned, and rested her hands on Will's shoulders. "A word with you, please."

He looked up, his grey eyes wide. "I meant no disrespect, Highness. I was just angry and kind of flailing about, trying to surprise folks. I mean, I know the truth, and I'm sorry."

She shook her head. "Will, that did surprise me, but that's okay. You had your back to her, but that shot took my great-grandaunt right between the eyes. Thank you. However, that's not what I wanted to talk to you about."

Crow cleared his throat. "Dranae, perhaps you'd stand me to a mug of mulled wine?"

"Wait." Alexia looked back at him, and then at the other two. "You don't need to go, because I'll freely say this in front of you or as many others as can hear. What you did back there, Will, was probably the most ill-considered, irrational, and impulsive thing you could have done. It was dangerous, and before this is all over, it could well be the death of you."

The thief slowly nodded and glanced down at the slush. "I know."

Alexia reached out and tipped his face up with a finger. "That's why it's also one of the bravest things. It was a *heroic* act."

He frowned. "How do you figure that?"

The princess smiled. "You saved a life in there. Kenleigh Norrington isn't the fated one. You read him right: he is stout of heart and limb, loves his mother and his country, and would obey her without question. In this battle, though, it's *not* enough. While he would do everything he was told to do, Chytrine would gobble him up and spit out bleached bones. In backing him down, you saved his life.

"And that's the essence of heroism, isn't it? Every one of us does all we can to avoid death. But a hero knows there are some people who can't protect themselves, so he steps in to protect them."

Will grinned. "Or *she* steps in."

"Thank you, sir." Alexia smiled. "The other thing about being a hero, Will, is that it's not birth makes you one. If it were, Scrainwood would be a hero. So would Kenleigh. Being a hero is something you learn, but it's mostly something you accept. Back there you acknowledged that being the Norrington is quite a responsibility, and you accepted that responsibility for yourself. That took a lot of courage. So, whether we're riding north to Caldeo or south or east or west, I'll be proud to ride with you."

The thief blinked for a moment, then snorted a laugh. "Me? Responsible? Who would have thunk it?"

Crow smiled and slapped him on the shoulder. "A fitting attribute for the King of the Dimandowns, don't you think?"

"I guess." Will shifted his shoulders and Alexia felt a shiver run through him. "Thank you, Princess."

"You're welcome, Will." She straightened up, then slid her left hand to the small of his back. "Now, get in there and warm yourself. Dranae and Princess Sayce, you, too. Order whatever you want and have it put on my account. Crow, I would have a word in private with you."

Dranae nodded and guided the other two into the building.

Crow looked at her. "Yes?"

"Upstairs, in my room, please."

He nodded his assent, so she led the way up the stairs to her room. Crow slipped in past her and she closed the door. He turned the wick up on the table lamp. She pointed him to the chairs by the window as she squatted at the edge of the bed and reached under the straw mattress.

"I believe this is yours." She pulled out a long, slender, cloth-wrapped package and slid it across the blanket to him. "I got it from Resolute and had to tell the Oriosans that you'd given it to me as a wedding gift to stop them from confiscating it."

Crow smiled as he unwrapped the sword. "Fitting it should be yours. You've made better use of it than I. You slew a *sullanciri* with it."

"*We* did that."

He nodded and slid the blade from the ancient, scarred scabbard. Though the scabbard and belt had seen better days, the sword looked as if it had just come from the forge. The long, straight blade had two edges and a thickened forte. In that reinforced area had been set an opalescent gem. It was shaped like a keystone, and that design had been echoed in the brass cross hilt decorations and the pommel cap. Stained leather wrapped the hilt and Crow's fingers caressed it lovingly.

She watched him, and something tightened around her heart. He concentrated on the blade, and the shifting fire in the gem flashed little rainbow lights over his face. His eyes grew distant, and she knew well that the simple weight of the blade—the feel of the leather and the cool metal of blade and pommel—could summon up hundreds, even thousands, of memories. She had no idea how much blood it had spilled, how many desperate cuts it had turned, how many gibberers it had cloven and vylaens spitted. Somehow, though, she was certain that Crow remembered only the faces of those he saved and, more sharply, the faces of those he could not.

The lines of that face, the hollows—the way that one lock of white hair fell across his forehead, crossing the scar that started there, then worked down his right cheek—all pleased her eye mightily. She wanted to reach out to brush that lock back into place, not because it needed to be cleared from his face, but because she wanted to touch it, to feel it between her fingers, and then her fingers deep in his hair.

"Princess?" Crow looked at her. "Is there something wrong?"

Alexia blinked, then shook her head and stood. "No, nothing wrong." She refrained from pressing her hands to her stomach to stop the fluttering there. "I, ah, just wanted to be sure that you had Tsamoc back as we rode north."

Crow nodded. "Thank you. You know that this stone is from the Radooya Bridge? We destroyed the bridge before we came to Svarskya. Actually, the bridge's *weirun* destroyed the bridge for us. This stone is all that is left of him. His name was Tsamoc. Once he removed this gem from his chest, he came apart, and so did the bridge.

"A friend of mine, Naysmith Carver, made Tsamoc and gave the sword to me. It saved me in Boragul and after, running from Chytrine's hunters, and countless times since." He resheathed the blade. "Tsamoc asked Nay to let him help destroy Chytrine. I've been doing all I can to help him since."

"And you've done very well."

"Thank you." Crow set the sword on the bed, then looked up at her. "And I owe you an apology."

"For what?"

"For spurning your effort to save my life. Scrainwood would have had me killed had you not come up with this solution." Crow twisted the gold band on his left ring finger. "For years I'd all but forgotten the sentence of death. Compared to how badly Chytrine wanted me dead, and then the trouble locating Will, it just seemed unimportant. I avoided Oriosa, grew this beard for a disguise, became Resolute's aide, and spent most of my time off in the middle of nowhere killing Aurolani troops. The Vorquelves knew who I was—many of them anyway—but they didn't care.

"When I was found out, the sentence crashed back down on me and..." He hesitated, then frowned and fell silent.

Alyx slipped forward and knelt on the bed. "What? Don't be afraid..." The seconds the words were out of her mouth, she realized her mistake. "Forgive me, I didn't mean to intrude."

"No, no, it's fine." His eyes flicked up. "I gave up. They had me, and I realized I was tired. Tired of all of it."

"But, Crow, you *were* tired. Your leg was broken and you didn't let Kerrigan heal it and we had been riding hard for days, of course you were tired. And then they beat you and left you naked and cold down there in that root cellar and..."

"Shhhhhh, Princess, please." Crow sighed. "All you say is true, but none of it mitigates the fact that I wanted to quit. And I would have given up, save for one thing."

He slid the ring off his finger and tossed it between her knees. "This. The elaborate measures you went to in getting it on my finger. You could have just broken me out of Tolsin. We could have been on the run, but you chose another route."

"You were the one who pointed out that running would have been difficult."

"Yes, but your action reminded me that this war with Chytrine is more than just a personal thing. Princess Sayce is right—time was wasted here, but good things did happen. There isn't a war between Oriosa and Alcida. You're not an outlaw, which might cause some countries to reconsider their support of the Okrannel campaign. This *was* the right way to do things, though what happened is hardly what we anticipated."

Alexia picked the ring up and flicked it back and forth against her thumb and index finger. "It was something you would have seen, given time, a lack of beatings, and rest."

"Perhaps." He smiled. "But now I don't feel tired anymore. I am ready to ride north, to deal with Chytrine and her people. You gave me the chance to catch my breath, and for that, I can't repay you."

"Sure you can." She tossed him the ring. "Keep wearing this."

"Princess, this charade..." His voice shrank painfully.

"Crow, listen to me. We are friends. I wish for you to have that ring." She listened to herself and found that what she was saying didn't come easily. The words were describing the truth, or at least a portion of it. *A fragment of it.*

"I dare not, Princess."

She arched an eyebrow at him. "Why not?"

"This ring, the way Kerrigan made it has all the same links as it would if we were married. If I fall..."

"I would know?"

"Probably not."

She felt a tightness in her stomach. *I would know.*

"If I fall, and war *is* a younger man's game, someone could take this ring and use the magick to trace it back to you. They could find you and attack you because I had failed."

A coldness pooled in her belly, then bled into her voice. "And the reverse would be true?"

"Yes, they could find me using your ring." Crow gave her a smile. "The chances of you falling, however, are remote."

"You mistake my question, Crow." Alexia shook her head. "If you fall, my ring would still be linked to yours. With magick, I could find the one who took it from you. I could hunt them."

He looked at her for a moment, then nodded and swallowed. His voice still came hoarse. "Yes. And I would do the same."

She stretched out, leaning forward on one hand, so she could close her other over both his hand and the ring. "Then keep it. Wear it. This is what I want."

"Yes."

Alexia raised her face to his and brushed her lips over his. That brief caress, barely felt, sent a thrill through her. It wasn't until that moment that she knew she'd intended to kiss him, and wanted to do so again.

Crow pulled back, his lips parted, his right hand coming up to caress her left cheek. "Highness..."

"Shhhhh, no talking." She rubbed her cheek against his palm, then turned her head and kissed it. Her violet eyes looked up. "Tonight I want, I *need,* to be held by you. I need your strength, your warmth. I need *you.*"

"Princess..."

"I said 'no talking.'" She smiled and kissed him again, properly this time. "The consort of an Okrans Princess would never think of contradicting her."

Crow wordlessly caressed her left cheek, then sank his fingers into her hair and pulled her mouth to his for a deeper kiss. Their tongues tangled, caressed, and explored.

Alexia broke the kiss reluctantly, but continued to smile as she pulled back to look up into his eyes. "Now, my consort, join me in my bed. Many nights I have been denied the comforts of my husband's arms and I desire greatly to make up for that lost time."

CHAPTER 33

King Scrainwood sat on his throne, watching Cabot Marsham lead Lady Norrington and her insipid son away to their chambers. *Good-hearted, nice, loyal.* Scrainwood found Kenleigh only slightly more tolerable than the sycophantic Marsham, but Marsham was so much more useful.

Scrainwood would house the visitors from Valsina for several days while he considered whether or not he would actually grant them the lands he'd given to the whoreget thief. The legalities of the whole thing mattered not to him. There were legalities and regalities, and he'd always found the latter took precedence.

"You might as well grant them the lands, Highness." Tatyana stepped from Linchmere's shadow. "The boy will be grateful, and his mother might well warm your bed tonight."

"If you read my thoughts so easily, you truly are the witch they say you are." Scrainwood snorted and looked at his son. "You may leave us. None of this will interest you."

Tatyana grabbed hold of Linchmere's sleeve as he started to retreat. "Highness, he should hear. There will come a day when he needs to know what passes between us."

The King of Oriosa looked over at his second son. The man's bovine brown eyes displayed little comprehension. He recalled when his boy had been keen and bright-eyed, eager to learn—a happy, laughing child. *Then his mother drowned and life drained from him.* "Very well, Linchmere. Stay. Learn. Say nothing, now or ever."

His son, silently and unceremoniously, plunked himself down on the floor and picked at the lacings on his shoes.

Tatyana moved forward, momentarily eclipsing the prince, then stepped onto the carpet and turned to face the king. "I have, of course, no more love for what has transpired here than you. The subversion of justice that resulted in Crow's release is only made palatable by the fact that the treason charges can later be reinstated and he can be detained at any time. That was very clever."

Scrainwood bowed his head. "I am not without resources when it comes to dealing with legalities, Grand Duchess."

"I see that, Highness." Her cold eyes glittered. "I would suppose that your use of this stratagem was in response to pressure placed upon you? Augustus threatened invasion? A regency for your son?"

The king shivered with recollection of the confrontation. "I won certain other concessions."

"Yes?"

"Indeed."

She looked at him intently, as if her blue eyes could compel him to tell her of the fragment of the DragonCrown now housed in the vaults of his palace.

He snorted. "No, Grand Duchess, nothing that should concern you, nor will it. Suffice it to say, Alcidese troops will not bespoil my lands. If Augustus' troops are to head north, they will do so by ship or a long march through Saporicia."

Tatyana laughed, then turned to look at Linchmere. "Learn from your father, for he is a master at playing both ends against the middle. Chytrine leaves him his nation because he has harbored her troops and allowed them some passage south. Augustus does not attack because of the fearful toll you Oriosans would take on his people. Were either to overstep the bounds of his agreements with them, he would turn to the other for succor. Well played, this game will retain his realm for him, and for you or your children."

Linchmere looked up, his mouth open and jaw slackened at her words.

Scrainwood put an edge in his voice. "Grand Duchess, speak to *me*. You freely accuse me of treason against the Southlands, but would not any other action consist of treason against my own nation? The news from Muroso is grim. Sebcia has fallen. Chytrine will have troops roaming into Sarengul, with Alosa and Nybal marshaling their forces on their mountain borders. She pours into Muroso. From there she has a choice, Oriosa or Saporicia, and I much prefer her fighting to the west than turning my nation into a long corridor to Alcida."

The grand duchess turned back toward him. A smile curved her lips but never escaped to infect the rest of her face. "Your grasp of strategy is laudable, Highness. So, the question becomes, then, if you will move your troops north, to Valsina, then drive west to choke off Aurolani supply lines. A sharp stroke north and west would close the Sebcian border, leaving Alcidese, Saporician, and Loquelven troops to crush her host against the anvil of your troops and Bokagul."

"Ha! And leave my troops caught between her retreating forces and the reinforcements streaming down from the north?" Scrainwood stood and shook his head. "I am not a fool, woman. I thought we had established that. What you suggest is the task to which heroes aspire. I have no such aspiration."

"I would do it, Father."

"What?" Scrainwood looked down at his son. "You would do what?"

"I would lead our troops to smash the Northern Empress." His dark eyes brightened. "We have very good troops, Father. We could march north and have them poised, just as she said."

"Have you heard nothing *I* said, Linchmere?" Scrainwood threw his arms wide. "There you are, intent on covering yourself with glory, without thinking for a moment of your nation. You want to be a hero? I have known heroes."

He looked at Tatyana. "I remember your grandnephew, Kirill. I remember him being a hero, and a grand one he was. He fought so hard, and he wept when we fired Svarskya. And he fought hard at Fortress Draconis, but what did it get him? He was slain; in an instant he was smashed against a wall.

"Is that what you want, my son? Do you want some divot in a wall somewhere to run with your blood? Do you want your mask, gore-soaked and stained with your brains, brought to me by ragged refugees fleeing the horde Chytrine would send to punish me? Because that would be how I remembered you as Chytrine's creatures hunted me. And all this just so you can be a hero?"

Linchmere looked down. "But Erlestoke is loved."

"Erlestoke is *dead*!" The king snarled, balling his right fist and slamming it against his thigh. "Have you come to gloat over that, witch? The alliance you offered, marrying your Alexia off to my Erlestoke, now cannot be. Even if she were not maintaining this fraud of a marriage to Crow, would she take Linchmere here? Of course not. Have you any minor nobles who would take him? No, they would not. So, the future of my nation is doomed, but I choose not to hasten its death with some futile act of heroism."

Linchmere lifted his chin. "How do you know it would be futile, Father? Our troops are good."

"Yes, of course they are good, son, very good." Scrainwood shook his head. "You are letting that little thief's words get into your mind, but he knew nothing. Less than nothing, in fact. How good our people are has no significance. Chytrine has dragonels. You have seen such things at Fortress

Draconis, I know you have. When you were younger they might have delighted you, but now you must know what they do. It is more than bowling a rock through ranks of lead soldiers. They tear people apart."

In an instant Scrainwood found the past merging with the present. Again he stood in the throne room, but the *old* throne room, the one he had changed so he could forget. He stood there, his mother's head in his hands. Her eyes stared up at him, her lips still working, as her blood dripped through his fingers. He tried to read her lips, wanting to know what her last words for him were, but he could not make them out.

He opened his hands and watched her head fall away. Her expression screwed up into one of pure rage, then her head hit the marble floor. It exploded as if it were rotten fruit. He leaped back, surprised that he could only hear the sound of his boots scraping on stone.

Tatyana looked up matter-of-factly, neither concern nor curiosity on her face. "What is it, Highness?"

"Probably your doing, witch." Scrainwood wiped his hands on his tunic, then glanced down at his son. "Leave us, now."

The boy—*what am I thinking, he is a man, has long been a man*—stood. "Father, I have never asked you for anything but this. Let me lead our troops..."

"Ha!" The king curled a lip back in disgust. "That fool of a Norrington might think Oriosans noble and kind, and the sort to soften at such a heartfelt appeal. In some faery tale, son, I would grant you your request. You would be victorious, then would return here and I would bless you for your efforts, but that is a fancy, Linchmere. You will lead no Oriosan troops. I will never grant you that leave. In fact, I expressly forbid it. Now, go!"

The prince stalked from the room, disappearing behind the folds of the mask-curtain. Tatyana watched him leave, then turned back to Scrainwood. "This is your course, then, to balance on the edge of a knife until circumstances force you to choose one side or the other?"

"There is no other course open to me, and you know that. I cannot stand alone against Chytrine. If she threatens to come into Oriosa, then we shall be overrun from the south and east. If I ally with her, the same thing will happen from the other direction." The king mounted the steps to his throne again and seated himself. "It is a sore position in which I am placed."

"It is a dangerous game you play, but one I understand." Tatyana's eyes tightened. "If you ally with Chytrine, Okrannel will hate you."

"Another burden. You have no nation, and what few troops you have raised are back in your homeland fighting beneath a Jeranese general. The hatred of your nation will sting me, but I will endure it." He paused. "Have you something to offer me, or shall I bare my back so you may scourge me as you will?"

"I offer you, once again, Okrannel's hand in friendship, Highness. I offer you a plan."

"Yes, and that would be?"

"Okrannel and Oriosa are held in pity and contempt. The Okrans people are the human Vorquelves, yet we are regaining our homeland with the help of others. We will be under an obligation to show our strength and our gratitude. What I propose is simple, and requires nothing but staying on your present course."

Scrainwood raised an eyebrow beneath his mask. "I am listening."

"The further south Chytrine drives, the longer her lines of supply. The situation you have seen is true; a deft strike will cut her troops off and let them wither to the south. But her successful campaign will demand more and more troops, which will leave her fewer and fewer with which to defend Okrannel. Once my homeland is free, my warriors will come here to Oriosa. Together our troops will strike, with my Alexia at their head. Together our nations shall destroy the Aurolani host."

"You suppose many things, Grand Duchess. There are many *ifs* before a *then* in your plan."

The old woman shook her head. "No, no, this is not supposition at all. Alexia herself will guarantee it. When she undertook her dream raid in Okrannel, she dreamed well. She dreamed of a series of battles that she would lead, in Saporicia and Muroso. They all led to a grand battle in which Chytrine's forces were crushed. She was exalted above all commanders, and glory was showered upon her and her nation."

The light flashing in Tatyana's eyes did surprise Scrainwood, for none of that animation made it to the leathery flesh of her face. He could tell that she fervently believed in the dreams, and the strength of that belief played into her voice. Her words almost made him believe himself.

"I fail to hear how Oriosa benefits, Grand Duchess."

Tatyana's eyes resumed their usual cold blue fire. "Her allies are lauded as well, Highness, and her dreams tell of bold masked troops intervening at a crucial point in the battle. Your troops, Highness, clearly."

Scrainwood thought for a moment, then snorted. "This is the new game, then? We have a Vork prophecy that starts everything, and now the dream of some Okrans princess will end it? And what lies between fantasy and dream?"

"Nightmares, Highness; horrible nightmares." Tatyana smiled thinly. "But there is always winter before spring, dark before dawn. Join with me, and the dawn shall be as bright as it can be."

Dawn. When we execute those who would play at treason. The King of Oriosa slowly nodded. "Through nightmares then, to awake again at dawn."

CHAPTER 34

With the thunder of the discharging quadnels echoing loudly, Erlestoke leaped through the smoke and fire. The sword had drained the world of color again, so that the crawl to his left had black ink splashing from two hideous quadnel wounds, not red blood. It heightened other perceptions. A vylaen fell back with half its skull blown off. The grey fluid spattering those behind soaked torpidly into their fur.

The first of the gibberers bearing the heavy crate his squad had come to steal looked up. Surprise registered starkly on its face; Erlestoke's saber slashed through that dumbfounded expression. As that gibberer reeled away and his corner of the ironbound oak case dipped toward the ground, Erlestoke's saber came up and around, then down, cleaving cleanly through the arm of another gibberer. It howled piteously and stumbled away, clutching the pulsing stump to its chest. The front of the case slammed into the ground, though two other gibberkin still held up the back end.

The Oriosan Prince leaped forward again, planting both feet on the case. The added weight bent the other two gibberers. The saber whistled down, opening the one on the right from mid-spine to crown. The other made to draw its longknife, but a quadnel shot blasted heavily into its chest, knocking it backward.

Erlestoke stepped lightly forward, as if he were at a ball. He could feel the saber's pernicious influence in the way he moved and what he was thinking. He had a mission, which was to steal the item in that case, and that was far more important than his life—or any life. The mission was as foolhardy as it was desperate, but it was even more vital.

Through the smoke, one of the cloaked figures came toward him. Up close it looked much bigger than it had before and, to complicate matters, the saber's magick appeared to be muted in its presence.

Doesn't matter. I was a warrior long before I had an enchanted sword.

The creature came on swiftly, not running, but with long strides that ate up ground. Behind it came a cadre of crawls, gibberers, and even a few vylaens. The human prisoners who had worked on the dig held back. Chained together, they could have done nothing anyway—though Erlestoke decided their reluctance to join in was more than just a practical consideration.

The prince closed with the cloaked figure and realized almost too late that it had to be nearly ten feet tall. He slashed at it crossways, looking to open its belly, but its left hand came out and down, sweeping from beneath the cloak. Erlestoke caught a hint of some sort of scaled armor on the forearm and expected the blade to shear through it.

To his surprise, it did not.

The creature's left arm came around and over, then its long-fingered hand closed over the saber's forte. With a single tug, the cloaked figure ripped the blade from his hand—so swiftly that Erlestoke's glove came with it. Then the creature's right hand emerged from the cloak and slammed an open-palm blow square into Erlestoke's chest.

A hideous crack rippled through him and the prince flew backward, landing heavily on Jullagh-tse as she dragged the case away. She went down hard and the case slewed around. She shoved Erlestoke from her, her clawed feet scrabbling for traction.

Erlestoke rolled forward and flopped on his back. His chest ached with each breath, and only keeping them shallow prevented the pain from spiking. He got his elbows under him and started to lever himself up, but his ribs cracked again, forcing him to gasp.

Behind him he heard the urZrethi. "Prize is clear."

The cloaked creature loomed large and larger.

"Go, go, go!" Erlestoke tried to shout, but only the first word had any volume. Digging his heels in, he tried to drag himself backward, but he could not escape the thing coming for him.

Both of its arms came up, opening the cloak to reveal a leathery scale armor that reminded him, vaguely, of a Panqui's armored flesh. Gold glinted in streaks and speckles on the green scale armor as it towered over him. Sharp horny knobs and spurs sprouted on the forearms and elbows. Clawed fingers rose to rake terrible hooked talons down through him.

Four quadnels spoke as one. Before the smoke hid the creature, Erlestoke saw one of the balls hit its broad chest and bounce away. Of the other shots he could not see what hit where, but the figure did stagger backward. The prince heard a mighty hiss and the thump of heavy footfalls.

Erlestoke rolled onto his stomach and heaved himself up, but his left foot lost traction and he crashed down again. His left shoulder hit the ground, jolting more pain through him. He cried out, then looked up at Ryswin, standing there, his silverwood bow drawn. "Go!"

The elf shook his head. "Hurry."

Erlestoke clawed at the icy ground and lunged forward just as the elf released the arrow. Behind him came a gurgle, then an angry roar that faded into a hiss. As Ryswin grabbed his left shoulder and hauled him upright, the prince hazarded a glance backward.

One of the quadnel shots must have shattered the cloak's clasp, for the creature had come through the thinning smoke naked. The armor Erlestoke had seen had not been clothing but flesh, and the hood had hidden a hideous head with spikes and horns. The face appeared almost human, though devoid of hair and covered in scales—save that a muzzle began to jut forward, and the lipless mouth displayed the lethal curve of ivory fangs.

The elf's arrow protruded from the creature's mouth. It coughed and grasped the arrow as crawls and vylaens came to its aid. Erlestoke saw nothing more as the elf bodily dragged him into the small passage they'd discovered, and down between rough-hewn walls to sanctuary.

Erlestoke gasped with pain. "Slow, I can't run. My ribs."

"We have to, Highness." The elf glanced up along their back trail. "We haven't stopped it, just made it angry."

"You know what it was?"

"Not for certain, no, but you recall my telling you about the *kryalniri*?"

"Nightmare creatures from long ago, yes."

The elf nodded solemnly. "There are stories, seldom told, of things that used to prey on beasts like the *kryalniri*. They are ancient and fell. The only things older are dragons, and the further we are from it, the happier I'll be."

Goruel knelt on one knee in the snow and spat out the arrow. A little greenish black blood came with it, staining the snow. It had not hurt him as much as it had surprised him. Even the soft flesh of his mouth had not let it penetrate enough to lodge. As he swallowed he could feel a slow trickle of blood running down the back of his throat, but the wound would soon close and the injury would be of no consequence.

One of the *kryalniri* came and knelt before him. "How can this one aid you, Lord-master Goruel?"

Goruel almost snatched the arrow up and drove it through the white-furred beast's lower jaw and into its brain, but the *kryalniri* needn't suffer because of his similarity to the elf. He forced his hands open, then turned the right one over and, curling the fingers inward, inspected his talons. In a whisper he asked, "Why is there no pursuit?"

The creature's eyes widened. "I thought to succor you, Lord-master."

Goruel rose to his feet, towering over the *kryalniri*. It quaked there at his feet, sagging back on its heels. It cast its eyes downward, yet still flinched as the shadow of his upraised right hand passed over it. "Fools who think thus deserve to die."

His right hand fell heavily in a crushing blow to the skull.

The *kryalniri* looked up, grey eyes wide as a vylaen collapsed next to it. "Lord-master?"

Goruel licked blood from his knuckles. "Prove to be more useful a fool than those vermin. Fetch me the sword."

The *kryalniri* scrambled away to do his bidding. Goruel advanced, following the case's track through the snow, right up to the blank stone wall where it ended. He sniffed, then flicked his forked, serpentine tongue against the stone. He closed his eyes and sniffed again.

There was something about Fortress Draconis that he had sensed from his arrival. It had strengthened, slowly, and had become especially concentrated and vexing. He could feel it where they sought the Truestones and in the aftermath of the *araftii* roost's crushing collapse. He had never sensed its like before, which did not cause him fear, but merely whetted his curiosity.

His minion returned with the sword and offered it up on flat palms with head bowed. Goruel took the blade and sniffed it. Delicately his forked tongue came out and he trailed the twin edges over the curved length of enchanted steel. In some places his tongue lingered, in others it returned for another pass.

He could feel the sword's magick and marveled at how insistent it was. It tried to mask his sight. It tried to paint those around him as fearful and, therefore, threats. It even offered advice as to how best it could be employed to destroy them.

He shoved this aside as one might toe away an inquisitive puppy and read more. He was able to taste its recent history. The blade related it to him in stark detail from the point at which it had been first drawn. Every bone cloven, every life taken, all of these came to him as subtly and fully as the nuances of spiced wine. He could feel the last wielder's hand on the blade, and got a strong sense of him. Before him, a woman, and before her, a *sullanciri*.

Goruel slowly nodded. *Malarkex.* That *sullanciri* had been slain in Okrannel, so the blade had traveled far. That it had been created for one of Chytrine's generals told him why the magick was strong enough for him to need to push it away.

Again he licked and found a slender thread of magick he had almost missed. The blade and its scabbard were linked.

Goruel gave the blade back to the *kryalniri*. "Use the seeking magick. The blade will lead to its scabbard, and that will lead to the fragment's thieves. Do it now!"

An unholy light wreathed the *kryalniri*'s hands, then played like lightning over the blade. It skipped and jumped down the curved length, then leaped in a scintillating ball that circled once, then bounced against the wall Goruel had recently examined.

He moved up, back and away as the *kryalniri*'s cry brought gibberers with sledgehammers and pry bars. They pounded on the wall and quickly breached it. A group of them plunged into the darkness beyond it, then howled. Vylaens entered, then the *kryalniri*. The purple ball of light slipped into the hole, then Goruel stooped and passed through its tight confines.

Deep and down they went. Most of the passages forced Goruel to crouch. At various points they ran into blockages, but the hammers and spells made short work of them. The lower they went, the faster blockades fell.

After less than an hour they reached a large amphitheater. The tiers for spectators had been decorated with the stone effigies of a variety of warriors, though these concerned Goruel not at all. He passed swiftly down the stairs and up again to the central platform. At its heart lay a square opening, and another set of steps heading down into darkness. He saw well enough into it, but the stairs ended at a corridor running cast, limiting his view.

He crouched at the platform's edge and picked up the scabbard. It had been nestled safely in a little depression, right there on the platform, which suggested deliberation. *And the only reason for that would be . . .*

The magickal sense he'd had of Fortress Draconis focused and spiked. A vylaen hissed and a gibberer howled, but Goruel did not need to turn his face to know what was happening. In front of him, all along the terraces, stone figures began to move. Slowly at first, as people might move when rising from a long sleep. Steadily, inexorably, they started forward, climbing down toward him.

The stone legion caught the fleeing gibberers easily. The figures could not move quickly, but there were so many that running through a thorny thicket would have been easy by comparison. Some gibberers struggled mightily to pull free, but at the cost of shreds of pelt hanging from clawed fingers.

The *kryalniri* mewed loudly and reached out for him as stone enemies grabbed it. Its claws screeched over the steps, scoring little white lines in the grey stone, then the creature evaporated in a mist of blood and floating wisps of fur.

Goruel retreated, though not in any way hurried or frightful. Behind him, the stairs had melted back into solid stone, leaving the platform a smooth killing arena. He strode to the center of the stone circle, shifted his spiked shoulders, then shook his hands out and cast aside the scabbard.

He roared once, defiantly, at the stone figures that crawled up the steps. Goruel licked the air with anticipation, and caught another hint of the magick pervading the area.

He nodded. "Yes, of course. I know it now and should have seen before. Very well." He waved the stone figures forward. "Do your utmost. Delay me you might, but defeat me, never!"

The heavy weight of the furred robes made Erlestoke's chest ache, but they kept him warm. He followed behind Ryswin, with Jilandessa trailing. She'd offered to heal him, but he'd refused. The spell would have fatigued her, and he could still move well enough.

Jullagh-tse Seegg led the way through tunnels that wound through the earth. They had long since left behind the corridors of the fortress and headed east, but because of the twists and turns they had no way of measuring how far they had come.

The urZrethi came to a place where she shifted her hands into digging tools and clawed her way up toward the surface. She angled the tunnel to make ascent easy, and before long cold air poured down through a hole, and snow quickly followed. The wind's howl could be heard, but not so loudly that they had to shout.

Erlestoke emerged from the hole with Ryswin's help, and clutched the blue-green DragonCrown fragment to his belly. The others climbed out, and the group made a dash fifty yards east to the tree line. Crouched there, leaning against a venerable oak, the prince looked back at Fortress Draconis.

The once-proud fortress had been shattered, and not even the snow could hide the damage. Walls gaped and buildings sagged. Whereas once the fortress would have been ablaze, serving as a beacon to warn Chytrine's troops away, now it lay dim and dark, like a phantom of fog drifting in from the Crescent Sea.

Verum, the weapons-master, knelt beside the prince. "I have my bearings. East for two miles or so, then southeast and we'll reach a storehouse. We can resupply ourselves there. After that, well, that's a decision for you."

Erlestoke nodded. "We have to keep this fragment from Chytrine, so we'll head south, right behind her troops."

"Not to question your judgment, Highness, but wouldn't we want to be going *away* from her troops?"

The prince gave the man a wink. "Oh, we know she'll be tracking us, so it doesn't matter where we run. Head south and we're closer to friends. Somehow, we'll have to hope they reach us before she does."

CHAPTER 35

Too much had been going right. Will growled as the small group came to Meredo's north gate. The day had dawned bright but cold, with a clear sky and small sun that promised no warmth. It was not the best weather in which to start a trip, but not that bad, considering the time of the year. Pushing the horses, they could make the trip in a week to a week and a half.

And the things that had gone right had been considerable. Kerrigan had returned looking a bit worn, with a hideous, half-naked green creature trailing after him. The innkeeper would have protested but for the fact that Vilwanese sorcerers had been looking for him, and the innkeeper had no desire to be turned into a frog or, worse yet, whatever it was the young master had following him.

Kerrigan didn't say much about his absence, other than to say he'd met a powerful sorcerer who was going to help him with a mission that was critical to stopping Chytrine. Bok, the malachite urZrethi male, was a servant on loan, and would accompany them on their travels. His master would catch up with them later.

The magicker did cast some spells to repair Will's blacked eye, then checked over his throat. He listened very intently to the story of Lady Snowflake. He thought for a long time, then gave Will a serious look.

"I don't know who she was or what she did, but it was powerful magick. You're healed, I can tell that. The spells I cast show there is nothing wrong with you, nothing at all."

Will had arched an eyebrow. "That would be good, wouldn't it?"

Kerrigan nodded, then reached out and lifted Will's chin. He turned his head left and right, then frowned. "The only thing wrong is this: those scars should have given me some sense of something wrong. Same with the feeling of cold troubling you. It's not a big problem, after all, since you can get warm, and the scars are not bad, and I sense no magick that would prevent you from being healed, but it is odd."

"Have you ever seen anything like it before?"

"No, and that is what is odd. When I checked Crow and worked on his broken leg, I also could see all the other injuries he'd had, including just getting old. Same thing with Orla. When I healed her from injuries, I repaired some other things. I cleaned up some bits of wear from age, so she wouldn't have those aches and pains. When I cast a diagnostic spell after that, there was *less* wrong with her than before."

Will nodded. "That makes sense. It would be like your spell comparing the injured person against who they would be in top shape and you fixing the differences."

"Exactly. In your case, though, the magick says that even cold and even with those scars, you are the best you can be."

"Could you fix the scars?"

The bed in Kerrigan's room groaned as he shifted his weight. "I could, *if* I could find them. I can see them, of course, but as far as magick is concerned, they don't exist. For me to set things to rights, there has to be a sense of wrongness, and there isn't here. Maybe if the spells that healed you interfered with each other, you could get this sort of mix-up. Maybe. I'm guessing."

Will smiled. "You, guessing?"

"Well, yes."

"And admitting it?"

Kerrigan's expression soured. "I see you've not changed in my absence."

The thief shifted his shoulders uneasily. "Only a little."

The two of them had left Kerrigan's room to join Princess Sayce and Dranae near the fire. There Sayce and Dranae recounted the exchange at the palace for the mage. Though they kept their voices low, Will knew the story would be flying through the streets of Meredo faster than the snow. While he knew that might not be a good thing, Will had put it out of his mind.

Until now.

A company of horsemen waited in the courtyard near the gate. They'd clearly been there for a while and, what was odder yet, each of them had a bare face. Their masks had been tied to their upper right arms, as was Will's.

One man brought his horse forward to bar their path. He had sharp features and dark eyes, which were accentuated by the fact that the flesh which his mask had hidden was noticeably paler. He looked straight at Will, ignoring Crow and Alexia. "You're the Norrington?"

Will nodded wearily and urged his horse forward, leaving Princess Sayce's side. "I am."

"You called the king a coward and said he wasn't worthy of the sort of stouthearted folk we have here?"

"Something like that."

"And in the Rampant Panther you said that we all need to be heroes to fight the Nor'witch?"

Will caught something odd in the man's voice. "Yes, I guess I did."

The man smiled. "Well, then, we're your men. Our ancestors, they took to wearing masks to hide who they were. But that's not serving us too well right now, so we'll be wearing our masks as you do, and we're adopting new names. We're the Oriosan Freeman Company, pleased if you'd be leading us to Caledo. I'm Wheatly."

The thief blinked and didn't know what to say. When he'd seen them, he had anticipated trouble. But before Will could get past his surprise, the Murosan Princess rode forward. "In the name of King Bowmar of Murosa, I welcome you, Captain Wheatly, and your men. Please, join us."

"Gladly. Thank you, Princess." Wheatly waved his arm and his group started to thread their way back through the Lancers to make up the rear of the column. Most of the riders gave him a nod, but two bringing up the rear refused to meet his eyes.

"Wait a minute. Stop." Will frowned. "Do I know you?"

The first man, whose soft shoulders mirrored his soft chin, shook his head. The second, looking young enough to be the first man's son, smiled confidently. Though a large man, and quite powerfully put together, his voice squeaked with tightness. "My brother doesn't speak much, Lord Norrington."

Will caught the voice and glanced at the man's hands to confirm his identity, but his thick mittens thwarted him. "Your name?"

"I'm known as North, my lord, and this is Lync..."

The other man looked up. "Lindenmere."

A shiver ran down the thief's spine. *Kenleigh* and *Linchmere, what* are *you thinking?* "You two should go home."

Lindenmere's voice shrank into a croak. "I have no home." The mask on his upper arm had a second orphan notch cut into it. "I was born to the mask. I want the chance to earn it."

"And you...uh, North?"

"As long as Chytrine is out there, no one is safe. Sooner we kill her, the less time I spend fearing for my family."

Will thought for a moment, then nodded. "As the princess said, welcome."

"Obliged, my lord."

Will reined his horse about and fell in with Princess Sayce as she led the way out of Meredo. Not many folks were out, given the chill. Those few who were stopped and stared as the company rode past. Will couldn't help but smile, given that the troupe had to be as odd a sight as had been seen since the last time a Harvest Festival had been held there.

Glancing back over his shoulder as a squad of Lancers rode out and along the road as foreguard, Will took a good look at the group. Alexia, Crow, and Resolute came next, followed by Dranae and Kerrigan. Lombo loped through the snow, looking as if he was having fun, and Qwc looped and swirled through the clouds of snowflakes that the Panqui would toss into the air. Bok loped along on impossibly slender stork legs, bearing a big wooden chest strapped to his back.

After him came a series of five wagons the princess had hired in Meredo, which had been fitted with runners for the snow. A big, boxy wagon led them and Peri rode in it. While she could easily fly in the cold, the air did get even colder higher up, and sometimes vicious winds blew. No one wanted her wings to get frostbitten, so they'd fashioned a rather cozy nest for her in the wagon. She had protested, but everyone countered that she was their secret weapon and she let that fiction mollify her.

After the wagons came a squad of the Lancers, all bright in their scarlet riding leathers. The Freemen company, which swelled to just over forty as other riders caught up, came next, and then the rear guard of lancers. The column stretched out over nearly three hundred yards and looked quite formidable.

Princess Sayce caught Will's eye and smiled as he turned to face forward. "I have to thank you for having your men join us."

"My men?"

She nodded and frosty breath trailed back as she spoke. "The Freemen."

"They're not mine."

Sayce looked at him hard, then white teeth scraped over a full lower lip. "You have no understanding of what happened at the gate, do you?"

Will frowned. "Princess, I may be the Norrington, but I was raised in the slums of Yslin. I'm a thief. King Scrainwood gave me a mask and a pat on the head and expected me to be his puppet. What happened at the gate was that a bunch of men who have decided they want to die have joined us."

Her blue eyes glittered for a moment, then she looked ahead. "In Muroso, Oriosa, and Alosa, for a man to bare his face before another is . . . Well, you only show your face to your family and closest friends. To show it to a stranger and to speak to you as Wheatly did . . . By removing his mask he was renouncing his former allegiances. He was, in effect, asking you to accept him as a vassal.

"They were, to a man, inspired by your words and your actions. Their masks used to define who they were. Now they want to be identified as your people. When you think they are worthy, they will expect you to mark their masks and let them don them again."

"Oh." Will took a deep breath and the cool air burned the back of his throat, making him cough. "Did I do it badly, then?"

She laughed. "No, not at all. That is why I was surprised you didn't know what you were doing."

"What about my telling Linchmere and Kenleigh to go home?"

Sayce looked over at him. "You must never call them by those names. Those are the names they had when they wore their masks. It's the same as it was with Crow. When he had a mask, he was Tarrant Hawkins. He lost his mask, he became Crow. They are now Lindenmere and North."

"And what did they think when I told them to go home?"

She pursed her lips for a moment. "You told them, in essence, they would have to work hard to prove themselves worthy of your mark on their masks. It wasn't a bad thing to tell them. North will watch out for Lindenmere, you know."

"I gathered, yes."

Will breathed in deeply, but more carefully, then raised his scarf to cover his mouth and nose. So much had changed. He'd gone from being a gutter-skulker to someone Crow and Resolute believed might be the solution to a prophecy. Then portions of the larger world began to see him as the solution to the troubles Chytrine was making. And now people looked at him with hope in their eyes, when a year earlier they'd have looked at him with contempt or fear.

And now I have people who want to fight and die for me. He shifted his shoulders awkwardly. In the time he had come to know Crow, Resolute, and Alexia—and the rest of the company—he had come to trust them. He would fight for them and with them. Their adventures had welded them together.

But the Freemen, they were entirely different. They weren't there because he was the Norrington. These men had heard his words and had heard of his deeds, and based on that alone had wanted to join with him. He'd have thought that maybe some of them were just out for adventure, but for an Oriosan to remove a mask was not an easy thing. As the princess had said, that was more than a spur of the moment decision.

Will looked over at the flame-haired Murosan. "Highness, I am now responsible for those men?"

She nodded. "Yes, you are. What they do is done in your name. You will pay for them, discipline them, and reward them."

"*Pay* for them?" Will looked back. "If I'd stolen the crown jewels, I couldn't pay for them."

"Lord Norrington..."

"Will, please."

"Will, you are required to pay those bills presented to you. Wheatly and Lindenmere, North and some others are not without means. You can tell that by their horses and their clothes. You will find that they will take care of themselves." She held a hand up to forestall a comment. "And, despite what you said before King Scrainwood, you will find the crown of Muroso will amply reward you for your efforts on our behalf."

Sayce stripped the mitten off her left hand, then worked a small ring from her index finger. She held it out to Will and he took it. It contained a small cameo mounted on a simple gold band.

He made to hand it back to her, but she shook her head. "You want me to have this?"

"I would be honored."

"Well, it is beautiful, but I doubt I could get enough for it to feed my men for a night."

Sayce laughed aloud and Will liked the throaty sound. Her eyes flashed brightly and almost as intensely as they had when she first found him. He remembered that, and her taking his hand. Heat flushed his cheeks.

"Will, that ring was from my father's mother. It represents an estate in western Muroso, near Lake Eori. The income from it, even in a poor year, will keep a dozen times that number of men."

"I can't take this!"

"But you must. You gave your lands away so you could come help my nation." Sayce smiled at him. "Now it is your nation, too. I don't expect that will make you fight any harder against Chytrine, just make the results of victory that much sweeter."

Will smiled, suddenly taken with having a new nation as his home. He removed his right glove. He slipped the ring on his index finger. "Thank you."

"The right hand. Your sword hand. Good."

"What?"

"It means you'll fight." The princess raised her own scarf to hide the lower part of her face. "Come, Lord Norrington, north to your new home. And death to our enemies."

CHAPTER 36

Had the journey from Meredo to Caledo been made in the summer, there would have been two choices of route. The longer journey would have taken them back to Valsina and then passed them south of Tolsin and northwest to Caledo. The great road there would have made travel quick, and easy accommodations would have been found along the way. The other route would have been to travel to Narriz, the capital of Saporicia, and then north on the road to Caledo. While that was the shorter route, the roads in Saporicia were not terribly well maintained, and much of the trade between Muroso and Saporicia actually traveled by ship around the Loquellyn headland.

But winter wiped any advantage of the roads, so the group headed straight north, intent on cutting through the Bokagul. The tall mountains dominated the horizon, and snow blanketed them. When winds had blown all the clouds away, snow could be seen drifting in long thin lines from the jagged peaks.

Alexia peered out through the thin veil she wore between the brow of her hat and the thick woolen scarf wrapped round her face. The veil helped dull the harshness of the light reflecting from the snow, and did keep in a bit of heat. Swathed in thick hide clothing and hunched beneath even thicker robes, she looked more a beast than the horse upon which she rode.

She did feel the cold and knew Will had to be miserable. But the thief didn't complain and that surprised her. The Will Norrington she'd first met in Yslin would have complained, and bitterly. Will had grown past that childishness now.

In camp the previous night, Will had joined some of the Murosans around a fire and sung with them various songs. He even offered new words for old melodies. One song, which he admitted was a poem he'd been thinking on for a while, involved the battle on the plains of Svoin, and featured her and Crow destroying the *sullanciri,* Malarkex.

His willingness to join in the singing impressed her, but less so than his acceptance of Kenleigh and Linchmere. Their presence among the Freeman Company had surprised her, and at first she thought they had been sent as Scrainwood's agents. She'd mentioned that idea to Crow, but he'd suggested that Kenleigh hadn't the temperament, and that Linchmere hadn't the guile needed to be a spy.

Upon reflection, Alyx agreed with Crow's assessment. She realized that Linchmere must have suffered a serious falling-out with his father to leave the comforts of the palace. Linchmere had been awkward in the camp, and mostly followed Kenleigh around, doing whatever the other man told him. Linchmere had begun to build a fire beneath a tree's snow-laden branches. The rising heat would have caused the snow to fall and smother the fire, but Qwc flew about clumsily and cleared the tree of snow. Linchmere did get dumped on, but had a smile for the Spritha's profuse apologies.

Alyx and Crow had retired together to a tent that had been set up a bit away from the others, though still within the camp. Whether people thought their marriage a sham or not, they respected their privacy. While the night was far too cold for removing all their clothing, they did huddle together beneath their blankets and share warmth.

There had been an urgency to their lovemaking in the inn—and an awkwardness. At first elbows hit where they shouldn't have, teeth clicked, and fingers tangled, but any mishap was greeted with a smile, a laugh, or a whispered apology. Soon enough, though, the actual words were of little use. Far more meaningful and expressive moans and gasps communicated all.

After they lay together, touching and caressing. She relished the tenderness with which Crow slipped his arm around her to pull her back against him, kissing her neck. That was something so welcome she gladly would have retreated into that embrace and never emerged. It was not so much that she wanted to escape the world and seek him as a sanctuary, but that she wanted, very much, to be there with him, sharing the peace of their coupling.

On the road he rode beside her, save when he checked on Will or talked to Resolute, or when she went to check on Peri. Even now, as she glanced over at him, his shoulders hunched beneath a huge bearskin cloak, he gave her a nod, and through his veil she could almost see his eyes twinkle.

During the time they were not alone, Crow had been solicitous, but also respectful. He would offer help, not insist on usurping those things she could

very well do herself. And if he needed help, he asked. He always had a smile
for her and remained attentive, while not demanding her constant attention.

Part of that distance, she suspected, came from the gap in their ages. That
first night he told her about Svarskya and having held her as an infant. A
tremor in his voice betrayed his uneasiness at being so much older than she.
As he made to apologize, she kissed him. "Our hearts don't care how many
times they've beaten, just that they beat together now."

He had accepted that with a smile. "Wisdom as well as beauty."

"Wise enough to know that when two souls are meant to be together, tri-
fling details do not matter."

Alexia smiled as their conversation echoed through her mind, but a keening hum filled the crisp air, demanding attention. Qwc flashed green against
the white snow, circling Will, Sayce, Crow, and Alexia, then hovered in the air
while pointing two arms off to the northeast. "Quick, quick, come quick. Important, *very* important." He began to drift up, then buzzed away, making a
beeline for the forested entrance into a little valley.

Crow's head turned in her direction. "A Spritha knows where it's supposed to be and when. We had best go."

Already Resolute had reined his horse around and was galloping after the
Spritha. Without a second thought, Alyx nudged her horse with her heels and
set off beside Crow to avoid most of the snow his horse was kicking up. Off to
the right, past Resolute, the Panqui sprinted through the snow, and behind
her she caught the sound of Will and Sayce joining the chase.

Off across a virgin snowfield they raced, then into a thin stand of pines.
Barely twenty yards farther, another field extended to a drop. To the north
spread a forested valley with a meadow at its heart. A stream split it and
wended its way south while, to the northwest, the grey granite walls of
Bokagul Mountains formed a border.

Resolute plunged straight down over the edge and disappeared from
sight. Lombo leaped into the air, his tail swinging to balance his flight. Alyx
saw him sink into the tops of pines, causing one to sway violently enough
that snow avalanched down from its branches. Crow's horse followed Resolute's, and she drove her mount over the edge just to Crow's left.

Snow flew, but the nearly treeless hillside gave her a good view of the valley floor. A small knot of people was beset by a horde of gibberers. A few
frostclaws circled, letting loose with their warbled hoots, while others clawed
bodies and tore at them with their terrible teeth. The people held the gibberers off as best they could and, from their awkward movements and coloration, she assumed they were urZrethi.

The steep hillside began to level out after ten yards. Crow reined back and
brought his silverwood bow to hand. He nocked an arrow, drew, and let fly.

The shaft sped past Resolute and took a gibberer high in the chest. It spun and went down, and a number of the gibberers looked up the hillside.

Which was right when Lombo pounced. He landed in the midst of them, crushing at least one beneath his feet. His paws flicked out, right and left, crushing bones or rending flesh with his claws. As he spun to face one threat, his tail shattered the legs of a gibberer driving at his back.

Another arrow arced down, this one leaving a temeryx thrashing out its life in a reddening snowdrift. Then a thundercrack split the air, echoing off the mountains. A gibberer jolted, then sagged to the ground, a hunk of his skull sprayed back in a little wedge over the snow, courtesy of Dranae and his draconette.

Then Alyx was among them. Halfway down the hill she had thrown off her heavy cloak, then freed her right hand of its mitten. It dangled from a thong at her wrist as she drew her sword and slashed down to her right. Bright red splashed the snow and her horse's flank. A gurgling gibberer crashed hard on the ground.

The snow made for difficult going, but horses proved far more agile than the gibberers. More arrows rained down and the draconette's thunder echoed again. Not every shaft nor every shot proved to be a kill, but the screams of a wounded comrade were as unnerving for the gibberers as they would be for men.

The frostclaws, with their quick steps and powerful legs, had an easier time of it in the snow, but Lombo seemed to take particular delight in slaying them. He was a fox among hens, streaking away from one broken-necked body to pounce on another, bear it to the ground, then wrench its head off.

Alexia parried a thrust from a longknife, then chopped her blade down on the gibberer's head. Bones cracked, then she kicked out at it, pitching it back. She reined her horse around and saw Resolute turning his horse within a circle of corpses.

Behind Alyx, Sayce was laying about with her saber while, rising in his stirrups, Will hurled the bladestars Resolute had created. Beyond him, a squad of the Red Lancers came riding hard. They drove against the thickest concentration of gibberers harrying the urZrethi, and the urZrethi took that moment to strike as well. Caught between them, the gibberers howled and wailed until they were all slain.

The remaining gibberers scattered as best they could, but the Lancers and Freemen rode them down. There hadn't been but thirty or forty of them, and a quick glance at their condition suggested to Alyx that these were stragglers and deserters who had banded together, and the small group of urZrethi had been caught at a most inopportune moment.

The princess trotted her horse over to the urZrethi. She counted ten of them, but several were wounded, and at least three urZrethi bodies lay in the snow. A female with flesh the color of red rocks, and long black hair plaited into a thick braid, stepped over to meet Alyx. The urZrethi had shifted her legs into spindly sticks, much as Bok had, and her forearms and hands had been transformed into a piercing blade and a horny mace.

"I bid you the peace of Bokagul." Her dark eyes shone with coppery flecks. "I am Silide-tse Jynyn, warden for this domain."

"I am Alexia of Okrannel." She looked over toward Will, thinking to introduce him, but saw him sitting astride his horse with an open wound on his leg. Sayce had dismounted and stood there spreading the rent clothes. The blood looked dark on Will's brown leathers and it steamed.

Alexia rode over to him. "What happened?"

"Nothing."

Sayce snarled. "I let one past. I let one get to the Norrington. It's my fault."

Qwc landed on Will's thigh, above the cut, then got down on all sixes and spat a wad of webbing into the wound. Will hissed and Sayce tried to swat the Spritha away, but Qwc darted back, then forward again, and deftly manipulated the webbing to cover the wound. The webbing did redden, but it also contracted, drawing the sides of the wound closed.

Wheatly reined up just shy of Will. "My lord, the gibberers are all gone. We've got them down to the last. A couple of our people are wounded, but nothing so's it would bother a man."

Will nodded. "North and Lindenmere?"

"North is fine, my lord. Lindenmere has a bit of a scratch, but he'll live."

"Good. Thank you, Captain Wheatly. You showed initiative; that's good." Will beckoned him with a finger. "Please, come here."

The man rode close enough for his right knee to touch Will's left. "Yes, my lord?"

The thief scraped his right index finger over his bloody trouser leg, then reached over and drew a dark stripe down the bridge of the mask on Wheatly's upper arm. "You may wear your mask again. You are now my man. You will serve as best you can, and you will tell me of others whose actions make them worthy of being mine."

The smile that blossomed on the man's face proved so infectious Alyx found herself smiling. "Yes, my lord. My duty, honor, and pleasure, Lord Norrington."

"And, Wheatly?"

"Yes, my lord?"

"If anyone needs healing, please send them to Adept Reese. I want live men, not brave corpses. Each scar is worth a story, true, but the ones he'll take away will be worth two."

"Yes, my lord." Wheatly tossed him a quick salute, then reined his horse about and started shouting orders to the Freemen.

Will looked up at Alexia, then over at the urZrethi. "How bad was it?"

Silide-tse looked back at her group. "I lost four and, depending, another may die."

Alexia looked up as Lombo wandered over and Crow joined them. "We need Kerrigan. Can you get him?" She'd been speaking to Crow, but the Panqui nodded and set off, loping up the hill.

The urZrethi sank down awkwardly on her heels. "Forgive me."

Sayce turned and dropped to a knee beside her. "Are you hurt?"

"Exhausted." She held up her mismatched arms. "Shifting can be tiring and we've not had much rest or food over the last week."

Sayce stood and whistled for one of her Lancers. "Find a way to get the sleighs down here safely. We'll camp here." She turned back to the urZrethi. "In no time, we'll have you some food and a place to rest."

Silide-tse smiled, then held up the mace. "No, no need."

The Murosan princess lifted her head and an imperious tone entered her voice. "We may be in Oriosa, but you will not refuse Murosan hospitality."

The urZrethi laughed. "Not at all. The offer of your hospitality is very welcome. Were we in Oriosa, I would accept." Silide-tse pointed to the northwest with her mace. "You see, this is *my* home. An hour further into the mountains, and I shall offer you *our* hospitality and our gratitude. Welcome to Bokagul. By your actions you have proven yourselves friends of the urZrethi, and in our realm, our friends shall want for nothing."

CHAPTER 37

The urgent need to help the wounded urZrethi quickly erased the ig-
nominy of being tossed over the Panqui's shoulder and hauled off
through the snow like a sack of potatoes. Kerrigan knew better than to
flail his arms or yell, since this was hardly the first time Lombo had carted
him off like that. Never before, though, had snow been dashed up into his
face so constantly that he had to swipe at it endlessly to keep it clear.

Behind them came Bok, with the chest strapped to his back.

Down in the valley, Kerrigan was deposited very much like a sack of potatoes in the middle of the battlefield. He rolled to his knees and surveyed the
situation. Three urZrethi were wounded, but their injuries consisted of minor cuts and scrapes. He crawled over to where two other urZrethi held a
third. The third urZrethi clutched at her swollen belly, and her companions
likewise pressed their hands to it.

There was a lot of blood. "Tell me how bad it is."

The copper-skinned urZrethi at the wounded female's feet shook her
head. She spoke in urZrethi, of which Kerrigan knew little and caught even
less. Another urZrethi, the one who had been speaking with Princess Alexia,
crunched her way over and squatted. "She says Sulion-Corax was slashed
across the belly by a frostclaw. Do you know what corax means?"

Kerrigan narrowed his green eyes. "She is allowed to bear children, yes?"

"Yes. She is Sulion-Corax Girscc and these are her sisters and cousins. She
is five months pregnant and the frostclaw may have hurt the baby."

Kerrigan exhaled strongly. "Oh, that complicates things."

"I shall make it worse for you. If you can repair the damage and save both, good. During that if you learn the gender of the child, say nothing. If it is a male child, and you cannot save both, however, save her."

The mage frowned. He knew enough of the urZrethi to know their matriarchy had little use for males—aside from breeding—but he thought that a bit harsh. "Don't worry, I will save them both."

He nodded at Sulion-Corax. "It will all be well."

Kerrigan closed his eyes and placed his hand on Sulion-Corax's. The urZrethi jerked under his touch, but the other urZrethi cooed soothing words at her. He set himself, then cast his diagnostic spell. Since it was elven magick, it flowed through her as if it were rootlets growing through the earth, slipping tendrils in and through her. The urZrethi, being a shapeshifter, had a nature that was highly mutable, but the pain she felt gave him tangible points of reference for his spell.

His awareness of her slowly sharpened, giving him a clear view of her injuries. The frostclaw had indeed slashed her belly and nicked her womb, but the child was yet small. Kerrigan redoubled his spell and fed the tendrils into the baby. He detected no injuries, but checked again.

Nothing. The child was not reporting pain, but something didn't feel right. The child's sense seemed diminished in some way. He feared for a moment that the mother's distress was affecting the child, so he cast a quick spell that dulled her pain and lowered her anxiety. The muted sense of pain she did still project coincided with her wounds, but this did not satisfy Kerrigan.

He pushed his awareness more into the child, and then ran out through the umbilical cord, tracing the link back with its mother. Halfway there he found it. The frostclaw had managed to slice a goodly way into the umbilical cord, cutting off the baby's supply of blood. Since the cord had no nerves, it could not report pain—hence his inability to detect the problem immediately.

Slowly, delicately, Kerrigan began knitting tissue back together again. He monitored the baby and felt the child become more vital. He checked once again to assure himself that the child was fine, then pulled back out. He repaired the cut to the womb, and then to the mother's abdominal wall. Finally, he sealed her skin.

He opened his eyes, then sagged back on his heels, before flopping on his side, breathing hard. The left side of his face lay in the snow, which burned a bit against his flesh, but he barely noticed that pain. What little he *did* notice surprised him, because his healing of the mother and infant should have been enormously painful. Every bit of pain Sulion-Corax would have felt while the wounds were healing had to be experienced. In casting the healing spells, he knew he could let her feel it, or he could accept it into himself. While he would not have wanted her to experience any of it, he never made the conscious decision to pull it into himself.

He considered and discarded the idea that the anesthetic spell he'd cast had taken care of the pain. Since the spell was commonly used, this little solution would have been learned long ago. Based on his conversations with Rym, he wondered if accepting the pain was some sort of brake Vilwan had imposed on magickers or if there was something else happening.

Lombo got his massive paws beneath Kerrigan's shoulders and pulled the mage into a sitting position. "More than bone-weary?"

Kerrigan blinked. "I'm fine, Lombo, thank you."

He looked around and saw everyone in the same positions they'd occupied when he'd begun the healing. Alexia looked down at him. "Can you help her?"

"It's done."

Will had ridden over and arched an eyebrow in surprise. "Done? You just barely touched her, then fell over. A heartbeat, maybe two."

"Really?" Kerrigan shook his head. He'd cast the spell the way he always did. *No, wait . . .* The obvious and urgent need of the situation had been what he focused on, so he wasn't concerned with himself and how he would do the casting. He quickly thought back to the spells he had cast when fleeing the pirates, both when leaving Vilwan and then leaving Port Gold. He had used incredible magicks, but their use had not exhausted him.

His weariness even now was not physical, but mental. What he had done was very difficult, even under the best of circumstances. For him to have accomplished it so quickly—his mind had clearly been racing, using the magick to repair the damage. That he had done it in so little time left him in shock.

And with a big question. *If I am not physically exhausted, the energy used to work the magick did not come from me. What, then, was its source?*

Kerrigan looked up and smiled. "Well, that gives me a lot to think about." He struggled to his feet, leaning heavily on Lombo.

The red urZrethi waved her bladed appendage toward the far mountains. "Please, all of you shall be welcome in Bokagul . . ." Her voice tailed off into a hiss as Bok came up, and she shifted to urZrethi. Of what followed Kerrigan only caught the word "bok" and it was said with disgust.

Kerrigan staggered through the snow to where Bok crouched with hands wrapped round his knees. He rested a hand on the green urZrethi's shoulder, then looked at the other. "Bok is my servant."

She tightened her eyes. "He is bok. He is an outlaw. You will keep him restrained."

Kerrigan patted his matted hair. "Of course."

Bok warbled placidly.

The urZrethi eyed him closely, then looked over at Princess Alexia. "It's not far, and you shall be most welcome. The Girsce family rules this duchy of Bokagul, and you will find their gratitude most lavish."

Silide-tse Jynyn did introduce herself to Kerrigan, then introduced him to the various sisters and cousins of the female whose child he had saved. It actually struck him that saving the child was more important than saving Sulion-Corax. As was explained to him, she had had a dream a week previous and had headed out with her entourage to gather snowberries from a particular grove. The dream had indicated that these berries would be the first solid food the child would eat, so the dream took on the command of law. The blizzards from the north had caught them away from Bokagul, and the Aurolani renegades had caught them on their return to Bokagul.

Getting the wagons down into the valley had proved less of a problem than Kerrigan would have imagined. With the urZrethi, Lombo, and lots of rope and horses, the descent went fairly easy. Peri did not remain in her cart for the trip down the hill, but instead was introduced to Silide-tse. The urZrethi warden gave her a message and directions on where to reach the entrance to the Girsce domain.

The journey northwest took four hours, and mountain shadows shrouded the valley as they made the trip. The bodies of the frostclaws had been tossed onto their sleighs as Lombo had not mangled them overmuch and they were reported to be good eating. Kerrigan had never tasted their meat before, but Crow gave him an encouraging nod, so he withheld comment.

At journey's end they drew into a narrow valley that twisted back and forth several times before opening into a slightly larger valley capped by a sheer stone wall. The cul-de-sac was large enough to fit their entire company, but only just barely. When riding through the narrow confines, Kerrigan had looked up and noticed that a small number of archers could harry any troops trying to lay siege to the entrance, and he was pretty sure this was a point not lost on the urZrethi.

The entrance to Bokagul itself impressed him. The sheer wall rose a hundred yards and glistened with ice that formed from melting snow above. At the base stood four figures carved in bas-relief from the grey stone. The two in the middle were smallest, and represented urZrethi. They stood small and squat, their hands touching the rune-decorated circle defining the entrance. Above them, and much taller, were two shapeshifted urZrethi who had the birdlike legs many used for walking through the snow. Moreover, their upper arms had been transformed into wings, which touched wingtip to wingtip over the entrance's circle.

Silide-tse paced beside him. "You know, Adept Reese, the urZrethi believe, someday, that the truly gifted among us will be able to shape wings and fly."

He nodded. "I have heard the legend. It is a wonderful dream."

"Yes, it is." She smiled. "Perhaps the child you saved will be the one with a light enough spirit to reach that goal."

"I should be delighted if it were so."

Silide-tse bounded ahead, but before she could extend a hand to touch the keystone, the massive disk rolled aside. Peri stepped back out into the cold, festooned with delicate gold chains and rings that sparkled with jewels, and cloth of gold that replaced the modest garments she normally wore. She was even laughing, which wasn't that rare an occurrence, but remarkable enough to surprise Kerrigan.

Pouring out of the doorway behind her came a host of urZrethi. They crowded around the cart that had once been Peri's home but had been given over to Sulion-Corax for the remaining journey. The urZrethi babble, which he could not understand, rose and fell with joy and sympathy, and was shot through with mourning for those who had fallen. As per urZrethi custom, the bodies were left where they fell and while the place of their passing would be noted, their bodies would not be recovered nor venerated.

Other urZrethi, to the last all male, came out to take the horses and guide the sleighs. They moved sluggishly and timidly, but went about their tasks efficiently. One even approached Bok to relieve him of his chest, then stood blinking when Bok growled. Silide-tse called that male off and gave him another assignment, which he undertook impassively.

Silide-tse drew the core company aside while other urZrethi directed the Lancers and Freemen to the billets awaiting them. The warden led them down well-lit corridors that were remarkably tall for so short a people. The illumination came from fat candles perched on metal stands. The reliefs carved along the walls were interspersed with colorful mosaics, all of which depicted men and elves in scenes with urZrethi. Kerrigan faintly recalled stories that might coincide with some of the scenes, but it struck him that these must have been taken from the urZrethi versions of the tales, since the urZrethi seemed to have the others at a disadvantage—which was seldom the case in man-tales.

Silide-tse led them to an inordinately large and oddly shaped room. A low, rounded corridor—low enough that both Resolute and Dranae had to duck their heads and Lombo was forced to crouch—opened into the first of two spherical chambers. The second chamber was smaller than the first, and its floor was set three feet higher, though their ceilings reached the same height. Opening into both spheres, small, round entrances led to other rooms, and just to the left of the corridor entrance the larger chamber had a huge hearth.

Silide-tse moved to the hearth and whispered a word, which started a pile of stones in it glowing like embers. She squatted before the fireplace, with her back to it, and opened her arms.

"This is a *coric*, and this is how we live. The lower chamber here is the common room and off it are the sleeping chambers for a family's males." She shot a hooded glance at Bok, who immediately retreated to a sleeping room near the entrance. "Male visitors, especially those who have come to get a daughter with child, are usually housed closer to the upper chamber. That is where our women reside. The Coraxoc, or matriarch, would have that central chamber. Her fecund daughters would have the chambers either side, and then the rest of us occupy the others."

Will counted heads. "Three women, eight men. Six chambers down here. It will get crowded."

Silide-tse shook her head. "The male chambers comfortably sleep six."

A snort sounded from within the hole housing Bok.

Qwc landed on Will's shoulder. "Qwc takes up no room. No snoring, either."

The urZrethi frowned. "You are guests. You are free to do as you please. If you wish to observe our conventions, this would please us."

Crow nodded. "We understand. Perrine, you shall be given the Coraxoc chamber."

Silide-tse's face brightened. "You *do* understand. Splendid. You will excuse me, then. I shall let you get settled and shall return with provender for all."

Kerrigan opted to share a chamber with Bok. The long, narrow room had a low, arched ceiling and no decoration at all, unless one counted unintended patterns worked at random in the plaster. He chose the stone pallet on the right and snatched a second straw-filled mattress to insulate him from the bed's chill.

Bok had shrugged the chest off and had set it at the head of his bed, while he curled up on the lower half of the bench. He'd already fallen asleep and Kerrigan was tempted to drop off as well, but a sudden clapping sound in the main room caused him to squat-walk over to the entrance and peer out.

Silide-tse had returned and had already shifted her shape back into something decidedly more human. She led a troupe of urZrethi who brought in a bunch of wood that was quickly fitted together into a low table. Others brought pillows to ring it. After that bowls, plates, cups, forks, knives, and spoons appeared, and every place was quickly set with far more utensils than any one person would ever use. Silide-tse, watching over the whole proceeding barked an order, and yet one more of each utensil was set out.

The urZrethi waved all of the guests into the main chamber and appointed them specific places around the table. As they sat, male urZrethi filed in, two behind each member of the company, and yet more came bearing tureens of soup and steaming platters of meat and heaping baskets of bread. Kerrigan's stomach immediately started growling and his mouth watered.

He and the others fell on the food as if they'd not eaten in a month, which they had, but only tavern fare and road rations, which might well have been mud in comparison. Oddly enough, Kerrigan noted that while spoons, forks, and knives were whisked away between courses, the plates and bowls remained. The servants shifted their hands to serve different courses, then retreated to wash their hands between courses. Kerrigan began to wonder if the urZrethi had little use for utensils since they could shape their own. As a result they supplied many and took them away between courses in lieu of having their guests wash their hands—which made no sense since they were not eating with them.

That sort of idle speculation was the height of Kerrigan's intellectual activity. He ate a great deal and drank more, since each dish seemed more delicious than the last, and each new wine had nuances he'd never tasted before. The food kept coming and in such quantities that even Lombo leaned back from the table and patted his distended belly right before letting loose with a belch strong enough to make the dinner table vibrate.

That did not so much end the meal as cap it, and everyone laughed aloud, including Silide-tse.

She clapped her hands and the servants departed, but the table was left as set, with enough food still there to feed the Freemen. She glanced at Kerrigan. "I shall leave this for your servant to clean up."

The mage nodded. "You are very kind."

"You are owed a debt. This is the least we can do to repay it." She smiled. "I shall return in the morning. Sleep well, all of you."

CHAPTER 38

Erlestoke wasn't certain, but he almost wished the day had not dawned clear and cold. The cold he could have done without. The frigid air managed to work itself into his clothes, and no amount of movement seemed to warm him. But then again, he wasn't moving all that fast.

That first night they'd found the storehouse that Verum had mentioned. The Draconis Baron had managed to scatter caches of firedirt and other supplies around Fortress Draconis, less against the need to retreat from it than for forces operating behind enemy lines.

Well, we're certainly behind the lines.

In that storehouse they replenished their supplies and drew winter clothing. The storehouse did contain a number of draconettes, but none of the latest variety. Still, the shot and firedirt worked in their quadnels, so they loaded up with enough for two hundred shots each. With clothing, food, and weaponry, every one of them moved out with an average of sixty pounds of equipment.

Only Erlestoke had been exempted because his chest still ached from the blow he'd been struck. Jilandessa had performed some simple spells and determined that nothing had been broken, but his ribs had been loosened in his breastbone. She offered to spell him back into shape, but he'd refused, figuring that if he lived long enough, he'd heal naturally.

The others split up his gear, leaving him to carry shot, powder, a quadnel, and the fragment of the DragonCrown. The fragment wasn't that heavy, so he was able to move along with everyone as they trekked south. The storehouse had yielded snowshoes, which did let them move more quickly, but any sort of hike through the cold was still pretty rough.

Their first day of travel had been through a snowstorm, which they actually welcomed as it hid their tracks. It did little to hide the signs of the Aurolani hordes and their passing, however. The carcasses of half-eaten animals, wagons that had been taken and then discarded when overworked draft beasts died, and even the frozen bodies of gibberers who had been slain by compatriots or the cold, marked the trail well. The presence of dead gibberers did not surprise Erlestoke, as winter marching was always taxing. It was actually the paucity of bodies that he found difficult to believe.

Ryswin shrugged when he mentioned this. "They come from the north. This weather is something they are used to. It might even seem mild to them."

"Which puts them at an advantage in a winter war." Erlestoke sighed. "How long do you think it will take Sebcia to fall?"

The elf's eyes narrowed for a moment, then he shook his head. "A lot of troops moved south. It's probably already gone. Muroso might be gone, too. Dragonels and dragons make Chytrine very powerful, especially against fortresses built to withstand conventional sieges."

Like the ones in Oriosa. Erlestoke had long resisted identifying himself with the nation of his birth. His father had embarked on a course that Erlestoke despised. The murder of his grandmother made him hate Chytrine, and made him determined to destroy her. It just terrified his father, and he did whatever he could to appease her. For that reason Erlestoke had traveled north to Fortress Draconis and begged his uncle, the Draconis Baron, to accept his service.

Despite that determination, however, the ties to his homeland still bound him. Just because he had no love for his father did not mean that he did not love Oriosa. He did not want to see Oriosans killed and their homes destroyed. Not only had his aunt been evacuated with his cousins there, but his own mistress and their child had gone south. It occurred to him that they must all suppose him dead, which only heightened his desire to return home.

If I can.

Their situation was precarious, and that was only if one was generous in assessing the dangers. The first day's snow likely kept Aurolani troops in Fortress Draconis, so there would be at least a day's gap between them and the troops moving farther south. That gap could be easily closed, but it provided them a narrow window of passage. Ideally they would move south, then cross the Tynik River and slip into Sarengul. There the urZrethi would provide them sanctuary or at least a route into Alosa.

Erlestoke wasn't certain where the fragment would be best hidden. If they could get as far south as Croquellyn, they could turn it over to the elves. Princess Alexia had done that with the Jeranese fragment when she'd stolen it from the Wruonin pirates. The elves of Loquellyn had set it away for safekeeping, but the prince wondered if that might not doom them in the long run.

Erlestoke's fears about a clear day meant they would leave a trail anyone could follow, but that eased as night fell. They ranged a bit to the east and in some hill country they found the shell of a crofter's home. Raiders had tried to burn it, but the fire had failed to consume the whole thing. Part of the roof remained, and all four log walls stood, though they were charred on the inside.

The nice thing about the cabin was that the walls did offer some protection against the Aurolani troops in the area, or so Nygal had said. Verum countered that they'd not mean anything if a dragon decided to finish the job. That sobered everyone up for a bit, then Erlestoke told them they could build a fire in the hearth if Verum said the structure was still sound.

The idea of being able to have heat brightened the prospects for the night. Verum assigned different jobs to everyone but the elves and Jullagh-tse since they'd have to take the night watches. Their ability to see in the darkness would make them perfect lookouts, and none of the men or *meckanshii* complained about the division of labor.

Erlestoke summoned three of the nonhumans over. "We are agreed that we strike south for Sarengul. Jullagh-tse, you're certain they'll take us in?"

She nodded, her grey eyes a stark contrast to both her rich red flesh and the dark of the heavy black wool cloak swathing her. "The urZrethi do not turn away visitors. I've been to Sarengul before—it is not that far from Bokagul, after all—and I even have distant cousins there. They may not welcome our having a DragonCrown fragment, but they won't search us or demand to know what we are carrying."

Jilandessa toyed with her long black braid. "Is deception a good idea?"

The urZrethi shrugged. "You would rather burden them with information they might not want? Yes, our entry will bring the war down on them, but they have no desire for Chytrine to reconstruct the Crown. Remember, urZrethi raise mountains and the dragons chase us from them. Our homes are unassailable otherwise. Let her bring her gibberers against us. Without dragons, they cannot hope to open our mountains."

Ryswin snorted. "Let us hope neither Turic or Runyk deigns to make a lesson of such confidence."

Jullagh-tse shook her head. "The will of the gods be what it may, destroying the urZrethi in their home is very difficult."

Erlestoke raised a mittened hand. "If we assume all that is true, the next question is where do we go from there? Princess Alexia left a fragment in Loquellyn."

Ryswin wrinkled his nose. "She would not have been allowed to leave

Rellaence with it in her possession. It was deemed unwise for her to bring it to Fortress Draconis. That would have put too much at jeopardy, and granted too much to Chytrine if she succeeded."

"That would have given her five fragments. She has the one from Svarskya, and one of the three from Fortress Draconis. We have one, the Jeranese fragment is in Loquellyn, and one more is gods-alone know where." The prince frowned. "How many fragments are there?"

Ryswin smiled. "You were the Draconis Baron's aide. Did he not tell you?"

Jilandessa snapped something at the Loquelf in Elvish. The warrior's eyes widened, then he blushed and nodded. When the color in his face returned to normal, he looked Erlestoke squarely in the eye. "You will please forgive me. Jilandessa has reminded me that you do have a right to information that has long been hidden from you. To the best of anyone's knowledge, there are seven fragments."

"Seven?" Erlestoke frowned. "I know of the five that men were given, and I have heard there was a fragment on Vorquellyn."

The Harquelf healer nodded. "That fragment was evacuated from the island, but vanished. Some say the Loquelves took it from the refugees."

"We did not." Ryswin lifted his chin. "I fought against Kree'chuc. I did not see the fragment, but had you been in Loquellyn at the time, you know our possession of it would have been lauded as a victory."

"That accounts for six." Erlestoke looked at his three companions. "What of the seventh?"

Ryswin opened his hands. "Though it was well before my time, the tale has it that a small group of adventurers were the ones who actually slew Kirûn. When they found the Crown it formed an open arc, not unlike some coronets. They'd not seen it before, and it was not until much later that stories arose that told of a seventh piece—the centerpiece. While each fragment is very powerful, as we have all seen, with the seventh, vast armies of dragons can be controlled. Its use is supposed to be exhausting, but when one can wipe out an enemy, the chance to rest comes easily."

The prince frowned. "So you are telling me that there were seven pieces, but only six were found and they were split up without anyone knowing that the central piece was missing?"

"It is true, Highness." Jullagh-tse Seegg nodded solemnly. "I am far younger than Ryswin here, but I have heard the same tales told in Bokagul. It was an urZrethi goldsmith who journeyed far and wide. She measured all the fragments and created an imitation of it, down to the finest detail. It was clearly incomplete, so she then worked out what the other piece might have looked like. The simple fact of the matter, however, is that we do not know where that other piece is. It is conceivable that Chytrine has it, and that she even stole it from the Crown."

Erlestoke sagged back against the log wall and winced. His chest hurt, and not just from the punch. "If all three of you know this information, why don't I? Why didn't the Draconis Baron?"

Jilandessa crouched beside him and rested her hands on one of his drawn-up knees. "It is because of the nature of men, Highness. Think of Fortress Draconis not as a place to stop Chytrine, but as a locus for power. All the nations of mankind, all nations of elves and urZrethi, pledged troops to and served at Fortress Draconis. But it was a man who created the plans, and men were forever the Draconis Barons. Men have a passion for power.

"When it was learned that there might be a seventh piece of the crown— one that would make it work—the elves and urZrethi were put in a curious position. All fragments save for one resided in human hands. It was thought possible that men might believe that we had lied about the number of fragments, and that we held one back because we did not trust humanity. That belief would quickly become malignant. Men would come to believe we held it back so we could gather all the other fragments and re-create the DragonCrown to summon dragons to destroy mankind."

Erlestoke shook his head. "That makes no sense."

The raven-haired elf smiled. "Highness, you have labored for the last five years at Fortress Draconis. You have worked with elves and urZrethi. You know us. You trust us. Ryswin is newly come to Fortress Draconis, yet you treat him as you do me because you have learned to trust elves."

Jullagh-tse nodded as well. "And, were the truth to be told, the idea of putting the Crown together again has been advanced. I've heard it mentioned in the halls of Bokagul. I imagine the same has been said in groves throughout elven holdings. Humanity encroaches on us. No one calls for mankind's destruction, but being able to drive men back . . ."

Erlestoke nodded. "I know the history. I know the men of Oriosa and the urZrethi of Bokagul have fought wars before, but we have fought side by side more recently. Still, your point is made. Those old wars still haunt the memory. Attributing evil to you would not be difficult."

Jilandessa sighed. "It is fairly safe to assume Chytrine does not have the seventh fragment. If she did, she would be much more powerful."

"Why can't she just make a new central segment?"

The urZrethi frowned. "The stones in the Crown are very rare. Some tales refer to them as Truestones, but I have no idea what is meant by that."

The elves shook their heads. "If their nature is known to my people," Ryswin said solemnly, "it has not been shared with me. However, if she had the skills to create a central portion of the Crown, she could make herself a new one. Something has prevented that from happening."

"Thank the gods for small favors." The prince leaned his head back against the wall. "We're still stuck with the same problem, when it comes down to it. Where do we go? If the elves are willing to hold another fragment, Harquellyn or Croquellyn are both likely places."

Jilandessa pursed her lips thoughtfully. "Harquellyn should be a second choice. I am different from my people, for we prefer to remain far from conflict. We would be welcomed, but in exchange for a pact of peace, they might give the fragment up."

"Ryswin, why did your people keep a fragment? Isn't that risking a lot given Chytrine's lust for the things?"

The warrior smiled. "My friend, it was the Loquelven ships that destroyed Kree'chuc's fleet and ruined his invasion. Chytrine hates us regardless of what we possess. We just could not have allowed that fragment to get into her hands."

"Croquellyn, then?"

The urZrethi nodded thoughtfully. "If we get that far south, we will be close to Tsagul. Depending upon where Chytrine is, we might even have to go further south."

The prince frowned. "There's not much more south there."

"No, Highness, there isn't." Jullagh-tse Seegg sighed heavily. "Somehow we shall have to hope it is enough."

CHAPTER 39

General Markus Adrogans nodded as he studied the model of the Three Brothers Citadel that warded the road through the South Gorge. "You've done a brilliant job, Duke Mikhail."

The dark-haired young man smiled, then bowed his head in thanks. "I like making models. It is to scale, of course, though the snow is just white paint and not mounded to the depth our scouts have reported."

The model represented a stretch of the road paralleling the Svar River as it passed through the South Gorge. On its approach to Svarskya, the river made an oxbow to the west and the road ran along the eastern shore. At the apex of the curve sat the centermost and largest of the fortresses, built up like a cake with one squat cylindrical layer upon another, decreasing in diameter as they rose four high. A round wall surrounded it. Opposite, in the center of the river, stood a huge tower, with an arched stone bridge connecting the tower and the fortress. From the tower, and between the tower and fortress, thick chains ran shore to shore to prevent boat traffic—something effective in the summer, but useless in the dead of winter since the river was thoroughly iced over and buried under snow.

To the south—the direction from which they would approach—lay the first of the two gateway fortresses. Each consisted of two rectangular structures paralleling the road for twenty yards or so, with crenellated walls all around, and plenty of arrow slits in the interior walls. Gates front and rear blocked the road, and any force that was successful in breaching the forward gate would be trapped in the fortress interior before they could get the rear gate open. Getting to the gate-opening mechanisms would require a lot of fighting and murderous close-range shots by archers hidden behind stout walls.

The smaller fortresses also had their river towers with arched bridges and shore to shore chains. Any attempt to cross the frozen river would be doomed since archers in the towers or on the bridges would have the advantage. Moreover, siege engines from within the fortresses would be able to hurl stones that would shatter the ice. The frigid water would kill soldiers faster than arrows, and the frozen bodies would be washed into the Crescent Sea at Svarskya.

Neither the gate-keeping fortresses nor their river towers had a line of sight between them, so they relied on the larger fortress to relay messages via a system of flags. The central fortress served as the garrison for the whole complex, with only a quarter of a mile separating one fortress from the other. It would send out troops to defend either gateway fortress, and the garrison in the farthest fortress could be summoned to help if needed.

"It is stunning work, but it does not give me heart." Adrogans slowly paced around the model, viewing it from every angle. Reaching out, he lifted the top layer from the central fortress. The interior walls had been painted in, and a black circle drawn to represent the central stairway. The details even extended down to indicating the privies with black dots, and notations about how many soldiers usually occupied each room.

"I wished to be able to complete the interior structure, General. Two of the Svoin refugees had served in Varalorsk, so were able to give me the details. They were helpful with the little brothers, Darovin and Krakoin." Mikhail shrugged. "After the battle, I shall fix things."

Adrogans smiled at him. "You are rather unlike your cousin. I could not imagine her doing something like this."

"Alexia?" The man laughed. "She is quite serious, and has no simple pursuits such as making models. This is fine, however, since she is the future of our nation. Not to take anything from you, General, for your efforts in ridding Okrannel of the Aurolani shall never be forgotten."

"Nor yours in riding with the Kingsmen." The Jeranese general's eyes narrowed a bit. "I think, however, you would be more at peace were you able to make models instead of war."

The duke shook his head. "While my nation is captive, I cannot know peace." He took a deep breath and lowered his voice. "General, you know what it is for one of us to make a dream raid, yes?"

Adrogans nodded, not betraying the fact that he found the whole idea foolish. "I have heard rumors of the procedure."

Mikhail half grinned. "Aunt Tatyana would have me flayed alive for telling you this, but it is something you should know. When I made my dream raid, I was with Alexia. Her dream, well, I will not betray a confidence, for she should not have told it even to me, but it bodes very well for the battle against Chytrine. But mine, General, it is very specific, and I must share it with you."

The duke waved his left hand at the model. "I dreamed of the Three Brothers, as you see them now. Thick snow, frozen river, a day so cold that if you spat it would freeze before it hit the ground. We were victorious that day. All three brothers in our hands."

"Good, very good." Adrogans clasped his gloved hands at the small of his back. "How did we win?"

Mikhail winced. "Dreams, General, are so seldom specific. But we did win, and I was there, in Varalorsk. I know this because I had drawn a sketch of the tower from my dream, then I spoke with the men from Svoin. I drew the map as they told me it was, and I compared the two. They matched perfectly. And, remember, General, that I have never seen the Three Brothers. I was born in Yslin, in exile."

"I am pleased to have the omen, then, as well as this model." Adrogans furrowed his brows, then replaced the top layer of Varalorsk. "Toppling these towers will not be easy."

"No, General. They have never been taken before."

The Jeranese general decided not to argue that point. The Three Brothers had actually fallen into Aurolani hands because they had been abandoned. Stories over the years had resolved themselves into a core fiction that indicated a noble had commanded the garrisons to come away with her and cover her retreat to Jerana. Some said it was Tatyana; others named various nobles, though no single story seemed to be verifiable. Tatyana had actually been in Yslin at the time of the retreat, and countless nobles had fled Okrannel, but none powerful enough to command the garrison to depart. Chances were the soldiers had just decided that fleeing was preferable to dying.

Had they ever been taken before, Adrogans might have had a place to start planning. As it was, the setup only had one defect, and that was that the three brothers could not see each other. Aside from that, they were nearly unassailable. The Svar River cut a deep gorge through the mountains at that point. The road was narrow and the approaches to Darovin were such that far too little siege machinery could be brought up the road and positioned to launch on the fortress. While a ram might do the job, the time it would take to haul it along the snowy road would give the garrisons ample opportunity to prepare themselves. The missiles from the fortress would be hideous and if they had dragonels...

"Beal mot Tsuvo's people said nothing about dragonels, correct?"

Mikhail shook his head, but pointed at two openings on either side of the gatehouses. "A generation ago these had ballistae in them that could rake the roadway. They have been opened a bit, and it is thought they might contain dragonels. The scouts did say the work was irregular, so I don't know."

Adrogans nodded and, dimly, felt Pain rake her fingers down his spine. The only way to find out what lurked there was to present a force that would invite an attack. Adrogans imagined men huddled behind mantlets, approaching as quickly as they could, being blown into bloody splinters by the dragonels therein.

The problem was that the Three Brothers had to be taken; otherwise, Adrogans' line of supply from Guraskya would be cut. It would have been possible for him to infiltrate his people through the mountains—killing many horses in the process—but they would arrive hungry and weak. Or, worse, the troops in the Three Brothers would be able to range south to the ford and cut off his supplies, if another blizzard didn't do that anyway or, worse, trap his entire army in the mountains so they would starve to death.

Taking and holding the Three Brothers would guarantee that no other Aurolani troops slipped in and attacked his army from the rear. Just because he knew of no other troops operating in the south did not mean there were none, or that none were on their way. Just over a century before, the Aurolani had undertaken the daring seaborne raid that won them Vorquellyn. A repeat of that action could land troops anywhere along the eastern coast, leaving them able to hammer his people against the anvil of Svarskya.

Mikhail pointed to six banners, four of which were located at Varalorsk, then one north at Krakoin and the other south at Darovin. "I painted them according to the descriptions given, and none shows signs of dragonels, but I do not know if Aurolani banners ever did. It would be six legions, though."

Adrogans nodded. "A garrison of six hundred, which is slightly less than the Okrans army used to use. Still, within those fortresses, they might as well be doubled, or tripled, even. They won't be foolish enough to come out after us as they did at the ford. The obvious approach would be the frozen river, but it is far too volatile."

"That is true. The water level is down to winter levels, but the river still runs deep. It did freeze over earlier than normal because of the weather, but the ice will not support siege engines. Were the river bed shallower, we might get a catapult down but . . ."

"The engineers would freeze." The Jerancse general sighed. "The river is just one broad killing field, and even if our people were able to rush past it and reach the roadway between Varalorsk and Darovin, what then? They would be trapped between and troops from Varalorsk would slaughter them."

Phfas entered the long, low building Adrogans had appropriated as his headquarters. He hissed as he saw what they were studying. "The Three Brothers. You know the history?"

Adrogans nodded. "Three brothers back in history stopped a Zhusk horde bent on pillaging Svarskya. They died there. The citadel was raised in their honor. That legend, uncle?"

The Zhusk shaman nodded. "An evil time." He glared at Mikhail as if daring the Okrans noble to make a comment, but the young man wisely held his tongue.

Adrogans smiled. "Why do you remind me of this legend, uncle?"

The old man smiled lopsidedly. "So you would know the Zhusk have no answer to this puzzle."

"Noted, thank you." The general shared a smile with Mikhail. "The Blackfeathers, the Rangers, and Beal's scouts will keep us informed about any reinforcements. It would appear, however, that the best approach—and I use that term advisedly—will be a frontal assault. It will not be pleasant."

The duke nodded. "The Kingsmen will request the honor of going in first, General."

"So anxious to die, Duke Mikhail?"

The young man shook his head. "These fortresses were raised to protect our home. How can we ask others to shed their blood first to destroy them? Only a coward would do that. Besides, I know we will win through, so I know I will not die."

"But you may be the only one to survive."

That comment sobered Mikhail for a moment, but his brown eyes dulled only for a heartbeat. "Then I shall be the one to scale the gates, slaughter the garrison, and lead the way to Varalorsk."

Phfas snorted. "Wake up, Svarskya. This is not a dream. It is a nightmare."

Pain's talons sank into the back of Adrogans' skull, but he shrugged the agony away. "It is indeed a nightmare, but one we shall find a way to push on through."

Mikhail smiled. "I have every confidence in you, General. I could only wish Alexia was here to help."

"I would welcome it." Adrogans glanced at Phfas as the shaman muttered under his breath. "Alas, even your cousin's vaunted talents might be stymied here. More blood than water will flow in the taking of the Three Brothers. Unless I can change that, the cost will keep Svarskya out of our grasp forever."

CHAPTER 40

For Alexia, the time spent in Bokagul had many dreamlike qualities, all of which conspired to push the horror of winter and the war into the background. Though she still felt the urgency to get to Caledo, the trip through the urZrethi halls and corridors—she could not bring herself to consider such places *tunnels*—went faster than expected.

The halls took her breath away. Having grown up in Gyrvirgul, she was used to living within mountains. After all, the urZrethi had created Gyrvirgul for the Gyrkyme, willingly courting the anger of elves by providing the winged ones with a home. There the urZrethi had created vast open galleries that were perfect for the Gyrkyme.

But had she been asked to predict the nature of urZrethi architecture, she would not have thought of the tall galleries as being something they would normally create. But it seemed the urZrethi built everything on a grand scale, with walls rising into gloom. Floor after floor of galleries and balconies, all decorated with ornate sculptures, soared into the shadows. The stone looked less carved than cultivated—trained the way gardeners worked topiary.

The whimsy in some of the decorations surprised Alyx. Her mental image of the urZrethi had rendered them dour and doughty, stout-hearted and humorless. But granted most of the tales she knew involved warriors who had emerged from the mountain strongholds for battle, and that might have provided a skewed view. She welcomed the chance to have her knowledge of them broadened.

Each night over the five days of their journey, the company was welcomed into a *coric*. Perrine always took the premier position by dint of the fact that she had what all urZrethi wanted: the ability to fly. Watching how the urZrethi reacted to Peri suggested that even if elves had offered to go to war over the Gyrkyme, the urZrethi still would have created Gyrvirgul.

Alexia shared a chamber with Crow at night and the others seemed to be happy for them—though Peri teased her as only a sister might. Alyx looked forward to the time she got to lie with Crow, whispering conspiratorially with him so as not to disturb any of the others. She loved tracing her fingers through his white hair, or down through the thatch on his chest and along the trio of scars that marked the right side of his body.

Occasionally she would forget the scars were there. One time, upon encountering them, her hand recoiled, but Crow's hand covered it. "It's all right, Alexia. They don't hurt."

"It's not that."

He snorted lightly and she could sense a smile forming on his lips. "You fear the memory would be painful, or could have been, but I was simply doing what had to be done to save my friends. When I did not break and when she could not trick me, Chytrine decided to kill me. The fact that I've lived long enough for these scars still to be there is a victory. There are few enough of those in the world."

Her fingers came up and raked through his beard. "We will have more, you know."

Crow's right hand came up. His index finger played along her jaw, then tipped her face up. "The same day Chytrine got the Svarskya fragment of the DragonCrown, she let you slip away. I think she will find that a very grave error."

He kissed her then and they made love. Softly, slowly, and quietly they joined, despite the urgency they felt. Desire flashed through Alyx. She wanted to touch and taste and caress. She wanted to feel him move under her and over her. She wanted to hold him very close and to be held closer, then have their worlds melt and fuse in passion until their unity was all that existed.

And, for a time, it was. In the time after that, sleep came, deepened by the feeling of safety in his arms. That struck her as odd, though, because she had never felt unsafe or insecure. She had just always felt that she needed to be on her guard, but with Crow that was utterly unnecessary.

That next day, the third in their trek, Alexia did manage to slip away and join the Communion of Dragons, while sitting back after a meal, listening to urZrethi singers present a melodic series of ballads she could not understand. Maroth met her at the slip and took her to the island, where she found the Black Dragon and two other individuals. One was female and appeared to be completely fashioned of ice. Alyx wondered if, for a moment, Chytrine had managed to project herself into the Communion, but she felt no malevolence coming from the woman.

The other figure was a man—or so she assumed since all she saw was the clothing he wore. From boots and velvet trousers to a heavy jacket and on up to a black velvet cap, it all seemed rather fashionable. At least she had seen some people in Meredo so attired. Of his flesh there was not a sign.

The Black Dragon greeted her warmly. "It is very good to see you. I had heard reports that you had gone north from Meredo, but nothing since."

Alyx regarded him curiously. "You are tracking me?"

"I will admit an interest in you, since I nominated you to join us, but I have not been hunting or spying. I assume you are traveling to Muroso? You left Meredo in the company of a princess." The Black's jaw dropped open in an approximation of a smile. "Prince Linchmere is missing from the capital, and many believe he'll be found dead with the spring thaw."

Alyx could not keep from smiling. "They will have to look well outside Meredo to find Linchmere. Just so you know, I *am* heading north. Right now we are moving through Bokagul. We are probably a week away from Caledo."

The Unseen Man sipped a cup of wine. "A week and it shall yet be there. Two perhaps."

The woman hissed. "Caledo will take far longer to fall, if it does at all."

"I hope, for your sake, Ryme, that your people fare far better than mine. The Aurolani would be at the gates of Caledo already save that the consolidation of Sebcia is taking longer than expected. The blizzards are in their favor, but they are slowing down troops and supplies. Sebcians have been laying their own nation to waste as they retreat."

Alyx nodded. "Your source is reliable?"

A hearty laugh issued from the invisible throat. "My dear child, I *am* my source. I fled Lurrii when it fell, and am now fighting on the peninsula. If no ships can be found, I'll die there, too."

The Black shook his head. "You'll not die. You're far too resourceful."

"My frostbitten toes—the few I have left—thank you, my friend." The clothes bowed toward the Black. "Chytrine's army is vast. Gibberers clearly breed faster than imagined. I have heard tales of other creatures in her armies, but have seen none myself. *Sullanciri* have been sighted, but again I have seen none. The push is on to Muroso, though."

The woman nodded. "Sebcian refugees have told terrible tales." She looked at Alyx. "My sister is safe with you, is she not?"

The princess frowned. "You know who I am?"

"No, but I would not be here were I not able to deduce that the Murosan Princess traveling north from Meredo is my sister. Her mission to bring the Norrington to Caledo was not sanctioned by our father. He will be pleased to accept help, but her departure angered him."

"Your sister is well, and is a bold warrior."

"A bit headstrong, but likewise heartstrong." Ryme's comment was made with some affection, but more annoyance. "The Aurolani have advanced on a broad front so you will never be truly safe until you reach Caledo."

"Thank you." Alyx frowned. Because she had learned about the Aurolani advance in the Communion, she would not be able to share that information with anyone outside. She would not be prevented from acting on it, however, and could direct things so that their guard would be up when they left the mountains.

She looked at the Black. "Anything from Fortress Draconis or Okrannel?"

He shook his head. "I fear the worst for our Communicants at Fortress Draconis. In Okrannel there is much secrecy, but Adrogans does appear to be moving against Aurolani probes in the Guranin Highlands. Beyond that I know nothing, though I do hope for the best."

"As do I." Alyx smiled. "I'd best be back to Bokagul. Until we meet again."

The Unseen Man raised his goblet in a salute. "*If* we meet again."

His words echoed in her head as she blinked her eyes and returned to the *coric*. Crow offered her a tankard of mulled wine. "Anything wrong, Highness?"

She accepted the wine from him, letting her left hand surreptitiously stroke the back of his right. "No, nothing."

"You seemed far away."

"I was, but I am back now. Come, sit beside me."

He eyed the choir. "Misery loves company?"

She winked. "No, lover, temptation demands it."

Will hunched his shoulders and pulled his cloak tighter about himself as the massive urZrethi portal rolled back. He squinted as light reflected brightly from the virgin snow. The company rode from a warm mountain fastness out to the shore of a huge lake in the northern reaches of Bokagul. Breath steamed, and ice began to form almost immediately on the muzzle of his horse.

Silide-tse Jynyn came striding up on his left, keeping pace with him and Princess Sayce. "The lake is Osemyr, which means lake of the stars. In the summer, on a moonless night, one can come here and peer at the lake. Its dark waters perfectly reflect the night sky. Constellations twinkle and stars streak to their death."

Will looked past her at a vast snowfield. "I'm sure it's beautiful. As beautiful as it is cold."

The urZrethi sighed. "My apologies. But our journey outside could not be helped."

For four days they had traveled through the halls of the urZrethi, passing from realm to realm. The whole of Bokagul was divided into duchies, baronies, and counties; cities, towns, and villages—which struck Will as incredibly odd because it was all underground. The routes they traveled were the equivalent of the kings' roads, save that a village might be above or below it, and therefore entirely unseen. The *corics* in which they stayed were guest lodgings, and delegations from the local nobility would come out to fete them. The idea, though, that someone could ride through a hallway and move from one realm to another just boggled Will's mind.

The reason they had been forced outside was Kerrigan's servant, Bok. His family name was Jex, and the next realm on the route was his home. Word of his presence had traveled quickly through Bokagul. Whereas most urZrethi just ignored his presence in deference to their visitors, the Baroness of Yreeu refused to grant them passage. That forced a detour out to the lakeshore and the biting cold.

Sayce looked over at Silide-tse. "It is not your fault. It is understandable that he would not be welcome there."

Will arched an eyebrow. "It is? What did he do wrong?"

The urZrethi kept her voice even. "He is a rebel against our society, Lord Norrington. He chose to live apart, so his return is not permitted."

"Um, you said he chose to live apart, but I thought he just decided not to be a slave. I mean, that's what I was told it meant to be branded a bok."

Sayce shook her head. "It is more complicated than that. Society has rules so that everyone can play their part. In Muroso, people are bound to the land, to work it for their liege lords. They produce food and livestock and generate income for their master and he, in turn, protects them. Your Freemen, when the war is done, will go with you to Eori and will begin farming until the time for them to rise and serve you as warriors comes again."

"But what if they don't want to?"

The Murosan Princess looked hard at him. " 'Don't *want* to'?"

Silide-tse cleared her throat. "I believe, Lord Norrington, human society might be different than ours. We have roles for our males. There are things that need to be done. When they do these things, they are fed and clothed and housed. They are well treated, but they are also delicate of mind and spirit. For one to rebel as the bok did is clearly a sign of abnormality."

Will twisted in the saddle and wanted to argue the point, but Bok took that moment to open his mouth wide and let out a belch that echoed from the mountains and might have triggered a small avalanche on the far side of the lake.

"Well, maybe that is the urZrethi way, but it's not the same for men." He glanced at Sayce. "Are you going to tell me that Muroso is different, too, or that being as how I was a thief, I'm an outlaw?"

She frowned. "I didn't mean to anger you."

"I'm not angry."

"The edge in your voice . . ."

"What edge?"

Sayce shook her head. "My mistake. No, Lord Norrington, I would not accuse you of being an outlaw, at least not in the sense we were speaking. Yes, as a thief you did work outside the law, but in accepting the mantle you have, you are preserving the very society you once defied. And it may be that you or your Freemen are not suited to being peasants, but not everyone else is capable of handling the responsibilities of danger and destiny."

"I can see that, but what is expected of normal folks, and what is permitted nobility are two different things, aren't they? Nobles are given the most responsibility, yet they don't acquit it."

Sayce shifted her shoulders. "I'm not sure I follow you."

Will sighed. "The crowns ruined Crow's life because they didn't want to take responsibility. King Scrainwood engineered things so that if Crow ever comes back to Oriosa, he'll find himself back on trial. There's so much deception, and it's not right."

The Murosan Princess smiled slyly. "You, a thief, complaining about deception?"

Will frowned. "Well, when I did it, it was honest deception."

"*Honest* deception."

He'd have taken offense at her comment, but mirth underscored her words, and he saw no malice in her eyes. "Thieves are supposed to deceive people. Leaders are not."

"Very true, but the complexities of the truth sometimes make it difficult for people to see what needs to be done." Sayce sighed. "While some people see that and can be shepherds, others can never be anything more than sheep."

He wanted to argue that point, but he stopped himself. Even in Yslin he'd seen sheep—human sheep, Vork sheep—and he'd seen the frostclaw that preyed on them. He liked to think of himself as a frostclaw. *Which means I accept what she's saying as true, as much as I hate it.*

Will sighed. "You might be right, Princess, but then I have a question."

"Yes?"

"How do you know who was truly meant to be a sheep? By your way of reckoning, I'd have been counted as a sheep, or something worse, but here I am leading men who aren't sheep, on a very unsheepy adventure. You might be right, but it could be that in every village of sheep there's one or two shepherds who never get the chance to be a shepherd."

She opened her mouth to reply, then closed it and frowned. Finally, she glanced at him. A wisp of her red hair lashed her cheek as she did so. "I need to think about that."

"Yeah, me too."

* * *

The trek took them a quarter of the way around the lake, then back down into the domain of the Seegg family. They were welcomed most profusely, both because the Seeggs and Yreeus had something of a rivalry going, and because several urZrethi from that duchy had served at Fortress Draconis, including one of the duchess' cousins. No word had been heard as to her fate, but everyone seemed hopeful.

Silide-tse explained that the next day they would complete their journey through Bokagul and head northwest to Muroso. "I will not be able to accompany you, but I will wish you the best on your journey."

Because she was going to be leaving them, the company made certain their meal in the guest *coric* was in her honor. Much food was eaten and much wine drunk, then various among them gave her gifts. Will presented her with a sapphire ring he'd taken from the castle of the Pirate Queen of Wruona. Resolute gave her one of his bladestars and Kerrigan took a piece of wood and magically shaped it into a bracelet that had a rune for each of them on it.

Perrine's gift was the best, however. She plucked a brown feather from the leading edge of her left wing and offered it to her. "With you as our guide, we have flown through Bokagul. When it is time for you to fly, I shall be *your* guide."

The assembled urZrethi all fell mute. Silide-tse's eyes teared up and her mouth quivered. She said nothing for a long time, then glanced down at the table. "Save for you, I would be long dead. My life is yours, so it shall be lived in your honor, my friends. I shall make you proud."

Will had to swallow hard, but managed to squeeze that lump out of his throat. He raised his cup. "You've called us friends. You've shared your home with us. I don't know about proud, but I couldn't feel more honored."

Everyone drank to that, then the urZrethi offered toasts and another choir started singing. Resolute, whose pained expression suggested he was close to killing something, suggested that in lieu of another song, perhaps Will would tell the tale of how he got the ring he'd given Silide-tse. He did, with Silide-tse translating, and their hosts were mightily entertained.

Exhausted, Will finally rose from the table and, from the state of his clothes the next morning, assumed he had fallen asleep before his body actually hit the mattress. The next morning, however, the condition of his clothing mattered little, for he woke with a furious thundering in his head. He clapped his hands over his ears by reflex and discovered two things.

His head did not hurt as if he was hungover, and the thunder wasn't coming from inside. He opened his eyes and rolled off his bed just in time to hear shouting. He poked his head out and heard another thunderous blast.

"That sounds like . . ."

"Dragonels, yes." Resolute growled as he emerged from his hole and strapped on his sword.

Just then Silide-tse came running into the *coric*. "Hurry, my friends; to arms!" She pointed back the way she had come. "The Aurolani have breached the Seegg gates. They have invaded Bokagul!"

CHAPTER 41

Though Neskartu said they would travel by traditional means from his Conservatory to Muroso, the seven-hundred-and-twenty-mile journey lasted less than a week. Drearbeasts drew their sleighs and pulled them swiftly through snow and over frozen ground. The massive ursinoid creatures, with their curved, daggerlike fangs, thick white fur coats with light blue striping, and long claws in flat paws, were feared by many—including most of the students Neskartu had brought with him. But Isaura had seen drearbeasts gamboling as cubs, so felt little dread in their company. As draft beasts they served strongly, though their prickly nature made them a danger to their handlers when either was fatigued.

The journey south did disappoint her in one aspect. Their little caravan swept past Fortress Draconis at night, during a snowstorm, so she never got the chance to see it. For so many years she had heard tales of it, and from childhood it had been the forward post of all evil, harboring troops who would someday stab northward into her mother's realm. That it had been brought low pleased her, and she would have liked to see it so humbled.

As they neared their goal, they found much evidence of the victorious Aurolani legions that had overrun Sebcia. They had been led by two *sullanciri*: Anarus and Tythsai, who had once been known as Aren Asvaldget and Jeturna Costasi. Myrall'mara had dealt with securing the countryside, and while there were pockets of resistance, Isaura was assured they were shrinking. The day before they reached the front lines around the Murosan town Porjal, one of the *kryalniri* was assigned to their company and gave them the news.

Isaura found the snow-furred mage pleasant company, especially when they conversed in Elvish. He called himself Trib, which was short for Retribution. Having been born on Vorquellyn, choosing such a name was his right—though, as he noted, that was quite a mouthful to shout in the midst of combat.

They reached Porjal, on the northern coast of Muroso, in the middle of the night. The city was located on the western bank of the Green River, which flowed from Bokagul to the Crescent Sea, forming the border between Muroso and Sebcia. As had the refugees before them, the Aurolani forces crossed over the frozen river with ease. They took up positions that cut the city off from the land and prepared to lay siege to it.

As the morning dawned, Isaura got her first glimpse of the city and was surprised at how small it seemed. At its heart were walls that rose up a hundred feet, with towers at hundred-yard intervals going up another thirty beyond. The walls formed a crescent that ran from shore to shore. There were many buildings outside the walls, but they mostly appeared to be slums. The lack of smoke rising from the chimneys suggested they had been abandoned.

Despite that, the pennants flying from towers provided a colorful contrast to the snow. Isaura, strolling along the lines with Trib, pointed to a cross-hatched banner in yellow and red. "That one is very pretty."

"It marks the presence of the Duke of Porjal. The red shows his blood ties to the royal family. His grandfather and the king at the time were brothers."

She regarded him in surprise. "You know Murosan history, then?"

The *kryalniri* shook his head. "You will see that Murosans take great delight in announcing their lineage before entering battle. At least, the mages do, and the duke's retainers are rather accomplished in that regard as well."

"I do not follow you."

Trib let his left hand shade his sapphire eyes, then pointed to pair of black basalt dolmen set on either side of the main road. "Throughout Muroso, you will see structures such as those. They are the stations where wizards stand before engaging in a duel. Our troops have engaged many wizards—some young, some old—who are defending their towns. They advance, announce themselves, then fight. I have lost several of my siblings that way."

Isaura rubbed a gloved hand over his shoulder. "I am sorry to hear that."

Trib shook his head. "I had many littermates, Princess, and the best have survived. Ah, look, here comes someone now."

A little door in the city gate opened and a single figure stepped through. He wore a scarlet robe belted with a white cord and carried a stick that was longer than a baton but shorter than a full staff. White breath trailed back from his mouth as he marched along the road. His blond hair appeared almost as light as the snow, and the mask he wore matched his robe in hue. Above and behind him a number of people peeked out through the wall's crenellations.

The man moved to the westernmost of the black stones and stood with his back against it. His voice came loud and strong through the crisp air. The gibberers in the camp quieted as he spoke, shifting around to watch him.

"I am Gramn Lyward, son of Con Lyward, Magister of Porjal. I am an Adept, learned in the ways of the Muroso Academy. I will slay all those who come to oppose me."

One of the *kryalniri* plucked her staff from the snowbank into which it had been plunged and started off toward the Murosan, but Neskartu emerged from a tent. The *kryalniri's* head snapped around as if she'd been roped. She bowed in the *sullanciri's* direction and drew back.

From within another tent two of Neskartu's apprentices emerged. Isaura recognized Corde and a slightly older man—his age was hard to tell, but white had begun to tinge his beard—named Parham. The man did not carry a staff, but instead had a set of five silver rings that were linked together as if a chain. He stretched them from left hand to right, locking them into a rigid column, then let them slide together in a ringing circle. One came free, though she could see no gap in it, and Parham plopped it over his head to hang around his neck.

Parham approached the battleground with confidence, but without swagger. He wore a bright yellow tunic and boots and trousers of black. Sunlight glinted from the rings while derisive shouts poured down on him from the walls.

Even at a distance, by the set of his shoulders, Isaura could see that Gramn Lyward thought little of his opposition. He twirled his staff with ease, bringing his left shoulder forward and letting the stick whirl behind him in his right hand.

Parham bowed, then brandished the quartet of rings that still remained linked. The third from the left glowed red for a second, then a sizzling scarlet disk arced toward the Murosan. The Southlands' mage flicked his left hand, launching a green spark that intersected it. Brilliant light flashed, as if lightning had struck when they met, and Gramn smiled as the Aurolani attack flew past.

From the wall, however, came gasps. The red disk had missed the mage, but had slashed at the dolmen, leaving a dully glowing scar. Gramn half turned to regard it, and when he turned back he seemed a bit less confident. His staff still twirled in his right hand, but more spasmodically, and his mouth tightened.

Parham twisted the rings, then let the chain of them swing around his right wrist once, before catching hold of them with his left hand and snapping another spell off. This time the second ring glowed gold. A fiery golden eagle fletched with lightning swooped in at the Murosan. Its talons reached for him, the claws growing longer as it approached.

The staff came out and around in a lemniscate of pale blue, catching the magickal bird and splashing feathers into the air. Then both sides of the loop began to twist tighter, drawing the figure eight into a thick cord that torsion made yet more tiny until it evaporated. It took every trace of the bird with it.

Trib nodded. "Neatly done."

Parham spun his chain, then grasped the four links two and two. He oriented them full on Gramn, as if their ends described a tube. The rings glowed and a furious gout of fire poured forth. The fiery column shot like dragon's-breath straight at the man.

Gramn took a step backward, but that was all Isaura could see before the flames hit him. She expected him to burn, but the torrent of fire exploded as if it were a stream of water hitting a wall. The flames roared as they blasted away from the Murosan, and even so far away the heat kissed her face like a summer breeze.

The fire failed when Parham staggered back a step, shivering with fatigue. The flames collapsed into a greasy black cloud, which ascended quickly into the air. Steam from the melted snow curled up lazily to cover the battlefield in a low fog and, for a moment, nothing could be seen of Gramn.

Then the Murosan rose from the mist. One end of his staff burned, but he quenched it in a puddle. His once-scarlet robe had been singed brown and black in places, and white smoke rose from the ragged cuffs and hem. His mask and blond hair remained intact, however, and a cold smile split his soot-stained face.

The stick began to spin again. Slowly at first, one rotation then another. Gramn eyed his foe and the staff picked up speed. A bit faster, then a shift in direction before it spun very fast indeed. The Murosan gestured casually with his left hand, striking a green spark, then snapped the staff hard along his right forearm.

Silver fire wreathed the stick, then shot out at Parham in a jagged bolt of searing lightning. The Aurolani mage let four rings hang from his right hand while he swept the remaining one up and off his neck. He stabbed it edge on toward the lightning, then dropped into a crouch and touched the ring to the ground.

The lightning bolt bent in mid-flight and struck the ring. Its argent fire played in little flames over the ground, consuming the vapor rising from puddles, then drying the puddles themselves. Though Isaura felt no heat from it, a tingle did run over her flesh. That spell had likely taken Gramn years to perfect, and yet its fury had been dissipated so easily.

As he knew it would be. She shook her head. Parham had never been a diligent student and had always sought methods that were quick to power instead of ones that could be built upon. It was not that the man was stupid, he had just been lazy and believed that because his intelligence let him do some things easily, that those which were difficult were not worth learning. Toward that end he had shaped his rings and had imbued them with enchantments that made casting a limited number of spells very easy and made those spells themselves staggeringly powerful. That Gramn had stood against any of them was a wonder.

Parham's death, however, was not a wonder. Parham had dealt with the incredible threat offered by the lightning, but had ignored the green spark. It had floated up for a moment, then resolved itself into the form of a hummingbird. The magickal creature shot forward, stopped, turned to the right, then flew into Parham's right ear and out the left side of his skull. The bird lost all shape, but so did the mage's head.

Great cheering arose from the walls as Parham flopped over in a clatter of rings. Gramn dropped to one knee and pressed his forehead to his left arm. Isaura was unsure if he were simply tired or was giving thanks to some god, but quickly enough he heaved himself to his feet and spoke his challenge aloud again.

Corde twisted her brown hair into a short ponytail and tied it with a piece of leather. "My Lord Neskartu, please permit me to answer his challenge."

The *sullanciri* waved her toward the battlefield. She headed out in Porjal's direction, then stopped and turned. "Yes, my lord, I know."

Isaura frowned. Corde wore a long tunic of white over black trousers and boots. Around her waist, a scarlet cloth had been wrapped twice and knotted at her right hip, so that the ends flopped down at her knee. She discarded her gloves as she went.

"Trib, she has no staff."

"No, Princess, she does not."

Corde reached Parham's body and pried the rings from his right hand. The one with which he had redirected the lightning still stuck in the ground, and she left it there. She examined the rings, giving each a raspy whirl against its mates, then looked up and bowed her head to Gramn.

The Murosan canted his head to the right. "Those trinkets did him no good, woman. Get your staff and we shall battle."

" 'Tis not the spell or the staff, but the sorceress, Muroso-*tuc*." Though Gramn might not have known what the Aurolani suffix meant, Corde's tone and the way she clipped it off made it clear that it was not a term of endearment. "I am prepared."

"Do your worst."

She shook her head as Gramn once again adopted the stance he had used to face Parham. "I shall do my *best*."

She fanned the rings and the third glowed scarlet. The red disk again flashed to life and arced in at Gramn. The Murosan contemptuously triggered the green spark that glanced it aside, this time knocking it up and out into a grander arc. He nodded at her, then twitched his finger in her direction, inviting another attack.

The rings rang and spun, then locked down into the fire cylinder. The flames poured out hot and fast. The stream was smaller, but flowed more quickly and drove Gramn back two steps as his staff came around. He spun it quickly, summoning a golden shield that splashed the flames high and wide. Through them Isaura could see him straining, but his spell held.

Corde yanked the rings apart, abruptly terminating the fire stream. Gramn rose from a crouch at the base of the dolmen, smiling. His staff was not burning, nor was his robe. The people on the wall cheered loudly, and that broadened his smile.

Then that smile froze.

The people's cheering sank into wails.

The scarlet disk that had been so easily deflected had arced back down. As had its predecessor, it sliced through the dolmen, this time fully bisecting the stone. The upper portion slid forward on molten rock. Its leading edge hit the soft ground and sank in until it hit frozen earth, then pitched forward.

Gramn spun and stabbed his stick against it. Blue fire shot from the staff's base and pierced the earth. The stone slowed, then stopped, held there by magick. Gramn's back bowed with the strain, but he held even as muddy ground oozed up and around his feet.

Corde rustled the rings against each other.

Gramn shot back over his shoulder. "You wouldn't..."

"No need."

The Murosan's right foot slipped in the mud.

The stone slammed down heavily enough to shake the earth even where Isaura stood. Thick mud streaked with blood splashed out. Brown water had darker tendrils seeping through it, and bubbles rose thickly.

The wails of horror from the walls lasted longer than the bubbles.

Corde casually wiped mud from her tunic, then tossed the rings away. They crashed loudly against the stone and lay there, shining on its broad black face. The sunlight reflected off them, painting four white rings over the walls of Porjal.

Toward the center of the Aurolani position, an order was shouted. Before Corde had crossed even a quarter of the distance back to her lines, dragonels spoke, splitting the air with fire and thunder. A dozen iron balls hammered the walls within those rings. Masonry crumbled, and people fell.

The conquest of Muroso had begun.

CHAPTER 42

Shouting from the *coric*'s common room brought Kerrigan awake, and he sat upright before a wave of vertigo hit him. Bok reached out to steady him, then dragged him from his pallet and propelled him through the small round opening. Silide-tse stood there, gesticulating toward the doorway. Resolute tossed Will a heavy pouch that clanked with bladestars. Crow slipped from the room he shared with Alexia, tucking tunic into trousers, and she followed several seconds later already clad in a short-sleeved coat of gold-washed ringmail that fell to her knees.

Thunder blasted from the hall, and Kerrigan's sleep-befuddled mind had a hard time handling the incongruity of thunder *within* the mountains. In a heartbeat he realized it must be the roar of a dragonel.

He raked fingers back through his hair. "Silide-tse, how did they get inside?"

"Traitors!" She spat another word, which sounded very much like "*kachadikta*," though he had no clue what it meant. "When our families moved south from Boragul, centuries ago, we left signs for others to follow. Those paths and entrances have long been forgotten as grander roadways supplanted them. Now our ancient sisters have brought the enemy!"

Resolute grabbed Silide-tse by the shoulder. "How many? Where? What do you need from us?"

"Kill the Aurolani; leave the greys to us. We need to hold them, slow them. We are retreating to the Grand Gallery." She glanced at Kerrigan. "They want him there."

The Vorquelf pointed at Bok. "You get Kerrigan there. Everyone else, kill things!"

Resolute's command struck Kerrigan as blatantly obvious, but it wasn't until he headed out that he understood its import. As they came into the Long Hall, small knots of male urZrethi keened and fled back toward the Grand Gallery. Female warriors with arms ending in sword blades, axes, or maces—with armored plating contorting their bodies and spikes sprouting everywhere—urged their males along and turned to face the oncoming enemy.

A flood of gibberers filled the hall and in their midst rolled small dragonels. At Fortress Draconis Kerrigan had seen how devastating dragonels could be. There Aurolani balls slammed into walls, bouncing high and long before coming back down and expending their energy. Here, in the close confines of the hallway, poorly aimed shots ricocheted from walls, bouncing through retreating urZrethi. One ball vaporized a male's chest, scattering his arms and head in a bloody mist. Others tore off limbs and crushed bodies, leaving their victims bleeding and screaming until more thunder drowned them out.

Lombo shouldered his way past Kerrigan, then bounded toward the advancing gibberers on all fours. He leaped, arms spread, claws flashing. His battle roar filled the hallway, and some gibberers gave way.

Behind them, however, a rank of draconetteers raised their weapons and pulled the triggers. A staccato cacophony of thundercracks accompanied the lancing of fire into the air. Lombo's body jerked and began to spin, then he crashed down hard. He smashed several gibberers to the ground beneath him, shattering bones, but lay still on his side.

A jolt ripped through Kerrigan as the Panqui went down. He stepped forward, willing his friend to rise again. He wanted to run to him, to cast a spell to check on his wounds and then another to heal them, but those spells required him to bridge that hundred-foot gap.

That gap into which flowed more and more gibberers.

Beyond Lombo's body the draconetteers began to reload their weapons. The gibberers' mouths hung open in satisfied smiles, their keening laughter piercing the din. One spat on Lombo as he worked, raising a powder horn to refill the weapon with firedirt.

Kerrigan balled his left fist, raising it to shoulder level, then shoved it forward and opened it. Green sparks, like a swarm of angry bees, rose from it. They shot straight out at the gibberers. Some hit the advancing warriors, stinging them and burning black patches into the mottled fur. Others dipped and cut, then reached their true targets.

One penetrated a powder horn, igniting the handful of firedirt at once. It exploded, taking the gibberer's paw with it. Others poured with the firedirt into the draconette's barrel, causing fire to flash out. One flaming jet seared a face, blinding that gibberer, while the others just leaped back, dropping their weapons.

Dranae shouldered his draconette and pulled the trigger. A small flash preceded a larger one, which was accompanied by a loud blast. The ball slammed into a gibberer's belly, dropping it to its knees before it flopped over and thrashed its life out. The man dropped back a step to reload. Alexia, Crow, Sayce, and Resolute tightened into a line, swords drawn.

Off from the right came an urZrethi with slate-grey flesh. The left hand had been replaced by a hook and the right by a knobby mace. Spikes had been sprouted at knee, elbow, and shoulder, but the armor remained thin. The grey moved with great agility, but hesitated as Silide-tse intercepted her.

The Boka urZrethi had shifted herself as if to form a smaller model of the Panqui. Thick, armored plates covered her broad back and formed bracers and rerebracers to protect her arms. The right hand had become a lance a good four feet long, whereas the left was shaped into a pair of thick spikes. Silide-tse's legs had become much shorter and splayed out broadly for balance.

The grey snarled and leaped forward, driving at Silide-tse. The hook raked left to right, trying to catch an ankle, but the Boka just rolled onto her back in a somersault, came to her feet, then thrust out low as the grey came in. The lance punctured the grey's left thigh, wrenching a screech from her throat. The right-hand mace came around and pounded on Silide-tse's left shoulder, but skipped off ineffectively.

Suddenly the Boka was well inside the grey's guard. The lance ground in the wound, then appeared to soften and waver. It thickened, then became a tentacle that grew longer. It slapped against the grey's back, then lashed across her throat, tightening. The hook came up to tug at it, but Silide-tse's left arm came forward, driving the paired spikes up beneath the grey's breastbone.

The grey screamed hoarsely, then stiffed once before a violent spasm shook her body. Silide-tse ripped the spikes free, then flicked the tentacle. The grey's body spun off and smashed against the hall's far wall while the tentacle smeared dark blood over the ground to the accompaniment of dragonel thunder.

Silide-tse turned back and smiled victoriously.

The crushing power of a dragonel ball erased that smile. Teeth scattered and clattered as her decapitated body crashed back onto its carapace. She somersaulted twice, the tentacle writhing like a wounded snake, then lay still. A widening pool of blood marked where her head had been.

Other balls had flown at the same time. Some skipped off the high gallery balustrades, peppering fleeing urZrethi with stone fragments. Some, knocked from the galleries, literally flew down. Their arms flapped furiously as they half transformed into wings, but did not slow their falls. Their bodies shattered against the hard stone. Some projectiles, with flatter arcs, caromed off pillars and bounced through the urZrethi. One ball, streaked with gore, spun madly in the center of the Long Hall, describing a little series of bloody curlicues.

And throughout the shots, the gibberers continued to advance. Kerrigan saw vylaens in their ranks, and a taller creature here and there. They looked more elven than anything, save for their snowy fur. He had no idea what they were, but he knew he'd not seen their like before.

Resolute and the others engaged the gibberers. Steel rang on steel, and blades swept round in skirling arcs that rent pelts and crushed limbs. To one such as Kerrigan, who had not been trained to combat, the ability to catalog blow after blow was denied. Combat became chaos punctuated by screams and roars, challenges and warnings, the heavy thump of a body hitting the ground, or the lighter thump of some lesser part doing the same.

A draconette barked. Princess Sayce spun, her mask half-off, her sword flying. She hit the ground hard, and her limbs flopped loosely against it. A great cry went up from within the gibberer ranks, but before they could press that advantage, Will Norrington leaped into the gap. He shook his head, flinging off blood from a stone-shard cut over his left eye. His face was half-masked by blood, and he brandished two bladestars, grasped at the nexus. He faced the horde with mere fistfuls of steel.

"No!" His growl sliced sharply through the din. "By my blood, you will *not* pass!"

Kerrigan had expected the fury in Will's statement, but not what accompanied the words. A wave of magick pulsed off Will with a force that staggered Kerrigan. The nearest vylaen screamed and vomited blood, while others reeled away in agony. The closest snow-furred figure slumped in a dead faint and—just for a moment—the battle ceased.

Then the push of the rear ranks knocked several gibberers forward, and the slaughter began again.

Peri stooped and picked up the once-spinning dragonel ball, then spread her wings and launched herself into the air. Kerrigan watched her for a moment, then pointed at Princess Sayce. "Bok, bring her. Now." The urZrethi darted forward and caught her up by the shoulders, then dragged her back.

Qwc circled him. "This way, this way!"

Resolute shouted. "Pull back!"

Farther down the hall, behind the surge of gibberers, a dragonel went off, but clearly something had gone wrong. Instead of a flash of fire, Kerrigan saw a jet of flame cutting across the enemy formation. Bodies flew in the air toward the right, then to the left, as the ball slammed off a wall and scythed back through.

More shrieking came from the Aurolani ranks, this time on the left. Kerrigan couldn't see what was happening until one of the snowy elves screamed and rose into the air as if flying. His back bowed, then cracked. Massive paws, one on his neck and the other on his tail, bent his shoulders to his hips, then cast the body aside.

With his tail smashing and his claws rending, a blood-streaked Lombo shouldered his way through the horde. One unfortunate gibberer turned to see who had bumped it. Lombo's head surged forward, and he bit the gibberer's face off and spat it at another.

Crow darted forward, cutting down a gibberer raising a barbed iron spike to impale the Panqui. One of Will's bladestars *thwocked* into a gibberer's forehead and Dranae's draconette spoke again, this shot blowing the throat from one of the snows.

Crow pulled Lombo back behind their lines, then the company began to fall back. The Aurolani troops pressed forward and were sure to overwhelm them save that something impeded their progress. It was as if there were iron bars running from floor to unseen ceiling. One gibberer pressed flat up against it, and another twisted, shouldering between the barriers.

Kerrigan frowned and cast a quick spell that let him trace magick. A crescent of little luminous dots glowed a ghostly green that matched the blood on Will's face. *By my blood, you will not pass.*

In some manner, Will's blood and his oath had combined to work a potent magick.

"Will, your blood!" Kerrigan drew a hand across his own forehead and flicked it off, as if ridding himself of sweat. Will looked at him oddly, but the mage just pointed. "Do it! Splash your blood on the floor. *Past* your blood they shall not go!"

The thief's eyes widened, then a cruel smile split his bloody mask. He swiped his hand over his cheek and dappled the floor with a flick of his fingers. Advancing gibberers ran into a tangle of impenetrable rods. Will danced farther right, wiping and flicking in a diagonal line that choked off the Aurolani advance. As they snarled, he laughed, then rained droplets on them as they clawed at him.

Those baptized with his blood howled piteously. It burned them as if it were molten rock. Their flesh sizzled, sometimes breaking into open flames and at other times just smoking as their bodies melted. Will laughed aloud, then licked his lips and spat at them, burning a hole through one's chest.

Though the gibberers could not pass, save where they could squeeze through the droplets, the same was not true of dragonel balls, draconette shot, and weapons hurled in anger. Resolute grabbed Will, dragging him backward as he painted more stone with blood. Kerrigan used his telekinetic spell to deflect one iron ball, then snapped to the left as a draconette shot struck his shoulder. The shot stung, but the bone armor had stopped it, leaving him with a neat hole in his tunic.

As they retreated to the Grand Gallery, a few gibberers squeezed through after them while others started to climb up to the upper galleries that ran along the Long Hall. Bokagul urZrethi retreated, unblocked by Will's blood. A few Bokas formed a rear guard and began to kill those few gibberers who did make it past the barrier.

They came out of the northern leg of the Long Hall and into the Seegg Grand Gallery. It literally formed the hub of the community, and rose to dizzying heights. The Hall itself only opened into the lower half of the gallery, but balconies ringed it for another four levels, and generous levels they were. Kerrigan had estimated previously that from floor to domed ceiling, the cylinder ran two hundred feet, and Silide-tse had confirmed that estimate when she pointed to the fountain at the center of the mosaic-decorated floor.

In contrast to the wails of survivors and the thunder of dragonels, the central fountain gaily burbled and gushed water high—cresting just below the ceiling. The fountain took the shape of two kneeling winged figures, pressed belly to belly, with their heads bent reverently and their wings raised such that the four tips converged a good thirty feet above the floor. From there the jet shot up, thick around as a man, then splashed down gloriously over the two figures.

Boka warriors guided the company toward the stairways that spiraled up and around the Grand Gallery. Kerrigan was ready to continue up past the fourth level—the one at the top of the halls that led to the Grand Gallery—but Bok handed Princess Sayce to Dranae, then tugged him along the wide balcony circling the gallery. Kerrigan resisted for a moment, then saw a group of urZrethi sorceresses.

One with onyx skin smiled at him. "We do not know what you did to slow them, but we could feel it here."

"I did nothing."

"Modesty; good. We need your help." She pointed to her fellows. "We have a way to stop them, but we cannot do it alone. Will you help us?"

Kerrigan nodded. "Tell me what to do."

She pointed down at the fountain. "The sculpture. I need you to destroy it."

"Destroy it?" Clutching the balustrade, he looked down as the last of the warriors started up the stairs. He cast a spell and caught the hint of an enchantment on the fountain that did resemble his telekinesis spell. There he used the magick to draw and lift something, whereas here it was used to restrain. It was really the same spell, just reversed.

As a dragonel ball skipped in from the Long Hall and bounced off the fountain's lip, Kerrigan turned his head and smiled at the sorceress. "I know what you want. Are you sure?"

She nodded, then turned to her confederates. "Go!"

Each of them grew long legs and moved to a position near the top of eight halls that converged on the Grand Gallery. The only entryway the sorceresses left unattended was the northernmost, through which the enemy was advancing. As one, the seven sorceresses grew their left arms long and reached up to touch the keystone in each of the other arches.

Magick rippled through the air, shifting and shapeless, yet tangible enough to send a tingle through his flesh. It began to move in a circle, starting at the southernmost position and flowing to the right. It came around faster and faster, building in intensity. It struck him first as a light breeze, then a hot summer wind.

At the entrance to each of the seven halls, the air began to shimmer. As the heat built the arched image wavered, then began to grow more opaque, filled with amorphous mist that thickened into a billowing curtain. Then that ethereal fabric tightened like a taut sail against the wind, sealing every hall, save that through which the Aurolani advanced.

The onyx sorceress took Kerrigan's right hand. "Now."

The human mage drew in a deep breath, then let his sense of magick flow into hers. Heat came back along the connection, as if their energies boiled against each other, but soon the current became smooth and quick. The tingle again ran over Kerrigan, then poured through his spine and up into his head. There it swirled around, tightening into a roiling spiral.

Kerrigan extended his left hand and found the statue's sense. His fingers closed and met resistance. He adjusted his grip, slipping it down farther toward the base, then tightened it. He caught a hint of surprise from the urZrethi, then exhaled, set his teeth, and yanked.

With a great cracking of stone, he tore the statuary from the heart of the fountain.

Water geysered through the hole, rising in a column ten feet in diameter to slam into the gallery ceiling and spray back down. A cold wave hit Kerrigan, shocking him enough that he dropped the statue and fell back. Then, sputtering, he stepped forward again to the balustrade and watched the water boil and froth.

As with fountains everywhere, the water came to it under pressure. The magick he had detected on the statue had restrained most of the water, only allowing that slender shaft to come up through the fountain's heart. With the statue gone and the spell broken, the flow was no longer plugged. It raced down through the tunnels that brought water to the urZrethi realm.

Already the water level of Lake Osemyr had fallen an inch. In a week, a river in Oriosa would run dry. By the end of that same week, a lake would form north of Bokagul, and a village that had once sat in a sleepy little valley would forever disappear.

But now, given only one outlet, the water cascaded into the Long Hall. The first Aurolani were in some ways the luckiest. When the wall of frigid water hit them, most were shocked into unconsciousness. Those who were not struggled against the rising flood, choking and sputtering until the rushing water propelled them into the shafts raised above Will's blood. The water's weight was sufficient to pass them through as if mud through a fine mesh screen.

Hundreds of thousands of gallons raced into the Long Hall, sweeping everything before them. Gibberers tumbled and bounced off walls. Water wrapped some around pillars, crushing them like eggshells. The dragonels were lifted and tossed about as if mere toys. Their heavy bronze barrels smashed the troops they rolled over. Shot moved down the Hall like pebbles in a stream, and firedirt was contemptuously swirled away in the flood's rage.

Farther on the water flowed until it reached the portal through which the Aurolani troops had entered. It burst forth in a torrent that sent those yet waiting in a little canyon scurrying for higher ground. The water filled the canyon, then streamed north to swell a rivulet over its banks and flood a valley.

Kerrigan shook his head, flicking water from the ends of his hair. "How long will you let it flow?"

"How long will it take for their stink to be cleansed?" The sorceress shook her head. "If Lake Osemyr must be drained, then so be it. Hours or centuries, this river of tears will run until we never need fear unleashing it again."

CHAPTER 43

William frowned as Kerrigan looked over at him. The thief raised a hand to the fine stitchery that Peri had used to close the wound in his forehead. "Really, Ker, it's fine. You just go on using your magick to fix up those who need it."

"It really would take no time at all."

Will shook his head. "Having a scar isn't going to be so bad. Be worth a drink or two when I tell how I got it."

"As you wish, Will." The mage shook his head wearily and returned to his work.

After the battle, the company was conducted to a new *coric*. In the lower common room, Kerrigan worked with Bok on Lombo's wounds. The draconette shots had done little more than stun the Panqui, though a few shots had drawn blood. Kerrigan had not had an easy time removing the draconette balls or repairing cracked bits of Lombo's bony hide—but mostly because Lombo hated being fussed over.

The Panqui's protestations had finally been enough to get Kerrigan focused on the others. After Lombo, the most grievously wounded had been Princess Sayce. Now Will cut across the lower chamber of the *coric* and up the steps to the woman's sphere. There he crossed to the rounded doorway leading to the princess' chamber.

He hesitated for a moment and his heart rose in his throat. Sayce lay on a soft pallet with a white sheet draped over her, tucked up to her throat. Her head lay on a satin pillow all but hidden by the flaming carpet of her hair. Her mask had been removed, but in its place she wore a light lace replacement. Like the sheet, it was white, and served to emphasize her pale skin.

For a heartbeat he feared she was dead, but her chest rose and fell slowly. Relief flooded through him. The idea that those eyes might never open again was something he couldn't countenance. Once he saw she was resting peacefully, he smiled and the tightness around his heart eased.

Will turned to leave, not wanting to disturb her, but she stirred. He looked at her, and slowly she turned her face toward him.

As she had lain there, he'd only seen her right profile, but the left side of her face was mottled purple and blue, with yellow at the edges. The lace courtesy mask stood out against that angry flesh. She snaked her left hand from beneath the sheet and raised it as if to touch her face, then let her arm fall across her stomach instead.

"Will?"

"Yes, it's me." Will's voice grew small and he swallowed. "I wanted to see how you were doing."

She snorted lightly, then winced. "My head hurts more than when a horse clipped me."

"I can get Kerrigan."

"No, no; don't." Her voice gained a little strength and a lot of urgency. "He's done enough for me. Come in. Sit."

"But you should be resting."

"I am on a stone bed in a rock hole, which is a lot like being entombed." Her right eye flashed brightly—far more so than her bloodshot left eye. "Feeling half-dead in a grave is not very restful."

Will smiled and entered the room. He thought for a moment about sitting on the edge of her bed, but it was narrow enough that she'd have to move closer to the wall. Instead, he sat on the floor with his back to her bed and looked up at her over his right shoulder. "I'm glad you're doing better."

"I was lucky. Dranae thinks the draconetteer didn't load enough firedirt or that it was wet, so only some of it burned. The ball hit the left side of my forehead. My mask helped. Still cracked my skull, but your friend healed that."

The thief shivered. Kerrigan had described it as a depressed fracture—which was the fancy way of labeling the big dent in her head. Kerrigan managed to get the bone out of her brain and fix up all the immediate damage. It had been a harrowing healing for Kerrigan, tired as he was from helping the urZrethi to flood the hallway, but he had triumphed.

"He can take care of the rest of it. You'll be good as new."

"Why don't you let him fix your face?"

Will shrugged uneasily. He didn't mind having a scar there—not that he thought Peri's handiwork would leave much of one. The scar would create a link between him and Crow, since they'd both earned scars fighting Chytrine. Heroes always had scars. In some ways it seemed to Will as if it were cheating for a hero to be unmarked.

"Kerrigan has better things to do than to make me better-looking." Will smiled. "As if that could be done."

Sayce smiled and let her right hand drift down from beneath the sheet to brush fingers through Will's brown hair. "You may be right there, Will. Making *me* look better would take a lot of work. The left side of my face is throbbing."

"You look fine."

"Is that some honest deception, Will? Stick with thieving. You don't lie very well."

"I'm not lying." Will frowned, and the stitches pulled a bit. A blush warmed his cheeks, then the frown melted into a goofy grin he was glad she couldn't see. "You look a lot better now than when I saw you fall."

Sayce nodded weakly. "I know what you did, Will. When I was hit, I didn't black out. Not at first. It's not like I remember events in order. I do remember your voice, though."

Her fingers idly played with his hair, but she turned her face to stare toward the dim ceiling. "I had been hit hard. I knew I was hurt. Badly. I was going to die. The shock...the pain...I couldn't see out of my left eye. I couldn't move. And then...then, Will, I heard your voice. 'By my blood, you will not pass.' My life had been slipping from me, but your order, it stopped me. I wasn't going to pass from this life. I couldn't. So I knew I would survive."

She glanced down at him again and smiled. "Earlier, Kerrigan came in and wanted to fix my face. I told him to go away. He sighed."

Will nodded, relishing the sensation of her fingers against his scalp.

"He said, 'What is going on with you people?' I asked what he meant, and he told me you refused to be healed, too. Kerrigan thought it must have something to do with being hit on the left side of the head." She twined a lock of his hair around a finger. "When I found out that you refused healing, I decided I would, too."

"But, Princess, you could use it."

"You don't understand, Will. Your men, the Freemen, they're willing to take a mask from you and wear your mark to honor you. Similar wound, same engagement. I'll wear this bruise to honor you for saving my life."

"But I didn't..."

She lowered her hand and pressed a finger to his lips. "Stop. You acted when it was needed. Think about any hero you know. Think about Crow. Heroes don't think about acting heroic, they just do. They see a need and they fulfill it.

"You know, Will, I never doubted you were the Norrington of prophecy. I might have wondered if you were truly the hero he was supposed to be, but no more." Sayce exhaled heavily and her eyes fluttered. "I'm sorry, I'm drifting back to sleep. I don't want to be rude."

Will stood slowly, taking her hand in his, then laying it on the edge of the bed. "Rest some more."

"You'll come see me again?"

Her question made his stomach do a little flip-flop. "Of course."

"Good." She smiled and closed her eyes.

Her lips moved again, but Will could not hear what she was saying. As quietly as he could he left her chamber, fingering the stitches above his left eye. He'd thought of it as a link with Crow, but now Sayce had forged it into a link between them. That idea pleased him.

He thought more about it, and let the events tumble back down into the whole myth he'd conjured about his life. Once upon a time he wanted to be known as Will the Nimble, the King of the Dimandowns. He wanted to be known as a rival to the Azure Spider. Resolute had accurately ridiculed that notion at their first meeting, then had led him off on an incredible series of adventures. He'd gone to Vilwan and seen dragons battle. He'd gone to Okrannel and had seen an Aurolani army crushed. He'd been feted and celebrated in Yslin and Meredo. He'd raided Wruona and stolen a fragment of the DragonCrown from the Azure Spider.

And now he had traveled the halls of Bokagul and saved a Murosan Princess from a horde of gibberkin.

Any one of his adventures would have been more than enough for a heroic song. He had, in less than a year, achieved far more than he could have ever dreamt of in his childhood. In fact, he realized, had he been born that very day and raised as he was, his hero would not have been the Azure Spider, but Will the Nimble.

Yet, in realizing that he had attained his childhood goal in less than a year, he discovered how hollow an achievement that was. Princess Sayce had been right: heroes did not think about acting heroic, nor did they dwell upon having been heroic. And while things he had done might seem heroic in hindsight, at the time they had to be done and, more important, if he had not done them, someone else in the company would have. His actions were not at all special in the company he kept.

Will smiled slowly as somewhere, deep down inside, the child he had once been screamed in outrage at the idea that he was not special. *The times, they are special, and they call for a lot from us.* He looked around the *coric* and nodded as Resolute entered and Kerrigan scolded Lombo into silence.

Qwc buzzed over and landed on Will's right shoulder. "Doing well, Will?"

"I am indeed, Qwc." The thief smiled. "I'm tired, sore, sewed up, and not looking forward to the winter trek to Caledo. I know we're going to get hurt, and I fear some of us will get dead."

"Does not sound like doing well to Qwc."

"But I am, Qwc." Will nodded solemnly. "The company I keep sees to that."

CHAPTER 44

Try as he might, General Markus Adrogans had not found a way to guarantee that less blood than water would flow in the taking of the Three Brothers. The arrangement of the three fortresses had thwarted enemies for centuries, and most of them had not had to contend with the frigid cold snap that had settled over the countryside. For while it brought no snow, it made the march north agonizing.

Adrogans had brought his troops down into position three days before the assault and begun creating two siege machines. He opted for rams, with roofs and stout sides to protect the men wielding them. That made them incredibly heavy and slow to move, but if Darovin *did* have dragonels, the rams' robust construction might shrug off a few balls. The question really became one of whether or not they could withstand enough shots to break through the first oak gate.

The Jeranese general had deployed the Blackfeathers to snipe at guards and keep them always on alert. While the river supplied no real attack route against the Three Brothers, its frozen surface did allow Beal mot Tsuvo and her troops to range north around the forts and along the road, setting up ambushes for any Aurolani reinforcements coming south to the Three Brothers.

Adrogans huddled inside a thick, furred robe, then pulled his scarf down and spit. His spittle cracked in the air as it flew. "At least Duke Mikhail's dream was accurate concerning the day's weather."

Phfas snorted. "You place too much trust in Svarskya and the Kingsmen."

"If this plan works, it will be because of them." Adrogans glanced back along the roadway. The ram slowly advanced thanks to the efforts of the

Gurol Stoneheart battalion. They sang a deep, lusty tune, rhythmic and guttural. With each repetition it grew in power. The ram, which looked very like
a covered bridge on wheels, ground forward. The heavy wheels crushed the
snow as it moved, while the ram itself swayed forward and back, side to side,
with each motion. The warriors had hung their round shields on the exterior
walls, so the bold devices painted in reds, blues, greens, and golds lent it a
fierce martial air.

The horses and liveried warriors of the Kingsmen waited around the corner from Darovin. Their horses stamped and blew out great plumes of angry
steam. The warriors all had lances. From the tips of some fluttered gay pennants. Anonymous in their heavy armor, they would not be easy to kill, yet
Adrogans knew that many of them would die. Any mounted horsemen
trapped in the citadel would be slaughtered, yet there had been no way to
deny Duke Mikhail's request to let the Kingsmen go in first.

As the ram slowly came into view of Darovin, activity increased on the
battlements. A few arrows arced out at the crawling ram, but none of them
hit. Out by the river, a few elven shots hit the tower from the far shore. One
gibberer did fall flailing to the ice below, but its body failed to break through.
The crusted snow cracked beneath it, and a light dusting of powder puffed
up and quickly floated down to cover the body.

Phfas pointed a finger at the top of Darovin. "They signal."

The yellow flag that had been flying over the first tower slowly came
down, then a red flag and a black pennant were raised. Across the river, elves
flashed mirrors to communicate what the flags at the other sites were doing.
Varalorsk acknowledged the signal by repeating it, then offered a green flag.
Darovin replied by lowering, then reraising, its red and black flags.

Adrogans smiled. "Red to report a threat, black to dismiss it and the offer
of help. The commander at Darovin is confident he can deal with the threat.
Good, very good." He turned to the signalman on his left. "Signal the Blackfeathers to advance toward the Darovin river tower."

"Yes, sir."

The signalman used his mirrors to communicate that order to the elves.
Mistress Gilthalarwin ordered her warriors to emerge from the brush on the
far shore and approach in a long skirmish line that began to tighten into a
semicircle as it drew closer. The gibberers launched arrows at them. While
their height did allow the Aurolani archers greater range, their lack of
accuracy—especially in face of the breeze—made their defensive efforts less
than effective.

The Darovin commander reacted by sending more troops running out
over the arched pathway to the river tower. The Darovin garrison should
have numbered approximately one hundred, and the river tower had enough
room for half that number of archers to be employed effectively. Even with

the elves' superior skill at archery, the chances of their doing much against the tower were nil.

"Signalman, tell the Warhawks it is time."

The man shifted and flashed his mirror at the mountain high above the Three Brothers. No light came back, no signal acknowledged the message, but this did not surprise Adrogans. Instead of looking upward, he shifted his glance to Darovin's river tower and, leaning forward with his hands on his saddlehorn, waited.

The first Gyrkyme he saw was traveling so fast that he was certain the winged warrior would never manage to pull out of his dive. The Gyrkyme had folded his wings in tightly and dropped toward the river, as if a suicide who had flung himself from the mountain. Nothing more than a brown streak, the Gyrkyme then snapped his wings open, twisted right, then left, and shrieked as he shot past the river tower. He swooped up abruptly, rolling in the air and gliding toward the river's far shore.

By rights that level flight should have made him an easy target, but the tower behind him was in chaos. The Gyrkyme, and those who flew in his wake, carried firecocks. The devices consisted of a crockery oil reservoir and a fusing mechanism that ignited the puddle of oil once the globe shattered on the tower. The resulting explosion launched balls of flame and black smoke into the air.

A half-dozen firecocks slammed into the top of the tower, instantly immolating the archers at the top. Several more laced fire onto the archway, cutting off both retreat and reinforcement. One Gyrkyme flirted with death as she streaked low and deliberately aimed her firecock at a lower level arrow slit. The device apparently made it through, as fire burst out the other openings and one burning body remained lodged in the slit on the tower's far side.

The flags atop Darovin immediately shifted. Down came the red and black. In their place rose two long green pennants.

Phfas cackled. "He demands two legions to help. Fool!"

The Kingsmen had advanced enough to be seen from Darovin and raised their voices in a cheer as they saw that signal. The Gurolans must have figured out what was happening, for their song redoubled in strength and the ram lurched, moving faster. The song pulsed power and Adrogans could feel Pain attuning herself to it, reading the ache of muscles, the creaking of sinews, the sharp tingling of frozen toes.

The Darovin ballistae launched their missiles. Adrogans took heart, since the heavy shafts with the foot-long blades had not nearly the power of a single dragonel ball. Even so, some spears did pierce the roof and Pain communicated to him the golden torture of the cold, steel head spitting a man.

The song faltered for a heartbeat, then resumed again, stronger and more defiant. The Kingsmen started forward again, but Adrogans held up a hand to restrain them. He read the urgency in the jingle of tack and the quivering of muscles, but shook his head. "Wait for the signal."

The two green flags flew down. When they rose again, a third had joined them. This green flag had three white dots on it.

Phfas' eyes narrowed. "Sorcerers."

Adrogans nodded. "As we expected." The elven scout on the far side of the river flashed a confirmation that reinforcements were moving up, including vylaens and the *kryalniri*.

The shaman threw off his robe, interlinked his fingers, bridged them, and raised them over his head in a stretch. The little charms hanging from his leathery skin stood out. Whereas Phfas normally wore rings of gold or other precious metals, this day he sported small stone amulets painted white, bits of bone, and two frostclaw feathers.

The general smiled. "Are you ready?"

"Yes."

"If you please."

Phfas' hands parted, but remained above his head. The fingers splayed out and quivered. Tendons stood out and veins twisted beneath his skin. Scars became almost luminous and wove themselves into a network that closely resembled a snowflake. They burned whiter than snow itself.

Then the shaman's hands convulsed into fists.

A crack sounded from the mountaintop. For a heartbeat after that there was nothing, then a slow rumbling rose in its wake. The rumbling built, quickly, swallowing the song, eclipsing the screams from the tower.

Phfas, like Adrogans, had bound to himself *yrûn*, though his closest ally was air. As his fists closed, air hardened on the mountaintop. It drove down solidly at various points cracking the crusted snow and pressing it into the softer, looser powder below. The snow began to slip and slide, passing quickly over a deeper, icier level. The rumble grew as it picked up speed, then the snow flew from the mountain in a white cataract.

Snow, so light that it would drift down easily from the clouds, hardly seemed a threat, but it poured off the mountain swiftly and heavily. Tons of it flew in a fluid sheet, mixing huge chunks of ice with a few trees and the occasional rock, pounding down onto the roadway between Varalorsk and Darovin with the fury of storm-driven waves.

The Aurolani reinforcements—all three legions—vanished in the avalanche. Snow landed twenty feet deep on the roadway, rising higher than the walls of Darovin itself. The swath of snow flowed onto the river and the ice cracked. The snow poured down into the dark hole and disappeared.

The ram continued forward and the Darovin ballistae shot more hurriedly. More men died, but soon enough the shots from the tower played back against the middle and tail of the ram. Archers lined the top of the gate wall and shot down, trying to drive their shafts through the roof, but to no avail.

Adrogans watched the aft end of the ram swing back, then forward. The first impact sounded like a giant hand knocking politely on the gate. Then another knock, heavier and harder, echoed through the valley. A third came, then a fourth, each insistent, solid and undeniable. With enough time, the gate would shatter.

Suddenly chaos erupted on the walls. Gibberers pitched forward, spinning from above the gate to bounce from the ram's roof. The gates opened, slowly at first, then more quickly, and the Gurolean song transformed itself into a cacophony of war cries.

Adrogans spurred his horse forward, with the signalman and Phfas trotting in his wake. He glanced back at the shaman. Phfas' skin had taken on a blue tone and the older man shivered, but his eyes still burned bright. He smiled even more brightly.

"You see, uncle. It worked."

Phfas nodded. "The Zhusk could have done this."

"The Zhusk did. They just had help."

Adrogans dismounted at the ram and, drawing his sword, ran in through the gate. The Stonehearts had already reached the far gate and opened it. A few of them ran out toward the mountain of snow cutting the road. A couple of gibberers lay broken on the roadway, or struggling to drag themselves from beneath tons of snow. The Stonehearts ended their misery.

The Alcidese general, Caro, begrimed but smiling broadly, met Adrogans in Darovin's courtyard. "It worked perfectly, my lord. Yes, more blood flowed than water, but that's because so little water flowed."

The difficulty in taking the Three Brothers really fell into two areas. The first was a need to lure troops out from behind walls so they could be slaughtered. The roadway offered an obvious killing ground, and the Blackfeathers could have slain many of the reinforcements, but they could only have done so from the river and there they would have been in the open and terribly vulnerable.

The second problem was a manifestation of the first: how to approach the fortresses unseen. At first he had considered having the Nalisk Mountain Rangers descend on ropes from the mountain, but that would still have left them outside the fortresses, and as vulnerable as any troops on the road. With the river frozen, nothing could be floated down to deliver troops, and they would have still remained outside the walls.

Ultimately Duke Mikhail had provided the solution. So exact were his models that he even showed the stone tunnels where the fortresses' offal flowed into the river to be carried away. Those tunnels provided a way in, but one that was guarded by twenty feet of frigid water.

More blood flowed than water because, fifteen miles upriver, Zhusk shamans whose *yrûn* were water summoned all their power and diverted the river into an old flood channel. While the river pooled into a lake, Caro's Alcidese King's Horse Guards, the Helurian Imperial Steel Legion and the Okrannel Kingsmen had traveled beneath the ice, in the frozen riverbed, to the effluent tunnels. They slowly snuck into the fortresses and then, when the avalanche thundered down, Caro's and Mikhail's men attacked Darovin and Varalorsk respectively.

A man on the top of Darovin called down. "Varalorsk just raised a green legion flag. Elves say reinforcements are heading to Varalorsk."

"Understood." Adrogans raised a hand and summoned the leader of the troops who had appropriated the Kingsmen's livery forward. "Captain Dmitri, have your people get that ram in here, then close the gates and man them."

The man from Svoin nodded, then turned and began to issue orders to his troops.

Adrogans looked at Caro. "Shall we make our way to Varalorsk?"

"After you, my lord."

With Phfas trailing them, the two generals hiked up over the hill of snow and back down to Varalorsk. The small sally port in the southern gate opened and filthy Kingsmen waved them forward hurriedly. Their urgency did not surprise Adrogans, as the green flag requesting reinforcements had been raised by the Kingsmen to lure Aurolani forces into the open. On Varalorsk's north wall archers who would slaughter the reinforcements would be hidden, and this was something to which all of the attackers had looked forward.

The expression worn by the Kingsmen was not one of glee. "Hurry, General, it is the Duke."

Adrogans slipped through the port and followed quickly. His guide led him through Varalorsk. In his mind Adrogans could see his route winding through Mikhail's models. Deep inside they went, then up and up to the top level. His guide indicated the door to what should have been the commanding officer's quarters, then stood aside.

Adrogans stepped over the body of a dead *kryalniri* and reached a wooden cot upon which an ashen-faced Mikhail lay. The dark brown clothes he wore hid much of the blood, but the fingers he clutched to his middle could not hide his wound. A hideous slash had opened his belly.

The Jeranese general turned to Phfas. "Get me an elven healer *now*."

"No, General." Mikhail's words came hissed and barely above a whisper. "There is no time."

Adrogans looked back at him and saw a thin trickle of blood trail from the corner of his mouth. One of the other men standing there dabbed at it with a red cloth. "We've taken the towers, you know. Your plan worked."

The dying Okrans noble nodded. "I know. It was as I dreamed."

Adrogans narrowed his eyes. "Did you dream..."

"This? No." He snorted weakly. "I am neither so brave nor foolish to walk into this. In my dream we won. We did. Then my dream ended. Now my life ends."

Outside the roar of the archers rose as they revealed themselves and slew the arriving reinforcements. Their cries would signal the other Kingsmen waiting to emerge, and Krakoin would fall.

Mikhail smiled. "General, you will take Svarskya. I know it."

"You'll be there with me."

"No, no I will not. I shall watch, though." Mikhail's eyes flared wide and white, then a spasm of pain shook him. More blood dripped from his mouth and stained his teeth. "A favor."

Adrogans leaned closer as the man's voice faded. "Anything."

"Tell Alexia dreams can come true. Tell her to trust her dreams."

"I will, my friend, I will."

Mikhail's body shook once more, then went limp.

Adrogans reached down and closed the man's eyes. He mouthed a silent prayer even as Pain raked her talons across his belly. He winced, then looked up at the other Kingsmen standing around the cot. They looked stricken and he could tell each one of them would have gladly given his life in exchange for that of the duke. *They even think his death is their fault.*

Adrogans let his eyes harden and kept his voice grim. "I would speak no ill of Duke Mikhail, but he lied. He *was* a brave man, the bravest, for only the bravest could have taken Varalorsk."

He hesitated for a moment as Mikhail's men looked up at him and blinked. He waited until they could truly comprehend what he was saying, and once he read that in their dark eyes, he continued. "The duke *did* foresee his death, but he knew it was the sacrifice that would win the Three Brothers. He knew it would let us win Svarskya, so let no one think his death could have been prevented. He offered himself for the rest of us, for Okrannel. I charge you with making certain the truth of his death is known. Long shall his courage be sung."

The trio of Kingsmen there nodded, then one met his gaze openly. "It will be our sacred duty, General."

"Then I shall leave the master of the Three Brothers to your care." Adrogans nodded once, then left the room.

Phfas caught up with him quickly. "Why lie for the dead?"

"Was I lying, uncle, or had Mikhail forgotten that part of his dream?" Adrogans narrowed his eyes. "His memory will drive them further than he would have alive. He wanted Svarskya free, and this way he will win it. He gave everything to this cause, and we shall make sure his effort bears the fruit he intended."

CHAPTER 45

For the barest of innocent moments, Princess Alexia's heart leaped when she first looked upon fair Caledo. The city of white stone rose from the snowy plains as if it had been crafted from the snows itself. Eight towers soared above the points of the octagonal city walls, each stout, each sheathed in alabaster flesh. Within the walls stood four more towers, each sleek and softly curved, with high arching bridges linking them. Beyond the city, Lake Calessa lay covered in ice and deep snow.

From the crest of the hills to the east of the city, only two elements spoiled the snowy vision. The first was the pair of black stones set near the eastern gate. Alexia had heard of Murosan mages meeting to duel at these stones, but she'd somehow relegated such tales to the realm of fancies. Yet here they stood, tall and imposing. Their stark contrast with the city itself, both in color and angularity, made them seem jarring and menacing. Alexia read them less as a sign of Muroso's strength than foreshadowing of Chytrine's onslaught.

The second divergent element was more reassuring. Bright banners of red and blue, green and yellow, purple and gold hung from tower windows. Pennants, long and bright, waved and snapped from tower tops.

Alexia reined back and studied the city, and the empty expanse leading up to it. She forced herself to memorize every detail: the city's majesty, its gentle strength and its unmarred walls. She noted the lack of carrion birds, and drank in the peace of the lakeshore city.

Snow crunched beneath the hooves of Crow's horse as he rode up beside her. "It is breathtaking."

She smiled and nodded. "I fear, given what will come, it will only be in our memories that Caledo lives."

Crow sighed out a plume of vapor. "Win or lose, Chytrine's invasion will reshape the world."

Alyx nodded slowly. She'd seen that in Bokagul, where the shock of the invasion had stirred the populace. The urZrethi had thought themselves invulnerable in their mountain fastness, but that illusion had been shattered forever. And while a debate still raged within that nation as to how many troops they should send to help, there was indeed resolution to act. Already small units were patrolling the mountains and heading toward Sarengul to warn others. Alyx felt certain that the Boka would send warriors to help defend Caledo since it had been Princess Sayce who had brought all of them to Bokagul.

I just have to hope they will get here in time.

The urZrethi had been generous in showing their thanks to Kerrigan and the others for their assistance in turning back the invasion. While the ability to shift shape had obviated the need for the urZrethi to use weapons and armor, their metalsmiths were quite adept at fashioning the same. Alexia had been given a thick-bladed sword with a reinforced forte and slightly curved blade of incredible lightness. The steel, which had an exquisite swirl pattern worked through it, was flexible, yet held an edge that was sharp enough to split a floating feather.

The Murosan troops and the Freemen had all been given light suits of mail that they said weighed less than silk. UrZrethi smiths fashioned new bladestars for Resolute, which he accepted with only a minor grumble. The others he'd been willing to leave behind; these he would have to collect. But, despite his protest, it was quite clear he was pleased. Peri had been given a winged helm light enough for her to wear in flight, Crow a sheaf of arrows with steel broadheads that would, it was said, pierce a dragon's scales. And, along with a light coat of mail, Will received beaten gold bracers, each set with a sapphire as long as his thumb.

Princess Sayce, Kerrigan, and Bok, however, received unique gifts. The Murosan princess was given a silver mask to replace the one that she'd worn when shot. The left side had been set with amethyst in memory of the purple bruise she'd worn. Despite riding into the cold, Sayce had chosen to wear it, and there was no denying it enhanced her beauty.

The urZrethi honored Kerrigan by presenting him with a wand made of a single long crystal circled at each end with a ring of gold that was set with a dozen gems. When he used it, various of the gems glowed, and their hues shot through the wand, threading themselves through any visible spell. Alexia had no idea what the significance of that was, but Kerrigan seemed delighted, so she took that as a very good sign.

Bok received the most peculiar gift of all. His presence had caused trouble for the urZrethi. They would have preferred not to notice him at all, but the fact that he had dragged Sayce clear during the battle could not be ignored. After much deliberation, the word "*bok*" had been removed from his name. In effect they accepted him back into their society, but everyone did seem to breathe a sigh of relief when he evidenced no desire to remain in Bokagul and instead accompanied Kerrigan northwest toward the Murosan capital.

The journey from Bokagul to Caledo had taken six days through foothills and valleys. The blizzards let up during their trip, but the snow that remained had made it tough going. Occasionally they met urZrethi patrols, and once ran across the aftermath of an urZrethi ambush of some Aurolani deserters, but otherwise they passed without seeing much of interest and not being seen themselves.

Out and around Alyx and Crow galloped a company of Sayce's Lancers. One of them had bound the Murosan Princess' personal pennant to the tip of his lance and carried it upright as he rode toward the city. Because she had learned of it in the Communion, Alexia had been able to say nothing about Sayce's father being displeased by her mission to the south. Sayce's dispatching of the squad to announce her arrival—along with that of the Norrington—might well blunt her father's reaction.

Alyx urged her horse forward again and down the last hill in the wake of the Lancers. "How long do you suppose it will be before the Aurolani arrive and lay siege to the city?"

Crow shook his head. "There's no real way of telling, but the signs suggest sooner rather than later. For Chytrine to have sent forces into Bokagul, she's probably already neutralized Sarengul. That secures her flank and pressures Scrainwood. She can take all the time she wants to conquer Muroso. She has any of a dozen ways to expand south from there, and that's well before summer, when the true campaigning will take place."

The princess had hoped Crow would see some flaw in her analysis, but the simple fact was that Chytrine was isolating countries and taking them one at a time. No single country could stand against the full might of her army and its dragonels. As the Aurolani forces moved south, they did venture into lands with higher populations, but that just meant there would be more refugees to send streaming south.

Alyx shook her head. "As beautiful as this city is, it is wholly unsuited to holding off Chytrine. The dragonels were made to shatter walls like that. Those towers will topple under her assaults. The Murosans are known for being valiant, but standing against her is foolishness."

"We can hope King Bowmar will be more reasonable than his daughter, but I doubt it." Crow shifted his shoulders. "There are things we can do to slow Chytrine down, however. And for now, buying more time is a victory."

Even before the detachment of Lancers reached the city, the eastern gate opened and a larger troop of horsemen rode out to greet them. The two groups—the smaller in red, and the larger in blue—met and mingled for a moment, then the bulk of the larger group rode east toward Alexia and the others. The Lancers continued with an escort back into the city.

Princess Sayce came riding up on Alexia's left, giving her a view of a silver profile. "This is not likely to be good. My brother is at the head of the riders. Let me handle this."

The slight tremor in Sayce's voice amused Alyx. "As you wish."

Snow splashed up from hooves, then flew apart in the breeze as the riders approached. One man, tall and lean, bundled in furs against the cold, moved out in front. The breeze caught the hood of his cloak, billowing it out, then blowing it back. Long brown hair streamed back from his head. The mask he wore was as large as the one Sayce had worn, but instead of red, or even the blue of his unit, it was black.

As black as the magestones marking the city gate.

The man reined back, slowing his horse to a walk. He raised a gloved hand in greeting. "Welcome, travelers. I am Prince Murfin, of the Murosan royal house. You would be Alexia of Okrannel?"

Alyx nodded, rather surprised that he'd not addressed his sister. "I am. This is Kedyn's Crow. You know Princess Sayce."

"Indeed. It is a pleasure to meet you both." Murfin did not even glance at Sayce, who had gone very still and quiet. "My father, King Bowmar, offers you his hospitality and his thanks at returning a wayward daughter to her home."

Before Alyx could offer any sort of reply, Will rode up. "More like she's the one who's bringing us here, not the other way around."

The prince smiled, almost as if he had been expecting such a comment. "And you would be the Norrington."

"Until someone better comes along." Will urged his horse forward until he partially eclipsed Murfin's view of his sister. "I've brought with me a company of Oriosan Freemen to fight for Caledo."

"Your contribution is most welcome. They can join the other Oriosans here. We're grateful for your help." The prince broadened his smile for a moment. "It is a great honor to have you all here, and things have been prepared for you in Caledo. Captain Twynham here will conduct you to the city and your lodgings. Once you have had a chance to rest, my father would like to welcome you all."

Alyx nodded. "We will await his pleasure."

"Splendid." Murfin glanced at Sayce. "Sister, attend me on my return."

She nodded and started her horse forward. Will moved to accompany her, but she laid her right hand on his left arm. "No, Will, just go with the others."

"But..." Will looked from her to her brother and back again. "You shouldn't ride into trouble alone."

"That thought will be all the accompaniment I need." She leaned over and gave him a soft kiss on the cheek. "From the moment I left, I knew what this would be like. I will see you soon enough."

With a touch of her heels to her horse's flanks, she started off and raced a bit past her brother. He set off, cloak flying, and caught up with her. Neither slowed, but neither did she try to elude him. Alyx thought she even might have heard laughter on the wind, but she couldn't be certain.

The King's Heavy Horse spread out along the column with a blond man, Captain Twynham, leading the way back into the city. He didn't say much, but rode tall and proudly in the saddle. Alyx and Crow followed him several paces back, with Will falling in behind her and Kerrigan coming up beside him.

Will grumbled in a low voice. "I'm not sure I like the look of that Murfin."

Kerrigan kept his voice soft. "You caught it, then?"

"Caught what, Ker?"

"The spell." The Vilwanese mage shifted in the saddle. "I almost didn't. Murosan magick has a different feel to it, but he cast a spell on the lot of us when he came up."

Crow turned. "When?"

"When he raised his hand in greeting. Takes a tricky man to say one thing, but cast another."

Crow frowned. "What kind of spell?"

"Just a moment." Kerrigan closed his eyes, raised his right hand from the saddlehorn, and wove his fingers through an odd little pattern of movements. "I am not wholly certain, but it could have been some diagnostic spell."

Alyx raised an eyebrow. "Checking to see if his sister was hurt?"

Kerrigan's eyes popped open again. "That could be it, yes."

She laughed. "Definitely sinister."

"I still don't like it." Will snorted. "He wasn't friendly to her at all. They should be thanking her."

Crow winked. "Don't assume they are angry. Being worried would be enough."

"Well, if they do anything to her, I'll..."

"What will you do, Will?"

The thief sighed in response to Crow's question. "No fair asking me to make good on empty threats. I just hope she'll be okay."

"I'm sure she will." Crow faced forward again, but Alyx still caught the full force of his smile. "Your friend will be fine, you'll see, Will."

* * *

Captain Twynham led the main company into the city and on up to the central quartet of towers. The easternmost pair comprised one building, the palace, while the other two were used by the Caledo Academy of Magicks and the Guilds Tower, in which most of the nation's guilds had offices. Once he'd taken them through the palace gate, they turned left and approached the South Tower. Attendants took their horses to the stables there, while body servants emerged to conduct the travelers to their own accommodations.

Alyx and Crow parted company quickly, as he went to see to the billeting of the rest of the company. She bid him a silent farewell, then followed a middle-aged woman with rosy cheeks up a spiral staircase to the small suite of rooms they had been given. The sitting room faced east, with the sleeping alcove off to the left, complete with a huge four-poster bed thick with quilts. To the right lay a toilet and bathing area. A folding screen decorated with painted wooden panels showing scenes from a hunt would allow privacy in that area.

A slender woman not quite as tall as Alexia was standing in the room as they entered. The servingwoman gasped and immediately dropped to one knee. "Begging your pardon, Highness, I didn't know."

The woman shook her head. "It is no matter, Meg. Leave us for a moment. Perhaps Princess Alexia would like you to fetch some food?"

Alyx caught a note of familiarity in the voice. "I'm not hungry at the moment."

"Very well, then." The woman's features were sharper than Sayce's, but close enough that the familial resemblance could not be ignored. She waited for the servant to depart before smiling. "Greetings, Princess Alexia. I am Dayley. I feel as if we have met before."

Alyx nodded, knowing full well that this was the woman she had met in the Communion. "So nice to make it a reality."

The Okrans princess offered Dayley her hand, and was met with a firm, warm grip. They shook hands, pumping each other's arms three times, but before they could release, something odd happened. Alyx felt herself shifting—there was no other word for it—as if moving into the Communion. Despite that feeling, she remained there, in the South Tower with Dayley.

But they were not alone.

Off to the east appeared a beautiful woman with snowy white hair and a soft innocence to her features and expression. Her eyes immediately caught Alexia's attention because, despite her being semitransparent, they glittered silver. Her mouth moved and Alexia caught pieces of words. "...Kesh, here things...victorious...casualties..." There was more, but the volume waxed and waned, with the words sometimes coming slowly and other times squeaking quickly.

When their hands parted, the vision vanished.

Both women looked at each other, then held hands again, but it did not come back.

Dayley frowned. "You saw it, of course. What was it?"

Alyx shook her head. "I don't know."

She shivered and Dayley caught it in her grip. "Something, Alexia. What is it?"

The Okrans princess frowned. "'Kesh' has to refer to Nefrai-kesh, Chytrine's general. Was she communicating with him? Warning him? Something like that?"

Dayley nodded, letting her hand slip from Alexia's. "Logical, but it was something else that made you shiver. What?"

Alyx shifted her shoulders uneasily. "In Meredo, Will saw someone, someone he said saved him from dying. She could have been the person he described."

"Someone in league with Nefrai-kesh saved the Norrington?"

"So it would appear."

Dayley sighed heavily. "I don't know what to make of that, if it is welcome news or not. If the gods are merciful, perhaps we have a chance to figure it out."

C H A P T E R 4 6

Kerrigan awoke with a start. Bok had clapped a knotty hand over his mouth, stifling an outcry. The mage clawed at the hand, but could not move it. The urZrethi's hand remained in place for a moment or two more than it needed, then finally moved away as Kerrigan stopped fighting him.

The young mage blinked his burning eyes. He'd not intended to fall asleep when guided to his chamber. He just lay down on the bed while Bok went for the luggage and shifted things around. He remembered yawning and deciding to close his eyes for a moment—then the hard press of Bok's hand on his mouth brought him back to consciousness.

Rym Ramoch, standing there at the foot of the bed, shook his head. "I asked you to awaken him, Bok, not scare him."

The urZrethi sank to the floor in a low crouch and mewed an apology.

Kerrigan pulled himself upright and banged his head on the headboard. "Ouch."

"Don't be doing that, Kerrigan. We can't have you dashing your brains out when we need them." Ramoch moved stiffly to an overstuffed chair near Bok's corner and seated himself. "I apologize for my absence, but when you detoured into Bokagul, reaching you was too difficult. Knowing your goal, however, I was able to come here ahead of you. I have learned some things that might be useful in your quest."

"Learning how to detect fragments of the DragonCrown?"

"The same. But first, however, I need to know what happened in Bokagul."

Kerrigan yawned as Bok slunk across the room to Ramoch's side. The elder mage idly tangled fingers in the urZrethi's hair and scratched him as one might a dog. The younger man smoothed a wrinkle from the blankets upon which he'd slept, then began to recount his adventures beneath the mountains. Rym Ramoch did not interrupt him, and because his face was masked and shadowed, Kerrigan had trouble telling if he was even listening.

When he finished his recital, the crimson-robed mage nodded solemnly. "The power you displayed is impressive. If you are able to harness that and direct it toward our goal, Chytrine will not be able to stand against you. And this thing with Will and his blood is surprising. You've seen nothing like this before from him?"

"Well, he curses all the time, but this . . . I could feel the magick pulsing off him. The effect his blood had on the Aurolani and their allies was horrible—and incredible. Even when we were leaving, after the hallway had been washed clean, I could still detect the magick. It would not surprise me if an *araftii* flying above that spot would not be stopped by the columns of power marking where his blood lay."

Ramoch drummed his right index finger on the arm of his chair. "Something must have happened to him. What was different?"

Kerrigan shrugged his shoulders. "I think maybe he likes Princess Sayce, and she had been hurt when he acted."

"A factor, certainly, for it lent power to the oath, but something else."

"Well, before Bokagul, while you had me, he had been bitten by a *sullanciri* and said a woman in white healed him. He has two burn scars on his neck and is always cold."

The elder mage's head came up. "You have examined him?"

"Yes."

"And?"

"And he seems normal." Kerrigan frowned. "Normal except that I can't detect the scars. They should be there and wrong, but his body seems to have accepted them."

Ramoch pressed the fingers of his left hand over his mouth for a moment. "That is fascinating. Watch for more symptoms, more signs."

"What is it? Is he okay?"

"I'm sure he's fine. More than fine, actually. Still, it will bear watching." Ramoch nodded. "Now, tell me, did you notice anything particular about his magick? Something that marked it as his?"

Kerrigan smiled. "I thought of that. Not at the time; we were too busy fighting. But later when I got a chance to examine the places his blood had fallen, there was something about it that had an essence of Will. It's very hard to describe. When I cast a diagnostic spell, I would get odd echoes in the back of my mind: hearing a word as he spoke it, or catching a flash of his grin, or even seeing him as he was in Yslin, running away from me."

That latter memory brought a frown to Kerrigan's face. Granted that had been before Will had known him, but Will had run from a gang of youths beating him up. Had the situation been reversed, Kerrigan would have waded in to help. *At least, I think I would have*. Will had apologized, and had since become his friend, but some bitterness remained because of that incident. *Because of it I was given the dragonbone armor to protect me*.

"This is good, Kerrigan, very good. You are sensing his essence. Your mind is relating that to memories you have of him. This indicates you are capable of perceiving a great deal more information related to a spell than most other mages."

Kerrigan smiled. "I've had a chance to think more on that, too, based on our previous conversations and what I noticed in Bokagul. I've identified at least seven different dimensions I think I should be able to find in a spell. They are: Person, School, Race, Nature, Intent, Influence, and Power Source. Person, School, and Race I know are there. I picked up on the difference between a diagnostic spell cast by Prince Murfin of the Caledo Academy and the one I would cast. Since I know it was a diagnostic, I guess I got Nature, and Intent, too. Influence I know about from you, since you said I have the taint from the DragonCrown."

"And Power Source?"

He frowned. "I have cast spells that draw on my own physical strength. That's how I learned to do things at Vilwan, but then there are some other spells I've cast in an emergency, like diagnosing and healing the urZrethi infant in the womb. I wasn't tired afterward. It was as if the energy for that spell was taken from somewhere else. I could guess my further training at Vilwan might have showed me how to access other power sources."

"Clearly, Kerrigan, you were shown those paths, but in a subtle manner so you do not have conscious control of those flows. Were this not true, you'd not have been able to draw from those sources." Ramoch waved his left hand idly. "That matters not at the moment, however. Your analysis is very good, and there are dimensions you have missed, but those are largely inconsequential—temporary things dealing with local factors at the time of the casting. Your further thoughts?"

"Well, I thought about how it would be possible to remove the taint from someone or some thing. The closest analogy I can come up with is thinking of the item as a piece of cloth that has a stain on it. You have to clean the item, dye it, or put a patch over that stain. Patching would be the most crude, but could take as little as laying another enchantment over the first. Wheele—the Aurolani mage who killed my mentor—did that sort of thing to hide a spell beneath another spell. I did that with my duplicate fragment of the DragonCrown. The problem there is that, if one looks closely, the patch can be detected, and then the real stain can be seen, as you managed when sorting the dragonbone armor from the DragonCrown taint on me."

"Your analogy will suffice, however weak. Overdyeing, then, would be a more integral form of patching. You would weave more magick through the item to draw a searcher away from the stain, making it appear to be part of some other pattern."

Kerrigan nodded. "I guess so, yes."

"And cleaning?"

The young mage shifted uneasily on the bed. "That I am not sure of. It would require getting into the fabric of the spell, separating out the tainted aspects, and substituting something else—which may or may not have its own taints. Just taking the time to get in to identify the taints and their parts and what they do in the spell would take a long time. Crafting replacements would take a long while as well, and then actually doing the cleansing, well . . . That would be very difficult."

"But could it be done?"

Kerrigan's shoulders rose and fell abruptly. "The trick is keeping other taints out. In a ritual setting, in an arcanorium where all was calm, where all ingredients were pure, where all outside influences were eliminated, it might be possible to minimize those things."

"And might it be possible to fashion yet another spell, a thaumaturgical simulacrum, that would actually insert trace influences such that your weaving could have the racial taint of an elf, or the training taint of someone from Caledo?"

The young mage's eyes opened in surprise and his head went back, banging off the headboard again. "Ouch!" He rubbed at the rising lump on his head and let the pain disguise his surprise. *If someone could do that, they could hide the intent of a spell, taking a mage off-guard completely. They could lay blame for something on someone else. They could do almost anything.*

"I guess that would be possible."

"It might be necessary. The question for you is this: are your spells identifiable as being cast by a human, or do your elven spells seem elven?"

"I don't know." Kerrigan frowned. "Why is that important?"

Bok grunted as if that were one of the most stupid questions he'd ever heard.

"In your analysis, you've forgotten one very important thing. It is this: how are you going to detect all these aspects of spells?"

"With a spell."

"Very good. Now, with the patch idea, you have a spell hiding aspects of another spell. What if the patch is reactive? What if the patch is a spell designed to send a different message back to the caster depending upon aspects of the spell being used to monitor it?"

"I'm not sure I follow."

"Take Will, for example. You can see the scars on his throat, yet the spell you cast on him does not reveal him as changed at all. Clearly, from the scars, from the magick that accompanied his oath and the spilling of his blood, he is different." Ramoch opened his gloved hands. "You used an elven diagnostic spell on him?"

"It's the best one I know."

"It's the only one likely to be cast on him in your company, isn't it?"

Kerrigan nodded slowly. "Human diagnostic spells work fine for assessing trouble, but the elven is better. UrZrethi would be another possibility, but unlikely."

"So, a spell masking what was done to him that reported back null results in response to human, elven, or urZrethi spells would effectively hide what was done to him. And any other dimensions of that spell that might reveal the identity and intent of the caster."

"Yes, exactly." Kerrigan slowly began to smile. "And any masking spell that was used to hide a fragment of the DragonCrown might similarly be tailored to deflect spells depending on the race of the person using it, the school of magick, or the very spell itself."

Rym Ramoch clapped his hands. "Splendid; you have it."

"Do I?" Kerrigan frowned again. "I'm actually pretty confused. I have the key to learning what happened to Will? I have the key to finding the DragonCrown? I have the key to hiding the taint on me?"

"Some of all." The crimson-robed mage pressed his fingertips together. "Among those dimensions you mentioned, there is some overlap. The taint of the DragonCrown is mostly tied to the source of your magickal energy. It is an item of power and has poisoned the source of your power. When you draw on your personal strength, it bleeds into the spells. When you are summoning other energy, there is much less of the taint. It is good you are here in Caledo because the magickers here rely on a ritual purification before working important spells. You will learn this from them, and flood pure energy into yourself. That should burn out most all of the DragonCrown taint."

"And the armor?"

"That should be the least of your worries. There are few who would recognize the spell, and the sense of intent you give it is entirely different from the previous user."

The younger mage stared intently at his new mentor. "If I heard you correctly, I could assume you were around when Kirûn was alive."

"You could, and you could be wrong. Recall my mention of simulacra previously. A simulation might not be exact, but sufficient for my purposes."

That defense, Kerrigan noticed, was not a denial.

"Your first job here will be to cleanse yourself, Adept Reese. Listen to what they tell you to do and follow their instructions completely. This is one spell you will not need to modify. Not yet, at least."

He arched an eyebrow. "But someday?"

"If all goes as planned, yes, but this is far afield from where we need to be now."

"And after that?"

"I would have thought it would be obvious." Ramoch cocked his head slightly to the right. "Mask spells identify searching spells through particular dimensions. Once they know what the spell is, they know what results to let it report. You need to fashion your own spell that will confound the masks and allow you past them."

"I can see that. With your help, I'm sure I can do it."

"You'll have to do without my help." Ramoch held a hand up. "No one can know I'm here, Kerrigan. Though Caledo's people are stalwart, there are those who are agents for the enemy. If Neskartu learns I am here, there will be yet more trouble than any of us want. I will come to you as I can, but my presence must remain a secret."

"But . . . If I need you?"

Ramoch stood and bowed in his direction. "You may think you need me, Kerrigan Reese, but you are wrong. All you need is already inside. I am but a catalyst—for now, anyway. Nothing you will face here will require more than your native caution and intelligence. If that were to change, you would have my help."

Kerrigan snorted. "So if I don't see you, I can handle anything I face?"

"Yes, that, or I've been slain by the enemy."

"That's not much comfort."

"I didn't mean it to be." Ramoch laughed. "There is little comfort to be had in these dire times. Accept that as a fact, then work to change it."

CHAPTER 47

Will shivered in the grand chamber the Murosans had given him. The one thing he'd liked about Bokagul was that the rooms had been small enough that he had been able to keep warm. While the coverlet on the big bed was quite thick, he wished the bed was closer to the fireplace, and that the fireplace was bigger and that a fire was already roaring away. The chairs nearest the fireplace did look comfortable, and he eyed the bed's coverlet and considered just wrapping himself in it and fashioning a bed of sorts from the chairs.

The servant who had led him to the room had wandered off, promising to bring back wine and some bread, so Will didn't even look up from his fingertip exploration of the coverlet's thickness when a faint knocking came at the door. "Come in."

"Forgive my intruding, Lord Norrington."

Will's head came up and he turned, having recognized the voice. As he saw her, however, he hesitated. He knew it was Sayce because of the silver-and-amethyst mask, but without that he'd not have identified her. Instead of her red riding leathers, she had donned a simple gown of deep blue and loosely belted it with a knotted white rope. Her shoulders had slumped slightly and her eyes were downcast. She bore a silver tray with a pitcher of wine and a single earthenware cup, along with a small round of bread and some cheese.

Will crossed quickly to her and took the tray. He set it on the table between the chairs at the fireplace and turned to welcome her, but she'd already sunk into one of the chairs. "What's wrong, Princess?"

She shook her head and her red hair veiled her face for a moment. Tears ran from beneath the silver mask and dappled the breast of her gown. Sayce pressed her left hand to her mouth, then swiped roughly at the tears.

"Please, Will, forgive me. I didn't want to do this in front of you."

"What is there to forgive?" Will sank to a knee before her. "What's wrong? Are you hurt?"

"Physically, no, but in my heart." She sniffed, then raised her gaze enough to look into his eyes. "My father, he was terribly angry with me for having gone off. He has accounted the deaths of each of the Lancers to me, personally. It didn't matter that they volunteered to go. I will have to apologize to all of their families—I planned to anyway, you know I would have—and I have been stripped of my rank. He almost disowned me."

The sorrow in her voice sank fangs into his heart. Will started to twist the ring she'd given him off his finger, but she closed her hands on his. "No, Will, no, you keep that. That estate was mine to give, and I am happy it is yours. I do not regret what I did, not a bit of it. I did what I did to save Muroso. You're here, and that is all that matters."

"Princess, I can't keep it." Will swallowed hard, scarcely believing his own words. Had he stolen the ring, he would have considered it his by right, and would have claimed to the grave that it had been passed down to him through generations and that any hint of theft was a gross insult. "Please, I am not suited to being a lordling."

Sayce smiled. "You are far more noble than those born to it. I have seen this. You have changed my way of thinking, you know." She shifted again, and her smile broadened. "And here, when I am despairing, you make me laugh. You make me feel . . . you make me feel happy." She gave his hands a squeeze. "Thank you."

"I didn't . . ." Will fell silent for a moment, finding himself tongue-tied. It was more than that, though. An odd flutter ran through his belly. Heat rose, and he could feel his cheeks burn. His mouth went dry. He stood slowly, drawing his hands from hers, both reluctantly and knowing, somehow, that he had to.

He turned back to the pitcher and cup. "Would you like some wine, Princess? There's only one cup."

Her voice softened. "If you would share your cup with me, I would be honored."

Will nodded mutely and poured. He didn't like the fact that his hand was shaking as he poured, and fought to hold back the tremor. He set the pitcher back down, turned, and, extending his left hand, offered her the cup.

She made no move to take it. Instead, her hands rose to the back of her head, where she slipped the knot holding the silver mask on. Sayce drew it off timidly, then looked up at him. "Will, do you think I am pretty?"

He could say nothing. The bruise on the left side of her face had faded to yellow, but in no way marred her beauty. Her straight nose, high cheekbones, and strong jaw combined with blue eyes, fair skin, and red hair to make her a vision of loveliness. When she had worn the courtesy mask while recovering he had seen much of her face, but its lace had hidden the playful spray of freckles over her cheeks and nose.

She immediately glanced down. "You don't have to say anything. Your silence says it all."

"No, wait, Princess...no." Will started forward and some of the wine sloshed. It didn't hit her dress, but drenched his hand and sleeve.

And then she was there, placing her right hand over his left, gently and firmly covering it, steadying the cup. Her left hand met his outstretched right. Her fingers wove into his and brought that hand to her lips. She kissed the back of his hand softly, and again.

"Princess..."

Her voice came breathlessly. "Will, you saved my life. You will save my nation. You have changed the way I think about life and the way of the world. I went to Meredo looking for someone to save the world I knew, and found someone who has given to me a whole new world."

She eased the cup from his left hand, then drank. She smiled, then kissed him. He tasted wine. Her hair brushed his face and her body pressed against his. The wine, her scent, the soft clinging of her dress to his legs, even the pressure of the belt's knot, joined the sensation of her lips on his to all but overwhelm his senses.

Will circled her waist with his left hand and drew her more tightly against him. More than just his body responded to her. For the first time in forever he didn't feel cold—he felt about ready to combust. And as her thighs shifted against him, she could not fail to notice his response.

In his mind, while this was sudden, it seemed so appropriate. He was a hero. She was a beautiful princess. He had saved her life. He would save her nation. Why would she not love him, not want him, not want to show her gratitude to him? That was the way of things. Such unions had been recorded in hundreds if not thousands of ballads and certainly would fit in the cycle of songs about Will, the King of the Dimandowns.

Yet even as part of him was seeing her affection as his due, another tiny part rebelled. He had already seen that life was not a cycle of songs. While he had saved her life, while he did like her, why would she like him? Because he was kind to his men? Because he shed his blood in her defense? Those things could be said of countless people, and the majority of them would have been citizens of Muroso. In some ways it made no sense, but the emotions and desires roaring through him gave him no time to think.

She deepened her kiss and they moved together away from the fireplace, toward the bed. How the cup ended up on the bedside table Will was uncertain, but her unburdened right hand sank fingers into his hair, her fingers redolent of spilled wine. They tightened in his hair, tugging a bit, getting him to lift his chin so she could kiss his throat and beneath his left ear.

Then the bed caught Will across his hamstrings and he sprawled back. He started to sit up, but Sayce pressed him down with a hand to his belly. As he relaxed, she withdrew her hand and her dress came off over her head, leaving her naked save for the loop of white rope slanting down across her waist.

He had thought her beautiful before but, standing there naked, she simply took his breath away. Delicate breasts peaking at rosebud nipples were dusted with freckles. From strong shoulders through the narrows of her waist and the flare of her hips, her creamy flesh seemed almost luminous. She brought her left knee up to the edge of the bed, and he marveled at the play of muscles on her thigh.

"Do I please you, my lord?"

Will nodded and fire spread through him. "Very much so, Princess."

"Good. It is my desire to please you even more."

With incredible care and delicacy, she removed his clothes and covered his exposed flesh with soft kisses and tender caresses. She bid him lay back as she crawled onto the bed with him, crawled *onto* him, and began kissing him anew. She moved up and down over him, her fingers, her hair, her lips, and tongue igniting every fiber of his body.

And then she pressed him into her and lowered her hips to his. Sayce kissed him heavily and deeply, tasting his mouth, stealing his breath as her body rocked forward and back, her hips rising and falling. Sometimes her body's urgency betrayed her, speeding things, but as his breath became ragged she slowed again, transforming quickness into fluid motion. She moved with him and against him, their bodies slipping over and past each other as the dew of exertion coated them.

Finally, after an eternity that ended all too quickly, Will's passion erupted. Sayce clung to him more tightly and sucked at his neck even harder as her own body shook and shuddered. His groans covered her moans, but he could feel them against his neck, and the vibrations from them echoed the rapid hammering of his heartbeat.

They lay there together, hard breathing slowly tapering into easy, restful respiration. At some point Will fell asleep. He did not know for how long, but when he awakened, Sayce slept with him, pressed against his right side, the coverlet pulled up over both of them. When Will sought to stir, she just burrowed more tightly against his side and murmured something. He could not understand the words, but the tone and the warm caress of her breath on his chest coaxed him back to sleep.

* * *

Just before dawn Sayce awakened him with a kiss, then pressed fingers to his mouth. "My dear, dear, Will, I have to leave you. I did not intend to stay here all night, but . . . but I could not bring myself to go."

He kissed her fingers. "You can stay."

"No, Will, I can't. If my father were to learn I had stayed with you . . . Oh, no, Will, it's not that. I can see the hurt in your eyes. No, my father has incredible respect for you. It's me he thinks so little of. He would tell you that I am unworthy of the affections of one so important."

Will blinked. He knew he was still half-asleep, but it made no sense for her father to think she wasn't worthy of him. *More like the reverse.* "Princess, your father can't think that of you."

She laughed a little and kissed his right shoulder—the one she'd slept on. "He does—right now anyway. He has in the past, but his ire will fade. Then, Will, then he can know, but not before. If he were to be really angry, he might send me away and I couldn't bear that."

"No, I'd not want that, either."

Sayce smiled broadly. "Will, when we see each other, we must be circumspect, but in private . . ."

"You will come back?" He tried to keep the disbelief from his voice, then blushed. He was fairly certain such a question was never asked, at least in that manner, by any of the heroes of epic songs.

"Come back? Of course. Oh, Will, were it not for my father, I could not be torn from your side. I think I . . ." She fell silent.

"What, Princess?" A knot formed in his stomach. He thought he knew what she was going to say. He found it exhilarating and terrifying at the same time.

"I think I am wicked for thinking about adding another burden to those you already bear, Lord Norrington." She kissed him softly on the mouth, then the forehead. "You are very deep in my affections, Will. Very deep."

"Princess, I . . ."

She pressed fingers to his lips again. "Say nothing, my lord. Say nothing. I know what is in your heart. That is enough."

Sayce dressed in silence, though she did smile when she saw him watching her. She filled the cup of wine, drank, then kissed him once again, hastily, before leaving. Will rolled up onto an elbow to watch her go, then collapsed forward onto his face as the door clicked shut behind her.

He didn't know what to think or what to feel, though he did know he felt very good, at least physically. The coverlet, where he nosed it, was full of her scent. He breathed deeply and her perfume quelled the riot in his head. Smiling, remembering, he fell asleep again.

* * *

His servant greeted him with breakfast, which Will took at the table near the hearth. The servant built up a fire, for Will's sense of cold had returned, and even a hot bath did not get rid of it. While bathing, Will dared not let himself think of Sayce, lest his body betray his feelings in the presence of the servant, but choosing not to think of her guaranteed he could think of nothing but, and specifically her joining him in the tub of hot water.

Though he had previously considered it a curse, the sense of cold helped him because it cooled his ardor and concealed all visible evidence of it. He emerged from the tub and dried himself off, then dressed as quickly and warmly as he could.

The servant had anticipated his needs and had set his clothes to warming before the fire. Will pulled them on and smiled. Fastening his belt around his middle, he fished a gold coin from the pouch and tossed it to the youth. "Thank you."

The young man, who likely was four years older than Will, caught the coin and stared at it. "Oh, my lord, thank you."

"You are most welcome." Will smiled and tied the mask onto his right shoulder. "I believe I'm ready to go."

"Yes, my lord, very good." The servant bowed. "It will be my pleasure now to conduct you to the king."

CHAPTER 48

Alexia smiled as Will was led into the small antechamber where the company had been assembled. "Good, we are complete."

The thief blushed as he looked around the dark, stone-walled room. "Were you waiting on me?"

Resolute grumbled and shifted on a rough-hewn bench against a wall. "We've all been waiting, but this is to be expected when the king receiving us has his nation under siege. But even that, I suppose, is nothing compared to what kept you waiting."

"I overslept." Will lowered his voice and his eyes, but his blush faded instead of rising, so Alexia assumed he was lying. "Nobody told me we would be summoned."

Crow smiled and clapped Will across the back. "We were all tired. We've been on the road for a long time. A soft, warm bed was quite welcome."

Alyx nodded in agreement. "Besides, we've spent the time discussing how we can help here."

Before she could elucidate, the door opened behind her. A man in the livery of the King's Guards smiled. Alexia didn't see any rank insignia on the uniform, but the grey in his beard, the scars on his hands, and the numerous ribbons decorating his black-and-midnight-blue mask suggested he'd been around long enough to have attained the highest of rankings. "If you will follow me, please."

Alexia led the way, wearing dun leathers with the Okrans winged horse rampant on her left breast. She'd been given a lacy white courtesy mask, which she had donned. Crow, who followed her, had not put on a mask, nor had Resolute, Lombo, or Qwc. Kerrigan had been given a mask of black lace, whereas white had been given to Peri, Bok, and Dranae. Will's mask rode on his upper right arm.

Their guide took them down a corridor, then up a staircase that doubled back and opened into a broad, shallow, rectangular room with a relatively low ceiling. They entered through one of the long walls, opposite a large hearth. On either side of it were set two other doors, both closed, and murals covered the walls. The rest of the walls had maps on them and had been furnished with a number of long flat tables that contained tactical models of areas in Muroso.

Alexia was well acquainted with such models. She'd studied them in Gyrvirgul while working out tactical variations on battles from the past. More recently, General Adrogans had used similar models in plotting out his Okrannel campaign. Each table had small wooden blocks on it to represent troops, each emblazoned with a paint scheme that identified the unit.

Attending these tables and the maps on the walls were mages. Each bore a slate that she assumed was an *arcanslata*. Somewhere in the field, other mages were scouting the enemy and sending information back to Caledo and King Bowmar. Provided the information was reliable, the reports gave the Murosans a great tactical advantage over the enemy.

"Your Majesty, here are your guests."

Alexia had followed the guide's glance to a particular table and expected one of the grizzled, older men to greet them, but instead a tall slender man dressed in the black robe and mask of a mage reacted to the news. His crisp gait made short work of the distance separating them. Close up Alexia could see several strands of white in his thick black hair and beard, but otherwise he seemed more Prince Murfin's match in age. *I could easily have taken them for brothers.* What surprised her was that, for as long as she could recall, the king of Muroso had been Bowmar, and the man before her hardly looked of an age to be Sayce's father, much less father to Princess Dayley or Prince Murfin.

She'd also not expected him to be a mage. She'd heard stories of his being a masterful tactician and had even studied a couple of minor battles he'd waged when one of his dukes had rebelled and tried to join Saporicia. He had showed a good sense of territory and deployment of troops. For that reason she had assumed he was a warrior, but clearly this was not the case.

"I am pleased to meet you all." The king smiled easily and his dark eyes did seem to reflect his smile. Not completely, but enough that Alexia did not feel wholly uneasy. "There will be a ball, of course, at which we shall all be formally introduced, but I know well who all of you are. I apologize for how you were brought here, but I do not regret your presence. You have arrived at a most critical time."

He turned from them, then beckoned them on with the wave of a hand.

They followed him to one of the sand tables. It depicted a city by a river. Au-rolani forces outnumbered Murosan units three to one, and the Aurolani had already taken the city. The Murosan troops were strung out on the road lead-ing south and some undecorated blocks had been used to represent refugees.

"This is the city of Porjal. A cousin of mine ruled over it, but now he is dead. Two of his sons have likewise perished, and a third is wounded and be-ing evacuated. His eldest daughter is leading the rearguard action as the refugees are evacuating west to Navval and beyond. You all know how diffi-cult a march that will be, especially in this weather."

Alexia nodded. "I am sorry for your loss, Highness."

"You are most kind, Princess Alexia. When I have the time I shall mourn their deaths, as well as that of my city. What concerns me most, now, is what the destruction of Porjal portends." Bowmar folded his arms over his chest. "Dragonels are the key to all this, of course. We met them as we would nor-mally do. Our mages fought theirs, killing a number, losing some ourselves. Despite warnings, however, my cousin took great comfort in Porjal's walls. Spells had been worked to reinforce them. They did take a harder pounding than Lurrii in Sebcia, but the walls fell nonetheless. My cousin had promised me a month; I got a week."

Crow nodded at the table. "How current are the positions?"

"Those positions came in at dawn. We should be receiving another report soon, by noon at the latest. If we hear nothing, we have to assume signal-mages are being lost. The slaughter would be incalculable."

Alexia studied the situation closely. Muroso's terrain consisted largely of rolling hills that sloped west toward the ocean, then rose again toward the Saporician Highlands and southeast toward Bokagul. Forests dotted the countryside, which made it more defensible than flat, bare plains. Even so, that the Aurolani were used to winter neutralized that advantage and created hardships for Murosan troops.

The majority of the population existed along the seacoast, save for those who lived in Caledo and, a bit farther south, in the city of Zamsina. The roads from Oriosa and Saporicia ran through Zamsina before heading north to Caledo and then out west to the coast. Coming in toward the capital they'd skirted the city and picked up the north road halfway between Caledo and Zamsina.

The defensive situation was not good at all. The Aurolani had two targets to hit. The first consisted of the coastal cities. They'd already taken Porjal and could roll into Saporicia, right to the border of Loquellyn. The advantage of doing that would be to allow them to ship supplies down by boat, which would be quicker than the long road past Fortress Draconis.

And they will be needing more supplies. If a city's walls can be reinforced, by stone or magick or both, the Aurolani will require more firedirt and shot to bring the cities down. In addition to providing the Aurolani another line of supply, taking the coastal cities would also cut the Murosans and the folk of northern Saporicia off from being supplied by sea. For those two reasons, rolling the coastal cities up made perfect strategic sense.

The other target was Caledo itself. Because it was the capital of the nation, it made a perfect political target. Taking Caledo would be the equivalent of decapitating the nation. Its citizens would lose heart. The nation would, in the minds of some, cease to exist. Some nobles would take advantage of that state to either ally themselves with Chytrine to save their realms, or otherwise proclaim themselves independent—until the Aurolani rolled over them and shattered their cities.

The very idea of failing to defend Caledo adequately was as bad as losing the city itself. If the coast went, the city could hold out for a while. But if Caledo fell, the chance at cohesive opposition to Chytrine evaporated. While the government might fall back to Zamsina, the loss of Caledo would let the Aurolani still take the coast, and Muroso's free zone would slowly starve.

King Bowmar looked over at Alexia as if he had read her mind. "It is grim. They feint at the coast, so we have to move to defend it. They feint at Caledo, so we have to defend the capital. I do not have enough in the way of troops to save both areas, and the loss of one betokens the loss of the other. Chytrine's dragonels will shatter our walls and kill our troops."

"Then we have to stop the dragonels."

Alexia looked over at Will. "Easier said than done, Will."

"I know, but not impossible." The young thief squeezed in at the edge of the table beside her. "Look, I've seen dragonels. The only way to stop them from breaking the walls is to build bigger walls, which I'd guess you're going to try to do, or prevent them from getting in range to hit your walls. Or, if you can't keep them out of range, you keep them from being able to hit so hard."

The king canted his head. "I'm not sure I follow you, Lord Norrington."

Will sighed heavily. "In Bokagul, Princess Sayce was shot by a draconette. Lombo was, too. Dranae figured some of the folks using the firespitters didn't put enough firedirt into them. The shot didn't hit as hard as it could have. Now it strikes me that if they've not got the firedirt, they can't use it, and since you know where their troops are, you could have some folks out there stealing their supplies."

Alexia smiled. She'd wondered at Will's sudden exposition on tactics, but once again he'd reduced a military operation to an exercise in thievery. "Very good, Will. I think you've got the half of it."

"I do?"

She rested a hand on his shoulder. "Yes. Highness, Will's right. The only way to slow the Aurolani forces down is to cut their supplies. This means that, as your people retreat, they have to destroy anything they can't carry off. It's winter. There's no living off the land and an army can't fight when there's only snow to fill their bellies. Despite the hardship it will cause, everything the Aurolani will benefit from must be destroyed."

The king nodded. "We've already begun the shifting of stores and live-stock. We've destroyed some bridges but, so far, we've not fired villages. We can do that, however."

"That will be good. The second thing that needs to be done, as Will suggested, is to keep the dragonels out of range of the walls. Your situational information makes this possible. We can set up ambushes and defenses at key points. We hit the lead elements of the Aurolani force, stop them, and wait for them to bring their heavier troops up to blast through. Our defenders fade before them, which means our people have time to destroy supplies while, at the same time, we force the Aurolani to wait on land where there is nothing for them."

King Bowmar ran a hand over his bearded jaw. "So elementary I should have seen it. We have taken pride in the strength of our walls, and the skill of our mages. Cities have become the focus for our defense, but when faced with a force that can overwhelm our cities, defending those cities is just waiting for destruction. I am not certain this defense in depth will defeat Chytrine, but it will slow her forces down."

Alexia shook her head. "No reason you should have seen it. This war is unlike any we've faced before."

"And yet all this was clear to you."

She shrugged. There was no way to explain to him that her entire life had been spent learning how to defeat conventional forces. From her earliest days she knew of the destructive power of dragonels, and knew they rendered any city into rubble. If a force was stationary, it invited destruction, so the only antidote to the dragonel was to be found in a highly mobile force that made the enemy's advance grind to a halt. Since she had always believed Chytrine would return, dragonels had to be accounted for and countered. Here, in Muroso, she had a perfect landscape for providing a solid defense.

"What we need to do, Highness, is to determine which forces you have that are best suited to their roles. We need a city force to defend and reinforce the cities. We need a mobile defense force that will hit, hold, slow, and fade before the enemy. And we will need..."

"You'll need your hunter-killers." Resolute's voice echoed strongly. "Crow and I will organize that force. We have spent a quarter century harassing Chytrine's troops. There is no one better suited to it."

Alexia smiled. "I have some experience at the kind of tactics you are talking about."

The Vorquelf's silver eyes locked on her and sent shivers through her.

"Princess Alexia, please do not think I doubt your abilities or harbor any doubts about you, but you will not be coming with us."

She tried to cover her surprise. "Why not?"

Crow smiled. "Because, Princess, only you know what you have in mind for your mobile defense forces. They will be your responsibility. If they are successful, you will know why. If they are not, you will make them successful. There is no other way."

Alyx caught the reluctance in Crow's voice and took solace in it. In her mind she'd seen herself off riding with Crow. They would be out there, free, slashing at Aurolani troops. People without nations attacking an enemy that would destroy all nations. But that freedom, the exhilaration, were illusions. She wanted to slip the responsibilities for which she had been trained and just fight at the side of the man she loved.

In his voice she heard that Crow did not want to be parted from her either, but she hid the smile that realization sparked. Both of them knew their own desires had to be subordinated to their duty. Until Chytrine's troops were defeated and she was slain, any peace and happiness they might know would be a fancy that could be easily torn asunder.

Will looked up at her. "Don't worry, Highness, I'll take good care of Crow."

Bowmar frowned. "I had thought, Lord Norrington, that you would remain here to rally my people."

"Probably not a good plan." Will sighed. "Chytrine wants me dead, so having me standing around in one place means that place is a target. I'll be with Crow and Resolute. Only thing worse for her troops than having me waiting for them is having me hurting them."

Crow glanced at Resolute, then shook his head. "That decision, Will, is not final. We will talk about it."

"I figured that, Crow." The thief shrugged. "We can talk lots, but it comes down to this: we have a plan to stop Chytrine and folks who can do it. Anything that stands between us and spilling blood is just a waste of time."

CHAPTER 49

The piteous notes in the screams echoing through Porjal were what unsettled Isaura. She fully understood the need to pacify the city. The siege had been successful, but the resistance had been fierce. Lord Neskartu had been forced to work hard to counter the magicks that rebuilt the shattered walls. The dragonels had to pound them into gravel and then dust before her mother's troops were able to enter the city.

Once they were poised to do that, a heavily armed force burst from the city and headed away, westward along the coast. The Aurolani troops entering the city had become overconfident, and assumed there would be no one left to fight them. In a sense they were correct, for very few people remained. Those who did, however, were clever, suicidal, and adept at setting up and springing ambushes and booby traps that mangled, maimed, and occasionally killed.

Given the casualties among the sorcerers Neskartu had brought south with him, Isaura found herself pressed into duty aiding the wounded. She joined Trib in trying to heal some *grichothka*. One had fallen into a pit that had been lined mostly with upward-pointing spikes that impaled him as he fell in. Others at the bottom of the pit pointed down, holding him as his fellows tried to pull him free. Yet others had arms smashed or severed, shoulders crushed and legs broken as stones fell, or logs rolled. Any number had their feet punctured by a pair of iron nails bent at right angles and welded together in the middle. With all points sharpened, they could be tossed on the ground and a spike would always point upward.

She'd shaken her head when first she saw a collection of the wounded.

Isaura had actually heard the pained puling and mewing, but not even that had prepared her for blood-matted fur, rent flesh, and eyes wide with agony. The weapons used against the gibberkin clearly had not been meant to kill them. The spikes in the traps were too short to stab all the way through. The traps were meant to wound, and that made no sense to her.

Trib, his white fur reddened up to his elbows and dappled crimson over his chest, explained carefully. "They have no desire to kill, my lady. A dead warrior requires only a hole in the ground. These require care and food and housing until they are recovered enough to go home or back to war. A corpse can be abandoned, but a wounded comrade must be rescued, often putting the rescuers at risk."

"But that is so cruel."

"This is why we fight them." The *kryalniri* looked about him at the living carpet of wounded. "If we do not stop them, they will do this to our people when they come for us."

Retribution and reprisals had come hard and fast. Much of the outer ring of the city had been reduced to rubble, but the interior and the seaside remained virtually intact. Squads had roamed through the city, flushing out humans and herding them into squares. Some had been burned alive, the thick, nauseating smoke swirling through the city, while others were crucified and left to suffer. Their cries lacked the shrieked urgency of the burned, but took on a hideous tone as they subsided.

And there were always more, stronger cries ebbing slowly to replace them.

She could understand the repression and punishment of the city's populace. If they were not discouraged, they would continue in their cruelty. While she could even understand their desire to protect their homes, their conduct—in the way they lived and in the way they fought—showed them to be lacking in the ways of civilized behavior. *It is not possible to reason with the unreasoning.*

Yet despite her understanding, the way things were being done did discomfort her. Children were being slain along with adults. Isaura accepted as fact reports that said children were leading the troops into traps, but certainly they were merely imitating adults. Lord Neskartu had chosen some of them to be borne back to the Conservatory, so they had potential for use in the future. She wondered if all the children could not likewise be redeemed, once they were showed the error of their ways.

This thought woke her—at least she decided this was what awakened her, not the dying echoes of a scream. She was tempted to use the magick Nefraikesh had given her so she could report her unease to him and suggest a plan to save the children, but she refrained. The last time she had reported to him, she caught a vision of two women, and it had frightened her—though she did not know why. It did make her reluctant, however—that late in the evening, with the wind howling outside—to speak with the king of the *sul-lanciri*.

Unable to return to sleep, she slipped from her bed in an unruined portion of the duke's palace. She pulled on a blue robe and belted it about her waist with a gold silk tie, then padded barefooted through the palace. She knew that with rebels about she was taking a risk, but she felt no fear. She was determined to find Neskartu and broach the subject of reforming the children.

Her journey took her deep into the main building, and high. Cool air bled into the upper corridors from shattered windows and one spot where a wall had been holed, but it still felt mild to her. She hurried past battle-weary *gri-chothka* on post on the lower levels. In the upper reaches of the palace, however, the gibberers were taller and stronger, wearing clean tabards, and *kryalniri* patrolled the halls.

No one questioned or stopped her, however, so she reached the modest chamber in which the duke had once held audiences. Eight pillars supported the ceiling, which did not rise high enough to escape light from the burning torches below. Scenes of myth, of hunts for giant serpents or temeryces, looked down on the four figures gathered in the room.

Lord Neskartu stood with the two other *sullanciri* leading the Murosan invasion. Anarus, who wore a wolf's-visage and had a thick pelt covering his body, curled a lip in a snarled greeting. He had neither seen nor heard her enter. His nostrils had flared as he caught her scent, and he meant the greeting to be pleasant, but a flash of lupine fang and a ripple of powerful muscles would require far more effort to seem welcoming.

Tythsai bowed her head, slowly, in Isaura's direction, but did not do so out of overt respect. As with several other of her mother's generals, Tythsai had entered Aurolani service after death. The crude stitchery that kept her head on her body was impossible to miss, as was the lack of a flesh-and-blood right arm. Isaura seemed to recall, decades previous, when that arm had likewise been sewn on. Later it had been replaced with the first of several mechanical arms, making Tythsai into a *meckanshii* of sorts. Her current limb appeared to be made of quicksilver, though quite ordinary except for that detail.

The fourth member of the group immediately dropped to one knee. Even when he bent his head, he remained taller than she. The black cloak he wore covered him from shoulders to floor, with the spikes on his shoulders, arms, knees, and back poking out at sharp angles. The broad face, even with its twin curves of ivory fangs and covered in dark green scales, appeared softer and more friendly than that of Anarus. His big, dark eyes blinked once, then he lowered his gaze.

"Highness, I am honored."

Isaura nodded toward him and her white-blonde hair slid forward past her shoulders. "Naelros, this is unexpected. You were at Fortress Draconis?"

Naelros kept his head bent and would not meet her gaze. "I have come south, Highness, for I have failed the empress. I have brought my troops to help here and to search. One of the fragments was stolen from Draconis. Others are out hunting, but there is a chance the thieves tried to come south. We will find them, but our strength is needed here."

It will be most welcome, Naelros.

Anarus snapped his jaws at that assertion. "Your strength may be needed, but you dilute *our* strength with your suggestions." The lupine *sullanciri* moved to a table upon which had been spread a large map of Muroso. Heavy silver candlesticks held down the corners, and up by Porjal wax had already spilled onto it. "The only course of attack is to drive on Caledo. Once we strike the head, the body will die."

Yet because this is the obvious course, Anarus, they will defend against it.

"What matter? They cannot stand against us!" The *sullanciri* hunched his shoulders and raked his clawed hands through the air. "We have the might— with or without your people, Naelros—to crush their capital."

Naelros slowly rose to his feet and walked to the map. He kept his gait steady and slow, but his long legs devoured the distance. The table touched his legs just above his knees and he had to bend down to tap a taloned finger to the map. "The coastal cities are easier to take. Once we eliminate them, we will be able to reinforce and resupply ourselves, and they will have nothing. We close the border with Saporicia and Muroso dies."

"Take Caledo, and the coastal cities will open themselves to us." Anarus turned and nodded toward Tythsai. "You concur, yes?"

The female *sullanciri* said nothing, but her right hand tightened into a fist. Her fluid metal fingers drove down through her palm and emerged as spikes through the back. The end of her limb thickened as the fist became a spiked mace. One long spike grew from the top of it and she tapped that against the map's representation of Caledo.

Neskartu reached out with a hand, letting his arm and fingers stretch out beyond all normal proportions. His fingertip played over the coastline. *These are the better targets.*

A low growl rumbled from Anarus' throat. "What is it you fear?"

Nothing. The toll taken on my students and your stores of firedirt, however, was greater than expected. If we have the ports we enrich ourselves and hurt them.

Anarus snorted. "This is precisely why you are not in command of this invasion. Do you think supplies will flow here immediately? Yes, we can send ships from Vorquellyn, but this invasion will be won with the supplies already flowing south on the land route. There is nothing that can oppose us."

Then you devalue the magery of Muroso.

"No, I count on you to rid me of their mages."

This shall be done. What of the Norrington? What of Alexia of Okrannel?

Anarus started to snarl again, but Isaura's gasp cut him off. "She is here!"

The wolf-thing's head snapped around. "Who? Your mother?"

"No, this Alexia." Isaura pressed her hands to her temples. When Neskartu had communicated the concept of Alexia, it merged perfectly with the image of the blonde woman she'd seen when speaking with Nefrai-kesh. "She is in Caledo."

"How do you know this?"

Naelros snorted a hint of steam. "Even I have heard rumors that the Norrington has come north to Muroso. Alexia travels with him. She will be a formidable foe."

"A foe without dragonels." Anarus glanced sidelong at Naelros. "A foe without your kin."

"They are not for you to command, but for the empress." The dracomorph's dark eyes narrowed and his voice lowered in volume with no loss of timbre. "Anarus, you took Porjal, but it took longer than any other city. In Caledo you will face even more severe defenses. You may receive help, but if you insist on attacking the southlanders where they are the strongest, the cost of your victories will slay the invasion."

"Were your prophetic visions accurate, Naelros, you would have foreseen the theft of the fragment. Your performance pleases our mistress not at all. Mine does, which is why I command here. I welcome your strength, but it is my vision that has brought us this far, and shall carry us further."

He tapped a finger on the map. "Caledo will fall. There is nothing a foundling princess from Okrannel or a bastard gutterkin from Alcida can do about it. It is our empress' will that Muroso fall, and so it shall. Before there is a hope of spring, this nation shall be ours."

CHAPTER 50

Will glanced through the open doorway of Princess Alexia's room, as if making sure she was alone before he knocked on the jamb. "I'm sorry to disturb you."

Alyx looked up from a chair near the fireplace and smiled. She had been preparing to enter the Communion to see if there was anything she could glean from them about Aurolani efforts elsewhere, but the apprehension on Will's face made it easy for her to set that aside. "No, that's fine, Will. What's the matter?"

The thief hesitated, then began slowly. "I was wondering...um, I need some help." He stepped into the room and extended the small parchment packet in his right hand toward her. "I got this message but, well, I can't read."

Alyx beckoned him farther into the room and he came reluctantly, which surprised her. He was more subdued than usual, and certainly more so than anytime since they'd started to put together the group that would attack Chytrine's supply train. "Crow could have read it for you, or Resolute."

He shifted his shoulders uneasily. "I would have asked them, but they're busy. Kerrigan, too. I mean, not that you are not, but..."

"No offense taken." She took the packet from him and turned it over one side, then the other. It had been sealed with red wax, but the seal meant nothing to her. The address on the reverse had been written in a clean hand and directed the packet to be delivered to Will Norrington in Caledo. Though there was no indication of who had sent it, Alyx was pretty certain it had been written by a woman.

The concern on his face suggested to her that he knew it was from a woman, too, which could have explained his reluctance to have Crow or Resolute read it for him. "Doesn't say who it is from, but it is meant for you. It was sent here to you in Caledo."

"So, it's not from here?"

"Here?"

"*Here* here, like from the palace or anything?"

"Probably not." She shook her head, then pointed him to the other chair. "You can sit if you want."

"I'll be sitting enough when we ride out. I'll stand." Will swayed a bit from side to side, then crossed from the door and rested his hands on the back of the chair she'd pointed to. "You can open it."

"I'll have to if I'm to read it, won't I?" She slid a thumb under the flap and broke the seal. She drew out two folded pieces of parchment and glanced at the bottom of the second page. "It's signed, 'The one you saved.' "

Will frowned for a moment and anguish washed over his face. "That's it?"

Alyx looked at the first page. "Dear Lord Norrington, Since your departure from Meredo, the city has been in an uproar."

The thief's anxiety broke and he grinned. "It has to be from Sephi!"

The princess frowned. "Sephi is Scrainwood's spy?"

"Was. That's why she said you and Crow were married. She wanted to help me, so I made her my spy." Will came around and seated himself on the edge of the chair. "What does she say?"

Alexia quickly scanned the two pages. "It's mostly court gossip. Linchmere's departure was noticed immediately, and folks are saying that he's with you, or that Kenleigh and he are off on a mission to Fortress Draconis to save Erlestoke and bring him home to the throne. Various soothsayers are spreading the story that Erlestoke is still alive, but she thinks they might be stalking horses for a group of nobles who are looking to overthrow the king. If they hold Erlestoke up as some paradigm of virtue, King Scrainwood looks even worse, so the people will be upset. One of those lords ended up dead, so she supposes there is a shadow war going on, which is not good."

Will shook his head as he frowned. "Oriosa, weak as it is, is better than no Oriosa. If it falls apart, Chytrine just pours through it."

"That's absolutely true." Alexia looked at the second page. "King Scrainwood, it seems, is keeping company with Nolda Norrington. I might suggest not letting Kenleigh know that."

"No, no, I wouldn't."

Alexia sighed. "This is not good. My aunt and King Scrainwood have plotted to have the leaders of the world meet in Narriz inside a month, to determine new strategies. Invitations have gone out and travel has been started.

King Bowmar has said nothing, so either he thinks such a meeting is foolishness or..."

"...or they never invited him, figuring he'll be dead by the time the meetings come off." The thief closed his eyes for a moment. "They're assuming that Chytrine won't just march on into Saporicia."

And if they assume she will... The implications of that idea surprised her. She could have believed Scrainwood would have set an ambush for his fellow leaders, but Tatyana? That made no sense. What did make sense was that somehow Tatyana had managed to twist Scrainwood around to the point where he saw an advantage in opposing Chytrine, and with the Aurolani horde poised to invade his nation, that wouldn't have been difficult.

"I don't know what they are thinking, Will." Alyx sighed and tried to let the flutter in her gut subside. "She closes with, 'You should know that the people of Meredo have taken your words to heart. Your Freemen have set an example. There are free militias preparing to defend the nation forming up all over. Refugees are being welcomed and housed. There are even those who think you should be placed on the throne if neither prince survives. I would add my voice to their cries, but it is best I remain hidden. Better to serve you and our cause, which I shall.'"

Will settled back in the chair and let out a big sigh of relief. "Thanks. I should write her back, I guess. I would, if I knew how to write and where she was going to be."

"That is a problem." Alexia refolded the letter. "Now, why don't you tell me the problem you came here to ask me about."

The thief's eyes grew wide for a second, then his expression smoothed into one as close to innocent as he could manage. "That was it, the letter."

"Will, you came here because you must have trusted me. Now the signature 'the one you saved,' applies to this Sephi, and to at least one more woman I know of."

"Two others could say that." Will shrugged. "One you don't know."

"And the other is from here, which also worried you. You thought this was from Sayce." Alexia rose, closed the door to her chamber, then returned to her chair. "Why would getting a note from her concern you? And what about it couldn't you ask Crow, Resolute, or Kerrigan?"

"Well, it's this thing, see. A romantic thing, so Kerrigan wouldn't know anything about it."

She smiled. "Will, I don't think I'm much better equipped than Kerrigan to deal with questions of romance."

"But you've, well, you've at least kissed someone." Will shifted painfully in the chair. "I mean, Crow has, too. He's kissed you, but he wouldn't know what a woman thinks. And Resolute, well..."

She held a hand up. "We are agreed on Resolute." Alyx leaned forward, resting her elbows on her knees. "I will help if I can, but it's probably easier for you to read this letter by yourself than it is for me to read someone else's feelings."

"Please, Princess, don't say that." The plea in Will's voice sank deep into her heart. "I can't...I don't know who or what or how, and with my going away and Sayce going with you, I mean...I don't know what I mean."

He hung his head and she reached out to stroke his hair. "Will, tell me what has happened."

He sighed heavily, then nodded. "Well, okay, it's like this. When we were in Bokagul I liked her. We were friends. She's closer to my age than any of the rest of you, except for Kerrigan, and he's okay, but there are times he's talking and I recognize words but I don't have any idea of what he's talking about. But Sayce didn't see me as some little thief, but as a hero, so she talked to me differently. I mean, you and Crow and everyone but Resolute talk nice to me, too, but I guess it was just different with her. I liked talking with her. I liked it a lot. And then when she went down, well, I was angry and bleeding and said what I said and I don't have any idea what it was or why it worked, but it did and she was saved. Then when I talked to her while she was recovering, she was grateful and she ran her fingers in my hair and, well, I liked that, too."

Alyx forced herself to keep a sympathetic expression on her face. She wanted to smile broadly because Will's angst was achingly innocent and funny, but to him it was anything but. "No reason you wouldn't like it, Will."

He nodded. "Okay, then on the ride to Caledo we talked more, and that was good, but then when we got here, well..." Will's expression got solemn and he grabbed her right hand. "You have to promise me you won't say anything, you have to promise."

"I promise."

"Okay, okay. So when we got here Sayce came to me. In my room, and she stayed with me. And she did that the next night and even last night. And, and...I think she loves me and I like her fine, but, I don't love her, and I think she thinks I love her and when I have to go away..." His voice shrank to a squeak. "I don't know, I don't know."

Alexia felt ice sluice through her midsection. She and Crow had spent the nights in Caledo together and had bravely acknowledged that their being apart was necessitated by circumstances. Each had fingered their rings, cherishing the link that gave them to each other. They remembered the pledge to avenge the other's death, but both felt confident that they would never have to do so.

The hopelessness in Will's voice just ripped open the sack of all the emotions she'd been tucking away. Fear of losing Crow, of never seeing him again, pounded her. Fear of his dying in pain, of her dying without seeing him, without having the comfort of his arms, lashed her. Just the sense of emptiness transferred from a cold, lonely bed into her heart made her gasp.

Will looked up. "What's wrong? What did I do?"

"Nothing, Will, nothing." She gave him a brave smile. "Is what you are asking, 'What do I say to Sayce when we part?'"

He nodded. "You have to help me." He pressed the heels of his hands to his eyes. "All the songs only deal with true love, where they can't bear to be apart and where you know they'll be reunited, or one of them will die really, really horribly and the other will die of a broken heart, or forever love the other until they're reunited in some other life or something like that. But, as for my situation . . . Nothing."

"Your situation is too real to make for a good song."

His hands came away and he stared at her. "Took me hours staring at the ceiling last night to figure that one out."

"I'm not helping, I know." She drew in a deep breath, then let it out slowly. "If you think she's really in love with you, wait . . . Are you sure you're not in love with her?"

"Well, according to the songs . . ."

"Forget the songs. What do you feel inside?"

He shook his head. "I'm all confused. I mean, I was confused about Chytrine and being the Norrington and everything, but by comparison, I've got that all figured out clean. Do you love Crow? How do you know? What do you feel?"

Alyx started to answer, but words froze on her tongue. A host of emotions tightened her throat, but brought with it a smile that sparked the hint of one on Will's face. "I feel everything, Will. Mostly, I guess, I feel as if he's the answer to questions I never knew to ask. Wants and needs I didn't know I had, he fulfills. He's as vital to me as the air or wine or food."

The thief smiled. "Now *that* is the kind of stuff mentioned in the songs."

"But not what you feel for Sayce?"

He shook his head. "I don't know. I mean, I like her. She is my friend and I like being around her. I'll miss her and everything, but . . ."

Alyx nodded. "Any chance you will come to love her? The songs talk about folks growing into it, as I recall."

"Yeah. I don't know. Maybe." He shrugged. "That's what makes it difficult, don't you see? She loves me, and if I say I don't love her, I break her heart and then if I do love her . . . But she shouldn't be loving me. Sometimes I don't think it's *me* she loves, but *the Norrington.* She loves the guy who saved her, who will save her nation. She sees a me that I don't know is me, you know?"

The princess smiled softly at him. "I know. When I meet my people, the Okrans exiles, they look at me that same sort of way. They expect much, learn to love their vision of the person who will fulfill their expectations. That's not me, but trying to change their minds would be impossible."

"So, you're saying that there's nothing I can tell her?"

"No, that's not what I'm saying." Alyx frowned. "What I'm saying is this: you and Sayce are each going to be heading out on very dangerous missions. There is no guarantee that either of you, or Crow or I, will survive. Times like these, we all need our friends. If she loves you, and if you could learn to love her, letting her think you love her isn't bad. There will be enough pain out there for all of us that we don't need to be creating more."

He raised an eyebrow. "I should lie?"

"You ask that question with a lot more ease than makes me comfortable, Will."

"Well, in the Dimandowns, truth was kind of squishy. Lying was just self-preservation."

"No, I don't think you should lie, but I don't think you need to close any doors. It could very well be that if we are successful . . ."

"*When* we are successful."

"*When*, yes, when we are successful, you could come back to that lake she gave you and raise a brood of children and live happily ever after."

Will grinned. "I like the idea of being the King of Oriosa better."

"I'd rather have you on that throne, too."

"But I guess what you're saying makes sense. If I die out there, or she dies out there, there's no harm in being loved or thinking you're loved. Might make things a bit easier."

"Hey." She leaned forward and caught a handful of his tunic. "No dying out there. Not you, not Crow, not Resolute, not any of you."

Will grinned broadly. "Okay, so no dying with you or Sayce or Kerrigan or Peri, right? Deal?"

"Deal." Alyx gave him a wink. "You'll need to figure out what to say to her and when."

"I know. I'll work on that."

"In the middle of the night?"

"Probably." He stood, then abruptly leaned down and kissed her on the top of the head. "Thank you."

Alyx stood and gathered Will into a hug. "Glad to be of help. Don't want you preoccupied when you're supposed to be out there stopping the supply of firedirt that's going to be used against me."

"Just make sure you don't let them get to my castle on the lake, okay?" He freed himself from her embrace, then shot her a quick salute. "If you need to use it, though, feel free."

"Good luck, Will."

The young thief shook his head. "Save the luck for yourself. I'm the Norrington, remember? I don't require anything more than that."

CHAPTER 51

The dawn came cold and clear the morning the northern raiding force was to set out. Will, standing on a South Tower balcony overlooking the palace courtyard, shivered beneath the thick hide robe he wore, but he knew it wasn't because of the cold. Out beyond the city walls the white plains stretched on to the north forever, and nothing seemed to be moving out there. The landscape looked sterile, and the idea that anything could survive the trek north seemed impossible.

He knew it wasn't true—both that nothing was moving and that nothing could survive. According to the reports from Murosan scouts, the Aurolani force had decamped from Porjal and were heading south toward Caledo. The refugees from Porjal had headed west to the coastal city of Navval and would be sent farther along the coast until they came to Paloso, the city near Lake Eori. Will didn't know if that choice had been made as an omen, or just because the next stop would be Saporicia and, with any luck, an escape from danger.

They run from it while we ride into it. Will shook his head, then smiled and nodded at a couple of the Freemen in the courtyard below who were preparing their horses. At his headshake they had begun to double-check what they were doing, assuming he was signaling displeasure. Once he nodded, they smiled and went back to work.

The Freemen, who comprised a legion drawn from Murosan refugees and Oriosan volunteers, were one of three units that would be in the northern force. To them were added a legion of Murosan Lancers—the Queen's Own Guards, whose chosen uniform was white with slashed red sleeves. Originally these two groups, comprising two hundred warriors, along with members of the Crown Company, as the princess' allies had become known, were all who were going to head north. While all of the warriors were skilled or enthusiastic, that didn't shield them from reality. Their mission would be very dangerous and would very likely get them all killed.

The odds improved slightly when a company of *meckanshii* rode into Caledo the afternoon of the day Will had spoken to Princess Alexia. Colonel Sallitt Hawkins led them, and all of them came equipped with draconettes. The colonel had spoken with King Bowmar, and it was explained to Will that these warriors were intent upon returning to Fortress Draconis or, barring that, "causing maximum discomfort to the enemy."

Nominally they were just traveling in conjunction with the task force, but Colonel Hawkins immediately began coordinating with Wheatly, integrating his supplies with those for the rest of the task force. Oddly enough, Lindenmere evidenced some skill for getting the supplies ordered and stowed—and likewise estimating how much of what would be needed for the campaign. North helped him with the lifting and toting, and a true affection for Lindenmere seemed to have grown up between the other Freemen and him.

And Lindenmere has become a bit harder and leaner, as has Kerrigan. Will watched the magicker move through the courtyard. He still had that gawky, awed look on his face that he always wore, but he stood a bit taller and had shrunk a bit around the middle. That wasn't to suggest he was even close to cutting the sort of figure that Dranae did, but in Kerrigan one could almost see someone who could be taken for Dranae's younger brother or cousin.

"What are you thinking, Lord Norrington?"

Sayce's question surprised him, primarily because she'd managed to sneak up on him. He turned slowly and smiled for her, which brightened her face and made his guts flip-flop. "I was thinking how much the war changes people, and how much they're likely to be changed. Lindenmere probably never did a bit of hard work in his life, but he's down there working now, and not shrinking from it. And Kerrigan, he's changing."

"And you?"

Will closed his eyes and nodded. "Not even a year ago I was slumkin, stealing anything I could lift and getting regular beatings from my master and my enemies. My world was a place maybe six blocks long and wide, and if you'd asked me then if I'd ever leave it, I'd have said no. And now, here I am, far north, volunteering for something that might get me killed, and certainly will get me hurt. Definitely true of those down below."

His eyes opened as Sayce approached. Up to that point she had hidden any public signs of affection for him, but with less than an hour before he'd ride away, she was throwing caution to the winds. She reached out and slid her hand over his shoulder.

"I've changed, too, Will."

"I know."

Sayce smiled and gave Will a look that he knew would haunt dreams and warm him on cold nights. "How do you think I have changed?"

He looked her straight in the eye, then gave her a wry grin. "You were raised as royalty, but young enough that you knew you'd never have to accept responsibility. You realized that you were not exempt from the duties of your blood, so you accepted them and have done your utmost to fulfill them."

Sayce's face froze for a moment, then she looked down. "You read me very well, Lord Norrington."

"You're not easy to read, Princess; I just know the story well and recognize it." His gloved right hand emerged from beneath the heavy cloak. He took her chin between thumb and forefinger and lifted her head until she looked him in the eye again. "These are extraordinary times and require extraordinary measures from all of us. Doing what we must is something in which we can take pride and even joy."

"Yes, exactly. I . . ."

Will pressed his thumb to her lips to silence her. "Sayce, you will be going with Princess Alexia and fighting to delay those on their way here. I will be going north. Neither of us knows what the future will bring. Out there we could be killed, which would be bad. Worse, we could be broken. Maybe they will make us into *meckanshii,* maybe not. We could be captured and tortured. We might even be made over into *sullanciri.*"

She blinked at him and tears began to gather in her eyes, but did not yet flow. "What are you saying, Will?"

Again he smiled for her. "What I am saying, Princess, is that our futures are uncertain, but our past, the time we have spent here—the time spent here *together*—it will be eternal. It can't be taken away from us. We don't know if we will ever be able to stand together like this—if after what we will go through, we would even recognize ourselves as the people who stood here— but we have. I won't forget. I can't. I don't want to. What I remember will be a great comfort in the coming days."

Sayce stepped closer and enfolded him in a hug. She pressed her right cheek to his, and he felt the burn of a tear. His arms went around her and he held her tightly. That surprised him, because while he knew he didn't love her, he didn't want to let her go. Not just yet.

So he held on to her and she clung to him. And, just for a little while, the horror of the future was held at bay.

Through the stable doorway Alexia could see Will and Sayce on the balcony. She watched them embrace and wished she could have heard what Will said.

If he was able to order his emotions, then something in what he said would help me order mine.

She'd given some thought to what she wanted to say to Crow on their parting, but that was only in the little snatches of time they were apart. They'd conspired to minimize them, to their mutual delight, but there were times when duty called them one from another. Just that morning she had been off listening to the latest reports from the north and had agreed to meet him in the stable, but Crow had been delayed.

"Princess Alexia, begging your pardon, but I would appreciate a favor."

She turned and the smile growing on her face slowed. She had recognized the voice in pieces. First she linked it to Crow, then realized who had spoken. "Colonel Hawkins, what may I do for you?"

The *meckanshii*, swathed in thick furs and wearing a mitten on his left hand, lowered his eyes. The silver of the mail used to replace the flesh of his face glittered around the right edge of his black mask. "I would ask you to introduce me to your husband."

"But..." She hesitated. "You already know him."

"That is not why I ask, Highness."

From behind her Crow spoke. "He asks, my love, because I've not spoken with him yet. I've refused."

Alexia heard pain in Crow's voice and watched it tighten Sallitt's expression. She turned to Crow. "Why would you refuse?"

"Because I have no family outside you and Will and Resolute." Bitter anger strained Crow's voice. "All that was taken away from me."

Sallitt's head came up. "And it was taken away from me, too."

"You still have your mask. You still have our family."

"But not our complete family." The *meckanshii*'s metal hand snapped into a fist. "Tarrant, you don't know how it was."

Crow snorted. "It doesn't take much to figure it out."

Alexia gripped Crow's forearm. "Give him a chance."

Crow nodded and the tension flowed out of his forearm.

Sallitt's metal hand opened slowly. "After the Okrannel campaign they brought me back to Valsina. That was before the Draconis Baron had figured out how to make *meckanshii*. I was useless. You'd had your mask stripped away, but for what I didn't know; and our father forbid us from mentioning your name ever. I knew you weren't dead and had I been whole, I'd have found you.

"Then the stories started saying you were dead and that you'd killed yourself. I couldn't believe them, but I couldn't prove them otherwise. Several years later, long before I ever heard a song of Crow, the Draconis Baron sent for me and made me as I am now. He gave me a purpose. I accepted my position at Fortress Draconis not, as some have said, to redeem our name, but to continue the fight we'd both been part of."

Crow said nothing, but a tremor began to run through him.

Sallitt's hazel eyes flashed from within his mask. "Some *meckanshii* suffer what we call 'metal fatigue.' We get tired of trying to be human because we so clearly are not. We try to forget who we were because our injuries carry with them a lot of mental pain. I had that, plus the way our father had changed, and the loss of my little brother. I was lucky, though, and met my wife—gods grant Jancis still lives. She brought my human half back, and it's that human half that makes me seek you, brother. To tell you I've never believed what has been said of you."

The man who had been Tarrant Hawkins looked up. "But when you were told who I was at Tolsin, you rode away."

"I did, yes, because I felt betrayed." Sallitt's eyes tightened. "We'd been long on the road together. You'd saved my life and yet you had not trusted me with who you were. Should I have known? You, traveling with Resolute, in the company of a Norrington, it all seems so obvious now, but it wasn't then. You were Crow, a living legend. Had you been Oriosan, you'd have worn a mask, so I never made the connection. But you knew who I was, and you didn't trust me. That hurt me and made me doubt."

Crow's lips pressed together for a moment, then he slowly nodded. "You're right. I did you an injustice. I'd spent so many years refusing to be Tarrant Hawkins that even though I knew you were my brother, I couldn't be your brother. Too much pain there, too."

"I guess I can understand that." The elder Hawkins chewed his lower lip. "No one in the family believed the charges against you. Even though Father would not speak of you, the rest of us did, secretly. I know he didn't believe them, though. I think after he took your mask, he learned the truth."

Crow shook his head. "Our father had his own reasons for doing what he did. How is . . . How are they?"

"Father died about six years ago. In his sleep. Mother lives with Ellice now. Everyone else is well." He smiled weakly. "We will have time to talk about them on the road."

"Perhaps we will." Crow nodded, stiffly at first, but easing. "I have spent more time being Crow than I ever did being your little brother. It will take time for me to get used to that role again."

"The day you left Valsina you stopped being my little brother. I saw it when we met at Fortress Draconis. A little brother I don't need. A friend and comrade I know and trust, on the other hand."

Crow extended his left hand and took his brother's flesh-and-blood hand in a firm grip. "Agreed."

Sallitt nodded to Alexia. "Thank you, Highness. I will leave you two. I have things to take care of. Good luck, Princess."

"And you, Colonel."

The *meckanshii* departed quietly despite being half-metal. Alexia smiled at Crow. "I think it is good you spoke with him."

"Why is that?"

"Because I know your family was important to you and renewing those ties will be good."

Crow sighed. "I hope you are right. Here and now, though, it is my new family that most concerns me."

"It made me happy to be included in it."

"You *are* it."

"No, you included Resolute, who can take care of himself, and Will." She reached up and tucked a long lock of white hair behind his ear. "Speaking of whom, Will might want to talk to you about Sayce. Do him a favor and listen."

Crow looked up from tightening the cinch strap around his horse's middle. "What is going on? What have I missed?"

"He and Princess Sayce have become close. Parting will not be easy for them." Alyx choked down a lump in her throat. "It's not going to be easy for me, either."

"I know." Crow nodded, then crossed to her and reached out to brush his left thumb over her right cheekbone. Alexia half closed her eyes and pressed her cheek against his palm. "Alexia, I have been dreading this parting more than I dreaded being executed in Oriosa, more than I have dreaded anything else in my life."

He gave her a thin smile and brought his right hand up on her shoulder. "There was a time—there were decades, in fact—when going out to do what we're going to do meant nothing to me. Not because I'm stupid or I was suicidal; it was just because that was what I did. It was the life I'd chosen—or the life that had chosen me, I don't know which. Resolute and I would just go out to harass Chytrine's forces and if we didn't return, it was another oath broken, another prophecy tested and proved false.

"I never thought my life empty until you came into it and made me want more than just Chytrine's destruction. I still want that, yes, but I want it because it means there will be a future for the world, for us, for our *heirs*."

A jolt ran through her. "You would want to have children with me?"

"After all this is over, Will should be able to take care of himself. Resolute will have a homeland to deal with, so I'll be at loose ends."

"Don't joke about that, Crow, please."

"Forgive me. I'm not joking."

Again his thumb stroked her cheek. It felt rough, but strong, like the rest of him, and Alyx knew their children would possess his strength and hers. They would stand tall, be brave and intelligent, relentless in the pursuit of that which would make the world better. Her right hand came up to cover his on her cheek, and her left hand strayed to her middle.

She immediately thought of how she had run her hand down her belly to shock her aunt. This time, though, she wanted to feel a swelling. She wanted to feel life beginning within her.

That shook her. Her entire life had been spent in training. She had been forged into a tool to liberate her homeland. Yes, she had thought of being married, having children, but that was always something that would occur *after* the liberation. As with many other nobles and warrior-women, she had an elven charm on an anklet that prevented pregnancy, because children would be an unnecessary complication in her life.

But now, *here,* with Crow, she wanted them. As she thought about their having children, she could see them all, at different stages of life. An infant sleeping on Crow's chest, a daughter astride a horse, shrieking with delight, her gold hair flying, and a son, too young to need to shave very often, but already tall and clean-limbed and dressed in mail, ready for war to defend his nation. All these visions and more came to her in an instant.

"Princess?"

Crow's soft inquiry brought her back. She blinked then, capturing his hand in hers, she turned her head and kissed his palm. "I want that, too, you know. I will have children by you, Crow, whether I'm the Queen of Okrannel or just a wandering soldier of fortune traveling with the man she loves."

His smile split white beard and moustaches. "Oh, we *will* have children, my love, as many as you want. And they will go on to do great things. What we accomplish will be as nothing compared to what they will do."

The truth of what Crow was saying struck her as undeniable, even though she knew that Chytrine, her hordes, and countless other forces stood in opposition to them and their dreams. Somehow, though, just his saying it created that future and it became an objective she would reach. No one would deny them that future.

"I know you are right, beloved." She squeezed his left hand, then slid forward into a hug. "I will miss you terribly. Only knowing that we will be together again, together to start our family and raise it, will make our parting bearable."

He squeezed her tightly to him and she sank into that warm embrace. "There's the trick of it, Princess. You and I, and everyone here, we're fighting for a future of hope. The only way you kill hope is to kill everything. There's little doubt Chytrine would be willing to go that far, but even she can't do that much damage."

"Unless she gets the DragonCrown back together."

A shiver ran through Crow. "Yet one more reason to stop her here in Muroso."

Alexia pulled back. "You will be careful out there, won't you?"

He nodded. "No unnecessary risks."

She gave him a stern look. "You have traveled with Resolute. What you two consider *necessary* risk would cause Kedyn's heart to quail."

Crow snorted and kissed her on the forehead. "I will be careful. You best be as well."

"I promise, beloved." Alexia gave him a sly grin. "After all, we'd best be setting a proper example for our children, starting right now."

"Exactly." Crow smiled at her. "I love you, Alexia. I will return to you. Ours is the future, and no one and nothing will take it away."

CHAPTER 52

For Erlestoke and his people, finding the northern gate to Sarengul shattered was both good and bad. On the good side was the fact that they could not be denied entry, and any shelter from the cold would be welcome. For two weeks they had traveled south and a little east, with hunting parties driving them on. The mountain halls of the urZrethi homeland would let them move faster and, with any luck, escape their pursuers.

But escape into what?

Jullagh-tse Seegg had followed signs invisible to Erlestoke and had brought them through a narrow mountain valley that led to the gate. Snow choked the small cul-de-sac and had there been bodies left behind from defenders and attackers, they had been firmly blanketed in white. Snow likewise decorated the carvings around the circular gateway, frosting the stone urZrethi warriors engaged to drive off a dragon. While that representation was hopeful, the fact that the gate lay broken beneath the arch undermined any good feeling.

Jullagh-tse stepped forward, tentatively, on her long legs. She peered into the shadowed interior, then came back to report to the others. "I see nothing but snow, smell nothing at all, and hear nothing but the light whistle of wind. This was just one of many traveler gates. Could be attackers are further inside, but the defenders could have cut things off."

The prince frowned. "But the fact that the gate has not been retaken, and that we see no signs of recent fighting, is not good. I don't really want to think about what it took to open the gate."

Ryswin pointed at the gate with his bow. "Strong as it would have been, enough pounding by a dragonel would have opened it."

"Might be," Verum offered. He pointed toward the high sides of the canyon. "By the same token, the Sarens would have emerged up there and slaughtered troops on the ground. That means the Aurolani took to the heights, ambushed the Sarens, then pushed on in. If they had urZrethi help..."

Jullagh-tse shook her head adamantly. "No urZrethi would betray his homeland."

"Don't need Sarens to do it, Jullagh-tse. You remember the old stories about the urZrethi left behind in Boragul forming an alliance with Chytrine?" Ryswin shook his head slowly. "They'd know what sort of defenses had been set up. They lead troops to the right places, and ambushes will succeed."

The urZrethi hesitated, then nodded reluctantly. "If that is true, if they had Boras to lead them and help plan, things could have gone badly. If the Boras came claiming to be escaped slaves, they would have been welcomed and could have worked from the inside to cause more trouble."

Jancis Ironside looked over at Erlestoke. "What is your plan, Highness?"

Erlestoke unslung his quadnel from his shoulder. "We'll leave fewer tracks in there than we will out here, and going through the mountains is preferable to going over them. The state of affairs in Sarengul is also going to be important to assess. We will need to send a report on it via *arcanslata*. They need to know down south what is going on."

The elven archer narrowed his blue eyes. "Given what we carry, is entering a realm where the enemy might be in control a wise idea?"

"Probably not, but moving through the mountains is even less so." Erlestoke looked around at the company. The three elves and one urZrethi had weathered the two-hundred-mile journey fairly well. Jilandessa had clearly had the toughest time of it, but that was because she was doing a lot to keep everyone else healthy. The others—old and young, human and *meckanshii*— had been sorely tested by the trip. Erlestoke could barely remember when he'd last felt warm, and he couldn't recall when his muscles didn't ache. Discussions over cold meals had become centered on hot ones, and spirits in the company had slowly begun to ebb.

The prince pointed his draconette toward the dark hole in the mountainside. "We've been running for over two weeks. We've been lucky in avoiding our pursuit, and Sarengul is going to give us a good chance to leave them behind. If we are able to kill some Aurolani and help the Sarens, I have no trouble with that. If they choose to help us in return, we are far better off than struggling through the mountains. We go in as a team, as we have done throughout."

The elf nodded. He and Finnrisia, the other elven archer, moved to the fore, stepping lightly over the snow and leaving no tracks Erlestoke could read. The rest of the company crunched after them, unlimbering quadnels. They fitted lengths of slow-match cord to the firelock, then let Verum ignite the ends so that the weapons were prepared for use.

The two elves mounted the steps to the opening, then Finnrisia ducked inside. After a couple of seconds Ryswin joined her. Jullagh-tse quickly entered after that, then the urZrethi reappeared in the opening and waved the others through.

The light reflected from the snow illuminated the hall, revealing small drifts and a few bodies frozen in death. Erlestoke spotted a couple of gibberers, a vylaen, two urZrethi, and a crawl, as well as enough debris scattered deep in the hallway to suggest that a dragonel or a charge of firedirt had been used to open the gateway.

As Verum directed warriors to secure cover, Erlestoke turned to Jullagh-tse. "Any suggestions for where we go from here?"

She pointed along the main hallway, which headed east. "This route will connect with one of the grand corridors. It will head north and south. I've been on part of it, but only coming up from the south. There it connects with the other major route that runs northeast–southwest, from Muroso to Nybal. It will be the most direct route, and the most likely place for us to meet resistance."

"Are there alternate routes?"

She nodded. "All along the grand routes there are villages and towns. Some have the grand routes running through them, so they are built all around them, above and below and to all sides. Other villages are removed from them, with their own roads. There are routes down to the mines, or to the springs. The mountains have a web of trails that are known, and probably an equal number that are hidden.

"The problem is this: invaders could move through the grand route without ever having to see any of the outlying villages, and those villages could block a tunnel so that it would take forever for an invading force to open it. With access to stores and water, a village could survive a siege for months, if not years, and would always have a route out to the skyside."

The prince rubbed a hand over his new-grown beard. "If someone decides not to let us pass, we could be trapped. Worse, we could be lured into a trap. Seems moving along the larger routes and seeking smaller if we need to is going to be our best bet right now."

Jullagh-tse nodded. "The heartening thing is this: we have not seen Aurolani reinforcements heading this way. Chytrine must think she has the Sarens defeated or contained. The Aurolani troops think there is no one coming in behind them, else they would have left guards. If we are cautious, we might get through this."

"It is something to hope for, yes."

The prince stood and signaled for everyone to move out to the east. He took pride as his soldiers moved from point of cover to point of cover, with the elves going first and the urZrethi bringing up the rear. As they moved deeper into the mountains the amount of light faded, such that elven vision was very helpful. The others moved up smartly, investigating homes and halls as they went.

The devastation could be easily seen. Dark bloodstained walls, and the stench of death permeated the air. Jilandessa used a little magick to see what she could learn about some of the victims, but all her spells told her was that they had been dead for a long time—not quite as long as her people had been on the road, but close.

The injuries inflicted, and the victims, testified to the savagery of the attack. Children had died clutched in the arms of mothers. One child had been killed by the same draconette shot that slew her mother. As had been the urZrethi tradition, the dead lay where they fell, but Erlestoke was fairly certain that the Aurolani assault would have made it impossible to recover bodies, even if that were the urZrethi way.

The Aurolani had not invaded with impunity. Bodies of their dead littered the hallways, but not nearly enough to make Erlestoke take heart. He'd kept a rough tally in his head of urZrethi warrior fatalities to those of the enemy, and the ratio proved depressing—overwhelmingly so when he factored in the civilian bodies. The Aurolani forces had come through, and an orgy of butchery had followed.

Once they reached the intersection with the north–south route, the numbers of bodies shrank appreciably. Erlestoke guessed that once the gate had been breached, alarms had gone out, and the people who lived around the grand routes were evacuated deeper into the mountains. By doing that the Sarens could avoid casualties and, if they were lucky, let the Aurolani pass through.

Late in the afternoon they found a small complex of rooms that had been abandoned. While the Aurolani had looted it, they had been haphazard. Jullagh-tse located some stores of wood, food, and wine, and they were able to seal the door. That night they enjoyed a hot meal and managed to get some rest in warmth.

A warm breakfast and good night's sleep helped revitalize the company. Morale was slowly climbing and remarks were made about pursuing the Aurolani instead of slinking away from them. Everyone replenished their provisions and the squad moved out cautiously.

That second day passed uneventfully. Erlestoke could feel how anxious everyone was to move quickly, for the route they took was wide, tall, and largely without sign of conflict. Yes, the Aurolani had taken to defecating on anything that could even vaguely be considered ornamental, but even having feces smeared over murals did little to spoil the majesty of Sarengul's Grand Corridor. The sculptures that decorated pillars and defined balustrades defied desecration. It made Erlestoke imagine that while the Aurolani might take control of Sarengul, they would never truly possess it—and that it would welcome those who came to liberate it.

That second day ended in another way station where they again found stores of food, drink, and fuel. It struck Erlestoke as a bit odd that those who had evacuated the area had not come back in the wake of the Aurolani advance either to secure or to poison these supplies. Jullagh-tse offered no answer as to why that had not happened, but the supplies proved to be untainted, so the group spent another night in relative comfort and safety.

On the third day, however, any illusion of safety vanished as they came upon the reason no urZrethi had ventured into the Grand Corridor. The route had run south and Jullagh-tse indicated they were getting close to one of the larger towns and an intersection with more roads similar to the one through which they'd entered. Even before the dim lights allowed them to see what had happened, they could smell it and, worse yet, hear things feeding upon the aftermath.

Little frostclaws, not much bigger than dogs, worried the bodies of the dead.

The huge, cylindrical intersection for paths from all levels of the mountains had roadways that spiraled up and down. Directional arrows carved in the stone pointed out the diverse destinations that could be reached over the broad avenues. Even though most of the intersection remained hidden in shadows, it was easy to imagine it as a place of much activity.

Now, though, the activity consisted solely of the flapping of flesh as greedy little temeryces crawled inside bloated bodies to feast on decaying flesh.

Erlestoke had little problem understanding what had happened. The urZrethi defenders had fallen back before the Aurolani assault. Chytrine's troops had pursued quickly and had not taken precautions against an ambush. When they reached the crossroads, the urZrethi hit them with a withering attack.

Unfortunately, they had not hit hard enough.

It could have been the presence of dragonels and draconettes that undid the urZrethi. He saw much evidence of the damage that both would wreak. A dragonel ball bouncing up and around one of the spirals would eventually lose momentum and stop, but it would harvest arms and legs as it went. Bodies of urZrethi magickers appeared to have been riddled with draconette shots, and their deaths would have made countering Aurolani magick all but impossible.

The crawls, it seemed, had won the battle, for there were very clear signs of their presence. Not only were bodies blackened and burned as the result of spells, but holes had been melted in walls. The sheer power of the magick astounded him, and the evidence of the cruelty with which it had been employed sickened him.

All around the walls, the crawls had been at work. Magick had melted stone, and survivors had been pressed into it, hand and foot. The stone then solidified, binding them there—in essence crucifying them. While the urZrethi should have been able to shift their shapes to escape those bonds, being battle-weary and, as most were, wounded, would prevent them from effecting any escape.

Crucifixion, Erlestoke knew, was not an easy death. Hanging there, the body would labor to draw breath. The very weight of the viscera on the lungs would shrink their capacity until the victim slowly suffocated. Cries for mercy would shrink to moans then mews, rasped breaths, and finally death rattles.

Jilandessa started to cast a spell, then shook her head. "A week ago this battle took place, not much more. The victims here lasted two or three days, five at the most."

The prince nodded. The cylinder would have collected the sounds of their dying and sent it through the mountains like an ill wind. No one knowing of the attack and hearing that finale would have ventured forth. The silence that came with their deaths would have been welcome, but would have encouraged people to stay hidden.

Jullagh-tse Seegg pointed south. "The Aurolani went that way. We will catch up with them soon if we follow."

Erlestoke frowned. "The first thing we do is find a place to hole up, then we backtrack and see if we can find a parallel route. If we can't, then we follow in their wake. They're not going to let themselves fall into another ambush like this, but what we see here doesn't mean they'll be unopposed hereafter. Our goal is to get through—and we will, somehow."

He took a last look at the walls. "We have to. If we don't, there are many other places where we'll see this and worse."

CHAPTER 53

Alexia had known this meeting was important even before both King Bowmars put in an appearance. The man she had first been introduced to as King Bowmar had, in fact, been Crown Prince Bowmar. When he was present with his father in the map room they could not have seemed more different, save for similar masks and almost identical robes. The elder Bowmar was shorter than his son, balding and stoop-shouldered and reminded her of her grandfather.

When he spoke, however, the true king seemed his son's age. He spoke with clarity and even wit. He—*they*, Alexia corrected herself—had a tactician's grasp on the state of their nation that few other rulers would have understood or accepted. The king did not shrink from the grim assessment of things indicated on the maps and models.

The crisis Muroso faced had forced the two Bowmars to undertake a most dangerous and radical exchange of spells. As it was explained to her, because of their consanguinity and long years of association, during which the true king had not only raised his heir but had instructed him in the ways of magick, the two of them were singularly like-minded. Together they worked a spell that was a variation of one that allowed magickers to cocast a spell that linked them very tightly. What one knew, the other did as well.

The crown prince said to her, "It is not as if we share a mind; we simply share memories. We benefit from each other's experiences. While one rests, the other works."

While Alexia understood the idea of the magick, the reality of it made her uneasy. Giving another access to her memories was something she could never do. It was a sacrifice of self that she couldn't even begin to comprehend.

But, then, I was raised to be entirely at the disposal of my nation, so am I really any different? She had accepted fully that her life would be subordinate to the cause of her nation—at least she had until she'd fallen in love with Crow. But in her case, at the very least, she had the illusion of free will, which the magick denied both kings.

The elder king studied the latest maps of the situation near Porjal. "Pursuit of the refugees to Navval has been cursory only. Reports do put the *sullanciri* as gathering their host for a drive south here to Caledo. This was not unanticipated, and our strategy to deal with them has kindly been supplied by Princess Alexia."

He pointed to a small unit located roughly sixty miles north-northeast of the capital. "Here are our Freeman Rangers, more or less. We have not had reports from them that betray their location, but we anticipate that they have reached roughly this area. They have made good progress, and as the Aurolani host moves south, they will be able to cut the supply lines."

Bowmar the senior picked up a small block of wood representing a military unit just outside the capital. "We will take these troops, the main bulk of our force, north along the Porjal road to the Green Dales and set up our first battle. We will let them know we are there, so they will set up to deploy against us, then we shall fade from that attack after inflicting some initial casualties. We will ambush pursuit to convince them they need to approach slowly."

Alexia nodded. The elder King Bowmar would not actually be with that force, which was comprised of four crack regiments. They had only one regiment of cavalry, but it was the best in Muroso, with three battalions of light horse for pursuit and one of heavy horse for devastating attacks. Of the three infantry regiments, one was comprised of scouts and rangers who would be able to form up in small hunter-killer groups to harry the enemy advance. The other two regiments were more standard and would be used to hit and hold the enemy when things became serious.

Crown Prince Bowmar would be in command of that force. Alexia had been told that his distance from his father would affect how quickly they could read each other's memories, so the elder would not be seeing what his son saw as his son saw it. They said the delay was something on the order of an hour per mile of distance. *Arcanslata* reports would come faster, but would contain a lot less detail.

King Bowmar's dark eyes flicked toward Alexia. "You, Princess, will lead this secondary force up the Navval road and keep it parallel with our force. You will be able to strike east and hit the flank of the Aurolani host."

She nodded. "I do know my role." It had rankled her a little that her strategy had been taken over by the Murosans and that she had been given a smaller force to command, but she quelled her unease quickly. She was a foreigner; young, and, in the eyes of many, utterly untested. For her to have been given the command she had—two regiments of cavalry—was a great honor. She wished she had her Wolves riding with her, but they were off in Okrannel fighting alongside General Adrogans.

The old man's eyes sparkled for a moment, and his son smiled. "Oh, Princess, we do know you would like to hit the Aurolani when they form up their column to march south again. If that appears to be something that would work, we shall permit it."

"It would hurt them badly, but would only be done if it would not pose undue risk to my command." She kept her voice even, and had to suppress a smile. Her use of the word "undue" had been deliberate to distance herself from the insane *unnecessary* risks Resolute and Crow would be taking.

The crown prince gathered his hands at the small of his back. "Princess Sayce has requested to be allowed to join your force."

Alexia frowned. "I thought she was meant to be part of my force since the beginning."

"She was, but I argued against her joining you." Princess Dayley glanced angrily at her brother. "Sayce has done more than enough."

Alyx rubbed her hands over her eyes. Dayley was using the tone mothers use when protecting children, and if Dayley was linked to her mother the way Bowmar was linked to his father, the implications of that were too much for her to want to contemplate. She blinked and remembered that Dayley was not a sorceress, just a member of the Communion. *If this were something of import that she wanted me to know about and say nothing, she could have told me there. I have to conclude, then, this is some internal Murosan matter.*

The Okrans princess folded her arms over her chest. "It is true that Sayce has done a lot. She ventured south, found the Norrington, and dragged him north. She fought well and almost died in Bokagul. With her nation facing extinction, however, I'm not sure anyone can determine if what she's done is *enough* aside from her. The warriors who went south with her were drawn from the King's Scarlet Lancers, and I have them with me. While I don't think they need her to lead them or even inspire them, she can do both, and do both well. If she is free to join me, I would like to have her along."

Dayley shook her head. "For her to go would put too much at risk." She looked past her brother at her father. "Sayce should be sent south to Alcida, or west if the Loquelves would accept her and keep her safe."

"Keep her safe?" Alexia frowned. "What are you talking about?"

Dayley's features sharpened. "My sister is pregnant with the Norrington's child."

Alexia's stomach just twisted down in on itself. "Was this all a charade? Did you send her south to seduce Will?"

The elder king shook his head. "We did not." He glanced at Dayley. "I sent her."

Crown Prince Bowmar had enough grace to look surprised, though Alexia would have preferred his being aghast. Dayley blushed crimson. Alexia looked from them to their father and back again. "I don't know what to say, what to think."

"You may think what you will, Princess, but I did what was necessary. If the prophecy is true, the Norrington bloodline is very important and I wished to secure it. Not for my nation, but for the future." King Bowmar's lips pressed together in a narrow line. "You have seen how inept my peers are at assessing the threat that is Chytrine. Sebcia is gone and no one has raised a voice, much less an army, to take it back. My nation is invaded and, aside from your company and renegades from Oriosa, there are no foreign troops here to oppose the Aurolani horde. I am not sanguine about the future of my nation in the short term, but I will do what I must to see the prophecy is fulfilled in years to come."

Dayley looked down at the wooden floor. "I was given the job of traveling south to find the Norrington and seduce him. My sister, who has forever been jealous of me, decided to head south and bring the Norrington to Muroso. She seduced him and consummated the seduction here, just to rub my face in it. That accomplished, she wishes to continue being a hero and go with you."

Alyx looked at the crown prince. "You knew nothing of this?"

He shook his head. "I have been preoccupied with the war and have not gone rummaging about in my father's head. Of that I am glad. I did not know, and would not have approved."

"Yours is not to approve, son. With the crown goes the responsibility. Were you in my position, you would think differently."

Alexia could not believe it. She remembered Will's turmoil when he came to talk to her. *He was worried about breaking Sayce's heart. He was worried she would feel used, and yet he was the one being used all along.*

She looked up. "What is wrong with you people?"

"I have a nation to think of."

Alexia batted that assertion aside. "You hide behind that noble idea as if no one can see the lies you've wrapped yourself up in. You're plotting revenge. If Muroso falls because no one else comes to your aid, you'll have the Norrington they need to save themselves. And don't try to deny it, because using subterfuge to get someone with Will's child—especially one of your own daughters—proves there was no altruistic motive behind what you did."

The elder Bowmar shook his head. "Secrecy was required so that Chytrine would not try to have the child killed."

"*That* lie is so flimsy a whisper would shred it." Alexia's violet eyes became slits. "You don't seem to understand: it's not *any* Norrington, but *the* Norrington. If it was the bloodline that was so important, Will would have been spending himself night after night to create a legion of Norringtons. I'd be carrying his child myself."

Something clicked in the back of her mind. She glared at Dayley. "Sayce doesn't know she's pregnant, does she? You had someone use magick to determine that."

"She knows."

"You don't lie well enough for me to believe you. If she knew, she'd not want to travel with me."

The true king watched her closely. "You know, however, so will you take her into combat with you?"

"And risk losing the child? Yes, but only to get Sayce away from you." Alexia raked her clawed fingers back through her hair. "King Scrainwood and now you. Is it the masks that encourage duplicity, or something else? I don't understand this and I don't want to. You complain about others playing political games and not helping you, but you do the same thing; and you play them with a young man who came north to save your nation. He's the young man who quite possibly *can* save your nation."

Before anyone else could reply, one of the signal-mages came over and placed a number of unit designators at the edge of the map, in Sarengul. One indicated the presence of Aurolani troops in the urZrethi stronghold. That did not exactly surprise Alexia, since she had supposed that the strike on Bokagul could only have been undertaken if Sarengul had been neutralized by conquest or alliance.

The mage placed another marker down, a small one with nothing to indicate nationality.

"Pardon my interruption, my liege, but this information was relayed from Alcida. A small group of people from Fortress Draconis have reached Sarengul and report the Aurolani have invaded it. Details are spare, but parts of Sarengul fell two weeks ago. The refugees are working south, but do not know what they will find or if they will make it through."

King Bowmar nodded. "Have a message relayed to them that they are to head here to Caledo if they make it through."

"Yes, Highness."

The elder Bowmar looked at Alexia. "The situation is yet more dire with the confirmation that Sarengul is gone. Chytrine need fear nothing on her march south, so her entire might is focused here. I do not regret any steps I have taken to protect my nation."

Alexia let her voice grow cold. "But you were a party to the discounting of Tarrant's story after the last war, weren't you? What did you do with the time you bought your nation?"

The elder king hesitated and the crown prince stared at him, stunned. "You knew, Father, that Chytrine would be coming?"

"It was conjecture."

The crown prince shook his head. "You can't lie to me; I have your memories of that time. You knew it was wrong, you knew she would come, and yet you did nothing!"

The king's shoulders sagged. "I hope, my son, that you will be wiser than I was."

The crown prince nodded. "I had better be, or the future—secured by a Norrington heir or not—will be short and bloody."

Alexia snorted. "It's likely to be short and bloody anyway."

Crown Prince Bowmar gave her a solemn look. "Then let it be their blood and their time. I will make sure you are kept informed of my activities. I am sure my sister will be safe with you."

"I shall do the same, and I shall keep her safe." Alexia glared at the king. "Not for the sake of your future, but for Will's. What you have done is bad. Let us just hope it does not become something worse."

King Bowmar looked up. "I fail to see bad or worse."

Alexia shook her head. "You were thinking to create another Norrington to have in case this one isn't *the* Norrington. But what if your grandson, by dint of his blood, now *is* the Norrington of prophecy? You've stripped Will of his import, of any power he might have had. As *the* Norrington, he might have been able to accomplish great things out there. Now, who knows? No matter what, Will Norrington will be doing everything he can for you. If your action has worked against him, you and your nation will pay dearly for your betrayal of Will."

CHAPTER 54

For Kerrigan Reese, the whole idea of a purification ritual being practiced by wizards seemed more theological than thaumaturgical. He could understand folks wanting to cleanse themselves before they went to worship a god, but Kerrigan felt no connections to any particular deity. None had claimed wizards, and wizards had not been inclined to adopt any deity. It did occur to him that Yrulph Kirûn might have been trying to ascend to the level of a god at one point in time; but even had he succeeded, Kerrigan doubted he would have had much of a following.

When you can daily play with the stuff of miracles, the gods somehow become superfluous.

In the week he'd been in Caledo, he had come to modify that initial opinion of the ritual. Prince Murfin had showed him how to do it—clearly skeptical that anyone from Vilwan would see value in it. Kerrigan, who was well used to learning from all manner of tutors, listened to the instructions carefully and followed them exactly.

And he had repeated the ritual each morning for the last five days. Heading down into the chamber beneath the palace the day he was to ride out with Princess Alexia and her force toward Navval, he felt the need for the ritual especially keenly. While he had never felt *cleansed*, he did draw a certain amount of calm from it.

In a small alcove he stripped himself naked and looked down. Because of his girth he'd never been comfortable naked. While he'd not had much contact with others his own age as he grew up on Vilwan, he could still hear sniggers and laughs when he wandered past. No one dared confront him directly, since they knew enough about his power to be afraid, but children still will be cruel to those who are different. Never having a chance to befriend them or change their minds, he had lived with his shame.

And to console himself, he ate.

He smiled to himself. He had learned, very early on, that his tutors would spend a lot of time with him, including at meals. He would be indulged in whatever he desired as far as food was concerned, since it would be used to reward him, or its withholding to punish him. By learning what his mentors wanted, he could reward them for rewarding him by selecting that sort of food, all the while enjoying it himself. Food became power for him, and his girth became a reason he needed more food.

Fat also gave his enemies an obvious target. Kerrigan had inured himself to criticism about his size—at least he hid the pain from his face, so no one outside could see they stung him. Such an obvious target satisfied most folks, however, so they did not probe any deeper for other vulnerabilities—ones with which he had not come to grips.

He ran his hands down his chest and confirmed again that some hair was growing in on it. He wasn't going to be as furry as Crow or Dranae, but no longer would he be as bare as a baby. While on Vilwan he had continually been treated as a child, but once away, once traveling with others, he had been accorded more adult status. *And my body agrees.*

Hair growing in on his chest was not the only change. He had indeed lost weight. He couldn't tell how much, but he did know he was smaller. By no means could he see his toes all the time, but he did catch glimpses of them a lot more often, and the belt on his trousers had been tightened a couple of notches.

Kerrigan moved from the alcove into the first of the ritual stations. The Caledo Academy, he had noticed, was fond of blending things in their spells and rituals. He knelt in a small box roughly a yard by a yard, and six inches deep. The sand and ash it contained crunched ever so slightly as he dropped to his knees. He scraped up huge handfuls of the gritty black mixture—the ash and sand representing the elements of *earth* and *fire*—and began to scrub it over his body. It packed dark beneath his fingernails and stained his flesh a light grey. He worked it into his hair and all over his body, dusting what he couldn't reach and working it into what he could until his skin tingled.

He smeared the last of it on his thighs, then stood in a tiny cloud of dust. There was no doubt about it; he definitely felt dirty and in dire need of a cleansing. He twisted his feet, burying them to the ankles just to make sure they were covered, then stepped from the box and moved to the next station.

Ahead of him lay a steaming pool of water, which had stepping-stones arranged in a spiral pattern. Four trails, each beginning from a spot designed with a rune for an element, curled out, the stones getting larger as they went.

A central stone stood a step away from the final stone on each spiral. Steam licked up in vaporous tongues and Kerrigan could easily feel the heat as he approached.

Steam: air, fire, and water. With the stones, we get earth, too. He started on the fire spiral just because he'd not walked it before. With each of the eight steps he took a deep breath and called to mind a specific thought. On the first stone he was supposed to recall his last meal, which he did with great ease, though it was not pleasing. Caledo had already begun to ration food, so he'd not been given much.

Once he recalled it, he sought to put it out of his mind. When he accomplished that, he moved to the next step, and the next, remembering things that went from the mundane to the exotic, physical to emotional to philosophical. Each time he put something out of his mind and moved forward, he shed concerns and let his mind become quiet.

At the penultimate stone, the largest on the fire path, he lowered himself to his knees. The stone was not soft, but as he sank back onto his heels and settled in, it did not feel all that hard on his knees and shins. He let his arms hang limply at his sides and closed his eyes. As he shut out the visual world, he could feel wisps of steam caressing and teasing him. In their wake came cooler air, which sent a chill through him, but soon the heat and steam coaxed a sweat from him.

When he knelt on the fire stone, Kerrigan's overwhelming sensation was that of being filthy. He wanted to be clean. He wanted his skin to stop itching. As he broke into a sweat and as the moisture began to ooze out of him, it eroded the dust and dirt. He could feel it dripping down him, dropping from his chin to his chest, running down his neck and collecting beneath the fold of fat that covered his lap. Sweat stung his eyes and tasted salty on his lips. It flowed into his ears and burned in the abrasions he'd created by scouring himself with the sand.

As the sweat ran, Kerrigan saw influences and evils, toxic thoughts and attitudes, the taint of the DragonCrown, flowing out with it. In wanting to be clean physically, he created linkages with things he wanted to rid himself of mentally. He just let them pour out of him with the sweat. Not all of them made it all the way, but enough did that he felt a growing relief.

Then, at some point, when he felt he had progressed far enough, he rose and stepped onto the central stone. It was the stone that Prince Murfin had called the birthstone. When Kerrigan had first stepped on it, the prince had told him to brace himself and Kerrigan wondered what for.

Now he knew.

He readied himself and raised his face toward the ceiling.

The icy water began as a slow trickle that played over his face as softly as a spring rain. Kerrigan moved his face, letting it wash sweat and dust from his eyes, then brought his jaw down and hunched his shoulders defensively, for what had begun as a trickle became a torrent. Frigid water splashed down over him in breathtaking sheets. One after another, they washed away all traces of dirt and sweat, puckering his flesh and leaving him sputtering. His skin burned and tingled. A huge shiver shook him, and water droplets sprayed from his hair over the pool.

Letting air hiss in through his teeth, he moved off along the earth spiral and reached another alcove, where he found a blanket that he wrapped around himself. Murfin had explained that the water used on the birthstone was cut as ice from Lake Calessa, then was melted by sunlight, so that Father Sun and Mother Lake would be the ones to welcome the newly cleansed back into life.

He let his hair drip and seated himself. The symbology was not lost on him, but just seemed overkill. He felt clean, and the cold water had certainly revitalized him. In the wake of the ritual he also found some peace and, better yet, was able to identify some of the elements of taint the DragonCrown fragment had left on him. They were certainly less than they had been when he had started the rituals, as if each cleansing eroded a bit more of it.

Examining the taint, however, had started him thinking on ways to detect the presence of a DragonCrown fragment. If what Rym had suggested was true, then anyone attempting to hide a fragment would be looking to cancel or fool spells sent out to detect the fragment. The defending spell would either have to conceal the fragment from the seeking spell, or would have to overpower the seeking spell and report back negative results.

The key thing to either of those approaches on the defensive side was that they had to recognize the seeking spell before they could defeat it. In his discussion with Rym, he had come up with all manner of dimensions to spells that would make them identifiable. The easiest one for a seeking spell would be its very nature. Seeking spells sought targets, then reported back with results. How long that took, and how good the results were, depended on a lot of factors. Often it took time, and the resulting information was less than useful.

Kerrigan had hoped that detection spells taught by the Caledo Academy would be significantly different from those on Vilwan, but they were almost identical. The spell created a general template that used information the caster put into it, then went out in the world and looked for something that matched. If Kerrigan wanted to find a cat, for example, he'd imagine a cat and would cast the spell. The more details he filled in, like age, name, hair color, scars, gender, and such, the more likely he'd get a perfect match.

Casting that spell, though, would overwhelm him with cat reports, and even if the specific cat he wanted was located, the time it took to report back could well mean that the cat had moved away and could never be found without more spells and a lot of searching.

Kerrigan noted an inherent flaw with detection spells and was pretty certain someone else must have noticed it before. If they had, however, they'd not fashioned a spell to take care of that problem. The flaw was this: the spells were slow and clumsy because they sought every object and checked it against the template, then evaluated how closely the thing matched. If it matched on enough of the parameters, the spell would report back that it had found the target. Thus, a statue of a black cat might fulfill the parameters of a search for a black cat, especially if the wizard forgot to include "alive" as an aspect he was searching for.

What Kerrigan had in mind to develop was a search spell that moved more quickly. What he would do was order the parameters he was looking for, and reject items immediately when they failed to match a parameter. For a DragonCrown fragment he would start with rejecting anything that was not magickal in nature, then anything that did not include a gemstone, anything that was of insufficient weight, and anything that was less than seven centuries old. In effect he would be turning search spells inside out and he hoped that would allow him to find the hidden fragments because concealment spells would not recognize the nature of his spell and react to it.

Even better than that, though, he decided to make the reporting back more exact. Once the spell had a match, it would trigger a secondary spell. The spell would shoot out two—Kerrigan wasn't totally sure what to call them and wished Will was around because he'd have a good word for them— two *heralds*. Each herald would go a half mile north or south of the target, then vector in at him. Because they would travel at a known rate of speed, and each would include vector and time information when it reported back, Kerrigan would be able to calculate how far away the item was and the exact location. Best yet, since the heralds would not contain information about the target per se, any spells cast to prevent such information from getting out— such as a spell that overwhelmed the detection spells and made them report back a lack of detection—would be powerless to stop them.

He didn't yet have all the details worked out on the casting. The heralds were ready to go, but setting up the hierarchy of match parameters and making that work was difficult. He felt fairly certain he'd have it ready to go inside a week, and would cast it toward Oriosa to see if the red fragment was still there.

Kerrigan smiled and sighed happily. He hoped Rym Ramoch would be pleased with his progress. *It's one step closer to stopping Chytrine, and if that does not make him happy, little else will.*

CHAPTER 55

For General Markus Adrogans, the battle made no sense. There, in the distance, barely a dozen miles away, lay Svarskya. He'd remembered it as a shining city of tall towers and stout walls, but now it sprawled broken and blackened, with smoke rising as if a siege had already shattered the defenders. In the harbor beyond it lay a fleet of ships, and he suspected they'd brought reinforcements.

In pushing north along the river road to the capital, he had progressed cautiously. More troops came in from the Guranin Highlands to garrison the Three Brothers. The highlanders had greatly enjoyed that idea, and the clans negotiated hard to get the tower they thought the most storied. Once he had his rear secure and his troops rested, he headed north and sent General Caro with the Alcidese Horse Guards ahead for reconnaissance in force, while the elves and Beal mot Tsuvo's people fanned out through the countryside.

Between the Three Brothers and Svarskya itself there lay only one good battleground where the Aurolani could hope to stop him shy of the city. The valley that the river had cut through the mountains spread out into vast coastal plains. To avoid the marshlands to the east, the road crossed the Svar River over a massive bridge. Known as the Svar Bridge, it had been constructed with fortifications at either approach, which would make it easy to hold against attack.

Caro and his heavy cavalry battalion arrived to find the bridge only lightly defended. Though infantry support would be days coming, Caro bravely took the bridge and made ready to hold it. Once word came back to the main body of troops that the Horse Guards were holding the bridge, the Alcidese

King's Heavy Guards infantry regiment requested and received permission to hurry ahead to support their countrymen.

Gyrkyme scouts and messengers had continuously flown back and forth to keep Adrogans informed, but the majority of their messages indicated that nothing was happening. Then, when Adrogans and the main body of troops were but a day away, the Aurolani marched a light infantry regiment south and staged a first attack on the bridge.

The Alcidese repulsed the attack easily. While they only did light damage to the enemy—estimated at less than a hundred killed or wounded—their casualties were even fewer. The Aurolani troops withdrew, then more troops headed south from the city, including a battalion of light cavalry on frost-claws and a regiment of heavy infantry including some hoargoun and the *kryalniri.*

What surprised and amazed Adrogans was that the Aurolani had positioned themselves farther north than necessary and had let the sunken road split their east wing from the main body of their formation. The east wing was then trapped between the road and the river, seriously limiting their ability to do much at all. Moreover, the Aurolani position allowed Adrogans to send his own troops across the bridge and form them up in broad lines.

The Aurolani were inviting him to engage in a set-piece battle, where he had the advantage in both numbers and terrain. The only way that would have made sense was if they had dragonels with them. That weapon's destructive capability could have done serious damage to his troops in formation, but without them, the outnumbered Aurolani forces were doomed.

Adrogans surveyed the battlefield. From the bridge, the land began a gradual descent through the plains to the city. Snow covered the ground, but it could not hide the depression made by the road as it cut its way through the landscape. Where the land swelled, the road might be as much as ten feet deep, and all but on the level with the surrounding terrain, but here it was a five-foot-deep gulf choked with snow snaking a white line through the Aurolani formation.

A slight breeze whipped pennants on lances and tugged at furs. Icy snow swirled up from the ground and rasped over helmets. Horses stamped and blew out great jets of steam, while across the battlefield frostclaws ducked their heads to groom white feathers on their breasts. The hoargoun slowly swayed from side to side with the breeze, like the mighty oaks from which they had formed their clubs.

Both sides stood ready, and Adrogans was content to wait. Since the Aurolani would be attacking uphill, he was happy to let them come. Maintaining the momentum of a charge was difficult that way, and once they stalled, his cavalry would charge. The Aurolani had chosen both the battlefield and their position on it poorly. He had no idea what they were waiting for, but unless they had the good sense to withdraw, few of them would be leaving the battlefield alive.

Then Adrogans saw it, above the city. It descended through the clouds as a fireball trailing a thick plume of white smoke. It slammed into the highest remaining tower and exploded there in a shower of flaming debris. A jet of fire shot straight up into the air, touching the low, grey clouds, and just for the barest hint of a second, he could feel heat radiating out.

The Aurolani host raised their voices as one, and their lines lurched forward.

That wasn't just a signal to begin... That was the arrival of Nefrai-kesh. Adrogans narrowed his eyes. The Aurolani general had stationed himself in a city tower twelve miles distant, but with a clear view of the battlefield. He had decided to watch his troops, not lead them—for reasons that were beyond Adrogans. But the Jeranese general did not mind. *I will give him something to watch.*

Astride his horse, Adrogans turned to his signalman. "Blow an alert for the Savarese Knights and Matrave's Horse."

The man raised his brass horn to his lips and blew. First he played a call-song for the Savarese horsemen, then another for the mercenaries. After that he blew the alert signal and followed it, again, with their individual callsongs. Flags went up in each formation to acknowledge the order.

The sunken road caused more of a problem for the Aurolani than Adrogans had anticipated. The whole right wing was lagging and its westernmost elements had a weak connection to the center. While that wing was made up of heavy infantry, their formation was losing its front and spacing as it moved through the sunken road, leaving it vulnerable.

"Signalman, blow left wing advance."

The man complied, and the left wing of Adrogans' formation began to move forward. It consisted primarily of the Jeranese Mountain Guards, which was a heavy infantry regiment. As their reserves, Adrogans had the Svoin Irregulars, but he was very reluctant to use them in combat. They needed seasoning, but this sort of battle was not the sort of place to get it.

The Aurolani host picked up the pace as it came uphill. They marched to the increasing beat of huge drums, and chanted loudly in tongues and cadences that sounded blasphemous. Adrogans could feel Pain sinking her claws into his breast as she clung to him from behind, but he ignored her. There would be enough pain for her to feast on soon enough, and he had no need of the special vision she would grant.

With the increase in speed came the increased dislocation and disruption of the Aurolani east wing. Adrogans signaled, and the readied cavalry units charged. Snow flew as hooves pounded down the road, and horses slammed full on into the infantry.

What had been pristine snow was now churned crimson, alive with twitching bodies writhing around broken lances. Horses, with their backs broken from a blow with a hoargoun's club, thrashed their hooves in the snow. The rime giants, skewered by dozens of lances, faltered and fell, some pitching over into the road, others stumbling back and crushing gibberers underfoot.

Kryalniri and vylaens cast spells, but Phfas and his Zhusk compatriots used the power of the *yrûn* to blunt most of these. The small contingent of Vilwanese warmages he'd been given shot their own spells. They specifically targeted the Aurolani magickers, forcing them to choose between self-defense and death. A surprising number chose the second option. Even as they died, they cast hideous fireballs that incinerated cavalrymen, or punched holes in the infantry line.

Gyrkyme laced the Aurolani formation with fire. Their swooping attacks released dozens of firecocks, which exploded against Aurolani troops or the ground. Three of them hit one hoargoun at the heart of the Aurolani center, turning him into a living torch. In his pain he crushed comrades, and his screams were enough to chill the blood of all who heard. Other firecocks wrought havoc amid the frostclaws. They killed some, and unnerved others enough that a panic swept through the Aurolani cavalry.

Cheers ran through Adrogans' troops as the Aurolani formation began to crumble. Their left had hit and held, such that the Aurolani center came forward. Its support, the east wing, had been shorn free, leaving the flank open for a crushing charge from the Alcidese or Jeranese Horse Guards. A textbook example of how a battle should be fought, things were going too well for Adrogans for him to be comfortable.

Then he saw it.

The burning hoargoun had been cavorting and spinning, but never trying to slap out the flames that engulfed it. Instead its thick fingers tore at the harness it wore. It was attached to a satchel of heavy canvas, not unlike those troops wore to carry supplies. *Save no one wears one of those into combat.* On a creature the size of the hoargoun, the satchel could have contained three bullocks, and it certainly bulged with whatever its cargo was.

Adrogans watched it for a moment more, and felt Pain sink her fangs into the back of his neck. He pointed at the hoargoun and shouted at Phfas, but it was too late.

The hoargoun's pack exploded.

The creature wearing the device literally became a crimson mist from the thighs upward. Fire blossomed for a second where its chest had been, then a thunderous blast rippled over the landscape, knocking warriors down, making snow dance, and even shattering ice over the river. A lethal spray of missiles shot out in every direction.

Gyrkyme were shredded, spiraling down with bloody feathers floating in their wake. Some of the Savarese Knights had swept around to the rear of the Aurolani center, catching the blast full force. Round lead balls and jagged pieces of bent iron punched through their armor. Sharp fragments of crockery sliced exposed flesh and the force of the blast itself was enough to send horses and riders tumbling.

But as much damage as the explosion did to the Savarese Knights, it did more to the Aurolani troops. It ate the middle out of their formation. Those it had not killed it wounded, and all the infantry had been knocked down. They struggled to their feet, dazed and disoriented, with many of them turning back to see what had happened.

Which is when Adrogans' troops hit them. There had been no charge blown nor any signal given. One of the balls had crushed the signal horn and the hand holding it, but these men needed no signal to know when to fight. They had been shocked and some hurt by the blast, but all of them had their blood up, and the enemy became the focus for their fury.

Fighting to steady his horse, Adrogans swiped at blood dripping into his right eye. Something had hit him, opening a cut, but the pain of it was nothing compared to the pure waves of agony his *yrûn* played into him. It swirled through him like a twisting column of fire, so he took hold of it, channeled it, then cast his gaze out over the battlefield.

There, on his left, another hoargoun was struggling with a pack. That creature was not burning, but a thin trickle of smoke rose from the corner of the burden it raised over its head. The creature's arms went back, preparing for a long throw that would plant the device deep in amid the Mountain Guards.

Adrogans stabbed his left hand at the hoargoun and let pain flow. He let pure agony wrack the hoargoun, locking its muscles and bowing its back. The satchel sank lower, then the creature toppled backward. It hit the ground in a cloud of snow, and the satchel bounced once before it exploded.

With that explosion, the Aurolani left wing evaporated.

So did the fire atop the tower in far Svarskya.

One of the other hoargoun, one that fell in the initial charge, had been fitted with one of the explosive devices. Someone decided it should be called a boombag, and for want of a better term, it stuck. Vilwanese mages and several weapons-masters hauled it off to a small hollow and opened it. Inside they found a cask of firedirt with a long fuse surrounded by shot, metal, and ceramic debris. It appeared the device was meant to be used as the second hoargoun had attempted to use it, though one warmage did note that the harness was not really conducive to easy removal.

Could Nefrai-kesh have meant the hoargoun to commit suicide? He looked north to the city. Lights burned, from the towers and broken walls, out to the city warrens that surrounded the inner, older city. *Is he telling me that we will face such things every step of the way?*

That prospect shook Adrogans for a moment.

Phfas came to stand beside him and look at Svarskya. "You take this as a warning, yes?"

"Is there another interpretation, Uncle?"

The wizened man nodded. "The dog that does not want to fight barks louder than the one that does."

Adrogans considered that for a moment, then nodded. "Even if those devices had worked, not enough damage would have been done to allow his troops to win. And if he had meant to use the boombags to win, he would have employed them against the bridge garrison. You're right; there is some other game being played here, and I don't know what it is."

The Zhusk shaman snorted. "He is foolish, if he plays games when we are making war."

"Yes, but perhaps he has a grander prize in mind."

"Will that stop you from winning yours?"

Adrogans smiled and rested his right hand on Phfas' shoulder. "No, but if I knew what his prize was, we might be able to win that as well."

"Excuse me, General, we have a report about the battle we are prepared to send to Lakaslin by *arcanslata*." The signal-mage gave Adrogans a piece of parchment, then cast a spell to make a light so he could read it. "Is it satisfactory, sir?"

The Jeranese general nodded slowly. "This will do for my private archives. Delete any reference to boombags and give all credit for the victory here to the troops on the field, not the devastation done by those things."

"But, sir, warning others of the devices..."

"I know, but they failed here, so perhaps they won't be used again." Adrogans gave the man a nod. "If we let others back home fear things they might never see, we contribute to the Aurolani effort. I won't aid the enemy that way."

"Yes, sir." The signal-mage bowed and withdrew.

Phfas smiled. "You see a glimmer of his prize?"

"Not really, but we both agree Nefrai-kesh was sending a message. I've just decided his message was meant for me alone." He scratched at the stitched cut over his right eye. "As such, it is unimportant to anyone else, but a message I shall take to heart."

CHAPTER 56

Will had known intellectually that raiding supply caravans would not be easy. The supplies and replacement troops Chytrine would need meant vast numbers of people and huge amounts of equipment would be heading south. Just the draft beasts and their keepers would outnumber the raiding force they had assembled. Had he been planning an equivalent strike on a gem merchant's caravan, he would have wanted the forces a lot more even and the strike to be on his own turf.

The experience Crow and Resolute had gained through decades of hitting and running, combined with the knowledge of the local area provided by the Murosan Lancers, gave them an edge. Unconventional tactics worked further in their favor, like dropping trees across the routes the Aurolani used, or switching the little marking stones around so a supply train marched off along a road that took them well out of their way.

Crow and Resolute set out definitive rules for how to attack the enemy in any of their ambushes. Magickers were always a target, and the best shots—be they archers or draconetteers—were assigned to kill them. Next were the draft animals. Sleighs that couldn't be drawn could not deliver their goods. If they could isolate a part of a supply train and steal the goods, they did that, but anything they couldn't get to, they burned.

And from the first siege of Fortress Draconis, Crow had learned how devastating a burning wagon of firedirt could be, so when fire-arrows played over the supplies, those were favored targets, and everyone got under cover when one was engaged.

The two of them even planned their ambushes in depth, setting a reserve and lines of retreat that would make pursuit difficult. After an initial rattle of draconette shots cut down sleigh drivers and mages, arrows would rain down from another direction, killing beasts. When the troops assigned to protect the caravan moved to attack the ambushers, they themselves would be raked with flanking shots.

In the six days they had been out, they had diverted four groups—two being parts of the same caravan that had gotten stretched out during a snow-storm. They hit one of those groups hard when the leader decided to camp for the night. That particular raid still sent shivers through Will.

That section of the supply train had been the lead element, and had decided to wait for the other half to catch up. In all fairness to the leader, the snow had started getting thicker, so traveling was not going to be easy. He chose for them to shelter against the lee side of a line of hills, so they got some protection from the wind. The terrain did force them to stretch the caravan out, and the storm meant the guards at one end of the camp couldn't see or hear those at the other end.

And all the while they set their camp up, Resolute and others studied the layout. They learned who was sleeping where and marked out what wagons were the most important. This section had very little firedirt, so instead of exploding it, the raiders decided to steal as much as they could to replenish the supplies of their draconetteers.

Though gibberers are normally nocturnal, the drive to get supplies south meant they had been pushing themselves hard. The storm came as a welcome excuse to rest. And had the howl of the wind not covered the raiders' stealthy advance, the rasped, rumble-growl of snores would have sufficed.

Will remembered watching Resolute drift soundlessly through the night to reach the first gibberer picket before the beast even knew he was close. The Vorquelf had approached from downwind, denying the gibberer a chance to catch his scent. The first it knew of his presence was the tight clasp of his hand over its muzzle. The second was the sharp, short stroke of a razored longknife across its throat.

Despite being half-metal, Sallitt Hawkins had reached the next guard equally silently. As it turned and sniffed at the scent of blood on the air, the *meckanshii* caught its neck in the *V* of his right arm. His left hand caught hold of the metal wrist, then he twisted and dragged the gibberer back over his right hip. Another twist from Sallitt, this one shorter and sharper, and the gibberer went limp and slid to the ground.

Will moved with them through the night, entering the camp as if part of a legion of ghosts. Knives and garrotes made short work of guards and those few hapless gibberers who ventured from tents to find water or relieve themselves. Resolute sliced through the wall of the leader's tent and stabbed one of his bladestars through the creature's chest.

While the raiders moved toward the middle of the camp, Will directed his Freemen to loot the firedirt sleigh. Without complaint and with a minimum of trouble, they accomplished their task and before long they reached the place where Crow waited with the Lancers. Will said nothing to him, but waited at his side. Finally, the others trickled in, with Resolute bringing up the rear.

Crow looked at him and whispered in a low voice. "No scalps?"

The Vorquelf actually smiled for a moment. "I only take them from warriors."

His words sank deep into Will and chilled him. Deep down he knew that the gibberers below were just as important to Chytrine's war as those on the front lines. Without the supplies, her army would grind to a halt. Without food, they would starve. Without firedirt, they could not break city walls. Every one of the gibberers they slew down there would hurt a handful of warriors.

The fact was, however, that most of the gibberers in the camp were not warriors. Some were old, some were young, others were clearly addlepated, but only a few could have actually qualified as warriors. Certainly, given a longknife they would defend themselves, but they were not trained for killing. They hardly represented the caliber of foe he'd fought in the past, and killing them as they had almost seemed like murder.

Part of him knew their deaths were necessary. What made him uncomfortable was being in a position to sit in judgment. Just because Chytrine had decided he had to die didn't seem to justify his being able to decide the fate of others. Then again, by killing them, he stopped her from killing him and his friends. It could be justified as self-defense, but had none of the clarity of self-defense wrapped in battlefield glory.

As the raids progressed, the raiders began to form bonds. Crow encouraged that by mixing units for specific missions, and assigning groups to aid others. That built trust and on those occasions when the depth of preparation proved necessary, everyone was happy for the help.

It started with the *meckanshii,* but slowly spread throughout the group. The Oriosan warriors from Fortress Draconis had left their life masks behind, so they had fashioned for themselves black masks that they did not decorate. Though no one talked about it, everyone knew the black masks were because no one harbored even the illusion that they would survive their actions. Wearing a black mask mocked death, and soon the Murosans and Will's Freemen made and donned them. The *meckanshii* even made black masks for Lombo, Qwc, Dranae, and Resolute. The four of them quickly adopted the masks.

There was no black mask for Will, and after he got over the initial pique at being left out, he understood why. Everyone there believed fervently in the Norrington Prophecy. If they were going to die, Will would die last. As long as he defied death, there was hope.

That afternoon, before they mounted up to stage another raid, Sallitt Hawkins approached his brother. In his metal hand he held a black mask. "We were hoping that you'd wear one of these and join us."

Crow, who had been settling his bow into his saddle scabbard, hung on to the saddle. His shoulders sagged for a second, then he turned with a grim expression on his face. "You know I can't take a mask. Mine was long ago stripped from me. I was judged unworthy, and that has not changed."

Sallitt stood there silently, the mask's ties floating softly on the breeze. Will watched the muscles bunch in his jaw and his eyes narrow. The silvery metal mail that fleshed the right side of his face contrasted sharply with his red hair and pale skin, but it flowed as if it lived, tightening as the man thought. Will actually saw a vein pulse at his temple beneath argent sheathing.

The elder Hawkins kept his voice even, but a tightness in his throat had lowered it. "We've been thinking on that. It was Tarrant Hawkins who was stripped of his mask. Events seem to have proven that to be wrong. But it's not Tarrant Hawkins we're offering this mask to. We're offering it to you, Kedyn's Crow. The past doesn't matter. What matters is that you've earned the honor of a mask many times over."

Crow started to shake his head and deny the honor.

Will stepped forward and took the mask from Sallitt's hand. He looked up at Crow. "In Meredo, you accepted that I was your liege lord. You accepted a mask from the hand of a Norrington before. Will you take this one now, for me? For this company?"

The white-haired man nodded slowly and dropped to one knee. Will stepped behind him and fastened the mask on, catching a hair in the knot. "It's not that this mask makes you one of this company, Crow. In taking these masks, they're all joining you and Resolute in your war with Chytrine."

The Norrington stepped away and untied the mask from his own right arm, then pulled it on. He reached back to tie it into place, but found Crow there. "A Norrington always has a Hawkins to help him, my lord."

Will smiled as he felt the knot snug and tug a piece of hair. "Thank you, Crow." He looked up and saw the other men, especially the Oriosans among them, smiling broadly.

Will aped their smile. "Well, now that's done, men, we have killing to do. Let's go. There will be a lot of it, so we might as well get an early start."

CHAPTER 57

Even before setting out for Navval, Alexia had seen signs that her strategy was having an effect on the Aurolani forces. Crown Prince Bowmar and his core of two heavy cavalry battalions had hurried north on the Porjal road and set up in the hill country. As expected, they skirmished with the Aurolani lead element, which withdrew and waited for the bulk of the army to come up. When the Aurolani general—identified by *arcanslata* as a *sullanciri*—entered the field of battle, the Murosan cavalry withdrew to a new line of hills, with the infantry to back them up.

The Aurolani made several attempts to bring their dragonels up, but this was a tricky proposition. If they came too near to the cavalry formation, a quick charge by the Murosan warriors could kill the crews and destroy the weapons. To protect them, the Aurolani leader only advanced them with sufficient infantry cover, and the cavalry before that. When the cavalry pulled back for the final time, they withdrew to hills where the infantry—aided by magick to unfreeze the ground—had dug in. There the dragonels would be shooting uphill against targets behind cover.

The Aurolani did have skycasters—short, squat dragonels that launched a ball filled with firedirt that exploded over its target. Will had dubbed the missiles thunderballs and they burst into a lethal spray of shrapnel. While they would be able to deliver their thunderballs on target, they had to be positioned relatively close to the hill they were going to be shooting at.

The Murosan hill positions were by no means invulnerable. Positions like that had been overrun from time immemorial. With enough warriors moving fast enough, a enemy could overwhelm the defenders and sweep over them. The cost would be frightening, but it was the only way to dislodge them.

Not the only way, Alexia reminded herself. A single dragon could sweep over the line of hills and burn the defenders alive. Alyx had seen firsthand the destructive capability of a dragon's fury. The city of Porasena in eastern Alcida had ceased to exist in less than five minutes.

Predictably, the Aurolani commander detached a part of his force to swing west through a gap in the hills to try to get around behind the Murosan position. Chances were that the two battalions of light cavalry would be insufficient to stop a full retreat, but they could slow it enough that the main force could come up. At the very least, the Aurolani light cavalry would be able to stop any supplies from getting through to the force astride the road, weakening that position.

The light cavalry rode under the banner of four crushed skulls, one each of white, red, blue, and green. Gibberers and vylaens mostly, with a few renegade men, the six hundred rode out under cover of darkness as if heading back toward Porjal, then came around the hills and moved swiftly west. With the night sky clouded and the moon no more than a sliver, the chances of their being seen by the Murosan defenders were minimal.

Alexia, on the other hand, had the benefit of a Gyrkyme scout who would be invisible in the night sky, but had sharp enough vision to return with a complete count of the force that was executing the flanking maneuver. The Aurolani detour would only be ten miles, which they could make easily in the night and arrive the next morning already set up behind the Murosan lines.

While that strategy was sound, it was based on misleading information. At the Murosan position were displayed all manner of unit banners, including those of the King's Heavy Cavalry regiment; a famed unit that actually was under Alexia's command. Yet while the King's Heavy Cavalry *was* in the hills, it wasn't in those hills.

It was, in fact, massed in the forested hills above the valley through which the Aurolani rode. The valley itself had been carved out by centuries of spring floods, so that, while narrow, it had a flat bottom through which a small stream ran. The stream had been completely covered by snow, and the snow, which was not deep, had frozen hard. The Aurolani, moving swiftly through the night, had no inkling of the disaster about to befall them.

Their first warning came when the Heavy Cavalry's First Battalion charged out of the forest to the north. The three hundred heavy cavalrymen came riding fast out of the tree line. They actually were heading for the last part of the Aurolani line, having waited until the rear guard passed them before they launched their strike. They started from five hundred yards away and came on at a full gallop; they would be nearing the end of their effective charge when they reached the frostclaws.

The Aurolani clearly knew the limitations of heavy cavalry. As the rear element shot forward, lengthening that range, the forward elements split north and south, to curl around and slash at cavalry flanks. The Aurolani outnumbered the Murosans two to one and should have had an easy time tearing them up.

The Aurolani had opted for the first of three possible reactions to this ambush, and Alyx had positioned her troops to take advantage of any scenario. In this one, the Second and Third Battalions attacked from the north and south respectively, hitting the Aurolani units in their rear flank.

While frostclaws were fearsome fighters, they didn't outmass by much a warhorse encased in armor. Their broken bodies whirling and feathers flying, crushed frostclaws squawked and gurgled as the cavalry pounded into them. Lances skewered gibberers, lifting them wriggling from saddles. Screams and shouts, shrieks and whimpers fought to be heard over the clang of metal and the crisp snap of bone and lance.

The rearmost element of the Aurolani, seeing what had befallen their comrades, raced forward, outdistancing the ambushing force. Alyx could imagine them believing they had escaped their doom. They pushed on west toward where the valley began to narrow again, doubtless intent on slipping into the forest to loop around and report back to their leaders.

The King's Heavy Cavalry had a fourth battalion. It waited for them, having been positioned there to stop the whole force had all the Aurolani decided to bolt. Alyx had left Sayce in command of that unit, and the young Murosan Princess waited until almost too late to launch her charge. The Fourth poured out of the woods and bore down on the Aurolani, smashing through them. The lead lancers blasted a furrow through the center of their formation, and the swordsmen behind them shredded what was left.

Sayce rode over to where Alexia, on the ground amid the Third Battalion, was cutting the four-skull banner from the broken standard. "They are all dead, Alexia."

"How many of ours are hurt?"

Sayce glanced back into the gloom. "Four dead; a lot of cuts and gashes, mostly from frostclaws. I have a dozen horses that probably won't make it."

"Get the worst of your injured up to Kerrigan. Let him fix them up enough so they can ride. Then I need you to pick four of your best riders and send them to your brother. Tell him what happened here."

Sayce cocked her head. "But we have *arcanslata* to send that message."

Alexia slid her dagger back into the sheath in her boot before straightening up. "And it is just possible that Chytrine has come up with some manner of detecting the location of *arcanslata* in use. I would like to avoid having our position spotted needlessly."

"I hadn't thought of that."

Alexia nodded. She had not given it overmuch thought herself until she'd made the mistake of asking Kerrigan what was occupying his time on the ride north. He'd explained how he was working on a class of detection spell that was unlike any other and how it would be able to figure out where anything was, like a fragment of the DragonCrown or any other magickal item. He noted, for example, that using her wedding ring, he could pinpoint Crow's location. At least, he thought he could. She then asked about finding *arcanslata*.

Kerrigan had smiled and rolled his eyes. "Possible, but only when they are in use. They're not very magickal otherwise. This spell will be for important things."

Alexia had not taken the time yet to explain to him how important *arcanslata* could be, but she assumed that anything Kerrigan could do, Chytrine could do, too. That assumption might have invested too much power in the Aurolani Empress, but Alyx would rather overestimate an enemy than not.

A soldier came up bearing the severed head of the Aurolani leader. Alexia gave him the banner and the man gleefully wrapped the head in it, then secured it with some leather bindings into a nice, tight little package. "All set to go, Highness."

"Thank you."

Perrine descended and folded her wings. "As nearly as I can see, sister, no one escaped. There are a few frostclaws about, but we can hunt them down in daylight."

"Thanks, Peri." Alexia pointed to the package the soldier was holding. "If you wouldn't mind, could you deliver that to the Aurolani commander?"

"With your regards?"

Alyx looked at her smiling sister and shook her head. "I don't want you that close to them."

Peri accepted the bundle, then stepped back and spread her wings. "They'll get your message, Alyx."

"And I'll await their reply."

Isaura felt Anarus' fury well before she ever heard the agonized wolf howl in which it was given voice. She slipped from the warm cocoon of skins in which she had slept and pulled on her clothes. She took her time dressing. She knew she would have to attend the *sullanciri*, but if she were the first to his side, he would focus his ire on her, and she wanted to avoid that.

Having delayed as long as possible, she wended her way through the labyrinthine passages in the command pavilion and reached the central room. Neskartu and Naelros had arrived before her. Of Tythsai she found no sign, but since the undead *sullanciri* neither saw with normal eyes nor had any need of sleep, she often spent the nights walking and watching.

On a table, lying on a wrinkled mass of sodden cloth, sat the head of a gibberer. Based on the designs painted in white on its face, Isaura took it to be a leader of some sort. Only when she looked more closely at the cloth and saw it had been a banner did she begin to understand the import of the head's presence.

Neskartu's face flowed around to glance at her.

Delivered by Gyrkyme—Alexia's pet. The flanking strike failed.

Isaura looked over at Naelros. He had suggested a stronger force to make that maneuver, but Anarus had opted for speed. Anarus, it struck Isaura, became hasty as the moon waned, and seemed more possessed of himself as it grew to full.

The dracomorph acknowledged her glance with a nod, but remained silent.

The wolfish *sullanciri* paced angrily. As he turned, he would look at the bloody head and snap at it. Half the time he would curse, the rest growl. His eyes blazed with an evil light, and snarls bared fangs with menacing regularity. Anger and outrage radiated off him like heat from molten rock.

Then his head came up and his ears flattened back. A long tongue came out and he licked his muzzle, then hunched his shoulders and gathered his clawed hands at the small of his back. "There are a number of things made clear now. First, the Murosans have learned well from the plight of the Sebcians. The only way to stop us from laying siege to their cities is to prevent us from getting at their cities. They do this by blocking the roads and confiscating our supplies. Soon enough, though, we will have more troops and supplies coming in through Porjal, so the troops they have out there now will be useless."

Naelros nodded. "If you desired, Lord Anarus, I could take my people and hunt down their raiders."

"No, no, that will not do." Anarus growled, but not savagely. "Your troops are no more suited to hunting than mine are. I do have a task for you, though. You will take your regiment and two others, along with a dragonel battalion. You will drive at Navval."

Is it wise to split your force?

The snarl directed at Neskartu came quick and dire. "Question me not, wizard. That force will be sufficient to threaten Navval. If our troops arrive to lay siege and no one comes to lift it, the people will lose heart and open the city to us. Without defenders, the dragonels will be enough to reduce the defenses to rubble. Our move will force King Bowmar to weaken the garrison opposing us here in order to defend Navval, or he will lose that city."

Isaura raised a hand. "My lord Anarus, the people of Muroso set great store in their wizards. Until the ones in Navval are eliminated, the people will not surrender."

"Of course, Princess; that is obvious." The *sullanciri* pointed a crooked finger toward the distant Murosan position. "They have not erected any of their black posts there, so they resist our invitations to pit their wizards against ours. Lord Neskartu and his students are wasted here. I will send them to Navval as well. You, Princess, may stay here or go, as you will."

She will come with me. Her safety is my charge.

"Then see to it well, my friend." Anarus turned and looked at the draco-morph. "You have questions?"

"How long do I have to take Navval?"

The *sullanciri's* ears flipped this way and that as he thought. "Two weeks should be sufficient."

"And have I enough firedirt and food to accomplish the task?"

"If you do not squander the first, and if you do not feast with the second, yes." Anarus' eyes narrowed. "You will be resupplied from Porjal, since it will be faster to reach Navval than wherever I shall be. My supplies will still come from the north, when they get through."

Naelros nodded. "And you will request more assistance from the empress?"

"Done, long since done." A growl rolled from Anarus' throat. "Come to me with news of Navval's conquest or do not come to me at all."

Something *ancient* moved through Naelros' dark eyes. Isaura did not know what it was, but it burned her senses. It had been equal parts anger and contempt, and yet more, woven in such a tight and complex pattern that she could only marvel at what little she comprehended. Naelros would obey the *sullanciri*—for now, at least—but what he did after he reported success, she could not predict.

Whatever that would be, Isaura was certain, it would not be as foolish as Anarus' hastily snapped command.

CHAPTER 58

Kerrigan Reese was finding the Conservatory students very annoying. They sat there in their encampment, at the heart of the Aurolani siege force, casting spell after detection spell. Not only were their detection spells cast in the old, sloppy style he now detested, but they were painfully easy to deal with.

Once it had been reported that a third of the Aurolani army had moved northwest toward Navval, Princess Alexia had marched her troops to the city ahead of them. While the cavalry formed a screening force in the direction of the enemy advance, the Zamsina Guards, a light infantry unit, hurried to Navval. Kerrigan had traveled with them and had been afforded chambers in the local Caledo Academy.

He had been tempted to ignore the Aurolani spells, but a conversation he'd had with Princess Alexia reminded him of a job he had done for General Adrogans on the Okrannel campaign. Kerrigan had prepared lots of documents that purported to be from a unit traveling covertly through the Okrans countryside. When the enemy uncovered this cache of documents, they sent troops out to hunt for these phantom warriors.

Thus Kerrigan had been introduced to the concept of disinformation. It was patently obvious that if the Aurolani thought there were more troops in the city than there were, they would be slower to attack—and vice versa. An underreporting of troops might lure them into an ambush, and an overreporting might even make them withdraw.

Kerrigan took some time to examine the Aurolani spells and realized they were looking to detect fires burning, swords, spears, arrows, and adults sorted by gender. Clearly each mage had been given a specific result to tabulate, and together they would provide a picture of just who and what was waiting inside the city.

Messing around with the results of every spell would have been difficult, so Kerrigan chose his targets carefully. He selected the best-cast spells with the tightest search templates, and those were the ones he played with. He examined them, learned the method of their reporting, and created two spells. One sought the reports and killed them; the other sought the reports and duplicated them.

Both spells worked well and validated Kerrigan's thoughts about how masking spells might function to conceal something from a search spell. *An* old-style *search spell*. He also created a spell to seek out counterspells employed to detect the spells he cast to alter information. Those never produced results, which actually disappointed him, even though it meant the enemy had no idea they were being tricked.

But what annoyed him about the Conservatory mages was their dogged persistence in casting their spells. He hardly got a chance to work on his detection spell for a fragment of the DragonCrown, but late in the afternoon of the second day in Navval, he thought he had it ready. Ignoring the search spells for a moment, he set himself, then cast his spell.

Kerrigan could not help but be pleased with himself. His spell melded a number of styles and aspects. It twisted and tangled like the organic weavings of elven magick, but before the tendrils thickened, they evaporated as might urZrethi magick. When they flashed into form again, they had the angularity of a human spell, but its sharp crusts burst as elven tendrils grew out through them.

He cast the spell toward the east and at the Aurolani camp. He'd planned to cast it toward Meredo, where he knew a fragment existed, but the distance would delay the report, and he was anxious to see if the spell worked. If the enemy had a fragment of the DragonCrown, he was sure to get a report quickly. He focused the casting to a narrow arc, which would, perforce, expand as it swept forward. He figured the rate of speed would be a mile a minute, with the rate slowing as the arc grew. At that rate, however, he'd have his report back from the Aurolani camp in seconds.

He waited.

Nothing.

Two minutes. Three. Time moved with incredible sloth. Four minutes and then five.

He frowned. He could imagine one of three results. First, there was no fragment of the DragonCrown in the enemy camp. Second—and he did not like this idea at all—there *was* a fragment, but a spell masking it had defeated his spell. Third, which he actually liked least of all, his spell just didn't work.

It was this third possibility that he had to address first. He reworked the spell. Instead of searching for a fragment of the DragonCrown, he opted for something a bit more simple. He picked a target suggested by Princess Alexia and decided to search for *arcanslata*. He recalled telling her that they could only be detected when they were in use, but he knew that wasn't entirely true. There would be a taint on them from the use of magick, but it would be hard to detect. Still, determined not to let that defeat him, he worked out the search parameters and blasted the spell out, directing it to the east and south.

If the Aurolani don't have any, I know the crown prince and the king do.

Within seconds he got three reports of *arcanslata*. One was located in the Aurolani camp and the other two were within Navval itself. The spell would take a while to get to the crown prince and to Caledo, so Kerrigan sat back and waited.

Before he got the heralds back from that spell, he got something else. It washed over Navval heavy and hard, blasting into the city with the force of a torrential rainstorm. It even felt like a storm, with magickal energies roiling and boiling. It raked through his mind like the screech of talons on slate, then built to drive a flaming spike into his soul.

His hands went to his head and he spilled out of his chair as pain shot through his body. Even wracked as he was, he retained the presence of mind to identify the spell and prepare a counterspell. Fingers twitched, and his lips began to move as he started to defend himself.

An inkwell, heavy and full, smashed him in the face and shattered. The bony armor rose, preventing injury, but the black ink poured over him like blood. Snarling, he rolled to his knees and looked at Bok. "Why did you do that?"

The urZrethi held a boot ready to throw, while his other arm, elongated, was seeking the boot's companion. "Soppit, soppit, soppit."

Kerrigan's hands went to his head again as the mage-storm shot lightning up his spine. His back bowed and he gasped for breath, then the spell released him and he flopped to the floor. He lay there limp for a moment, then found Bok squatting near his head.

The urZrethi dabbed at the ink with a corner of the blanket from Kerrigan's cot. The mage wanted to push the foul-smelling creature away because he was still furious with him, but the tenderness of the gesture made it hard to sustain his anger. "Why, Bok?"

"Soppit."

Kerrigan closed his eyes and shook his head. His mind slowly began to clear, and he started sorting things out. Someone in the enemy camp was a powerful sorcerer and had cast a wild spell toward the city, but it was a spell that would only have had an effect on magickers. While it was painful, distracting, and annoying, it really wasn't designed to do any serious damage. In fact, it was a spell that was easy to defend against—a variation of a nuisance spell all students learned to use when sparring against other apprentices.

And since we are all used to detecting and defending against that spell, we recognized it and cast counterspells to deflect it. Kerrigan's eyes shot open. "Help me up, Bok."

The urZrethi lifted him, then crouched at his right shin, smiling up insanely.

Kerrigan nodded to him, then set his face and cast a spell. It swept through the area seeking the sort of reports that Conservatory spells sent back. The air was alive with them. Each one reported the presence of a sorcerer who had defended himself against that attack.

The Vilwanese Adept shook his head. "We were like children. He casts and we react, pinpointing how many mages there are in Navval and giving him a good idea of just how powerful we are. I'd have done exactly that except for you, Bok. Thank you."

"Bok bok." The urZrethi bounced at Kerrigan's side, then loped off to his corner and curled up in a pile of hides.

Kerrigan finished wiping up as much of the ink as he could, then washed his face and hands. All the while he mulled over the sensations from the spell. He probed its dimensions and got a sense of the sorcerer who had cast it. Because it was a simple spell, there was not that much creativity involved. Even so, there were distinctive dimensions to it; it had definitely been cast with a Conservatory taint.

There was something more, though. Beneath the veneer of Conservatory magick he found a solid Vilwan base. And, between them, almost so slight he missed it, there was something else. Had it not been so powerful he would have missed it. It formed a boundary between Vilwan and the Conservatory, marking a sharp and radical transformation. He'd not felt its like before.

On a hunch he rooted around in his things and came up with a wand—not the gift of the Bokas, but something far more ordinary. The Conservatory magician Wheele had said his master had given it to him specifically so it could be used to kill Orla, Kerrigan's last tutor. Kerrigan carefully trickled a spell over it and almost effortlessly he discovered the same taint on the wand as had been on the annoyance spell.

He sat on the edge of his bed and felt his blood go cold. *A sullanciri cast that spell. Neskartu, the one who had been Heslin. He's out there, and he knows how many and how powerful are the sorcerers here in Navval. He knows about everyone but* me.

Kerrigan's grip tightened on the wand as anger flared through him. Neskartu had enabled a half-trained magician to kill Orla, a fully trained Vilwanese warmage. The desire for revenge flashed through Kerrigan. His failure to save Orla, and the virulent nature of the spells that killed her, fueled that desire. What he wanted more than anything else was to tear Neskartu apart.

He smothered that thought shortly after it was born. He was no more suited to going to war with a *sullanciri* than he was to lifting a mountain. He was powerful, and the fact that Neskartu didn't know he was present in Navval gave him a certain element of surprise, but even that didn't come close to guaranteeing a victory. Nothing would—but not even to try would mean that those mages who did would be killed.

What to do was a problem Kerrigan wrestled with until he fell asleep. Neither awake, nor while dreaming, did he find a solution. And his sleep, which was fitful at best, ended abruptly. As he came awake and his blanket slid down the mound of his stomach, he sought that which had awakened him, hoping it *was* a solution to his problem.

It was not. Instead, it was another problem, and one that took his breath away. He threw off his blanket, pulled on his trousers and shirt, and went running through the tower. When he reached the door he realized he had no boots, but didn't go back for them. He streaked through the streets, reaching the ducal palace, and was granted admission, despite the fact that it was midnight.

Huffing and puffing, he climbed tower stairs and pounded on the door to Alexia's room. He got no response and pounded again. "Open up . . . it's me, Kerrigan." He leaned heavily against the door. "It's important."

The door jerked open and he stumbled inside. Peri steadied him. Alexia finished gathering a robe about herself and knotted the sash. Though she had clearly been sleeping, her violet eyes looked alert.

"What is it, Kerrigan?"

"I cast a spell before, trying to find pieces of the DragonCrown. I was testing it and cast it toward the Aurolani camp. It came up empty."

"That's good." She frowned. "You should have told me this before."

"No, no, you don't understand." He straightened up, drew a deep breath, and pointed east. "The spell actually worked. I found a fragment out there. It's traveling in the open, no masking spells or anything. It's in Sarengul. If Chytrine doesn't already have her hands on it, she will very soon."

CHAPTER 59

Will ducked beneath the cut of a gibberer's longknife, then rolled his hip into the creature and pitched it forward onto its face. He landed on the gibberer's back with both knees, then used both hands to punch the jagged remains of a broken longknife through its leather armor. Snow muffled the snarl that went from savage to mewling, and as Will ripped the hilt side to side, the gibberer's struggles likewise faded.

An arrow hissed past Will's left shoulder, so close he could feel the rush of air against his cheek. A solid *thwock* resounded behind him, followed by a gurgle. Will spun and saw another gibberer thrashing its life out with one of Crow's arrows pinning its heart to its spine.

Freeing the longknife from a nerveless hand, Will stood and parried a cut low. Before he could reverse his grip and slash back up, Lombo's left paw swept out in a grand arc. It caught the snarling gibberer on the right side of its face and cranked its head around. Bones snapped like a thundercrack. Will didn't know if it was the neck or skull and didn't care.

"Thanks, Lombo."

More arrows hissed through the air as the ambushers paused in their retreat and feathered gibberers. Some went down, but others kept coming, stuck through with shafts. They were intent on their prey and dogged in pursuit up the wooded hillside.

From the left came a series of flashes accompanied by the rattling crack of draconettes. The fusillade ripped through the gibberers, spinning some around, dropping others as if hammerstruck. A few turned to face this new avenue of attack, which would require them to traverse the hillside, but another wave of arrows swept over them. The shafts slew some and wounded more. Along with the draconette assault, it killed the gibberers' momentum and those who could began to withdraw down the hillside.

Will and the other raiders continued their ascent—though Lombo appeared very reluctant to let the enemy go. "C'mon, Lombo. There will be more to kill later."

The Panqui grumbled. "These break good."

"Yeah, Resolute would take scalps from these ones."

The particular ambush that had resulted in the hillside fight had really been the result of luck on both sides—and the raiders had just been a bit more lucky. They'd buried a cask of firedirt in the snow at the base of a hillside right up tight against the road. They set up signs to misdirect a caravan and got a small one—one that appeared to be separated from a larger one. When the most heavily laden sleighs drew parallel to the cask, the raiders detonated it. While they would have hoped for more, the sleighs they targeted were clearly carrying a lot of food.

Or so they thought.

But it appeared that the Aurolani had decided to set a trap of their own for the raiders, and had created the little decoy force. The sleighs, all highsided and covered with canvas, had not contained food but concealed combat troops. Had the raiders attacked in their normal fashion, the combat troops would have hurt them badly.

Fortunately, the cask's explosion blew apart two of the sleighs, toppled two others, and generally disrupted the caravan. The guards, who likewise were warriors of the first order, had driven hard and fast at the raiders. Here Crow's preparation had proved itself. As the raiders withdrew, archers and draconetteers had cut down their pursuit.

While they had been successful in eluding the gibberers, the advent of decoys was not a good thing. They had known all along it was just a matter of time before the Aurolani sent troops after them. It was a further diversion of Aurolani resources, and they all took pleasure in that, but active pursuit would seriously limit their ability to further disrupt supplies.

Will patted Crow on the shoulder. "Thank you for that shot."

"My duty, my lord." Crow let his voice mock Will, but the wink he gave him through that black mask, and the smile that went with it, made it okay. "Thanks for bringing targets close enough for me to hit."

"Is that what I was doing?"

"I hope so. Anything else would have been stupid."

Will readied a barbed reply, but held it as Sallitt Hawkins and Resolute came to join them. Crow's older brother's mouth was set in a grim, flat line. "Given where we are, I'm fairly certain they're boxing us off. There is probably a unit north of here, and one south, both moving east. They sent in this bait train hoping it might kill us, but I'm sure there is a larger force directly west waiting for word."

Crow nodded. "They probably were relaying messages via *arcanslata* on a regular basis. The lack of a message will do just as much to alert the other forces as a full report. Apparently we've angered them."

"And we'll keep them angry." Resolute grinned. "The force south of here will have pushed itself harder than the one to the north. If we angle back toward Caledo, we might miss it, or be able to find it, track it, and hit it from behind, then withdraw to the capital."

Will frowned and tapped his mask. "I thought there was little chance we were going to get out of this raiding thing alive."

Sallitt smiled. "Just because we invite death, Will, doesn't mean we have to welcome it."

Will would have just as soon told it to go away, but in the back of his mind he knew he was doomed. The cold he felt, part of it anyway, was death nibbling away at him. He wasn't certain *how* he knew that, he just did. It could have been, in part, that the heroes of songs seldom came to good ends. Very few of them lived happily ever after. While Will had never considered what his life would be like after, say, thirty years of age, now he figured he would be lucky if he made it thirty weeks more.

Maybe even thirty days...

He glanced at Crow and marveled at his chiseled features, the wrinkles and scars age had given him. The same was true of Sallitt, whose half-metal face made him seem yet more ancient. Even Resolute, though his flesh had the ageless youth of all elves, had a distant, aged quality to his silvery eyes. All three of them had seen more of life than Will ever had, and likely ever would. They had done things and endured things truly worthy of heroes, yet they would go unsung because they had no prophecy wrapped around them.

And they will live happily ever after.

A chill ran down Will's spine. That was it, then, the element that separated everyday people from heroes. Everyone wants to live happily ever after. People want to prosper; they want to see their children and grandchildren grow up. They want to live their lives as well as they can, and make things better for others. They work hard to do that.

But heroes work harder. Heroes are willing to sacrifice their own lives so others—people unrelated to them, people who have never even heard of them—can live their lives to the fullest. Heroes are willing to invest their lives in the lives of others, using their lives to shield others from evil, even though the people they save may never be aware they were saved.

Will looked around the vale into which they strode. Men and women were gathering their gear, saddling their horses, helping each other. There were spare horses and empty saddles, for the raids had not been without risk.

There were those who had died, those who were injured badly enough that they might not survive, and others who would bear the scars of their encounters for the rest of their lives, no matter how short that life might be.

Every one of them was a hero. The black masks proclaimed them so. Each one of them had chosen to abandon his or her life to head out on a mission that, if Chytrine won, would be deemed foolish at best and an utter failure at worst. If Chytrine won, their efforts would be cursed, and those who survived to flee farther south would say that all could have been saved if the raiders had tried harder.

But who could say we did not? The *meckanshii* all gathered together and Will watched them with wonder. They were men and women who had been horribly disfigured in combat and allowed themselves to be put back together through magick that welded metal to their bodies. Sallitt's right arm had been mangled by a blow from a *sullanciri*'s ax. Somewhere he had gotten it hammered back into shape, though Will could see some residual twists in the metal. He had no idea what it would have felt like to have a smith pounding those crooked metal bones straight again, but the idea that anyone could think that what a *meckanshii* endured in order to fight again was not enough of a sacrifice astounded him.

As for his own Freemen, he wondered what possessed them to leave their homes and follow a boy into another nation to fight against a foe that was devouring *all* nations. He looked at his half brother, who didn't need to be here, and Linchmere, who could have had all the armies of Oriosa between him and Chytrine's troops. Anyone who could suggest that these men were not heroes was insane.

When he first met Resolute and Crow, the Vorquelf had ridiculed him for desiring to be a hero—at least a hero on the scale he had been thinking of. Will believed heroism consisted of the actions recalled in songs, but the heroes he modeled himself on, he realized now, were hardly worthy of the title. While he knew heroes sacrificed mightily, he had focused on the glory.

He shivered. Being cold and hungry was hardly glorious. Being cold and hungry was hardly heroic, either, since countless people were both every day. The difference, he decided, was that they were enduring the cold and short rations for a good cause. It wasn't that the ends justified their means, but it elevated their circumstances. Anyone could go without food, but how many could do it while fighting an army?

How many would volunteer to do that? Will hugged his arms around his chest. *How many would die in such an effort and count themselves lucky to have done so?*

The arrival of a signal-mage bearing an *arcanslata* interrupted his reverie. "Crow, this just was relayed from Caledo. Two pieces of news. The first is old:

Sarengul is under assault by Aurolani forces and may have fallen to them as much as two weeks ago."

Crow nodded. "It seems that heading east and fading back into the mountains isn't an option. Your plan may be it, Resolute."

The signal-mage shook his head. "It gets worse. A fragment of the DragonCrown is located in Sarengul. There are a number of people in there from Fortress Draconis. We don't know if they have it, or if they are hunting it, but a piece of the crown is buried in a place crawling with Aurolani troops."

The *meckanshii* tapped a metal finger against his chin. "Has to be in possession of the people from Draconis. If the Aurolani had it, they would be headed north. If our people were tracking the Aurolani troops, we would have been told to send people to help retrieve it."

Resolute nodded. "And if they said nothing about having it, it was because they didn't want spies alerted to its presence. How did they learn the fragment is there?"

The signal-mage shook his head. "It was not stated."

Crow and Will spoke at the same time. "Kerrigan."

"If it's Kerrigan, I'm willing to trust the report." Resolute's argent eyes became slender crescents. "We have to assume it's moving. They need to keep us informed of its location. We can find it and them if they do."

"Wait a minute, Resolute." Crow jerked a thumb west. "If we head into the mountains, we bring pursuit with us. We could find the fragment and then have to face them."

"True, though if we flee before them, they might not pursue as aggressively. They want to stop our raids, after all."

Will raised a hand. "What if *they* learn of the fragment?"

"I doubt they will want us *more* dead." The Vorquelf shrugged. "Their motivation doesn't matter; they'll die all the same. The mountains will just make us a bit harder to find, and we'll have to hope that will make enough of a difference."

CHAPTER 60

Erlestoke hated the feeling of being stalked. For close to a week his team had moved through Sarengul. They had intended to keep as close as they could to the Aurolani forces, and if there was another Sarengul attack that created an opening, they wanted to break through the lines to what they hoped would be safety.

Their plan, however, had been predicated on what they thought of as logical behavior for a military force. The bulk of the Aurolani troops had continued to move south along the main route. They fought little skirmishes here and there, but the Saren attacks did not amount to much. The Aurolani forces pushed on, and Erlestoke followed them, ignoring side passages off the main line.

Then the Aurolani leader made a classic mistake and split one group off his main force to follow a sideline. Erlestoke's people had missed the signs of that departure, but quickly became aware when that unit came back into the main route. They hunkered down, hoping the enemy would return to the main body of the Aurolani force, but they never did.

The main Aurolani force had started acting much more intelligently, too. Erlestoke's group could find very little in the way of supplies left behind. What they did find was occasionally poisoned and often booby-trapped. For the first several days he had no reason to suspect the Aurolani were doing anything more than looking for urZrethi stragglers, but after four days, the hunting became more diligent and his people had been forced to flee into the byways and smaller passages.

Jullagh-tse had explained how villages and towns existed up and around the main routes, but Erlestoke had never quite grasped the idea until he moved into some of them. They could be built around a cylinder, with the doorways to *corics* opening onto that central circle, or as a maze of *corics* that were chopped into rock as miners followed the serpentine twists of an ore vein.

Erlestoke and his people were moving through an ore town. Its narrow roads broke off at odd angles. They rose, then curved and dipped sharply before coming to a broad stairway that slanted upward and cut to the right. Facing down that stairway were the empty black pits of windows, but at any moment archers or draconetteers could pop up and the stairs would offer his people nothing by way of cover. Worse, he couldn't see the entrance to the building, so even if they got up there, getting in to kill the snipers would be difficult.

While he knew they were being pursued, he couldn't be certain that some of the enemy hadn't gotten in front of him to wait in ambush. The village's abandonment only added to his sense of insecurity. The lack of any indications of a massacre was a good sign, but there could easily be a lot of blood splashed over stone walls before any of them got out.

If any of us get out.

Being pursued didn't bother him as much as having the sensation that his pursuers knew what he was carrying. He would have expected any Aurolani troops cutting across his band's trail to follow—that made sense. What would drive them on faster was knowing he had a piece of the DragonCrown with him. He had been hoping, however, that the journey through the bowels of Fortress Draconis would have been enough to throw informed pursuit off.

It further disheartened him that their pursuers did not come after them pell-mell, but seemed to be moving deliberately. The gibberers should have used numbers to compensate for a lack of sense, but they hadn't. While Erlestoke still felt that he and his people were making their own choices in terms of the path they were taking, the enemy force clearly was cutting off all avenues of retreat. They could only go forward and, at some point, the enemy would be there waiting for them.

Erlestoke crouched at the base of the stair, then turned and pointed Ryswin and Finnrisia to the stairs, indicating they should mount them. He then signaled for Jancis to come up so both of them could shoot into the windows if any targets showed themselves.

It was a desperate tactic that could have turned out badly in any number of ways. While the two elves could take cover at the base of the wall, avoiding easy shots by the snipers, it could be that off to the right there were more lurking who would catch them in a horrid trap. Still, there was no choice, so hefting their bows, the elves swept past him and sprinted up the stairs.

The stairs did not really rise that sharply, but the steps were just long enough to force a break in the elves' stride. For urZrethi who could shift their legs to be any length, the steps wouldn't prove a distraction, but they cost the elves time.

Erlestoke raised his quadnel and aimed it at the rightmost window. A sniper lurking there would have an easy shot at Finnrisia as she raced up the stairs. He strained his eyes, looking for any movement in the room. Was that something? Was *that*? He had to be certain because the sound of a shot would undoubtedly bring pursuit through the village maze.

He waited and waited. The smoke of the slow-match stung his eyes, but he dared not blink for fear he might miss something. In his mind he ran over what he would do if he saw someone in the window. He could see a gibberer archer drawing a bow. Erlestoke would steady the draconette, squeeze the trigger, and hope, after the weapon flashed and boomed and the smoke thinned, that he'd see Finnrisia, unhurt, at the top of the steps and a splash of black blood dripping from the window.

Finally, after what seemed an eternity, the elves reached the top of the stairs. Without a moment's hesitation the two of them cut right and sprinted away. Erlestoke listened for the sound of any fighting. When he heard nothing, he turned and waved the rest of the crew up the stairs. They raced past, leaving him and Jancis acting as rear guards.

And there, emerging from the darkness, he *did* see something. Something he remembered very well from the past. His chest ached as he swung his draconette to cover it. Without glancing at the *meckanshii*, he squeezed the trigger. The hammer fell, the priming flared white, then the quadnel roared and bucked, vomiting fire and metal.

With his left hand he snapped the cocking lever forward and back, rotating the barrels. He drew the hammer back, primed the new barrel, and sighted down it. There, twenty yards distant through thinning smoke, the huge cloaked figure of the creature that had hit him in the chest had dropped to one knee. It steadied itself with one hand on the roadway, while the other arm that had been held out for balance now appeared as only a stump beneath the cloak. Beyond it, a knot of gibberers had gathered, one flopping on the ground from Jancis' shot.

Erlestoke shot again, then stood. His second ball had hit the cloaked figure and knocked it back onto its tail. The cloak flew open enough for him to see that, indeed, the right arm had been severed at the elbow. The left leg, also now exposed, appeared lighter in color than the rest of the creature's body, and thinner, as if it had been withered because of an injury.

"Jancis, pull back."

She stood and shot, then recocked her draconette. Her shot had crushed the skull of another gibberer. "That barrel always shoots high."

"They don't know that."

They both withdrew up the stairs at a steady pace. Erlestoke brought his third barrel into position and primed it. He kept it trained down the stairs as he slowly backed his way up. One gibberer peered into the stairway and hooted, but pulled back before either one of them could shoot.

The *meckanshii* glanced over at him. "They'll rush us now."

"I know." Erlestoke smiled as the howls rose from below, then the two of them turned and ran up the remaining stairs. At the top they stopped, and each snapped off a shot into the group. One gibberer went down, tripping up two others, but it did nothing to stem the onrushing tide.

Calmly they each cocked and reprimed. In a couple of heartbeats, they could thrust the muzzles of their quadnels into the faces of their targets. That would kill two or perhaps even more if a ball carried well, but before they would know the results of their efforts, longknives would have carved them into quivering slivers of flesh.

From above, through the windows, a rattling of shots blasted back down the stairs. Gibberers spun and jerked as holes opened in pelts and leather jerkins. Erlestoke did stab his weapon forward and pulled the trigger, flash-burning a face as the ball blew out the back of its head.

A gibberer also made it to Jancis, but she saved her last shot. Instead, she parried a weak lunge with her metal left arm, then stabbed stiffened steel fingers into the gibberer's throat. It reeled back, choking, tripping over the bloody body of a comrade, then slid back down the steps.

Quickly she and Erlestoke cut into the passage to the right. It narrowed, then swung left and up, to a small courtyard. A door on the left led into the building with the windows. Three more shots rang out, and Ryswin announced, "They got it."

Erlestoke ducked his head in through the doorway. "Don't count on it staying down. I've shot it twice."

The elf frowned. "What is it?"

"I think it's the thing from Draconis, the thing that was guarding the fragment."

"It's still moving." Verum raised his quadnel and triggered a shot. "It's down. Again."

Erlestoke turned to Jullagh-tse. "I have the feeling it wouldn't have pressed us so closely except we're being herded toward a trap. Do we have options other than to continue down this road?"

The urZrethi nodded. "It's an ore town. We might. You won't like it, though."

Verum shot again. "It's not steady, but it's hearty."

"Right now, there's not much I won't like if it includes putting distance between us and that thing."

Jullagh-tse pointed up. "This village is fairly high up, so to get water, it's going to have its own cisterns. This high up, we're looking at a quarry where snow melts and flows down in. We have to find the internal reservoir here, where the trickling water will collect, then break into the flow tube. We crawl out and we're on the outside."

"How big a tube are we talking?"

She shrugged. "The thing chasing us won't be able to follow."

"But can the rest of us get through?"

"I don't know, Highness."

Erlestoke rubbed a hand over his mouth. "But you could shift your shape enough to get out, right? No question of that?"

"Yes."

"Okay, here's the plan. Let's find this way out. If we can all make it, we do. If we can't, the fragment is yours. Get as far away as you can." Erlestoke laid his hands on her shoulders. "And none of this brave, 'I don't want to go.' None of us want to go, but we'd all do it if we had to."

"Yes, Highness, I know."

"Good."

Another shot sounded and Verum cursed. "Dammit, Nygal, give me your draconette."

Erlestoke looked at the heavyset weapons-master. "Did you miss?"

The grizzled warrior shook his head. "No, I hit it dead center. Mistake I was making was giving it a chance to stand up before I shot again." He raised the borrowed quadnel and triggered a shot.

"Got it. Broke its left leg, I'm sure of it." Verum nodded. "It's crawling away from the stairs."

"Good, maybe that buys us some time."

Jilandessa glanced at him. "Will it be enough?"

"Who knows. Right now I'll just settle for more." The Oriosan prince gave her a confident smile. "What we do with it will decide if it is enough or not."

CHAPTER 61

Isaura clapped her hands over her ears to shut out the screams of the burning mage. The Murosan sorcerer who had opposed Corde collapsed in a flaming mass. People on the walls of Navval shrank back or reeled away.

Seated there before Naelros' pavilion, which had been set up barely five hundred yards from the city, Isaura could not smell the roasting flesh. For that she was thankful, for at least that was one aspect of the display she could escape. Being Chytrine's daughter, there was no way she could avoid watching, since all of Lord Neskartu's charges saluted her, their master, and Naelros before marching off to do battle. For her to absent herself would greatly affect morale, so she sat there.

And there was a part of her that did not shy from watching her mother's enemies die. She would have preferred to see them led to see reason, but it was obvious that having an army camped outside a city was hardly something that would encourage compromise. As it was, they opposed her mother, so they were a threat that had to be neutralized.

Death duels between the wizards was accomplishing that rather well.

Isaura admired the courage with which combatants from both sides approached the battleground. Though they were mortal enemies, they still showed respect for each other. Neskartu had been very careful in selecting the opposition for his mages. He had previously cast a spell that allowed him to assess the strength and number of the sorcerers hidden in Navval, and he planned accordingly.

The Aurolani had fared very well in the combats. While a handful of the *kryalniri* had been killed, and two of Neskartu's Apprentices had been slain, a full dozen of the sorcerers from Navval had been destroyed—including the last four in a row. Corde had dispatched two of them by herself, one after the other, and gave the appearance of remaining for a third. While that did seem a bold move, the Murosans had the habit of sending their strongest mages out first and working down.

Neskartu, who was able to sit without a chair, was a varicolored presence between Isaura and the dracomorph. *They are reduced to Apprentices, all of whom will be swept away. Naelros, you will have little opposition from the realm of sorcery.*

The dracomorph nodded slowly. He, likewise, used no chair but instead squatted back on his heels. A hooded cloak covered him, but Isaura could still see his large eyes glittering from within the hood's shadow. "There is no haste. The longer we wait, the less powerful they become, and the more time we have to build our stores of firedirt."

His assessment came firm and even, yet sent a chill down Isaura's spine. She had seen Porjal fall, and its subjugation had been savage. Anarus' assault had concentrated the dragonels such that they collapsed a section of wall; the army then poured through the breach. The slaughter had been horrifying and the city was taken in short order.

Naelros, however, had been given two weeks to take Navval and showed signs of using every minute of it. The dragonels had been laid such that they would shoot over the walls and destroy buildings within—proving the walls to be ineffective protection. That could suffice as inducement for surrender and might allow him to take the city with the walls intact, which would make it very difficult for anyone to retake.

Isaura realized their strategy would save Aurolani lives, and she applauded that idea. What she hated was the visiting of the war on those who were not warriors. She had seen the same thing in Porjal, but it had resulted in the bloodlust frenzy of the city's storming. Here the death would be random and its only purpose would be to terrorize the people so badly they could not think of resistance.

She wondered, though, if such random slaughter might not stiffen resistance. She further wondered why Naelros couldn't see that as a possibility. Being a dracomorph who likely was centuries old—though this mind might only possess decades of consciousness—he doubtless had a differing view of humans than she did. She was even willing to consider that her interaction with Neskartu's Apprentices had inflated her view of their capabilities, since his students were drawn from the smartest of the humans.

When she had raised this point with Naelros, the dracomorph had thanked her for her words. "I shall consider your ideas, Princess." His voice rang with sincerity, but he commented no more on what she offered. Instead, he concentrated on his preparations, and seemed not to have altered things one bit.

The small mageport in Navval's gate opened again. A heavyset, dark-haired youth squeezed through it and strode toward the battleground. He wore a simple robe of dark brown that had been secured around his bulbous middle with a length of white cord. He tried to stride purposefully, but a trick of wind lashed him with the smoke from the burning woman. He side-stepped awkwardly, stumbled for a moment, then caught himself against the black dolmen and slowly straightened up.

Laughter and hooting sounded from the Aurolani lines, but it did not appear to daunt him. He straightened his robe, then lifted his chin. "I am Kerrigan Reese, Adept of Vilwan. I come in challenge."

His right hand came up and forward. His fingers were curled into a fist around the middle of a wand. His hand glowed blue for a moment, then that glow sprang off into a soft sphere. It bounced across the snowy ground between Navval and the Aurolani lines. It took short, high hops, and some long ones as well. It leaped over warriors, then rolled for a bit before coming to rest before Lord Neskartu.

The *sullanciri* flowed down to one knee and scooped a hand beneath the spell. His fingers contracted, raking through it. A similar color played through him. In an eyeblink he was standing full upright and the colors quickened as they flowed through him.

Most curious.

The dracomorph lifted a hand to suppress a yawn. "How so?"

He was undetected in the survey of Navval. And the wand he is carrying is one I created and gave to Wheele. Wheele used it to slay an old acquaintance of mine.

Isaura studied the youth. The brown robe indicated his area of expertise was conveyance magick—though she admitted it could just have been the only color robe he could find. That he was from Vilwan and in a Murosan city was a bit of a curiosity. His moving into the dueling circle, which was a Murosan custom, was unusual, and his daring to challenge a *sullanciri* remarkable.

Young and very foolish, or young and wise beyond his years.

Corde, who yet stood in the circle, turned to face the youth. "I am Corde of the Aurolani Conservatory. I will face your challenge."

No, Corde. Neskartu's command barely brushed Isaura's mind, but she felt a tingle. One *kryalniri* who had the misfortune of standing between the *sullanciri* and Corde caught the full brunt of it and fell twitching to the ground. It hit Corde hard, shaking her badly, but she bowed and withdrew to her own lines.

Naelros peeled his hood back and looked at the *sullanciri*. "You will accept this challenge?"

I have no reason not to. He possesses that wand and clearly wishes to avenge Orla's death. He cannot stand against me, and if he uses that wand, it will be his certain death. Without another comment, the *sullanciri* took a step forward with his left foot. In an eyeblink he was there, ten yards from the Adept, his colors rippling down his body in tigerish stripes.

Naelros shook his head. "So foolish."

"That is not certain."

The dracomorph's forked tongue flicked out through the air for a moment. "Ah, you refer to the boy. I do not."

Isaura watched Kerrigan intently. He was obese and awkward, yet there was something about him. Not anything attractive in any sexual sense. Some of the Murosans had intrigued her in that way, but in Kerrigan she had not the least flicker of interest. She realized, after a moment's reflection, it was less because of his appearance than another sense she had of him.

One of kinship.

They were linked in some manner, but that feeling was completely outside her ability to understand. She felt as if she were trying to hear a color or taste a song. She had no means by which to identify what she was feeling.

Neskartu let his thoughts seep out in a circle. *You are the youth. You may strike first.*

Kerrigan shifted his shoulders, then clasped his hands on the wand at the small of his back. "I issued the challenge. Yours is the first strike."

More laughter pulsed from the Aurolani lines.

Naelros' nostrils flared. "I do smell fear from the boy, but not enough. Not nearly enough."

Isaura shook her head. She could feel the power gathering around Neskartu. The *sullanciri* pulled from pure, strong flows, but only skimming bits and pieces of currents. What he was gathering would be strong, but merely a fraction of what he could have drawn were he open to the reality of magick. Neskartu's right hand rose slowly, and his fingers flowed through a series of forms before he pointed his hand at Kerrigan and cast his first spell.

The argent brilliance of the attack did not surprise Isaura, for she knew the *sullanciri* would try to overwhelm his enemy at a shot. A jagged bolt of lightning as thick as her thigh sizzled through the air, crossing between the combatants in a heartbeat. Pure power burned the air, and snow melted into steam.

The bolt never hit the youth. It skittered wide, then curled back around, spawning smaller bolts the way a vine might sprout thorns. They stabbed at him with little silvery blades. Some curled and hooked, trying to rake over him, but none touched him. The lightning swirled around him faster and faster, tightening as if to crush him, but the silver slowly evaporated in an ec-toplasmic fog that revealed Kerrigan unrumpled, unmoved, and unharmed.

Isaura reached out and could feel the dissipating energy of Neskartu's spell, but she caught nothing of what Kerrigan had used to resist it. As a rule, like would have had to meet like. While a skilled magician might be able to block or deflect a spell using a lesser spell, that was a function of the de-fender's superior knowledge of magick.

Which means he is so far above Neskartu that... No, that could not be pos-sible.

Kerrigan nodded slowly. "Please, you were a Magister on Vilwan. Out of respect for that position, I offer you a second strike."

The colors running through Neskartu danced as if they were drifting on the surface of a storm-wracked sea. Both his hands flowed wide at shoulder height, then descended and rose again. As they did, so did the power gather-ing around him. The mist from the snow began to gather and creep toward Kerrigan. It flowed up his robes, frosting them. Quickly enough he would be entombed in ice. Deprived of air, he would collapse, and Neskartu would let him smother.

That was the intent of the spell. In reality, the vapor rose and some did frost the hem of Kerrigan's robe, but it never got past his knees. The vapor did continue to flow upward, but it kept going, higher and higher, until it be-gan to curl back around in a mushroom shape. The cloud above him contin-ued to boil until the *sullanciri*'s arms fell and it all vanished.

Naelros' dark eyes blinked. "Now I smell much fear."

"From the boy?"

"No."

The Vilwanese youth bowed his head to Neskartu a third time. "You knew my mentor. You caused her death. I will allow you a third strike, but no more."

Neskartu's anger radiated out wordlessly. Even Isaura flinched, but the youth did not. The *sullanciri*'s body shifted as his fury built, and he gathered in power. Neskartu grew and expanded, rippling with shadow muscle, sprouting huge dragon wings. Colors raced, bouncing within him as if trapped in a closed vessel, melding and shifting. Incredible amounts of power poured into him, more than Isaura would have ever thought he could contain.

The *sullanciri* twisted, lifting a wing past the dolmen behind him, and grabbed the stone. He yanked it side to side, as if it were a tooth to be loos-ened in the jaw, then tore it free. Muddy clods of dirt dripped and fell from the thick end. He raised it over his head, then smashed it down on the Adept.

Isaura caught no sense of Kerrigan employing magick in his defense. Un-gainly and jiggling, he danced aside. The stone slammed into the ground hard and heavy. Isaura could feel the earth shake even where she sat. The impact bounced Kerrigan back and dumped him on his fat backside.

He slumped against the black stone and grabbed at the edge with his right hand.

Mine! Neskartu's triumphant mindburst made her breath catch in her throat. The hulking *sullanciri* bent over, grasping the stone again. Muscles rippled over his back and arms. Colors intensified to outline them. Once more the stone would rise, once more it would fall, and Kerrigan would be pulverized.

The stone did not move.

Calmly, despite the violent effort shaking the *sullanciri,* Kerrigan rolled to his knees, then levered himself up with his hands on the stone. Though the stone had landed in turf softened by spells and melting snow, Neskartu might as well have been trying to uproot the whole of Navval. All of his efforts were for naught.

Kerrigan's voice gained a bit of an edge. "Enough. You have had your third strike. You had one for being challenged. You had one for what you had learned. You had one for what you have done."

Neskartu's clawed hands released the scored stone. The *sullanciri* straightened, but kept his wings unfurled to make himself larger. The colors no longer raced through him, but flowed in bright, twisting sheets.

And now you would have your strike?

Kerrigan nodded slowly and brought the wand to hand. "My strike, yes."

The *sullanciri*'s colors quickened. He had said that Kerrigan's use of the wand would bring certain death. Isaura did know that Neskartu graced the most promising and treacherous of his students with gifts like that wand. While these gifts enhanced the ability to cast magick, they were not without danger. Through them the *sullanciri* could destroy a rebel.

Isaura found herself wanting to shout a warning, but she could not. Her mother had told her that she would be betrayed, and the words came back to haunt Isaura. *I will not be the one to betray her.*

A heartbeat later, she knew neither the warning nor the betrayal was necessary.

The youth looked up at the creature towering over him. "I know two things. If I cast through this wand, you will kill me. If I *use* this wand, I will kill you."

Power flowed so quickly into Kerrigan that Isaura could feel currents warping to fill him. Neskartu began preparing defenses against any number of combat spells, but they mattered not. The *sullanciri* had missed the most important clue about his attacker, and had he spotted it, he might have been able to prepare correctly.

Isaura doubted that would have saved his life.

Kerrigan was not a combat mage. He did not cast a spell *through* the wand, but *on* the wand—a wand Neskartu had enchanted himself. The spell hyperaccelerated the wand. In the blink of an eye it went from motionless to a blur.

Like an arrow, it punched through Neskartu's chest. It tugged at the flesh of his back, tenting it between the wings. The wand lifted the *sullanciri* so quickly into the air that his arms and legs streaked out behind him like streamers. The wings collapsed around him, and his body followed, until he had become nothing but a dark line ringed with angry colors. Then Isaura heard a thundercrack, felt it ripple through her chest. The end of that line snapped forward to the front, then it disappeared into a puff of white vapor high in the sky.

In the thundercrack's wake, silence reigned. Shock showed on all faces, save that of the Adept. He looked mildly curious, then rubbed his hands over the thighs of his robe. He frowned as he looked at the stone, then gestured almost blithely and it floated back into its original position.

Off to Isaura's right, a fire captain snarled an order. A spark was set to the firehole of a dragonel. Smoke spurted upward with a hiss, then a moment later the weapon roared. It belched fire, and an iron ball arced out. It bounced once, splashing water and grasses, then bore down on Kerrigan.

The youth froze. The ball struck him solidly in the chest, tumbling him back two dozen feet. A great cry rose from the Aurolani lines and the dragonel crew heartily congratulated itself.

Then the Adept struggled to his feet. He wove unsteadily, but appeared to draw strength from the cheers of the spectators high on the walls. He staggered over to where the ball lay steaming on the ground, then lifted it awkwardly. He waddled off with the thing suspended between his knees.

Naelros shot to his feet and snarled at the dragonel crew. The gibberers mewed and hid themselves behind their weapon. The dracomorph turned his head and looked at her. "He will use the metal from the ball to shape wards to deflect anything with a similar content, will he not?"

Isaura nodded. "If all the balls are from the same crucible, or the ore was mined in the same place, they would be effective."

"But not wholly."

"After what I saw here, I could not judge."

The dracomorph nodded slowly. "This changes things." He settled back onto his heels. "This changes many things."

The calm that bled into his voice surprised her. "He has slain a *sullanciri* and is very powerful. You cannot be thinking to continue the siege."

Naelros fixed her with a dark stare. "He is powerful, but not the *most* powerful. He has changed things, so shall we. With proper aid, your mother shall be pleased, and Navval will be mine."

CHAPTER 62

Svarskya lay before Adrogans, broken and old. Houses sagged. Towers had collapsed, crushing buildings and raising stone scars across the landscape. The outer city had once been beautiful, and the walls surrounding it almost ornamental. Those walls remained largely ornamental, having been long since overgrown and covered with snow. So many gaps had been worn in the outer ring that one could not easily follow its line with the eye. It would have been simple to mistake it for hillocks.

Nothing moved in the outer city. That, Adrogans reminded himself, did not mean nothing waited there. The sprawl stood a half mile thick at its narrowest point, and quadruple that at its widest. In the quarter century since its conquest, the streets had shifted as new buildings were raised and old were razed, but the various routes to the old city were still obvious.

The old inner city, which had grown around the docks, still boasted towers and tall walls. Prince Kirill's evacuation of the city had let the Aurolani take it without requiring its destruction. Consequently, Adrogans could easily imagine its splendor in the previous era, but he doubted he would ever see it look so grand again.

General Caro rode up. "We are ready to go when you are, General."

Adrogans snorted. "We might well wait forever then, for I do not know if I will ever be ready." He glanced up at Nefrai-kesh's tower, where flickers of flame flashed from windows with a certain regularity. "What are you thinking?"

Phfas laughed harshly. "A question you should put to him when your sword is at his throat."

"If we can get that far, Uncle." Adrogans' constant companion, Pain, of-fered him nothing. She did not cling to him or claw him, but merely rested against his back as if she were a tired child given to his care, not the embodi-ment of physical torment. With combat looming, she should have been at her most fierce, anxious for the orgy of agonies.

The potential slaughter had Adrogans' mind racing. Any of the snow-covered hovels could have been packed with firedirt. If he sent tight forma-tions into the city, an explosion would kill hundreds. If he spread them out to forestall that from happening, concentrated Aurolani forces would over-whelm his thin lines and slaughter his warriors. *And if he has enough firedirt to make all those hovels explode, my entire army will die.*

On the one hand, the Aurolani hardly needed to defend the outer city since the walls of the inner city still held. Adrogans' swift advance had out-stripped the chance of any siege machinery being brought up. And while the outer city would yield enough lumber and rock to build such things, that would take time. Since the Aurolani could be resupplied by sea, time worked in their favor.

It could have been that Nefrai-kesh desired nothing more sinister than buying time. The problem Adrogans had with that was that Nefrai-kesh could have bought a lot more time by the proper use of troops in previous battles. If he had strongly garrisoned the Svar Bridge, taking it would have won time *and* chewed up a lot of Adrogans' troops. *And if boombags had been used there, there would be no counting the cost. Come spring, he could have crushed what was left of my forces.*

There were many contingencies for which Adrogans could not account. While *arcanslata* reports did keep him informed in general terms about the eastern front, he had no true sense of how many of Chytrine's troops were being diverted there. It was quite possible that Nefrai-kesh would not be re-inforced. In fact, it could have been that his troops were being drawn away to be used in Muroso. The conquest of Sebcia could have hurt Chytrine much more than anyone knew.

He looked over at Caro. "Does his giving us the outer city make any sense to you?"

The Alcidese commander shook his head, then tipped his helmet back. "All the discussions we have had have failed to explain his reasoning. My greatest fear is that he wants us in the city because it cuts down our ability to maneuver and he can infiltrate troops among us. Worse, if we are drawn into certain lines of attack and he is able to bring a dragon to his side, we are un-done."

Adrogans nodded. "But after the last dragon was slain at Fortress Draco-nis, Chytrine has not used one. Her control may not be good, or there may be few she can control with as little of the Crown as she has. If one were to be employed against us, though, it would have been used at the bridge or the Three Brothers. Still, you have a point. If we see one, we must push our forces into the Aurolani forces and make it hesitate."

Phfas cackled. "He did not hesitate with boombags."

Caro winced. "A good point. Nefrai-kesh seems fairly intent on killing us by whatever means."

"I would accept that but..." Adrogans gestured boldly at the outer city. "There is not so much as a flag flying outside the inner city walls."

"I like the paradox no more than you do. It suggests he has a surprise in store."

"The only surprises I like in combat are the ones I create." Adrogans sighed. He glanced right at the new bugler. "Signalman, general advance."

The horn sounded and the army of liberation started forward. Adrogans had arrayed it in a wide line. He had his infantry set up in ranks five deep, which meant they had a greater frontage than normal. The Svoin Irregulars actually ranged out in front of the professional soldiers. They moved in a ragged line, clearly eager to enter the capital.

Behind the infantry came the cavalry, and it maintained its tighter formations. When Nefrai-kesh sprang his trap, Adrogans wanted to be able to hit hard with a mobile force. The cavalry oriented on the larger roads, and Adrogans assumed that if there were going to be boom traps, those would be the most likely spots for them. That's where he would put them were he defending the city, so Adrogans had to hope the infantry screen could locate and destroy any traps before the cavalry would ride into the city.

Everyone moved forward smoothly. Adrogans noted no alarm or extra activity on the inner city walls. Banners fluttered and sentries marched. If they saw anything, or heard the bugle call, they gave no sign. A few spectators did appear on the walls to watch the advance, but they appeared calm.

The Irregulars entered the city. As they had been ordered, they slipped into buildings and moved through them, hunting for anything out of the ordinary. The Svoin survivors had spent so much time lurking in the warrens and byways of a dead city that Adrogans knew they would feel right at home. They crept through it like mildew growing up a wall and signaled back as they cleared each block.

His infantry moved in next and secured roads. Squads searched for signs of traps, but Adrogans didn't see anyone deploying the red flags that would indicate danger.

Then, as the cavalry reached the outer walls he saw it. A figure in black, a small man, came walking up the street from the inner city. His cloak flowed out after him as if made from forty yards of diaphanous black silk. Little pieces of it seemed to snap in a breeze that did not exist.

The figure stopped, then bowed, and the cloak shifted from black to white.

"Tricks to amuse children."

Adrogans smiled at Phfas. "A sign of a truce. Nefrai-kesh offered the same at Svoin."

"That is not Nefrai-kesh."

"No, but it is his herald." Adrogans glanced at Caro. "Care to ride with me once again, General?"

"Of course, my friend."

Phfas made it a trio. They rode down into the city and nodded to the troops who had entered it. Warhawks flew above them and landed on the roofs of buildings near the large intersection where the herald stood. Adrogans waited to feel the breeze that was making the white cape flow, but it never touched him even as he drew close.

The figure sketched a bow. He wore a black mask, and the flesh beneath it had a corpselike pallor. His eyes, however, remained alive. They literally burned, with flames licking up from the sockets. He clasped his gloved hands before him, appearing more a solicitous tavernkeeper than a creature of power.

"I shall boast, my father is your host; in the tower he resides. He wishes you no harm, no undue alarm, until the morrow's battle tides."

Adrogans nodded. "You are Nefrai-laysh. You're the Norrington's father."

"'Tis a mistake you make, my role to take, and give that gutter whelp. When all is done, and we have won, he will have been no help." As the *sullanciri* spat out his verse, sparks flew. "Speak not of that son, for he is but one and nowhere near. But here we are, in Okrannel's star, let us make things clear."

The *sullanciri* opened his arms to take in the whole of the outer city. "We have laid in for thee, a feast, you will see. Wine, bread, and meat, enough to eat. Warm houses to keep, tonight you will sleep. Spend a safe night, rise to the fight. Tomorrow you die, widows cry, soldiers bled, join the dead."

The Jeranese general frowned. "That's it, then. Your father sent you to tell us he will feed us then kill us? We have a night of peace before slaughter?"

"What you have heard is entirely his word. Here you will dwell. He wishes you well. Without fail, on epic scale, tomorrow forces flail, but tonight peace and torment surcease."

Phfas snorted. "Words and games."

Will things be poisoned? Does he want my troops drunk and sick? Adrogans glanced up and beyond Nefrai-laysh to the tower in which his opponent dwelt. Nefrai-kesh appeared in a window and gave Adrogans a salute.

Pain remained quiescent and asleep at his back.

Adrogans nodded. "We will accept this hospitality. Thank your father."

"From your mouth to his ear, have no fear." The diminutive *sullanciri* smiled easily. He waved a hand and his cloak wrapped tight around him, then exploded into a hail of snowflakes. They spun up into a funnel, then danced back to the inner city and disappeared, carrying Nefrai-laysh.

Caro had a concerned expression on his face. "You can't actually mean to eat their food and drink their wine."

"I don't fear poison. Nefrai-kesh is trying to do the honorable thing, and I will accept that. I think the reason he's trying to be honorable, however, is because tomorrow he won't be." Adrogans sighed. "And *that,* my friends, is what I fear unto death."

CHAPTER 63

Alexia stood in the window of her tower chamber, unconcerned that the light behind her silhouetted her for the Aurolani dragonels. She had to admire the Aurolani leader's calm deliberation. After Kerrigan killed a *sullanciri*, the city's mood was jubilant. The Aurolani sent no more sorcerers forth, and the magick duel had been counted a solid victory for Navval, despite the frightful cost in personnel.

Kerrigan had explained the importance of the pilfered iron ball. Smiths had already shattered it into more than a dozen pieces. Kerrigan and others used them to create spells that would deflect shots directed at the city. Plans were advanced, from shields to loadstones that would concentrate shots in one area. It all sounded promising, and since supplies of firedirt and shot were being cut by Crow or diverted to the siege at Caledo, hopes were high for success.

The Aurolani commander clearly had a different view of the situation, and Alexia could not fault his analysis. As dusk fell, the Aurolani dragonels began to speak. They roared defiantly and spat their iron cargo at Navval. The waiting sorcerers used their magick to deflect shots and divert them, rendering them all but harmless. Efforts to blast the city were futile.

But the Aurolani commander just stepped up the rate of shots, keeping them flying faster and more furiously. Dragonels went off in volleys. And where a single magicker might have been able to handle a single shot, now he had to choose among a flight of them. The more he tried to deal with, the more strength it required. Balls arced by untouched as exhausted sorcerers collapsed.

Moreover, her opponent's crews heated the missiles in fires until they glowed cherry red. When one of those shots made it into Navval and crushed its way through the wall of a house or granary, it ignited whatever it touched. From her vantage point, Alyx could see dozens of little fires burning. With a cadre of magickers, they might have been able to keep the fire in check, but too few magicians were being forced to do too much.

And the shot was not the only weapon employed against the city. Just the constant booming of the weapons was enough to fray nerves. Alexia was awake at midnight because she needed to study what her enemy was doing, but others were awake because they could not sleep. For all they knew a thunderclap was the only warning they had before an iron ball bashed their home into burning splinters.

Already people had begun to stream toward the docks.

Alyx frowned. She was confident that the enemy had neither enough firedirt nor shot to sustain the assault for long, yet their profligate expenditure seemed to contradict that. The commander facing her was a fool, a daredevil, or had more supplies and support coming and was not worrying about running out of charges for his dragonels.

Her obvious strategy for dealing with that problem would be to send a force out to raid his position, but she did not have enough troops to hit the Aurolani hard enough. While they could hold the city in bitter fighting, they were incapable of lifting the siege. Moreover, if she were to charge out with a mounted force aimed at taking the dragonels, a volley by draconetteers or, worse, a leveled volley by the dragonels themselves, would be devastating.

She hated having to sit and wait, but she had no choice. As long as the Aurolani had diverted part of their force here and were using up a lot of supplies, those same troops and supplies were denied the forces closing on Caledo. King Bowmar's messages from the capital were rather sanguine. He labored under no misapprehensions about Alexia's being able to hold Navval. He just wanted her to delay the loss for as long as possible.

A knock came at her door, but before she could turn and invite whoever waited there in, the door opened. Three men and one woman, all of middle age and masked, filed in. They had donned fine clothes and clearly had discarded their cloaks elsewhere—all save Duke Thow, in whose palace she was standing.

The woman, whom Alexia was certain she'd seen before but could not recall, stepped from the group of her fellows and extended a hand. "For the love of the gods, Princess Alexia, you must listen to us."

The duke grabbed the woman's other arm and restrained her. "Princess, we regret this interruption, and we mean no disrespect, but we must speak with you." He nodded toward the window. "As you have seen, the precautions we thought would save us are for naught. The city is burning. People are homeless. People are injured; they are dying."

"Your city is under siege. Casualties cannot be avoided."

"Granted, Highness, but we must do something."

Alexia sighed. "I have been considering that very thing. The Aurolani will cease their shooting. They have not enough supplies to keep it up. Our sorcerers will rest and be able to do more."

The duke shook his head. "They have too much to do. All the fires..."

She snarled. "Magick is not the only way to deal with fire, my lord. I have detailed troops to help organize firefighting efforts. This will leave our mages free for more important duties, like stopping the enemy."

Alexia continued, not letting the duke get a word in edgewise. "I have considered a raid, but that would leave us worse off than before. It would sap our strength, so that when they came to take the city we could not oppose them. The slaughter would be unspeakable. Is that what you want?"

The woman tore her arm free of the duke's grasp. "No, we want to avoid that. This is why we have come to you. We want you to negotiate a surrender."

"What?"

One of the other men opened his hands. "You said yourself that the Aurolani are not shooting at the walls to preserve them against a counterattack. We could negotiate and let them come into the city. We would let them have it in return for the safety of our citizens. Surely they would see the wisdom of that exchange."

Alexia snapped her mouth shut, then shook her head. "Do you know what you are saying?"

The woman's head came up. "It will stop the slaughter."

"You are insane. I know what it is for a city to be overrun by the Aurolani. Svoin was so poisoned that when it was liberated, it had to be burned. This city is home to twenty thousand souls, thirty perhaps? As it is now, so Svoin once was. When General Adrogans liberated it, fewer than five thousand people remained."

The duke waved that idea off. "That was after twenty-five years."

Alyx fixed him with a hard stare. "And you assume someone will come save you before another quarter century has passed?"

"No, we expect the Aurolani will abide by any agreement we make with them."

"And why would they do that? If you surrender this city and *if* there were troops around who could rescue you, they'd not waste their time. They would just bottle you up in the city with the Aurolani, and when the gibberers ran out of rations, then you'd see just how long your agreement would last."

The fourth man, a white-haired magistrate, let menace slip into his voice. "We have other things we can turn over to them. Valuable things."

"Such as?" Alexia's violet eyes narrowed angrily. "Me? The killer of a *sullanciri*? What are you saying, Magistrate?"

"You know very well what I am saying."

"I don't, Magistrate. Perhaps you'd better tell me!" Sayce stood in the doorway. Pure fury burned through her words. "Are you suggesting you would trade to the enemy two people who have come here of their own accord to save you?"

The magistrate looked down his long nose at her. "Princess, you would be safe."

"Not with you, I wouldn't." Sayce strode through their midst, placing herself between them and Alexia. "You would sell me once the others had not been enough, and then others would sell you."

The woman pleaded. "The alternative is death."

"*Yes*, it *is*!" The Murosan Princess' hands rent the air. "What are you not understanding? The Aurolani have come here to destroy us. They swept through Sebcia like a summer storm, and why? What did the Sebcians ever do to Chytrine? Nothing. It is the same with us. We have done nothing to invite this invasion save to have a good nation with stouthearted people who work hard to make the best life they can for themselves and their families.

"Look at yourselves. You wear masks, but do you think you are truly worthy of them? Your ancestors would strip them from your faces, then peel back the flesh beneath them. You have become the very complacent sort of people we overthrew when our ancestors took the mask."

The duke's spine stiffened with indignation. "You mistake us."

"No I do not, not at all, Duke Thow. I see you for what you are. Just as you are willing to sell Princess Alexia or Kerrigan to the Aurolani, claiming it is for the sake of the people, you would sell the people for your own sake. You would count that a suitable price to pay, and would praise those making the sacrifice, but would deem yourselves too important to the nation and the city ever to offer yourselves to the enemy."

Sayce's unbridled anger cowed the gang of four. Blood drained from faces and the woman covered her mask with her hands. Her shoulders shook as if she were sobbing, though Alexia thought the gestures exaggerated.

"This is what we are going to do." Sayce's lips peeled back in a fierce snarl. "I will guarantee your safety, since you are clearly worried about it. I will have some of my Lancers guard each of you. I assure you that if there is any chance that the enemy would take you, you will be slain and avoid the humiliation of a painful death."

The magistrate's eyes widened. "You cannot threaten us with murder!"

"No?" Sayce's head came up and she crossed her arms beneath her breasts.

"Better a threat of murder than a charge of treason. It is your choice. I prefer the latter, since then all your lands will be forfeit to the crown. Your children will be reduced to paupers, but at least they will be alive."

The duke snorted. "Let the crown have my lands. Chytrine will have them soon enough."

Alexia stepped forward and laid her left hand on Sayce's right shoulder. "There you have it, Duke Thow. Chytrine will have your lands, your city, soon enough. The question is how much of a price will she pay for them? You can give them to her and you will get no gratitude in return. Or you can join us in opposing her. If you were to kill one gibberer you would be selling your life more dearly than you could ever imagine, and the price she would be charged would be greater than she will be able to bear."

The flame-haired princess nodded. "There you have it. Live up to your mask and the fidelity to your nation it demands, or bare your face and slink into obscurity. Better death while free, than an eternity as a slave."

The four of them—pale and meek—stared blankly.

Sayce pointed to the door. "Be gone."

They filed out quietly, without a bow or an apology.

Sayce looked at Alexia. "I am mortified for my nation that you witnessed this."

"You mean witnessing you tame a pack of cowards?" Alexia smiled slightly. "This is a new side of you, one I had not taken into account."

The smaller woman nodded. "I know, when I arrived in Meredo, that I made a bad impression. You were not what I expected. Will was not. Nothing was what I thought it would be. You have, however, showed me that you are more than I could ever have expected.

"Will did as well, and Crow." Sayce looked down, and her voice became wistful. "I heard whispers of you all before I came to Meredo. The raid on Wruona. The evacuation from Fortress Draconis. I imagined a band of heroes, but not the way you are. It's less a band than a family. It hurts you to be apart from Crow, doesn't it?"

That question surprised Alexia more than the duke's suggestion. "I don't like being separated from him, no."

"He is all right out there, isn't he?" Sayce glanced sidelong at her. "You would know if he wasn't, wouldn't you? Love is like that?"

"I feel I would, yes, and he would know if I were in danger here."

"I'd know the same about Will."

Alexia kept her face impassive. Sayce's comparing her feeling for Will with Alexia's for Crow made no sense. Sayce might say it to engage Alexia's sympathies, but to what end? They were both trapped by the same army in the same city, with enemies outside the walls and vipers within. Any differences they could possibly have would be rendered insignificant by their situation.

The only reason that makes sense is... Alexia felt a chill run down her spine. "You really *do* love him, don't you?"

The Murosan Princess looked up, then nodded quickly. "My sister was supposed to go to Meredo and seduce Will to get him to come to Muroso. I hated that idea, so I went myself. I was prepared to offer myself to him if need be, but I wanted to convince him to come of his own accord. I thought he would be so different: like his half brother in form, with Resolute's brash attitudes. He wasn't any of that. He was quiet and funny—and so very kind when he came and sat with me as I recovered. I hadn't expected..."

She brushed away a tear, then smiled, though the corners of her mouth quivered. "Listen to me, I sound like a girl with her first crush. But I dream of him, you know, and I worry. The past several mornings I have woken up positively sick. And now that they are heading into Sarengul, I don't know what to think, what to hope."

"What to fear."

Sayce nodded. "That's the worst."

"I know." Alexia slid her left arm over Sayce's shoulder. "I think we fear what they fear. Yes, never seeing us again, that's a big one, but greater is dishonoring them with failure. I know Crow won't let that happen."

"Will won't, either."

"So then that fear is useless." Alyx hugged her across the shoulders. "As for not seeing them again, well, the only people who will prevent that are the army out there. And that's good enough reason, as far as I am concerned, for making sure they don't succeed."

CHAPTER 64

With the new morning, Adrogans forced from his mind the incongruity of the previous day. The food provided by the Aurolani had been a bit plain but filling. The wine had been very good, much of it rescued from cellars in Svarskya or shipped in from Sebcia. Adrogans disliked drinking the spoils of battle, but toasts had been raised to the Aurolani defeat. As Caro had noted, better they drink it than any Aurolani troops and he found himself unable to argue with that logic.

Morning had come early and painfully—though not because of any hangover. His mistress, having slept the previous day away, now rode him with claws and spurs. There would be much discomfort meted out in the coming battle. If he did not concentrate, pains would impale him and cut at him, as they would countless others.

But concentrate he did, for his task was not a simple one. The ways into the inner city were limited. Two breaches in the walls had been created during the original siege. Barricades had been raised to block them using timbers and other debris from Svarskya. The one to the west of the main gate was impassable. To the east debris formed a causeway to a wide hole. The barrier there seemed less well built. Whether that was intentional, to be used as bait to lead them into a trap or not, he had no way of knowing.

That breach, however, was the weakest point in the inner city's defenses.

The main gate stood open as its massive doors had been smashed down decades before. More debris had been arranged there, forming a series of small walls across the main road. While the soldiers stationed there would not survive long, the presence of the walls meant troops would have to slow to cross them. This would leave them very vulnerable to archers and dra-conetteers.

Adrogans also wondered about skycasters, thunderballs, and boombags. Their judicious placement would devastate his force, but he had no way to discover or disable them. And if he approached cautiously, as if they existed, and they did not, the assault would take far longer than it should. Yet, if he went in recklessly and they were employed, his force would be slain. There was no middle ground.

I must win with blood what I would have preferred to take with strategy.

Nor was it a good day for battle. Before dawn a cold north wind had be-gun to howl through the streets. Snowflakes started to fall. Though not thick, the wind drove the snow south, so his men would be marching against the wind. Worse yet, their arrows would be shot into it and, worst of all, the clouds to the north crept toward the city, promising much more snow.

"Signal the advance."

The signalman blew the advance and other buglers picked it up and re-peated it. Above the battlefield his remaining Warhawks flew. They dove re-peatedly at the wall above the main gate. Their firecocks exploded brilliantly, their spears and arrows skewering soldiers. Burning oil sent fiery streamers down the wall and his men cheered as if that were an omen of victory.

Onward the soldiery marched. In thick, swollen ranks the infantry ad-vanced. Aurolani troops at the main gate rose and shot arrows or threw spears. Some men went down, but the arrows and spears that flew back scat-tered the opposition. Those who could retreated and scrambled back toward the inner city, and the front ranks of the Helurian Imperial Steel Legion reached the first wall. They crossed it and pressed on, though another hail of missiles tore at them.

Over to the east, Beal mot Tsuvo led her clan's dozen companies in a sui-cidal charge up the causeway to the breach. Adrogans had not wanted to give her the honor of that position. He viewed it as dubious, especially in light of the fact that the first troops in there would almost assuredly die, but she de-manded it. While her role in the march to Svarskya had been vital, she and her troops had been spared in major engagements and their highland blood demanded the chance to prove themselves.

There, arrows flew thicker than snowflakes. Warriors rushed upward, round shields raised and festooned with arrows. People slipped and fell, some never to rise, others to struggle up and keep moving forward. As the Guranin warriors drew close, grapnels on ropes flew, catching on the barri-cades. Stout warriors grabbed the ropes and pulled, though the arrows that greeted their effort killed many. As a gap opened in the barricade, warriors surged forward. They leaped over tumbling timbers and batted aside thrown rocks, then fell among the gibberers opposing them.

Adrogans waited for a boombag to explode, reducing the clan warriors to meat and ghosts, but nothing happened. Then he waited for dragonels to blast, splitting the morning with thunder and bright light. Scattershot would rip through his troops, anointing that gap with blood.

The infantry had drawn closer to the main gate. The Jeranese Crown Guards had slipped through the thinned ranks of the Steel Legion and driven forward. They'd taken the second wall and the third, with one remaining before the barrier at the main gate. There, or deeper in, or just on the other side, dragonels and archers could rake his troops. Boombags could leave smoking craters where they had been.

He sought for signs that his other efforts might have borne fruit, but he saw nothing. The Okrans exiles had raised a battalion of light infantry, and he'd combined it with the Svoin Irregulars. He had infiltrated them into the city's sewers, in the hopes they could slip in and attack the defenders from within. That, too, like Beal mot Tsuvo's charge, was suicide, but neither group had shrunk from it. As if it would make them invulnerable, they murmured to themselves "dreams can come true," and accepted their assignments.

Pain rippled jagged sensations through him as warriors fell. He could sense the panic of people drowning in frigid sewer water. The hopelessness of a dying soldier trying to stuff his own entrails back into his body came to him with piercing clarity. More things, from burns and cuts to crushed limbs and implements, flooded into him.

This was the sort of battle he hated. There was no fast or easy way to do things. Until the barriers were cleared, his cavalry could not move. And even when they could, he didn't know what they would face.

Whatever it was, it wouldn't be good. No matter what, Adrogans could not shake the feeling that he had already lost the battle. *All the blood is being spilled needlessly and yet for a purpose of which I know I will not approve.*

He glanced up at Nefrai-kesh's tower and the fire burning there. *I am defeated, but I know not how or why.*

Suddenly, over to the west, a firecock exploded against one of the barriers. He smiled and pointed. "Our luck may have changed."

Caro followed his line of sight, then nodded. "I shall see you within, then."

"Yes, good hunting." Adrogans reined his horse around and rode west to where his Horse Guards waited with the Okrans Kingsmen. As he neared the cavalry and the Gurol Stoneheart Battalion trotted toward the burning barricade, he saw fighting behind it. Somehow, the Svoin Irregulars had won their way through the sewers and were attacking the Aurolani forces at the breach.

The Stonehearts raced up the debris hill and met little opposition. They, too, used grapnels and ropes to haul burning debris aside. As the lead ranks parted, the trailing legion surged forward and fought its way through the gap. The other legions widened it further, then Adrogans and the cavalry started forward at a trot.

With every hoof-fall Adrogans waited to see that mountain of debris become a volcano. He sought through the driving snow for the first hint of light and some sensation of warmth. He waited to see men begin to topple as the midden erupted. He knew fire and stone would shred them, then a rock shower would crush his horsemen.

Closer and closer they rode. They got close enough that he could see warriors grappling with gibberers and spitting vylaens. Axes rose and fell; longknives flashed. Bodies—man and animal—reeled away leaking and torn. Screams and howls echoed louder than war cries, but war cries still could be heard. As his horse started up the slope, he shouted as well.

"For Duke Mikhail!" Adrogans drew his sword and leaned forward, urging his horse on. Powerful muscles bunched as the beast propelled itself upward. Rock tumbled, but the horse kept his balance, leaping forward, cutting sideways and up. Foam flecked beast and bit and, finally, they reached the summit.

Adrogans had a moment to survey the heart of Svarskya. He had expected to see fire-blackened ruins, for the walls and the bits of towers that rose high enough to be seen had given that impression, but his expectations were dashed. Streets were clear and buildings, though they lacked for paint and plaster in places, appeared in good repair. After Svoin and the outer city, he had not been prepared for such order.

If one did not look too closely, it would be easy to imagine this place never having been touched by battle.

But he did look closely. As his horse descended, signs of battle were everywhere. Blood ran thick in gutters and bodies lay twisted on cobbled streets. Some corpses burned and others were in pieces. The wounded twitched, cried, and scrabbled for cover or weapons or anything that might succor them.

The Horse Guards poured through the gap behind him and inside the inner city they cut to the east. Riding fast, with the Okrans Kingsmen behind them, they reached the main gate quickly. There they found Aurolani infantry massed to oppose the charge that would be coming through the main gate. The cavalry slammed into the rear of one battalion, riding soldiers down, slashing madly and driving forward into another battalion.

The Kingsmen sheared to the left and obliterated the last two battalions that had been waiting. The city streets trapped the Aurolani troops and only allowed the rear ranks to run. They could not run far, however—and certainly could not escape the vengeful warriors who, after more than a generation in exile, had come to reclaim their homeland.

Dismounted warriors flew up stairs and into the chambers above the gate.

Any Aurolani therein would be able to rain molten lead or boiling oil down on troops riding through. They could even have had a boombag ready to detonate. But the Horse Guards, bloody swords in hand, burst into that chamber and bare minutes later returned triumphant.

Adrogans directed other men to clear the main gate, which they did, then Caro and his Alcidese Horse Guards rode through. They fanned out through the city, hunting and killing. Farther east the Savarese Knights and Matrave's Horse rode in through the gap Clan Tsuvo had cleared.

Despite the success, something was wrong; Adrogans knew it. He had lost people, but not nearly as many as he should have. There were no dragonels— not in the city, not used at the bridge or the Three Brothers. There were not enough troops. And the city was pristine.

Phfas appeared at his side. "The tower."

Adrogans looked to the top of it and saw the fire burning there, then it rose into the air. The two of them, father and son, rode together on a horse with dragon wings of fire. They galloped into the air, circled the tower once, and headed off to the north and east.

Nefrai-kesh threw Adrogans a salute.

Nefrai-laysh's laughter mocked him.

Once they had secured the city, Adrogans entered the tower with Caro, Phfas, several other of the Zhusk, and two of the men who had attended Duke Mikhail at his death. The group made the ascent carefully. They watched for traps and proceeded as if each step would betray them.

Pain again slumbered, so Adrogans had no fear.

At the top of the tower, in a chamber half-open yet somehow immune to the weather, they came to a banquet table laden with food still warm. The candles there had burned halfway down, and had they entered the tower immediately upon the *sullanciri*'s departure, it would have made for an elegant scene.

Phfas sneered dismissively. "Too many chairs."

Adrogans moved to the head of the table. There, instead of a plate being set, a sheet of parchment had been stuck to the table with a dagger. The script had an easy flow, but the general found the dark brown hue of the ink unsettling.

Blood. Its being still a bit moist unsettled him more.

Adrogans leaned heavily on the table, holding himself up on straightened arms, and read aloud. "My dear General Adrogans. I congratulate you on a campaign fought brilliantly and well. Neither I nor my mistress thought you capable of waging a winter war. Because of this, I have been caught without reinforcements or supplies, all of which were required in the east.

"You have won the freedom of Okrannel. I was here to see it fall and though it saddens me to fail my mistress in losing it, I do not begrudge the Okrans people their homeland. They now will know a peace that I have not known, nor am likely to know.

"With profound admiration, I am, Nefrai-kesh."

Caro stared at him. "That cannot be what it says."

"Read it for yourself."

The Alcidese general frowned. "We won because we dared push at a time when she had her troops elsewhere?"

"A fiction. The dragonels used at Lurrii or Porjal could have been shipped from there to here in five days, easily. The same for troops. It has been nearly a month since we took the Three Brothers. This city should have been teeming with gibberers."

Caro sighed heavily and stared out the window that overlooked the wall. "Why the pantomime? At the bridge he could have hurt us. Here he could have hurt us. Why?"

Phfas reached over and pulled the leg off what appeared to be a chicken. "Does why matter? The witch has lost the city."

"You're wrong, Uncle. She didn't lose it." Adrogans frowned. "She traded it to us. But for what?"

The Zhusk shaman shrugged. "Time will tell."

"It will." Adrogans shivered. "I just don't think it's a tale I want to hear."

CHAPTER 65

In some way, Erlestoke reflected, it was unfortunate that the Aurolani arrow had not been poisoned. It had taken him through the right thigh. Jilandessa said it hadn't done too much damage, so he didn't let her do more to it than stop the bleeding and close the flesh. Her skills were needed elsewhere, on more grievous wounds, and he was able to limp along as he was.

But had the arrow been poisoned, he'd be dead. That would mean his nose and cheeks, ears, toes, and fingers wouldn't be burning with frostbite. He'd not be consumed with fear about the DragonCrown fragment falling into enemy hands. He wouldn't feel hungry and tired or any other of those things that differentiated the living from the dead.

Their escape had not been without casualties. Jullagh-tse's plan had functioned well, and they'd made it into the trickle tube easily enough. As they started to exit, though, Verum volunteered to stay behind. Erlestoke still heard shooting when he left the tube, so he allowed himself to imagine that, somehow, the *meckanshii* might still be alive somewhere in Sarengul.

Jullagh-tse Seegg led them through the mountains on a course that ran south and a bit west. She was angling for a pass with a chasm spanned by a rope bridge. It had been years since she had gone that way, but all of the landmarks remained in place to guide her. The chasm literally split one whole duchy in Sarengul, and if the Aurolani were going to use the internal tunnels to get ahead of them, they would have to go far out of their way to do so. They all hoped that the Aurolani forces had not yet penetrated that deeply into Sarengul.

To fully escape pursuit, all they would have to do is reach the bridge and cross over, then cut it behind them. Jullagh-tse had also described the chasm as being huge and bottomless. In the back of his mind Erlestoke considered it a possible dumping place for the DragonCrown fragment.

The Aurolani did pursue them, and relentlessly. At dawn the Aurolani had ambushed them—killing three and wounding four, though none of the wounded was crippled. His group had gone from a dozen to seven, which, given all they had done, was rather remarkable. Still, being tired, falling into that ambush, and losing people so close to their final escape took the heart right out of him.

Wind whipped through the mountains, driving snow south. Erlestoke much preferred the wind at his back, but it made watching their back trail painfully difficult. Out through the shifting sheets of snow he could see gibberers. Some were on the ground, following their path directly, while others moved up into the rocks. The wind neutralized arrows, but that didn't stop the Aurolani from launching them.

And, as always, trailing them, came the cloaked figure. It walked awkwardly, but kept advancing. The wind tugged at its scarlet cloak, but it never stopped. It never hunkered down against the wind, nor raised a hand to shield its face. What seemed worse to Erlestoke was the nagging sense that what had been a severed arm two days previous had, in fact, grown back somewhat.

Jullagh-tse pointed south and then to the right. "There, you can see the opening to the canyon. Not far now."

"So they will have to make their move if they don't want to be cut off, right?"

"Yes." The urZrethi looked down. "Highness, I am best equipped in the mountains..."

"Yes, of course." Erlestoke made to shrug his way out of the harness that held the DragonCrown fragment. "Take this and head out, fast."

She laid a brown hand over his mittened right hand. "No, Highness, what I mean is that you should move quickly and let me hold them off."

"It's not happening that way." He looked back at the others. "Let's move fast now. Speed will be our friend. Once we're over the bridge, we're safe. Rys, Finn, go!"

The two elves led the way through the narrowing canyon and off on the twisting crosscut that would lead to the chasm and their salvation. The wind muted the cry of a gibberer high on a point, but others heard it and began to come on faster. Other cries came from the high rocks, and Erlestoke surmised that more Aurolani troops had arrived from inside the mountains.

Jullagh-tse helped him limp back as best he could. He held his quadnel in his left hand and had his right arm draped over her shoulders. His right leg wasn't working that well, so his foot dragged along, leaving a long, serpentine trail.

A couple of black arrows fell here and there. Ryswin snatched one up, fitted it to his silverwood bow, and returned it to one of the gibberers.

Onward they raced into the western canyon. It narrowed to twenty yards at the tightest point and twisted back and forth twice, making it easy to hold off pursuit, even if for only a moment. Inside the canyon itself the wind died. Erlestoke could hear the crunch of feet on snow and the hissed grumbles of his wounded comrades as they worked their way west. Anticipation grew as well, for the canyon began to widen and took one more grand, sweeping turn to the south.

There they would find the chasm and the bridge.

They did—but things were not quite as predicted.

The chasm itself was much as Jullagh-tse had described it. The canyon sloped slowly down to it, barely five hundred yards distant. When she'd seen it last, it was in the summer, with meadow grasses providing a verdant carpet dotted with the reds, yellows, and blues of flowers. Grey stone showed where ice and snow now clung in frozen sheets. The chasm itself, which was easily two hundred yards across, had its own coat of snow and ice on the edges, almost suggesting a dark trough between two snowdrifts.

Erlestoke looked over at Jullagh-tse. "When you said you'd not been here in a while, exactly how much time were we talking?"

"Seventy years or so. At that time they were only talking about doing this, and they'd been talking about it forever." Her flesh lightened to a streaky tan. "I had no idea."

The rope bridge that was to be their salvation had long since been replaced by a strong, proud arch spanning the gulf. Heavy blocks had been used to create it, and marble to finish it. In the urZrethi tradition, it was decorated with wonderful running sculptures and tableaux. Though snow did cling to portions of the span, the majority of it remained clear. Wide enough to let four horsemen ride abreast, it featured welcoming stone sentinels who greeted the travelers with broad smiles.

Erlestoke shook his head. Even using every last ounce of firedirt they possessed, they couldn't have loosened a single block. "And it's too wide to defend against what is pursuing us."

Ryswin, who had stopped twenty yards on, looked back at him. "What do we do?"

Before Erlestoke could answer, an arrow slanted down from above and tugged at the elf's shoulder. Blood splashed on the snow, but Ryswin did not go down. The arrow had only grazed him. He twisted out of the way of another shot, then danced back as he nocked an arrow of his own.

He drew and shot as everyone else began to run for the bridge. Behind and above them came the hoots and howls of gibberers. Arrows flew. Most went long or wide, though one did hit the quadnel and get caught between barrels. Ahead someone went down with an arrow in the back of his thigh.

Erlestoke gave Jullagh-tse a shove. "Get Nygal."

The prince turned, drew a bead on one of the leading gibberers, then squeezed the trigger on his quadnel.

Nothing happened.

The priming dust had blown out of the hole. He eared the hammer back, drew his powder horn, and calmly reprimed. The gibberers howled and shrieked as they rushed forward. Longknives gleamed in the air. From the right Jancis snapped off a shot that dropped one gibberer, but that effort would fall far short of what was needed to stem the tide of onrushing troops.

Even if my every shot counted for ten . . .

He squeezed the trigger again. The hammer snapped. Priming powder burned. A heartbeat later the quadnel thundered and bucked against his shoulder. It ejected smoke and fire.

A running gibberer fell.

And then another.

The thunder built, echoing from the canyon walls. There, either side of them, waiting in the rocks, were draconetteers. *Meckanshii!* Erlestoke couldn't believe it. *How did they get here?*

A tiny winged shape buzzed in front of him. His four fast-moving wings dispersed the smoke as he hovered. "Quick, Highness, quick, come quick." He grabbed Erlestoke's left shoulder and pulled.

The prince turned and started running as fast as he could. Behind him, gibberers howled, but from frustration. Glancing back, he could see them retreating, leaving a dozen or more bodies in reddening snow.

A man reached him. Though the man was wearing a black mask, the prince recognized him from the scars on his cheek and his white hair. "Crow. How is it you are here?"

"The Spritha, Qwc. We knew a fragment of the DragonCrown was heading through Sarengul, and Qwc knew where he was supposed to be. We just followed." Crow turned and pointed with a silverwood bow toward the bridge. "The rest of our men are on the other side, along with our horses. We deployed our *meckanshii,* and have the rest holding the way out."

From around the edges of the valley the *meckanshii* began to pull back. At the northern end, the gibberers had drawn together into a group. They appeared to be reluctant to advance again.

Then the cloaked figure entered the valley. The gibberers drew away from him. He came forward, ignoring the draconette shots that spat snow near his feet. He stopped well shy of the corpses, raising his left hand and holding it out expectantly. "Very well, your lives for the Truestone. You have earned that much."

Will came up beside the prince. "What is that?"

Erlestoke shook his head. "I don't know, but it has followed me from Fortress Draconis. It's been shot and worse, but nothing stops it."

Crow patted the prince on the shoulder. "Let's move." He turned and signaled the others. "Let's go!"

The cloaked figure spoke again. "A second time I offer you your lives. Harken unto me and you need not die."

Erlestoke straightened and threw back his cloak to reveal the blue-green stone in the harness that had been fashioned for it. "Your life, not ours, for this stone." He closed his cloak again and turned toward the bridge.

Already on it were a handful of *meckanshii* and a man he'd met in Crow's company at Fortress Draconis. He pointed his people to it. "Let's go."

From behind the prince rose a keening wail filled with longing and fear, but also an incredible amount of power. It froze Erlestoke's guts and cut at his knees. He slumped heavily on Crow, and felt the other man begin to go down, too. That sound conjured fears with the numbing power of childhood nightmares and left him quivering.

The pain of sinking to one knee shocked Erlestoke's mind to clarity, and he wished it had not. When his head came up, he found himself looking at the bridge. Then a vast, cruciform shadow passed over him, the edges of it rippling against the canyon's stone walls. From overhead a creature drifted into his vision. He had seen its like before, but never from that angle. And never had he felt so much like prey.

The dragon, its horned, serpentine head flashing a coppery red in the sunlight, soared lazily forward with the ease of a hawk. Erlestoke could feel the touch of its gaze like a lash across his back. If it wanted to take him, it could, and there was nothing that could be done to stop it.

The dragon's mouth opened, affording a momentary view of massive ivory fangs before a boiling gout of fire obscured everything. Thick and furious, the red-gold flames splashed over the center of the span. The stone sentinels at the nearest end melted like candles left too close to an inferno. For the blink of an eye Erlestoke could see Dranae and the others in silhouette at the peak of the span, then they and molten rock poured into the chasm.

The dragon's passage pulled the fog of melted snow in its wake. It passed over the chasm, then folded its wings and perched on a cliff beyond the far side. Talons clutched stone, crushing sheets of ice that fell below. The creature settled itself, then swathed itself in its wings.

Its eyes blinked, then it spoke in sibilant tones. The words rekindled Erlestoke's fear. They twisted maggotlike over his flesh and inside his skull. He did not know what they meant, and was certain they would always be beyond his comprehension. And he also knew that were he tortured for a year and a day, he would not sink to the depths of despair he felt at that moment.

From behind him, the cloaked figure spoke clearly. "Gagothmar says he would like the Truestone. It would greatly displease him if he needed to cleanse it of your ashes."

CHAPTER 66

Kerrigan's eyes burned as though they'd been soaked in oil and lit afire. He'd not slept in more than a day. After slaying the *sullanciri,* he returned to Navval and began to work on ways to defend the city from dragonel shots. Better magickers were given fragments of the ball he'd rescued and used them as foci to deflect incoming shots. Other pieces were made into attractors that drew the shot to certain targets, such as piles of rubble, where they could do little more than reduce stone to gravel.

As the magickers' efforts to deflect and direct the shots took effect, the Aurolani had begun to direct spells at the city's defenders. Kerrigan had to leave off working on the dragonel shots and diverted his energies into defending the other magickers. Fortunately, the Conservatory spellcasters worked individual spells, which spread them out enough that he could react to each in turn.

When he had been at Vilwan, the idea of defending so many people against spells from so many magickers would have daunted him. Wizards' duels so often came down to casting the perfect counter. If your spell could not match the energy in the attack, you could get hurt. Since very few magickers were good enough to measure the energy of an incoming spell, all too often defensive efforts used too much energy. If one wizard had the initiative, strength, and kept attacking, the defender could exhaust himself.

Spell dimensions provided a different way to defend. He stopped offensive spells by casting counterspells that hunted particular dimensional aspects. When his counter located that aspect, it clung to the spell and told the other spell that it had hit its target. The spell then discharged its energy harmlessly. It had worked against Neskartu and his students alike.

He worked hard through the night, despite the booming of the dragonels and the crackle of fires. The shouts and screams of victims likewise tugged at him, but he forced it all away. With his eyes closed he focused and projected his awareness into the ether around Navval.

Spells approached from the Aurolani camp sporadically. Some came in quickly, burning like dragonel balls. Others drifted like butterflies slowly seeking a blossom. Once he found a spell, he countered it. Most spells accepted the targeting surrogate and discharged prematurely. A couple were a bit more sophisticated—and all the spells began to double-check targeting information by mid-morning, so he actually had to designate alternate targets. The spells did discharge into them, killing a variety of vermin that Kerrigan had sent Bok out to collect for use as targets.

Exhausted and pleased in equal measure, Kerrigan had breakfasted lightly in mid-morning, right after the dragonels had ceased their pounding assault. Some buildings still burned, and a good number of others had been crushed, but the walls remained strong. The resolve of the people likewise defied the Aurolani. Spectators climbed up onto the walls to jeer and shout defiantly at the enemy.

The enemy spellcastings had stopped, but Kerrigan knew enough of warfare not to see this as something other than a sign of surrender. The Aurolani mages had to be as tired as any magicker in Navval. They would retire and rest, as would their counterparts, to be ready to oppose each other again when the coming siege began.

Despite the existence of warmages from Vilwan, and the martial tradition among Murosan sorcerers, magicians traditionally played a tiny part in warfare, save for dueling. The magickal assets of one side tended to neutralize the assets of the other side. Spells could certainly gather information for a general, but the actual fighting usually came down to steel on steel.

Not to mention that an arrow or a sword was usually more than enough to end a sorcerer's military career.

Given his discussions with Rym Ramoch, Kerrigan wondered for a moment if the present manner of doing things was the way it had always been. Yrulph Kirûn had been powerful enough that he had created the DragonCrown, and commanded an army of dragons. Then he had moved south to try to conquer the world. Was it just the dragons that gave him an edge, or was he able to win battles through the use of magick? Did the martial tradition in Muroso harken back to those days, before Vilwan had been pacified, or had it been adopted as a way to prepare against the return of more militant mages?

He found no answers to those questions as he munched on stale bread and drank watered wine. Neither suited him, but that was what Bok provided. What he really wanted was a chance to sleep, but before he could crawl into bed, he was summoned to the ducal palace and Alexia's side.

With Bok in tow, he entered the upper chamber of the northern tower. Alexia was resplendent in her golden mail, and he could not help but smile. Her long hair had been gathered back into a single thick braid. The black lace courtesy mask barely hid her features, but added enough mystery to make her that much more alluring.

With her were Sayce and several other local military commanders. All were clustered around a map spread on a low table in the center of the circular room. In the background stood several signal-mages with *arcanslata*. A balcony ringed the tower, with access provided by east and west doors. Against the north wall, by the window, a stairway moved up to a trapdoor that would allow access to the crenellated tower top.

Alexia looked up and smiled. "There you are, Adept Reese. You should know—no matter what happens from this point forward—that but for your efforts, Navval would have fallen hours ago."

"Really?" He couldn't keep the disbelief from his voice. He had known that she wouldn't lie to him, but the nods and expressions of thanks on the faces of others surprised him. "I didn't think I did that much."

Light chuckles met his comment, though Alexia did not laugh. "There were some individuals who felt that by morning, there would be little of the city left. They wanted to surrender it to the Aurolani. Your efforts did not go unnoticed nor unappreciated."

One of her advisors, a Murosan Magister who had killed two Conservatory mages the previous day, nodded solemnly. "I have not the skill or knowledge to describe what you have been doing, Adept Reese, but if a mere Adept from Vilwan can do what you have done, there is yet hope for the world."

"Oh. Thank you. I did what I could."

Alexia waved him over to the map. "I know you'll need rest, but I have been thinking. In combat, wizards normally neutralize wizards. Would it be possible for you to cast spells that appear to be powerful and lethal, to make their mages defend against them, while the others here can direct their magicks against specific targets?"

The portly mage crossed his arms and stuffed his fingers in his armpits as he thought. "I guess it would be possible. It would require layering a mask over a fairly simple spell. The mask would present itself as an even more powerful spell. I could do some other things, too, to make them think they were Conservatory spells coming in and, oh, if I were to modify the herald spell, then cast something past them and have it launch a masked attack spell, I could make them think they were being attacked from the east, as if we have troops behind them."

Alyx raised an eyebrow. "That would be a *yes*?"

He looked up, then nodded, his jowls shaking. "I can do it. I will need some time to prepare things. And to sleep. And I'll need to eat something substantial."

Sayce nodded to Alexia and immediately headed out of the room.

The Okrans Princess smiled. "I don't know how much time you will have."

A great wailing from the east pierced the chamber. Kerrigan couldn't identify it, though it sent fear pulsing through his guts. He had a sense that, were he not so tired, he might have been sharp enough to figure it out. *Then again, had I all my wits about me, it would probably scare me silly.*

The wails and screams of people suddenly mingled with, then drowned out, the original sound. The company moved out the east door and onto the balcony. Kerrigan drifted in their wake and found himself on the south side of the tower, beside Alexia, looking east.

A dragon whose deep purple scales were edged with gold landed toward the rear of the Aurolani camp. It furled its wings, then swept its head back on the end of a long, lithe neck, and looked over its left shoulder at its back. Humanoid figures, a half-dozen of them, slowly dismounted. It was not until they reached the ground and gained perspective that he realized they were hoargoun, and positively huge.

Which means that dragon is enormous.

"Ah, Highness, before you ask, 'no.'"

She smiled at him. "As much as I respect your skills, Kerrigan, were you fed, watered, rested, and studying for weeks, I'd not ask that question."

From the command pavilion, a tall figure walked through a forest of unit banners. It appeared to address the hoargoun first, for the frost giants began to move forward, and gibberer formations began to line up. Then the figure reached the dragon.

The dragon brought its head down and laid it on the ground. It appeared almost docile. Its tail curled around to cover its side, and its hips and back shifted as the dragon settled in. Wings furled and adjusted, then lay flat. Then the figure pointed toward Navval and the dragon's head came up.

A signal-mage walked over to Alexia. "Caledo reports a dragon has joined Anarus' forces. Shall I tell them of this one?"

"Please. Tell them we will advise of conditions once we see what is happening, but that it does not look good."

"As you wish."

Suddenly, the dragon reared up. Its wings spread wide, its head rose and let out a ghastly shriek—equal parts outrage and hatred. Its head came back down and its gaze swept over Navval. Kerrigan found himself holding tight to the balcony's balustrade, wanting to flee, but too terrified to do anything for fear he would be noticed.

With its forepaws clutched to its chest and wings stretched up and out until the tips almost touched above its head, the dragon lumbered forward. It moved as a fowl might, swaying from side to side, its tail jauntily bouncing behind it. It knocked over a few banners, and squashed a few gibberers, but those were just the ones who had been upset by the pounding of its heavy tread.

The dragon passed in front of the Aurolani lines, then hopped almost as a vulture would, approaching Navval as if the city were carrion. A few arrows arced out, but they bounced harmlessly off thick scales. The dragon loomed larger, the battleground dolmen barely reaching its breastbone.

Its head lowered again, but any hints of benign intent died as its eyes hardened and its mouth opened. Kerrigan actually felt the heat before he saw flames, then all he saw was a roiling torrent of living fire. It struck the eastern gate and wall hard enough that masonry cracked and stones shifted even before they began to glow. The massive oaken gates blew in like shutters before a cyclone and then, in an eyeblink, became ash stains spread deep into the city.

The people who had been on the wall had begun to run, but it mattered not at all. The dragonfire sought them and herded them. Tendrils curled around them, turning them into living torches. It sprang to find another victim and another. The flame ran along the lines of joinery in the stonework, nibbling at block edges, making them drip turgidly down the walls.

The roar that accompanied the flames came as a blessing, for though it assaulted the ears, it eliminated the terrified screams of the dying. After far too long, the roar slackened into cold silence. The dragon's head came up and its jaw opened in what Kerrigan could only take to be a grin.

At that moment the mage felt certain of only two things. The first was that he would not live to see the end of the day. The second, and far more important, was that he'd never seen a more beautiful sight in his life; for the dragon's smile abruptly shrank and its head dipped below the line of the half-melted wall. The body jerked back, hopping clumsily, and it turned with the same craven posture as that of a whipped cur.

All from a shadow passing above it.

As big as the purple dragon had been, the cruciform shadow that passed over it was able to darken it entirely. Kerrigan looked up and caught sight of a black form, then the sun blinded him. He ducked his head and rubbed at his eyes, then looked to the south, following Alexia's pointing finger.

The new dragon soared effortlessly to the south and Kerrigan thought, for a moment, it might be heading to Caledo. Then one wing rose and the other fell, bringing it around in a lazy turn. It leveled out and pumped its wings once, speeding north again. Straight toward the city. *Straight toward* this *tower!*

The Black Dragon slowed as it approached and spread its wings wide. Red stripes curved from its belly up the edges of its midnight hide. Huge claws reached out for and grabbed on to the palace's south tower, crushing stone as they closed. Debris fell to the ground, ricocheting through the streets below. The dragon closed its wings around the tower and clung to it tightly.

Kerrigan found himself pressed with his back against the tower wall. His terror would have shamed him, but Alexia stood beside him and Bok was crouched, peering out through the stone posts in the balustrade.

The Black's massive head loomed over them. A red forked tongue licked out. Tiny droplets of spittle did flick off and one burned a plum-sized hole in the stone next to Kerrigan's head.

The Black opened its mouth, but no fire issued forth. Instead, in a voice far too tiny to belong to such a creature, it spoke to them.

"I am Vriisureol. I can resolve the problem here."

Somehow Alexia found her voice and took a half step forward. "You can rid us of this other dragon?"

Vriisureol's eyes blinked. "If you see Procimre as the only problem, Alexia of Okrannel, then songs do not lie in telling of Okrans courage. No, I would rid this man town of Procimre and the army. At a price. My price must be met."

The princess' chin came up. "And what would that price be?"

Vriisureol's eyes half closed. "I require Kerrigan Reese."

CHAPTER 67

Will turned slowly and deliberately showed the dragon his back. "Hey, you, you have any idea who I am?"

The cloaked figure gave no sign he'd heard the question.

Crow growled. "Will, what are you doing?"

"I'm fixing to get good and angry." He glanced at the older man. "I don't know how I did what I did in Bokagul, but would it hurt if that happened here?"

"You're not bleeding, Will."

The thief drew a dagger. "I can remedy that." Flicking his left hand down, he shucked his mitten off, then wrapped his hand around the dagger's blade. He looked at the cloaked figure again. "I'm the Norrington. That's *THE* Norrington. You know the prophecy. Now do you and Gagmar want to be tangled up with that?"

Laughter came from the cloaked creature, and sibilant echoes of that laughter slithered back from the dragon. "This does make it more interesting, Norrington—infinitely more interesting. It does not change the outcome, however. Turn the Truestone over, and you will live to play out your prophecy. Perhaps."

Erlestoke straightened up and shrugged his cloak off. He pulled off the harness with the fragment of the DragonCrown and let it dangle from his left hand. "This is what you want, right?"

"Throw it here."

Will's mouth went dry. "You wouldn't."

The prince smiled at him. "You can bet your mask on that."

Erlestoke let the stone fall to the crust of snow. The light played a green-gold cross through its depths. The cross gave Will the impression that he was being watched. He could feel power pulsing off the stone and felt something inside himself begin to throb in sympathy.

The prince cocked the quadnel, primed it, and pressed the muzzle to the stone. "Gagothmar might not have wanted to clean ashes off this, but how will he feel about piecing it back together?"

The thief grabbed Erlestoke's left arm. "You can't. Don't do it."

"We can't let them have it, Will."

The cloaked figure shrugged. "Do it. Even one of the vaunted dragonels couldn't shatter a Truestone, not in that setting. When it was fashioned into part of the Crown, it became even more vital than it was before. These mountains could fall on it and it would survive."

Crow rested his left hand on Erlestoke's right shoulder. "I don't think he's bluffing, Highness."

"Alas, neither do I." In one smooth motion the prince raised the quadnel, aimed, and the firelock fell.

Will ducked from the blast. As the white smoke cleared, he saw that the cloaked figure was down. The gibberers had broken and were running. "Great shot!"

"For all the good it will do."

Will couldn't understand the resignation in Erlestoke's voice until he saw the figure slowly struggling back to its feet. "What is that thing?"

"Relentless." The prince sighed. "We all really appreciate your traveling this far to rescue us. I dearly wish things would have worked out better."

"If you have to die, I guess dragonfire isn't a bad way to go." Crow shrugged.

"No! We're not dying." Will drew the dagger across his palm and hissed as pain followed the stroke. Blood sprayed out in a line, dappling snow and fragment alike. Snow blossomed red, but the blood sank into the stone and disappeared. More power pulsed from it.

Will dropped to his knees and pressed his bloody palm to the fragment, then clutched it and raised it high. "You will *never* have this!"

Power pulsed again, heavier and harder. An elf in Erlestoke's company gasped and doubled over. A number of Resolute's tattoos lit up, and the metal limbs of *meckanshii* spasmed. The dragon hissed menacingly, and even the cloaked figure appeared to stagger.

It didn't fall, however, and very little pain bled into its voice as it spoke. "Your efforts will avail you nothing." It stopped speaking in human words and instead gave voice to a wail similar to the one that had summoned the dragon.

Will whirled, the fragment still clutched in his hand. Blood continued to drip and the stone grew warmer. The pulsing flowed into his skin and inched along his forearm.

Gagothmar spread his wings and launched himself forward. The wind of his passage swirled snow from hillsides. Lower and faster the dragon flew, with copper highlights slithering over his scales. The shadow played over the ground, drawing ever nearer the chasm. His mouth opened, fangs flashing, and Will braced for the fiery torrent that would consume him and his friends.

Lunging up from the crevasse, a gargantuan dragon of a deep verdant hue closed its jaws on Gagothmar's breastbone. The copper dragon shrieked in pain, and sprayed the sky with fire. His wings beat furiously against the green's snout. Blood gushed, black and steaming, from the copper's breast. The massive jaws opened again, lunging and closing again, crushing the chest.

With one whiplash flick of its head, the green sent Gagothmar's body tumbling back to the west side of the chasm. It rolled in a tangle of wings and tail. Fire trailed from his mouth and burst out through the hole in his chest. Wings cracked crisply in the cold air, but even that sound was drowned out by the gloriously loud crunching as the green gobbled its enemy's flesh.

Slowly, sinking talons through the snow and into the stone beneath, the enormous green dragged itself up over the chasm lip. Black blood ran from its jaws. Sunlight sparked off golden flecks deep in its scales as the serpentine creature heaved itself onto the valley floor. It tried to rise, but slumped heavily to its left, triggering a small avalanche of snow that half buried it.

With one eye it looked at Will. The stone pulsed a bit more weakly, but still sent a trickle of energy up through Will. The spots on his throat burned, and time began to slow as an awareness of shapes and powers, influences and currents—of time and portent—flowed around Will.

I know you!

And I, you.

Will almost felt as if he was watching himself. While the green had slain Gagothmar, the cloaked figure had not been idle. It had run forward, as fast as it could. The scarlet cloak had flown off, allowing the creature to increase its speed. Its left hand reached for Will, intent on rending him to win the prize he clutched.

Will spun away from its lunge, twisting around to his right. His left hand came out in a long looping strike. As the creature's hand shot through empty air, Will slammed the fragment against the right side of its skull. He could feel the bones crack, reducing its head to a sack of mush, then watched as the body spun limply through the air to crash through the crusty snow and slide from sight.

Will found himself on his knees, staring after the creature.

Crow looked from him to where the body rested under a slowly drifting cloud of snow. "That was, um, how did you . . . ?"

"I don't know." Will shook his head and pressed the fragment to his own chest. He pointed his right hand at the green dragon. "We have to dig him out. He can't take the cold in his condition."

Erlestoke shifted his shoulders uneasily. "We owe that dragon thanks, but . . ."

"No buts; he's a friend." Will stared at them. "Don't you get it? That's Dranae."

The effort to dig Dranae from the snow was aided by the dragon himself. As Will drew closer with the fragment of the DragonCrown, the pulsing started again. Will tucked it up inside his coat, without letting go, and as his fingers warmed up again, Dranae opened an eye. A tremor ran through one wing.

Dranae heaved himself up, letting snow slide from his head and neck, then shook. Sheets of white blinded everyone for a moment, then when it drifted down, in the heart of a huge, dragon-shaped depression, sat Dranae, as naked as the day Will, Crow, and Resolute had first found him.

They hustled him into a small cavern the *meckanshii* had discovered while setting up for their ambush. Various individuals donated pieces of clothing, but he refused everything save the cloak that the scaled figure had worn. He swathed himself in that and shivered for a bit, then smiled at Will.

"Our debt is canceled."

The thief blinked in surprise. "I owed you a debt?"

Dranae nodded. "When you were bitten by the *sullanciri*, the poison was neutralized."

Will's eyes widened. "You're Lady Snowflake?"

The dragon in manform threw his head back and laughed loudly. "No, no, not at all."

"Good." Will blushed, remembering some of the dreams he'd had. "But she did exist?"

"Yes. She came to you in that room. I watched her clear you of poison."

Crow frowned. "But Qwc had chased all of us from the room. He was in there with Will alone."

"No. I did not join you. Because I desired it, your minds assumed I did." Dranae sighed. "If you will recall, I was in the hall, behind Will, and caught him when he fainted. It was not my intent to deceive you, but I knew forces were in play that required me to remain where I was if Will was to live."

Will raised his bandaged left hand to the round scars on his throat. "Did you do this?"

Dranae nodded slowly. "It was the only way to save you." He brought his right hand out from beneath the cloak. His thumb and middle finger grew sharp talons. As he turned his hand, Will detected the scars from small puncture wounds in the pads of the thumb and middle finger. "I cut myself and mixed my blood with yours, Will. I was able to repair the damage the venom had done. There have been some lingering effects, like your chill, and for that I am sorry."

He swallowed hard. "I guess I would have been a lot colder in a grave."

Crow crouched beside Dranae. "I, ah, I don't know how to ask this but ... what are you?"

The talons shrank again as he gestured toward the valley. "I am what you saw come up out of the chasm. My name, among my kind, is Dravothrak. By your reckoning, I am old, very old, but among my kind, my age is roughly similar as my age appears to be in this form. I was old when the DragonCrown was formed, unlike that pup I slew out there."

Erlestoke pointed outside. "And the thing Will killed?"

"Dracomorph. A life stage. To you quite formidable, but among my kind, barely worth the waste of a name."

"Wow." Will smiled, then glanced over at Resolute. "You knew all this?"

The Vorquelf shook his head. "My knowledge of dragons is limited."

Dranae looked up. "Still, friend Resolute, you suspected. I called myself by an ancient man-name, not knowing it had passed from use."

"I found myself curious, Dranae, but other things demanded my attention."

"Of course." The dragon smiled. "You would like to know why I am here, why I opposed Gagothmar and why I oppose Chytrine?"

"Yes!" Will glanced around. "I mean, we would like to know that, right?"

Crow laughed. "Yes, Will, we would."

"Not all dragons, as you know, can be commanded by the Crown, even when it is complete. Vriisureol, the grand Black who intervened at Vilwan, fought as Kirûn's ally. He was not subject to the Crown. Even in pieces, the Crown can exert influence, though most of those who answer its call now are young. What Chytrine cannot compel, they offer willingly.

"The elders with whom I am associated deemed it important to send their own ambassador to the world of mortals. They helped me learn and work the magick that allows me to transform—though one of them, in her wisdom, caused me to forget my true nature when I transformed that first time. When you found me I knew nothing more than my name. As I traveled with you, I learned what it was to be a man, though I do not think even she imagined I would fall in with such extraordinary company."

Erlestoke nodded. "By becoming a man, you could understand our fears and desires, our hopes, strengths, and failings?"

"Yes, and to report back so we could decide on which side to enter the fight."

The thief wrinkled his nose. "So you were testing us? Even though you knew you might end up eating us or something?"

"Not testing, watching. I watched you deal with the tests presented by others. And, had you any question, I had long since determined I would remain with you and fight at your side." He smiled carefully. "And your action, with the Truestone, Will, proved to me the wisdom of that choice."

"What do you mean?"

"I had been coming to realize my nature, day by day. I was able to draw on it to save you in Meredo, but the spell that had stripped me of my memory had the unfortunate consequence of blocking me from the means to complete the transformation. On the bridge, Gagothmar blasted me and the stone. His breath was insufficient to destroy me—no more than Resolute's rebukes could destroy you, Will. I fell into stone that had been made molten by his breath. It encased me and I felt comfortable. There are points in our lives, such as when a dracomorph transforms into a drake, where being cocooned in stone is a part of the process. I would have remained there, taking comfort, save that your blood and the stone woke me to urgency.

"I remembered who I was, who you all were." Dranae snorted. "I remembered the insolence of that pup in thinking he had killed me. Primarily, though, I felt your refusal to surrender. Your spirit, my blood, the stone, the prophecy—all of these things brought me back to myself and I was able to act."

"I'm glad you did." The thief flexed his left hand. "But how did I manage to kill the dracomorph?"

Dranae laughed. "Part of your nature, Will. You and I are linked. You stole some of my strength and my awareness, so you knew he was coming, and you were able to deal with him."

"And this link, because of the blood, is why I was able to do what I did in Bokagul?"

"That I don't know, Will—which is what brings me to my next task. I need to report back to Vael, to my superiors." He sighed heavily. "The debate that ensues could decide the fate of the war and the world."

Crow nodded. "I cannot think that the mortal world will have a better ambassador to dragondom than you, my friend."

Will nodded in agreement and slapped Dranae on the shoulder with his injured left hand, then groaned. "Yeah, just don't tell them that some of us can be stupid at times, too. We will miss you."

"No, you won't." The cloak dropped away and muscles rippled as Dranae stood. "After all, you're going with me."

CHAPTER 68

Alexia took another step forward, despite the reptilian scent wafting off the Black Dragon. "I will sacrifice no one."

Vriisureol turned his head slightly, watching her closely. "And were I to ask for Alexia of Okrannel? Would Alexia be sacrificed?"

Alexia started to answer, but Kerrigan shoved himself from the wall. "No. It's me you want. Fine, then take me. My death doesn't matter if it's going to save the city."

The Black's wings spread, then snapped forward. A blast of air buffeted the both of them as the dragon launched itself into the sky. Alexia clung to Kerrigan, steadying him. They both watched as Vriisureol gained altitude, then began to soar in playful circles over the city.

The princess took the mage by the shoulders and held him out at arm's length. "What were you thinking?"

He looked up at her sheepishly, and not a little bit hurt. "I was thinking the deal is good enough to save Navval. You were going to offer yourself, weren't you?"

"That's different."

"How?"

The question made her shiver. She grabbed the back of Kerrigan's neck with her right hand. Drawing him close, she rested her forehead against his. "It's different because it is my life. I'm the one responsible for Navval's defense, and you'll be a lot more useful to the world, given all you can do, than I will be."

"I *might* have been more useful." Kerrigan pulled back and pointed toward the Aurolani camp. "But as strong as I am, I couldn't have done that."

The purple dragon had slunk on its belly back to the Aurolani lines. Its claws had ripped great furrows through the snow, bringing up black earth to mark its passage. It glanced back over its shoulder, lifting its chin from the snow and hissed, but fell silent as Vriisureol's shadow passed over it again.

The Black came in low and snapped at the purple dragon's hindquarters. The grounded beast yipped, then rolled onto its side, exposing its throat. Its quivering tail curled in to cover its belly.

The cloaked figure that had spoken to Procimre moved through the camp and flung off its red cloak. It towered over the fleeing gibberers. At least one caught itself on a hooked spike on the thing's forearm. With a casual gesture the bleeding beast was tossed aside and the figure continued on its way without a break in stride.

It passed in front of the Aurolani lines, then called out in a keening tone that undulated into inaudibility.

The Black's course shifted when the thing called out. Though she would not have thought it possible, Vriisureol turned in the air and swooped back with the ease of a Gyrkyme at play. The Black replied and they exchanged words, though Alexia could make no sense of the hisses and shrieks.

"Kerrigan, have you any idea what is being said?"

The mage shook his head. "Not a clue. I don't know what that is, or why it speaks dragon. I hope it won't negotiate a better bargain."

Alexia shared that wish and wondered, just for a moment, if Vriisureol could read her thoughts. On the very next pass his tail came through and batted the figure into the air. With a powerful pump of his wings, Vriisureol surged forward, then rolled. His right wing curved and cupped the broken figure, then swatted it to the left. The left wing popped it back right, then the Black's head came up and snapped the thing out of the air. Teeth flashed quickly and the figure vanished into that massive maw.

A great cry arose from the Aurolani camp. The purple dragon continued to slither forward, then stopped with its snout at what had been the command pavilion. All around it, gibberers and vylaens scrambled and ran. Hoargoun lumbered as best they could, using their long legs to retreat quickly toward the south. *Kryalniri* joined them—save for one leaving the command tent in the company of a slender woman dressed entirely in white.

Alexia shivered again. Even at that distance she knew her. That was the woman she had seen in her room in Caledo, when she first met Princess Dayley. *Who is she?*

The *kryalniri* walked the woman to Procimre's left forepaw, then steadied her as she climbed up. The woman worked her way to a position between the dragon's wings and tied herself into the harness that had held the hoargoun.

She sat there with her back against the creature's back, as if in a carriage for a leisurely ride.

The *kryalniri* stood back and waved. Procimre gathered his feet beneath himself, then flapped his wings once, hard, to lift from the ground. A wingtip casually hit the white-furred creature, exploding him into a red stain upon the snow.

Vriisureol dove and snapped again at Procimre's tail. The purple dragon shrieked in protest, though that protest quickly became a frightened mewing. He beat his wings more hastily and turned toward the ocean. The Black chased him out over the water, then drew up and with several pumps of his wings, arced skyward.

Alexia had spent most of her life in Gyrvirgul. She had watched countless Gyrkyme fly. The precision and power she had seen in the Warhawks, or the artistry of the Swifts, they had defined for her grace in flight, but this dragon reduced the Gyrkyme aerial artistry to panicked flutterings.

Vriisureol came over in a loop. His head and neck described an elegant arc, then one wing came up, the other down, and he rolled into a long swoop passing right over the Aurolani line. Alexia waited for him to open his mouth and release a fiery flood that would stretch a burning line from the ocean to the road to Caledo.

He did not. As he reached the middle of the camp, his wings flared forward and beat hard once, letting him hover. Vriisureol's head came down and his jaws opened. He vented his rage over the command tent with a loud roar that was equal parts triumph and contempt.

A puddle of fire rolled from that spot. Burning wave fronts, like ripples in a pond, pulsed along, quickly overtaking gibberers, vylaens, and the frost giants. The smaller creatures just vanished as the liquid flames poured over them. The hoargoun made it several more steps, burning like torches, before they flopped forward into the incandescent lake.

Flames washed over the lines of dragonels. Some exploded, others just vaporized. Tents and tools, weapons and sleighs all evaporated in the rolling conflagration. Drearbeasts and frostclaws burned black in a heartbeat and disappeared.

The heat from the dragon's assault and the force of the wind it created did push Alexia back. Kerrigan gestured and some of the heat abated. Bok had moved in at Kerrigan's legs and clung to her as well.

The fire seeped across the open field that had separated the Aurolani from Navval. People on the walls below—a few guards and the foolishly curious—began to run. It looked as if the burning tide would splash against the walls. Alexia expected they would erode them as ocean waves gnawed at castles of sand, but the dragon's fire stopped short. Pennants and flags did ignite, but beyond that, little damage was done.

Vriisureol swooped through the flames, curling them in his wake, then drifted south and east. At various points his head lunged, and little bursts of fire exploded against the ground. He came around in interlocking loops, spitting more fire, then finally flew back toward the city.

He landed once again on the south tower and more of it crumbled. He thrust his head toward Alexia. "I have done as I said I would. The enemy is no more."

"I see that. Why did you let the other dragon go? Who was the woman who escaped with him?"

The dragon snorted. He looked from Alexia to Kerrigan. "Kerrigan Reese, it is time for the honoring of the bargain."

The Adept frowned. "The least you could do is answer her questions before you kill me. It would be polite."

Vriisureol cocked his head to the side. "A lecture in manners. How... mortal."

Kerrigan shrugged. "Well?"

"I said I would eliminate the enemy. Procimre was reduced to a beast of burden and sent away. The woman Procimre took was not your enemy."

"But she was from Aurolan."

"Alexia of Okrannel is wiser than to assume unanimity in any group." Vriisureol straightened his head and looked at Kerrigan. "Is Kerrigan Reese prepared?"

"I guess so." He turned and gave Alexia what was supposed to be a brave smile. She decided she would remember it that way and ignore the quivering of his lower lip. His voice came in a whisper. "Let the others know... Good luck to everyone."

She nodded, then leaned in and kissed him once on each cheek. "I will. May the gods bless you in your next life."

"Next life?" Vriisureol's eyes narrowed. "This common tongue lacks nuance. I am not going to slay him. I have been sent to provide transport. I am to bear Kerrigan Reese and Bok to Vael. There are those who wish to speak with the Adept."

Alexia blinked. "You came to get him? If you are just transport, than why did you...?"

The dragon's head came up. "I was told to see to Kerrigan Reese's comfort. I chose to see Procimre and the Aurolani as a discomfort. Do not question such fortune, Alexia of Okrannel."

Her hands came up. "No, no, no question. I just wondered... the seeming gravity of what you demanded..."

"A lack of nuance." Vriisureol extended his left wing to the balcony. "Come, Kerrigan, climb onto my back."

He shook his head. "I don't understand. Why are you taking me to Drag-onholm?"

"The struggles of mortals have not gone without notice. Certain efforts have attracted attention. Kerrigan Reese will be examined and decisions will be made."

"Ah, wait." Kerrigan's brows knitted together. "You were to see to my comfort, yes?"

"Yes."

"Well, I won't be comfortable unless Princess Alexia comes with me."

Alexia's guts began to boil. "Why do you want me there?"

He regarded her with innocent eyes. "You just told me about responsibility. If they are going to try to decide something based on me, I'm far from a good example. You are. If someone has to represent us mortals, you're better for it than me."

The sound issuing from the dragon sounded remarkably like a groan. "As desired, but that is it."

"And we will meet you outside the city. We have to get our things and put our affairs here in order." The magicker's eyes narrowed. "Um, isn't there something else you want to do, like fly south to Caledo and drive that dragon off?"

Vriisureol raised his nose to the air and sniffed loudly. "No. Marimri has never been an annoyance. I shall wait over there." With that he took off again and drifted to the blackened landscape that minutes earlier had been home to Navval's second most dire threat.

Kerrigan's expression reflected how guilty he felt as Peri blinked her big eyes at him. "I am sorry; I didn't think. I was tired. I should have included you as someone I needed."

Alexia hugged the Gyrkyme tightly. "I am sorry, too, sister. I wouldn't go, but this could be a chance to bring more help like Vriisureol."

"If I am not there, Alyx, you will not be safe."

The Okrans Princess held her sister tighter, feeling the soft down against her cheek. "I will be safe, sister. I know it."

"Said without conviction."

Alexia pulled back and met Perrine's sad stare. "You have to trust me, Peri."

The Gyrkyme frowned. "I do trust you. You know that. I just don't like being apart from you. Kerrigan has Bok. Who have you got?"

"Who will Alexia need?" Vriisureol snorted at Perrine, ruffling feathers. "You need not fear for her."

Alyx smiled despite the dulling of the light in her sister's eyes. "I will be fine, Peri, and we will return quickly. Vriisureol has promised to bring us back."

Sayce, her arms crossed over her belly, nodded solemnly. "Very fast, I hope. The news from Caledo is not good. The dragon there took down part of the city wall. It seems to be resting, but there is nothing we can do to stop it."

"Marimri." Kerrigan smiled and tugged on mittens. "Vriisureol said her name is Marimri. She's young, so she'll have to rest for a while before melting another wall."

"So Caledo's life can be measured in days, not hours."

The dragon lifted his head, glanced at where Bok was tying a chest into the harnesses on his back, then looked at Sayce. "Marimri likes pretty things. Bribes will work. And songs; Marimri likes songs. If the songs are pleasing, Marimri will listen for as long as they are sung."

Alexia nodded. "Then you bring the troops here to the east, hit any supply trains heading south from Porjal, and hit the rear of the army."

Vriisureol nodded. "Bring bards. Have them sing loudly."

The redheaded Murosan looked surprised. "That might work. I will see what my father thinks. That might just work. Thank you."

Alexia smiled and gave Sayce a hug. "Take care of yourself. We will be back as soon as we can."

She gave her sister a final hug, then followed Kerrigan to the dragon's paw. She mounted behind him, steadying him. She seated herself opposite him and tied into the flight harness. The dragon scales, while quite hard, were smooth enough that they'd not be too uncomfortable.

Vriisureol craned his neck around to inspect his cargo. Apparently satisfied, he came up on all four feet. Muscle rippled beneath his flesh as his wings unfurled. With one tremendous downbeat, the dragon left the earth and Alexia laughed aloud. For the first time in a lifetime, she could feel what her sister felt when flying, and despite being where she was, she was happy.

CHAPTER 69

From Procimre's back, Isaura was able to see the disk of winter's always-night curving sharply down over Aurolan's white tundra. North they had flown, over the Sebcian peninsula, past Vorquellyn and the ruins of Fortress Draconis. Over the Boreal mountains they went and yet farther north. As the day died and darkness overswept the world, the purple dragon began to descend into the valley in which her mother's castle sat.

Isaura shivered, but not with cold. The heat from the dragon's muscles took the edge off the air. She had also never thought of her mother's realm as cold, but seeing it shrouded in shadow, it suddenly seemed frigid to her, and part of her wanted to avoid this homecoming.

The rest of her immediately rebelled. Her mother feared betrayal, but she would not be the one to betray her. *She trusts me, and I owe her everything.* The young woman steeled herself for what she feared might be her mother's displeasure, and sought those things that might brighten her mother's outlook.

There were not many. Neskartu had been slain by a child. The dragon Vriisureol had destroyed the rest of the Conservatory students. The entire army besieging Navval had been eliminated. Naelros had not been a favorite of her mother's, but the loss of any allies hurt.

Trib's death had saddened Isaura. She'd beseeched the *kryalniri* to join her and escape, but he had refrained. He knew Vriisureol would permit only her escape; his presence would put her in jeopardy.

The dragon landed before the black citadel, then reared up and rested his chin on the balcony. Isaura unhitched herself, scaled his neck, passed between his horns, then slipped off his nose and onto the stone. Without so much as a hiss or murmur, the dragon withdrew, and Isaura did not regret his slinking departure.

The grand chamber she entered had been changed somewhat, but it took her a moment to figure out how. Some of the furnishings had vanished, though from the smashed piece of a bench leg near the hearth, she supposed they had been broken up and fed into the flames.

Opposite the fireplace, an inky blackness stained the wall. A couple of steps into the room she realized it was not paint, but the flaccid flesh Neskartu had last worn. She saw the limp limbs and the withered wings. It hung there from the wand, which appeared to have been driven into the stone to half its length.

Isaura fought another shiver, then smiled happily. "Mother, it is good to see you again."

Chytrine's head came up and, just for a moment, Isaura caught the last of a venomous expression as it bled away. A smile replaced it, though not as broad as the one she wore. "Daughter, you are come home. Had you not arrived within the hour, I would have sent Nefrai-laysh to find you."

The smaller of the two *sullanciri* sketched a bow. "Within the hour, the skies I would scour, to find that shining star which, dear Isaura, you are."

"My lord Nefrai-laysh devalues the stars."

"He thinks too much of them, you mean to say, daughter." Her mother's blue-green eyes narrowed slightly. "You were seen home safely?"

"Yes, Mother. Vriisureol allowed me to come north." She hesitated and bit her lower lip. "He destroyed the army at Navval. He killed Naelros."

Her mother waved that report away. "That army never should have been there. It was useless, and remains useless. The fall of Caledo will render that loss insignificant."

"It pleases me that you are not disappointed, Mother." Isaura smiled again and looked at the other *sullanciri*. "And you, Lord Nefrai-kesh, how goes the war in Okrannel?"

"It is done, Princess." Nefrai-kesh smiled politely.

"You defeated Adrogans?"

"By no means. He has taken Svarskya and Okrannel. He has won his prize."

Isaura frowned. "I don't understand."

Chytrine laughed lightly. "It was necessary for Adrogans to succeed in order for us to succeed. We have given them back a ravaged country, while we have made great gains in the south. When Muroso falls, we will be farther south than we were before, and Oriosa will not be an obstacle."

"But, Okrannel..."

"Isaura sweet, you do not understand. In Svarskya are hidden the seeds of the Southlands' destruction." Chytrine's voice took on an edge. "Okrannel's loss did come sooner than I had intended, but other events conspire to make up for this setback."

Nefrai-kesh dropped to one knee and bowed his head. "It is to my mortification that I have failed you so, Empress."

"A minor failure, pet, and one worth nothing compared to your victories." Chytrine reached a hand out and lifted his chin. "You will not fail me again, will you?"

"Never, Mistress."

"Good. There are important tasks to which we must attend. You, Nefrai-kesh, shall remain here to coordinate things. Your son has been given his assignment. I shall be taking Myrall'mara and Ferxigo with me. Anarus shall press the siege. Things are working to my satisfaction."

"What would you have me do, Mother?"

Chytrine regarded Isaura with wide-eyed innocence. "You, child? I would have you remain here and learn from Lord Nefrai-kesh."

"But is there nothing else I could do?"

"Oh, sweet child, what is it?"

Isaura started to speak, but her throat thickened. *How can I tell her that I feel she does not trust me?* "Mother, I did not mean to fail you."

"Fail me? Oh, no, child, you mustn't think that." The Aurolani Empress moved to her daughter and embraced her. "You have seen much in the south, and I wish you a chance to know peace again. To know peace before I call upon you to help me once more."

Chytrine took her by the arms and pulled back to look up into her silver eyes. "I have minor tasks to attend to, and so I shall deal with them now. There is the matter of the ruby fragment. It is not lost to me, and may well be had for a reasonable price."

Isaura's face brightened. "That is wonderful, Mother!"

"Yes, child, it is. Three pieces are so much more powerful than two, and the ruby especially so. Even if the others were gathered to oppose me, the balance of power would leave me with the advantage on the ground."

Isaura glanced at where Neskartu's flesh hung from the wall. "What of the youth who did that?"

"A vexing problem, yes, but one we shall work upon." Chytrine reached up and caressed Isaura's left cheek. "Fear not, daughter, the enemy's victories shall sour in his mouth, and what he swallows will poison him. The course may not be the one plotted, but our destination shall remain the same."

Adrogans rubbed his left hand over his face. "Read that to me again, please?"

The signal-mage's exasperation filled his voice. "My lord, if you do not believe me, you can read the reply yourself."

The Jeranese general spitted the man with a furious glance. "It is not you I disbelieve, it is the message."

The signal-mage clutched the *arcanslata* to his chest. "You do not understand, sir..."

"READ!"

His bellow made the man jump back and brought a smile to Phfas' face. Both Gilthalarwin of the Loquelven Blackfeathers and General Caro managed to keep their faces blank, but he knew they were mulling over what they had heard.

"From King Stefin of Okrannel to General Markus Adrogans. We have heard of your victory and our heart knows great joy. The debt owed to you by the Okrans people can never be repaid. Your victory is the greatest ever won in our nation and shall be sung of forever. You will ever be revered in our nation, and we shall always consider you a friend of the highest order.

"From Queen Carus of Jerana to General Markus Adrogans. I convey to you my grand admiration at your feat. Six months ago the liberation of Okrannel was but a dream, and one many said could not be realized. You have proved them wrong, and proved yourself the greatest military mind alive. While nothing would please us more than to have you join us in Narriz for the Council of Kings, we would not trouble you to overcome your aversion to traveling by water. We bid you remain there in Svarskya until you are called forth again."

The signal-mage looked up. "It has all been authenticated."

Adrogans nodded. "I believe you. Leave us now."

The signal-mage withdrew from the chamber that had previously housed Nefrai-kesh. Adrogans waited until the man was gone, then Phfas invoked his *yrûn* of air to swirl about the tower and prevent the words spoken from being overheard.

The Jeranese general sat back in the high-backed wooden chair at the head of the table. "That's it. We are thanked and told to wait: no word of reinforcements or redeployment."

Caro nodded. "I do not know if I should take heart that King Augustus did not send a message of congratulations. I wonder if there is dissent in Narriz over what should be done in the future?"

"I have no doubt there is, my friend." Adrogans shifted his shoulders as Pain stabbed long talons down either side of his neck. "Things would be much worse if our leaders knew the full import of this victory."

In searching the city, several important discoveries had been made. There had been boombags rigged to explode, but their fuses had never been lit. Other searchers had located a workshop where firedirt was formulated.

Equally important, a ship that had been scuttled in the harbor had not sunk in deep water. At low tide men had gone out to it and discovered a cargo that included dragonel shot and a number of dragonels in watertight crates. The common soldier took it as a very good sign that their advance had been so rapid that Nefrai-kesh had not been able to use those weapons.

Adrogans was well aware that the weapons *had* been deployed. Ever since Chytrine had introduced the first dragonel a quarter century before, the secrets of their manufacture and the production of firedirt had been sought after. Dothan Cavarre, the Draconis Baron, had jealously guarded that secret and refused to share it with the nations of the Southlands. He feared that once they had a weapon capable of bringing down castle and city walls, wars would rage in the south. When Chytrine came again, there would be no one to oppose her.

And now they have given me these secrets. He shook his head. Here he was, a victorious general who had just been given weapons that would guarantee his invincibility. He already had Okrannel. Jerana was his nation, so he could just declare Okrannel a province of a Jeranese empire. Gurol and Valicia would fall quickly enough, then an alliance with Alcida against Chytrine would allow both nations to descend upon and divide up Reqorra, Helurca, and Salnia. Were Adrogans to let Alcida become the battleground where he fought Chytrine, he would have that nation, too.

Gilthalarwin gave Adrogans an easy smile. "I wish I could imagine your leaders as being shrewd enough to see the dragonels for what they are. I fear they will just see them as a means to dominating their neighbors. You are right to conceal this information."

Caro shook his head. "There is a problem, however. This information will not remain secret forever. Once someone—let us use King Scrainwood as an example—learns you have the dragonels, he will point to a conspiracy against nations that do not. He could choose, then, to accept Chytrine's offer of protection against you, and there are other nations that would do likewise to avoid destruction."

"Fools who deserve her," Phfas hissed derisively. "They flow from fear to fear."

"That may be true, Uncle, but do their people deserve it?"

"If their people allow it."

The Loquelf frowned. "And if they do not, they attack their leaders and overthrow them. More chaos and Chytrine to benefit."

Adrogans sighed heavily. "We are congratulated, but told to wait. For what, we do not know, and that will destroy this army as surely as the dragonels would have."

The Alcidese general nodded in agreement. "Our army needs to be active. I would like to put them to work rebuilding the city's defenses."

"Yes, we want them to think we are going to make sure Svarskya does not fall when the Aurolani return." Adrogans looked at the Loquelf. "I wonder,

Mistress, if you and your people would be willing to engineer a deception for me?"

The elf's dark eyes sparkled with amusement. "How much of one?"

"I want to send your scouts out, both to the east toward Crozt and northwest toward the mountains. I suspect there are Aurolani troops operating in the east. If there are not, or they are insufficient to threaten Svarskya, I want reports from the west indicating that Aurolani troops are gathering for a strike on Svarskya. I need the reports to hold this army together."

"And to convince those in the south that they should not call their units home?"

"It is a mild deception. The Aurolani will interpret your scouting as preparation for an invasion, which will tie up some troops."

"And if we find nothing to the north and west?"

Adrogans smiled carefully. "Chytrine gave us the dragonels in hopes that we might create an empire. She expected Okrannel might be the northern reach of it, but the Ghost March exists further north. It's been a quarter century since King Augustus took an army through it, and he never had dragonels. I may carve out the empire she wants, but just not the one she expects."

CHAPTER 70

In the end, it was the vote of the Oriosan Freemen that decided things. Dranae was only going to take a limited number of people with him to Vael. That list came down to Will, Crow, Resolute, Erlestoke, Lombo, and Qwc. The Panqui, as a race, were favorites of dragons, so Lombo's inclusion was a foregone conclusion. As for Qwc, since there was no way to prevent him from coming, Dranae invited him along. The other three came because they had been Dranae's companions, and Erlestoke because he actually possessed a Truestone.

Those who were left behind were placed under a joint command of Sallitt Hawkins and his wife, Jancis Ironside. Exactly what they would be doing had started a debate. The Murosans wanted to return to Murosa to continue to harass Aurolani troops, even though their chances of surviving were dreadful. The *meckanshii* wanted to head back toward Fortress Draconis—especially after learning there were other survivors there. Jullagh-tse Seegg struck a middle ground and pointed out that if they went back into Sarengul, they could help crush the Aurolani occupation army. The Sarens would then move to strike at the Aurolani, which would give them much more strength for hitting supply trains than they had now, *and* Sarengul would become a refuge for people fleeing the Aurolani armies.

A return to Sarengul would also mean a chance at finding Verum, and the idea of locating a lost comrade meant a lot to all assembled.

The Freemen held a meeting and discussed things. Wheatly came to Will and asked what he thought, but Will just smiled. "You've earned the command of this unit, Wheatly. You know their minds and their hearts. Whatever you decide, I know it will make me proud."

Wheatly then announced that the Freemen were all for entering Sarengul and fighting the Aurolani therein. While the Murosans weren't wholly happy with that idea, a supplemental plan to lure their pursuit into the mountains and use the byways of Sarengul to destroy them did suit.

No one found leave-taking easy. Will said good-bye to each and every one of the Freemen. Each wished him well; they each took from him a small snippet of the bloody cloth that he had wrapped around his left hand before Jilandessa healed the wound. The Freemen sewed the brown patches onto their masks, below their left eyes, which is where they would cut an orphan notch if their father was dead. He knew why they did it, but the idea that a group of hard-bitten warriors would choose to see him as some sort of father figure astounded him.

Crow had a hard time saying good-bye, too—leaving his brother and his sister-in-law, to whom he had just been introduced. The Freemen and others also made a big deal of his departure and told him to keep wearing his mask. "If you're going to represent us before the dragons, Crow, then you have to be attired proper" was the oft-voiced sentiment.

Erlestoke had it rougher, though. He was leaving behind his squad of soldiers, without whom neither he nor the DragonCrown fragment would have escaped Fortress Draconis. The mission they had chosen to accept was one that would very likely kill them, so the good-byes they said could easily have been forever.

Toughest of all, though, seemed to be having to part from his brother. Will had been saying good-bye to Linchmere when Erlestoke came by. The elder prince's jaw dropped in surprise, then a smile blossomed on his face. "Linchmere?"

The younger prince stiffened and blood drained from his face. "You're alive! You're alive."

"Yes, very much so, and very happy to see you." Erlestoke embraced his brother, then glanced at Will. "Why didn't you tell me my brother was here?"

"Well, we were dealing with Dranae and everything and, you know, it's been a long day."

Linchmere pulled himself from his brother's embrace and smiled. "It's because, Highness, no one here knows who I am. To them I'm just Lindenmere, one of the Freemen."

Erlestoke's eyes flicked up and Will was certain he caught the knowing glances from other Freemen milling about. *All* of them knew who Lindenmere really was. "Well, I never would have guessed. You've come with them from Meredo, have you? Father must be furious."

Linchmere shrugged. "He'll be more surprised to see you back from the dead than to see where I've gotten."

"Pity if it's true." Erlestoke's smile broadened. He clearly couldn't believe the changes that had been wrought in his brother. Though Linchmere had only been a Freeman for just over a month, he'd lost weight, made friends, and earned some scars. "He won't recognize you, that's for certain."

Linchmere's return smile burned brighter than dragonfire. As the brothers embraced, Will withdrew to gather his gear for the trip. It struck him that, in many ways, Linchmere had been like Dranae, only it was the crucible of war, not a bath in molten rock, that had awakened him. Likewise Kenleigh had taken on an edge. In combat he'd proven quite stalwart, but content to take orders rather than give them. That didn't mean he didn't exhibit leadership capabilities. He did, very much so, but he was the sort of man who led by example instead of command or force of personality.

When next Will saw them, the brothers were laughing together. Linchmere was helping Erlestoke work on the riding harness they'd use on Dranae. Having met them separately, Will never would have guessed they were brothers, but here he could see it. Moreover, he could see they were friends.

With many promises of future drinking, feasting, and wenching being exchanged, those bound for Vael clambered onto Dranae's broad back and nestled down in the valley between his shoulders. They roped themselves into the princes' harness and waved to their compatriots.

Will was glad the rope harness allowed him to crawl forward to where Dranae's neck joined his body. While the air was cold enough that Will couldn't remain there for very long, he got to watch the landscape below. He could see the way rivers flowed from mountains down to lakes or the sea. Forests spread over the hills and plains, save where men had chopped them back to feed fuel and building material into villages and cities.

And villages and cities were easy to spot because of the rising smoke. From most it was from cookfires, but the flight took them near enough to Caledo to see that part of the city was burning. He hoped Alexia, Kerrigan, Peri, and Sayce were still alive, and would be able to defeat the Aurolani or escape.

"Dranae, can't you go down there and kill the Aurolani before we go to Vael?"

"No, Will." The dragon hooked his neck back to watch him. "There is a chance I could be killed, and the DragonCrown fragment would then go over to Chytrine. More importantly, there is another dragon down there. My intervention could trigger a larger battle, which would be to Chytrine's benefit."

"The first reason I get, but not the other." Will shrugged.

"In due time, Will Norrington."

Night fell before they left Muroso. The thin sliver of moon complemented the stars and Will saw lots of them. He half expected Resolute to take the opportunity to drill him on how to navigate by the stars, but being aloft and surrounded by darkness seemed to take an edge off the Vorquelf.

He did point to one chain of stars. "That is the Flail of Raisasel. He was a grand elven hero, from Vorquellyn. Back then, Vorquellyn was just part of the elven holdings. Everything from Loquellyn to Croquellyn and Harquellyn were all part of one grand elven nation."

Will picked out the curvy line of seven stars. "What did Raisasel do?"

"He did many wonderful things, and the songs sung about his exploits are legion. He slew dragons and fought battles with the *kryalniri*—the real thing, not these ghosts Chytrine has created." Resolute actually smiled, and for half a second Will thought he might sing one of the songs of Raisasel.

Then the Vorquelf's eyes narrowed. "Songs to entertain children who never expected to have to fight."

The Panqui extended a claw, dug some flat white wormy thing from beneath a scale, and popped it into his mouth. "Lombo likes star-songs."

The thief smiled. "Do the Panqui have a song about Raisasel?"

"No flail. Seven sisters river floating." Lombo's grin revealed a small morsel of squirming worm. "Not child's song."

Erlestoke smiled. "In Oriosa, those are seven merchants and the moon is counted a thief. When it passes through them, it steals their light."

Crow nodded, then looked to Qwc. "What about the Spritha?"

"Spritha sing not of stars." He looked around at his companions. "Holes in the sun's hood, just holes. Why sing, why?"

"Dranae, do dragons sing of the stars?"

The dragon looked back. "People create stories about what they fear as a means to define and control the threat. Raisasel slew no dragons, but elves feel safer to think that one of their number did. Dragons have no fear of the stars because we know what they are."

Will frowned. "So do the Spritha, but I don't think they are holes in some hood the sun pulls on."

"No, Will. What would they be, then?"

He hesitated. "Well, I've not thought about it much, but they look like gems just scattered up there. If we could fly high enough, we could get them."

Dranae laughed and a tiny bit of flame jetted from his nostrils. "The Spritha are closer than you are, Will."

Crow smiled. "What are the stars then, Dranae, if that information can be shared?"

"Stars are just like the sun, but very far distant from here."

But that can't be. They're so small and the sun is so big. Will looked at Crow and Erlestoke, then the three of them broke out laughing. "No, Dranae, that can't be. Sparks from the sun maybe, but suns? Not possible."

Another fiery snort accompanied a smirk. "Doubtless you are right, Will."

As they flew west and south, the sky began to lighten in the east. The sun stole over the horizon, and long shadows began their retreat from its light. Will crawled back up to his vantage point, rolling onto his back to watch the dawn, then onto his belly to see their destination.

Vael sat in the southern portion of the Crescent Sea, due north of Gyrvir-gul and northwest of Vilwan. Thick jungles covered it so well that as night's veil was lifted, Will could still see very little. Occasionally a brilliantly colored flock of birds would rise, swirl above the leafy canopy, then descend and dis-appear again.

Several dark grey peaks thrust their way up through the vegetation wreathed by thin white clouds. The tallest sat in the middle of the island, but Dranae did not make for it. Instead, he flew toward the northern end and dipped down into the jungle. They drifted down into a misty valley with steep walls covered in mosses, and overgrown with deep green plants and vi-brant blossoms. Water poured down in frothy cataracts. At the far end of it, Dranae lifted his left wing, banked into a turn, then landed effortlessly on a greensward before the opening of a massive cave.

"We have arrived, my friends." Dranae lay down on his belly and extended his right forepaw to give them an easy way down to the ground. "Isn't it beau-tiful?"

Will was ready to agree with that assessment; the valley had been breath-taking. But Dranae was nodding toward the cavern mouth—which seemed only a cavern mouth, devoid of decoration.

"Am I missing something?" he whispered to Crow.

"If so, I am missing it as well, Will."

Dranae's eyes half lidded. "I had forgotten that you do not always see as I do." The dragon extended his neck, opened his jaws, and breathed out softly. His exhalation flowed like fog over the stone. Then color flowed into it, painting the rocks in soft, chalky layers. Blue rivulets flowed down, carving the rock, enlarging the opening. Watching the process was hypnotic. In bits and flashes plants grew up, blossomed and died, animals came and left in an eyeblink. Rocks shifted and melted until the present opening remained and the colors bled away.

Will blinked. "Wow. What was that?"

"A little dracomagick." Dranae canted his head slightly to the right. "Every event in the world produces echoes—not of sound, but resonations that travel in time. Dragons can see those vibrations and make sense of them. With some magick, we can provide them substance so that others can see. To me, when I land here, I see what you just saw, but on a larger scale. To me the cavern opens as if the rock were a curtain. It welcomes me home."

Crow nodded. "I can imagine that is indeed beautiful. I have a question, though. If what you say about actions creating resonances is true, then dragons have access to everything that is happening."

"Or ever has happened, since those resonances still flow through the world." Dranae nodded. "Your question is preface to wondering why, with such knowledge, we have not intervened before on behalf of Chytrine's enemies—even if just to inform them of what is happening elsewhere."

"You anticipate me well."

"Your question contains pieces of things that have long been debated. First, however, it is possible to use magick to kill resonances before they are born, or to alter others, so the information is not always reliable. Second, imagine hearing a hundred birds singing. How do you pick out the notes of one specific bird? And then expand that to all the notes ever sung by every bird that ever lived? How do you know which to listen to? Dragons may pick out a line or two to follow, but it is for their own purposes and amusements. As spying goes, we are hardly efficient."

Erlestoke smiled. "And Chytrine has her resonances damped?"

"So I have been told, yes." Dranae stretched and adjusted his wings, then lifted his right forepaw and gestured toward the mouth of the cave. "Welcome to my true home. As you welcomed me into your world, so I welcome you into mine."

Will led the way into the dim cave. Luminous lichen did provide some soft green light, reminding Will of Oracle's cave near Gyrvirgul. He wished Dranae would use more magick to reveal things, but even without it, the place was stunning. The pillars of stone had all shades of color streaming through them, and small creatures moved through the stalactites and stalagmites both. Will wished he could be looking everywhere all at once.

Crow grabbed the back of his jacket and yanked him back right before Will stepped off into an abyss. A wall of heat rose from the depths. Down there, moving slowly, molten lava with dark islands floating on it flowed toward the north. The islands broke apart and sank, with flames flaring here and there. Watching it was almost like watching the dracomagick at the entrance, and for the barest of moments Will just imagined what it would be like to see that river with the mystical layering.

"Watch where you're going, Will."

Dranae came up and lifted each one of them across. "Forgive me. I lose perspective of size sometimes."

They continued on, but Will lagged back to remain near Dranae. "That thing you did with the entrance. Does it work for other things?"

"An example, Will."

"Well..." The thief shifted his shoulders uneasily. "People?"

The dragon nodded sagely. "Living things, yes. Creatures are studied to determine things about them—feeding patterns, migrations, breeding habits..."

"Breeding habits?" Will blushed heavily. "Even *people*?"

"Yes, Will, though we find that about as interesting as you might find watching dogs mate."

"Oh, so you haven't..."

"No, Will." Dranae eyed him carefully as they moved into a tunnel that sloped downward and moved to the left. "You specifically were interested in seeing resonances of someone?"

The thief nodded. "I was wondering if, maybe, you could let me see my father from, you know, before he became one of *them*."

"Why?"

"Well, because, okay...Back in the mountains I saw Crow with his brother, and despite all that's been done to Sallitt, they looked a bit alike. And Erlestoke and his brother, I could see the family ties there, too. And I guess I know my father used to make rhymes, the way I do sometimes. I know he's my father and all, but I can't *see* it."

"If I were to do that for you, Will, you would have to realize two things. The first is that it wouldn't be a seeing-thinking model of your father. You'd be watching him as if he was a ghost. He wouldn't see you. He wouldn't talk to you."

"Okay, I guess." Will shrugged. "What else?"

"He could end up *haunting* you."

"Haunting? Like a ghost?"

"Precisely."

"Wow." Will tried to remember if he'd ever seen a ghost or not, but didn't think he had. The prospect of having his own personal ghost made the hair stand up on the back of his neck, but he decided to chance it. "I'm still willing to try."

"Then I will perform that service for you, gladly." Dranae paused beside the company as they waited in a large, round intersection. "We will go left here, to my family chambers. You will rest while I report to my masters, then we will see to your needs until you are summoned before the Congress."

Erlestoke's lips pressed together. "Congress?"

"Our ruling council." Dranae's mouth opened slightly. "It is they who will decide if we will oppose Chytrine, or enter this war on her behalf."

CHAPTER 71

Will really got no sleep. When they reached Dranae's family holdings, a number of dracomorphs guided them to guest chambers that were located off a central antechamber. To everyone's great surprise, they found Princess Alexia waiting there for them. Crow shouldered past Will and swept her up into his arms, hugging her tightly. Her arms went round his shoulders and she hung on as he spun her around. He couldn't hear what they were saying to each other, but the smiles told him it must have been good.

The rest of them all turned away, letting their gear slip from shoulders. Will wanted to pepper the princess with questions about how she'd gotten there, but a quick look from Resolute kept him quiet. He grabbed his stuff up and carried it to one of the doorways off the antechamber.

By the time he returned, Crow had released his hold on the princess, though he still had his arm slid around her back. She smiled broadly, greeting everyone and even letting Qwc settle onto her right shoulder. Quickly enough she told them about the battle before Navval and how she had come to join Kerrigan at Vael.

Will clapped his hands. "Princess, that was nothing compared to what Dranae did. He *killed* another dragon, just took a big bite out of him. You see, we were..."

Erlestoke rested a hand on Will's shoulder. "There will be time for that story later, Will. I think we all need some rest."

"No, I'm fine, really."

Resolute cleared his throat. "Will, we all need to go lie down for a bit and collect ourselves."

"Oh, right." Will nodded, finally comprehending. "Okay, well, I'm just going to go to that room over there. If anyone wants to hear the story or anything, that's where I'll be."

Alexia nodded. "Sleep well, Will. It warms my heart to see you again."

"Mine, too, Princess." He wandered to his room and sighed. Everything had been scaled to dracomorphs, so to get into the bed, Will had to climb up the foot, then launch himself onto it. He landed in a thick down mattress that almost swallowed him.

Will lay there in the big bed and suddenly felt very alone. The look in Alexia's eyes when she saw Crow was the same look he remembered from Sayce's eyes. *I wish Sayce had come with her, too.*

That realization surprised him. Growing up as he had in the Dim, love was something that happened only in songs. He'd seen a lot of lust in his time—his mother had made her money on her back. The liftskirt trade was a staple of the Dim, but certainly couldn't be mistaken for love. And families— which he didn't really know, other than by observation—often seemed to be together because it was easier to survive that way than if they were apart. Marcus and Fabia certainly had that sort of relationship.

In songs, of course, love was something of burning intensity. It was fated; recognized instantly. What he felt for Sayce hadn't been fated or recognized instantly. He'd begun, slowly, to enjoy her company. And when he was saying good-bye to her—even with the reservations he'd expressed to Alexia—he really didn't want to say good-bye.

When he did get to sleep, he dreamed of her. He saw her and Peri in the forests of Muroso, hunting gibberers. They were driving the enemy before them and out of Muroso. As the two of them watched the Aurolani troops flee, he awoke smiling.

Will dragged himself out of bed and pulled on his clothes. He left his coat off, as he didn't feel that chilly in Vael. In some ways the heart of the mountain felt like home to him and he began to explore. He didn't get far, though, before a dracomorph found him and agreed to conduct him to Dravothrak.

Dravothrak lay resting in a large, domed chamber. He opened a blue eye and his head came up. "You do not look rested."

"I couldn't sleep much." Will shrugged. "I was wondering if you could..."

"I believe I can. While I rested here I sifted through impressions and I believe I have found him—a piece of him anyway." Dravothrak motioned him closer. "Will Norrington, meet your father, Bosleigh Norrington."

The dragon's breath blew soft and cold, congealing into a translucent shape. Edges took on hints of white and slowly filled in, revealing a young man a bit taller than Will, but not much heavier. He had an open face and slight smile. He paced, looking through Will, moving toward him, with one hand on his chin and the other behind his back.

Will stepped away from the ghost's line of march and heard his father's voice. "Yes, yes, those lines will do. It will be a grand poem. I'll call it 'How to Vex a Temeryx.'

> *"How to vex a temeryx,*
>   *It's not easy, no*
> *Temeryces, if you please,*
>   *Live in ice and snow.*
>
> *Build a fire, perhaps a pyre,*
>   *To warm its darkling heart.*
> *Or with a knife, take its life.*
>   *Hitch it to a cart.*
>
> *Into its tail drive a nail,*
>   *Or perhaps a spear.*
> *Fill its head with boiling lead,*
>   *That will inspire fear.*
>
> *On a bet, use a stout net,*
>   *Bind it up all nice.*
> *Using a mace, strike its face,*
>   *More than once, try twice.*
>
> *With a snare you trap a pair,*
>   *Feed one to the other.*
> *Stuff its nose with dirty hose,*
>   *And then let it smother.*
>
> *With a rope, cut off all hope,*
>   *Tie it to the floor.*
> *Feed it lice, perhaps some mice,*
>   *Make it beg for more.*
>
> *You may vex a temeryx,*
>   *If stout of heart are thee.*
> *But take care, for if you err,*
>   *its luncheon will you be."*

Will laughed aloud. "Again. I want to hear it again."

Dravothrak smiled. "That might be beyond my control. I can try, but what I would have to do to the magick could make him remain with you. Right now I can dismiss him, but I might not be able to later. Do you want to risk that?"

"Sure, what could it hurt?" The thief smiled, his eyes sparkling as he watched his father move. A happiness showed on his face, beneath the mask he wore. Will did read a hint of arrogance there; still, this was his father, and not the thing Chytrine had turned him into.

Dravothrak blew again. The figure froze, then began pacing once more. Leigh Norrington repeated the poem, then began the cycle all over. Will concentrated and by the fourth recitation had the whole thing memorized. By the fifth he was beginning to tire of it, so he waved his hand in front of his father's ghost.

"Enough, already."

The ghost walked toward him and Will's hand passed straight through him. A chill ran through the thief, then the ghost vanished. "What happened?"

Dravothrak laughed. "It's your blood. He's there, behind you. No matter how fast you turn around, you won't see him, but he's there. Nothing to worry about. He should fade in a day or two. Until then..."

"I'm haunted; I know." Will shrugged and closed his eyes. He brought his father's face to mind and heard his voice again. He could see himself in those features and catch elements of his voice in his father's. Connections began to form.

Prior to that, he had been the Norrington because he had been told he was. Oracle told him, and used magick to prove it. Chytrine trying to kill him, Crow and Resolute finding him, Sayce seeking him out, even Scrainwood giving him a mask, all of those things were external signs that he was the Norrington. And Will had accepted that mantle because it was a responsibility he could shoulder.

Until that moment, however, he'd never truly believed he was the Norrington. He was willing to play the part, and he'd done it well. Seeing his father, though, hearing his voice, confirmed the Norrington Prophecy. Not only did he accept the job, but he now knew he was *meant* to have it. He *was* the fulfillment of the prophecy.

He opened his eyes and felt cold for a moment, then looked at Dravothrak. "Thank you."

"It was nothing."

"No, it was everything." Will smiled and laid his hand on one of Dravothrak's toes. "I *am* the Norrington. I will redeem Vorquellyn and I'll kill the scourge of the north."

"Yes, the prophecy." Dravothrak's voice hummed with power, sending vibrations through Will's chest.

> *A Norrington to lead them,*
> *Immortal, washed in fire*
> *Victorious, from sea to ice.*

Power of the north he will shatter,
A scourge he will kill,
Then Vorquellyn will redeem.

The thief smiled. "It sounds much more powerful when you say it."

"The power comes not from me, but from the prophecy itself, and the people it has drawn to its fulfillment."

Will nodded. "Well, I was pulled out of a burning building as a child, and the raid on Wruona would be our victory at sea. I guess I just have to lead folks north to the ice, to defeat Chytrine, and then we can redeem Vorquellyn."

The dragon's head rose, towering over Will. "The work of a lifetime. Even a dragon's lifetime." Dravothrak looked past him, then hissed.

Will turned and a dracomorph stood there, with his head bent forward. He hissed back at Dravothrak, but in a very polite manner. A returning hiss brought the dracomorph upright again and he waited.

Dravothrak spoke from behind him. "Will, please accompany this small one to the Congress Chamber. The others will join you there, including Kerrigan. I must travel another route and take my place in the Congress."

Will craned his neck back. "What will we be doing?"

"Answer questions as they are asked. Just answer truthfully and all will go well. Chytrine has few friends in the Congress, and even they suspect her motives. If we succeed, you will have allies in your war against her."

"They'll be welcome." Will nodded. "Thank you again."

"It was my pleasure, Wilburforce Norrington."

Will wandered from the chamber in the wake of the dracomorph but did not wonder at Dravothrak's full use of his name. He did want to turn and ask the shade following him if he had chosen such a horrid name for him, but he wasn't sure he'd get an answer. Given that his father had gotten him on a whore during a drunken binge in Alcida, he wasn't sure his father had known he'd been conceived, much less had anything to do with naming him.

Besides, his father then and his father now weren't the same person as the shade. The shade was happy and free. None of the tragedy that had shaped his life showed at all. The poem he recited was fun and playful, and Will imagined him that way. *That's what I got from him. That's the foundation that makes me the Norrington.*

The dracomorph led him to a semicircular shelf of stone that jutted out into a lake of fire. Will walked up to the edge and saw a line of runes ringing it. He couldn't read them, but he could feel power humming off them. He looked past them and at the way the heat from the fiery lake made images shift. Will breathed out as Dranae had at the cavern entrance and saw his breath mist briefly in the invisible barrier holding the heat back.

He smiled, then looked past the edge and deeper into the lake. There, at various points—on tall, flat rocks, tall towers, and niches carved in the far walls—he saw dragons. Lots of dragons, and some of them were looking at him. In the distance, he saw Dravothrak settle into place, but he held back from waving.

Qwc zipped past him and, for a heartbeat, Will thought he was going to sail through the barrier. "Qwc, be careful!"

The Spritha stopped short of the wall, then turned. "Hot, hot, Qwc knows. Very hot."

"Yeah, really, really hot." Will winked at him, then turned and smiled as the others joined him. "I was talking to Dravothrak. As soon as Kerrigan gets here, we're supposed to answer questions when they are asked of us. If we do things right, we might get help against Chytrine."

Crow stared at him and paled. "Will, what is that thing behind you?"

"You should recognize him. He's my father. Dravothrak made him appear. He'll go away soon, but I heard him recite his poem 'How to Vex a Temeryx.' "

The older man shivered, then shook his head and chuckled. "That was going to be Leigh's most magnificent poem. I'd love to hear you recite it, Will."

"Sure, tonight, after all this is over. It'll be fun." Will let his voice sink. "Sorry if seeing him was unsettling. I just needed to prove that I am *the* Norrington."

Alexia raised an eyebrow. "Was that ever in doubt, really?"

Will shrugged. "Never hurts to have more proof?"

Crow patted him on the shoulder. "None of us has ever doubted it, Will. You've proved it over and over again." He looked past Will and at the dragons. "And here you'll have a chance to prove it yet one more time."

CHAPTER 72

Despite his having dozed on Vriisureol's back as they flew to Vael, Kerrigan hardly felt rested upon his arrival. Two of the ten-foot-tall dracomorphs guided him and Bok to the chambers they would occupy. The cozy suite reminded him of an urZrethi *coric,* though it had been built to more human proportions and had only three rooms off the main chamber. He occupied one, and Bok took another.

Kerrigan was uncertain how long he had slept, but the scent in his nose and the rumble in his belly seemed to decide between them it was more than long enough. Out of the clothing Bok had unpacked and laid on a shelf, he pulled a tunic and trousers, then stamped his feet into worn boots. He knew he looked nothing like a mage, but that didn't matter to him. He was hungry.

Still, the ease with which he shed his concern about what was proper raiment for a mage, and the distance he felt between himself and Vilwan, marked how much his experiences had changed him. Some of it, he knew, was the fellowship he felt with Will, Alexia, and the others. He was more a part of their group than he was a citizen of Vilwan. On Vilwan he had been a thing to be trained, a weapon to be honed—though exactly for what purpose no one ever bothered to tell him. *But, then, Crow does not tell his sword what he intends to do with it.* To his friends he was more than an object, and to him they were more than dulls who had to be tolerated.

Another piece of it was because of the revelations Rym Ramoch had made about Vilwan and the nature of magick. He'd seen more of that in Muroso. Vilwan was not the wellspring of all magickal knowledge. Even the Conservatory in Aurolan had found other ways of approaching things. That all made sense in a way it never had before. Kerrigan never would have supposed there was only one way to make a chair, or only one thing that would function as a chair, so why would the same be expected of a spell? *There are many paths to the same result.*

In a very short time, he'd learned more about magick and how to handle it than he had after years at Vilwan. Granted, his training on Vilwan had made him able to see and master these new things, but Vilwan's encouragement of inefficiency struck him as totally wrong. They did that so mages would be less powerful and easier to control, but in making them so, Vilwan made them less able to deal with a mage who might actually be more efficient.

He wondered for a moment if that was what Kirûn had seen. But the simple fact was that Kerrigan now could do more than any of his contemporaries, and he had a working spell that could detect the presence of DragonCrown fragments. With that spell, he could help undo what Kirûn had done so long ago.

Smiling, he shoved himself off his bed and wandered out into the main chamber. There he found a round table set with a steaming ham, fresh bread, cheeses, vegetables in sauces, and a host of other things that he did not recognize per se. It all smelled delicious and his mouth watered before he could even dream of where he would start.

All of that quickly went by the board, however, when he saw Rym Ramoch emerging from the suite's third room. "Master, when did you get here?"

"It seems as if I've been here forever, Kerrigan."

"*How* did you get here?"

Ramoch laughed. "Vriisureol is not the only dragon on Vael, you know."

Kerrigan nodded, and waited for his master to take a seat at the table. Ramoch strode to the far side, drew the chair back, and sat. He seemed a bit more animated than in the past, but the excitement of being in Vael could easily explain that. The crimson-robed mage waved Kerrigan to his chair, and Bok appeared from beneath the table to slide a heavily laden plate in front of him.

The young mage looked down at it. He couldn't tell if it had been picked over or not, but the rumble in his stomach told him that it really didn't matter. He smiled, forked a small strip of ham into his mouth, then closed his eyes and moaned. "Very good."

"Good, good. The thralls do as they are told, but one does not always know if they understand the orders they have been given." Ramoch nodded slowly. "Your work on the detection spell, and your actions at Navval, were impressive. You amaze me."

Kerrigan smiled, and in between mouthfuls explained a lot of what he had done. In fact he became so engrossed in the discussion that he left off eating entirely, shoving the gold plate aside so he could lean his elbows on the table as he pondered the many questions Ramoch asked.

The questions were not easy, but Kerrigan tackled each one happily. He realized that he'd greatly enjoyed fashioning the spells, and that he'd been happy they had worked. But here, for the first time in forever, he had someone with whom he could discuss his work. Rym Ramoch understood what he had been trying to do. His previous mentors, save Orla, had only been interested in making sure he mastered whatever they were teaching him. While some casual conversations might nibble at the edges of the theoretical, most of his mentors failed to have a broad grasp of magick. They knew their specialized areas, but without a generalist's grasp of things, they had no hope of understanding the connections between the underpinnings of the various disciplines.

He remembered how Orla had seemed surprised when he re-created for her the staff she'd lost. He'd used wood as a raw material and woven several different spells together to get it right. For him it had been effortless. It was a spell he'd created so he could replace things he'd broken, but to her it was a minor miracle. Ramoch, while he might be impressed with the spell, was capable of understanding *how* Kerrigan did what he did.

Their discussions continued through the morning and past lunch. Kerrigan picked at food as they talked and noticed things disappearing beneath the table from time to time. Bok's rolling burps confirmed where these items had gone. Ramoch ate nothing, but Kerrigan did not find that terribly remarkable since the man still wore his mask and was thin enough that he probably didn't eat more than once a month.

In the middle of the afternoon, a dracomorph with ivory scales and red dots over breast and back came and spoke to Ramoch in hisses and snaps— all quite respectful-sounding. The mage nodded, then shooed the creature away with a gloved hand. "We have been summoned, but we have some time before our appointment. I would show you some of Vael, if you wish."

"I'd like that. I think Princess Alexia would, too. Shouldn't we get her?"

Ramoch pressed his fingertips together. "She is otherwise occupied, I'm afraid. Much of your company from Meredo arrived this morning before you wakened. You'll see them soon enough, but the princess joined them straight away."

Kerrigan smiled. "Will and everyone else?"

"Yes, including Dranae. He is a dragon."

"A dragon!" The young mage thought for a moment. "Was he the one who healed Will?"

"Partly, I believe. There were likely other influences." Ramoch stood and smoothed his robe. "We shall investigate properly later. First, I want you to see some of Vael. Come, Bok."

The urZrethi slid from beneath the table and followed the two of them out of the suite. They exited onto a path perhaps ten feet wide, with columns of stone spaced every dozen feet or so. On the right side the wall was solid, but on the left, it was open to a large gallery. Kerrigan could see other walkways as small as this one, then much larger ones below. The walkways themselves, while smooth, dipped and climbed like termite trails in wood.

Ramoch led the young mage along. "These pathways were built for the thralls and dracomorphs. They are, in essence, servants' corridors—though they serve humans quite well. I hope you are not offended."

"No, Master."

Ramoch nodded. "You know, of course, that dragons and the urZrethi are enemies. The urZrethi raise great mountains, then dragons dispossess them of their hard work. Vael itself was once a much larger place. Alcida never had a coast and the urZrethi home bordered Loquellyn. In ancient times, the dragons and urZrethi fought a grand war over it. When the dragons destroyed it, all but Vael sank."

Kerrigan glanced at Bok. "Is he safe here?"

"Bok? Yes. He is known to be my companion, so my friends are his friends. You are under similar protection." Ramoch opened his hands. "You have seen Bokagul, so you can imagine what the grand halls of Vareshagul must have been like. Alas, no more. Since it was lost, no urZrethi construction has risen so high, nor been so ambitious."

The young mage puffed his way up an incline. "Why did the dragons destroy Vareshagul?"

Ramoch shrugged. "Who knows the mind of dragons? It could be they thought this would be a wonderful place to live. Or some of the more sinister tales could be true."

"Such as?"

Bok hissed.

Ramoch petted the urZrethi's head. "Dragons have been around since the founding of the world. There are legends that suggest they fought a war with other creatures, which were even more terrible than they. The dragons won and forced those things deep into the bowels of the earth, imprisoning them and their evil. Those creatures created the urZrethi to raise mountains and dig deep enough to release them."

"Who, then, created elves and men and the other races?"

Ramoch looked at him slowly. "These are all legends, Kerrigan. The source of the conflict between dragons and urZrethi is hidden in the mists of antiquity. It is just important to know the conflict exists. Origins that distant mean nothing today."

"But if we knew how it started, there might be a way to establish peace."

Ramoch laughed. "Eliminate Chytrine and you might be able to accomplish the impossible and establish peace between the urZrethi and dragons. But first things first."

The three of them moved through Vael at a leisurely pace, but always down and deeper. Kerrigan looked for hints of what had once been urZrethi construction, but it eluded him. Everything appeared to be natural stone, despite the fact it clearly had been shaped. The columns were spaced so evenly that nature could not have played a part, which meant magick had been used to guide things. Even so, he did not get the impression it had been done hastily. Instead, he imagined spells that would allow the stone to flow naturally, building the columns. It would take lifetimes, he calculated, then amended his thought. *Human lifetimes.*

For a dragon, that would be nothing.

Finally, Ramoch led him into a chamber so enormous, it was beyond his ability to truly grasp. It could have housed all of Navval, and perhaps even Caledo and Lake Calessa. In fact, the chamber had a lake of molten rock as its basis. The edge of the rock shelf onto which Kerrigan emerged had been worked with odd sigils in an arc. They pulsed with power and he assumed they were what prevented those standing on the shelf from bursting into flame. Above the lake, a huge stone arch held the chamber's roof in place.

The lake itself had a number of tall stone formations with craggy sides that rose like flattopped mountains. Elsewhere, cut into the rock walls were other perches, large and small. The ones above the shelf remained empty, but those on the lake and surrounding it had dragons sitting or lying on them. Dragons of every size and color were present. Some were missing toes or eyes, others had broken horns and tails and jagged scars devoid of scales. Kerrigan noticed some appeared to be asleep, and one or two, he could have sworn, were actually just stone statues tucked into a niche.

Kerrigan took all that in before the shouts of others brought him back to the world. Lombo scrambled over, and Qwc circled him happily, then returned to a place at the apex of the shelf's curve. Alexia was there with Crow, both of them looking very happy. He recognized Prince Erlestoke of Oriosa, and saw he was carrying a fragment of the DragonCrown. Resolute stood beside him and had a hand resting on the hilt of his sword.

Kerrigan smiled and waved, scratching Lombo behind an ear. Seeing them all made his heart swell. Throughout his life he had always felt he was an outsider, but these people accepted him and even liked him. He saw the joy he felt reflected on their faces, and that made him happier yet.

Will, bright-eyed, came running over as Lombo withdrew. "Kerrigan, have you seen this place? It's huge, like Bokagul, but huger!"

"I know. My master was giving me a tour." Kerrigan looked hard at Will, for the ghostly shape of a man was clinging to him like a shadow. "Will, what is...?"

"That?" Will jerked a thumb over his shoulder. "A thing Dranae did with dracomagick. He's a dragon, you know. He's the one who healed me, using dracomagick; that's why your spells didn't quite figure out what was going on. He's called Dravothrak here. That's him, the big green one, right over there."

Kerrigan nodded, but the green dragon gave no sign he'd seen him.

Rym Ramoch took a step toward Will, then looked over at Dravothrak. "Dravothrak, have you any idea what you have done?"

The green's head came up, but the ghostly form flowed from behind Will to eclipse the dragon. The phantom went from translucent white to black, fire erupting from its eye sockets. *I've seen him before!* Ice flushed through Kerrigan's guts. *That is Nefrai-laysh!*

Nefrai-laysh's left hand darted forward, fingers stiffened into a blade. He plunged his hands into Rym Ramoch's chest with a great snapping sound and the tearing of cloth. As the *sullanciri* ripped his hand free, the sorcerer collapsed on the ground, his arms and legs twisted unnaturally. Worse yet, the hole in his chest let Kerrigan see that Ramoch was nothing more than a huge wooden doll. The mask had been knocked askew when he fell, revealing a blank face.

The *sullanciri* danced back, holding aloft a glowing ruby stone. It pulsed with life strong enough to radiate light through Nefrai-laysh's black flesh, outlining his bones. The *sullanciri* gathered his feet beneath him, then leaped back and away from the crowd, landing gracefully on one of the flat perches above the shelf.

"Hark unto me, dragonkind; my mistress would have you know her mind. Things here, you will debate, and your decision rests much on fate." Chytrine's herald laughed aloud. "Discuss as you must, discuss as you will. Discuss wisely and I won't have to kill. Listen to them, listen to me, then the world's fate decided shall be."

CHAPTER 73

Nefrai-laysh spoke in a dismal rhyme, but Will barely heard his words. He looked from the broken manikin and up at Kerrigan's face. Shock and betrayal dragged at the mage's cheeks, and they drained of color. His eyes began to glaze over, but Will grabbed two fistfuls of his tunic. "I'm sorry, Kerrigan, I'm sorry, but I need you here. This is bad and we have to fix it."

Bok reached out, his arm transforming, and swept Will away. The thief spun and fell, landing on his butt not ten feet away from Qwc. As his head came up, he saw Nefrai-laysh on the shelf. His form had become completely black save for the fire burning in his eye sockets and his flaming cloak. He held the glowing gem aloft as if he were going to throw it down and dash it into a million pieces.

A large dragon, with dark blue scales striped with lighter blue, shifted on his stone pedestal. "This Congress would accept testimony from a representative of the court of Aurolan. You need not threaten Rymramoch that way."

"Alas, parity with them I desire, those before the lake of fire." The *sullanciri* pointed at Erlestoke. "A Truestone has he, so even are we."

The blue tilted its head to the right. "We would treat you with equanimity regardless. You are all guests here, and are bound by the Peace of our Congress. Violence one upon the other is not permitted. Violate the peace and earn our ire."

Crow pointed to the broken puppet. "This was not violence?"

Another dragon, this one a mottled grey with one broken horn, pointed its muzzle toward a dragon resting in a niche. The one he indicated had red scales, but their color was muted, as if it lay beneath an inch of dust.

"Rymramoch is not a guest and Rymramoch put Rymramoch in jeopardy. Foolishness paid is foolishness bought."

Dravothrak spoke. "And totally beside the point. I was sent to travel among men and so I have. We have been told that men mean to collect the Truestones and re-create the Crown to force us to abandon our duty. That is not true. They have held the pieces apart to prevent Chytrine from re-creating the Crown and using it to destroy all that lives."

The grey snorted two jets of flame. "There is a problem with the extermination of men? We created the Panqui to keep men away from our homes, but they still encroach. Chytrine does us a minor service in pursuit of a greater one."

A black dragon with red stripes spoke, and Will realized two things. The first was that he'd seen that dragon before, at Vilwan. The second was that the wall between him and the lake not only served to keep the heat out, but was functioning to translate the hissing of dragons into words they could understand. *I wonder if Resolute hears them speaking Elvish?*

Vriisureol's voice rumbled through the invisible wall. "For how long does she serve us? Now she offers to be our ally. She uses the Truestones in her possession to summon some, then lets them offer her their service. She has enslaved no one, but will this always be the way?"

The blue replied. "The Crown is ever a threat as long as it exists. Chytrine says that when she gets all the pieces and fits them together, she will unmake the Crown, freeing the Truestones and us of their tyranny forever. She *is* gathering them for this purpose."

"Yes, yes, that is right. She gathers them with all her might, facing death and mankind's spite." Nefrai-laysh pointed at Erlestoke. "His stone, give it to me. I'll bear it to her, you see."

Resolute drew Syverce. "It will be your death to take that stone."

"You're part of the plot, deny it not, Resolute so bold." The fire in the *sullanciri*'s eyes flared. "Soon not to be bolder, not to be older, but just very much cold."

The blue's nostrils flared as gold flame licked from them. "Do not use that sword, elf, or it's not cold you'll be."

Resolute glared at the dragon, but did not return Syverce to its scabbard.

Will picked himself up off the shelf and stared at the blue. "I'd like to be heard. I don't know if it helps that I've got dragon's blood in me, or that I've bled on the Truestone the prince carries, but I think there's a way you can see the truth of things pretty easily."

The blue's head oriented on Will. "Pray, tell us."

"Well, it's like this: I'm a thief. If I'm going to steal things, I figure out where they are and then I go after them. Now, Chytrine took Vorquellyn a long time ago. Maybe there was a stone there, maybe there wasn't, but she stayed there after she took it. And then, twenty-five years ago, she tried to take pieces from Fortress Draconis, but she didn't. Still, she had forces far south of it, and my father knows that, because he made up a poem about fighting them long before he saw a Truestone."

The *sullanciri* hissed. "Tell your lies, you who was whelped 'tween poxed thighs."

Will snorted. "You were there before I was."

Fire shot in jets from Nefrai-laysh's eyes, but he remained silent.

The thief continued. "And then she went to Fortress Draconis and sent folks to Lakaslin to get fragments. She got one from Fortress Draconis, the prince has a second, and a third is hidden. And the one from Lakaslin is hidden. But, still, her troops are heading south even though she doesn't know where the pieces are."

The grey snarled. "Is there a purpose to your recitation?"

"Well, it's this. If she wanted the fragments—if that's what she's been going after—she'd be stopping when she knows she can't find them. But instead, her troops continue south." He pointed at his father. "And you already know she enslaves people and makes them do her bidding. If you look at what she does, not what she says, I would be thinking you don't want her to have that Crown any more than we do."

The blue considered things for a moment. "Your point is taken. The request for possession of the Truestone is denied."

The *sullanciri* raged. "Hear my plea, do not fools be! They come here in heroes' guise, concealing venom in honeyed lies. It is plain to see, they are no friends to thee. But mistress mine, the magnificent Chytrine, has your best interest at heart. Keep not the crown apart. Give us the stone, merely a loan. Then with four, she will gain more. Her goal will be at hand. Dragons will rule the land."

Will blinked. "Four? Four? She has two, this would make three." He looked at Crow. "The ruby! We left it with Scrainwood. He wouldn't!"

"Not if we stop him."

The thief turned back to the blue. "Get us to Meredo, and we'll bring that fourth stone here. You can keep it, along with this one. That way you'll know it will be safe." Will smiled. "In fact, if Chytrine really had your best interests at heart, she'd bring *all* the fragments here and let you keep them."

The grey snorted two gouts of flame. "The thief uses wormwords to convince us to gather the stones in one place so he can steal them."

Will's head came up. "I'm very good, but I know I couldn't get them out of here. Neither could Chytrine."

The blue looked at Nefrai-laysh. "You will convey to your mistress our desire to have her deliver her Truestones here."

The *sullanciri* laughed aloud. "You have no grounds; you overstep your bounds. Your request she does deny." With his right hand he reached behind himself and circled a finger through the air. An oval hole opened in nothingness. "You have earned her ire, and in consequence dire, one of you must die."

Nefrai-laysh drew back his left hand to throw the ruby stone. As his arm came forward, he jerked. A spear passed through his body, lancing down from left armpit to right hip. The haft caught his arm, abbreviating his throw. Instead of the Truestone flying straight out into the heart of the fiery lake, it spun end over end in a long, high arc.

Will watched it fly. He watched it spin and began to run. Light flashed from the heart of the stone as it tumbled, falling faster and faster. Will measured the arc, reckoned where the stone would land, and dove.

His fingers closed on the stone's smooth surface. His body twisted. He threw the stone back toward the shelf and saw it was going to fly true.

"Qwc, get it!"

As Will's body passed through the magick wall, he saw the Spritha dart for the stone. The little creature wrapped all four arms around it and hung on tightly.

Then the heat hit Will and he was no more.

CHAPTER 74

The appearance of the *sullanciri,* the revelation of Rym Ramoch as a puppet, the spear, the sharp war cry of a furious Gyrkyme, the ruby's glittering arc as it spun through the air, and Will's dive all left Kerrigan stunned mindless. He saw Will grab the Truestone, spin, and throw it. His eyes followed the stone's arc and saw the Spritha's flight intersect it. He only caught the explosion of flame in the corner of his eye.

He couldn't look. He couldn't confirm that the new fire in that lake was Will. He opened his mouth to shout, to scream, to do anything, but he couldn't breathe.

Then he saw Qwc flailing and falling. Kerrigan's left hand went out and triggered a spell. He caught the Spritha softly, then whisked him over to Alexia, redoubling the spell to restrain her from lunging after Will.

Back above him, on the ledge, Nefrai-laysh snarled in anger. "Oh, you can all be dragon-hearted, but my wrath shall not be thwarted!" He gestured with his right hand, and from it burst a golden sphere the size of a ripe melon with little tendrils of golden lightning racing around its surface. It shot forward, piercing the wall, and veered straight for the blue.

The blue snorted, and a magickal shield smashed the spell away toward the grey. With a flick of a claw, the grey sent it spinning farther into the Congress Chamber. The dragons, like adults marveling at a child's invention, invoked spells to send the *sullanciri*'s attack skittering between them. The spell lost none of its lethal fury, but this seemed only to amuse the dragons.

Lombo let go of an explosive roar and charged the cliff beneath Nefrai-laysh. In two huge bounds he reached it, then scaled it fast and furiously. The *sullanciri* half turned to face the Panqui, but the haft of the spear caught on the edge of the magickal doorway. A spell began to gather in his right hand, but before Nefrai-laysh could finish the casting, Lombo tackled him, sinking fangs into his left shoulder. Both of them tumbled into the portal, which snapped shut, trimming head and butt from the spear, and shaving a tuft of black hair from the tip of Lombo's tail.

The *sullanciri*'s disappearance did not affect the spell, which the dragons still batted back and forth. Then the golden orb swerved straight up, slamming hard into the apex of the roof arch and spitting rock everywhere. It burned its way up higher, golden sparks drizzling down through the hole. Then a huge gout of red-gold fire shot down and touched the surface of the lake. The spell's detonation shook the entire mountain, spilling everyone to the landing save for Crow and Alexia, who cradled Qwc between them.

Above the dragons, red cracks spiderwebbed through the ceiling. Chunks of stone began to fall, splashing into the molten lake. Hot rock splattered the shielding spell and dripped down like rain. Some stones crashed into the rocky pedestals, and one dragon spilled from his perch. His scrabbling claws gouged stone, but they found no purchase and he pitched screaming into the liquid rock.

His screams defied translation, yet their meaning could not be mistaken.

Dragons breathed and gestured. Wave after wave of magick flowed out and up, bolstering the roof, but rock still fell. Tremors shook the ground. The entire mountain was coming down and, as powerful as the dragons and their magick were, not even they could prevent that.

"Kerrigan!"

The mage looked over at Crow. The man had drawn his sword and stood over Alexia. Kerrigan shook his head. "I can't do anything! The whole mountain is falling in."

Crow pointed his sword toward the hole the *sullanciri*'s spell had created. "Get this sword in there. Now!" He tossed the blade into the air. "Go, Tsamoc. The promise will be completed!"

Kerrigan reached out with a spell and plucked the sword from the air. He drove it past the shield and saw the metal begin to glow. The gem set in the forte was also glowing, with opalescent highlights pulsing. It almost seemed as if the gem was shifting and melting, for the closer it got to the hole, the larger and more solid its light appeared.

As the blade ascended into the hole, the gem exploded into a round, flat disk, then it curved down into a milk-white bowl alive with flashing lights. In places, the bowl twisted as more rock fell, but no stone pierced it. Then the bowl expanded, pressing up against the shattered ceiling.

The light bled up into the mountain, leaving the chamber as dark. Above, the rumbling ceased and the earth stilled itself. Then the light reappeared, pouring down through the central hole. Eight luminescent lines shot out. Two ran down the original arch, while the other six ran at angles to it. Rock cracked ahead of them, as if they were plows splitting crusty earth, then stone oozed out through the furrows. It swelled like rising bread, then solidified.

Four gleaming opal arches now supported the Congress Chamber's vaulted ceiling. And there, at their heart, an angular, eight-sided cone of rock pointed down. In it, Kerrigan saw something moving, something vaguely manlike.

He shook his head. "What was that?"

Crow swallowed hard and swiped a tear from his left cheek. "The *weirun* of a bridge in Okrannel. It destroyed itself to stop Chytrine's marauders, but only after we promised to let it fight against her. A friend bound it into my sword, and we did wonderful things together. This, however, is what it was meant for."

Peri landed next to Alexia. "Are you all right, sister?"

"I'm not hurt." Alexia's face came up, with tears etched in red reflections on her cheeks. "But, Will . . ."

Kerrigan looked over at where Will had gone through the wall. *Where he went into the lake.* "He's gone. Just gone."

Rym Ramoch's wooden limbs clattered as Bok collected the Truestone from Qwc and stuffed it back into his chest. The puppet clambered upright, but made no attempt to adjust the mask. The left-hand glove had come off, exposing the hand as wooden bits linked by spring-and-leather joints.

"Yes, Kerrigan Reese, your friend is gone. His sacrifice, however, will not be forgotten."

Erlestoke dusted his hands off. "It best not be. If this has not shown you how little Chytrine can be trusted, then you walk blindly into the doom she'll bring you."

The grey, settled again on his pedestal, snorted. "We *walk* nowhere."

"Fly, then, and the quicker into doom for it." Erlestoke shrugged off the harness with the DragonCrown fragment. "As Will said, I'll leave this piece here, to show you we have no desire to re-create the Crown."

The blue's azure eyes half closed. "Pity, for only by bringing all the parts together can the Crown finally be split asunder. When it was created, we were complicit in its making. At that time it seemed wise, but events conspired to make us question that wisdom."

Alexia stood. "If that is true, why haven't you collected the pieces?"

Rym opened his arms. "Complications, Princess. We knew where five of the Truestones were, as you did. Three in Fortress Draconis, one in Okrannel, and one in Jerana. There had been one on Vorquellyn, but it is lost. Of the seventh, we have no report. Without being guaranteed success in gathering them all, we chose to wait. In our reckoning, it has not been that long."

Erlestoke frowned. "My original point stands, however. You now know that Chytrine cannot be trusted. You should help us gather all the fragments together and stop her."

The grey curled a lip back. "Chytrine cannot be held responsible for the actions of a subordinate, especially since he was attacked here. That was a violation of our peace."

Crow arched an eyebrow. "But Nefrai-laysh was in the act of attacking Rymramoch."

The puppet held up a hand. "There are nuances of our ways that complicate the situation, Kedyn's Crow. Allowing myself to be as I am now, I have placed myself in jeopardy and no dragons are compelled to save me. In fact, most here would have been pleased to see me pay for my foolishness. The Peace of the Congress Chamber did not extend to me. But the Gyrkyme's attack on Nefrai-laysh violated that peace."

Peri screeched defiantly. "Evil reveals itself; rules do not."

Kerrigan looked at his mentor. "You're saying Will died for *nothing*?"

"No, his death—his *sacrifice*—counts for much." A cold tone entered the puppet's voice. "I am not without influence in this assembly. And we shall not pretend, shall we, Vriisureol, that you did not lead this Gyrkyme here? Or shall we be led to believe you failed to notice her trailing in your wake?"

The Black Dragon's mouth opened in a bit of a smile. "Why would I be concerned with something that could neither catch nor harm me?"

"Would you deny giving her magickal assistance to find this chamber? You always seek to be too subtle, Vriisureol." Ramoch looked in Peri's direction. "Perrine was lured here so she could intervene. While her action violated our law, Perrine did not act wholly of her own volition."

Peri screeched again, angrily, at the Black. Vriisureol, presumably having heard her curse translated into his tongue, widened his eyes for a moment, slowly closed them.

"So, it is this way, my friends. The violation of our peace here will be used by Chytrine's allies to justify their support of her. Conversely, Nefrai-laysh's attempt to bring down the mountain will justify the position of those who oppose her. As those forces are currently balanced, dragonkind shall remain neutral."

"Neutral?" Erlestoke shook his head. "She already has dragons as allies, and dracomorphs as well."

Rym Ramoch pressed the wooden hand to the hole in his chest. "Individuals, yes, as do you. I have helped Kerrigan, and shall help him even more. Dravothrak has helped you, and Vriisureol, well, he plays his own games, but so far they have benefited you. And there are others here who will feel compelled to aid you. To most, however, you and Chytrine are in a race. Whoever amasses the majority of the Truestones first will be the side for which we shall intervene."

The Oriosan Prince crossed his arms over his chest. "You play a dangerous game. If you support the wrong side, you will be denied the Crown. If you come into the war too late, the same thing will happen."

The blue raised his head. "Lecture us not on politics, for that is what is being played here. While we do not all move to intervene, some of us do. The factions here who win will win much, and those who lose will lose even more."

Kerrigan's hands balled into fists. "But this isn't a game. It isn't a race. It's a *war*! People have died. Orla died. Will just...and Lombo...Who knows...?"

Grief suddenly overtook him. His stomach shrank in on itself, and Kerrigan folded around his middle. He sank to his knees, then curled up into a ball. In his mind he saw lightning play through Orla's guts. He watched Will burst into flames.

He wished his tears could have doused that fire, could have healed Orla's wounds. He knew, however, that they could not—that all the tears that had ever been cried could never heal anything.

And yet, even with that realization, he could do nothing but cry.

CHAPTER 75

A lexia shifted in the bed. Crow's body pressed against her back, with his left hand on her stomach and his arm under their shared pillow. She slid her fingers from his, then rolled over to face him. His hand slid onto the small of her back, and her arm circled his chest.

She pulled herself tight to him, needing to hold as much as be held. She kissed his forehead. "You're not sleeping."

Crow, his eyes still closed, shook his head. His hair rustled against the pillow and his beard brushed the top of her breastbone. "I keep thinking back to the night we first found him. He was soaking wet, and so tiny. He'd been punched. He looked so helpless, just drenched and bedraggled, a feral little thing.

"And then today. I saw the expression on his face when he threw the Truestone. He knew Qwc would be in the right place. He'd changed so much, grown so much. The Will we found would have gone for the stone, but only because it was a gem, and he never would have thrown it away. No, he would have gone into the fire, clutching it to him, staring into its depths."

Her hand came up and she sank fingers through the white hair at Crow's left temple. "I know, Crow; I saw the changes. The way he dealt with Scrainwood and the Freemen. The way he dealt with Kenleigh. Once he left the Dim, he grew up a lot."

"And now he's gone."

"He sacrificed himself so Rymramoch could live."

Crow nodded. "He died well, yes. I can but hope I will die that well. We were so certain, though, that Will was *the* Norrington. Were we wrong? Was the prophecy wrong? Was Scrainwood right? Is Kenleigh a Norrington? Is he *the* Norrington? Is the Norrington out there dying in Sarengul?"

Alexia shivered and Crow hugged her a bit closer. "Crow, Kenleigh may not be the heir to the Norrington bloodline."

He pulled his head back. "You're not talking about his brother are you? What *are* you saying?"

She frowned. "After you left Caledo I learned that Sayce's family had determined she was with child. At Navval, she was beginning to suffer morning sickness..." Another shiver shook her. "Oh, by the gods, how will we tell her?"

She could feel the gooseflesh rise over Crow's back. "You're telling me that she is carrying Will's child?"

"Yes. *And* she is in love with him. She does not *know*—at least, not yet—about the child. She will soon, of course, but she's probably leading an army to attack the Aurolani host sieging Caledo even now."

Crow groaned and his body sagged. "Will is dead, and the other Norringtons are in harm's way."

"There are two *more,* father and son."

"They would never betray Chytrine." Crow shook his head. "It's Leigh and his issue that concern the prophecy; his father is no part of it. As for turning Leigh against Chytrine, that might be possible, but he could never stand against his father. No matter how powerful Chytrine is able to make the *sullanciri,* she cannot cancel out their innate flaws. Nefrai-laysh's action in the Congress Chamber was pure Leigh. It was one of his fits of pique. What Will said stung him."

Alyx pressed a finger to Crow's lips. "Lover—husband—I know your mind is racing off on many paths, but there is one you avoid. Will's death is a great loss to the world, and the world should mourn. It will mourn. But you, too, must mourn. He's been as a son to you..."

Crow's lips pressed together into a flat line, and tears welled in his brown eyes. "Not a son. A nephew, perhaps, and another chance with Leigh. My father helped raise Leigh's father and taught him how to be a great warrior. He helped raise Leigh. And Leigh was my friend and I failed him. I failed him horribly. The sword he possessed—the sword that possessed him—came with a price. Its owner would be invincible, save that in his last battle he would be broken. Leigh was, and I did the breaking.

"But Will was his son, and I could teach him. I could give him the benefit of all the mistakes I'd made, all the mistakes his father had made, and all the things I had learned fighting Chytrine. Through Will, I thought I could atone for the evil I'd done his father and his grandfather."

She grabbed a handful of his beard and tugged his chin up so she could look him square in the eyes. "And let's not forget that Will was the world's only hope and you managed to keep him safe from Chytrine and her minions. You weren't acting selfishly; you were acting for the world. Had you not found him and had things not moved as they did, Chytrine would have five pieces of the DragonCrown, the dragons would be her allies, and we would all share Will's fate."

He nodded quickly, then turned his face upward. Tears rolled down the side of his face. "It hurts, Alexia. It hurts to feel hope die and . . . Worse, when I saw him running, I wanted to shout at him not to do it. But then, I saw the look on his face, and I was so proud of him. He'd gone from a feral child to a man, and made a man's choice. And I couldn't stop him; I couldn't . . ."

As Crow's voice trailed off into silent repetitions, Alyx slipped her arms around his body and clung to him. She buried her face against his neck and felt tears splashing down onto her cheek. His body shook, wracked with sobs, and she held on all the tighter. She held him until his body ceased jerking and his arms enfolded her, and she held on even past that.

Finally, as Crow sniffed and swiped at tears with his left hand, she kissed his neck, then pulled back. She came up on her left elbow and pressed him onto his back with her body. She slid herself onto his broad chest and settled her shins along his thighs as she took her weight onto elbows and knees.

Her fingers brushed hair back from his face, and thumbs smeared tears before she kissed his cheeks. "Crow, there are two things you have to know. The first is that I love you more than life itself. You did not fail Will, and you have not failed the world." She lowered her mouth to his and punctuated her comment with a firm kiss.

Alyx's head came back up and Crow tangled a lock of her white-blonde hair around a finger. "Second, my love, I believe in the prophecy, and you were right about Will. Sayce's child, Kenleigh, or Nefrai-laysh may now be the Norrington by default. There is one other possibility, however."

"And that is?"

She smiled. "That what Will has done has actually already fulfilled the prophecy. His death and all the things set in motion by it will make the prophecy come true. What we have to do, then, is to make sure everything comes together, and the threat of Chytrine is ended forever."

It didn't really surprise Erlestoke to find Resolute sitting out on one of Vael's external landings. Though far too small to support one of the grand dragons, the opening was large enough to permit dracomorphs access.

The Oriosan Prince looked at his comrade. "Couldn't sleep, Resolute?"

The Vorquelf's head came up. "I have not had a good night's sleep, Highness, since before your great-grandfather was born. Tonight, though, sleep eludes me completely."

"We seek the same quarry and it escapes us both." Erlestoke sighed loudly and glanced at two silhouettes flashing past the sliver of moon. "I envy Perrine and Qwc their ability to fly."

"They are no more successful at hunting than we are."

"But perhaps they can stay ahead of despair." Erlestoke met Resolute's cold silver stare. "Don't tell me you don't feel it."

"Last I knew, Highness, I was not of Oriosa, therefore not subject to your commands."

"I know you're upset. I can understand..."

The Vorquelf rose from the rock upon which he sat. The moon's cold light sank him into a silhouette save for his silver eyes. "Upset? You understand? You'll forgive me if I choose not to believe that you understand what I am feeling. I have been without a home for well over a century. You may hate your father, you may have chosen to live apart from your nation, but I do not have that luxury. My family was slain, and my homeland taken from me. All I have ever wanted is to go back, so I could be bound to the land and have a normal life.

"Will was the key to that. When Crow and I found him he was nothing. In his mind 'right' meant anything that pleased him, and 'wrong' was someone else's useless sense of morality. His duty was to himself, perhaps to friends, but no further. He, like you, wanted to be king, but his kingdom was a five-acre slum that spent half the day underwater and awash in sewage."

Erlestoke shook his head. "That's not the Will I knew. That's not the Will who died here today."

"Exactly. That *wasn't* the Will Norrington who died here today. We trained him, we gave him a sense of duty and obligation. At least, we pointed him toward them, and he accepted those burdens. He wasn't perfect. He had lapses. There were times I wanted to take him back to the Dimandowns and leave him there."

The prince nodded, keeping his voice low. "But then there were the times he rose above. My brother told me how he faced my father down, and how he accepted the Freemen. I saw how they looked at him, and spoke to him, when they took their leave. He had earned their loyalty. No gutterwhelp could do that."

Resolute shook his head. "No. None could have and, had he lived, he could have done so much more. It's over now. The prophecy is broken."

"Do you think so?" The prince scraped a hand over his jaw. "Perhaps it just needs to be reinterpreted."

"Oh, it will be." Resolute pointed east toward Saporicia. "When we arrive in Narriz tomorrow and reveal that the Norrington is dead, it will be reinterpreted by everyone. Some will debate the words in the original Elvish, others will twist phrases and clauses and make up stories about the other candidates to make them fit. Perhaps the Norrington just means someone from the Norrington holdings. And there are other Norrington families in the world. Perhaps a cadet branch. Genealogies will sprout like mushrooms in manure, as anyone who wants to be a hero manufactures himself a Norrington pedigree."

"Getting rid of them will be a bother, but..."

The Vorquelf shook his head violently. "You've been at Fortress Draconis too long, Highness. The Draconis Baron kept everyone there focused on Chytrine. When I was a child she took Norvina and Vorquellyn. When you were a child she took Okrannel and tried to destroy Fortress Draconis. The pattern, as Will pointed out, is clear. Now she has Sebcia and soon will have Muroso."

"And the nations of the world will band together to oppose her."

Resolute's barked laugh echoed off Vael's tall peak. "Tell that to the people of Norvina. Tell that to Vorquelves like me. The nations of the world use every excuse they can to avoid doing anything so bold. In a grand conspiracy, they broke Tarrant Hawkins, branding him a liar and traitor, when they knew full well that your father was a puling coward and that Hawkins' message from Chytrine was correct. Just imagine, Highness, what will happen when news spreads through the leaders at Narriz?"

Erlestoke felt a chill run down his spine. "Factions will gather around various Norrington candidates, splitting the effort to oppose Chytrine. Nations that feel vulnerable will form alliances against neighbors, and some will treat for peace with Chytrine. My father will, certainly."

"And so it is all undone. Even if she is content to wait for another generation, she will not lose. With fertile lands like Sebcia and Muroso, she will harvest food, feed her armies, and they will swell until they become irresistible." Resolute fixed him with an argent stare. "Your child will never sit on the throne of Oriosa if Chytrine is not stopped now."

The prince considered for a moment, then nodded solemnly. "Then we will have to convince them of that."

" 'Twould be easier to bring Will back to life."

"That doesn't mean we can't do it." Erlestoke started ticking things off on his fingers. "Alexia and I can speak with the politicians and try to convince them. Kerrigan can rally Vilwan to our side. You and Crow can speak with the military folks. Perrine can recruit an army of Gyrkyme. You draw the Vorquelves, and we'll have dragons: Rymramoch, Vriisureol, and Dravothrak. Even Bok might be useful, and we have the Freemen helping free Sarengul, so we'll have other urZrethi allies. We could put together a formidable army."

The Vorquelf's eyes half closed, and he actually smiled, which Erlestoke did not find exactly comforting. "That plan is not without merit."

"But its chances of success are minimal?"

"They are, and any little thing could cause its collapse." Resolute's smile grew a little. "It will also make a lot of people angry. But given our alternatives, it's probably the best plan we'll find."

Kerrigan hated the expressions of shocked disappointment and betrayal on the others' faces. "I said, 'I'm sorry, I can't go with you.'"

Erlestoke stared at him. "But we need you. You can show the Vilwanese how to locate fragments of the DragonCrown. You can teach them how to fight Chytrine's troops."

The portly mage shook his head. Bok squatted with him at his left side, and Rym Ramoch, in a new scarlet robe, stood on his right. "I have a lot of things to learn here. My master is going to teach me some dracomagick that should help me refine my spells and make them more effective. If I go with you, I won't be as valuable as I will need to be. I won't be the ally you're going to need."

Crow slipped from Alexia's side and pulled the mask from his own face. He rested both hands on Kerrigan's shoulders. "Kerrigan, I don't doubt that you feel you need to stay here. It makes sense."

"Thank you." Kerrigan glanced down, refusing to meet Crow's stare.

Crow's right hand came over to his chin and tipped his face up. "But, before we go, before we let you stay here, I want to know the *real* reason you're not coming with us."

Kerrigan opened his mouth for a moment. A denial sat on his tongue, then he shut his mouth. He could feel his jowls quivering. He clenched his jaw lest their quivering make it to his chin and lips, then shake tears from his eyes. He sucked his lower lip in between his teeth and bit it, hoping the pain would keep the tears back, which it did. It let him swallow past the lump choking him, too.

He began in a small voice. "I could have caught the Truestone. I could have caught Will. I could have saved him. I could have slammed Nefrai-laysh through that portal before Lombo got there. I could have saved Orla."

Crow squeezed his shoulders. "None of that is your fault."

"No, Crow, not my fault." Tears began to burn their way down his cheeks. "But I could have *prevented* it! If I had more training. If I thought faster. And..."

The man finished it for him. "And you don't want to fail us and let us die, too."

Kerrigan shook his head, unable to speak.

Crow drew him into a strong hug. Kerrigan hesitated, uncomfortable and desperate, then grabbed handfuls of Crow's tunic and gripped them hard. He hung on tightly as Crow gently stroked his back.

"You listen to me, Kerrigan Reese. I know Orla told you to listen to me and to Resolute. She wanted you to stay with us. She wanted you to learn from us, and as she lay dying, she made you our responsibility. And we kept you with us until we left Caledo. Not because we thought you'd be in danger with the Freemen, but because we knew you would be far better employed with Alexia in Navval.

"And you were. You saved lives. You did things that saved Prince Erlestoke and kept yet another DragonCrown fragment away from Chytrine. You defeated a *sullanciri*. The great things you did just confirmed what we had known: you are a good man, with a huge heart, and woe be to the enemy that you choose to fight."

Crow released him and stood back. "So, if you think you need Rymramoch's training, then you should stay. But when we need you..."

Kerrigan nodded. "I'll be there. Thank you."

Crow looked at the puppet. "You train him well, and keep him safe."

The puppet cocked its head. "You'll forgive me if a weaponless man's threat sounds a bit hollow."

"I remember where I left my sword. I don't think you want me coming back for it."

"No, indeed." Rymramoch's puppet bowed to all of them. "Travel safely and well."

Kerrigan waved as his companions turned and climbed onto Dravothrak's broad back. The green dragon gave him a little nod, made certain everyone was strapped in, then spread his wings and launched himself skyward. The young mage remained there, watching, until the dragon was but a small, dark speck in the morning sky.

Rym Ramoch's gloved left hand landed on his right shoulder. "Crow was right. You were right. What you learn here will make you the most powerful mage in the world. We will be able to find the missing fragments of the DragonCrown and then, ultimately—with Bok's help—we will find Chytrine herself."

Kerrigan glanced down at the green urZrethi. "How are you going to help us, my little friend?"

"By sharing with you, Adept Reese, everything I know about her and her ways—which actually is considerable." The urZrethi smiled as he straightened up and stood, cultured words pouring softly from his mouth. "After all, I *am* her father."

About the Author

Michael A. Stackpole is an award-winning game designer and author who has gone into hiding for fear of being lynched because of the ending of this book. (Note: if you read this bio before you read the book, you are expressly forbidden from reading the last chapter first. I will know if you do.)

While being sequestered from normal society, he is madly at work on *The Grand Crusade,* in which all questions will be answered, all issues tackled, and all desires satisfied (unless there's something that would lead into a really neat sequel).

His website is www.stormwolf.com.